D1430076

Walton Street Publishing is an independent publishing house located on th... of Madness represents the first title by the publisher, and the author: Robbie Rimsky

Mr. Rimsky was born in 1979, in Chicago, Illinois. Son of a metalworker and loving mother, he continues to make his home on Chicago's West Side, in a 4th generational family brownstone that is more or less falling apart, with his fiancée, Kimberly, and their dog, Poa.

Do note: we've left some empty pages in the back of this book, in case you need to write shit down, or draw. Feel free to go crazy back there—nobody is going to judge you.

Walton Street Publishing
Chicago, Illinois
60622

1523 / 3500

check us out!

Front Cover Design: Ryan Antonio Karey
Rear Cover and Spine Design: Jane Kathryn Cornell
Editor in Chief: Joshua James Sopiarz

Written, Designed, Printed and Bound in the United States of America
This book has been manufactured using Post-Consumer Recycled Materials
www.waltonstreetpublishing.com
ISBN: 978-0-615-44144-3

Thank you for buying the First Edition—

Many thanks Robbie

1

Walton Street Publishing Presents:

A Mild Form of Madness

A novel—

To my family and my mates:

I'd be nothing without you—you've taught me everything about life and living, and made me free. Thanks for letting me know what it means to be real. This is for you guys—

All my love and cheers to the good times of the past and future

Robbie

If there's anything funny about this, it's that I shouldn't be speaking with you right now. See, I'm supposed to be working. I started a new job earlier today: 'A new, *exciting* opportunity,' to be precise. Those are all I seem to hear about these days—that's what everyone is looking for. The same old new and exciting bullshit everywhere you look. How's that aphorism go? The one unremittingly uttered throughout every office, every machine shop, every classroom, in every household and on every street corner—that one statement— the eternal justifier of our finite reality twisting into the infinite realism of *grind*ing it out. From seconds to minutes to hours to days to y*ea*rs, grinding it until suddenly you realize that the millions, the *bill*ions of breaths you've breathed—those run out man. They run out real fucking fast. The end of the finite reality is the infinite certainty, indeed, indeed.

So again, how's that aphorism go? That we just, "Do what we gotta to do to get by,"—is that it? Listen man. What you h*av*e to do is eat, drink, sleep, and breathe. That's the mandatory. Aside from that, what you do with your time is your call. And I don't know about you, but I can't stand doing what I don't want to do—I hate it. I try to avoid hating things as often as possible, but really, I hate obligatory involvement in uninspiring activities. Life strikes me as too fleeting to squander as vast a percentage on such as contemporary creatures hold a propensity to do. Thing is—and you probably know this as well as I—a very basic set of problems tend to arise when you try to abide to the code of living your life in whatever far-gone style you choose. My current problem is the one I've always had. I'm broke to the point of having to do what I gotta do to get by. I gotta work, just like you, likely. That realization, man, it's beautiful and inestimably fine if happenstance you're doing *ex*actly what your heart holds the most robust and fervent love for, but if this is not the case, well—I get sick to my stomach just thinking about it. That not only am I going to get up for work to*mor*row, but I'll have to get up the next day, and the day after that, all next week, the rest of this month, all next quarter, the quarter after that, all next year, the following three, five more maybe, when I'm ill, when the weather is perfect and I long for wild non-premeditated immersion in such—when I want nothing more than to lay alongside whomever the hell I happen to be awaking beside, when I'll want to climb the highest peak available and jump right the fuck off, right off and into a relentless game of speed chess—my body, those trees, these skis, every move counts, no mistakes please—on all the days I'd prefer to be doing something, *any*thing besides going to work—I'll have to go. The realization that you'll be getting up to work in an environment that you detest for the rest of your life is plain dreadful. And this—this is why I quit jobs for a living.

Leaving that gig this morning wasn't the most brilliant move of the decade, but truth is, I just couldn't do it. The place was just too disheartening—the people, the concept, all of it. Can you i*mag*ine selling insurance for a living? Calling thousands upon thousands of people, relentless as a cockroach—"What do mean you're not interested? What? Do you think you're going to live for*ever*? You could get sick any day now—might be tomorrow, might be to*night*. Time is of the essence sir, it really is." You got that right pal, and that's basically why I left.

Thinking back on it, I came pretty close to not showing at all. The office was located on the twenty-first floor of the Fifty-Five West Monroe building. I didn't need to be there until eight, but found myself freezing outside the entranceway by seven o'clock. I'd awoken a touch earlier than needed, dead frozen, and could not fall back asleep. I have a tough time sleeping when I've got too much on my mind. I wanted to sleep more than

5

anything in the world, but all I did was lay in the dark while attempting to discern the revolutions per minute of my ceiling fan from the cadence of its creak. I do weird stuff like that while my mind is roaring off on uncontrollable tangents. I'd probably sleep better without the distraction, but the creak provides the added anxiety that the fan will crack from the ceiling, crash through my tent, and fracture my face. The possibility of such allows my mind to skedaddle from my legitimate or more plausible apprehensions, and stew upon the fan. It's a simple escape, and I enjoy it.

At twenty past three my focus switched from the fan to my heart. The young ticker was noticeably irregular. She ticks odd beats if my nerves are too fried. Problem may be that my perpetual series of downgrades has recently kicked into overdrive.

I live in a moderately suitable neighborhood on the Near Northwest Side of Chicago, alright. If from this city, or any major metropolis in the free world for that matter, I'm certain you can fathom the framework of the scene—'tis ten percent trendy, young urban professionals, prettified according to new-fangled fashion formulas of meticulousness, who reside within preen, decorated-to-the-nines apartments or recently refurbed condos—ten percent middle-aged, triumphantly successful family units locked tightly within devilishly manicured, half million dollar or more, single family fortresses—thirty percent middle class, average income, penny-pinching citizens struggling to subsist within a financially average neighborhood in a financially above average city—thirty percent predictably impoverished, coupon cutting people's people, polite and handsome as a consequence of their pecuniary imperfection and the ensuing ramshackle tradition of furrowing eight persons into a two bedroom apartment or an overtly oxidized, four door Chevy Caprice Classic during Saturday afternoon excursions to the local Village Outlet—ten percent elders who have steadfastly remained within the community and the buildings of their birth with the consistency of the shrill eastern breeze off Lake Michigan in the early February morn—and finally, ten percent tumbledown-type, unhinged, mentally deranged individuals for which armed robbery, assault and battery, and rape or murder ain't no thang. Then there are an exceedingly tiny percent of photography, writing, roaming and observation-obsessed persons who sleep in a two-man tent in a petite, heatless, windowless garage within this afore mentioned neighborhood, which of course is I.

Beyond the obvious weirdness, living on the low in an inner-city glacial garage is fairly unpredictable. Bums, random manic cunts wobbling up the alleyway all cockeyed-like, tumbling into the aluminum garage door in a half-gassed stupor, eerily echoing domestic squabbles, strong armed stickups, occasional initiation beatings, sporadic drug deals and intravenous drug use three feet from my hat-enveloped head as I lay motionless and incessantly on edge within my cozy nylon Coleman, staunchly affixed to my no-noise code of living and mostly non-amenity way of life. Urban camping—'tis a crazed existence for sure. I can go on for days, months about the details of this experience—the necessary adjustments of working for assorted Fortune Five Hundred businesses while fully dependent upon public resources to maintain a preferential outward appearance and the painstaking effort to keep family, friends and acquaintances in the dark about the fact that you're living in the dark. I could go on, but I'm not in the mood to speak these details just yet.

Anyhow, on this morn, after an exceptionally erratic sequence of heartbeats I unzipped my sleeping bag, sat up, pressed my blue-green knitted woolen mittens hard against my eyes, hard enough to see a white flash, and made a hushed verbal plea with my mind to chill the fuck out. For unobvious reasons, I've had trouble relaxing as of late. The most difficult part is carrying on in public settings without letting on that you're on the verge of, or currently, freaking out. A select few of my friends have an idea of my problem, but most do not. The ones who do know—they confided that they encounter those same problems, after which I told a small sampling of them that I do as well, and all without explaining my main reasons for feeling anxious. I would never tell somebody I had a problem before they told me one of their own, and even after someone has confided I usually keep my own issues tightly bottled. I'm a secret keeper at heart. What happens with me is that if too much is on my mind and I am in a public setting where a vast conglomeration of halfwits are carrying on with unrelenting botheration, I can't breathe. I don't know if it's an asthma attack or if I'm claustrophobic or what, but when it happens it is very imperative that I leave the scene and greet with fresh air immediately. I've come close to blacking out on quite a few occasions where unsullied ventilation and ample space were not readily available. People often laugh about how often I disappear from a given locale without appropriate notice. Unbeknownst to them, this is the reason. The problem is more recent than erstwhile, and I wish it would go away.

But yes, this morning—I slipped out my sleeping bag, jumped from the inertly cold, concrete floor, unzipped the door to my tent, asked my bladder to please, please do not explode, shook off the creeps with a steaming gush of warm breath into my cupped, frozen hands, lit an array of eight non-scented candles and a single stick of incense with a blue tip, strike anywhere match struck off my crumbling brick partition, sparked a puff with the nearly concluded burn of the same matchstick, addressed my innermost emotion by hitting play on my boom box, and *Kind of Blue* hummed all gentle-like, barely audible and entirely temperate through my earth-brown, poorly insulated, crumbled plaster, brick-lined garage. Next, I fired my propane stove, placed a pot of slightly frozen water upon the burner, eagerly awaited liquefaction, got my blood moving with a few hundred pushups and sit-ups, shadow boxed for another few minutes, and poured my boiling water into a well-worn green thermos, fresh cup of tea on the brew.

I subsequently nabbed a hunk of not quite stale, not quite frozen French bread off my makeshift plywood countertop, gnawed it down with the sideways chomp horses use to chew heavy wet hay, undressed, took a sub-zero, makeshift shower which I currently do not wish to describe, and dressed expertly. I unplugged my boom box, threw the straps of my old ski pack 'round my shoulders, blew out the candles one by one while casually observing the accumulation of additionally indistinct smoke with each rout of radiance within the room, and took a brief, final glance about to make certain all was in order before devastating the final flame between my just salivated thumb and index finger, and sneakily sailing out the side door of my $75 dollar per month domicile to mingle with the windswept world of supposed normalcy.

Skipping to the fore, I caught the eastbound bus on Chicago Avenue by six thirty, and found myself standing outside the office an hour early like I said. I noticed a coffee joint adjacent to the lobby and decided to snag a Joe—the jitters were lacking. A polite girl with stick-straight brown hair and pallid blue eyes poured my drink sportily quick. Gawking upon a nearby table and awaiting my fix, I spied an individual directly to my left who according to the modern code of value, likely held significance. And so there, scone and latte in hand, leather portfolio spread neatly open to a series of charts and graphs and an impeccably tailored tweed suit jacket lain neatly and spread upon the back of his chair, away he went with the ruthless efficiency of Francisco Pizzaro, measuring profit and yield, making eye contact with all who cared to notice and speaking in overwhelming lurid and shrill tones on his cell phone that served to imply: it shant go without recognition that I have more, and you have less—nearly every single quality of his mind-set building within me an oft felt affection for silence.

"Here you are."

"Cheers." I snagged my Joe, undid the lid, gave the cream and sugar a good spin, a good twist, all that—got that perfect, gentle soft brown color spinnin' round and round, dribbled a nibble of sugar, twisted the tan tornado of deliciousness southern hemisphere style, crushing the Coleuses effect, counterclockwise above the equator and all that, capped the cup, flipped the stick, thought about going upstairs, almost made the move, but cruised out the revolving door and back into the frigid morning air. I decided I'd stroll to Chase Plaza and think things over.

In case you're not from Chicago, Chase Tower is this crazy-looking building between Clark and Dearborn. She's the tallest building in the Loop proper—two hundred and fifty-nine meters of concrete and steel concave through the soil and flex toward the heavens. She's reminiscent of the GE building in New York in lots of ways. They're the same height, both sport popular sunken plazas, and both are located in the heart of their respective business districts. A four thousand square foot mosaic depicting the four seasons—*Four Seasons*, a Marc Chagall creation—occupies the Plaza length-wise along Dearborn. If you ever get the chance, take a close look at the hundreds of thousands of glass protrusions and stone tiles working in harmony to create the countless images on the mosaic. You'll appreciate the madness of Chagall's mind. He went berserker on it, must have taken years. No matter how many times I look it over, his creation always seems to show me something previously unnoticed—I dig that. Another thing to do with Chase Tower—stand at the base, place your foot upon one of the concaved piers, and focus your eyes upon the vanishing point in the sky above. As my blues focused upon the sloping façade and crisp sky on high, the usual illusion that I could tear right up her face did not disappoint. I gave it a shot, but as was proven many moons ago, blasting up the façade via foot tis a permanent no dice.

I stood momentarily still, smoking on the sly, trying not to think, not to move, and my eyes shifted from the fresh blue sky to the petrified marble staircase across the way. As my heels echoed through frozen marble plaza and past the non-active fountain, my body felt delicate, like if I stepped too hard, my whole torso might shatter. I concluded clicking halfway up the double staircase on the south end, sat, leaned the small of my back against a large slab of cold marble, stretched my legs across the stairs, drew a new drag deliberately deep within my chest, and exhaled a long stream of clean, white smoke, through my raw, wind-chapped lips. As a sliver of midwinter early morning sunlight refracted off my face, not a hint of warmth was felt. The whole scene was a brightly blue sky, a brisk eastern breeze, and a traditional midwinter sun of sharpness and softness—one which casts glaring light while providing little heat. Had it been summertime, gobs of people would've been cramping my style. People have a tendency to congregate in the plaza when the weather is fit for human habitation. And that's what is so nice about the harshness of winter—it gives you the chance to fly solo in scenes that are normally bustling with maniacs—makes you feel like you can take it, and they can't. Much like the feeling of sprawling in the middle of a busy intersection in the middle of the night, you expect to be run over at any second, but the lights keep changing and the traffic never comes. If you've never tried that, you should. It's a startlingly peaceful feeling—much like I assume sitting in an electric chair during a power outage to be.

As I sipped my Joe and dragged my way through my tightly packed handcraft, the pace of people plowing paths to work was cruelly high-pulsed. It's obstinate sound—that of people plowing, sickly so. The frozen marble walls of the sunken plaza served to sharpen the sound. Watching them pass, listening to them plow, my mind was stuck on the subject of the past twenty four months of my work experience: eighteen original gigs. Nice and steady, quit by quit, I'm burning bridges at reputable companies as hastily as hiring managers will allow.

Digging through my bag in search of my temporary building ID, I stumbled upon the last known photo of my father's father. I keep it on me wherever I go. It's a pretty simple photo—just him on the couch, looking exhausted, and ready to die. I didn't grasp it at the time I clicked the button that snapped the shutter, but in all the time I knew him, that was the only moment in which his passionate blue eyes held an articulation of defeat. I developed the film two weeks later, a week after he died. As I stood statically in the indistinct red light of a darkroom in the Chicago Photography Studio, my hands were visibly shaky. I pressed the button on the timer and exposed an eight by ten sheet of matte photo paper in soft, mildly filtered light for sixteen and one half seconds, removed the blank paper from the tray, and slipped the .matte-styled mystery into a large tray of D76 developer. Slowly, silently, stoically, as I held my breath deep within my body, my grandfather appeared on the paper. Upon comprehension, a taut tear collapsed from one of my furious blue eyes, splashed upon his conquered image, and a series of ripples spread slowly outward. I gently rinsed the paper in lukewarm water, hand running over his face, whispering, "It's okay, Gramps, I promise everything is cool," placed the photo into the fixer, walked into the frigid night air and sat quite quietly, with my back leaned against a parking meter, thinking of what could be done.

Stumbling upon the photo this morning, I was fairly keen on heading home and forgetting the gig, or better, just plain forgetting. I removed the mitten from my right hand and in accordance with their odd shade of white, my fingers were stone frozen. I positioned my hand an inch before my eyes and marveled at its formlessness—it was illuminated in the heatless, ultra-bright sunlight refracting from the rounded windows of Fifty-Five West. A crescent-shaped cut overwhelmed the third knuckle on my right hand. I probably needed stitches—two, three at most. The wound wasn't that fresh, forty hours old, and after accidentally scraping it upon the rough staircase while stabilizing my sit, thick beads of blood began slowly seeping, dripping out of my body, and freezing upon contact with the worn marble staircase. Two, maybe three drags later, a crackling sound and the distinct smell of burning flesh lead me to believe the cut was permanently cauterized. Bic lighters, though slightly less precise, are far less expensive than the price of a needle, six inches of thread, and the trained hand of a human seamstress. I stood, gritted my teeth, blew a mixture of skin and ash from my knuckle, completed clicking up the frozen staircase, furrowed in to the flow of people plowing eastward, clicked across Monroe, and spun myself though a revolving door and into the lobby of Fifty-Five West.

***

Fifty-Five is pretty loaded with law offices and whatnot—bustling big shots are the mainstream. I wasn't jibing with the beehive vibe, but what could I do? Get stung and ignore it, that's about it. I was a little worried—I was hired fairly short notice for this gig, early last week. The chap that hired me issued a temporary building ID when I accepted the job—as to where tis, your guess trumps mine. Cat gave me a madman congratulatory handshake, I

9

pretended to care, he slipped me the temporary building ID, told me not to lose it, I said I wouldn't, and, five minutes later, t'was gone for good.

A menacing posse of guards spread throughout the lobby indicated the lack of ID to be a slight predicament. I had an excuse figured, but upon closer inspection—one guard was guarding his nostril, two were guarding the Suntimes, and the last guard, a Sasquatch if I've ever seen one—he was guarding a businesswoman's bosom in a style that said he and some sex offender database went back to prepubescent incidents of extraordinary perversion. I squeaked through the scene all sly-like and before I knew it I was solo in an elevator, floor twenty-one ablaze.

As the brass-coated doors slammed shut and my feet pressed hard against the floor, my stomach became queasy. The crazy thing—despite this being my eighteenth career in two years, I still get the first day jitters. There's just something about introducing myself to a large number of unidentified individuals that makes me nervous. The sheer volume of lies I have to tell to get my foot in the door doesn't help matters. I mean think about it—every person I meet, every s*ingl*e person I encounter in a new office, I have to deceive them. Lemme tell you something man—that's a lot of lying, a *lot*. I'd show you the W2 forms to prove my story, but I usually burn those the same day I receive them. W2 forms make great kindling. You can count on the ensuing fire to feel e*x*tra cozy. Throw on some jazz, brew some green tea, spark a nice spliff, and knock back a few pints—whatever your vices, enjoy them in this moment—lay out some blankets, call your girl and re*lax*. It sounds silly, but seriously, you should try this sometime—this is a favorite holiday of mine. I neither support the system, nor take from it. I live as an animal roving the planet, because that is exactly what I am.

* * *

As soon as I stepped from the elevator I began wishing I hadn't shown in the first place. I would've turned back, but the doors opened smack into the reception area of the insurance joint and I was trapped—they own the entire floor, that style place. The secretary's desk was a stone-throw away from the elevator and the rail-thin blond-headed woman behind it was wolfing some poor guy's ear about, "Why the *hell* is the water dispenser empty?" The guy she was screaming at was ancient, prehistoric almost. He looked too frail to move a pack of st*a*ples across a d*e*sk, but she went ahead and gnawed his face off about the water jug anyhow. I hate seeing old guys getting hassled, but I felt especially bad for this one. It felt like the incident was a microcosm of his entire life—like he hadn't stuck up for himself within the past sixty-four years. The guy shuffled his worn brown boots across the black tile floor to break his back with the water jug, and the skinny witch addressed me before I had a chance to offer assistance.

"Yes? What is it? Do you n*e*ed something?" she asked all brash. My suspicion was she maintains one of those diets where the main exertion of energy consists of spewing calories out of her mouth via excessive, fully unnecessary screaming, resulting in a slim, scant frail frame of oxygen and raw, scathing vocal chords.

"Sure, yeah, this is my first day actually—I'm Anthony Riedie, the new District Sales Manager." This place Pensury hired me to be in charge of two hundred insurance agents, a mistake, obviously. I worked for a similar insurance company previously, Peltip Insurance, and held a similar position. Point being, after an agent sends in an application or a claim, before it gets underwritten, it goes to the District Manager's attention. The *rea*son it was a mistake to hire me for that position is because it's quite easy to make some seemingly insignificant changes in specific aspects of claim paperwork and medical records before they are sent to the underwriting department that shall ensure the *insur*ance company will not be able to wriggle out of large medical payments or rider the major medical concerns of their clients. *Tech*nically while in this position, I was supposed to ensure the opposite. I, along with the underwriters, was supposed to unearth any feasible reason, each reason later identified as a rider, for which the insurance company can fuck people on subsequent health insurance claims. 'I have heart problems and need medical insurance, fast!' Sure, we'll insure you—everything *but* your cardiovascular system—five eighty a month. It disgusts me, American healthcare—I'd get rewarded for hanging people out to dry, basically. What I accomplished at Peltip was the same thing I had planned for Pensury—to insure the shelling out of large sums of cash to and coverage for those who, according to certain industry *ru*les, didn't deserve it. "Sorry friend, preexisting conditions are not covered by your insurance. That knee condition, that heart condition—next time you find yourself gimping along with a racing heartbeat and need to hit the doc it's coming out of *your* pocket—unless of course preexisting is changed to nonexistent. Delete, whoops, delete, whoops, lemme just move this to there and—boom, *swish*—I'll send this on to underwriting then and you'll be all set.

Fact is, on average, as is proudly reinforced in meetings, insurance companies pay no more than twelve cents on the dollar of all premiums collected—and, obviously, the *rea*son they collect such obscene profits is the fact that they wiggle out of paying claims—unless of course I'm working there.

"So? So what are you saying?" Carol asked—the entire room, despite smelling overwhelmingly of disinfectant, felt very impure, very contaminated.

"Okay, well, I'm not really sure where I'm suppose to be and, you know like I said, it's my first day and I was hoping you could point me in—"

"Where's your license?" she asked, "Let me see it. You're a United States citizen I take it?" I thought of telling the cheeky bitch that no, I'm a bleedin' Eskimo, but I gave her my license and shut the hell up. I wasn't in the mood to start things off on the wrong foot. I just tried to picture her old, frail, and midway though a fall that would inevitably shatter her hip into billions of miniscule pieces.

"Is this address *ac*curate? That address on Walton? Is it up to date or what?" She made sure to physically *point* at the address with her index finger—in case I didn't know what was printed on there, or, more likely, to show off her slightly too crimson, quarter-inch too long, nails.

"Yup, that's it, that's the one—on Walton, between Western and Oakley, three blocks north of Chicago Avenue, one block south of Augusta. That's where I live, you betcha."

"Do you realize the time? It's quarter 'til eight. Wasn't seven thi*r*ty the sugges*t*ed time to arrive?" The craziest thing of all was some poor bastard slid a wedding ring on her finger, nice one too—a clean, square cut *rock* centered perfectly upon a clean, platinum band. Some cat fixed her up proper, ten stacks on that rock, easy.

"I'll be honest with you Mrs. Moon—I guess I missed the part about—"

"It's *Ms.* Moon, *Ms.* This is an en*gage*ment ring," she said, sticking it up my nose practically, "I'm not married yet."

11

"Well alright then, *Ms*. Carol Moon," I said. There was a gaudy golden trophy shaped like an enormous smiling face, combined with a proclamation of "Outstanding Customer Service" placed impressively upon her desk—hence, I knew her name. "Like I said, I didn't catch the seven thirty part. The guy who hired me, Mr. Monahan—he said *eight*. I didn't catch anyth—"

"Well you *should* have. You should have caught it—you would have if you'd *lis*tened. All I deal with around here are people that don't listen to *any*thing. If you're going to be working here we need to get some things straight right off the bat. Do you have *any* idea about how much time I put into my company-wide emails? How many times I check to make sure they're *per*fect before I send them out? How much effort I exude to make sure everything is *crystal*-clear? And what do I get? *Ques*tions! Thirty different people asking me *ques*tions when I've already explained the *an*swers in the *orig*inal letters and *orig*inal statements. The last thing I need is another person working here that doesn't know how to *lis*ten." Misery takes serious effort. I could tell she wasn't just having a bad morning. Carol Moon was the type that earns their misery one miserable moment after another.

"Listen Carol, I understand that's frustrating, but I'm coming off three obscenely raw days, I'm not in the mood for a lecture right now—I was simply being honest. How 'bout you just give me my ID, tell me where I need to be, what I need to do, and I'll do it. I'll get out of your hair and go on my merry way. It'll be much easier for both of us that way, it really will," I said, nice as pie. It's funny how often after speaking with someone directly and openly, they give you this look like you're being an asshole. Carol gave me that type of look and sent me on my way. She directed me down the hall and told me to enter the third door on the left. The third door was supposed to lead to the training room. She told me I'd find the rest of the members of my training class—the ones who had been on *time*—seated in alphabetical order. A nametag would point to where I was supposed to seat myself. She said our trainer would arrive no later than eight thirty and that I could twiddle my thumbs until he arrived. I thanked her, sauntered down the hall, and opened the third door on the left. Sure enough, the third door opened into this stuffy-as-hell training room jam-packed with punctual motherfuckers. I made myself laugh a bit because I opened the door rough as hell and everyone in the room jumped out of their seats—they thought I was the goddamn trainer.

***

My seat was way the hell in the back because of the alphabetized accommodation. I'm pretty used to sitting towards the back by now, and prefer to do so. The first thing I noticed after sitting down were six of those motivational plaques all over the walls. The kind with slogans regarding '*Suc*cess' coined beneath photos of stone walkways and shit like that—the kind that make you want to quit everything. I care naught for such, and less for the people who write them. My only hope is that some loon scrawls those verses on a pornography-ridden bleached wall in a dingy basement via candlelight and laughs his ass off at all the self-sanctified rascals who rewrite the slogans on their forearms with Indian ink at the start of their work days.

Two seconds after I was situated, the maniac on my left identified himself as Phil Stantillo, and introduced himself with an overly dramatic—let's be best buddies—type of handshake. Phil was a middle-aged guy who looked like he'd fallen for about six obvious scams in the past two weeks—each time he blinked it looked like he was trying to crush his eyeballs or mash eyelid fleas, I couldn't tell which. His oil-black hair was worn in a three quarter part, and excess pomade congealed at the tips. The head had an overall impression of being a fire hazard. His articulation held a hint of a stutter, and his breath, a hint of bologna. After cracking the hell out of himself with fourteen various knee slappers, Phil changed the subject to insurance.

"You know Anthony," he said, eyes jumpy as hell, "I'm telling you, people will always need to buy insurance, *al*ways. They'll always need it and that's nothing but a cold fact, a cold fact of life. I mean people get sick, people get injured, people catch bad breaks, people get ripped off—what can you do? Nothing, absolutely *no*thing. And that's why insurance is the *per*fect industry to get involved with." I feigned interest and he stammered ahead. "It's just, I'm—I was in a real jam awhile back. A *r*eal jam, boy, I'm telling you. When I think about it, geez. You ever—I mean, ah, nevermind, forget it. But you know what I mean?" I could only guess what he was thinking about—something terrible, I'll bet. I was catching one of those looks that invite somebody to say, 'What's wrong?' or 'What happened?' and then the guy says—'Nothing,' gazes into the distance all deep, and says, 'It's just—' and off they go about some maddening slew of problems. I don't know what it is—the way I look, how I dress, the fact that I always try to look directly into someone's eyes while they're speaking with me, the fact that I pay attention to the details of what people say, I don't know. Whatever it is, people tell me all sorts of weird information about themselves. A safe estimation would say I've had nine hundred and sixty unfamiliar people purposely disgorge highly confidential or highly peculiar information about their personal life into my ears during the past two years. Standing in line, seated on the L, at the Lakefront—wherever I am, randoms find me and spill madness. Like while waiting for the bus this morning—while I was waiting on Chicago and Western some middle aged guy with a patchy beard and an original Bulls Starter jacket strolled up and asked me if he could ask me a question. I said yes, he asked if I owned an answering machine, I said no, he said he did, I said cool, and then he told me he's had eight purposeful personal phone calls in the past three years, two of them pranks. But fortuitously, he said, he speaks with dozens of people per year who dial wrong numbers because his number is only one digit away from that of Club Micky. He became very quiet and so I mentioned a close friend once told me that as long as you try hard and don't kill yourself, everything will work itself out. He didn't say anything and: "What happened to your eye?" I asked.

"I got mugged by some *tee*nagers."

"Well, like my Uncle Norm says: it's a violent world—you gotta stick with it. Come prepared, man, and don't take shit—that's all ya can do," I said.

"What's he do for a living."

"He draws depictions of violent offenders from the words of innocent victims."

"Here in Chicago? For the PD?"

"Yep."

"Maybe you could talk to 'em about this." No doubt he has a lot of knowledge, my uncle, he taught me a load—the truth, plain and direct, raw as it stands—know what I mean? After the Auto Show, he and my dad would always sneak me into this seedy joint south on State, down by Area 1, and I'd sit spying sociable hookers while listening to detectives tell wild stories, my mouth silent and mind awed at the world. I learned lots as a lad, sitting with those guys and soaking in rays with a fishin' pole at my fingertips—like the fact that millions of these sorts exist: lonely mice chomped up and shat out by society like wet hay, ready to rot in an empty field by their lonesome before being devoured by flies, one bite at a time until again being shat in lesser magnitude and spread evenly over the meadow—shit from shit, its whole existence inane and futile.

I didn't respond and he continued speaking, just a touch quieter for each freshly arrived individual at the stop, brown eyes holding my blue with desperate intentions until the bus came, by which time he was speaking so quietly there was not adequate reverberation for response, just an O so lonely eyes and the feeble lip movement of an individual so unsure of where to begin, he wanted to end. The sixty-six screeched up, he said thanks for listening, I said sure, and the two of us crammed into the already crowded bus, and never spoke again. What do you say to statements like his? Not much, I suppose.

I tried to ignore him, but Phil Stantillo was one of those people who don't pick up on the cold shoulder too well. I could just picture the guy getting high for sake of talking himself down—he would not stop rambling. After answering eight rhetorical questions he said, "And the *best* part is we'll always be covered! We'll have to be—we'll be working for an in*sur*ance company! What? Don't you get it?" Yes indeed, indeed I do. You could tell he was disappointed when I didn't laugh with him. He cracked an awful cackle and paused with this big sigh at the end to allow time for a sympathy chuckle, but he didn't get one. That's the thing—if I say something and you don't find it funny, don't fucking laugh. I'll listen to whatever you have to say, comprehend every syllable, sit on the edge of my seat with my fingers crossed and a hand on my balls if that's what you want, but don't expect me to pretend to be amused if I'm not. Who the hell enjoys sympathy laughs? Lots of people, unfortunately, but nobody I comprehend. And as much as I usually try to avoid doing it, I wind up feeling guilty when I don't chuckle—then comes the dreaded guilt-laugh—it's even worse than the sympathy.

The stale bologna on Stantillo's breath didn't help the situation, nor did several oblong chunks of mystery meat crammed between his stained teeth. Anyone who eats bologna for breakfast belongs in hell, case closed. There'll be thousands of them in a giant room with bologna floors, bologna walls, shackled by and bound to a bologna chair, and it'll be woefully humid and all anyone will be allowed to do is chew profuse, tumor-ridden chunks of sweating, decaying bologna. Those are the types of thoughts Stantillo's pungent breath made me think—it was that rank. As he obnoxiously slapped his hand on the table and reared backwards with a loud, openmouthed roar, I couldn't help but imagine myself vomiting my coffee and stale bread straight down his esophagus—just fire a hot curdled stream of coffee, bread, and digestive acid down his throat, real gourmet-like. I looked Phil S. dead in the eyes and said, "Hey Phil, I don't mean to not be speaking with you, it's just that I have a *really* sore throat. Actually, I have so much m*u*cus in my system that I was, well—if you keep making me talk, I'll have to ask you to take a look at the back of my throat and count off the weeping sores. My entire head feels like it's about to explode—can you let me chill?" My throat wasn't sore, obviously—I just needed him to zip his trap. Today is not the day. He jabbed his head off for another five minutes before he started speaking with the unnerving sloth sitting to his right—had the exact conversation with that guy, too. Same jokes, same timing and everything, and they both laughed loud as hell about the having to be covered by insurance part. Horrible. Barring a temporary brain hemorrhage, there's no way the guy didn't hear Stantillo use that precise line two minutes earlier. He didn't laugh then, but all of a sudden— whatever. I don't want to think about it. I'd noticed a boisterous greenish-yellow nose-bat lynched from one of Stantillo's coarse, jet black nose hairs minutes before, and I was mainly hoping the guy beside him was laughing about that. Upon closer inspection, the guy with whom Stantillo was speaking—he had what looked like unsystematic bits of hardened nonsense spackled upon mouth, his lips—he had crap everywhere, all over his face, like somebody smashed a handful of dampened oats on his mug just before he got on the elevator, and a gargantuan hairdryer greeted him upon exiting. I live in a ga*rage* and maintain an unsoiled survival and these—fuck it. I found the image as grotesque as Stantillo's snot, genuinely contemplated leaving, but the guy in charge of training waddled in and I got stuck.

***

The trainer, man—guy went by Robert Reinstrudle, no joke, and doubtless he was a demon of unworkable duplication. The Rein didn't arrive until quarter past eight—guy stormed in wildly, face red and sweating like a mule—eighteen degrees and he be streamin'. Besides that, he was wearing a pair of these steamed up child molester-type spectacles that creeped the hell out of me. I felt like running to Macy's and buying the guy a new shirt, but like I said, I'm flat broke. His dress shirt was restrictive to his torso—one of those stylish pink oxfords with a white collar—problem was he'd either missed, or broken a crucial button in the middle of his abdomen. Two lonely, curly stomach hairs were poking all over the joint and his bellybutton was exposed. I imagined his stomach to look like a wooly dartboard—bellybutton bull's-eye surrounded by perfectly ringed stretch marks. I don't know—if I were an awkwardly sweaty kid I'd probably think about wearing an undershirt or smearing my gut with some goddamn deodorant or something. The Rein had no qualms regarding his leak factor. But the worst thing about the Rein—aside from the wart clusters on his earlobes—he lugged one of those ancient brown satchels into the room. You know the kind. The kind you see nervous wrecks drag through the Loop all the time. The point is they're dying to maintain the illusion that they're on the verge of breaking the big one or lugging around fifty pounds of magical mathematical formulas destined to result in reasonably priced cold fusion power production, but the truth is those satchels are jammed with betting receipts from some filthy dog track in the middle of Iowa, or apple cores, at best. It's why they're never opened in public—tis a bluff. Rein stashed his big brown in the corner and took nervous glances in two minute rotations, as expected. I felt rather horrible for the guy, and wished he wasn't so.

"Welcome welcome welcome!" He said, clapping his thick mitts together twice per welcome, "My name is Robert Reinstrudle and b*o*y does this look like a hungry group! Hungry for suc*cess*! You know what I love to see? Hungry faces ready to tackle the world! And judging by instinct, it seems that's ex*act*ly what we have here. Is it? Am I right? Is everybody excited?"

"Yeah!" Everyone screamed, louder than expected, but not loud enough, apparently.

"I said—is eve-ry-bo-dy ex*cit*ed?" Rein asked, rocking his syllable-styled claps once more. He'd plopped himself in this rolling chair and a pair of extra-wide, tassel strewn black dress shoes propelled his body across the room. He was pretty smooth, I admit. A roll chair legend, could teach a class: Making It Hurt 101. Rein was leaking away and wolfing for wind like I couldn't believe, rolling along at roughly three miles per hour, cornering like a dream, through the rows, is he foaming at the mouth? Nope, t'was a smeared pastry scenario. "I'll ask one more time. Is eve-ry-bo-dy ex*cit*ed?"

"Yeah!" Everyone screamed yet again. After the unison cheer settled, ole boy Phil—he stood.

"I know it's probably not my place to ststand and interrupt," he said, face flushed to hell, hands quivering a bit, "But I just want to say that I'm *ready*! I'm ready to be suc*cess*ful! I've spent my entire aaadult life as an elementary school principal at The Lady of Our Mother and, and—I don't really ever want to talk about wah-what I went through, I mean about education and wah-what kids, I mean—nevermind. I'm just saying I'm ready to re*rest*art my life and tackle the business world! Who's with me?" And, astoundingly, everyone in the room went bonkers about how ready they were to be suc*cess*ful. I should have eyed Stantillo as a broken principal from the get go. It was pretty obvious the students from The Lady of Our Mother mangled Phil's confidence something fierce. His face was terror-stricken when he brought it up. He reminded me of my elementary school principal in that regard. Whatever his scenario, there's no chance Stantillo experience at The Lady of Our Mother rivaled the cruelty of my elementary school. Minds came into that place as optimistic, gleaming beacons of hope, and, eight years later—departed as heartless, cynical machines, proficient in the art of malicious mocking aggression, equally experienced as both victim and antagonist, blind to authority, and eerily wise to the ways of the world. Nobody came out of that joint scared to fight man—*no*body. Any sign of weakness could be used for years to come, so backing down from confrontation was never an option.

"That's *j*ust the attitude we're looking for!" Rein said, "And I won't be surprised if you wind up as the most successful individual in this entire class. Remember that name people, Phil Stan—Standstill—I'm sorry, what's the proper pron—"

"It's Stantillo!" I said.

"Thanks Anthony, right, remember that name, class—Phil Stands*tilla*. Because that's ex*act*ly what we need, lots of Standstillas. We need 'em by the *h*undreds—people who l*i*ve to achieve, l*i*ve to be superstars! People who l*i*ve—just like Pete here," Rein said, waving a fat finger in Stantillo's direction.

"It's Phil."

"Whatever. Does anybody think they'll be a better agent than him? Do you? If you honestly think you have a chance, let me hear it! Go ahead, Phil had the machismo. What are you people bringing to the table? Anything? C'mon folks, let's get some energy flowing, positive juices people, we hired you for *pos*itive juices. Well go ahead folks, let loose!" And, incredibly, everybody went wild about all sorts of exaggerated nonsense. It took forty seconds for everyone to stop whooping it up. By the time the proles settled down, The Rein had rolled himself behind his walnut desk in the front of the room. He accidentally propped his stomach on the ledge and the remaining buttons of his shirt held on for dear life—the scene was almost too agonizing to observe. Rein snagged a Snickers bar from the top drawer, his stubby hands tore it open with the ferocity of a caffeinated chipmunk attacking a late season acorn and, after swallowing a mouthful of spit, he jumped back into his spiel—

"Wow! I mean, wow-*wee*! Can I just say I have ne*ver* seen a training class like this in-my-life! I haven't, that's the dog-gone truth. I'm *so* excited to be a part of this, *so* excited to welcome you all to the team, and *so* excited that all of you are *so* exc*i*ted!" he said, and people start hooting all over again. "I want to start things off by telling you a little about myself, a little about how I came to work at Pensury Insurance—twenty years and counting," he said, standing, rising to his tiptoes for the 'twenty years and counting' part, throwing a wink towards the class, mouthing the second half of his Snickers bar and crashing down upon his chair as though his femurs had instantly shattered upon his effort to stand. "When I'm done with *my* story, we'll go around the room so all of you can share *y*our stories—interesting personal facts maybe, and how you decided to choose Pensury as the institution you'll dedicate the rest of your *lives* to." I winced. "Okay, I'm sure you're all *d*ying to know my story, so—"

So Rein went ahead and droned on with his life story, his favorite parts at least. He frenzied himself on his love for women's volleyball, rare leather, being a party king and, of course, the love of his life: networking amongst insurance industry professionals. Good times good times. Upon the fastening of his face our focus settled upon Abraham, Hank—some chirpy-looking cat in the first row. I watched this fellow the whole time Rein jabbered along. It was pretty obvious Abe was just *dying* to talk—his legs were bouncing all over the place during the Rein's speech. Hank Abraham was first alphabetically. People who've spent their entire lives atop alphabetical lists are usually impatient as hell. I went to grammar school with this one guy, Bill Budrift, whose face always turned bright red if a teacher decided to do something reverse-alphabetical. It'd ruin his entire day—he'd yack about the decision at recess, in the hall, during gym—it was like, hello? *N*obody cares—in a high-flung opera voice—*nobody ca*res, *noooobody caaaaares*—who cares? Not me. But yeah, HA reminded me of Budrift—I could tell he went through the roof when Rein went standard-alphabet. He pumped his fist beneath his desk—a serious, yet not unexpected, ouch.

Rein indicated Hank could speak from his seat, but HA insisted upon speaking at the *pod*ium. He opened his speech with the resolution that *he*, not *Phil*, would head the class as Pensury's top producer. He carried the prediction into some predictable story about how he'd been *d*ying to get involved in insurance sales since he was ten years old and how this 'exc*iti*ng opportunity' is a dream come true. I was in the mood to pronounce—rumors indicate the long awaited blowjob convention arrives at McCormick Place next week, do register—but didn't bother. I never bother saying jazz like that aloud. Someone usually utters something in that regard four minutes later and everyone goes wild about what a 'funny guy' they are. I prefer not to be known as a '*f*unny guy'—I don't want to be known at *all*, actually. After Budrift part deux stopped chirping along, the telephone game picked up twenty-six similar stories before settling upon my head at ten o'clock.

"Actually folks, I'm surprised this has worked out as fittingly as it has," Rein said, "Well, almost so. I wanted you to introduce yourself last, Anthony, but it appears you trump Stantilla from an alphabetical standpoint. Would you mind if Stantilla introduces himself before you?"

"Not at all."

"See folks, Anthony Riedie, the guy with the sandy blonde hair before Stantilla there—you might not be able to read his nametag," Rein said, chuckling a bit—I'd doodled random caricatures all over the thing.

"Sorry about that—doodling is such a silly nervous habit of mine. They're never very good," I said, flipping the name tag facedown on the table. Nobody said anything, so I said, "Well, hello everyone. Yes, I'm Anthony Riedie." I forced a painfully gigantic smile to appear on my face, and without desiring to, wondered how long it would take my body to explode upon the cold ground below had I opted for a soaring leap out the plate glass window. I wondered what I would think about on the way down, wondered if the people in the room would remain working there, or be forever turned off.

Rein smiled even wider and said: "Mr. Riedie comes to Pensury h*i*ghly-touted. Mr. Monahan, V.P. of sales told me—what has it been? You've been in the insurance industry for only four years but met twelve years worth of quotas while working as an agent?"

"Something like that."

"Something like that? Ha! Look at this guy! Talented *and* modest. That's a great recipe for success, as I'm sure you know full well," Rein said, throwing a genuine grin and a double thumbs-up in my direction. Man, did I feel confused. As I glanced around the room and noticed all the new hires looking at me, each of them smiling big, sincere smiles, I felt—I felt my throat seal and couldn't get a breath past my chin. A white flash carried itself through my vision and my heart began hammering away with uncontrollable irregularity. As Rein continued, I was on the verge of passing out—

"That's three hundred percent per month, people. Three *hun*dred percent per month for four years. That's forty-eight consecutive months, as all you mathematics majors will have me know, of sheer *d*omination. So in a sense, it's like he hit one hundred percent of goal as an agent for one hundred and forty four consecutive months. I'm sure anyone who has been involved in business of any sort understands how huge those numbers are. Anthony has an astounding track record—and this is why we've hired him to manage you all. We hired him to make you the best because he *is* the best. He was the best candidate out of a pool of two hundred great ones. What is going to happen is he's going to go through the same training class as you all, so you'll get to know each other quite well before working together in the trenches, you as agents, and him as your district manager. So yes, do you mind if we save you for last and let Stantilla introduce himself before you? Is that alright, Anthony? It's just—Dan has told me such great things."

"Those were all lies."

"What?"

"I said I'm not surprised."

"O—well is that alright then? If Stantillo goes first I mean?"

"Yeah, sure, that's perfect Robert." I was surprised at how unhealthy my voice sounded, hearing it aloud. It sounded as if I were about to cry—with the word perfect, my voice cracked, and thankfully, no one else seemed to notice. I cleared my throat, ran my hand through my hair, over my face, paused and pressed my eyes hard enough to envision a white flash, and said, "Actually, my throat is pretty scratchy right now. You mind if I run for a glass of water before I speak? Stantillo and I have already met."

"Okay yeah, sure. But don't be too long, huh? I want to get things moving along as soon as possible. We have a lot to cover this morning."

"I understand completely." I stood, snagged my frayed navy pea coat off the back of my chair, placed it over my shoulders, grabbed my bag, and walked to the front of the room. Surprisingly, nobody seemed to find it odd that I would choose to wear my coat and bag to grab a glass of water. As I placed my hand upon the silver doorknob, I figured I'd say something in case anybody was suspicious. "Anybody else want any water or coffee or anything? I'd be happy to grab some for you. Chips? A candy bar or anything?" A modicum of declarations indicated that water and treat were not needed, so I opened the door and split through the threshold. I spun around at the last second, said, "I'll be right back," and shut the door gently behind me. I walked hurriedly, half-consciously down the hallway, major focus being my breathing, psyche tearing onward: you fucking promised you wouldn't do this, you swore you would work. What is wrong with you man?

I stopped abruptly at Ms. Moon's desk. "Carol? Carol! Ms. *Moon!*" She tried to wave me off, but I wasn't having it.

"Listen, I told you, I have to call you back. Be*cau*se. A new hire is standing here and he needs something. No, he's standing here. I have to call you back. How many times do I need to tell you? For the eightieth time, I don't *care*—you decide. Lis—you're not *hear*ing me! Good*bye*. Yeah, you too," she said, and the phone went slam. "What do you need, Anthony?"

"When you see Reinstrudle, I don't know. Just tell him I'm sorry, okay? Tell Mr. Monahan sorry as well. Tell him he hired the wrong guy, could you? He seemed like a nice enough guy—couldja tell him that? Couldja tell him that I'm sorry? I just can't do this anymore."

"Do what anymore?"

"I don't even know," I said, looking past her, "And hey, I really hope I wasn't an asshole this morning. All I needed was a little help, and I sincerely tried to treat you politely." I inhaled a deep breath, turned, and my heels clicked half way across the cold tile floor before I abruptly stopped, exhaled, and circled back. "And you know what, Carol? That janitor, the one I observed you deride so inconsiderately about the water dispenser—I know I don't personally know him or anything, but you know what? Don't do that anymore. Just because he doesn't stick up for himself doesn't give you the right."

Upon uttering my suggestion, a small shouting match ensued—Ms. Moon did the shouting, trumping her decibel level on a sentence by sentence basis, and I stood unusually immobile, patiently eavesdropping on the strained vocal chords of a lifelong screamer. "Finished?" I asked, when she'd finally run out of breath.

"Just you wait," Carol said, and as I walked toward the elevator the phone receiver was expediently placed to her ear, and a four digit number dialed with the crimson tip of her right index finger.

After what seemed ages, the elevator doors opened, I got on, and upon their closure I observed the brassy reflection of minor tap dancing movements while enjoying an uninterrupted ride to the lobby. Not surprisingly, upon the opening of the doors, I was greeted by a beefy, paste-white, cross-armed, leaned-back fellow with a shaved head and was advised, "Name's Earl McManus. I'm head of security in this building, been that way every-single-day for the last ten years, bud—every-single-day. Don't even think about getting any wise ideas, pal. Ms. Moon called in while you were waiting for elevator number four. We heard about the ruckus you caused upstairs, and I had to interrupt the eating of my bacon, egg and cheese sandwich to rush over here and greet your ignorant-ass." His breath was hotter, more wretched than Stantillo's had been, so I walked quickly toward the main entrance, obstructing the airflow from his mouth by twisting my head down and to the side. "Don'tchu even think about stepping foot back in this building, ever, bub, and that's a warning you *bet*ter heed, cause if you don't—" The 'thuh, thuh, thuh', of the revolving door masked my consequence before the opportunity to not care presented itself. Be it mid-morning, early February, post brainstorm: probably shouldn't have quit the job, Anthony—in case you forgot, you possess zero dollars—I deduced circumnavigation of the Loop via stroll in the company of uncontrollable tangent-styled thoughts to be my best option.

I took a very, very deep breath, gazed at the crisp blue sky once more, and began to stroll. "My, what a good day for a walk outside—deep breaths," I said to myself, "Deeply inhaled, dramatically exhaled breaths of air is all the medication my mind needs in order to mend these tattered, threadbare thoughts of what shall become of someone, anyone, everyone, everything for which existence is currently granted. Streetwalk thought of: is this for naught?—feelings fraught and intentions forgot—just might take me a sweet, non-involved walk—just gaze at the trees, their wafting dead leaves—but how foolish I was in pretending to be, the least bit capable of non-comparative deliberation between the lifecycle of leafs, and wayfaring me.

The mid-morning scene showed little difference than that of daybreak. Mother Nature was frigid and ruthless. And the city, our city, with its typical style of half-beauty, half-horror—hug me, or crush me? Kiss me or kill me?—she seemed in the mood to devour any and all creatures at their first sign of weakness. The only people around were those obliged to be: blue collar peeps groovin' their grind—white collar peeps tryin' t' save time—destitute cats beggin' for dimes—completely different stories, completely different minds. And that—in the midst of our respective wanders, our meandering moseys, all that jazz—that's when you and I caught one another. So yes, it's quite nice to see you. Not to offend, but you look a touch less than magical at the moment. But I guess this is what it's all about: random steps in random directions at random times. They determine our dissimilar destinies and make life worth living. Thing is, most people never step *any*where—and if they do step, it's on eggshells. I'm glad you're not one of those—we wouldn't be here had you been. And so now that we're here, just you, me, this bitchin' ass jukebox and a little bit of flame—let's get to it. I'll tell the story, you pick the grooves. I'll try not to disappoint mate—here goes.

1

The steady sound of sirens cutting through the cold winter night meshed rightly with the cursed, shadowy face in the bricks staring down upon me—I would sleep on my left side to avoid eye contact with this Cydonian outcropping of crumbling plaster and stone, but in accordance to ice pick sharp pains felt within my shoulder, I'm fairly certain that collar bone was slightly cracked in a bicycle accident long since past—laying to the left is a no go. I twist-turned, producing a crunching sound from the plucked frozen feathers knitted within my dual folded sleeping bags, and skeletal trees hissed in the swirling winds of unoccupied February darkness. Being that the cold, cold world of Chicago and her winter had unleashed a fearsome wrath, the time had come: nights of no one—not a soul for blocks and the only sound is that of your own solitary footstep reverberating lonely and crooked, commencing as it will with the compressing charge of ice crystals going *crash*—each isolated pace carrying the weight of lonely thoughts and lonelier actions. Walking in the stoic, silent, desolate night, Chicagoans know—every pebble stepped upon, every hint of ice, every crunch of snow sneaking behind thee is to be scrutinized for mal intent.

It was slightly past midnight on this latest Friday morn that sleep was scuttled by the sound of a man standing upon the frozen cinderblocks littering the gangway of my garage— perpetually pacing the imperfect tightrope between them, was an unknown urban predator. T'was a keen acoustic observation of the nervous, involuntary habits of a mammal stalking its prey, made all the more gripping because I had no idea of what the guy actually looked like. One thousand imagined hateful faces and various races filled the hypothetical void connecting chin and cranium, as this creepy individual concealed itself in the shadow of my abode and continued hiding, lurking in the silhouette of the garage—presumably waiting for a profitable target to stroll past.

As the soles of his shoes rustled sharply upon snowy gravel, cig after cig was flicked tersely off the aluminum door, each more forcibly than the last, presumably to match an inner rising frustration from the lack of available game. Foolish of you, I thought, to leave behind such an abundance of viable DNA blueprints via saliva born residue—didn't think this through, did you?—and his high pitched, child-like voice intermittently squeaked to itself, all the while mentioning illogical non-sequiturs before growing quiet with the echo of distantly approaching, heeled footsteps.

He tapped his feet quickly and without distinct rhythm, perhaps in an effort to generate warmth, and I imagined a speedy, lean, spry sort of fool who would be difficult to corral. Moments later, after the presupposed casualty never materialized, he plopped down heavily against the brick wall with a heaping exhale, and I pictured a hefty sort of fellow, intent on smothering his victims with a Haus-like maneuver.

Uncertain of what to do, I shivered hard, base layer slightly damp with sweat from the exertion of laying irrationally still—the last thing I wanted was to make a peep and have this menace ascertain the fact that I was mere inches away. Surprise is strategically crucial across all elements of life, especially aggression—I figured while he was busy plundering his victim, I could easily sneak up from behind and end him with an accessory.

My bladder was brimful and in an effort to cross my legs as an auxiliary twist-tie, I accidentally kicked the hatchets. Sharp iron edges clanged clumsily shrill. I breathed deep, held my inhalation, and exhaled slowly, steam tumbling out my nostrils as my heartbeat implored this motherfucker to scram.

Within arms reach I keep a small Gerber throwing hatchet for a left-handed huck at the upper torso, you know, to control the destiny of my personal wellbeing, and to provide distraction and immediate pain, followed by the bulky, weighty, nameless hammer/axe in my right hand, and its devastatingly accurate strike through the center of the skull—but no, none of this was necessary. Slow motion, momentary silence was severed as the individual in question, seemingly spooked—he suddenly stood, and the back of his nylon coat went chafing up the frosty brick wall with a brusque swoosh. He lingered for a moment, unzipped, and took a long, wide-strewn leak off the building next door before staggering all short-stepped down the ice-strewn alleyway, and heading for a different roost. I suddenly couldn't help but wish for an uncontaminated conscience and the right to judge and execute, but a multiplicity of fault-laden incidents renders this first strike line of reasoning staunchly hypocritical, and thereby moot.

I squeezed my numb, balled-up-in-the-glove hands between my thighs and shuddered uncontrollably. As was truth, I felt as though I was freezing from the outside in, extremities icing over and immobilizing by the minute—cold reaching inward like a spider web—only a small matter of time before wrapping its placid grasp round my heart and freezing it solid. I ignited a black Bic, illuminated the zipper to my front door, exited the tent, put on my moccasins, jumped around real fast for a few tics, snuck out the side door of the garage and tiptoed 'round the corner, deployed a territorial pissing, slipped back indoors, put on two more zip-up sweaters for a total of five, and dove back onto the sleeping bags and under a posse of quilts like a maddened bear, curled up and ready to go dark.

Breathe, beat, shiver and dream.

Not quite dawn, some drunken fireballer whipped a bottle off the neighboring garage door on three, four separate junctures, until it finally shattered, resounding sound of which jolted me awake with a start. I was then subjected to a smattering of late night, helter-skelter heckling bounding off brick, and an ode of: "Fuck this city! Do you hear me? Huh? Fuck this city!" The slurred words of what sounded to be an angry, middle-aged Caucasian male faded southbound with his galloping gait. I speculated his folly and closed my eyes—the room was just as dark as it had been with eyelids open.

Breathe, beat, shiver and dream.

The faint sound of sirens fading south on Western Avenue, a jet engine, screeching, decelerating breaks, enthusiastically accelerating engines, rust-strewn, wind-shoved swings, adult, middle name included orders and scattered, pursuit-orientated, childlike laughter made their way through my aluminum garage door and my mosquito-netted tent. And O, yes—overwrought, enlivened sniffing—probably from the same goddamn dog that habitually sniffs his nose through the tiny crack at the bottom of my garage door—his nose had gone wild, a scant thirty-some inches from where my head lay. I don't know why it is so, but this dog has a tendency to sniff this garage for extended durations each and every day, just shy of six in the morn. The owner just stands there, feet having come to a crunching halt, and now planted firmly upon the ice-speckled gravel: "Whatcha smellin girl? What's in there girl? That's a good girl, go*o*d girl!" the voice goes, as I hear this big ole terd plop just beyond my nose. Poop goes unpicked and I long to yell, "The number one food source for urban rats is dog feces, pal!" My curdling, empty stomach knows it shall be less than ten minutes before it is cringing at the distinct sound of excited rat claws upon cold, icy concrete, and the ensuing sound of sharp jagged teeth tearing into a crunchy, frozen on the outside, mushy warm on the in, defecated rodent delicacy du jour—swank baby, swank.

"I'm fucking out of here, man," I said to myself.

When I leave the crib, I'm out early and absent from the premises until well after dusk. You can't have people seeing you walk into a garage and not come out until the next day—old Chicago neighborhoods are filled with all sorts of suspicious motherfuckers, as should be the case. If you make a habit of listening to the police scanner while leaned back on an ole Sherlock, you'll die about some of the circumstances people ring in: "The guy in the apartment above me—he's just using the toilet way too much. Can you send someone over?" It's endless—better storylines than television, and good exercise for the imagination—mixed with calls of graphic, substance fueled violence, there rains a huge slew of weird spies incessantly lusting to bust you, me, anybody and everybody for the slightest misgiving. Victims, witnesses, perpetrators, dispatchers, cops, medics—thousands of their stories air in a given night—strained emotion funneling their voices into occasional corny humor in an attempt to assuage the chronic desperation—so many lives, so many life events, right here, right now, frolicking wild under the tacit, unspeaking night sky of assumed lucidity. See, this is why I try to come and go quiet and unnoticed—I long to live off the grid, and people are wary weirdoes—but then again:

I popped out the tent, pressed play, and in the background pumped lightly audible proper licks and jazzy drums from the 'Birth of the Cool'. The initial track—'*Move*'—set me in motion as fresh socks, crisp drawers, and my woolen hat sat elevated above the Coleman camping grille, resting across a small pot of evaporating water, preparing to greet my chilly, recently awoken head. You can only run the grille for a handful of minutes so as to avoid an excess of carbon monoxide build up and subsequent suffocation in this unventilated, rectangular domicile, so I try to blast it fast, move around, and hit the road.

I seized the least rumpled 'business casual' outfit I could find in one hand, and snagged a short lifetime worth of writing in the other—twelve extended journals filled with bona fide tall tales of fable-like creatures of localized fame, and a semi-associated manuscript—I jammed the whole of it all snugly inside my bag, right beside a Ziploc pouch of hygienic materials, pocketed a pen, set the earth alight, double checked that I had all I would need for the entire day, killed the stove, sent an ace up my sleeve, buttoned my coat cuff to prevent accidental slippage, and exited the side door dressed in as many layers as would be needed for an extended hike.

2

Cracking the door, I stole a look at what the morning presented: an enlivened, crimson civil twilight had caused a few meager wisps of clouds to catch fire. "Nice," I said to the sun, still a degree or two below the horizon, "C'mon round n' light her up—set this blue sky ablaze," and looking down, I noticed a mass of smoked-down-to-the-filter Newport cigarettes, and a collection of footprints the size of a goddamn yeti. I was glad I didn't wind up having to fight that heap of a cunt down to the death—glad he moved on without incident. I imagined having to explain my activities to a harebrained detective—"What do you *mean* you were sleeping in the garage when—" a whole slew of cops digging through what little I have, excavating my pockets, reading my material—"Ay, ay boss, read this paragraph—I think we might have a premeditated *killer* on our hands," busy eyes pouring over my photos—"What's with all this?" I told you, this is my office, and my home—I'm living like this because I'm trying to be terribly frugal and creative and I absolutely flat out refuse to work for people or institutions I don't respect unless I'm purposely decreasing their profit margin according to self-appraised principals while fulfilling my own, separate work, on their premises at the very same instant. The only way I can save up the loot and produce proper, strong material to create my own institution for manipulation is if I live as an urban survivalist for a minute, and I'm doing so—it's fully logical.

This flash meditation in the books, I locked the door and turned around—flush into the face of a heavyset woman with a bent cigarette smoldering in a crooked smear of burgundy lipstick, and short, spiky hair, dyed nearly the same color as her mouth.

"Well! How are *ju* this morning?"

"Whoa! Hi there—quiet down, Jesus—you practically scared me to death right there," I said, trying to think of something normal to say. I recognized her voice. The people across the yard, neither of whom I had laid eyes upon—they often have loud, early morning arguments about money—their lack thereof. The woman has a heavy Latina accent and the guy sounds like a fairly busted-out white dude in his fifties—likely a lifetime smoker from the sound of his merciless hacking cough. Whenever he yells I visualize the face of a guy I rode my bicycle past on Ashland and Blackhawk last summer—this busted motherfucker in his late forties, with an old, rutted up mug and rusty colored hair, stringy like random crops of twisted wires sprouting from a flaky orb of bleached concrete. His sticky, bent figure was dressed in beaten down, dirty garb and he was smoking a square all harsh in the dense humidity, leaned back on a bench, waiting for the #9 south to 95th. His sweaty face leered angrily into my own while a severely dehydrated, golden rainbow, launched skyward from somewhere deep inside a tangled bush of gnarled black hair and spattered the scalding asphalt in loud drops, just past the tip of his tattered boots.

"Are ju okay? Are ju frozen?"

"What do you mean?"

"What ju th*i*nk I mean?" she asked.

"O, I get it—you think?—you think I was? O no, it's not like that—I'm not a bum or anything. I work for a publicly traded company—that sounds corny, I know, but it's not like I'm living in there. I just wanted to make the right decision and not drive drunk last night. I rent this garage legally."

"Ju do?"

"Yeah—from ZTZ Properties—you know, same jerks as you."

"And ju got a car that fits in there? I never seen no tire tracks in the snow."

"Well—you know."

"Don't worry—a secret safe with me, baby." She was suddenly gazing at me with a look of wanton hunger about her face. "I live right across the way. Apartment 2R. I'm always home during the day—I got nutting much to do."

"Well, maybe I'll see you around or something. I have to get to work."

"Wait—I'm Esmeralda"

"O—well, my name's Keith. Keith Swinehart the 3rd—like I said, maybe I'll see you—now that I know exactly where you live." I almost screwed up and said some shit like: hey, by the way, don't tell anybody you saw me come out of the garage, and maybe I'll swing past—but I didn't. Never end a conversation by placing secondary emphasis upon an initial presumption that perhaps you're up to no good—it immediately places you at a power disadvantage. What you do, if possible, is think of human nature—look a person dead in the face while employing a ridiculous, authoritative sounding surname, and try to subtly insinuate, with both your eyes, and tone, that you might, just *might* be willing to burn their house down and coldly wipe their seed from the earth if you're improperly fucked with—and then you leave cordially.

3

I exited the little side fence on Iowa, crossed Western, walked east for a block, and beyond the wind driven snow, the view that was captured by my eyes was that of a prim Chevy Tahoe recreating a south-facing lean-back on Oakley. A semi-fractured-looking individual was all up on the driver side window, speaking just a decibel or two too loudly about grams and whatnot. "Keep it fuckin low nigga, or I ain't gonna' be rollin' up here f'drops no mo. We can't do this 'round my crib cuz all.'em new blue lights, so be cool." I sauntered past with my head dead noon, relaxed and lighthearted. Whenever you stumble upon drug deals in mid swing I feel it's best not to deviate from the natural flow. If you continue past but turn the face away, you look suspicious. Turn toward and you look nosy. Turning completely full-round to avoid the situation is far too abrupt and obvious, and the suspect is liable to assume you obtained their license plate and that you're going to call the cops, which of course may result in several quantifiable problems for your wellbeing. That's why you simply stroll past, unperturbed and not gawking, like a possible client. Gravy.

I paced on and driving tactfully down the potholed street in an old piece of shit was a plucky fellow with a rusty shovel bungee corded atop a banged up trunk. A gleaming mound of snow upon his rooftop was in the process of a measured reduction with each jolt of his front end, and his windows were wide open. I was walking at roughly the same speed, just an arm's length away when the final movement of Schubert's String Quintet came to a harmonious halt, and Grape's illustrious voice came over the airwaves and stated, "The time is precisely six twenty-nine."

"WFMT?"

The car stopped, an old pair of bushy grey eyebrows went aloft and, "Glad you know it, young man!—classical music is very lost on much of today's youth. You been to Orchestra Hall? Do you listen to classical music on the radio?"

"Yes and yes—my whole childhood and forever after."

"Wow, that's great—take care now!" he said, and he quickened the pace of his pistons to that of a speed walking Lincoln Park mother in her thirties, late for a latte, and eager to gossip. He hand signaled ninety degrees at the stop sign, tumbled westbound on Rice, and symphonic overtones recoiled against the old walls of the jaw dropping, don't build 'em like that anymore, edifice of St. Nicholas. Its Byzantine-Slavonic style and the thirteen copper onion domes, weathered to green, push their crosses high into the limitless sky in representation of Christ and the 12 apostles rising to a place called heaven. Along the north side of the building, a color splitting stretch of stained glass windows had set the daybreak of the icy alleyway to that of an insanely intricate kaleidoscope. The colors sent me drowning in memories—drivin' past at sunset, sitting front seat in my grandfather's heaping soda truck on the handful of special occasions that he took me along for an afternoon of deliveries in hard-bitten locations. I couldn't help but feel like a big man then, feet hangin' high above the floor, watching the toughest guy I knew violently revolve a steering wheel bigger than me as we toured Chicago streets. Strolling on, I wished he could have hung around a few years to watch me grow big—at least a few more cold weeks in '85 to have finally seen the Bears win the Superbowl, but, you know, those bells ring at the oddest times.

I continued south, passed a hotdog stand, and turned the corner on Chicago Avenue to the sound of traction-less tires whirling in place upon ice-packed pavement. Muffled orders of an older man to "Go! Go! Go!" cracked sharp, and he shoved with all his might, tendons quivering along the lower rim of his neck and, "Aw damn it! You woulda got it! We practically had it! Why'd ya let off the gas?"

The smell of burning rubber and a squall of steam filled the newly sunlit, frozen air as an old lady peeked her concerned face out the salty driver's side door of an old Buick Park Avenue and asked, "Is it out?"

"Of course not! You let off the gas too early—how many years do we have to go through this? How many winters? Jesus friggin' Christ!—I swear this city is gonna' kill me." The old man was exasperated and breathing very heavily—his face was pink and he made me chuckle. "I'll dig a 'lil bit more around that back tire—maybe then we'll be home free."

I tossed my bag against a heap of snow and said, "Yo—hey sir, you want a hand bustin' out? I bet we could push her outta here easy, man, you and me, if we give her a big go together."

"Couldja? Aw, that'd be a big help—you're a big help. Ay Maude! Ay!" She again peeped a head of pink curlers stiffly out the window, and her eyes looked tired and cold. "We got a 'lil help now. Now listen—when we get it rockin', don't lay off the goddamn gas 'til she's out. You blew it last time—but don't go blowin' her up, either—that's the last thing I need. Just try and keep her steady at about three thousand RPM's, no more, n' don't let off 'til I yell or we're free."

We lined up, each on one side of the bumper, like sprinters ready to charge out of frozen blocks, and he yelled, loud enough for everybody to hear, "Okay—one, two, thr*ee!*" Wheels whirring, the man's face banged into the bumper with an awkward clunk. The palms of his black leather gloves slipped off the cold metal trunk with his initial push, and I strained to move the old, weighty sedan. I got it to rock, just a hint of a hint, and the lady compressed the gas, good and consistent—the old man jumped back in the game like a wily old bottle rocket, grunting, shoving rearward with his ass against the bumper, hot blood leaking from his nose, down his lips, and gently dotting a small circle of ashen snow to look like the closed wings of a contented ladybug.

I pushed with all my might, leaning hard with my shoulder—and eyes rolling backward the sky appeared watery blue and lightly patterned with thin, fragmented, lava red clouds, steadily windswept and clean and tearing apart—

—*Whurr!*

"She's loose!" he yelled, "Cut it Maude! Cut it!"

"Woo! Alright, man," I said, patting the old chap's shoulder. He pulled his glove off his hand, ran a stark white finger below his nostrils, shook his head at the deep hue of red, quickly gathered his shovel, threw it in the back seat, and opened the driver's side door.

"O my gosh! Honey! Are you okay?"

"Well Maude, you were right—we shouldn't have parked on Chicago, goddamn it! Plowed us right in. Move on over, I'm drivin'—O! And hey," he said, hanging out the door, waiving back at me, "Thanks pal—once again, thanks a ton. You mighta just saved me a heart attack—unless I'm strung up at the doc's in an hour or two."

"Heh, hopefully not—ain't no thing, though—have a day."

4

As I pondered the odds stacked against attaining old age, I picked up my bag and progressed eastward. Passing Leavitt, a little girl—full body enveloped in a puffy purple one piece—her bubbly red head was seated quite contentedly in a matching Radio Flyer, and she flew up the snow covered curb in wild fashion. Her lilac, mitten covered hands clapped madly at the effort to overtake the snowdrift, and she smiled widely in acceptance of the risk of capsizing. It made me glad that such behavior was being imparted to her as admirable by her father. He chuckled hard and hauled on through the dawnlight shadows at a rapid clip.

Still rather cold and in need of relief, I figured I would jog to manufacture some semblance of heat. I quickly built up steam and breezed past the wild assortment of mostly Latino, mom and pop shops dotting Chicago Avenue between Damen and Ashland. An emaciated, balding Caucasian man in a plain white T standing outside a recently graffitied condo building just west of Walcott was demanding entrance, waving his hands wildly and threatening the woman at the door with a flathead screwdriver. Ashen vapor gushed off his quivering, hairy shoulders as he defiantly yelled, "You'll live to regret this!" before hailing an approaching Yellow cab, and launching his body stiffly through the rear door.

Continuing on past the remarkably defunct Viva Plaza and shuttered Alvin Theater, two thirsty-looking fellows in their fifties wearing blue-green workman overalls stood casually in front of the Downtown Tap Room. A dirty, impatient, sun-soaked face said, "This is the problem when seven in the morning is the beginning of your evening—everywhere ya go ya wind up at least fifteen minutes ahead of schedule."

"You don't work in a steel mill on Cortland Avenue, do ya?" a man asked, eyeing me up.

"Nope," I said, "I don't."

"Good, kid, you got it good—don't ever apply," the man retorted, face discomfited as he slowly stretched his arms above his back—they both had a chuckle and I moved along.

Next door down, a husky young G with sagging pants cheerfully whished me, "Good morning!" as he gruffly pushed open the unwilling to budge, oxidized chain gate protecting Mucho Fashion, and prepared to get an early start on business. "Yo man—we got some new Sean Jean last night—mad sick," he said, "You can get first dibs—come on in."

"Thanks mate, but I ain't with it."

"Well, if you know somebody who is, do me a favor n' drop the *word* B!"

"Sure thing."

Ahead of schedule, I hung a right on Ashland and ran two blocks to the crusty gas station on the corner of Huron. Standing outside, a couple of young Latino kids in salty Timberland boots were rocking a roe shambo to see who'd buy the cigarettes. Rock smashed scissors twice and I walked in ahead of them, held the door, grabbed a pack of gum, and got in line behind two working men in their mid thirties, a good handful of years older than me. "Why can't you jus get a 'lil scratch saved and get outta town two weekends from now? We'll go up to the Dell's er some shit—nobody'll be 'round n' they got some decent strip clubs up there. Plus them lonely Wisconsin broads are probably desperate n' willing in the winter. We'll roll up all big city-like n' get our smash on, man!"

"Shit, I got probation fees, court costs, lawyer fees, gotta get my whip fixed—"

"Shit, you sound like me last month," retorted a man with hands like hams, and then, "Lemme get foteen on three and a Swisha, a single—I got some good," he said, refusing to mince words regarding his intent. "You think our lungs are black, man?"

"Shit, prolly—"

"And hey, man," he said to the deadpan Arab face behind bulletproof glass, "Where you hidin' them Auto Weekly's? I'm gonna' snag one on the way out."

"You *still* lookin' for a good price on a white Cadillac?"

"'Til the day I die."

The Arab pointed to the rack, they moved along and I shoved a random pack of wintergreen chewing gum and two dollars beneath the glass. "Sun-Time or Trib?"

"Just the gum, man."

"New York Time?"

"Not today."

"We got special on Long John. Three for a dollar."

"Nah, just the gum."

"We got healthy snack, too, now—Clif Bar and Harvest Bar."

"Nah."

"Fresh banana?"

"No man."

"We got special on coffee. One dollar for sixteen ounce. I charge you?"

"It's burnt. This whole room smells like burnt coffee—so no."

"How 'bout for seventy five cent?"

"How 'bout hitting me back my change and easing up? What? Is there a script on your lap? How 'bout next time you quit tryina up-sell me like I'm lost in some Bedouin bazaar, okay? I'm not from out of town."

"How 'bout fuck you—no next time!" His piercing voice shot through a toothy mouth and steamed the glass as an oddly small hand shoved my change angrily beneath the bullet proof glass.

"Fine with me! Jesus—all I'm tryina do is quietly buy some goddamn gum and move along! Is it that difficult? You have enough maniacs in this neighborhood contemplating coming in here with a gallon of gas and lighting you afire to warrant additional, needless instigation highly fruitless. Remember that, or you'll fuckin' burn someday." One of the young Latino kids broke into giddied laughter, and the other used the distraction to shoplift a Mars Bar. I turned, threw the door open with a charge, didn't pay attention to what was being yelled, stuck two sticks of gum in my mouth, shivered hard, and walked north to Chicago, chewing rapid and annoyed. I needed to get my hands on some coffee and wash up.

5

I crossed the busy, energy infused, sunlit intersection of Ashland and Chicago, jogged eastbound upon the slippery, cracked sidewalk for two more blocks, passed the mad randomness of Jerusalem Broad Spectrum Merchandises, and traversed Noble. It was here, just before entering the little café across from the aged, oft maniac-infested waters ala le Ida Crown Natatorium that I stunted my stride to tie my boot beneath a blue awning and its steady protection of a long abandoned storefront, two doors shy of my target. I steadied myself against a tarnished, not opened in ages, black iron chain gait, and lazily gazed through a chain link fence protecting the empty lot next door. There, on an old mattress, slanting sunlight reflecting from a broken window struck half opened eyes, providing instinctive facial recoil in the morning fog of startled initial inertia. An old man with a thick cardboard coverlet encircling his feet grimaced painfully before coughing mournfully in a quiet but mostly uncontrollable series of rolling grunts. Clouds screamed past in sudden shades before recurrent blades of sunlight overtook and ripped into his shadowy, secretive face. He groaned as if he were about to die, so I said, "Yo—yo man—you need me to call somebody, man?" He slowly rolled his head over, growled contemptuously, and said nothing.

I stood, marveled at the nightly low limits of such exposed survivalists, walked two entrances east, entered a little black door and immediately made for the bathroom. The scene was very crowded and bustling for seven in the morning, and the line for sustenance was rather long. I figured I'd wash my face and brush my teeth—get myself at least half way ready for work.

I pushed open a door in the rear of the structure, locked it, threw my bag on the doorknob, immediately disrobed from the waist up, twisted an old time faucet to its maximum release, cupped my hands, and splashed my body with hot, steaming water. Iridescent halogen light illuminated the massive temperature inversion provided by gas heated, rapidly tumbling molecules of hydrogen and oxygen upon my cold, dry skin by emphasizing gentle condensation climbing in miniature, unpredictable loops before diffusing and disappearing mere inches from the launch pad—this felt remarkably fine.

Operating quickly, I removed the shoe and sock of my left foot—the pinkie toe of such, a previous victim of mid-grade mountain orientated frostbite, was deeply red and purple, rather swollen and burning. "You weak little bastard—you always have to give me a hard fucking time, don't you?" Impressing with flexibility, I placed my foot under the faucet and liquefied what felt like a hard little BB of frozen blood congealed along the side and in the tip. I examined my face in the mirror, and its expression and general appearance gave no indication so as to suggest a grand subnormal fraction of my daily activities to be covert or disjointed. "Amazing," I said, shivering hard and powering my way through my breathtakingly warm sink-shower.

An unknown individual tried to get in the door, so I yelled, "It'll be roughly three minutes—sorry." I dried off with paper towels, threw on some deodorant, wet my hair and unsnarled it via frantic waves of five fingered combing, brushed my teeth vigorously quick, threw my sanitary belongings back into the Ziploc, re-dressed in a dash, and split. I opened the door with a bit of a jerk, and the woman waiting appeared startled. "Sorry for the wait."

"That? That was nothing—O, hey," she said, pointing to the corner of her mouth, "I think you left a little toothpaste at the bend."

"Thanks," I said, wiping away, "I appreciate you not being afraid to mention it."

"No problem—I admire your dedication to maintaining a healthy mouth."

"It's a constant battle, you know how dental plans are—the deductible is a killer."

She smiled at me as if I were some extra-spiffy specimen of fine linen and hand carved, platinum silverware, and she said, "You're so right—I think I'm going to start brushing after my morning coffee. It's commendable. See ya around." I couldn't help but chuckle. It's funny—people don't assume I'm living like this. I'm white, see, and the fact that I am lean and strong helps matters because fairly alright-looking white people are never assumed to be living on the fringes in such a manner—that's just a fact. Were I to fit a different description, where would the odds rest on her complaining to supervising powers that I was using the bathroom of the establishment as my personal cleaning quarters? The query left me curious.

6

As soon as I joined the line to order, the voice of a waxy-smiled real estate agent with a greasy forehead speaking to a wary older couple implored, "Just read the literature— like I said, I promise you won't have to flip *anything*! The market is flush with opportunity and, like I said—I mean, if you have some capital to play with—if we have some *chips* to play, what I can do for you is—well, it's endless really. We can make all sorts of moves, see, again, all you have to do is give me the money, commit the capital and—"

I impeded his voice with an imaginary anvil, but to no avail—he kept wailing away, leaned frantically over a myriad of papers and graphs and maps, and I sprightly imagined him dead and gone. What will he leave behind? Quiet. Ah yes—happy, blissful quiet. I wanted to seat myself at the table and tell the couple to save their money and be easy, to simply breathe and live and enjoy their lives and mutually loving interaction frugally—to wriggle off the line before they're drowned, gutted and served—to tell the real estate agent to please leave and quite possibly get bent—but something in their old, frantic eyes seemed to insinuate they'd already sold themselves, and were thereby unable to perceive the realtor's obvious desperation.

"Hi. I want a half egg and cheese sandwich, a cinnamon raisin bagel with extra cream cheese, two scones, five miniature muffins, and a large, whole milk hazelnut latte with three extra shots of espresso." The woman ahead of me in line was pale and soft and oblong and in possession of a haircut not much unlike the tight, white-boy fade this pimp slash traveling barber once issued me in Grant Park, post Blues Fest. I had extremely long hair at the time, and a small group of us and his old buddy passed three bottles of cheap wine and smoked several joints in the time it took for him to chop me, free hand, by way of dim, shadowy streetlight—waking the next day I was shocked that, inebriated and wearing shades, ole boy made certain that not a single hair was out of place. Best chop of my life right there, son, put it on the record.

The woman's phone began ringing an obnoxious, out of tone version of 'Raindrops Keep Falling on my Head', and her hand dove digging through her oversized, designer purse, which was of course loaded with an enormous smattering of consumptive bullshit—just like her body. Age-wise, she was in the summer of her life, but health-wise she appeared as if she was rapidly approaching winter—the cold winds seemed to be blowing on account of her own doing. She didn't reach it in time and she yelled, "Shoot! Hey, you know what, actually—I was good yesterday—why don't you it make ten of those mini muffins instead of five. I was *so* good yesterday. Why not? If I can't finish 'em now I'll eat 'em with lunch, so why the heck not?" she chuckled. I breathed deep, exhaled, and pondered why it is that nobody replies: because you're more than one hundred pounds overweight and frankly I'm in shock that your heart has not seized of yet—you're goddamn killing yourself, one bite at a time, and the joints in your legs can barely support your torso without ripping to shreds—that's why! You can hardly move! Your order contains enough energy to march twenty miles uphill with a fifty pound sack of potatoes. Step back from the edge Ms., please—because once you fall you most certainly will not be getting back up, and I wish you a long, happy, healthy life.

I turned away, sort of saddened, and against the window, a silver-haired father in his mid fifties adorned in blue, vertically striped slacks that stood in staunch contrast to a yellow and white, horizontally lined shirt, and a red, circularly patterned tie was having a conversation with an adolescent daughter he seemed to know very little about. She pulled her long black hair behind her ears, bit tentatively at blue fingernail polish, and he asked, "Do you have a roommate?"

"Yeah."

"Are you friends with her?"

"I like my suitemate, but not my roommate. She has, like, an obsession with the color pink—it's bizarre, she's out of her mind."

"Uh-huh."

"So I hear you're getting married again."

"Your mom told you?"

"Yeah."

"Well, it's true—we had discussed it, and *I* was the one who was supposed to tell you, but yes, it's true. I think it's going to be really fun. Now that we have a place in New York, there's just so much less stress—the distance makes me feel healthier."

"What's she like?—your new fiancée?"

"She's great, you know—your mother just wasn't the right person."

"And neither were my next two step-mothers, were they?"

"I flew in specifically to enjoy some coffee with you, dear. Must you?"

They gazed into the sunlit street for a moment, maybe at the black, shadowed bark of the two naked, motionless trees across four slush and saline-speckled lanes, and she said, "So is pretty much everyone coming to the wedding?"

"Basically—your brothers and sisters, your aunt, nephews, like ten of my friends, a handful of hers—and of course you if you want." He closed his sagging eyes and took a long drink from his steaming cup before asking, "So, do you plan on coming, or not?"

"Sorry, but I can't answer that yet," she said, pushing the base of her palm upon the bridge of her nose and thrusting her thumb and middle finger outwards, across her slim, dark eyebrows, "I'll have to think about it, dad. In some ways, I can't stand to imagine seeing you getting married again, for the third time since mom, making these dramatic vows that you'll only wind up breaking. I mean—how many times over the years have you said you're going to spend time with me, only to cancel and not be heard from for months? Frankly, I doubt I can stand seeing it again—and the only reason you're here drinking coffee with me is because you flew in for business in the Loop today. Let's quit pretending to one another, okay?"

The father gazed at his watch and examined his Blackberry, and just beyond him, a little frozen finch outside the window made a single flap, 180 degree turn atop a parking meter that if played back in slow motion would have shown his little bony feet stick a landing upon ice strewn iron in a style that mauls most Olympic highlights. His eyes met mine, a golden beak chirped twice, and suddenly he raised high into the pin oak across the way, delicate body bounding precariously in the hollow winter wind.

My turn to order had come and a friendly, middle-aged woman with merry eyes, dark hair, and grinning cheeks posed, "Mornin' hun, sorry for the wait—what can I get ya?"

I reached in my bag, handed her my steel thermos, and said, "Hey, mornin'—just a dark roast with a 'lil room if ya could."

"Sure thing—is that all?"

"That n' two pieces a' pumpernickel bread, toasted plain—jam on the side." It was so cold in the garage last evening that after I gathered two singles, six quarters, a dime and a nickel, mentioned, "Keep the change," and dropped the sum into the amicable lady's pink, course, workwoman palm, she subsequently flinched, and said, "*Ooooh*—your change is so cold! These coins are frozen—my gosh!"

"Yeah—it was a cold one last night."

"What?—ya got problems with the heat er somethin'?"

"I guess you can say that," I said, and she handed over the thermos, filled dark and rich, one half inch below the brim, "Which is why I've been looking forward to your delicious, belly warming coffee the whole way here. Thanks a million."

I walked around the counter, mixed my Joe good and proper, and she handed me my toast, hot and crisp, fresh out the coils, "One order of pumpernickel bread, and blueberry jam on a glass plate."

"Nicely done—certainly one of the finer things in life—I appreciate it."

"No problem," she said, and I ascertained a single, concise seat at a table directly in the midst of the idiosyncratic madness.

As soon as I sat, I took a big bite of bread and tried my best to avoid gazing upon a pair of ghastly legs located just a scant ways off to my right. A young girl likely near my age, dark hair pulled firm and knotted behind a bored, tired face—her legs were so ghastly from non-use that really I was having a difficult time *not* looking at them. Atop this, I had two sloppy little kids running wild and screaming up a bloody tantrum to the side of me. Their mother was driving folks mad by catering to their whims at each and every turn—I felt like turning around with a set of crazy eyes and an overly full mouth and proposing that they please shut up, *now*, but naturally, for sake of being civil, I refrained. What she was trying to do was play the part of the new, cute young mother and such, but in all truth the act was dreadfully annoying. She baby-talked more than her babies did, and the only time she cut it was when she made several uninterrupted attempts to make eye contact with a successful-looking man in is his mid-forties, ordering coffee—she was a far way pregnant, ready to drop another, ready to ruin it as she whined on with varied frivolous complaints to an uh-huhing friend who appeared to be chillin' on some corny cloud nine fantasy of her very own.

A woman at the table behind me mentioned, "I feel *so* sick—I don't know what's wrong with me, but my throat is *killing* me," and she coughed all crude and uncovered like a slink-necked bobble head in the direction of a table of two.

"Put a lid on it, will you please? I have a weak immune system," mentioned a latent homosexual man with a crooked sneer gashed into his unhealthily gaunt, frail face.

The clock tick-tocked for a handful of beats, and a woman with spiky blonde hair posed, "Are you worried?"

"Am I *wor*ried? No! I am fucking heartbrokenly angry and exhausted and sad." He coughed viciously and his watery-white, bloodshot eyes glared at me from deeply set black holes burrowed between pointed cheekbones. I felt bad for having unconsciously gawked, but I couldn't help it. He had become a spectacle of sorts—won't be long now, I thought—I wonder what that reality has you thinking, dreaming, wishing and screaming when you're all alone. What imagined negotiations and infeasible scenarios have charged through your head as you've observed yourself shrinking, decreasing, and fading away? I'm uncertain that I'd ever want to know.

I shivered hard and sipped my coffee and my ears got sucked into a conversation two tables away. A young pharmaceutical rep and her boss—a soft, pseudo-man with an artificially certain sounding voice and pleated brown slacks littered by fluffy white crumbs from an organic blueberry muffin—on they articulated, discussing the best methods to go about convincing disease mongering doctors to prescribe copious amounts of prescription drugs, th*ei*r drugs, to children who may, or may not need them. The duo seemed quite enamored with touting their own sense of exaggerated professionalism, ceaselessly seeking to outdo one another in their qualified effort to explain simple problems with as much needless complexity as they could muster. I thought of the man I had seen slinging product from the prim Chevy Tahoe and felt his practice to be more forthright, despite its illegality, and after listening to the cute, freckle-faced girl debate what bistro a certain depression specialist would likely prefer, I pressed my hands vertically firm against my face to the point of seeing a white flash and: fucking people, I thought—who can stand them?

"Wear your favorite outfit, workout that day, feel confident,"—such was the advice being distributed by two girls at the table ahead of me. They were speaking very expediently to a slightly awkward, shy sort of girl seated at their side: "And make sure your hair isn't flat, make sure it is not flat and sweaty and sticking to your forehead." The receptor stirred in its seat, eyes staring rigidly into space, and as she nervously tried to remember it all, her face coiled into the concentrated pose of a fraught fisherwoman trying to hook the final conger eel to have survived the Dead Sea—and onward her friends continued with varied infinitesimal advice on the dos and don'ts of inter-gender courtship: "And make sure your cheeks have some color—"

"But not *too* much color, you don't need to look like you own a rouge company or anything cra*zy* like that—"

"No, you don't need th*a*t, but you don't want to look like a mannequin, either." Life can really be just plain tragic at times, man, it really can be. It's like, what are you trying to do here? Dupe the guy into loving you for goodness sake? He either loves you or he doesn't. He can either live without you or he can't. If that isn't the case, if he isn't dying inside without you, then forget him—he'll always be looking, and eventually, he'll saunter on— simple as that.

"When are you due?"

"I'm *not*—I had my baby over a year ago."

"O, I a*pol*ogize—I thought I heard you were d*ue* again!"

A fit woman in her fifties went ahead and made this inquiry to a woman in her mid-thirties, waiting on a large green tea. You could hear in the voice of the younger woman that she was rather annoyed by the assumption. "Well, it was nice seeing you," the elder said, and then proceeded to place her sunglasses firmly upon her head before walking taught and snappy out of the café.

I thought about grabbing the paper, but an oily sonovabitch in his late thirties wearing a black beret and John Lennon shades upon a fanatical face making a heated, unsolicited speech to a girl in her early twenties—he was standing by the rack, barking down upon her. The girl wore a checkered bonnet and sat calmly cross-legged, drinking her Joe as he leaned in and carried on, "No, really, that's what I said—I said you're gonna' have t' pay me *more*, or else what I'm gonna' do is—" drop dead. I chuckled lightly aloud, imagining the angle in which his face would have suddenly twisted had she said it, and I didn't bother to overhear the imaginary repercussion.

Near the rear of the room, it went: "O—did I tell you? Jane says Paul isn't attending class this semester, and he says he doesn't plan on returning."

"He's not going to finish college, then?"

"I mean—he can't afford to finish right now."

"Correction—he can't afford *not* to."

"I don't think his parents have enough money, and he's not willing to indebt himself to such an obscene level—DePaul is really expensive, you know?"

"Did they go to college—his parents?"

"No."

"And therein rests my case. She'd be an *i*diot to marry somebody who isn't striving to attain a degree."

"Yeah but he's always reading all sorts of books and studying on his own."

"Is that supposed to mean something? What's he going to do? Walk into an interview and list all the knowledge he attained on his own? Knowledge doesn't mean a th*i*ng without that paper—not a damn thing."

I eased back in my chair, laughed a good, full sum about how often I had heard that last line of late, downed half of my coffee in a series of slow gulps, and longed for the ability to float soundlessly skyward—up, out and away. I was still rather early for work—my shift didn't start until nine—so I left my bag at my table, walked outside, and breathed a handful of deep, cold breaths. It felt good to concentrate on nothing minus deep inhalation, and subsequent wind blown condensation.

American Taxi #256 roared up to the curb, the driver ran in, came out in less than two minutes time, and off he drove with a fresh Joe and the Trib—good luck today, man, I thought, my hope is you make it home unscathed and alright.

Walking slowly westbound from the STOP sign at Ada, an African American man gently held the hand of a little girl in yellow rubber boots as she busied herself by analyzing her infinitesimal footprint in the powdery, firm snow, as compared with the broad tracks produced by her fluffy golden retriever. She suddenly broke loose from her father's grasp and leapt headlong into a large snowdrift, and the dog barked and panted excitedly while licking wisps of soft white from her tiny brown eyebrows. She rolled off like a wiggle worm and carried forward in my direction, quite obviously proud to be standing, this little girl, and she yelled, "I'm gettin' hot chocolate!"

"Good! Hot chocolate is good!"

Her father had a chuckle and said, "Sorry—don't mean to bother ya, man."

"O no bother, she's great," I said, as he tied the dog's leash to a parking meter.

"You wouldn't mind just keepin' an eye on our dog while you're out here, wouldja? My daughter always gets real concerned when we leave him alone for a few minutes." He leaned in, winked, and whispered, "You don't really need to watch him, but if she hears you say that you're going to, that'll save me a headache n' prevent her from dashing out the store t' check up on him while we're in line."

"O, of course," I said, obvious and loud, "I'd love to keep an eye on—"

"Mac!" she yelled.

"Definitely—I'll make sure he's just fine," I mentioned, patting him on his rump, "All you have to worry about is getting that hot chocolate."

"Thanks a lot, man," the man said, laughing, and they entered the café.

7

A filthy police car rolled up, parked illegally in an adjacent tow zone, and the officer, speaking on his cell phone, carried on in a heated fashion, occasionally pounding the steering wheel with the bottom of his gloved fist. Two seventh grade-aged, wiry boys with backpacks and thick winter hats strolled eastbound, in the direction of their school, and one said, "I think I wanna be a cop when I grow up."

"Why?"

"Because you get to carry a gun and kick in doors, dude, why else?" I felt like saying, don't plan on coming to my crib, man, because you won't be leaving—uniform or not. Fucking cops—it's a tough job and there are some great ones, but what percentage of those behind the badge hold this mentality dear to their heart? What percentage lives for the live action over the actual attainment of justice? Shit—if not most, it's damn close.

Gazing out the corner of my eye whilst brushing Mac lightly beneath his maw, I observed the officer close his phone, slam the dash with a leather-gloved fist, address a dispatcher on his radio, exit the vehicle, pull up his pants, slam the driver's side door, nearly slip and fall, and, directly beside me, his radio crackled, "Don't work too hard."

"I never do," he retorted. I'll bet, I thought, and I chuckled softly aloud. He snap-turned and glared at me as if I were an untold crime to notice.

"Can I help you with somethin', bud? Somethin' humorous to you?"

"Not particularly."

"*What?*"

"I said not par*ti*cularly." The instant escalation minus reason sent my heart dashing: here we go, I thought.

"Let's see some ID, eh? What exactly are you doing here?"

"Standing still, taking a break and seeing what's happening."

"Takin' a break from what?"

"Walkin'."

"Where?"

"Around," I said, digging in my pocket, handing over my ID.

"I hope, for your sake, that you're not lookin' t' give me fuckin' attitude, partner."

"I'm just sta*n*din' here, man—"

"*Man?*"

"I'm just standing here, *sir*—I'm early for work and I have some time to kill. What's the problem?"

"Nothin', yet—but if you make one more snide remark, I'll have no problem takin' you down t' 26th n' Cal n' makin' you fight for your life in a holding cell with a bunch a' bangers for the rest of the day. Feel up to it?"

"On what charge?"

"Disorderly conduct—whatever else I can find that'll stick."

"I—"

He cut me short by snapping his fingers once, three inches from my nose, and his chin quivered as he stared violently into my eyes. I imagined how many times he'd likely found satisfactory release via brutalizing invalid arrestees past the point of necessity, and he said, "I'm warning you—don't. In fact, go ahead n' put your hands on the fuckin' hood." I complied willingly, heart thundering, knowing better than to call his bluff, and he went ahead and kicked my feet apart slightly harder than was necessary, began frisking my legs and pants pockets, and he told me not to move. My palms, hot from the warmth of the combusting engine, conflicted with the topside state of wind whacked, red rawness, and, perhaps sensing injustice, Mac began barking wildly, jumping up in the air, and snarling at the officer.

"If you don't get your fuckin' dog t' calm the fuck down, I'm gonna' take it into the pound. You hear me? Shut up!" he yelled, seizing his Billy club, raising it high in the air as though he were about to strike him down.

"Whoa! It's not my dog! I'm watching him for some people inside, man, just calm down—you're scaring him. I'm complying with you, ma—"

He got right up on the side of my face, held the Billy club close and screamed, "If you call me man one more time you're going to get it! Got me? Don't move!"

"Yes, sir." I felt like assisting humanity and introducing him to the ace up my sleeve, but doing what you feel doesn't always work out for the best lest you're looking for a lifelong prison sentence.

He leered at Mac with the eyes of a life long animal abuser, spit near his front paws, never bothered to finish the pat down, said, "Stay right where you are," got back in the car, slammed the door, and went about checking my record and searching for outstanding warrants. Unbelievable, I thought—just another human being, not much older than me, but he, not you, repeated an oath to an assumed authority figure, and I am now at the whim of his budding power.

Just then, the man and his daughter exited the coffee house. Their facial expressions insinuated surprise upon observing me fixed rigidly to the metal hood of the police car. The little girl took a big, smiling sip from her hot chocolate, and asked, "Is he a bad person, daddy?"

"I don't know, baby."

"This is all just a silly miscommunication, guys—it's ridiculous. I kept watching out for Mac, so you know."

The father looked at me as if I were a complete and utter maniac, untethered the dog, and ushered his daughter away from what he viewed as a possibly combative setting. A handful of seconds later, the officer exited the vehicle, and his radio crackled, "Ten thirteen, I got a report of people fighting with chains over at Grand and Wood."

"Maybe we should let them fight it out and let a bus snatch the remains when they're finished—besides, I thought people don't start fighting with chains until after ten o'clock," he cracked back, "I'll take a look."

"Don't lemme be seein' too mucha you, smart guy," he said, and he flipped my ID past my foot and into the petrochemical waste-styled slush of the gutter, got back in his car, and rolled off in no particular hurry.

8

Emotionally stuck in the contradictory arrangement of being amazed but not surprised, I retrieved my dirty ID, reentered the café, finished my coffee, got a free refill, asked for five singles for an old Abe Lincoln, dropped a dollar in the tip jar, put my gloves on, reclaimed my bag and split. I walked east on Chicago, crossed Ada, hung a right, and, walking past the sunlit, laughter filled concrete yard of an old elementary school, a young kid yelled, "Hey, wait!" A warmly dressed little fellow with big blue eyes and white blonde hair poking out the bottom of a Chicago Cubs beanie casually strolled over to me, pulled a matching blue scarf below his mouth, and said, "My name's Sammy—there's a big bully here at my school!"

"There *is*?" I asked, not breaking stride.

He was holding his slightly smaller sister's hand, taking fast, certain little steps, and they answered simultaneously, "Yeah!—Yeah!"

"Does he give you or your sister a hard time?"

"No. He doesn't start trouble with me because he knows I keep a big rock in my pocket."

"Is that right?

"Yeah."

"Can I see it?"

"Sure! But do you promise not to tell anyone?"

"I promise."

"Swear to God?"

"Swear to God," I said, hand over my heart.

"Go over to the recess yard, Alyssa," he said, and, after some hesitation, she paced disconsolately toward a group of five chitchatting girls, standing in a semicircle. I stopped walking and he informally popped his little collar high like an old time gangster, gazed discreetly over both shoulders, and out from his pocket and into his miniature right palm rested a dense little lump of cracked concrete. "See?"

"Who taught you to do that?"

"My grandpa."

"He's obviously an extremely intelligent man. You listen to a lot of the advice he gives you?"

"Yeah—he tells me all kinda secret stuff. I always listen. I know more than two hundred secrets, and I never told one! He told me never tattletale on my friends, too."

"Anything else?"

"And to never start a fight, but if somebody monkies with you—don't be afraid and let 'em have it," he said, making two, hard little fists, and holding them beside his face like a future warrior of the Chicago Golden Gloves circuit.

"Well, keep it up, kiddo—you'll turn out alright."

"I found one of his guns hid in a Little Red Riding Hood video cassette one time, too," he said, eyes large and deliberative.

"What'd you do?"

"I gave him back the gun and asked him where the tape was, and he didn't know. I never saw that one."

"It's a good one—it teaches you to be smart n' watch out for scary wolves, but it seems like you've already learnt that lesson. Keep up the good work, kid."

"Wait! You want to see the car I'm gonna' buy?"

"What grade are you in?"

"Third grade—wanna see the car?"

"Sure." His little hand dove in his other pocket and pulled out a compacted fold of paper upon which faded ink was faintly visible. Circled in washed-out red smack in the middle of the page was a 1987 Plymouth Gran Fury.

"I'm gonna' be a Plymouth collector someday."

"How long have you been carrying around this ad?"

"More than one year. Want to buy it for me? It's only one thousand two hundred, and it has a lotta' power and many new parts. It was an old police car in Wisconsin, so it might have neat stuff hid in the trunk. It says firm, though, and grandpa said that means the guy ain't gonna' bargain with ya."

"I wish I could, kid, but not yet. Maybe someday I'll do alright and if I see ya again I'll get you something nice. Be go—"

"Wait!" the chatty little fellow said, "Do you keep anything in your pocket? I'll sell you this rock for a dollar if you need one—I got more."

"I keep my toys up my sleeve," I said, popping open the button of my coat cuff, allowing the sharpened on one side, blunt on the other, oxidized head of a sawed short, shop made rock hammer to slip into my hand. His mouth spread wide and engrossed, and I said, "My Gramps made this little guy—kept it up his sleeve when he made deliveries. I've got good company for long walks, so I don't need the rock—but here's a dollar for the sound advice. Add it to the pile of secrets."

"Thanks! I never got paid for advice before!"

"Take care, Sammy, and always watch out for your sister," I said, and I walked off. Kids are crazy—all you have to do is love them, teach 'em to stand up for themselves, make certain they read a heap of various material, implore them not to wrong good people for no reason, avoid quashing their beautifully random curiosity, get them outside, running around, and generally, they'll turn out alright. How has fulfilling these few simple objectives become so vehemently complex?

9

I sustained my southbound advance at a quick clip, walked past a few dilapidated HUD, low income homes with an objectionable number of smashed knickknacks littered about the front lawns, and I backtracked to Noble. I got to thinking it would be a good morning to walk through the West Loop and the warehouse district on the way to the office, as I find the uniqueness of sunlit, iced over, urban decay, irreplaceably intriguing. I was trying to decipher how many moments a tersely strode shot east on Lake, across Michigan and on over to 303 East Wacker might deduct from the seventy-five I had available to get myself to work when I noticed a rusted, lumbering brown van with a red stripe make its second slow pass of my person in less than a block. "Fuck me," I said, under my breath, after peeking out the corner of my eye and becoming ware of the fact that the madman sitting shotgun was sizing me up through an open window as if his foremost concern was using my body for target practice.

They pulled up right close with a quick rumbling jolt of the old V8, and the passenger yelled, "You a *Gent* man?"

"I ain't shit man, I'm just passin' through." I held his brown, alert eyes straight and sincere and heard my heart ramming in my ears. He rapidly reached into his crotch and displayed a blued steel revolver, and before I could run, my coffee plummeted to the ground and splattered my pants. The possible shooter burst into laughter and feigned toward me, "Fuckin' pussy-ass bitch!" he yelled, exposing yellow teeth that had been hidden beneath the beginning yield of a sparsely emergent, adolescent mustache—he was the exact sort of kid with whom you'd prefer to avoid an altercation: a burgeoning banger, young in the game and unschooled on the extensive possibilities allowed by life—barely old enough to drive but lookin' t' represent by throwing up a sign and shooting you in the face over nothing, not even bothering to rob you—just lookin' t' pull the trigger and blow his load with a big bang, just to see what it feels like, if nothing else.

A lightning quick reflection of innumerable unrealized personal conceptions was suddenly broken by the swell of firing pistons as the chubby Caucasian driver toured on at a leisurely pace, saying nothing. I stood irrationally still, mouth suddenly bone-dry as the van lumbered 'round the bend, set off east on Erie, passed Fitzpatrick's, and disappeared out of view. I heard a 'thwack!' and jumped back as an old man exited the front door of an adjacent single family home, gazed casually in my direction, yawned, and bent gingerly to pick up the frosty, freshly delivered Sun-Times laying upon his icy doorstep. He stretched easy—face flooded in cold winter sun—glanced at the front page, and returned to his dwelling.

Outwardly, I possessed an insouciant attitude of the incident—internally, I marveled at the lightning speed with which proper weaponry can tilt average odds into a damnable circumstance. Remember: never brandish a modified hammer, hatchet, blade or brass knuckles in a gunfight you can possibly avoid unless you can be sure to land a decisive, brute force initial blow to the neck or temple, else it's over. "Fucking Christ man—fuck," I said, quietly aloud, and onward I oozed upon disquieted legs, paces enshrined with involuntary mental echoes of what could have been had a mood been askew. Repeatedly, my mind reran the erupting coffee splashing steamily into the sunlit, frigid air, and I imagined the way red hot blood would have looked little different exploding warmly out the exit hole of a grievous wound channel at the back of my head, had he decided to pointlessly pull the trigger, as possibly he had done before, and most certainly he'll wind up doing in some future moment of incomparable finality. Their laughter lingered in my mind and I shivered hard while thinking that it's good to dress non-flush when embarked upon long urban strolls.

10

Continuing south and headed toward Huron, I kept my head on a swivel. I stopped suddenly, listened in the quiet, cold air, and thought that I heard the same timbre of an engine high throttled, returning 'round the block, and getting closer. I ran at a dead sprint, feet obedient to my mind's urge to churn faster, passed a deeply red, allway STOP sign that stood in stark contrast to the white-bricked building and blue sky beyond—no shading, no blending of the borders, just stark red, white, and blue in sharply angled patterns—and I crossed Ohio. There, adjacent from an old convenience store and a red bricked, rundown building on the southeast corner, I leapt an old iron linked fence and took refuge between a large, rundown motorboat, half-way sheltered by a tattered blue tarp, and the getting-on-in-years, hand painted picket fence protecting an adjoining yard. A split second consideration of calling the cops was quickly quashed as I imagined the same power hungry maniac coming to my aide, only to rob me himself, or hook me on a different offence of his own choosing. Besides, I thought, even if he would help, I'd prefer to die with my pride intact and on my own rather than rely on the public service of such an ignorant, foul hearted prick like him.

I quickly concealed my backpack and its booty of self production beneath an abundance of recently fallen snow. The last thing I needed was for my long accumulating work to get jacked. I could care less about being stripped of money, technological luxury, or moderate physical injury as compared to the sense of loss I would feel if my written material and the multitude of negatives I had in my bag were thieved—such would doubtlessly be the end of me. I laid flat upon the ground, shivered hard, and reduced my height to enable my eyes to spy right between the algae coated, turquoise bow of the cabin cruiser and the meadow of snow.

Sure as shit, within fifty seconds, after likely having taken Erie east to Ada, Ada south Grand, and Grand back west to Noble, the old van lumbered northbound, stopped at the corner, and backed into a tow zone with yellow blinkers pulsating not more than forty paces from where my warm chin melted a neat little resting place, concaved and hard in the newly compacted snow. I felt they likely hadn't seen to where I'd fled, so I settled in and breathed easy. Still though, I was immensely curious as to whether their reason for returning so quickly 'round block was to confront me personally, or if in fact they were hoping to stalk a separate, unknown member of the human herd. Returning so quickly to a location in which they had just recently flashed a gun showed a combination of ignorance for repercussion, defiance of logic, enthusiasm for the hunt, and inexperience in getting caught. I also noticed, to my amusement, several upbeat stickers affixed to the rusty rear bumper: Mothers Against Drunk Driving, an Honor Roll student shout out from a local high school, and, lastly, support for a local organization that staunchly encourages non-violence. What a classic smokescreen, I thought.

As I laid shuddering from the steadily liquefying gathering of ice granules that had snuck their way up my shirt, I sort of hoped that the passenger would get out of the car and enter a nearby residence so as to allow me to come to possess the ultimate trump card of knowing where he lived, thereby permitting me to seek retribution on his turf, and according to my own terms, if ever I found myself in the mood.

Nobody moved for a minute, and as the blue tarp slapped lightly against the white fiberglass, the incontestable smell of the nearby Burger Beacon and varied mealtime fabrications roasting greasy on the grille stirred my recently quashed hunger. I honestly contemplated digging into my DaKine pack, obtaining my phone, dialing the directory service and ordering a delicious breakfast sandwich to be picked up within five minutes, but I didn't risk stirring about. If only I were capable of fulfilling childhood daydreams and floating lightly to the scene of freshly baked scrumptiousness like Tom or Jerry, I thought, this current predicament would be finished. Nearly twenty-five years old and still this classic animation provides timely amusement in moments of full on upheaval.

It was then, just as I attempted to quash my coldness by imagining I was laying in a grass-filled grove shrouded in splintering sunlight and encircled by the combined harmonic fragrance of blossoming cottonwoods and deep, freshwater overtones, that I heard vivacious footsteps rising in proximity with each southbound pace. My angle was obstructed, but thumping echoes led me to believe that a well heeled male subject was approaching the intersection of Noble and Ohio.

I slid over a touch and peered between the deflated, treadless tires of the trailer and the rusty props of the dual engine outboard—directly at the corroded door hinge of the van as it whined unevenly ajar and, at the same time, crunching paces grew closer in range. My heart pounded in my chest and the hot blood circumnavigating my legs promptly thawed thousands of trampled snowflakes as I suffered the awful luck of recognizing the fact that somebody's daybreak delight was about to be spoiled by an angry juvenile empowered with a revolver, long before they did. I pondered, ever so briefly, shouting a warning aloud, but the split second deliberation was quashed as my mind projected a simple armed robbery, and hopefully no bloodshed. I felt no reason to complicate things and get us both shot dead.

The kid stepped slowly from the van, body language astoundingly relaxed, and, after mentioning something to the driver, he strolled casually across the street with a style that did not grant much warning of danger to the impending victim.

"Alright, freeze ma'fucka—don't move or say a fuckin' word. Gimme your fuckin' wallet, bag, your cell phone, that fuckin' Ipod pumpin' in your ears, n' your topcoat—do it fuckin' fast or I'll blast a ma'fuckin' hollow point through your heart, bitch—don't tempt me." He said it just barely loud enough for me to overhear, smartly restraining what must have been an inclined desire to instill fear via an ardent yelling at the cost of alerting the neighborhood—he allowed the dark, rifled hole of the muzzle of the gun to do most of the hollering via an ugly, all-inclusive insinuation, and I changed my opinion to suppose he was not as new in the game as I had presumed.

View obstructed from their waists on up, I observed shiny brown loafers toe to toe with a pair of purple and green high-tops, standing pat upon the dazzling, icy sidewalk.

Hesitation—seconds of indecision felt like years and I feared imminent gunfire and loss of life over insignificant manmade fabrics and greenbacks. A purple rubber sole hastily stepped forward, followed by four shrill cracks of steel against bone, and the man, after being wordlessly pistol whipped, threw the requisitioned objects to the ground, and went running westbound with a jagged, concussed sprint down Ohio.

Plump pallid boy maneuvered the van with a sweeping three point turn, trans sounding overly strained, and the passenger promptly knelt, jammed his piece into his waistband at the small of his back, scooped the haul, jumped in the passenger side door, and the beastly vehicle went thundering southbound on Noble as though a dirty old man late for an appointment with an open-minded call girl was resolutely at the helm.

41

The last thing I needed was to loiter around the crime scene and get questioned as a witness or pinned as a goddamn lookout or something ridiculous—I jumped off the ground, brushed myself off, dug out my bag, snuck slowly toward the south end of the lot, past the front end of the trailer and its support of a single, crumbling cinder block, and, using five little trees as cover, I leapt the fence in a single hurdle, eager to continue on with a hassle-free stroll to what I hoped would be the last day I would ever arrive to work for an organization I did not personally control.

11

Back on Noble, I immediately broke into a trot so as to fully amputate my association with the area. Done navigating the Great Lakes and a proud old river, I crossed Grand Avenue and, gazing toward the luminous Loop, my eyes spotted a rigid homeless man in turquoise hospital pants thrusting a diversely filled shopping cart through the shrill eastern breeze—stunted stride signified severe pain in his legs and feet, and I thought: what will become of him? What will become of anyone? Older I get, crazier I feel at the realization that perhaps I'll never possess the empyrean answers—even after—and this in turn melts my mind.

I continued south toward Hubbard, turned east, maintained a seven minute mile pace into a fire-red, West Town sunrise sneaking past the beautifully black, shadowed Hancock, and carved between charging Friday traffic on Ogden without breaking stride. I hustled on upon the snow-caked roadway for another hundred meters or so, slowed, reached into the secretive zippered compartment on the fore of my left shoulder strap, removed a recently prepared handcraft, sparked a flame and breathed deeply, happy of my morning's good fortune of awaking in the land of the free, with no upstanding governmental orders instructing me on how I should, or should not be using my time. Amazing, I thought, that the majority of the people breathing upon the earth at this very moment lack the basic, fundamental right of self-rule—how do so many allow this to be?

I exhaled white smoke into the bright, empty street, and smiled at the sight of two belligerent-looking, giant snapping turtles swimming deep below the surface of a blackened sea of esteemed predatory peril—this specific fifteen foot high by ten foot wide painting marks the commencement of the west end of the 'Say Goodbye Gallery'. Stretching nearly a mile, from just east of Ogden, all the way over to Des Plaines, and brushed upon colossal concrete canvases that serve as support for thousands of tons of Metra traffic rolling between the Westside train yard and the Loop, it is certainly one of the most underappreciated combinations of urban artwork and activism I am ware of—most illustrations embrace endangered species, rollicking joyful in their natural settings, set to the backdrop of the most beautiful skyline in the world. Many artists have worked on the projects over the years, and each time I travel past I ease back and wish for the chance to shake the hands and grant gratitude to the rapturous work of the insane unknowns who furnished beautiful originality upon the barren cityscape before the time I took my first breath.

I stomped hard, trying to regain feeling in my toes, and two men working on removing a city-issued, bright yellow boot from the front left wheel of their ride just shy of Racine cussed softly under their visible breath. A nearby sneeze startled me and I turned quick to notice a decrepit dude settled under the adjacent rafters of the same intersection, body tranquil, face staring blankly into isolated shadows.

Two sullen-looking railroad men with hardhats attended to unknown business in the razor wired slit between Carpenter and Aberdeen, and I swaggered on, continuing to enjoy the gallery. A few meat trucks driven by burly fellows bounced past and a sign fastened to a light pole said: East to Downtown, like you couldn't tell by the two mile wide prominence of the manmade Mount Massive gleaming conceitedly in the distance—heavy white vapor rose tall into the sky from the exhaust of an enormous, rumbling blue beast blasting its horn, and the steady exhale of wheel on rail met my ears as Metra tracks chugged suburban sprawl into the maddened fury of a skyrocketing metropolis jammed full bore with the taste of untold lives lived and died. I breathed deep, exhaled, gazed about, laughed lightly and thought: damn, I'm from here!—my family, my friends—this is our city, our space, our place, and god*d*amn it's fucking beautiful right now. The sky was blue enough to burn a hole through your eyes and I thought of how many times I'd been on the road, and returning home, whether driving in on the Kennedy, the Ryan, the Stevenson—there is no mistaking that feeling—that deep-seeded, biotic love that wells warm within upon glimpsing the undeniably raw vision of steel, brick and concrete rising through the clouds as an irrefutable testament to the illimitable inventiveness of free minds conjuring unimpeded for the benefit of free society. Chi man— you're either from here, or you ain't—fucking period, I thought.

12

I reached in my bag, checked the time on my phone, and realized that at forty-five minutes 'fore nine, I had to hustle. I stuck my combustible waste in a pocket, bent down to tie my shoe, and two men from the water department in florescent yellow vests went digging in the sewer at the intersection of Hubbard and Milwaukee—a single, filthy, duct taped orange cone encouraged raging drivers not to kill them. One man got down on all fours, twisted tangled wires with scratched up, pained hands, and, dropping his entire head into the sewer, he shouted an angry, echoing noise of no distinct resonance. His partner bent down with his ear to the hole as though listening to fresh water drain deep into the soil of a parched potted plant and, equally flustered and red-faced, they both stood, situation seemingly unresolved.

"I can't fuckin' bel*ie*ve we been at it fer tree n' a half hours already—motherfuckin' Ch*r*ist al*migh*ty!" The man's wide head looked bloated from all the blood that had likely rushed to his brain during the past three hours of subzero inversion—he was goddamn angry.

"Tell ya what we're gonna' do—let's barricade 'eis goddamn ting, get some breakfast, n' figure out how we're gonna' fix 'eis mess. Sometimes it's best t' step away from a tricky job fer a minute n' tink it out. I know a real good joint west a' here you prolly never ate at."

"Any good?"

"Shit, dey got the best Kaiser rolls 'eis side of Berlin!"

"Ya don't gotta tell *me* twice—let's go!"

They crossed on Hubbard to the east side of Milwaukee, pacing tired and sore to where their cumbersome truck was parked, and I set off swiftly southeast on Milwaukee, to Halsted, to Lake Street, and then dead east. A guarded-looking guy near my age approached from twelve noon, and posed: "Yo—can you slim me a square, B?"

"Nah man, I'm flat."

"Well hey—you wanna take a look at somethin' right quick?"

"I mean—not really man."

"Check it, yo—check this Palm Pilot," he said, removing a black rectangle from a coat pocket, holding it lovingly in his hands like an expert presenter on 'The Price is Right'.

"I—"

"It's like two point something giga pieces, man, fast as hell. It can hold all sorts of—"

"No man, really, I'm cool," I said, pushing past.

"You don't even wanna know what I'm chargin'? You st*u*pid, boy!"

I marched on into the fearsome wind tunnel as though my face was undergoing an extensively studied aerodynamic test, and I felt like a small, oval-shaped ice cube had been surgically inserted between my eyes. I stopped briefly on the Lake Street Bridge, turned my face to the side, leaned over the edge and gazed southward upon all the other drawbridges traversing the frozen River. The packed Green Line pounded deafeningly eastbound above my head as the distinct smell and sound of high voltage electricity shoved Westside proletariat toward the fulfillment of their varied endeavors. The span shuttered at the combined weight of the train, cars, buses and hustlers bouncing above the inflexible tributary. Plump plumes of snow plummeted pockmarked-white iron tresses to the beat of steel wheels crashing across the small gap in the tracks at the direct middle of the conduit in a perfect fulfillment of some goliath iambic pentameter, paper and pen be damned.

Continuing to breathe and gazing southward upon the stunning succession of burly drawbridges negotiating the River, I inspected the uncompromising flow of citizens marching eastbound upon the Randolph, Washington, Madison, Monroe and Adams Street bridges like a new-aged army prepared to slit as many necks as was necessary to hold precious, financial high ground. Sunlit steam rose in a swift windblown flurry from a small area of open water, and thousands of hectic sounds exclaimed good morning to the grind by knocking tiny tufts of light powder off individual rusty rivet heads so as to provide the passing appearance of a mountain blue sky distributing an implausible, abrupt snow squall.

I thought of all the folks I made an effort to observe in the careers I'd recently quit, and I pondered: doesn't anybody long for a self-contained destiny? Who are these people who simply 'show up' to places they can't stand for years on end, producing just enough mediocre yield so as to scarcely avoid getting axed—day, after day, after *day*—and this is what they do! Forever! Far too many spend their greatest years of keen health and unlimited potential slaving, the fuck, away, for institutions they detest. And still, s*t*ill economists wonder why it is that great sums of businesses fail to produce innovative, quality products for public consumption, and wind up going under. Hello? More than half the staff doesn't want to be there in the first place! And aside from simply not wanting to go, they come to view this job as the j*a*il they're stuck in for perpetually indebting themselves upon similar, mid-quality products such as those they produce themselves: products whose success or failure are mainly dependent upon unique marketing plans to convince people to go ahead and make unnecessary expenditures, founded in credit, that, in the end, will only wind up costing non-replenishable time, and dignity.

I thought of screaming: please, don't do it, baby!—why buy what you do not need with capital you do not possess for sake of impressing those who do not matter? Why listen to radio or television personalities as they implore you to venture from the home you can hardly afford and on over to the mall to spend more?—ever think of asking why? Why should I? What is so wrong with decreased consumption? Why such a push to get people to splurge? This practice, you see—this practice is madness! I remained stationary, watching hundreds of faces pass, and the majority of them looked worn beyond repair. I wanted to stop them and say: listen, I promise, it doesn't have to be this difficult! Please, don'tcha do it, don't work this hard year after year to have nothing left over—break away and set yourself free—bound off the bridge if need be—dive right in, crash face first through the ice—because freezing solidly deep and alone in tribute to free will is better than melting into the enslaved effort to compensate for the foolish expenditures your entire life span has become enslaved for—no more!

13

Shadowed streets embraced me and I paced on to the scrape of shovels lifting sand, the tap of trowel on brick—a silent sense of delight about the scene that yes, yes it's us who're out in the cold, steadily constructing this shit.

A hellaciously big man on the northwest corner of Lake and Wells clobbering through the sidewalk with a jackhammer suddenly cut it and yelled, "Fuck—hold off, eh? My forearms been gettin' all cramped up a' late. Damn. We're gonna' have to cool it for a minute—I keep forgetting to eat my bananas—they're a good source of potassium—prevents dehydration."

"Heh, funny," said his cohort, "I keep forgetting to eat pussy—it's a good source a' cold sores—prevents close-talkers," and they both laughed big and loud—white steam went roaring out of their broad mouths and tumbling through a gentle slice of morning sun in burly gusts. Stuck at the stop light, traffic eking slowly southbound on Wells, I listened in:

"Ay—know somethin'?—they ain't givin' me my raise. Found out on the first."

"What'd ya do about it?"

"I called in a few and came in a 'lil drunk a coupla times."

"Good move."

"Yeah, I'm over it now."

"What was the reason?"

"Wasn't in the budget, ya know?—sucks, but a'sa-way it goes."

"Ay—you used yer extra time n' took a vacation 'fore Christmas, right?"

"Yeah."

"Where'd ya go, anyway?"

"Talla*h*assee."

"Not so classy?"

"Every time I farted I was blowin' over somebody's shanty shack."

"Heh—why were you farting so much? You shoulda held back if that was the case—fuckin' chemical warfare n' shit—that really necessary?"

"You ever ate the food in Florida? You ever tried t' go out fer a decent Italian dinner down der? I was explodin' the whole w*ee*k."

"Yo what kinda Chicagoan goes to F*lor*ida in search of a decent Italian fuckin' meal and expects to find one? I don't order Italian food south a' Tinley Park. Unless you're in New York or fuckin' Boston or some real city wit real fuckin' Italians, man, you cook for yourself. What's wrong witchu? And Tallahassee? On vacation? Who goes from Chicago to Talla*has*see on vacation in the first place? Jesus."

"My wife—she has family down der."

"No wonder she's such a nitwit."

"Tell me about it," he retorted, kicking hard with a beaten boot at a clump of accumulated grime upon the squared steel head of the jackhammer. "Ay—I tell ya? Me and 'eis guy Minich—we were out last week n' we were havin' a good time when—"

"Ay, tell ya what—let's get this done first 'n then tell me. Foreman said we need t' get 'eis over wit 'fore break n' I'm fuckin' starvin', man."

"Sounds good—you ready?"

"Yeah, I'm good, let her go," and the jagged sound of the jackhammer shattering cold concrete reverberated between granite buildings with an intensity that should have fractured the frozen, rust-strewn steel girders sturdily supporting the snarling Brown Line as it twisted northbound toward the Merchandise Mart, rumbling slow and mellifluous. The light turned green and an out of state corroded Suburban with Michigan plates made the mistake of trying to cross Lake at the red. He jammed the entire intersection like a long ignored hairball wedged firm in a drainpipe, and dozens of irritated Chicagoans laid on their horns and cursed wildly at his lack of foresight.

The corner of Lake and LaSalle saw clouds of steam pouring from the mandible of a whistle blowing, arm waving, order shouting traffic director who mostly looked like a primed workhorse standing in a luminously cold, asphalt field, with a bag of hot oats strapped tight 'round its mane. As I waited to cross, I gazed south upon the unrivaled view of the soaring, hard physique of the Financial District. She insists that you look but pays no mind as though an amplified version of the empowered women striding her streets tall and lean, invoking dirty daydreams in the hot, sweaty summer sun.

A random man at my rear disrupted my reflection, mentioning, "Ah yeah—the good times—the good times 'er killing me, not softly, but viciously, n' I can't explain jus what I mean, b'cause I'm too fucked up." I turned around in time to view a vile yellow snot get sucked back inside an overwhelming nostril, and the same voice posed: "Ay Joe, can you reach for me? I'm only short a buck, man."

"I need what I got, man."

"Shit, thanks anyways n' shit—no mo drinkin' this month, no. I feel extremely close t' dyin', n' I ain't ready t' go jus yet. I need jus one mo blue skied summer, man, jus one mo long stretch a' fine days n' I'll die good n' glad." Not wanting to down him, I thought: in late March you can sort of feel it, like spring is right around the corner and you might just make it, might live through the Mother's attempt to steal you away—you got a good ways t' go 'fore you make it to those times, man.

He ran his hand down his face and: "M' wife—she took the eternal sleep some years back. I was drunk n' I crashed n' she jus went t' sleep right in my arms. I jus been kinda loss since 'en, like, jus *ti*red n' sad kinda—it's alright cuz I'm feelin' I'm gettin close t' fallin' in a black sleep a' gigantic comfort, like, hopefully this year n' such, so, you know, I'll be wit her 'en—I'll be glad."

"Shit, well—enjoy the rest of it man, the rest of the journey 'fore ya sleep."

He continued east at the change of the light and I rolled south, out of the way from where I needed to go but walking very fast in order to make up for the extra distance—I just didn't feel like listening to him.

I passed the State of Illinois Building and walked all the way down to the corner of LaSalle and Madison, where I encountered an old weathered white woman sitting tightly balled together in a green plastic chair on the northwest corner, holding a sign that read:

'Everything stolen from me.
Family *kill*ed!!
Your donations really help…'

She had an old, beaten down scarlet scarf pulled tightly over her face, and her body sat awkwardly hunched over the Big Gulp cup that was serving as the depository for her donations. I felt like asking her if it were true, the news her sign so candidly spouted, but how could I? All you could do was hope was for a repugnant series of karmatic events to come her way if in fact they be lies, and carry on.

The man standing beside me, he addressed his fine-creased mate, and stated, "My sister, Ms. Moneybags, I certainly don't feel very rich compared to her."

"That her?" I asked, tilting my head toward the exhibition at our side. He looked at me, confused, and I said, "Then stop grumbling, governor."

"Excuse me?"

"You got it," I said, crossing the street.

"You priggish prick! They'll come a day!"

"I'll be waiting," I said, winking, smiling, continuing east—and off he strode toward the fulfillment of his depressing, comparison-based destiny, twice leering back with aggressive overtones he dared not implement. Winking is one of three top-notch options you can use to flip the hell out of someone already furious with you. Winking, blowing a kiss, and laughing are the three best options. I usually go with the wink, laugh on the inside, and get ready for the person to try and take my head off with an easily avoidable, telegraphed haymaker. Those options have a serious tendency to push people over the edge—blind fury style. People get much angrier when their anger is countered with calmness. Aside from that, refracting calmness makes angry lunatics appear decidedly unstable—and, until somebody blows my head off, that's the fun part.

Waiting to cross north from State and Madison—the true zero/zero center to which every random address tallies away from—the man standing beside me was creating a low buzzing sound, too low for screaming, too vociferous for humming, and I casually stared straight on, observing the curving reflection of his germy face upon the salt strewn windows of a passing bus. I had another few minutes to kill so I followed this greasy, longhaired, crazy-bearded, methed-out motherfucker as he walked like a zombie through red lights on State Street all the way back north to Lake. I felt sort of like a ghoul focusing upon him to such an extent for a full quarter mile, but odds were he was going to get struck by a vehicle, and I was eager to see if his trancelike expression would perhaps finally change after colliding with an eight ton bus packed with post holiday purchasers eager to get to Macy's. He didn't modify a single stride in his stroll, and each time he nearly got rolled he seemed to prove the point that angels, if they exist, seem to spend the majority of their time flying quick meaningful circles around the useless and damned.

At Lake and Wabash, yet another deafening intersection that sees traffic from the Green, Brown, Purple, Orange and Pink Line growl around the bend at this, the northwest corner of the Loop in a persistent clip of sustained daylight pulsation, an equally persistent man finally got me to stop and listen after speaking into my ear for a full half block. "See, we need to secure another $50,000 for our church, for the deposit." He handed me a piece of paper with a big diagram and hypothetical images of what it would eventually look like. "That's the preacher's office, back there," he said, pointing a manicured, glossed fingernail at the blueprint.

"Looks swank, man."

"Edwin—m' name's Edwin, but O, O yeah, it's gonna' be real nice, I hope. Another preacher friend of mine, he got his church set up real plush last year. I'm hopin' for the same, really."

"Part of the reason I honestly don't care, I'm sure." He narrowed his eyes and stared blankly, surprisingly devoid of emotion, pupils set onto my own. "My hope is that you appreciate my honesty. I'm not pretending I have no money, I'm not saying, okay, maybe next time—no, not when we both understand that to be a falsehood, okay? All I'm saying, flat out, is that I could honestly care less about your prospective church. I hope you can appreciate that, Edwin," I said, handing back his flyer.

"Figures you'd say that," it came, under his breath.

"Come again?"

"I said figures you'd say that—white guy like you."

"White guy like me? Just how is my disinterest assumed to be racial? You think I'm supposed to feel some sense of guilt for your plight because I'm white or because your solicited requisition is conjoined with God? That judgment right there shows you're an imposter. I try not to feel sorry for anybody, pal, least of all those who attempt to distribute unanalyzed, blanket-guilt, for reasons of their own benefit. Had you been white, I'd be even more inclined to spit and say no. You have zero conception of how I live, what I do, what I own and why, and yet—'*Shi*, it figures, white guy like *me*'—amazing! You ain't no preacher, man—you're a fat liar and a heretic, and you'll be shitting your pants when finally you're about to die, with the deep seeds of your hypocrisy finally germinating into a venomous garden of inbred self-hate, churning, raging glumly through your guts as you gasp helplessly for a second chance. Enjoy the terror, big man, 'cause you ain't gettin' one."

14

I spit hard and walked east, unconsciously measuring the breadth of persons worldwide and across all faiths who utilize 'God' in their ardent, non-genuine effort to raise funds in the name of 'virtue', only to wind up self-deceived, forever frolicking stout and 'holy' in the unspoken name of 'God-given' greed. The thought of millions of such folk raking billions of dollars from truly respectable, uncompromised, hardworking men and women of underprivileged position placed me in the status of having to focus hard upon obstructing a violent craving fostering within. The blood chosen clerics, politically positioned priests and ravenous rabbis—and the same with overbearing, thieving government entities endlessly seeking to take what is rightfully yours in the name of the state—how do they sleep at night? Soft and sound and surrounded by the best sheets such extracted affluence can procure—flawed logic washing over the purblind public in waves of culpability, therein promoting false shame as the machine successfully implements a policy of subconscious derision, one bloodless kill after the other.

Such soundless shakedowns lead me to scream please—please cease feeling blameworthy for nothing, brothers, for lest you guard against this false guidance, you shall become yet another guileless puppet interweaved and paralyzed by the strings of assumed, unsubstantiated superiority—and this, this is a terrible place to exist, not much unlike the exact place I was heading toward: the twenty-third floor of the office building standing in the near distance. For within those walls the level of sophistication with which what is becomes spun into what is not and vice versa sends my mind out of sorts—the vital force of my inner self burns enraged by the ways of premeditated, corkscrewing soothsayers and their endless effort to profit from unguided, easily swept up, sycophantic souls as they are sentenced to drown under the guise of: a higher education.

I kept my head down and subconsciously counted my elongated paces as I marched through an impromptu, windblown-white dust devil, tight coil of which nimbly leapt from an alley to the sidewalk to the street and upon me before rising bright into the sky, splintering into thousands of glistening shards, and falling lightly back to earth—sudden spindrift devoured by eerie stillness.

Crossing a messy Michigan Avenue, I glanced north upon the sun drenched and luminous Wrigley Building as I waited upon the salted, concrete median, for a break in the northbound flow. After jumping at my chance, I skirted north to South Water, turned east, continued underground, and ambled beneath the entirety of 233 N. Michigan. The hypnotic hum of a massive, piston pounding fire truck firing up the ramp and returning to its residence shook a group of grubby shirkers from their slumber. A penetrating glance from a man clinging to his coffin-like incision in a subversive air duct said: come no closer. He rolled over, face turning away from the punitive wind, hands grabbing flustered and pell-mell at a soiled shroud so as to blackball the bleak reality of the dome beyond his dome, as he retreated silently to his insane foxhole.

15

Up the ramp and diagonally past Columbus, I revolved my way into 303 East Wacker, beeped my ID card upon a transmitter, repeated "Good morning," to a good-natured security guard, and made my way to the elevator bank. The middle-aged lady who shared the ride but continued on smelled like a mixture of stale Cheerios and band aids, and I wished her good day upon my departure on twenty-three. A quick check of the time defined my status as: fourteen minutes early. I rolled into the bathroom and quickly changed from a hoodie and jeans into more suitable slacks and collared shirt, brown boots still present, and like a phantom I scanned myself into the admissions arena and snuck over to my desk without getting stuck in a single, unnecessary conversation.

I chucked my bag beneath the workstation, sat and leaned back in my chair—my legs felt stiff from the five mile walk, and the heat provided by massive, unseen furnaces burning hundreds of cubic meters of natural gas felt great. Still shivering, endless blathering blazed over the cubicle wall and into my head despite a staunch effort to embrace silence.

A prepubescent-looking, sorority orientated, recent Big Ten graduate out of northern Ohio turned snappy, young Chicago business professional by the name of Caroline Gannon peered her face 'round the corner, sat upon my desk and said, "Meow! How was your morning?"

"Weird enough."

"What happened?"

"I woke."

"Are you shivering?"

"A little, I guess."

"Maybe you underdressed—I can't tell the temperature until I go outside."

"Funny how that works."

"My place—there must be something wrong with the heat because I had the thermostat set at seventy-four and it didn't get above seventy-one last evening. I froze!"

"Gnarly."

"Yeah, I mean—can you imagine how bundled up I was? I *still* haven't warmed up. I gotta talk to my mom and dad and be like, 'Buy me a place for three fifty'—they want to buy me a place for three hundred thousand, but in looking I've found that the difference between what you can get for three versus three-fifty is quite large. I'm not about to go living in some d*u*mp—know what I mean?"

"Not really."

"It's just—Old Town is sort of expensive."

I leaned in slow-like, and said, "Maybe you should get yourself a shotgun, a little persuader of sorts and roll out to four thousand west—out past Cali, past Sacramento even— maybe hit up something plush around Madison n' Cicero—so long as you have a piece in every room and you're ready to use lethal force, you can get an entire goddamn building for that price n' have yourself a good ole time."

"Eew, I wouldn't go west to Cicero! I never go further west than Ashland! *Eew!*"

"Well, alright then, if you don't mind I'm—"

"I'm so th*i*rsty this morning. I think I dehydrated myself from bundling so much."

"Want some water from my thermos? I just filled up in the sink."

"The s*i*nk? Um, no—I only drink b*o*ttled water."

"Well, thirty percent of humanity drinks out of virtual latrines—maybe you should embrace the peril. It might tear down those walls of awkwardly predictable normality."

"Um, I'd rather n*o*t," she said, preening her nose with a light swathe of foundation. The reflection of her large black eyes peering into a miniature mirror made her face look a little like a busied fly, "Who k*n*ows where that water comes from?"

"I'm pretty sure it comes from that giant, frozen Lake out the window—the one filled with melted glacial water that stretches north for the next four hundred miles or so."

"I prefer bottled, n*a*tural spring water, I really do."

"Fine with me, but do you mind letting me unwind for a second? I'll have a hard enough time hearing my voice all day to start off like this."

"What? Is something wrong? I'm not b*o*thering you, am I?"

"I can't understand it, I'm beat—you'd think that after such a dramatically extended sleeping session one would be lively to the nines and ready to operate with the crushing functionality of an expertly formulated, model piece of machinery—but nope, not me, not today," I said, lifting my feet from the floor, extending them straight ahead, tightening my stiff quads until they quivered a bit, leaning forward, touching my toes, rocking back and reaching my arms to the rear as far they would bend whilst leaving go of a deep, primal yawn—I was really beat.

"O no worry—it's almost time for the Rah-Rah!" She turned up the toes of a foot dangling from a crossed leg and twirled a strand of her excessively highlighted hair around an index finger and prolonged nail, hue of which did volumes to broadcast her ditzyness to the world.

"Great, see you there."

Caroline carried along and behind me a daft troll walked past an overly cologned cohort and mentioned, "Wow, that's a power tie!"

"Well, I'm a power tie type of guy!" it retorted, pulling up its pants and winking its eye like a car salesman with innate knowledge of all that is wrong with what he is striving to sell as polished and like new. I rolled lazily into the aisle, breathed deep, spun 360 degrees, and half way through the revolution I got an eyeful of unglamorous asscrack as the woman behind me bent over, urgently in chase of a Pop Tart that she reluctantly threw in the trash. She looked at me crookedly, out the corner of her eye, and I could tell from the glimpse that the item would have been eaten had there not been a witness. I almost mentioned: why care what I've seen? If you want to eat it, go ahead already! Good Christ, you're a grown woman and you're still worried as to whether or not an outsider shall spread rumors regarding the level of your edible hygiene?—I camp in a goddamn tent in a garage, okay? Do you really think I'm about to judge you on whether or not the ten second rule applies to this blueberry Pop Tart? Do *you?* I. Don't. Fucking. Care!

I slammed back toward my workspace and flipped through a large, yellow, nearly full steno pad. So tired, was I—and looking at my doodles, I thought, I used to be able to draw so well—what happened?

One of the only positive things about the joint was having my main timepiece be the clock face upon the Wrigley Building. Indeed the impending embarrassment of the Rah-Rah was a short seven minutes away, so I took a moment to read my scattered, written thoughts from the previous day:

9:12 in the A.M. and a morning meeting is taking place. I am not paying attention at all. It is a close-knit meeting with Petra leading myself and three others through varied tricks of the trade. Her satisfied eyes lend credence to the fact that she's impressed with the quantity of 'notes' I am taking—right—no matter, allow her to experience a false sense of professional extolment, and continue to exploit.

She is speaking with us while at the same time applying lacquer to her fingernails—additionally, I am having a hard time not vomiting as I observe her eating a grossly over-saturated cream cheese bagel while at the same time viciously smacking her pink lips, which are of course outlined with small globs of glistening white rubbish. Wow. I'm trying to describe her aura, but really I find myself drawing blanks aside from the fact that she is a supremely cracked-out, horribly disorganized, sloppy, unintelligent and whorish individual—I hate to give off a spat of rude descriptions such as this, but really—really they're true. Yet another person enamored with dramatic entrances for sake of discussing obvious, tired subjects—extremely slow-minded, man, incredibly—which of course allows her to perform very well at a job that involves reading scripts and ignoring repercussions.

'What are you doing?' she just asked. 'Sometimes I head-bang while I write—who doesn't?' she rolled her eyes and continues along—she looks like a fish—a blooper, actually—a blooper with a pointy nose—her shirt is far too tight and her stomach extends further than her breasts by about three and one half inches and then sucks into a vicious hole where her belly button is located. The entire sight is extremely unappealing. 'See, that's unfortunate,' Petra just mentioned in response to a COW of hers who, after speaking to me last evening, has decided against attending the University. She dialed and placed him on speaker phone in an effort to show us the most proper style with which one should flip the Switch, but I already drained the power supply—O my, she's quite angry. 'Who in the *hell* is CW

51

Martino?' she yelled, after hanging up. Her face, as viewed from this sideways angle, is amazingly foul. I can just picture her snorting all sorts of crusty substances into her head, and then falling to the floor for sake of an insane series of seizures and convulsions, blood streaming from her nose while at the same time a thick yellow paste spews from her twisted mouth, as she stutters, 'Like, I-I'm c-c-c-ch*ill* man—'

Caroline just leaned over and posed: 'Did you hear what she just said?'

'I haven't been paying attention whatsoever, nor do I plan to,' I whispered, and she looked at me with an expression that implied anger at my unwillingness to share the 'great knowledge' that had just been imparted upon us—such being the eternal babble of the background, of course—methinks ye should know this be a straightforward answer, not sarcasm serving as an evasive stance on my monopoly of overheard uselessness.

Ah yes—the meeting is finished. I rode in this morning—a beautiful, albeit sleeting morning, filled with speed, near misses, and utter elation.

And now 9:46 and still soaking wet—deeply cold—wouldn't mind fadin away to a calm cliff as a pastel blue eastern sky brightens slowly, low fireball of sun breaking a horizon of charging, sparkling water, yep—would be nice. Zybarsky needs to borrow my bike this evening and I'll likely have to walk tomorrow. Perused an abandoned Trib and Skilling says it's supposed to be sunny—is good.

After only six weeks on the job it has become fully obvious that, despite tearing this institution down a little at a time, I can no longer st*a*nd being here. I think tomorrow will have to be the end—I'll try to make it another week, another check, but I don't know.

The over-talkative Latina from financial aid that just walked in here smelled as if she were trying to hide a raging menstrual flow with an equally horrid, musky perfume—the combination was fully nauseating, man, really. What makes this even worse is that I am starving. I am starving and again I want to vomit. This is a terrible combination.

It felt really nice to get back to the garage and go black last night. Whisky and wine put me down like a tranquilized monster—ice cascading upon the iron roof like thousands of miniature meteors woke me from a deep, dark sleep, slate fuckin clean n' empty like I'd never been born—just woke and was. And this is what I'm doing? Wow boy, wow.

My entire mouth is in loads of pain right now—too much speaking. Making calls feels somewhat painstaking—having to speak, this is what is most difficult. I simply wish to—mad flock of soaked geese flying in an eastbound arrow past the window—you're back too early, boys!—that or you're too late!—but yes, I simply wish to sit silently, thinking, reading, writing, drinking coffee, tea, and listening to music. I have no need to hear my voice spouting loud and ever-present.

10:08 and I just called some hillbillyish cat named TL Bower: 770.535.4016 'If you're in the south, boy, it is c*o*ld, too cold!' said his answering machine. He is being force-fed a vicious conglomeration of poppycock so as to ensnare his family's reality with the swindle this 'educational institution' has to offer. He's not my student—belongs to T. Kramer—he is trying desperately to hoodwink and unpeel his onion, but after I get him on the line, this effort will be quashed.

I am now looking out the window, gazing upon the four ant-like folks strolling the salty sidewalk of the Columbus Drive drawbridge above the frozen River, some eighty meters down below—I imagine what it must feel like to be a fighter pilot or a gunner on an AC-130 Spectre—what feelings do they experience when pushing a button or pulling the trigger, destroying entire realities into finalities from on high? I hold doubt as to whether it can truly seem real, with the intensely hot visual of the explosion shrouded by high altitude silence—

The entire River is frozen solid minus the open water directly beneath the drawbridge—it remains devoid of ice for sake of nasty street salt that tumbles through the steel mesh, thawing and polluting.

10:22 and falling asleep. The woman seated behind me, Shauna, after patronizing a prospective student about their lack of education as if she held the slightest comprehension of Socratic Method-styled reasoning—she is now speaking about this gig as if it is brain surgery. 'That's interesting,' I just stated, in regard to a subject I did not find interesting at all, a subject I did not really hear to begin with. Fuck this place—

10:29 and I wonder when I'll die.

And in the distance—'I'm just trying to think outside the box *too*, Mr. Friar.' I simply am having a difficult time handling these people—they're not *all* bad, no, I deem some are fairly nice—it's just that few, if any, stand up to what they know to be wrong, and this disheartens me greatly.

10:41 and still soaked. What I wouldn't give for a hot bath. I think I'll sneak into the gym this evening, work the heavy bag, rattle the speed, lounge in the sauna, and take a blazing shower. That I've been attending one of the more exclusive gyms in Chicago for four months without a membership astounds me.

10:46 and I wonder *how* I'll die.

A short twenty minutes later and my throat feels as if it is constricting and my mouth feels infected. I can no longer speak with those for whom I do not hold care. 'Can I get the corporate headquarters? Thank you very much. Dan Mandeville please. Yes, Man*d*eville—thank you,' I say. Do you see how mad this is? I suddenly feel so very tired. But relax, Anthony, you don't need this job. Last as long as you can, but remember, you don't really *need* it—minus awaking with a heartbeat and lungs breathing, you don't need anything really.

And now eleven minutes to twelve, according to the sturdy old watch atop the Wrigley Building—rode quick for Joe at half twelve and I'm enjoying it quite much—snagged me Joe from that small, independent joint just north of Lake, crossed the street and used my clean privilege to steal a banana for a poor beggar outside Starbucks. He was happy, and so was I. Methinks if you refuse to pay your farmers a living wage, I may as well continue lifting bananas and occasional half sandwiches from as many of your stores as is possible for sake of distributing them to those in need. They're always happy, and so am I.

Three to twelve now—puffy-pant Latina just rolled back through and her odor was intoxicating. The air surrounding her appeared momentarily wavy. She struck a conversation with me, I smiled and exchanged respectful small talk, and finally, after divulging several diaphanous details of circumstances that did not concern me whatsoever, she walked on—a kind lady, she be, but I need not inhale her fumigation at this moment.

Two twenty-three and the voices continue to drone
My glands are so very swollen
You don't need this
Just write
Write, observe, create, save, destroy and remain unaffected
Allow nobody here to know you
How can you possibly hold care for this?
Easily
You
Can
Not
Be easy
Remain unaffected, create and destroy
So go—

"Hey—A*n*thony! Let's go—it's time for the R—"

"I know what time it is. I'll be there in a second, alright?" I stood, peeked over the walls of my cubicle to make sure nobody was within earshot, again dialed ole TL Bower, and the line chimed busy. Fuck—I wonder if he's been on the phone with financial aid—could he be? This early? I best not be too late. I hung up, sat, ran my hands through my hair, and leaned back in my chair for a moment. A river of hot blood roared from my head to my feet, and the usual beginning of the day Rah Rah-type reverberations echoed through the corridor.

I stood, shambled up the sterile, cubicle-lined passageway, and joined my energized teammates: The Untouchables.

16

Arriving at the northwest corner of the office, the view through the window was stunning. Across the River, NBC Tower rose to my fore—blocky, dense Art Deco shaped concrete rocketing into a crisp, clear blue sky—I wanted to gawk, there was so much more, but The Untouchables, be them thirty, had encircled a man by the name of Joshua Friar, our Director Of Admissions, along with his aids: Gloria Prendercast, and Petra Nudwigler, and the entire group was clapping in unison, slowly at first—male cheerleader-like—and then came the firm, steady escalation—"Who are *we*?" Mr. Joshua asked in a whisper, his initial stanza of madness—his usual—face growing redder by the moment, as though his feet were the base of a thermometer stuck under the tongue of an impermeable giant with a blazing fever.

"The Un*touch*ables," everyone whispered back, clap cadence increasing, eyes all wide, saliva on the rise—

"*Who*?" Josh bawled, staring everyone down with an expression that seemed to assert we were reproductively challenged—

"The Un*touch*ables!" Yes, that's right, you heard us!—went the expressions—the harmonious clap rounded turn four and thundered down the straightaway at breakneck speed—

"I *can't* hear *you!*" Mr. Joshua screamed, torso bent backward at a sixty-five degree angle, veins in his temples quivering to the cadence of his twisted, thundering heartbeat—

"The un*touch*ables!" everyone screamed, frenzied like firecrackers, clapping faster, harder, faster, harder, *fas*ter, *hard*er. We have penises—we have vaginas! Right on Joshua! Who do you think we are? We're changing lives, O yes!—we change lives one person at a time, O yes!—we perform mi*r*acles—do *you* perform miracles? I didn't think so! Fuck with us! Just *try* to fuck with us!—went the expressions—and the crazy high five exchanges—they were fritz-wild—on the side, up high, down low—uh-huh mate, too fuckin' slow—*ja!*—we're: The Un*touch*ables!

The enrollment coinsurers, they were freaking hard—and then came the chest bumps. Grown men and women, howling like they'd been raised by wolves—I did a summersault and a half-assed cartwheel and the whole building went shaking—

"Yeah Anthony—*yeah!* Do another cartwheel, do the No Roof! Yeah! Do the No Roof! Yeah! Yeah do it!—yeah man, *yeah!*" Someone was screaming.

Mr. Joshua agreed. "We need a h*u*ge day Anthony—you es*pe*cially. I don't know what, exactly, but something is very wrong with your numbers—all this enthusiasm and no en*roll*ments? You and I need to have a chat later this afternoon, anyhow," Joshua said, pointing a finger in my general direction. "As far as the rest of you—we missed our enrollment goal by thirty-nine percent yesterday. Thirty-*n*ine percent, people! And the COWs—your CO*W*s were down by forty-*s*even percent! It is not possible to attain an enrollment with securing a Contract On its Way, okay? Why are you here? Why do you people show up every day? If you're just coming here to simply collect a p*a*ycheck, you might as well leave right now," he said, exploding his rosy palms apart from one another, slowly shaking his head and its blond porcupine swoosh of a spike from side to side, "Just clean out your desks and walk out the darn door! Unless you're here to change lives, unless you're here to perform *mir*acles—get out. We need a no roof day—a h*u*ge one." A no roof day? Sure thing, bub—ain't no roof on my crib—ain't no roof on the number of people I'll convince to not enroll—ain't no roof on the number of leads I'll ruin, nope—no worries mate—I'll burn the whole fucking house down.

I jumped into the circle and grooved a flying worm right off the bat. It was out of hand, seriously man—my façade, she was way over the top. I jumped to my feet and my eyes—they were crazy for sure—everyone getting the stare down. "I can't hear *you!*" I proclaimed—and the flying summersault—I'm Jessie White's prodigy, boy, tumbler in the first—they fly me into Beijing on the weekends, ya heard?

I leapt out of my follow-through and carried into a second, more deliberate version of the flying worm, my usual, ridiculous face included. I whooped it up, frenzied flames and spread the inferno with the hot breath from my mouth—people were going crazy, my soul was ablaze—"*Roof* or no *roof?*" I screamed.

"*No Roof!*"

"*I* can't *hear you!*" I pointed a finger at Todd, in the newest employee's face, did the Hulk Hogan winding hand to my ear like I was deaf, and his easily coerced persona yelled a predictable slew of frat-boy-sort nonsense into the electrified atmosphere. Maintain the illusion, Anthony. Maintain the illusion—one more worm? It's probably your last, ay? Let's make it a good one. I was soon flying, breeze in my hair, my hands hit the ground and my body flew above my head, slowly, deliberately—my back cracked loud like a white ash baseball bat snapping on high inside heat—I'm so sick of this. I sprung from the floor, danced an Irish jig, progressed into a wampum pompum rain dance and screamed bloody murder: "*Roof or no roof?*"

"*No roof!*" The forty year old woman with the puffy hair and fake, infected-looking nails—the one in the flower dress—is she having a seizure? Let's find out—

"*One-more-time!*" My entire body crooked rearward, the window and blinds are actually quivering—I pointed at her—this woman—you should see the way she does it—gal needs a calculator to figure out how many nickels she needs to buy a bag of spicy Cheeseits from the vending machine, but when she's on the phone with a prospective student—you should hear what she says, the way she talks down to these people, belittles them, the way she goes out of her way to be discourteously manipulative and offensive: 'You can't take the loans and earn your degree because *why*? Because your mother is s*i*ck and you don't have the time or money right now? Well healthcare isn't free, you know, it takes *m*oney to heal people. How can you make money without a college education? Easy answer, sir—you *ca*n't make money without a college education. Well, sorry—I'm sorry your mother is sick, but that's just a fact—all I'm doing is giving you the facts.'

"*No roof!*" she screamed into my face, spicy breath causing my eyes to temporarily tear, if only trace. The façade, she was complete—execution-style. Damn, you people are marvelous, deliriously marvelous, and I own you.

17

"Alr*iii*ight," Mr. Friar said, "Best Rah-Rah of the week, and great way to start a Friday—way to get the ball rolling, Anthony."

"Thanks Mr. Joshua, I wasn't sure if I had it in me, I really wasn't." As time had worn on, I insisted on calling Mr. Friar, Mr. Joshua, and more and more people began to follow suit. It had quite nearly morphed into an official nickname, and I could tell he internally despised me for it.

"Way to push through, Anthony. You'll be a leader someday, just like Rich Knaffey, head of marketing—he's a winner. Alright people," Joshua said, clapping his hands together syllable-style, Rein-style, "You need to listen up and listen up good! In case you haven't realized, this is the last week these people can enroll into the upcoming semester." As you might expect, as with any sales organization, 'semesters' begin on a monthly basis. Admissions advisors are advised to leave that fact out of the conversation with a prospective student for sake of creating urgency—they're advised to leave that, along with many other details out of conversations for sake of urgency, among other sakes.

"Alright, I'm going to get right to it because we have a *h*eck of a lot to cover this morning. I know it's the last day of the month and you probably want to be on the phone, pounding away, but you'll be happy to know that you can stay as long as you want this evening, all the way until eleven o'clock if you feel the need—we cleared it with security," he said, giving a double thumbs-up.

Removing a small square of paper from the back pocket of his blue Dockers, he said, "First off, found written upon yet another bathroom stall was:

'Exemplify love
With your harrowing toil and
Elaborate stratagem—
Wreak revengeful havoc
Upon the anemic rovers of
Unwarranted savageness
Toward the ignorant'

"Now, let's be clear: when we find who keeps writing this, they are going to be charged a steep cleanup fee for all this nonsense, and fired immediately, get me? We know it's a man who is responsible because it has only been found in the men's stalls, so half of you are presumed innocent—the women, I mean."

"What does that even de*n*ote, exactly?"

"What it means, Caroline, is unnecessary distraction for the workforce—we don't need people sitting in the stall trying to decipher cryptic messages between wipes, alright? We need you pounding the phones, and enrolling students. I'd like to say forget I even brought it up, but upper management has issued a decree: if you happen to be in the bathroom and smell permanent marker from an adjoining stall, wait and see who exits. The powers that be have agreed that whoever succeeds in capturing this churlish culprit in the act will be due a two hundred dollar bonus." Joshua's stern face stared grim and accusatory in the direction of each and every male Untouchable, and stated: "Every single one of you is susceptible to suspicion."

Uncomfortable, first date-like silence ensued, and then: "What about the other teams? There are twelve other teams with roughly thirty workers per squad. Have they been placed under the same supervision?" posed an apprehensive face in its mid thirties that went by the name of Craig, "Is there reason to specifically say that an Untouchable is behind this? I mean—it can't be possible. I personally know of two people on the Marauders that speak negatively of their work—fellow smokers, I hear them gossip out front during break—I'll tell you who they are after the meeting if you'd like—they're under suspicion as well, right?"

Static faces stiffened squeamish, stone-like and stigmatized by the open-ended condemnation, and Gloria said, "I always said it's great to be a woman!" her heavy lisp emitted a small conglomeration of foamy discharge, roughly the size of a lemon seed, which therein landed soundlessly upon the blue carpet, mere inches shy of my feet. Expressions of: I'm scared—were silently answered by a rotating stare that insinuated: you *should* be.

"Everyone—and I mean everyone is suspect, including me." Frightened eyes glared about as though belonging to a neighborhood of East Berlin narcs eager to supply fresh, accusatory information to the Stasis. "Alright, now that we've covered this claptrap, let's get into more important things. Whatever the reason, according to the numbers, we've been losing people left and right of late. There has been a steady deterioration of enrollments for the past month and a half—students send in their application fee, you file their paper work as a fresh COW, and, for whatever reason, in between the time they're filed and the time they're pushed into financial aid, something goes horribly wrong, and we can't get them back on the phone. Understand: this is com*plete*ly unacceptable—completely! What'd we tell you during training? You need to acclimate your students to the idea of success. Have you been doing so? I'd like to think that if this was the case, our current state would not be the prevalent reality of shrinking numbers. Every *single* one of you for whom a previous comparison of results exist—all of your numbers are down. Why is this? Any ideas?"

"Maybe—has the quality of the leads deteriorated?"

"What? What was that? Who said that? Our leads are *flush* with the opportunity to change lives—whose opinion was that? I didn't see who spoke."

"I didn't mean it negatively, Mr. Friar, all I meant wa—"

"No, that's good—I'm glad you brought it up, Pauline—it's a fair question. To answer: who can tell me where our leads originate? Any guesses? Pauline?"

"Don't some of them come from people who fill out information requesting specific information about our programs? People who click upon the ads we place upon news and job boards and things of this nature?"

"Yes, very good—that is absolutely, one hundred percent correct. Roughly twenty percent of the leads you are asked to convert originate in that precise fashion. But more importantly, where to the additional eighty percent originate? Any takers?"

"Do we purchase them somewhere? From some sort of company that sells information?"

"Ah ha!—a member of the Untouchables has actually shown a susceptibility for re*mem*bering something—well done, Craig! As your Director of Admissions, I'm rather proud. We *do* purchase the remaining leads from information slingers, yes, but most importantly, what sort of key particulars are the people on this list associated with? Any takers?"

"Is it a list of people who are known to have not earned their diplomas of yet?"

"No, Shauna, it is not. To my knowledge, such lists are not in existence—don't get me wrong, they'd be nice to have, lists like that, but what you have at your disposal is even better. Any last guesses as to whom the eighty percent is comprised of? Anybody at all? No? Well, I'll tell you then. Eighty percent of those you speak with on a daily basis—their information has been procured from companies who keep track of people who are in a sense:

behind on their bills. The lists are a combination of people with poor credit, and people who are trying to be reached, successfully or not, by debt collectors—and that's why you shouldn't necessarily take offence when, at the first instant you get them on the phone, they're on the defensive. Our number, just like that of debt collectors, shows up on the caller ID as a toll free line. Such is why, often times, you're treated with such immediate hostility: they believe you're about to badger them about a bill, not chime in as the solution to the long litany of little mistakes that have compiled into the heaping weight representative of their current predicament," he said, expression gratified by the sheer simplicity of the psychology behind the sale.

"Now—and who was it that stated: 'Perhaps the quality of our leads has been diminished?' Who was that?"

"Sorry Mr. Friar, it was me, I jus—"

"No, no, *no!* Do *n*ot be sorry, alright Pauline? It's good of you to examine our process to an extent—when doing so accentuates students' underlying motives, thereby providing you with the recipe needed to release the tumbler and unlock the limitations imposed by not possessing a degree, okay? Now—can someone tell me *w*hy this is a huge advantage? Why is the fact that the prospective clientele we are contacting—what are some reasons as to why it is advantageous that they are currently deluged by debt, blinded by bills, and wearisome to the point of delirium from the effort of simply trying to maintain?"

"Is it because they're desperate for help?"

"Yes—I mean, that much should be obvious, Mr. Rothschild—and I'm only calling you Mr. on account of that tie you're wearing today, very impressive—but give me something more specific. Anyone in this position—and let's not pretend this status does not relate to some of *y*ou, too—but yes, anyone who has overbought to the point of losing the luxurious dream of free time included in their daily activities—why should our program fill the void of confused stagnation of achievement?"

"Is it because a degree will bolster their standing at work?"

"Assuming they're employed, yes Petra—this is *o*ne reason. The degree one holds is an alluring allusion to its intelligence. Don't you see how, after dangling this carrot to somebody in dire financial straights—the id*e*a of completing one of our programs—don't you see how, for people who cannot pay the bills, the idea of education is all the more enticing? Do you see how this works, Petra? The aggregate of their reality is ensnared with struggle," he said, grabbing Pauline by her rounded shoulders and, using his hand as an imaginary bar code scanner, he physically swept her across the beam, said, "Beep," and pretended to pile her upon an invented heap of recently enrolled cohorts. "See? It's that simple—from failure to success, just like that—and on with the next call."

Words twisting my stomach into a caustic soda, Mr. Joshua carried on in unfailingly philanthropic overtones, pious body language seeking to amalgamate the laymen into an amorous cohesion of sorts, stark reality of what was happening altogether impounded by a false sense of freakish healing of the hopeless.

"I'd love to end this meeting right here and allow you to have at it, but Rich and I, we—"

"What's Rich's background in, just curiously," I asked. Knowing how effectively his deformed agenda had been implemented upon prospective students, I was curious to see if he possessed special military training in Psych-Ops.

"Mr. Knaffey? He's a hell of an entrepreneur, a former class president,"—and off he went for a second, stating, in a sense, that, after studying the basic tenets of human nature, Mr. Knaffey went sailing on an ego trip long ago, and has since circumnavigated the globe several times. Mr. Joshua continued to rain praises of production on a man for whom, much to my mortification, immediate dregs of respect emanated throughout the assembly. "That's why we were excited to hire him as the head of our marketing department. He'd been so successful in his work for the mortgage broker, I mean—he was able to entice all *sorts* of people into buying new homes that otherwise might never have had the oppor*tunity*—management figured it is not that different from the *idea* of education—you know, the *idea* of wanting to become a homeowner is not fundamentally dissimilar from desiring to graduate from our esteemed University—see, in both cases, the parties in question are longing for su*ccess*, and the road that leads to such is intertwined—and, thankfully for all of us, management was right. As you can tell by the way our numbers have skyrocketed over the past few years, Mr. Knaffey—he knows how to push peoples' buttons and, whether they are ready or not, his marketing ideas get people interested in bettering themselves." The trouble with such tactics, I thought, is that nobody is there to take a Polaroid of the unprepared proles at the very moment their minds have to greet with all the problems that occur when hope meets reality. Everyone feels real brave and proud of themselves at the moment they're coerced into leaping from the high dive—it's what they look like after realizing they've plummeted into ice water—that's the shot I'm looking for—the image of their eyes when the cold reaches in and rips the oxygen right out of their lungs—I always imagine unimproved students opening bills and having their faces contort into an updated version of Edvard Munch's painting: 'The Scream', as it finally sinks in: 'O—we *actually* have to p*ay* for the way we're living and the resources we're using? You mean our life*style* includes repercussions? But, I mean—we can't afford it!' Well who woulda fucking thunk it, ay pal?

I don't know who I loathe more—those who've been duped, or the dupers themselves. Either way, in the end I'm just another frugal, independent motherfucker who'll be stuck paying for both ends of the rope that'll eventually loop in the middle and hang me. I squeezed my eyelids tightly together, released them, and thus continued to be fascinated by the forthcoming deliriousness.

"Anyhow, as I was saying, he and some others in upper management—we got to speaking, and we feel there are a lot of key points you are not harpooning. Remember what you need to be doing, okay?—technically you sell education, but in reality, what you sell is the dream. You need to make this the focus during every-single-conversation. Tell your prospective students—tell them to fasten a Post-It note upon the refrigerator with their graduation date so their entire family will see how successful they are. This works, trust me— it works like a gem. You see, that graduation date is an important aspect to the lattice of eagerness we're attempting to weave, people. Again, more than likely, these people are struggling. What you need to do—you need to get these people to put that possible graduation date somewhere that ensures everyone in their entire family will see it—on the fridge, the mirror in the bathroom—wherever everybody will see it. I hope you people understand why that's the first step. I *ce*rtainly hope so—we go over these reasons twice per d*ay*, and yet I often hear them excluded from the pitch—what is being misunderstood? In case you forgot, the r*e*ason this is key is because for them, for these people, that date—it's like the light at the end of the tunnel. What that date represents, at least in their mind—that graduation date represents the first day of the end of their suffering. And who knows? Maybe this education will help them, and maybe it won't—the honest truth: probably not always," Joshua said, extending his arms sideways, turning his palms upward, heaving his shoulders and eyebrows toward the ceiling—his usual expression of assumed innocence, "But as long as you get them thinking that m*a*ybe—that maybe it just m*i*ght—*w*ell then. If you can just get them thinking it m*i*ght, you'll have your fish on the line. You get them thinking it might help—trust me," he said, body hunched over a pretend fishing pole, slothfully recasting his line time and time again and, bending over, squinting, scrutinizing his imaginary bobber—is that a nibble? And now whispering, "C'mon now, c'mon—and wham!" he yelled, hands strangling a pen, body rearing backward, pretending to set the hook deep in the lips of the hungry victim, "You've got your fish and they're hooked nice and solid!—straight to the point that the optimism within their own minds won't allow them to wiggle loose. And this—this is the point—when they've begun selling them*selves* the dream, okay?" he said, reeling the catch toward the shore, "Such is the point—where they're selling them*selves*—this is where you need to bring each and every person—the ex*act* frame of mind you need to breach," he said, pretending to pull the fresh meal out of the lake, gaff deep in the gills, his mouth again forming into an upward wedge as he feigned measuring a sizable yield with an imaginary yardstick.

"Remember, we preach schoolyard rules—we play to k*ee*p—play to win here—we play to *win* or we don't play at all. We have a process, a sales process. Each one of your prospective students needs to follow it, *p*eriod. But they can never, *n*ever feel as if they're being sold an education. Never, *e*ver. They need to feel as if they're selling *y*ou. If they don't feel that way, even for a minute, you'll lose them—I guarantee it."

Caroline's white, undernourished feet shuffled around in her slightly too large red pumps for a second, flexing tendons tremor thin and brittle like overused, bleached chopsticks on the verge of tearing through a thin sheet of white, recycled paper, and she asked, "What's the best way to turn up the pressure? Without being overbearing, I mean."

"If you want your numbers to be plenteous, you need to have these plebeians make a pledge, okay?—say: 'Okay, listen to me, Johnny'—and your voice needs to sound very, *v*ery sincere at this point. If there is any shilly-shallying in your declaration, forget it—you *w*ill lose this individual. Remember—strength in timbre infers sincerity and truth. Art*i*culate, *enu*nciate, be elegant, coherent, and clear. You need to explain: 'Okay Johnny'—and, after addressing his specific litany of blunders, what you do is—you draw an imaginary line in the sand, and tell the prospective student that they need to make a decision—that: 'Listen Johnny, the juncture of success and failure has arrived, okay? It's time to decide if you're going to be one of the successes, or one of the failures. Upon what side of the chronicles is your story going to be told? I have a lot of successful people waiting for their chance to be qualified, and I don't have time for games—what's it going to be?' See? It's that easy."

As he spoke I could feel beads of sweat beginning to break through my scalp and saturate my hair, and I thought: they graduate as many useless zombies as they can, at the highest price point, as fast as possible, you know, to promote suc*c*ess. It was full on maddening. The guy to my left, Doug, was a fairly new employee, three weeks in, and typical of the workforce: a young father in his early forties with a high school education—he was extremely eager to 'try hard' simply because somebody 'gave him a chance'—elbowing me in the ribs, brown eyes beaming with belief, he whispered, "Mr. Friar—he's just so smart—*so* smart—he's only thirty-six and he already owns five apartment buildings. That's the difference between people like him and people like us."

"That's not the only one."

"You're right, you're so right," he whispered, nodding whilst simultaneously shaking his head from side to side, "I should have known that—I did—I mean, you know, he's just head and shou—"

"You have an opinion on something, Doug?"

"Um—I was just, ah, thinking, Mr. Friar, um—what if they don't have the money?" he asked, mouth visibly relieved to have verbalized a coherent query.

"If they claim they don't have the money or can't afford the loans, tell them: 'That's because you didn't go to school and pay your due diligence to acquire intelligence. This is your chance, right here, right now, to whirl that shortcoming into an advantage.' Tell them exactly that, and do not deviate," he said.

"Great, Mr. Friar, thanks—I—" the way a crowd tends to function like an organism with its head chopped off sent me imagining halved necks bleeding hot red, and thereby blocked my mind from absorbing the specific, intractable praise raining upon Mr. Joshua. The fact that the thesis being thrust out of his maw seemed visually scintillant from the sheer coldness associated with using somebody's greatest weakness against them in as vicious a variety as possible—under the guise of betterment—with a smile on his face and a bulge in his pants, no less—this had me feeling as though even the shadow cast by his propagandist persona was polluting. I placed my left hand over my mouth and felt the muscles beneath my ears bulge whilst involuntarily clenching my jaw in order to avoid screaming: what an incredible institution of higher learning this really is!

"What is it, Anthony?"

"What?"

His words sent my heart flying faster than it should—beating harder than I presumed it could, and he posed, "Do you have something to add? You're staring into my face like you're in a trance." I had quite a few topics on my mind. Maybe I need to change my taciturn ways and shatter the groupthink, I thought—should I just come out with it all? Should I unleash upon these people?—but what would I even say? Where would I begin? I mean— what? Is everybody in this entire room sedated? Do you hold zero competency of quality? Wake up! I looked around and thought: where are these people's heads? What are they on right now? What crazy, fucked up places are these people visiting? Some of them have to be with me, right? They can't honestly be taking all of this in, can they? Are they actually as they appear: standing eagerly in wait of their chance to 'give their best crack' at achieving these afore stated principals? Some, yes, perhaps most, but others—others are simply stuck trying to survive, to not die, having to do what they hate and know to be wrong in order to feed their families, just as is the case with many millions of humans across the globe— different languages, geographies, governments, climates and cultures, and yet: same ole bullshit—good, smart people stuck bowing down to yet another unsound yes-man in an inadequately tailored suit. Why is this? And what are they thinking about? Bills. Chores. Running up another bill to pay for a new, improved product that will allow them to complete a new, complex chore with greater efficiency. Food. Sleep. Celebrities. Bills. How they can do well at work for sake of paying bigger bills faster and allowing more time to complete the more complex chores. Food. Bills. Sleep—precious sleep—I inhaled, mind unable to extemporize proper argumentation so as to irradiate all that was erroneous within the institution and, after exhaling, I temporarily curbed my freedom of expression, and said, "Um—I felt as though I had something rather dead on spot to mention, but it seems to be eluding me now." Staring into his face, each little hair within his goatee in its prim and proper place, my resentment remained internal and pinned to a central point in the middle of my chest, constricting tighter by the minute.

"If the prophecy revisits, raise your hand and spout it out. I welcome any and all input in these meetings."

"Great," I said, wondering what he *actually feels* in his soul when alone.

"Now, before we break—what I want to do—I want to take it from the top, from the very *instant* you get a prospective student on the line," he said, voice low and bombastic, "As stated, as a prelude to your success, on the first call you want to be Colombo—you remember that show, right? Colombo? You need to be an incredible investigator. Thinking back upon where eighty percent of your leads derive, what should you assume is the basic motivation behind the prospective student's desire to enroll? Well? C'mon, *quick*—*somebody!*"

"To get their degree—wouldn't it be?"

"*No*, Mr. Rothschild! I mean—yes, but—think deeper! The reason, quite simply, is financial *freedom!*—such is the basic motivation behind the prospective student's desire to enroll. If you think knowledge is the main reason, stop kidding yourself. That's what the local library is for. We instill *some* knowledge, don't get me wrong, if they study on their own, they'll learn a little, but for most people—think about it. What do they write about in their entrance essays? Financial freedom! They might not write it with the elegance of Emerson, but if you simply ignore the spelling errors and awkward presentation and focus upon their complaints—I mean, the main problem, quite simply, is that they're poor! Such is the impetus that drives them to enroll—and that's ex*act*ly why you need to bond with these people about hope-induced, far-flung dreams of procu*re*ment. This is an easy desire to propagate into further urgency, okay, but to do that, you need to build *trus*t! Establish yourself as comrade—'Hey buddy, we're in this to*gethe*r—not only am I your admissions advisor, but hey, I'm *here* for you pal—I'm here the whole-way-through—we're going reach your goals to*gethe*r.' Remember: bond, build trust, establish rapport—bond, build trust, establish rapport—every minute, every day, every week, every month, every *single* phone call," he said, smacking the back of his right hand off the palm of his left, once per word. "Again: bonding, building trust, establishing rapport, bonding, building trust, establishing rapport—now, everybody repeat that five times aloud," he said.

It felt eerily similar to a request to: 'Please stand in a showing of patriotism.' Peer pressure and mob mentality swept away caution. As thirty sets of lips fell into motion, I could see that when the mob mentality takes over, even the perpetrators may not comprehend what's going on. Content rarely mattered—intelligence was measured in how loudly or rapidly one spoke. Observing the motorized movement of adjacent faces, I thought—when you hear that somebody has become trapped in machinery, there is no need to ask: is it bad?

"I'm sorry, but that chant simply wasn't thunderous enough. Understand—that mentality—that mentality is *cruc*ial! Es*sen*tial to meeting your goals! I can't begin to stress how crucial this is—give it to me again, louder this time."

As throats quivered at the unrestricted effort of vocal cords attempting to reach their zenith of decibel output, I almost laughed aloud. The level of manipulation was quite extraordinary. It was interesting to observe the way people who had been broken down from years of improper suggestion were willing to do nearly anything to remain 'employed' and in 'good standing' in the eyes of their 'superiors'—it was sickening really.

"Do you know what these students are? Deep down, students are professional procrastinators. And this is why you need to be the instigator, of the motivator, that breaks the cycle of procrastination! Go ahead and repeat that for me, everybody, once aloud—what do you need to be?"

"The instigator, of the motivator, that breaks the cycle of procrastination!" They all yelled, religious sloganeering rebounding off the low slung ceiling.

"Very good—now, define recommendation for me," Joshua asked, "I want to hear your personal definition of a recommendation. Why would you choose to recommend a student for admittance to this university? Anyone? You, Todd—answer the question," Mr. Joshua said, pointing at another new guy, the heedful-looking, waspish, waddling songster with buzzed, red hair—same one whose vitriolic attack upon improperly qualified pupils had, after a few short days, vexed me to the point of imagining vivid cataclysms affecting his welfare and safety. "Granted, this is your first week and you have limited-to-no experience on the sales, er, admissions floor, but I want you to answer. I want to hear what you have to say—reason being, you're fresh out of training, hence, you haven't had the time for the bad habits of others to morph into those of your own—which is, by the way, likely the reason you have the most COWs on the board since Monday."

"My definition of a personal recommendation?" Todd said, gazing his victorious eyeballs all overly perplexed-like toward the ceiling.

"Yes, what is it? Define the type of student you'd personally recommend for enrollment," Fryer said—this is a trick question, a favorite of his—every new person to join the team is asked the same question, and the answer is spun into a spectrum of spiritual and constitutional obligation.

"Well," Todd started, "I guess I'd recommend, you know, someone whose entrance essay is focused on good rea—"

Friar's ensuing laughter held an edge of hysteria. He caught his breath and grinned, pleased. "Okay, stop right there. What you all need to understand is that you have a moral obligation to enroll these individuals into this program. It's their right to attend this university. I hope you understand that what we're doing is, to an extent—it's miraculous. Who determines if they're going to be accepted? You do, or so you lead them to believe. There is no acceptance process at this school. There is, but at the same time, there isn't—unlike other schools' admission committees, we're not here to judge. So long as they have the money or qualify for student loans, they're in. As American citizens, it is their fundamental right to attend this university—we do not thwart dreams and we do not discriminate." A key feature of the process was that a radical core of individuals used legitimate issues ambiguously—concepts such as 'knowledge' and 'success' were thrown about without comprehensive analysis as to how, why, or if they would be earned. This served to generate warm 'feelings' in the stomachs of advisors, thereby manipulating a large mass to achieve goals most had yet to fully fathom. This, intentionally or not, feeds the pride, the power they believe they have, and helps to mask what is via the fledgling desire to 'assist' their 'fellow man' in confused gratification for playing a lead role in the 'greater good'—

Mr. Joshua crouched low to the floor, placed his face in his hands, stood quickly, and, his voice swelling with an authoritarian tones, he said, "Pretty simplistic, people—see, if you're assuming that you're going to enroll that prospective student—an assumption you better be making—you need to unpeel the onion. Unpeel that student's soul. At the center you'll find their pain—you'll find some type of pain, guaranteed, and the solution to that pain needs to be this education. We are their salvation—understand this fact. Enrolling them in classes is an agenda. It's our agenda, your agenda, and our agenda must be spun into their

63

agenda, *period*. Remember, somewhere deep inside the onion lays the belief that they're lifelong failures. Our objective is to make them believe they'll remain as such, that is, until they receive their diploma. It's not a hard sell—by no means should you be looking to stuff this down anyone's throat, that is, as far as they know—that's why it's a smooth force."

"Like a Tony Kukoc dunk?"

"If that's what works for you, Craig, then yes, like a Tony Kukoc dunk—think of your own metaphors, people, anything that helps. Again, the main objective is to make the student feel like we're looking out for their best interest. Once that has been accomplished, once you've earned that trust in the manner I already described—wh*a*m—they'll be *b*egging to enroll. I mean—doesn't anyone remember training? Todd," Joshua said, torso leaned forward, hands motionless, roughly the width apart one might have expected if he were in the midst of telling a story about the largest bratwurst he'd ever devoured, "You can make a name for yourself working here, a really, *r*eally big name for yourself—but if you want that to happen, you have to follow *p*rotocol," he stressed, face radish-red, voice vaunting the extolment of outside admiration. "Now—who can tell me what technique has been most responsible for vaulting average advisors into the limelight of developing into a member of the High Achievers' Club? Petra? Do you have an answer?"

"Is it the *S*witch?"

"See, now I'm *r*eally impressed. Twice in one meeting an Untouchable has shown a predisposition to remembering a major crux of our philosophy. Yes folks, indeed, Petra is correct—don't take it as a coincidence that she has joined us for a fabulous, all-inclusive vacation as a member of the High Achievers' Club for the previous two years. Petra understands that we use a reverse sell—that's our sales technique, and we call it the *S*witch. The Switch is the crux of our sales system—but before you can flip the Switch, you need to erect the infrastructure, okay? This in turn puts the student in the position of having to sell *you* on th*e*ir ability. I'm getting very, *v*ery tired of constantly going over this, but I'll run through it one last time for all you minions who have yet to comprehend," he puffed.

Indeed, Mr. Joshua was correct in his assessment. The 'Switch', like it or not, is the brilliantly employed modus operandi which allows hundreds of unthinking proles to compel tens, hundreds of thousands of additional unthinking proles to enroll into an overtly expensive institution whose curriculum imparts little wisdom, knowledge, or intelligence—this approach is first imposed upon the preferably, overtly yielding-type perspective representatives hired for the sales force—used against them during the hiring process and training—and then, the same series of psychologically mindful, scripted steps is used with masterfully premeditated, and sickening success upon pitiably poor, prospective students.

"Once we determine the student has money or the ability to obtain money, the only aspect that determines whether or not a student will be accepted is a recommen*dat*ion. So you say: 'Johnny, if we b*o*th decide we have an education match, I will then walk you through the paperwork you'll need to fill out in order to apply, and, only after a *r*igorous interview process will we decide if your educational history and future aspirations warrant a recommendation," Joshua said, his eyes tightly closed, brow line tense with frustration.

"It's a matter of being consistent with the play on their emotions. You're the advocate, then you throw up an obstacle to their acceptance, a constant game—it is all about being consistently inconsistent—advocate, obstacle, advocate, obstacle, and so on—you can never let them feel with any type of certainty that getting accepted to this University is actually possible. This will form the foundation for an eruption of self-doubt and erode the feeling of relative insulation provided by confidence, okay? The last thing you need to do is make this person feel as if they're capable of self-reliance—dangle the carrot, allow them to lick it a bit, but do not let them devour—not until their loans have been granted. At that point it is too late for them to backtrack—we're devouring them. Well, not devouring exactly, but we will have fulfilled our objective, and you will have earned your paycheck. You know what I'm saying, I'm sure. Questions?"

"What is the best way to get them to open up about themselves? I mean—what if they're reluctant to get into details? What'll really hook 'em the best—get them talking the most, I mean?"

A pressure wave of impatience sent his eyes bleary with exhaustion, and he said, "Please Shauna, all of you—understand—our approach is systematic, okay? There is not necessarily one specific portion of the practice that trumps all else—if you want to be certain that the person on the other end of the phone will enroll in the upcoming semester you must master each element of procedure. Our pitch is designed to sympathize with the student's pain, the pain at the center of the onion, their soul, as stated. Make them feel as though they need to overcome millions of obstacles—to provide a window of hope, ask open-ended questions that cause the student to inform you of an instance when they overcame an obstacle, you know, maybe they needed to make a phone call to a relative in a hospital but didn't have any change, so they scraped up a haul of aluminum and resold it or stood at an intersection and washed windows for however long it took to obtain thirty cents or whatever a phone call costs these days—who *knows*? Maybe they work at the Gap and fold jeans faster and more crisply than any of their coworkers—just funnel the conversational flow so as to enable them to describe several small victories."

"Like what? What's another example we can use?"

"Like, well—moving their vehicle in time to avoid a street cleaning ticket, maybe—see, I don't care what *angle* you use, just make them feel as if they're capable of something, okay? And, just as importantly, perhaps more so, as soon as you've affirmed that capability, tear it down! Shift the conversational flow toward reasons they have yet to achieve their degree and harp those reasons *mer*cilessly!" Joshua said, throwing his hands into the air, insinuating hallelujah-type obviousness for the reasons behind this tactic. As if out of sheer perversity, speculative pessimism was pounded into students' heads with ungodly persistence. "And as soon as you've torn them down to the point where they don't believe they'll be accepted, build up the reasons that they might, just m*i*ght be accepted once again—remember this is a very, *very* delicate process. I think you'll see that when the build-up tear-down is engaged effectively your students will eat from the palm of your hand—they'll believe you to be their sole human source of salvation."

The funny thing about this—the build-up tear-down approach is the exact process the education corporation uses upon their salespeople. Upon arriving in the morning, as you've seen, the day begins with a 'Rah-Rah'—management, on this day less than usual, builds the esteem of their sales force, praising their every trait, describing what a wonderful job they've been doing, and things of this nature. Then, when two o'clock rolls around: bam—the 'Reality Check' ensues. The purpose of the 'Reality Check', as you might suppose, is to tear down the esteem of the sales people and imply, that basically: 'Your effort has been mostly worthless, your further employment is non-essential, and if you do not dominate prospective students into enrolling for the remainder of the day—if by chance you don't exceed your lagging numbers—well, let's just say that we're always looking for salespeople who are hu*n*gry. There are a *lot* of hungry people out there, in case you forgot.' Just as with students, it causes many salespeople to heel, to beg, to consume whatever rotten fodder is laid before them without questioning.

"Your job is to motivate and inspire, to *s*ell, not to be judge and jury—to think, but not to think *too* much. Short on details and long on broad strokes, people," Joshua said, expression stark as he pretended to heave flowing waves of paint at an adjacent, white wall, "You need to follow the script, just nice and easy. Just memorize some dialogue, use a bit of voice inflection during key phrases in the script, and personalize it towards each student's source of pain so they deem you care about them—it is not difficult, just ignore the details to a certain extent and dial the phone." I raised my hand, eager to speak, but Joshua continued.

"Further—Rich Knaffey, he made a suggestion earlier today. Has anybody in this room ever watched a performance on Broadway? Fact of the matter is actors on Broadway live the role. They live it, and that's why you pay money to observe their performance. Night in, night out, paying spectators view actors and actresses put on a routine-orientated performance for the first time, and, and every-single-evening they have their minds blown. These actors perform for their guests with the same unspeakable intensity every-single-night. That is ex*act*ly how you need to live the role of a National Admissions Advisor, *p*eriod. The question is simple—are you believable, or aren't you? Do the students believe what you're telling them? If they do, you'll enroll lots and lots of students, make lots and lots of money, and win lots and lots of trophies. We give rewards here—huge trophies, and, as likely you already know, the trophies are actually shaped like Oscars. There's a *r*eason for that—if you want to be suc*c*ess*f*ul, you have to live the role. If you don't, if you're unsuccessful at—"

The speed with which the shadow of the ceiling fan went waving across Joshua's trim face conflicted with the dense, humid stillness of the room, and alas I still felt cold. I breathed deep, glanced out the window at the white, icy River lingering below, and held tight the feeling of swimming underwater with breath drawn for many years to be the sole means available for properly avoiding the endless scent of bullshit so thoroughly permeating our air. I exhaled, glanced around and found there's a certain frantic face people tend to make whilst entrenched in an unshakably fervent, non-admittance of what is. Feeling modestly dizzy, I closed my eyes and concentrated upon taking long, slow breaths, imagining what it would feel like to float up, out, and away—

His empty, threatening words carrying forward, I smiled at how easy it is to see how management uses fear as a tactic. When you're not afraid and do not care for invented repercussion founded upon false external judgments it's easy to see how *m*ost organized foundations use fear and confusion as central tactics to prompt actions. In Mr. Joshua's case such were used much the way politicians and media outlets act so endlessly se*n*sitive in an effort to shock, to jar, to distress the public about the possibility of dis*a*ster. It's a relative tactic used thoroughly in each phase of human interaction—especially within corporate America—with the key effect being the nauseating fatigue brought about by incessant scaremongering.

I opened my eyes and felt I was looking at people—it appeared as if from their first surrender to such scrambled, unorganized fear, lines of apprehension quickly chiseled themselves into their once adolescent faces, as if even then, even then in the days of their youth, their fresh mugs must surely have been compromised by images representative of the newly weary—and from these contours, invisible I-bolts were long ago inserted and strung with fishing wire hooked to the thick, greasy lips of three pound bullheads that, after having been sent hanging ever so tactfully dead, dying and flopping from the visages of the newly browbeaten, each and every time this person gave into external, unsubstantiated paranoia, a colossal, imperceptible, mangled hand gave the serrated fins a taut little tug—hanging from beneath the eyes, under the chin, from the earlobes, eyebrows, in the middle of the forehead and in the corners of the orifice, these rotting, diseased fish were surely hauled upon with knowledge-bound proficiency—lynched from whence first giving in to trepidation, the burdens have been sited upon folks with ever such delicacy, until finally, after years upon years of unrelenting submission, the weight has finally composed a corrupted, disgruntled façade in a sickeningly accurate arrangement so as to display a final masterpiece—a final ode to a decomposed life lived in incessant demoralization.

Speaking in cadences like a fundamentalist preacher, Mr. Joshua continued his spiel, "Further, why do you think our script runs the course as it does? Why do you think after all the questions, the multiple hours you've spent on the phone with this person, all the hours you've spent unpeeling the onion—why do you think the last question flows as it does? Do you think it's an accident? Do you have any idea of the sheer number of minds that have gone into the writing of that script? That script is water*t*ight, people—it's water*t*ight the whole way through. Do *n*ot deviate from that script—it's fl*a*wless. If there's any flaw it begins with your own deviation. The script, the entire process—it cost hundreds upon hundreds of thousands of dollars to create. We paid dozens of psychologists to create that script. Shall I remind you of some simplistic keys to execution?"

A stiff, stably irritated fellow—a type of guy who says, 'One, two,' after you say you need three seconds before you help them out—by the name of Timothy Kramer interrupted, and said, "I've been speaking to lots of people who've been laid off of late—do you have any specifics on how to pique their interest?"

"Very good question, Tim—if you'd have broken my flow for some nonsense, I would have been angry. Understand, folks, this is only going to become more prevalent as time drones on, and the economy worsens—and, frankly, unless some of your numbers should happen to rise, you just might find yourselves in the same position as those I'm speaking of, so pay close attention." Silent apprehension rose like UV-induced evaporation from a hot puddle of oily water in a parking lot, and he said, "Now, what you say in this situation is: 'Johnny, you're in a group of very talented people, it's not *y*our fault that you were laid off— but just think how much better off you would be *if*—how far ahead of the competition you'd find yourself if—*if*—'"

Fucking *if!*

"See how that works? What I'm doing—I'm giving them a little ego pat, and telling them: 'Johnny, I'm sure you are a remarkable talent, just one of many exceptional employees trapped in the current ordeal, stuck in the nightmare of having external forces limit your potential—if *o*nly you had your deg*r*ee—think of what an advantage that would be!' See?" They discard the why and how, but accept its consequence, earned knowledge, as if it were a self-evident primary requiring no blueprint en route to the secondary construction and eventual presentation of such, thereby leaving the student unable to compete in real world situations. Really it's as though expecting an untrained artist to read about art, recite what he's read, gaze upon a handful of secondhand photos of famous paintings, and then, after being commissioned to complete a complex masterpiece, he is to be somehow capable of conjuring one, as if out of thin air, without ever commencing with the initial stage of a physical apprenticeship.

"Say: 'I understand your feelings, Johnny. I've had others who've felt the same way, and what they've found is that'—and go from there. Tell them a success story, real or invented, of an individual who made gobs of money after taking loans and earning their degree. This method is called—*feel, felt, found*—and if you don't understand the mentality behind that by now, people, the mentality behind empathy being the ultimate dealmaker—I— if you don't understand this by now, I suggest you prance back to your cubicles, pack your belongings, and leave expediently. Understand—most people who've recently been laid off are holding on in vain hope for something, *a*nything that will improve their abysmal situation—the ship is sinking and they need a raft. That's why you say: 'What better flotation device is there, Johnny, besides knowledge?' Posing this query only adds ballast to the argument that they need to hurry up and send in their fifty dollar application fee, see?" I'd often witnessed how unemployment and lack of exposure to foreign ideas make people ripe for the picking for such well conceived banditry—so easy.

Doug, practically drooling, again poked me in the ribs, and his wide mouth whispered: "God, is he incredible or what? He has the answer every time—for every-single-question asked—Mr. Friar has a quick answer. It's no wonder I've had such a hard time getting a decent job for so many years, considering I'm up against brains like his— incre*d*ible."

An involuntary instinct almost fired a synapse that would have released a sharp backhand to his pathetic lips, but I checked myself, and whispered "Yep, he's fairly fucking incredible." Observing Doug bouncing 'round the room for the past three weeks, asking roundabout advice from every ruffian temporarily barking from the rostrum, I realized he was yet another of the unable to relax or focus, scattered personalities so mercilessly observed by my eyes, and I wondered what, if anything, he will ever contribute to the world aside dithering static. Further, I thought: what organic foundation of philosophy is he imparting upon his children? Simply because you have mastered bi-pedal locomotion doesn't mean you comprehend how to th*i*nk—are you making them strong and independent, or needy and weak? Are you expanding them to be aware of the illimitable possibilities of a freethought life, or contracting them into the disgusting funnel of collective passivity? I mean really, what lessons are his three young sons being trained upon? What sort of rotten baloney are they consuming? Lord what an unstomachable cycle!

"Some crucial, final keys for you to remember: first, and perhaps most importantly—always keep notes! Write down and remember their hot buttons, reiterate multiple bonding points—it's a qualitative solution, people—and, just as importantly, earn re*s*pect, not friendship—the impression of friendship shall place you in a power disadvantage. So again, think of the purpose for our last question: 'Johnny, a few minutes ago, you said'— whatever he's said—just repeat whatever the center of the onion unveiled, his pain. This is the genius of it—you say: 'Based on what you just said, Johnny, I have another question for you.' This new, incre*d*ibly im*po*rtant question, when stated, is the summation of his onion, of his entire soul. See, if you've done your job correctly, he already spilt it for you—his entire history of problems, right? Again, you *n*eed to take notes, jot down their problems, their essence, and repeat their own problems to them. Understand—it is very easy to discredit or attempt to not worry about your own problems when you are the one speaking of them—this is much more difficult to accomplish when somebody *e*lse is explaining all of your problems *to* you. Your tone of voice when repeating all of their problems into their ears—*v*ehemently concerned! You must make them feel as if they are on the verge of drowning! On the verge of going under—forever! After you've made it seem as if they are slipping away into the black depths, that is when you have to make your offer appear as if it is the only flotation device capable of saving them—but again, you're not certain if they deserve access to it. This is why, after repeating all their problems to them in a saddened, hopeless tone, they'll assume you've been hanging on their every word. This—this is the *exact* time you ask the last question: 'Johnny,'" Mr. Joshua began, tone a masterful duplication of one you might expect from a funeral director addressing a weeping column of weary mourners, "'After all we've spoken about, after all the time we've spent learning about one another—you've told me why you *n*eed to earn your diploma—you've told about all the reasons why your *f*amily is dep*e*nd*i*ng on you—the reasons why th*i*s opportunity—you've given me the excellent reasons why this opportunity will change your entire l*i*fe. I know you've given me all the answers, Johnny, but what I want—what I want is to hear the reasons you feel you de*ser*ve to be accepted. There are hundreds, tho*u*sands of individuals vying for a spot in our institution this upcoming semester—the competition is fierce. I'm going to put you on hold for ten minutes, Johnny—what I want you to do is write down the reasons why you think y*o*u de*ser*ve. When I get back on the phone, I want to hear all the reasons, in order, of why you imagine you deserve this opportunity to right your wrongs.'"

In order to avoid an eruption, I closed my eyes, and thought: it's okay, breathe—the most effectual parasites never disturb their hosts—you're not here to have fun or make friends or relate to people. This is your job—to produce as little for them as is possible to remain employed and continue to reduce the production of others while, at the same time, via random displays of unique knowledge and counterfeit effort, showing a scheming sort of insinuation that I hold the type of untapped potential that noble middle managers insist they can launch to stardom—it's okay, breathe—a decepticon pawn is a dangerous entity—for this gambit in turn continues to slash vast sums of profit over time—because nobody would dream that a person would purposely get hired at a company that produces sub par product for the sake of making the public aware if its inefficiencies—nobody checks that premise, it's not in the application, or in the personality tests—it's the antithesis of greed, hidden in inverted overachievement, and is therefore not comprehendible by the powers that be—and this is the fucking beauty of it.

"Do you people see the utter *genius* of th*at*?!" he exploded, "Do you see what position the prospective student has been placed *in?* What you've said, basically, is that his answers weren't good enough! And that, th*at* my friends—it is this transfer of responsibility that defines the Switch. It is at this very instant that the obligation of you having to sell them on our University is vanquished. At this instant, the obligation has switched to th*e*m being placed in the position of having to sell *y*ou on th*e*ir ability to be worthy. This change in responsibility makes them feel they're on the verge of not being accepted! Again, I can not begin to stress how key this is—especially given the fact that, if you've unpeeled the onion correctly, you've uncovered *mul*tiple faults in their educational, personal, or financial background and harped those faults to the point to which the prospective student feels as though this education is their final opportunity to right themselves. See, the entire time you've been telling them the reasons why our University is wonderful, they've been debating whether they're smart enough or not, whether they can afford it or not, and now, *n*ow they've been placed in the position of having to sell you on the reasons they're worthy of *us!* The genius is outlined in its simplicity. It's utterly brilliant—as stated, we paid a lot of psychologists a lot of money to write that script, so stick to it."

I looked into this man's eyes and saw no wisdom, no knowledge—all he knew how to do was add and subtract numbers from objectives he did not create in the first place and heap generic praise or disparagement upon those who did, or did not fulfill those presupposed parameters—he reminded me of most sales managers I've interacted with, fully—all except one—an intensely moral martial arts expert by the name of A.J. Wilder who would have gladly snapped Friar's neck and done the Moonwalk up the wall had he caught wind of this bullshit.

Mr. Joshua leaned casually upon the edge of a wooden desk, placed his arm horizontally upon a plain grey cubical wall, and chuckled, "Heh—you know, it was almost a waste of money, if you really think about it. I mean—do any of you remember Stewart Smally? Remember that skit from Saturday Night Live? Remember Stewart's catch phrase? 'I'm good enough, I'm smart enough, and doggone it, people like me?' Remember that? It's the same mentality really, only *this* time—this time it revolves around education, and money—the student's lack of both. As I like to say, again: officially we sell education, but what we really sell—we sell the dream. So never forget: advocate, obstacle, advocate, and then, after all the unpeeling, that specific question we just covered serves as the final obstacle—you put Johnny on hold for exactly ten minutes and, you know, do what you want during this time. Go for a smoke, snag some coffee, use the can, whatever—but be certain you're back on that line in exactly ten minutes. If, up until this point, you've done your job right, it won't matter what you're doing because Johnny will be sitting on the other end of the phone, writing the best reasons he can think of as to why he deserves, and his stomach will be quite unsettled, and the answer of your recommendation will serve as either the plug, or tap." He exhaled a long, relaxed breath of deep satisfaction and said, "As long as that Switch is complete, they'll believe this program, the online graduation program we offer—they'll believe that, in the long run, it'll make them wealthier, ease their problems, and solve whatever additional, unspoken issues reside at the center of their onion. As soon as they're forced to iterate their own problem aloud to themselves for sake of earning their way into this solution—*boom!* This is the exact moment when the fish is on the line for good—and that, friends, that is the essence of flipping the Switch—one of the best feelings in the whole-wide-world, no doubt." His lapidary last words stirred overawed expressions upon the majority of faces amongst the Untouchables, and this served to harden my resentment—I felt an immense desire to vanquish the whip hand, but fucking how?

18

"Ms. Prendercast, do you have anything to add?"

Waddling into the midst of the circle, each time her foot hit the ground it expanded sideways to look like a fleshy pink pancake struggling to balance the mountain of consumption teetering above it. She reminded me of an ugly flight attendant droning through the safety inspection with a facial expression consisting of bored, horrible amusement—not unlike a middle-aged prostitute riding the diseased, mutilated cock of an insatiable regular for the millionth time and finding a sort of enjoyment in it for some strange reason, indiscernible even to her.

I poked Doug in the ribs, and, speaking loud enough to hear, but quiet enough to deny, I mentioned, "She looks like a pale bean beetle jammed into that ballgown dress of hers—I hope she doesn't walk to work too often, because the amount of madly rank material that will build up within that twenty inch deep ass-crack will certainly be vast." Judging by his silence and the horrified—please don't include me in your subversive speech-look upon his face—he seemed to find the observation inaccurate.

A short-lived pause of the corruption became broken as the scaly spoonbill opened her beak, and shrieked, "Before I begin—great meeting, Joshua, incredible—just wonderful! How 'bout a round of applause for Mr. Friar?" she said, and most advisors lauded him as though he'd just done the flying splits, oohing and aahing and proving once again that the lengths people will go to pretend to care are horribly extraordinary. "Boy, did we ever need that! I don't have loads to say, team, but remember, it's early February—just what did most people in this country do at the start of last month? Well? Anybody have a guess?"

"Make a New Year's resolution?" Timothy tooted.

"Exactly, very good—the majority of adults in this country made a New Year's resolution only a few short weeks ago—this is especially true of the general base of people you're seeking to enroll—people in dire straights, okay? Now—what percentage of people do you think have already slipped off the wagon of what they swore they would accomplish? What percentage of people who said they were going to hit the gym four times per week and give up smoking?—what percentage has already nixed this plan? How many of them laid around last evening and had a cigarette with their coffee this morning? Well?"

"I'd bet most—or at least half," Caroline guessed, expression eager, not realizing both suggestions were of equal value.

"I agree—at *least* this many—and that's why, when you get them on the phone, somewhere in the middle of the process, during the second interview perhaps, you should tell them to make their New Year's resolution to: become *brilliant* this year," she said, literally frolicking in a circle, pleased as she was with her unique little angle. "What you do is you ask them how good it will feel when, at this time next year—ask them how they will feel after they answer a complex question posed by a complete and utter stranger and, after the stranger asks, 'How on *earth* did you know that?'—ask them how it will feel to exclaim: 'My New Year's resolution was to: become *brilliant* last year.' That's one of my own, you see?—feel free to test it out."

"Not to interrupt, Gloria," Mr. Joshua began, expression genuinely surprised, "But can I just say—I think you've already accomplished this goal—what a wonderful piece of advice! I'll be sure to tell Rich about your contribution—that's one of the best ideas I've heard in *months!*"

"O thank you, Mr. Friar, thanks, really—a compliment from you means a great deal to me—it truly does," she said, full cheeks blushing red. "Ahem, anyhow, remember, besides this, you need to plan for objections—have your Objection Tool Box at your side. The Objections Toolbox is designed as a panacea for all excuses—I know Mr. Friar covered some of these things, but there are other options. For instance, if a shortsighted student says they can't afford to take the loans and your initial response doesn't work, try this: 'You may have made your decision to not take the loans, Johnny, but I feel I *owe* it to you.' See that? See what I did there, folks? I owe it to tell *you* what *I* know—and go from there. Remember, not only are you the advocate, you're the *expert*, the *guru*—this technique insinuates you're required to look out for that person's best interest—you owe them! That's a key spin people, as key as it gets. I mean—what do you think these people will wind up doing for the remainder of their lives if they don't get their degrees? Anyone?"

"Digging 3,700 miles to the center of the earth from the surface, only to break down and burn?"

A few chuckles broke out and, "I don't know if the situation is that extreme, but you know what? Maybe, Anthony, may*be*," Gloria lisped, "I'm glad you understand why you're required to overpower their reluctance with an assorted assault so as to eventually propel them from the category of failure to success—I mean, at this stage, if they are not striving to attain their degrees, they may as well be digging to the center of the earth—that's actually a good metaphor to shock a student into action during the most inauspicious circumstances—and this—this is just another example of the fact that no one in this room is smarter than all of us—collaboration is key. Very good, Anthony," she said. I looked at her and, noticing beads of dirty sweat beginning to pop out of the fat-hump located just below the advent of her neck, I smiled wide at my internal surprise that she was of yet undiscovered and not cast for a leading role in the most fucked up, insane independent film a twisted, sick mind could possibly conjure.

"Now, if that doesn't work, use the take away: 'Your con*cern*s and qu*e*stions have brought concerns on *my* part'—see that spin? See that?' Not only have you refrained from answering a single question, you've refracted the heat onto them. Continue: 'Unless you can con*vince* me otherwise, I can*not* recommend you apply here'—see? That's a win-win situation. It's essentially the Switch combined with unpeeling the onion. A key maneuver for Admissions Advisors to remember—that twist served as my foundation for many an enrollment. Todd?" she asked, wobbling right close to him, "Do you consider knowledge to be power?"

"Yes—abso*lu*tely."

"Just a little extra tip for the next time around," she said, winking a lazy eye that may or may not have been looking into his own—I wished she had refrained, as the last time she made this suggestion, back at the beginning of the month, the entire subsequent week saw the whole floor echoing—'*Do you consider knowledge to be power? Do you consider knowledge to be power? Do you consider*'—ignorant vassals sending this sound bouncing around with never-ending metallic reverberations, as if the entire office had been shrunken and shaken and placed within an empty can of cream soda, rattling wind-blown up an abandoned alleyway in a dizzying nightmare of repetition that quite nearly gave me an asthma attack on the days where I had a few too many drinks and some smoke while observing Loop weirdness over roving lunch hours—wow, man, losing it—feeling quite short of air—I need to drink some cold water and splash it on my face and drink some more. Damn. Easy man, this is almost over—just let it out. Finally exhale and relax. Okay, there it goes—damn, my nose is cold! Just calm on down, you aren't dying—and even if you are, it's fine, fine—okay—simply stop forgetting to breathe!

"If that doesn't work, create urgency: 'Johnny, classes are *c*losing!—they're almost filled!'" she yelled, reinforcing another tactic used to frighten their victims and further ensure compliance, "'If your stance is that you cannot afford to enroll now, understand tuition will only in*crease*! The Acceptance Committee looks at procrastination as a possible lack of moti*va*tion! Don't you understand that the quicker you start, the quicker you will grad*u*ate?' And yes folks, I understand our classes do *n*ot fill, that there is no limit on the number of students we enroll in a given semester—this is a beautiful element of online universities. People never realize—hello? Isn't this an online university? How is it possible that classes fill? Exa*c*tly—so long as we don't run out of bandwidth, it isn't possible! How in heck would they know how many people are attending class? Easy—they don't know. All the student does is sit at their computer, log in, click through the PowerPoint presentations, repeat the same process time after time for nine months, write a couple basic papers, and wh*am*," she yelled, spanking the top of her fisted right hand into her left palm, "They're the first person in their entire family to have earned a degree and walked across the virtual podium, and wh*am*," she yelled, repeating the previous action, "Everyone is very proud of them. This is a beautiful thing, folks—a beautiful thing, indeed—we created this entire process from the ground up, and now—you, we—we are changing l*i*ves!"

"But if we tell them classes are closing, maybe they'll feel too pressured, and they won't want to enroll—I'm not lookin' t' give 'em too hard of a time or anything, you know?" Ole boy who posed this query, Orville, was wearing a sweater that displayed two wintry mountain ranges and three large evergreens in the front, and a balmy, beach scene sunset on the back—lots goin' on. His aura was what I had always expected an Orville to be—he was thick and burly and black and had a handsome baritone voice and a great pounding laugh—starts out real slow and gradually raises louder and deeper and louder still—an overall nice guy just trying to stay employed, trying keep hot food on the table for his family with few other options in the current global condition. It was subtly evident that he hated doing what he had to do to get by.

"Orville, I, like you, understand classes ne*v*er fill. I understand that fact as well as I understand that the Acceptance Committee—you, me, and Mr. Friar—all the other DOAs and their Advisors—we understand we could care l*e*ss about how much someone procrastinates. Of course, for sake of your sales numbers, you would obviously pre*f*er that they did not procrastinate, but obviously, so long as they are eventually successful in taking out loans, well—of course we'll let them in! Do you think we're going to turn down forty-five thousand dollars because they procrastinated? We can care less!—I understand all of this. What *y*ou need to understand is—these methods—these methods are *t*ools, cr*u*cial tools you'll need to master if you're planning to be suc*c*essful while working here. For instance, if you have somebody on the fence this morning, say—and say this in a sorrowful tone—but say: 'Today, Johnny—today is your only chance to get accepted. If you don't act today, you'll be placed onto a wait list. The list is long and by the time your turn has come, well—tuition will possibly have increased by *ten* percent.' Say that—and remember, this is crucial—when you explain that tuition will rise ten percent—and th*a*t folks—that is *n*ot an exaggeration. Tuition *is* going to rise ten percent—it's risen between five and ten percent every year since our induction as a university, sometimes more. Remember now, despite explaining the fact that, yes, tuition will rise, do not—absolutely do not—never, *e*ver provide hard numbers in terms of the cost of this education. They'll ask, O they'll ask a hundred times if they ask once, but just keep them focused upon the dream. The only hard numbers you should reiterate is the percentage of the rise of the total cost they do not comprehend that will occur if they do not act now. Reinforce this fact, get them to send in their fifty dollar application fee, accept them, refocus the conversational flow on the fulfillment of the dr*e*am, and transfer them up to financial aid as soon as possible. It's pretty simple, people."

"Why do you suggest this?"

"If you explained that those nine months of online schooling—if you mention it costs forty-five thousand dollars, Caroline, expect a click on the other end of the line. You'll lose them faster than you can blink. Remember this: NUTT—Never Underscore The Total. If they crack the NUTT, you won't get a sale, period."

"But what if they insist on knowing?"

"If they re*fuse* to stop asking questions about cost, Shauna, revert back to: 'Your con*cern*s and *ques*tions have brought concerns on *my* part—remember Johnny, you are nowhere *n*ear being accepted as of yet'—see? Use that spin again—refract the heat onto them: 'You want to earn your degree, don't you, Johnny? How many classes did you *f*ail in high school? Can you give me that number again? And what was your overall GPA? Really? Wow. I must have mis*h*eard you the first time. Maybe we shouldn't even be having this conversation at all,'" she said, face twisting into a sad lie of false apprehension. "Understand—an estimated ninety-three million American citizens make up the consumer market for this and other organizations of similar substance. I mean—this is a l*a*nd grab, people! The number of cash strapped adults out there who have yet to complete their college education is nearly nine digits long! Heck, we gave you cards, didn't we? The best advisors understand they're never off—if you're at the pub on a Saturday evening and overhear somebody speaking of how they're interested in returning to school: 'Hey Johnny, nice to meet you, I don't mean to interrupt, but I happened to overhear—I am an admissions advisor at an incredible, regionally accredited university—I don't have time now, but here's my card, give me a call sometime—I think we should have a talk," she said, walking close to me, pretending the setting was indeed that of a watering hole. Looking at her close, I couldn't help but think of the dozen-odd times she mentioned: 'I pr*a*yed last night that I'll get thinner'—and in the next breath, took a hulking bite of a huge Reuben to be washed down with fried enchiladas or a hot pastrami, you know, like God is planning to sneak into her body in the middle of the night and run seven minute miles along the Lake from midnight to predawn so as to erase her own lapse in judgment.

"It's pretty easy folks, pretty simple. Everything is all mapped out—just read the words. All we ask is that you maintain control of the conversations, don't get caught up in details, be sympa*t*he*t*ic to these people's problems, use plenty of voice inflection, take notes, and dial the phone. It's an easy job and we pay you well. These people—often times their past is nothing short of a litany of mistakes, a comedy of errors—their inner ego is a factory of false hopes just waiting to be set alight—your job is to ignite the furnace, turn on the lights, and illuminate the dream—whatever it may be. Actually, remember that line: their inner ego nothing short of a factory of false hope just waiting to be set alight. It's because of that fact that they'd give anything for a solution to erase that litany of mistakes. Make sure they understand: th*i*s education is th*a*t solution—it has to be. And remember—buyer's remorse sets in within seventy-two hours. That's a *c*rucial figure to focus upon—after they complete the loan paperwork, just get them through that first seventy-two hours, keep that dialogue flowing, keep selling the dream, stitch them into the dream of graduation and harp on those dreams, people—h*a*rp!—you can *n*ever let them stop dreaming. Do that and I assure you— you'll be incredibly suc*cess*ful here, a High Achiever in no time. And also, remember—these prospective students, they're pro*fess*ional procrastinators. Thus, you need to be the instigator of the motivator that breaks the cycle of procrastination! I want to hear everyone aloud—one more time—what do you n*e*ed to *b*e?"

"The instigator, of the motivator, that breaks the cycle of procrastination!" everyone yelled.

"And how long does it take before buyer's remorse sets in?"

"Seventy-two hours!"

"Very good—beautifully done!" Mr. Joshua interjected, hands flying out of his rear pockets and halting at shoulder height whilst simultaneously balling into fists, like he'd just sunk a long, winding putt at Augusta under severe, late Sunday pressure, "You must keep these two facts in mind if you want to cajole them into sustained action and avoid a trust deficit. Anything further, Gloria?"

"Okay—you know that thing we talked about, Joshua?"

"If you have the confidence, Gloria, go right ahead—dive in."

"Alright folks, I'll tell you what I'm going to do for you all, just this once—Joshua, who had the most phone calls yesterday?"

"Um, let's see here," he said, noisily flipping through his folder and, eventually gazing at a white print out, he ran his finger down a list of names, stopped, smiled broadly and spouted, "With a whopping one hundred and ninety seven calls, our winner looks to be: Timothy Kramer!"

Everybody clapped and Gloria said, "Well done, Tim—your consistency of effort is thrilling, it really is. What I want to do—just to demonstrate the fulfillment of my own inherent confidence in the script and what we've covered in this meeting, is call a student of yours, whatever student has proved most difficult of late—most hesitant of enrolling in the program—whoever's been the toughest nut to crack of late. Somebody you already recommended who is now balking. Who would that be?"

"This guy TL Bowler—definitely." In answering, Kramer appeared as he always had: a touch too short, subconsciously nervous and awkwardly tight—movement of body and head and face never quite seeming fluid for some reason, always jagged, moreover premeditated, forgotten, half-remembered and thrown into action in a jumbled tizzy—each time I observe him I feel like he just got done angrily asphyxiating his wiener in a bathroom stall, and he's afraid the whole world knows about it—very much outwardly awkward, this cat.

"What's his story? What point in the process have you reached?"

"He's just your average, middle-aged, family guy in his forties, with two kids and a blue collar background," he said, inadvertently irksome, handing over a handful of notes on the guy, "Overall, he plays it close to the vest—I unpeeled his onion a little bit, but he was less than forthcoming. I know he's employed and not making much, that's about it. I asked him the final question, put him on hold and eventually gave him my recommendation, but he didn't seem to care all that much."

"And his educational credentials consist of?"

"He's either a high school graduate or possesses his GED—I can't recall which."

"No matter, same difference—and where is he from?"

"Yeah—he's from the south. I think this is part of the reason we haven't bonded, really—I don't think he likes me. I never seem to bond with southerners—I think I talk too fast."

"Understand, Tim—all of you—when spending a day calling Mississippi, Alabama—you spend a few weeks in Deep South Mode, and you'll hear some wild excuses, it's only natural. What I've found that you have to be a bit more subtle with southerners, okay? You need to adapt your pitch to the student's style, not the other way around. As it goes: when in Rome—you know?—throw in a slight twang and explain that your family moved north when you were in high school, which in turn made it very difficult for you in some respects—with how fast and impersonal these damn Yankees tend to be. Pick a small to midsized city in the south, study it, memorize certain demographics, local sports teams, pro and college, other random facts, write everything upon on a blank sheet of paper, your Southerner Sheet, and when you make a call south of the Mason Dixon line, wh*a*m—ya 'll were born down th*ai*r, *too*," she said, evoking a chorus of easy laughter. "I mean—have some *fun*, folks! When we insist for you to live the role, that doesn't mean you should play the same one every time—quite the opposite—the *goal* is certainly the same, but in many ways, the path is always different. If he's blue collar, so are you, white collar, just the same, unemployed, as were you for a time, proud parent, nothing better—if nothing bonds you, invent something! You'll rarely, if ever, be blessed with ideal candidates who lack objections—hence why you need fabricate certain bits and pieces of your own character so as to bond and thereby make them such. Tim—anything else I should specifically know about?"

"Not really—he's a little self sufficient, though, which has proved problematic."

"You think he needs deflating in some respects?"

"I do."

"Alright then, gather 'round, folks, and prepare to take notes."

"I like to take notes, anyway," Todd interjected, "Because it helps me keep track of the little details," the big brain beneath his bristly red burr of a skull toiling tirelessly so as to disgorge such clinching mastery of the obvious.

"Great point," I said, flashing a blank, unemotional stare into the needling neophyte's eyes so as to source a small uprising of confused discomfort.

Temporarily making use of Orville's cubicle, Prendercast said: "We're going to do this on speakerphone, so if anyone should have to sneeze or cough, make certain you scamper away in time—listen carefully now, and don't make a peep." She flipped through Tim's notes on the possible COW as the group huddled close and, ever the showman, she moved about as though preparing for a final, long rehearsed orchestral recital, dialed the phone with great flair, looked around and, before the initial ring she lisped, "Welcome to Changing Lives 101, I am your professor, Dr. Gloria Prender*cast*."

Smiles and laughs zipped shut as the guy answered the phone, sounding like he had half a fish in his mouth—"Hell*ow?*"

"Good morning, is TL Bowler available?"

"This is TL," he said, swallowing hard and clearing his throat, ready, it sounded, to tell her: 'Thanks but no, for the last goddamn time, I'm not interested!' "Who've I got, here? This someone from that school again?"

"Yes, Mr. Bowler, this is Gloria Prendercast, an admissions coordinator with NVH Online. I'm calling you this morning—"

"Hey Gloria, you know yer connection sounds a little funny—there's an echo. I ain't on a speakerphone, am I? I ain't about t' go talkin' on some speakerphone with a bunch a' people I don't know about personal things, am I? That's not the way I like t' operate—I don't talk on speakerphones, nope."

"Of course not, Mr. Bowler, it's just you and I here. Do you have a minute?"

"Not morn'a couple," he said, drawing his breath together spasmodically.

"Well, to get on with it, Tim Kramer and I, we got to speaking about your educational aspirations and how this oppor*tuni*ty—it seems to be a great fit for your needs— we were about to enter a discussion with the director of admissions in a few hours here, in regard to Tim's recommendation and, with any l*uck*," she said, twang ever so slight, "Your acceptance to the university. Unfortunately, we've encountered an obstacle—the problem is: why haven't you sent in the application fee? Why haven't we seen that?"

"I'm in a real band right now."

"Meaning?"

"Well I'm just kinda tied up with a lot different things I got goin'—"

"Sure, sure—"

"My daughters are in school—"

"Sure, sure, sure—"

"I mean grammar school—"

"Sure."

"So they're real busy learnin' n' I'm tryin' m' best t' help 'em learn while at the same time workin' at three different jobs, you know, takin' any shifts I can—"

"Sure, sure, sure—"

"Plus I do a lotta' side jobs—"

"Sure, sure—"

"And I—hey, why in heck are you sayin' sure so much for?"

"I just want to provide positive feedback and let you know that I understand you."

"Well cut it out. You sound like a damn Chinamen. Anyway, as I was sayin', you know, it's a real strain, sorta, all this, but I guess I'm pretty lucky t' even have morn'one steady job when so many got none, so I might as well do it while they're around—take as many shifts as I can get n' save 'fore they go on n' get shut down like everything else seems t' be doin'—that's why I don't think now's a real good time for me. I'm in a real band, understand?"

"Do you not think that a higher level of knowledge and a certified college degree would help ease some of this hardship?"

"It's not that—I mean, educatin' yourself further n' everything—it wouldn't hurt, that's fer sure—I just, you know, I'm pretty swamped is all."

"Do you think you'll be less swamped as your girls grow older and become more involved in various activities and need more money provided to them so they can do what it is they dream to do? I mean—do you plan on providing them with the opportunity to attain their degrees?"

"I mean—I hope to. I would love to, you know, give to them the most I can—I'll always give 'em the most I can. So far as them gettin' their degrees, I mean—I'm plannin' on it, givin' 'em a chance, I mean—I'm certainly plannin' on it."

"Or are you just planning on it without a plan?"

After an elongated pause, Bowler cleared his throat, and went: "What're you sayin'? That I'm a bad father? That whachur drivin' at here? That I'm makin' mista—"

"*No!* Goodness no, Mr. Bowler! All I'm saying is—we all do it. We all say, 'O, I'm planning on completing a huge project someday, one that I start from scratch, all on my own—I'm planning on seeing the world while I'm still young, with my body moving free and unwounded by age—I'm planning on making certain my family will always have everything they need, so when my children reach my age, they won't have to work as hard as me or be bound in a cage of untrained, non-awakened talent.' Nearly everybody is planning on something, Mr. Bowler, but how many have laid out the schematics and determined the best route to get there? Go ahead, Mr. Bowler, what in your opinion is the percentage?"

There was a long, silent pause, and, a little sadly even, he said, "Heck, I don't know—thirty percent maybe? Thirty percent er less?"

"Looking at your daughters, their dreams ahead—can you honestly tell me you're part of that thirty percent? Have you figured out how you're planning to pay for them to participate in every activity they want to be involved in, throughout Jr. high and high school, and then, on top of that, have enough saved to send them to college—have you solved this dilemma?"

"I mean—maybe not yet," he sighed, "Probably not, really, to tell ya the truth."

"You and how many millions of others?—*m*ost, TL, most are in this position alongside you—as was I, for a time, until I changed my life by getting my degree," false squared—no life changing, no degree—same as ever, she anticipated every possible counterplea, always ready to place herself in an equivalent reality of the student, whatever the situation, languorous course of lies running smoothly through whatever roadblocks the prospective student enacted, bonding, building trust, and establishing rapport, "Which realizes the obvious point: none of us are bad parents, TL—not in the least. My children—" of which she had none, "I can finally state with full confidence that f*i*nally, after *y*ears spent worrying the night away over how I would acquire the necessary wealth to provide them with the greatest level of opportunity—after tightening my belt, getting l*e*an, and acquiring my degree, I can now say those days are *o*ver, TL."

"I mean, that's what I'm hopin' for, really."

"This is America, Mr. Bowler, and, as you know, as the economy has become more global, more interdependent, more complex—it is not as easy to make a living for yourself as it once was—nor is it getting any easier—yet still, despite the downturn, credit crunches, and new-aged hardships—to this day, there is no other country to which the great masses seek to flock to for sake of all the opportunities—just like this. How old are you, curiously?"

"Forty-four."

"So, like me, you're rapidly nearing the graceless stage of upper-middle age. In our fathers' generation, TL, all one really had to worry about was showing up on time, maintaining a positive attitude, and working hard. I wish it was so easy."

"Well—I mean, I suppose that's true, unfortunately. My pop wasn't Einstein er anything, but he was pretty handy, and a good, honest, hard worker—he busted his hump in the mill for years on end, n' it was enough to take care a' me n' my mother n' brothers fer all our upbringing."

"Is that mill still in operation?"

"Nope—it closed in the early 80s. He got real lucky n' was out by then, retired with a pension—it didn't work out so well for a lotta' people."

"Did the town become recessed?"

"N' then some. Most everything shriveled away—n' if it didn't shrivel all the way up, it at least got dried out pretty bad. A good lot worked at the mill, probably one third of adults 'round here, n' the others, most of 'em worked fer companies that supplied the mill's industrial goods, er else at stores where the mill workers n' suppliers shopped fer other types of things—clothin', groceries, doodads, knickknacks—you name it. A little bit of everyone died when that mill did."

"Be honest with me, TL—do you feel like you're up to date on all the newest communication devices being used to exchange complex information at the speed of light in this new, digital age?"

"I mean—no, not really. I just try n' do what I can. If someone needs some extra handiwork 'round their house, some carpentry maybe, a new floor put in, a water heater, some piping, you know, I try n' keep my ear out, work hard n' collect a couple bucks here n' there, whenever I can, really, n' I try not t' spend too much on myself."

"Do you understand, TL, how rapidly things are changing? The world of business is changing every day, becoming more advanced, higher paced, and less dependent upon antiquated workers who lack the technological expertise or business savvy needed to keep pace in the race for personal success in the twenty-first century. Even handymen, Mr. Bowler, need to acquire fresh skills that will allow them to market their old ones to their target audience. Simply, as you say, 'Keeping your ear to the ground'—this old fashioned sort of thinking doesn't get people very far these days. As you've likely seen, Mr. Bowler, nobody is waiting up for you—nobody is willingly lending you a hand, helping you to your feet, and shouldering the load—that's why Mr. Kramer called you and attempted to extend the arm of knowledge. My question is: why have you refused to embrace such a timeworn element of strength? Am I asking you to be overly persuadable by insisting you take on the responsibility of continuing your education without breaking into perspiration?" A query that personifies the personalized angle that admissions advisors employ to decompress the current standing of self in the mind of the prospective student—this in turn works well because the argument in itself *is* valid, and thereby blinds this individual to the fact that the solution, their version of education, could quite possibly be disingenuously simplistic, and thereby worthless so far as true, veritable self-improvement would be concerned. The wrongness of it all was so blindingly total.

"I mean, think of what you're passing up here. Time is of the essence, Mr. Bowler, it really is—Tim had already explained your situation, albeit with a fraction of the depth you've gotten into here this morning—I mean, from the way it sounds, it was the fault of many external forces that prevented you from getting your degree at this point. That's a big key to life—not thinking about things you can't control. But now, TL—now that this opportunity is being presented to you, and you alone, as the captain of your family's destiny—if you choose not to align your bearing toward the stars, if you choose not to pursue this dream, understand: you shall remain without your degree and in poor financial standing because you never committed the necessary time and effort to attain it, and the fault will be entirely yours."

"I mean—I agree with everything you're sayin', really, I do—it's just—I don't really think now is the best time."

"I understand how you're feeling, Mr. Bowler, I do—I've had other students who felt this way before enrolling, and what they found was that this opportunity proved to be the gateway to financial freedom they had always been searching for. Another laborer, a carpenter, in fact, out of Western Kansas, a Great Plains man—I guided him through the admissions process for our degree in Business Administration four years ago, and the numerous pointers he picked up and expanded upon turned him into one of the most envied new businessmen in Cheyenne County."

"Was he successful?" he asked, trapped in the thicket of fictitious comparison.

"Of course he was successful—he's made a million dollars!" went the comment spewed from her mouth, thus seeking to shove the desperate into perhaps the most elaborately illogical, get rich quick scheme of all time, under the premise of logic, "If, by the time you're finished with the program, you have yet to develop your own business, you'll be happy to know, TL—of those who've gone on to suc*cess*fully fulfill our expectations, our job placement rating is in the ninetieth percentile—people come to us as handymen and, if they don't leave as executives, they've certainly earned the potential to be one—I see it all the time," she said, whipping off statistics from her left tit, tenaciously misconstrued research backing the data—for what she didn't explain was if a student simply keeps their old job, or gets hired for something not related to their new field—like, say, flipping burgers at minimum wage—this constitutes a 'career placement'—yet another deliberate and careful misrepresentation to confirm the old adage that if you ride a river from commencement to conclusion, you're bound to experience all sorts of things, including some that will make you wish you would have drowned at the get go. Tis a simple, effective tactic—if you can't use what is offered, the offer, by definition, is without worth—or so it shall seem to this individual. Hence why, smartly, dozens of references to unattainable jobs are mercilessly harped upon, and the best means of unlocking the door is always a commencement from this 'University'.

The empress of half truths took a deep breath, held the index finger of her right hand firm to her lips, smiled with a nod at the silent encouragement of the adjacent, wheedling warlocks, and said, "Listen Mr. Bowler, you need to understand something. Mr. Kramer and I—we are going to b*a*t for you. At this point, if anybody's butt is on the line, it's not yours, it's mine. *We* are the ones sticking our necks out for y*o*u. Therefore, it is im*per*ative that you decide—are you going to be a part of the success stories, or a part of the *fai*lures?"

"I mean—how much does the program actually *c*ost, anyways?"

Mr. Joshua, circling the group like an ole Doberman—he snuck up beside me, poked Doug in the ribs, looked animatedly at both of us, and murmured, "Look at how she's smokin' 'em outta his h*o*le." Todd, having overheard, giggled ingratiatingly, and I closed my eyes and nodded my head, yes, yes, relax boy, just take a moment to consciously breathe—be easy, easy—

"Mr. Bowler, you haven't even been acc*ep*ted, yet, okay?" she stressed, subconsciously ducking her head in an incredible evasion of the responsibility to explain, "We have to study your high school transcripts, your application letter, all sorts of things, TL, but before this happens, before we can even consider you, we need that fifty dollar application fee. In fact, I'm shocked that I've gone to the point of offering my recommendation without seeing it—this is not standard protocol, TL—to be frank, the fact that I know you're a good family man, the fact that I've been there my*s*elf—it's helped a great deal."

The other end of the line saw a long, wheel-turning pause followed by a deep breath, and, "Well—I appreciate that you're takin' the time hear me out, Gloria—I mean—that hospitality—that ain't lost on me, no, it goes a long way—I can tell *y*ou care, too."

"I do—and that's why, at this point, sending a check will take too much time—even if you were accepted, you'd likely be waitlisted another semester or two, and by that time, tuition will have increased." She took another deep, concerned breath, prepared to pace her words perfectly, and explained: "To be fr*a*nk, TL, it's not my habit to contact students directly and explain all this—it's just, after speaking with Mr. Kramer—your situation struck so close to home for me, as a reflection of my own previous hardships—moving to the north from the south, raising two children in this troubled economy, grinding it out, little by little—it's just— I felt I *o*wed you this call—I know what it's like to come from a family of self-sufficient southerners, Mr. Bowler, which is why I wanted to bring you abreast to the fact that time is of the essence, and that without your degree, life will only become more difficult, because the days of inexpert self-sufficiency are fading away." Over and over, it kept ringing in my head: 'We play to win in these parts—we play to *keep*'—just try to breathe man, try to breathe—I closed my eyes and accidentally imagined him running at breakneck speed, holding the hands of his daughters, three sets of bare feet pulsating softly through a big fresh field in the fall, charging hard en route for an ample heap of multihued leaves serving as the beautifully soft and comfortable cushion of financial freedom and newfound knowledge, only to have their screams of joy be overtaken by the sharp sw*oo*sh when diving upon this deep pile of dry, air-filled leaves, and falling at terminal velocity into the keenly disguised black hole of misassessed dept and depression lingering below.

"We take Visa, MasterCard, and American Express, Mr. Bowler—rest assured that I'll personally run it through for you, and stand behind you with all my strength in recommending that, with any luck, you get accepted here and succeed in taking the first, precious steps toward changing your life. What's it going to be?" she asked, whirling around, placing her thumbs and index fingers together and blasting her hands apart in a violent, halting rainbow, as though a foreign guest conductor of the New York Philharmonic Orchestra asking the ensemble for silence, precious silence after a stunning performance, not a peep to be made before validation or condemnation from an uncertain, hulking audience of one—

An impetuous sigh on the other end of the line, and: "Well, hell, my pop always said you can't win the pot if you don't throw in your chips from time to time."

"Was he a good card player?"

"The best—you said you take AMEX?" Mr. Joshua took to writing down the number as Prendercast took an official, silent bow, and closed out the call by stressing the dense odds stacked against his acceptance, thereby fostering the final obstacle before eventually fulfilling the quest of extracting a superprofit from the working class. An early afternoon call, she stated, would deliver the status.

"Un*bel*ievable!" Kramer shouted, honestly awed, "Gloria, that was so unforced, the way you flipped him—he didn't come *close* to feeling himself being turned over! Assuming he enrolls, I mean—will I still get credit?"

"You bet," Gloria said, "Such will be your reward for having the most calls yesterday—hard work pays, people. Your job, Tim, is to get him through the next seventy-two hours, and to complete the stitch in as his loans are getting approved. Remember, the point of a stitch-in is to stitch them into the dream of graduation"—to complete the web of lies, basically.

"*Wow!* Alriiiight," Mr. Joshua interjected, jumping in middle of the circle like a horny quarterback eager to huddle, "Let there be no doubt of the level of excellence possessed by your colleagues—remember, if you stick with what we've covered this morning, you are all capable of the brilliance displayed by Ms. Prendercast. What an incredible note to close on—a perfect place to stop and let you have at an initial power hour—bring it in close here, guys, let's go get 'em, let's pound these phones—bring it in tight now, c'mon, circle 'round—ready? Give it to me loud—let's get after it today, everybody now, let's crush it—c'mon now: who are *WE*?"

"The Un*t*ouchables!"

19

Brain buzzing and feet feeling numb, I immediately walked down the corridor, grabbed my hoodie and sweater from my workspace, continued into the atrium, and hung a quick right into the bright, white walled, blue carpeted emergency stairwell. I pulled shut the heavy steel door, and as it locked behind me, I took a moment to consciously breathe. A long line of slow moving organizational associates streamed out of the admissions arena all loudmouthed en route to the bathroom and elevator bank, and I embraced the sort of subconscious, quiet paranoia that occurs when entering weird spaces such as emergency stairwells or secretly inhabited garages under the assumed gape of spying eyes. I had written TL's number in a small black rectangle at the base of my palm—it was sweat smeared, but readable. I yanked my phone from my back pocket, turned it on, jogged four and a half floors below so nobody could overhear, blocked my number, and dialed: busy. Second time, third time, fourth time: busy. "Fuck me!—if this poor bastard can't afford call waiting, a good five figures of elevated interest loans for naught could well stand out as the unsmiling interplay between a once steady saneness and the grating sort of anger that slowly bends the mind into a state of brittle, snapping violence."

Thoroughly aggravated, I sprinted up to the top floor, counting in twos and occasional threes before a few dozen stories above I touched the bottom of the rooftop with my palm, exhaled mightily, flew down to ground level, forty odd stories below, breathed deeply, and, after collecting myself, I slowly exited a large steel door into the main lobby. Encircled by floor-to-ceiling glass windows, the lobby always felt cold and drafty—I ignored a line of cohorts descending an escalator that led to the Pedway and Dunkit Doughnuts, twisted my face sideways, passed security, spun out the revolving door and was blasted by cold, bone chilling air charging south from across the River. "Ay boy!" I screamed at the biting breeze, "How the fuck are you feelin'?! You feel good, you know that?" A suited man curious of whom I was addressing gazed in my direction as I elevated my hood. I jogged toward the expanse, soles crunching hard upon ice and oblong pools of hard, blue-green salt scattered about six lanes of an empty East Wacker. Thinking of what I would say if TL answered his line, I counted forty-eight clangs down the slick, petrified iron stairway that lead to Columbus Drive, and forty-two more as I dropped farther down to the unpopulated, flurried River walk lingering below. The hour long meeting had seen the azure sky cloud over, and she now spit specks of nimble, accumulating snow in swirling braids of no succinct classification.

I reached into my favorite pocket, removed a secondary handcraft, set it aglow, crunched carefully to the water's edge, exhaled and thought: Lord, man—this is what people do in life—I mean, on the whole, this is what a large percentage of the population actually, fucking, *does!*—this is their manifesto, man!—slinging bogus, unnecessary product— coercing folks to spend vast sums of money they don't possess upon that which they do not need for sake of securing exaggerated accolades from similar corporate zombies—how goddamn motherfucking disheartening!

I smoked harder and leaned against a pile of snow. The dry cold upon my ass sent me imagining the River walk months ahead, during a thunderous spring storm perhaps, with round drops of warm rain pounding hard enough to knock red rose petals from their green, thorny stems, steady River traffic rumbling past: 'Chicago's First Lady', a beautiful vessel, she be, loaded with slink-necked tourists gaping upon buildings their eyes could not quite believe—I felt warm, if only for a second, but was quickly cast back to reality by the harsh northeast wind cutting through my pants and the related sound of slashed, cracked ice stirring ever so slightly, filling the air with an eerie, sharp echo rebounding off the bottom of the steel drawbridge as though thousands of serrated blades were slitting one another to pieces in an ocean of trashing chaos.

Fifth time: busy.

I turned around and took a hard, luscious drag, exhaled white, gazed up toward 303 East and tallied row after row of black windows until I hit twenty-three—and how tiny, it seemed, the place I had just been, a body-sized square now blocked by a pinhead, just as the River had appeared from on high: a thin, white vein, lacerating the concrete jungle with a silent, haunting stillness that, up close, was not quite as still or serene as from on high it had seemed—t'was voicelessly vicious and cold and ready, in a way, to swallow you whole, unmoving and unblinking, a hushed happiness of the fact that if or when you slip and go sinking, the steady undulation of breathing and beating shall snap straightline and be mine, all mine, and you, as with every generation old, are now forever mum.

Sixth time: ring, ring, ring—"Hell*ow?*"

"Hey, is this TL Bowler?"

"And who is this? Whur are you calling from?"

"Ay TL, it's C.W.—I'm under the bridge, downtown," I said, exhaling a huge white cloud of hot breath, mind laughing lightly at the ease with which you can go around setting little things straight, if so inclined.

"What's this? Some fuckin' pr*a*nk?"

"You just got off the phone with Gloria Prendercast, didn't you?"

"Alright, who the hell is this?"

"C.W."

"C.W. who?"

"C.W. Martino—I'm calling to let you know that your new friend is a fraudster, trust me."

"Come again?"

"I said you just got pl*aaa*yed, son!" it went, in a hilariously high-pitched tone that served to both infuriate and confuse him—I now had his attention.

"What the hell is going on here?"

"Before you go bonkers, just hear me out for a second, alright? My name is C.W. Martino, and I work for NVH Online. The entire call you just experienced was played out live in front of thirty salespeople via speaker phone, for use as example of how to best convince prospective students that they should indeed enroll in a curriculum that involves little else minus basic regurgitation of sub average material. I was there as you spoke with Gloria—when she told you made up lies of family and struggle, and so on—I have since stepped out of the office and, after ringing busy on my five previous attempts to reach you, I have settled in on some smoke under a bridge, downtown, and I am now speaking to you for sake of divulging this, and other information—basically, I'm calling to sabotage her attempt to dupe you, feel me?"

"Is this the goddamn Twilight Zone?"

"Nope—but yes, too." There was a long pause. The LSD drawbridge looked imposing to my right, and an Ambulance traveling northbound across the top stage of the Michigan Avenue Bridge was the most noticeable sound minus all three levels of Wacker drive traffic humming wet pavement to my rear as I faced the swirling wind, feelin' newly relaxed.

"I'm gettin' real upset here, pal—just what the hell is goin on?"

"Listen to me now, try to relax—this NVH Online joint is a locus of psychosis entrenched ideals whose admissions process insists for people to refuse to adhere to rationalism. It all happens without you even realizing it."

"How's that?"

"Don't you think it's odd that some college just started hounding you, seemingly out of the blue, for sake of insisting that you better yourself?"

"Well, I—I don't know—I guess I lost track of whur everything got started in the first place."

"How long have they been calling you?"

"I guess a little morn'a month."

"Did you make an inquiry of the program somewhere?—on your own, I mean—did you request information?"

"No."

"Are you behind on your bills?"

"Ex*cuse* me?"

"Just tell me, TL, I'm not tryin' t' be a jerk—do you have creditors calling you?"

After another pause, he said, "Well, I guess—but just one guy about one bill that's still in dispute from a long time ago. I'm not some deadbeat—get that straight."

"No, I understand—but that explains it. See, NVH Online procures lead lists from credit agencies. It is assumed that the persons upon this list are trending toward unmanageable debt, and are therefore ripe for the picking as a result of financial desperation—you were on one of those lists, and thereby deemed an ideal prospective student."

"I'm not goddamn desperate, pal—get that straight."

"I understand that—please, T.L., I'm on your side, I assure you—what these people want is for you to get that feeling about the day like it's crushing you—like you have no options. Was Tim Kramer the first person to call you?"

"He was."

"Alright, Mr. Bowler—I'm sorry to say that the reason Gloria called to close the deal today was a reward for Tim having made the most sales calls on the team yesterday."

"What're you saying?"

"What I'm saying is an acceptance process at this school does not exist. Every single person who qualifies for student loans gets accepted. When Gloria told you that she and Mr. Kramer were meeting with the acceptance committee for sake of presenting your entrance essay this afternoon, what she *should* have told you was that she was meeting with his sales manager for sake of conjuring the best way to psychologically ensure compliance with this strong-arm robbery. Like I said, man—you've been fooled. A bunch of us were forced to listen to the conversation so as to acquire fresh sales tips. This is all a numbers game—you're just another widget—another potential victim in the name of education. I mean—do you have any idea how much all of this costs, and what it entails?"

"Well yeah, but—not completely—I got caught up worryin' on gettin' accepted all of a sudden—not wantin' t' lose that application fee—they said it's not refundable if I get denied."

"So how many times have you received a straight answer on cost?"

"I mean—none, I guess. They keep telling me not to worry about that right now."

"Of course they do! Think about it—how quickly were you redirected from this query? Was the pressure not immediately spun back upon your credentials, or lack thereof—was this the case, or not?"

"I mean, in a way—I guess it was."

"Tell me if this sounds familiar: each time you asked for the total price of the education, ole boy Tim Kramer went on and made it seem as if getting accepted to this University—he made it seem as if this is an extremely intricate and delicate process. He evaded your inquiry and posed that being rejected is a serious possibility, and further, he insinuated that the only solution to your blight of having failed classes in the past was to allow the windfall of receiving his recommendation to carry you over the basin of your current problems. Sound familiar? He's doing this to throw you off-kilter, okay? Don't go falling for it."

"This is about the craziest goddamn call I've had in my whole *life!*"

"Yeah man."

"Tim n' Gloria both said they were going to develop me into a business leader."

"Development is an ambiguous term—further, you don't need to pay for that."

"But what about the application fee?"

"It's gone TL, sorry."

After a deep breath, he said, "Ooh!—if I could get my hands on that little weasel, boy! I'd squeeze 'em 'til he went blue, boy, I'm tellin' you! Fifty bucks is a lotta' money t' just shit away like that!"

"I mean, fine, they duped you for fifty bucks—it's over, let 'em have it. But whatever you do, don't let them turn it into more than forty-five grand at a thirteen percent interest rate over the next twenty years, because that's what's next. Understand, Mr. Bowler—there is no acceptance process here. All that matters is that you're approved for the loans and that you sign on the dotted line that ensures you've committed to them. If you take out those loans, what you'll literally wind up doing is paying more than $80,000 over the course of twenty years for sake of clicking through nine months of nicely styled PowerPoint presentations, okay?—eighty grand worth of busywork, that's what you'll be paying for. Do you realize how much money that is?"

"Of course I realize!"

"You know what PowerPoint presentations are, right?"

"Yeah—I don't use 'em really, but yeah, I'm familiar—like a high end slide show, right?"

"Right—that's what you'd spend forty-five large on over the next nine months: clicking a mouse through such presentations, flipping through boorish slides and writing single page, double spaced papers in regard to the contents of such on a bi-monthly basis. That's all it is—a colossal waste of your time and energy—like most, it's a degree based on busywork. Total nonsense—I mean—I was there on that call, man! I heard you!—you build things—you're a doer, just like my pop, all the men in my family, most of my friends, their fucking folks—you produce, man! Most of the people who work here—not only do they lack their degrees—I mean, if you asked them to tile a floor, it'd wind up looking like a crooked jigsaw puzzle drunkenly stomped into place by fat, dirty feet!—they couldn't install piping, drywall—none of this, not a chance! They're goofballs!—almost all of them!—and Gloria—she doesn't have kids, a degree—none of this! She's not from the south—all of those statements were lies, man! She's creepy enough to make your armpits itch, trust me. You have hard, durable skills, Mr. Bowler—if anything, all you should do is keep working hard and head to the library—pick up a handful of sharp business books, power through them, take notes, pick up some more, rack your brain, save your scratch, bit by bit, job by job, incorporate and start getting your name out there on a grassroots level. Each time you do a project, a bathroom, bedroom, a patio—whatever it is, man, just do a great, quality job of it, make some proper business cards, be courteous to your clients and, slowly over time, your name will get around as a quality contractor, and you'll earn a nice little nugget for yourself, doing what you enjoy. I mean—that guy in Kansas, that story—that's all bullshit, man, every single word—big fat lies out of a big fat mouth. I mean, hell, there's probably some cat who made out good for himself out there, but not on account of this joint, that's for sure. You'd become swept up in a swirl of assessments that will conclude in little to no improvements. That's exactly what would happen, I'm telling you."

"Why in the world are you doing this?"

I glanced upward and caught the image of a fatigued fellow in his early forties silhouetted black against the grey sky as he walked north upon the filthy Columbus Avenue Bridge. I wondered if he liked what he was doing or simply had to grind whatever scrap was available for sake of his family. He leaned into the biting wind as the Trump Tower, rising to his rear, soared until being swallowed in thick grey. "Some live the dream, some serve it, and others—others burn it. I've always been a bit of a pyromaniac—in reality, I have many reasons, so, you know—fuck them. Just don't feel like just another fool who didn't look before they jumped—this was a carefully orchestrated subversion. In a way, this is almost an attempt to keep you dumb and confused—not that you are, of course."

"No—Jesus Christ, I know whachur sayin'. It's like—you know how it went? I heard the word school and, assumin' you're involved in the process, you figure, one way or another, you'll get smart—but I guess that's not how it works."

"No, that's not how it works at all—but that's a perfect description of how it's played on people. There is no cognitive approach. Everything is based on feel—you'll feel smarter when finished, but in reality, you won't be, that is unless you take the time to learn things on your own, which, obviously, should have been done for free in the first place. Remember, people always feel very safe saying, 'O, well, you know, I'm in school.' Just what does that mean, TL? Are you not supposed to learn and advance and examine what is, every single day, classroom or not? You need to make it your own obsessive compulsive nature to constantly seek the whys and how comes lying in wait behind each is and every was—know what I'm saying?"

"Yeah—I thought I did, though. I just don't know how I got fooled—I thought they were accredited."

"They are."

"With the same kind of accreditation as the University of West Virginia?"

"Yep, Regional Accreditation—the same level as Yale."

"How is that even possible?"

"That's my question, TL—but think of how much money they're bringing into financial institutions via interest. Break out the calculator and go: thirty thousand students or more, per year, at nearly fifty large, with steep interest on that total over twenty years—I mean—there's a lot of zeros at the end of that equation, TL—loads of people are getting rich off this—the multitude of people across various industries getting a cut is deep, man. People not technically associated with the program have even more to lose than those running it—

they profit at a level that is difficult to tabulate. In reality, the institution was designed to be psychologically violent and coyly corrupt from the very get go. It's not always easy to spot propagandists—the fact that the whole shtick revolves around education is the ace in the hole, really."

"Hell, it must be—why else would Gloria's words move me to get involved?"

"Gloria used a slick, invented tale of evasion to lure by blurring the context of what you would have actually been in for, understand? In the end you'd realize an inverted outcome because the light she speaks of at the other end of the tunnel is really a train racing to run you down."

He paused, and said, "And that train is called debt."

"Ex*act*ly—I'm glad you see."

"Do you know how hard I've had to work to remain debt free, CW? *V*ery hard, I'm tellin' you—we been real frugal down here."

"And because of this, you're at a huge advantage. Those things she said—to a degree, they were right. It's true that nobody is lending you a hand—that production in today's world is more global, and therefore the opportunity to simply put your head down and grind a manual labor gig from nine to five for fifty weeks per year, pile the family in the car, and vacation for two—this isn't as simplistic as it once was. There are too many causes to name, TL, and, like she said, nobody is lifting you to a higher, more comfortable place, okay?—the only one who can do that is you, hear me? But you also have to remember that it is not necessary to pay tens of thousands of dollars to learn new material or advance old skills, okay?—not nearly. Doing so is a big mistake in a lot of ways. Once you're indebted to the system, it's really difficult to get their hands off of you."

"I figure, hell, if I'm gonna' trade my time for finances, I sure as hell am not plannin' on spendin' the profit in a frivolous style that'll lend all the work I done into nothin' more n' an even wash. *Heck* no."

"That notion right there puts you well ahead of the game, okay?—that's precisely what enrolling in this program would result in—an even wash, only worse. By celebrating consumption rather than conservation, the GDP encourages the unsustainable depletion of finite resources—most especially *y*our money."

"Spending ain't always easy to avoid, though—my daughters are startin' t' want a lotta' silly stuff."

"You'll simply have to be tough and tell your daughters no—get them into art, get them into creating things—buy them fifty dollars worth of colors, a stack of paper, and tell them if they don't want to amuse themselves with this, then go out, run around somewhere and breathe air. You can't be soft on these kids, or they'll run you. A lot of these people losing their homes grew up accustomed to getting whatever they wanted without having to work for it. 'O, I want a house and nice things to put inside—all the things I see on TV—give me credit cards and a fat fuckin' loan, please'—no, TL, keep the television turned off and borrow books—the problem is if you're linked to the world, you're literally being asked to spend money upon that which you do not need on a near *con*stant basis—it's a fucking deluge of suggestive chum the whole family gets stuck swimming through, and then you give in and go broke. Ignore it and remember the best way to learn how to do things and develop is simply by doing them—you've already discovered this—if you put all the money you would have spent upon poor product toward where your love lies while at the same time, living it— you'll make it. You're a strong, self-made man, Mr. Bowler—you don't need little conniving weasels telling you what to spend and where, how to learn, or what defines happiness. If you can avoid borrowing from these people, you'll be free—truly free."

"I'm going to be—I am, really."

"Good—I'm glad we spoke. I don't like to preach, but—hardworking people like you need to take heed of the heels treading upon their faces—the problem is that a bunch of heavy, backwards motherfuckers learned how to tiptoe real soft-like, okay, and suddenly great sums have woken with empty pockets and no viable options, pondering: just how has this happened? They never realized their brains were getting stomped into a bleeding purple mash, one tiny little footstep after the other. Enjoy your life, your morning coffee, and think about what we've discussed—self-educate, TL—good day."

With supreme derision on my lips I hung up the phone, relit my J, took a big tear, looked up toward the tiny row of black squares on twenty-three, exhaled and smiled a big fuck you into the sky. I sat upon a thick copper rope hold, weathered to green, sprouting from the concrete break wall, and thought: all throughout history and in every walk of life, that's all it's ever been—people ruling people and people allowing themselves to be ruled. I closed my eyes, leaned back and embraced the wind—through the black I felt like I was flying down a steep, burned out mountainside, high above the valley, alone and free and forever humored by my unfathomable smallness.

20

After sitting for a moment I scuttled up to street level and back to the office. A good lot huddled at the elevator bank, but the only duo associated with NVH Online was that of Rich Knaffey and the Team Leader of The Marauders, Brit Greer. I raised my hood and lingered at the back of the crowd. "You know, Brit, I've walked quite a few paces around the floor in the past few weeks, and I can se*n*se it dropping off—their enthusiasm, I really can—their sentences—the downward voice inflection is all but gone."

"No, you're right, Rich," mentioned a glistening mouth, "It seems as though many advisors are asking per*mis*sion to speak with students. You can *n*ot wrap sentences with upward voice inflection—it'll terminate High Achievement," she went, glaring upon her prim reflection in the brass-coated elevator doors just before they opened. "They're forgetting a top rule—end sentences on the way *d*own—you're going to attend school here because I sugg*est* it—you'll only be accepted if I s*a*y *so*—down, down, do*w*n—how advisors can develop a poor habit like that?—God only knows."

"Brit—crises are always moments of truth because they relentlessly expose both the strengths and weaknesses of all players involved—advisors need to ask themselves: am I strong? Or am I w*eak*?" I imagined a stone-faced man dressed in black saying this in a thick, Soviet accent—far more intimidating.

About fifteen of us crammed onto the lift. I stood at the back and, hood raised, my ole man-like voice, grumbled: "Forty-e*igh*t, plea*seee*."

Brit stood at the front, lit my button, and continued speaking: "If we don't have a serious, I mean *serious* chat with them, Rich—the upward voice inflection may morph into an addiction, their actual way of speaking. Numbers will fall though the floor, guaranteed—they already are. We're losing far more COWs than usual for some reason."

"Are you going to send a management-wide email about it?"

"No—you send the email. Set a Team Leader meeting for twelve-thirty—I'll work up an outline on voice inflection tips. Offhand, I can think of a whole slew of people who could use a refresher."

The doors opened on twenty-three, Rich insisted Brit exit first and gazed down upon her ass as he asked, "Can you put this down into a final action item as well?—have all the Team Leaders compile lists of five items they would like to discuss—assemble what you feel to be the top twenty questions, and I'll get to work on the solutions tonight. Let's get together briefly after work and go over it." I imagined all these Mr. Joshua-type fools licking their lips all weekend, throwing balls of scratched up paper into the trash, so dearly hoping to hear their questions posed in the next Team Leader meeting, and I felt tired and sad.

Their heels faintly echoed up the hall, doors shut, and my feet pressed hard against the floor. Up top the doors opened and closed and I rode along for a couple additional trips, confusing people with my statue-like posture and blanket lack of motivation for why I might be riding the elevator with them—

"What floor?"

"None in particular—anything higher than you is fine." Expressions insinuate I might as well have an atom bomb in my jock strap.

And back to twenty-three, I scan myself into the arena and momentarily rove. I pass a series of private offices, including a meeting place called 'The War Room' where a shaved headed, mildly homosexual man was in the midst of politicking a precarious line of questioning in a work-related performance review.

To his right, just on the other side of a thin pane of glass and awaiting her turn like a third grade girl outside the principal's office, was a pasty woman whose perfectly manicured hands shook as they slammed food toward a face that twitched like an overfed finch bobbing beneath tables, bombarded with superfluous crumbs in a crowded courtyard.

"Yes," I said quietly, "I feel quite fucked up. I need some water. I need to drink it and splash it upon my face."

Bathroom: splash, splash, gulp, splash, gulp—ah, alright then, all is well.

Back into the Admissions Arena and again past the window, the performance review continued. The thirty-something woman at the helm seemed to enjoy the user-friendliness of her power—her facial expressions whence sitting through answers conveyed a slightly too exaggerated sense of disappointed frustration. Her flat face floated slowly from side to side at the high flanged explanative conclusion of: an email issue. Her hands pushed firmly upon the end of the table and her body racked back in a halo of dissatisfaction as the gay man flailed for an excuse to an unheard question. I thought: is this what you people aspired to be? Terrified of one another over such silliness? Not only do they not have the answer, they don't even ask the question—and I think *I'm* crazy? Lordy.

Back to the desk—sit, lean back, breathe. Be. Breathe. Not so hard, see?

"Ugh! This is *so* annoying—this straw will *not* stay bent!" Why is Caroline's head popping around the corner of this cubicle like an insane frantic skeleton that almost dares to admit the impending endgame?—the dust and such—all that it loved, gone—forever gone— "Did you hear me? I said this str—" I'd like to say I've observed very few people to complain at such a degree of petty continuance, but that would be false.

"Is it really *so* annoying?"

"In fact yes, it is." Well bend your skinny neck another couple inches and keep it to yourself, please! "I just made a call and left no message with Morris Periwinkle."

"Fabulous."

"I already left voice mail script number one and two, so this time I just hung up. I don't want to scare him off."

"Doesn't that sound funny, making that statement aloud, when you put it next to the context that you're an admissions advisor, at a supposed college? Do you not feel odd?"

"What do you mean?"

"Isn't it obvious?" I asked, leaning over my pad of paper.

"What are you doing right now, anyway?"

"Impressing upon paper the unique aspects of this preposterous experience."

"You're strange sometimes."

"I appreciate that—but to be serious for a second: be gone with you now."

She squirmed back around the cube wall and Petra could be heard attempting to clink together three dollars in nickels and pennies for a bagel—amazing—I can just envision her pad being loaded with all sorts of sloppy, unnecessary bullshit. She tramped up the corridor, holding a vase, stopped as our eyes met, and said, "I couldn't find my handbag this morning—I found change in my desk, but: do you feel like buying me a bagel this morning, Anthony?"

"Nah."

"I figured asking wouldn't hurt."

"You were right."

"But hey—aren't these nice flowers? Willie sent 'em to me—it's our three month anniversary."

"Hmm, pretty nice—red and white roses in a pretty glass vase—but isn't that the guy who locked you in the house and threatened to keep you with him forever last week?"

"Yeah, but—you know. He didn't really mean it."

"Well, I suppose you're standing here so, up until this point, that's technically true."

"See? That's what I told my mom when I mentioned I'd forgiven him."

"Yeah—still though, I'd stash a little blade between the mattress and box spring if I were you—maybe an old, rusty letter opener—you could just reach over and shove it through the hole at the bottom of his neck as he comes down on you—it's just: there are heaps of violent psychopaths roving out there. Heaps, Petra."

"I already told him we can't play the choking game during sex anymore." She said it with eyes like she was trying to turn me on, but in truth the thought of some crusty fool named Willie jamming it home as he squeezed her windpipe made me woozy.

"Way to plan for your future—anyhow, I'm tryin' t' chill here. Caroline will buy you a bagel—I'm certain of it—go ask." I grabbed my thermos and split for water. The kitchen was littered with typical office warnings: 'If you use the microwave, please clean up after yourself! If you finish the coffee, make a new pot! The refrigerator will be cleaned out every Friday—no exceptions!' As usual, five or six middle managers were hanging around the Joe, talking earnestly, make believing as though they were having a 'meeting of the minds'. In one corner, two women were speaking about closets, and closet designers, and in the other, a girl with a hulking jaw was chewing a wad of mash on the side of her mouth like Popeye, looking directly through me, as if embalmed.

Kramer walked into the room and looked at me. His headset was still on as he placed a plastic bag in the fridge. "So, how's your month?"

"Pretty dead."

"That's too bad—I've been on par, actually."

"Any tips?"

"A practiced master never provides a young apprentice their most precious tricks of the trade, you know," he said, chuckling playfully.

"Funny, you sound like me."

"*I*—sound—like y*ou*? I mean, hell, my numbers might be down a little from previous High Achievement, but y*ou*—you don't have a s*i*ngle enrollment this month!"

"I know—it's terrible, ay?"

"I guess what it comes down to is: are you believable, or aren't you?

"I'm pretty believable."

"That's not what the numbers show."

"You think?"

"Yes, I do."

"That supposition substantiates everything I'm trying to do here."

He walked out, befuddled at the cryptic reference. I closed my eyes, rinsed and began filling my thermos as a man who looked as though he has been devouring an average of eight to twelve buttery flapjacks per morn, for many a decade, said, "Let's see, here." Solo before the vending machine, he was apparently too busy pondering how many dimes it took to buy a bag of Pizza Combos to recognize that one-eighth of his ass-crack was in view. Stomach hanging over his belt like a slab of melted rubber, he pounded hard upon and fogged the glass like an angry Ape at the Lincoln Park Zoo, eager to disperse a group of ghetto school kids from making faces and screaming obscenities when his purchase leaned over the coil, and refused to plunge into his grasp.

"Easy mate—from nothing whence ye came, and back to nothing ye shall someday return."

"Who the hell do you call to get your money back from this thing? Does anybody know who you call to get your money back? Who has seventy cents?"

I exited the kitchen to the thought of a firebomb when Mr. Joshua caught me by surprise. "Anthony—if I let you walk past with an untucked shirt, everybody'll want to walk by with an untucked shirt."

"Well, we don't need that sort of anarchy. I'm on it," I said, tucking hard as hell.

"By the way, how many appointments, COWs or applications did you bring in yesterday? What were your numbers?"

"Triple zero."

"Nothing?"

"Nope."

"Wow."

There was an awkward silence after he said—*wow*—and for a moment, I almost felt curious enough to pose: 'Wow what?—I would like a precise explanation—wow what? I feel like a laugh'—but in the end I went with silence, allowing for a false assumptive conclusion that my silence somehow represented a deep inner-centered concern about my lack of personal production. Much like truing a wheel, this is a delicate procedure—you have to act desperate and obtuse to a degree so as to disallow the realization that you're quietly rolling over their Adam's apple. Personal fear of failure based on their standards was obviously far from the case, but in executing this ruse, I have provided him a false sense of power via

91

pretending to be subservient to his mind and motivation, and henceforth I will continue to exploit the organization.

"Actually, no—I'm wrong—I had one COW."

"You know—can I see you in my office for a second?" I followed him into his office and he closed the door. "Take a seat." He gently slapped my shoulder as he strolled past and quietly sat himself—

I took a protracted blink and the leather chair I was sitting in was so hot that I felt as though I were seated upon a breathing calf, legs chained tight by barbed wire, heart pounding in rapid succession from the concerted effort to sustain balance beneath my weight as sharp steel slashed at the arteries of the lower extremities. I opened and closed tight my eyes and tried to remind myself that: no, no—tis hide, precious hide—just a long cloth softened and dyed after being ripped clear of his muscle, tendon and bone. I hoped it had been pulled clear after his throat was already slit—not before blood teemed from the gash red and hot, not unlike dark potent liquor lingering upon my lips on a steamy evening—no suffering, no suffering—sedation, baby, sedation—and I need to stop seeing all things for what they be— living beings ripped and mutilated by machines—men and women with skin fleshed via frantic factory farming—the extreme crowding and confinement, deprivation, non-anesthetized castration, branding, tail-docking and dehorning—the crushing transport and slaughter—fats and bloods and organs reused as needed through various bureaucracies and industry—but the skin of the animal represents the most economically important byproduct of the process for sure, I reminded myself, sinking my rump deep into the soft, tan hide, sprawling out and appealing to my mind for quiet, quiet—just skin 'em alive and let 'em keep working while we enjoy the fruits of the flesh.

"So do you think you'll be able to bring in that COW, or not?"

"What?"

"That COW you lassoed—are you going to drag it through the gate, or what?"

"That COW. Yeah. You know, I'm sure hoping to—it's a little up in the air right now—I'm looking forward to using some of the new tactics to grab 'em by the horns—but then it would be all bull, wouldn't it?"

"What do you mean precisely?"

"Nothing."

"What percentage would you place upon on capturing it?"

"About fifty—actually, maybe seventy—or probably eighty-five, really, after that great, tip-filled meeting, I'd say."

"Good—that's a good positive outlook—and that's the thing—we absolutely love your positive outlook and energy—" he bent down beneath his desk to scratch an itch and got a puff of whip cream in his hair, just above his left ear, after ever so slightly dragging his spiky head across the crest of his brimful latte. I didn't mention anything and he carried on, professional as hell: "It's just—you don't have the numbers yet. They'll come, I mean— they'll have to come if you want to continue here—I envisioned you as a future High Achiever when I hired you."

"That's huge—hearing you say that—it's a huge lift."

"You have to promise me to really focus upon tearing down objections today."

"Good call."

"What time is the COW's acceptance scheduled?"

"2:15, Mr. Joshua."

"Mr. Fryer is fine." He paused, and gave me a good look. It was the first time I'd referred to him as Mr. Joshua in a one on one situation, right to his face like that—it was real evident that he was bothered by it. His expression went: is this kid fucking stroking me, or not?—how it irks me that I'm not really sure! "Why is it at the same time as the Reality Check? We're to leave that slot clear, remember?"

"It was the only time he was available—and plus I was hoping, well—you know how Gloria made that call aloud this morning? Can I try that during the Reality Check?—to show what I learned and help invigorate the team with a successful call? I can be, like, the comeback player of the day or something—really get people going crazy."

"Wow—that's an interesting idea, Anthony. The only reason I'd say no is that I don't want any poor habits to infect the team. I was all for Gloria because she's by the book—a true pro."

"I absolutely will not deviate from the script. I'll focus and incorporate as many of this morning's lessons as possible—it'll be a memorable call."

"If so," he said, drawing his breath, "Then yes."

"Great. You won't forget it—really Mr. Fryer, I'm sure."

"What time is it now, ten forty?" I nodded. "Okay, Gloria's going to sit with you during the phone-a-thon for extra help. We're going to have a power hour from eleven-thirty until half noon."

Wrong—not on my last day—can't do it—maybe normally, for sheer hilarity, but now? No—fuck no—I felt like roaming, and maybe tasting a scotch—"You know I'm splitting midday for that dental work, don't you?"

"Um—no, I didn't."

"Yeah, root man—I got a dead root way in the back n' they gotta yank it or drill it or something—a whole show. I think the oral pain is part of the reason I've been letting people off the line too early, anyhow. Check this," I said, leaning across the desk, opening wide and exposing a large black hole in the back bottom left of my jaw.

"Jesus. Think you're in too much pain to argue?"

"In a way, maybe," I said, sitting back, "The doc is really suave though—I told him I have a big sales call, and he said I should be back on the phone this afternoon, drugged up and feelin' gravy."

"What time are you leaving?"

"11:15."

"What time will you be back?"

"One forty-five."

Two *point* five hours is a little long, isn't it?—went the expression. "Isn't that cutting it close?"

"Nah—we finished here? I want to get as many calls as possible before I go."

"Sure, Anthony—but bear in mind, that COW is important. We need a really big day out of you."

"Yep."

21

I sat back at my desk and checked the time. Fifteen of eleven. The only reason I said I would be leaving at fifteen past, is that those of us who were issued live checks were to obtain them at 11:00. I wanted it cashed green and in my hand before the Reality Check. I figured: leave when you get it, cash, relax, come back when you're about to quit, do so, have a real fun evening, wake tomorrow and get to work—the real work—nice and simple. I abruptly zoned on many thoughts of future actions when Petra walked past and, through a mouthful of bagel, said, "Are you going to answer that?"

"What?"

"The phone, on your desk—it's ringing."

"Whoop, so it is—thanks," I said, waving her away, "This is Anthony."

"Yo man."

"Joey?"

"Yep."

"Yo—fuck—nice surprise—what's good, man?" I said quietly.

"You first."

"You know—same old over here—just slowly blood-letting these thieves toward deprived health n' livin' the dream."

"You been writin'?"

"I've been gettin' it in, man—some decent work, I feel."

"How much longer is it gonna' take."

"A couple months—I'll snatch this last check today—I get it in about ten minutes, actually, and after I cash it green I'll be all set to live lean, roam and crank it out for the next while. I'm feelin' fuckin' ready t' go all in."

"Just pull some scratch together, print a few copies, and see how things go."

"Well that's the plan, son."

"Good man, I'm proud. You've been at it a long while. Still camping?"

"For the most part—fuck all that though—what's good witchu, man?—good hearin' your voice—I'd kill to hit a joint with a juke and dive in on a big tab. Where you at?"

"A rundown Bucharest office building."

"Meeting?"

"About to be—last of the day and I'm early."

"So this call is simply to kill time?"

"Not fully. I had been killin' it by betting on elevator doors with the gypsyish fool who runs the front desk here—which one's gonna' open first."

"Do alright?"

"He took me nine to one—didn't stop smiling—eventually noticed him peeking down just before the bet—figured he had some damn hidden sensor back there—quit then—we were only bettin' dollars, but, you know, I can tell he's gonna' have a big weekend now—this is Romania, after all."

"You ever think you should be institutionalized?"

"All the time—I can't talk much longer—I'm about to run up on this meeting with a broke former communist—but hey, real reason I called: I'm comin' home tomorrow."

"Really?"

"Yeah man—I fly out early."

"For how long."

"Two days."

"Are you bringing anything back?"

"Just two bottles of Absinthe and a bad temper."

"Nice man. How's it been over there, anyway?"

"I used to think I hate Americans, but now I know I just hate people—all I know is I'd love to go alley walking in the cold Chi. I need her—if I spend one more weekend in a former Soviet satellite state or the Middle East I'm gonna' crack, man—I'm not fooling."

"Fuck yeah, boy!—forget it, you're coming home now. Nothing else matters."

"You're right—I'll catch you in a bit then—ring the boys, have a few twisted, and get ready to get down."

"I'm already there man."

"And hey—make sure you have something good waiting for me."

"I will man. Peace." I hung up the phone and felt glad. I dialed five numbers and left five messages whose summation went: "Yo, it's me—JC is rollin' back into town for the first time in a half year tomorrow. He's only in for the weekend. Be ready to cut loose."

Jazzed at the news, I stood and began roving the scene: none of this matters, I thought, but at the same time, it fucking does—so many institutions such as this, weakening humanity from within—Americans bilking Americans so in the end we can borrow ten figure sums with stiff interest from the Chinese—sickening—I passed between teams and caught little snippets on my way: "You're still interested in getting your deg*ree*, aren't you?" went a woman whose tone insinuated the person on the other line would be an absolute *mo*ron if they weren't—never mind the fact that yesterday, I heard her say, "So like, *tech*nically, America was founded by whom and why, exactly? I get mixed up with that seventeen-hundred stuff."

I continued to move and a squishy woman from Human Resources by the name of Misty led a prospective employee about the office, and said, "Ex*act*ly, Rodger, motivation is a big key with us—like this Video game system, for instance—that's a little motivator—if you meet your numbers, you can have some fun." Misty was my initial interviewer, and she was very easy to fool by way of fronted enthusiasm for the cause. NVH was the only job I didn't have to invent fabrications for—I explained that, on the side, I had been working as a tutor for illiterate adults before applying. This was a true tale. "Anthony—this is Rodger, an applicant—what do y*ou* think about working here?" asked Misty, eyes wide in their insinuation that I best promote one of the accepted axioms.

"We change lives." I said so oddly slow and in a tone like a cheap movie phone automaton—I gave the guy a subtle look like: dude, spare yourself if you can, really—and he seemed to catch me.

I made another lap around the office and returned to my desk. 11:07 and still breathing—"Okay, now where is Kristen with this goddamn *loot*?" I whispered, "She normally can be seen making the rounds by now." My body felt horribly dry—my hands and mouth especially. I ran my hands over my face and: "Goddamn it, I need to get on out of here—fucking now. Really." Panic rose and I began to feel as though I were somehow trapped, held hostage by way of a paycheck—doors welded shut, I would now be forced to sleep in the stairwell and coexist with these people fifty hours per week in an insanely sober version of: 'Panic at Needle Park'—I would have to keep coming back here, or someplace like it, until I had enough to barely keep up on rising costs, which would be never. Holy fuck! This was a horrifying feeling. All I could do was sit staring at the clock with the static impatience of a currency exchange worker eager to stop counting money and cashing food stamps. Get. Me. The fuck. Out of here.

A girl with a remarkably flat ass walked past with the manager of 'The Eliminators', Jason Faun, and she said, "I figure if I bring him in I can get a nice purse. I need a nice purse—I need one for every day of the week. I lack Monday. I switch it up though—sometimes I start the week all hot, and then lay off on Wednesday." She walks with the strangest gait, man, I'm telling you—like a Warner Brothers cartoon character steamrolled and unpeeled, striding all awkward before being inflated afresh.

"What's his name?"

"Who? The COW? Ed Giordano—fast Eddie, he goes by—but he's not so fast—lazy, just—I feel you could twist him more easily than I. He's a bit of a chauvinist, and he won't listen to me—but you can't use an Asian last name with him. Jason Faun?—he'll never go for it. Say your name is Jason Rocco something or other and that you used to fix old hotrods, but now you prefer to *drive* them. I'll give you half of the commission if you help pull him in."

"That works."

"Hey, Anthony, how are you? How's your month going?" flat ass spoke this directly through me. I did not answer—we had spoken a few times before, but I was frozen, zoned on thought. Mistake—when I began the job, I just didn't speak all that much. In some ways it's a bad habit, not speaking. People hold a tendency to become strangely curious, and excessively suspicious of people who keep to themselves. And it's not like I didn't want to get to know people—there had to be some normal, cool peeps working here, but—I just hate having to answer life-related questions like: 'Where do you live? Where did you work before this, and why are you here?' With questions come answers, with answers come lies, with lying comes anxiety, and with anxiety—stress—stress includes dealing with stress, and to deal with stress, I revert to my vices: foremost of which is being out of control to a certain degree. Just say hello next time and there will be no worries—breathe.

"Meow—it's 11:11 make a wish! Well? I mean—so what did you wish for?"—a sharp blade and a trip to the sanitarium—good Lord!

"I try not to wish for things, Caroline, especially when people ask me to."

"Well, *meh*!" She made a mediocre-reality-TV-star-pretending-to-be-appalled-by-a-mid-grade-insult-type of face, and said, "By the way, you'll never guess what the guy on the line just told me. He said, 'This ain't all these nice words you're usin', I can see through your bullshit,' and then he hung up on me."

"He was a smart man."

"You're pretty negative considering how crazy you go in the Rah-Rahs."

"I guess I've a complex personality—either way, I'm dying to get to work."

"Funny—last night my friend Alex asked me how I'd like to *die*—I mean, what a horrible question!"

"What was your answer?"

"I said I would like to die in the shoe department of Neiman Marcus, with a Nalona Blahanic slipped gently upon my foot."

"Really?" I hope I die an excruciatingly painful death so as to allow others to fear their fate less—fighting 37 angry weirdos in a burning alley, something fun like that.

"By the way—do you have jumping jacks in your pants, mister? I haven't seen you seated, and making calls—not once this whole morning, in fact. How many calls do you have so far?"

"Few."

"You better get going—I already have nineteen cold calls on my tic sheet."

Where is this fucking *check?* Caroline zipped it, and I tried to ignore everything, but this one lady up the aisle, Kelsey—she found it necessary to recap every fucking conversation with whoever happened to be within earshot. If I were her husband I would have killed myself miles ago. Perhaps the worst part is that she was extraordinarily kind and polite. She is super kind, compassionate, all that shiza, and she was still succeeding in driving me mad with her mundane take on reality. Driving. Me. Fucking. Crazy. She closed a call with: "O my God, this is *awesome!*"—this statement along with, "I am really going to push for you, really—I think the committee will just *love* this!" The worst part was that she completely believed it.

I tried to write but all I could hear was: "You know what they say about the cold? When the wind blows—you're only happy when—well, something—I forget the gist—" Kelsey shouted this jumbled metaphor loud as hell at Orville, and I was able to see Orville cringe. I like Orville—he prefers to keep conversations on the low, whereas Kelsey prefers to, whether they're interested or not, speak with everybody around, all at once. What a fucking joint this is. "I was—I mean I *am* in so much debt that I pray—every single day I pray that God will give me an idea of how to get me out of debt." I almost asked her if God mentioned that it would be a good idea to stop spending gobs of money in a frivolous nature on a daily fucking basis, but I somehow held myself back from inquiring about the details of her visionary conclusions. Fuck. "That's why I enrolled in school here, my*self*—once you graduate you're eligible for middle-management." Sadly, this was true, thereby lending her reality to one not unlike the ironic incongruity of the original electric chair being constructed by convict labor for sake of creating a more civilized arena for executions. Like any typical shoe-leather force, the identity of those they were killing was eerily reflective of their own reality: she was now an indentured servant, a laborer under contract whereby if she met her sales goals for the upcoming year, and enrolled ten students per month—go: ten by twelve, by fifty thousand—she is now earning the company six million dollars per year, and further, paying the institution fifty grand herself, all to possibly make six thousand additional dollars over a standard of forty-five K salary, for a total net loss, after taxes, of roughly twelve thousand dollars, interest not included—plus mad credit card debt on clothing, a car payment, and a mortgage—she will now live the remainder of her life for payment, and die—but she'll have that fucking deg*re*e, boy, framed front and center—you can count on th*at!*

Back to my pad I started to draw a big hole in the ground when I noticed Tim Kramer pacing the floor. He spoke to Gloria and Mr. Joshua in a terse tone, returned to his cube, made an impassioned phone call and again walked through the hall with an expression one might carry if trying to speed walk and simultaneously squeeze turds into diamonds before allowing them to jet out the rectum via a single, horrifyingly deliberate, touching of the toes. Maniac. Pure. Unadulterated. True blue maniac. I could not help but feel a great personal acrimony for his boundless ego. I mean—it's difficult to take yourself seriously, let alone the other cunts doing so in such merciless concentrations.

After two more laps, he suddenly stopped and yelled: "Now they're fucking with my mo*ney!*" You could hear in his voice that his heart was racing. He quickly glared around like a tough guy, eager to see who took notice, which of course was most of the room. Mouths appeared utterly 'sh*o*cked' by the 'vul*gar*ity' of the moment.

I almost started to laugh, so I looked up and asked: "Any particular reason why you're acting like an absolute maniac basket case?"

"Don't talk to me right now. Nobody talk to me." He went into Mr. Joshua's office and closed the door.

I again stood and began to move.

I walked past a guy I had exchanged a few good conversations and regular hellos with over the past few weeks. His name was Heffe—he look up at me and: "Wow—that was pretty cool."

"What? Kramer's meltdown?"

"No, I missed it—but the guy I just called—he's a janitor at a cloning facility."

"You should ask him to send a few terminators over here. T-1000s—shape changers."

"That and a lot of gasoline."

"No shit—ay, you seen Kristen with those checks yet?"

"No, but I wasn't really looking—I use direct deposit. She might be around."

"Right. I need to get that check and bounce for a few, pronto."

"Sneak past her office and see if she's in."

"I will—say—you haven't been enrolling anybody besides cunt jagoffs, right?"

"No—not even them, really. I don't have the heart. I just called this guy Yuri Ivanov for what was likely the twentieth time since I arrived in this office—he answers, 'Yuri,' and then I usually just hang up the phone on the guy. It makes absolutely no sense whatsoever, which is fine with me."

"Good. How many more checks before you split?"

"Two n' I'm gone—I'm gonna' have a go at my own shit."

"Good man, be proud of yourself. Catch ya."

I walked past Kristen's office and she wasn't there. A man in management I did not know or care to asked how my day was. I said it was fine. He said his day was not so fine. I said fine and continued to look for Kristen. She was nowhere in sight. On the way back to my desk I glanced out the window. Snow was falling or rather tumbling down horizontally with a mad easterly gale—the mind went: I think I am going to shut down and cease speaking to people altogether. I will not pacify normative expectations by participating in small talk. Kelsey walked up, stopped me and said: "This is a good bag—I got it from Sears, and I kept my walking shoes in here two days in a row now."

"O really?"—see? I just felt obligated to reply: 'O really?' to this pointless statement uttered a few short seconds ago—no—I will no longer cater to such silly comments—doing so sets a dangerous precedent that subsequently allows others to feel it acceptable and thereby necessary to inundate me with their near endless chatter and noise about virtually nothing of importance or actual interest. Lord. Above all else, interacting in this style has me apt to simply work on my own.

I sat down at my cube and began to write. I could not concentrate. I tried to focus upon a specific character from the novel but could not. Tim Kramer stomped through the premises without stopping and again returned before tearing off yet again. His ears were unusually crimson. They looked more wind burnt than sun burnt but in reality it was pure frustration. He entered the 'War Room' and spoke to Gloria. I overheard Bowler's name mentioned several times. I couldn't help but smile. I wondered what he had said to Kramer and how he had said it—I wondered if maybe he had threatened to kill him. I hoped that he had.

I again stood and moved about. On the other side of the office, an unknown soldier was frantically flipping through miscellaneous papers—"Darn—I can't find my notes on that last COW," it said. Something in its tone or dress reminded me of a cattle trader in that on the Exchange, cattle aren't considered 'live' until they're fleshy enough to be slaughtered and sold. I stood in silent observation for a handful of moments, thinking: little boys trick one another all of the time—it's fun to watch it play out, it really is. I decided to return to the stack of papers once he was gone.

I continued moving and, in reference to available seminars in an upcoming semester, an advisor told a student: "It's all listed right there online, but whatever you do, don't print it out because, you know, it's just *too* many pages,"—like she was doing the person some huge favor—because the last thing you want to do is waist fifteen cents worth of ink and paper when soon you'll have fifty thousand dollars worth of pointless chores to pay for.

I again walked into the kitchen. Two inveigling imbeciles were going crazy about a silly TV character and the 'audacity' he showed in speaking 'that w*a*y' to his 'wife'—'I mean, to his *wife* for God's sakes!'—I felt compelled to pose: "Television is fake—you know that, right?" They both pulled their hair back behind their ears and stared at me. I smiled and went for water. There were no cups. I bent sideways and drank below the faucet. Water roared through my lips. I swallowed rapidly and did not care what they thought. Where is this check?

I exited and strode back to a large counter littered with bins—in front of each team, one sign said: COWs—and the other: Enrollments. I bobbed between teams and grabbed three thin-medium piles of random COWs, folded them small, and placed them in my fore pocket. From behind, some supercilious sucker snuck up and said, "What are you doing?"

The voice surprised me—I knew from the pitch that it was Rich Knaffey. Had he seen me crotch the COWs? In microseconds I focused upon acting naturally, extra-lax even, as if this was precisely what I was supposed to be doing. I pulled 'round and said: "Come again Sire?"

"I said why are you digging through all these papers?"

"I'm looking for information on my COW."

"What team are you on?"

"I'm an Untouchable."

"The piles you are poking through are for the Marauders and the Keep 'em Coming's. This isn't even your team—The Untouchables are on the other table, over there with the Big Shippers and the Infrastructure Constructors—why are you digging through this pile?"

"I'm trying to round up a misplaced COW—figured it might have stumbled onto a different ranch."

"What's your name?"

"Anthony Riedie."

"Well further, Mr. Riedie, it's after 11:30—have you noticed the fact that most everyone is seated at their desks? We're five minutes into a Power Hour—how many calls do you have."

"Zero."

"Well," he said, "Get on with it then! Take up this matter post 12:30 or I'll have to speak with Mr. Fryer."

I walked away. Fucking 11:35 and no check—I walked down a dull, cream-colored aisle beleaguered by bludgeoned bodies slumped in various postures of death. They spit phony tones as dialing fingers baited the world to taste a mouthful of knowledge in the upcoming semester. Almost to my desk, a voice called from behind, "Anthony, you're still here?" It was Fryer.

"Um, yeah."

"I thought you were leaving at 11:15."

"I was."

"It's twenty minutes after that."

"I'm leaving shortly—I was just doing some extra research on my COW."

"Great—that won't go unnoticed." I sat back at my desk, unfolded and looked over the papers. I figured I would give the COWs a ring in a while, and have a chat.

Gloria, swooping in like a spectre, came from behind, looked over my shoulder, grabbed a paper off the desk and said: "Drawing on the script like this is piggish behavior." For a second my heart jumped—she swept in so quietly. I thought she had caught me. How the niggling wench did not feel an itch from the ball of blackish-yellow ear wax on the verge of tumbling out the side of her head, I do not know. I found it sad that any single person would possess a feeling of intimidation or respect for this woman, this Gloria—it amazed me how people adjusted their behavior by regard of what she said to them. Why was it so easy? Why did vast sums bow to her conjured affront of power?

"What's a' matter Ms. Chipper Jolly? You don't like my drawings?"

"If you want to take art class, maybe you should sign up online—enroll yourself, Anthony—do so and you'll get rid of that goose egg on the board." Her mouth pulled wider. The subtle jab was very satisfactory to her. She spun the script back into my lap and: "Are you here for the power hour, or not? I was told that you wouldn't be, and now I see you sitting here, doodling or writing in that pad again."

I figured I'd wait ten more minutes for Kristen—I did not want Gloria to sit in on my calls. "I'm leaving shortly."

She unhooked the phone, "I want at least ten calls beforehand," and walked away.

I decided to comply to a degree. I was a titch paranoid. People were wound up. With Kramer tweaking about Bowler, they had to know a person in that meeting made a phone call. I had figured my finances very carefully, and I needed this one last check to jumpstart the publishing company—just comply for a minute.

I clicked up my day's fresh lead list, and dialed the first number. It rang to an auto auction, Frasher Auto Auction, in Salt Lake City, and when I got the candidate on the line, this Jay Frasher cat, I told him a slew of stories about how I needed an armored luxury vehicle that could withstand RPGs, AK-47 and SKS rifle fire. I told him that I came from a 'well to do' family and that things were 'pretty hot' right now. He said he was quite, quite sorry he couldn't help me, I adjusted his phone number in the system so as to ruin the lead, and we left it at that.

Still no Kristen.

The next man I called had inquired of the program on account of his freewill. He had seen an advertisement, and he figured it was time to 'get serious'. "So then, what do you want to do with your time?"

"Hell, I ain't sure. I guess something that I can be at until I retire. I don't know. I mean—that's what I been prayin' for at least. If it ain't in God's will fer me t' get some big job, well, then I guess it just ain't my fate."

"You know if you leave it up to—I don't know. Would you mind if I asked you a few questions about your educational background?"

"Nah, that ain't no major nuisance er nothin'."

"Alright—you definitely seem as if you're interested in educating yourself further than your current—"

"I ain't necessarily worried bout *ed*ucatin' myself further—don't go sumin' that. Education's great—I ain't knockin' it—but what I'm worried 'bout is gettin' my *de*gree. Once I got that degree, everythin' else'll take care of itself."

"Do you understand that when you go in and try to get hired at one of these jobs, you'll be expected to display knowledge that substantiates the degree? The knowledge is much more important than the piece of paper—do you understand that?"

"That ain't quite true because the paper proves. That's what the paper's—ain't that why they mail it to you? To prove ya got it n' whatever—all that knowledge? That's how ya get yer foot in the door."

"Yes, but—I'm just saying that the classes in this program might be a little bit basic, you know? There's not a lot of testing and they're a little on the eas—"

"*Hell*, the easier the better! I wanna take the most painless route, understand? I got kids, a fam—" He kept talking and I imagined the smell of his breath to be not unlike that of a cross country train I once took——an Amtrak on New Years Eve—the California Zephyr heading west—I assumed it would be a great party but it was in fact mostly filled with depressed people and their odd possessions—only one girl was up to drink with me, a pretty partial runaway in her late teens, and when she popped a bottle at midnight, I swore any number of people had just done themselves in with a Derringer—most were running from something, many of them speaking of how: '*This* year—this year it would be different—by this time next year we'll be—' and I wanted to ask: why do you really think it's going to be any different this time? What's your reason? What's the fucking plan, Jack?—but each time I creased my lips to talk my mouth got jammed full bore with the smell of a million sorrows gone by.

"I'm just saying that when it comes time to actually be interviewed, when you have to display your aptitude to a hiring manager—you have to do a lot of outside research, man, you have to attain knowledge on your own, without being told, you have to read up on all sorts of—"

"I hate readin'—I just don't like it. Never have, never will."

"Let's just get on with it then."

I was leaned back and looking at the ceiling when he said, "Ya know, I tole my family 'bout how I'm lookin' n' thinkin' 'bout gettin' my degree n' stuff."

"What'd they say?"

"They was amazed! They was totally amazed."

"Is that so?" Long and short was he wanted to know if he could be a surgeon in less than thirty months, on*l*ine. Dead serious when he asked me—thirty months, surgeon, online—said he heard it somewhere. Guy's probably been walking around for the past three weeks after having heard it somewhere, imagining what his life will be like once he's a surgeon, how sweet it'll be—a real life saver, boy!

"So you help place 'em in hospitals afterwards or we gotta do that ourselves?" That's what the guy asked me, just like that, dead serious. I mean, what am I going to say? I pretty much felt like hanging up and leaving, man. It was too ridiculous. I poked about his scenario—no GED, zip, dropped out in eleventh grade—and in a way I want to tell this guy that it's great that he has all these crazy aspirations to be a surgeon and whatnot, but man, you've yet to finish the eleventh grade and you're forty-one years old! So, sadly, I overhear my voice explain to the guy that he has to get his GED, and then complete regular college before entering a proper medical school. He says, "Yeah, I been meanin' t' get that high school wrapped, but man, I jus can't stand math n' science." Just can't stand math n' science, he says, but he wants to be a fucking surgeon. So I tell the guy, you know, that 'math n' science' are a pretty mandatory part of the GED and college, let alone med school and whatnot, and the phone got real quiet. "Guess I never thought about it." The phone went silent again. I Googled a local GED operation—"Shoot, lemme grab me an ink pen here,"—provided such, and he said thanks and everything, but I could tell he didn't write down any of the information. It was depressing as hell really—this guy, like so many tens of millions similar to him, was just a body for the most part, breathing and beating and eating and shitting its life away, one tic at a time.

Swish, swish, swish—it was then that I finally heard the stride of she who I'd been searching for—le check woman, Kristen Pluck. I stood and peered over the cube wall as she entered the arena. She walks with such resistance, this one—her thighs brush together with fire igniting friction upon the completion of every stride—some consultant guy entered at her side, some pencil mustache cat who, according to his nametag, was named Yuri—two Yuri references in one hour?—how improbable. He spit small talk, took notes, and generally succeeded in making it hurt as efficiently as one could have predicted a narrow-mouthed pencil-mustached consultant named Yuri to do.

Kristen scanned for a place to sit, marched toward a spot at the conference table across the room, dumped her rations onto the table and, after briefly composing herself, set off on wolfing a sandwich thorough her triple chinned, waxy face. Between bites she rested her palms tight against her thighs—purposely or not, she kept wiping slight hints of sandwich grease into the starched crease of her green pants. Her eyes looked as though she were secretly wearing an explosion-tight girdle—so tight, in fact, that her heart had been squeezed uphill and into her throat, compressed and constricted into an oblong, irregular shape as it lunged past her Adam's apple, thumping haphazardly and jagged before finally colonizing directly in the flush-middle of her face, hammering away red and furious and clogged with a lifelong accumulation of gook.

I stood and walked over. "Hey Kristen, do y—"

"If it's about the checks," she said, oxygen-deprived palm formed into a stop signal as she swallowed hard, "They won't be here before 2:00—the storm is holding things up." I turned around without saying anything, grabbed my things, and went.

22

The air outside the office was fucking delicious. I put on my shades, blocked out the world and went: "Well, alright, this is it—almost there—after I quit I'm never doing anything like this again. Once I get this check, and hell, even if I don't—fuck it, man—I'll thieve from an unjust and split the profit with someone in need to adjust karma if I have to—there will be no more of this working for people, ever again, in my entire goddamn life. You best respect that fucking promise, or starve." Walking from the building, I was released—I subconsciously counted my paces and thought: why does it always come down to numbers? Everything seems to: how much you made, lost, spent or still have—number of breaths that are left—fact of it all feeling so fucking fleetingly finite—a flickering wave of deep green in sunbeams as she lurches for more food on that late season, northerly breeze—let me drink that sun, Mother, because winter's comin', she's comin' down quick—start subtracting and soon I'll be bare.

I walked the top level of Wacker west, a hint quicker than two working men in hardhats. One with flecks of grey creeping into his grizzled black beard, asked: "Who the Bullies playin' t'night?"

"Fuckin Knicks—"

"At da Garden?"

"Nah, on Madison."

"Aw yeah? Nice," he paced on and: "Ya know, Mick, I don't tink I could make it as a Chicagoan in New York—I'm just too proud. If I ever moved to New York I'd probably spend half my day sayin': you fuckin' New Yorkers, you don't know how to do it right. I mean what kinda dumb bastard engineers wouldna' tought t' build alleys? Fuckin' trash inna front, whole joint smellin' a' dirty piss—it's only supposed t' smell like dirty piss beh*ind* yer house—didn't nobody tink about dat? Good Christ."

"Ain't it?" The guy chuckled as he tilted his head to the right to block the wind as I passed them by. I continued a couple blocks to the southeast corner of Michigan and Wacker and looked out while waiting to cross north. Partially covered in snow, several thin brass plates mounted in the sidewalk said: SITE OF FORT DEARBORN. A big group waited to cross and I decided to wait through a few lights and watch the world go. Via my eyes my mind felt like a live time-lapse exposure—the only stationary things seemed me, the buildings and the massive sculptured counterweights of the Michigan Avenue Bridge—many different types crossed the span in varied moods and velocities as snow piled steadily. The midday bustle was sloppy but clean. Cars were caked in dark slush and dress shoes and boots were swamped, but untouched areas were fresh white. A black man with long dreads seated on a crate jammed high notes on his sax to coincide with an unknown rhythm section playing off an old cassette tape spinning in his boom box.

The ground shook beneath my feet as two double-carriage buses blasted past—hard to believe that Michigan is simply a raised road right there—seems like she was simply bored down to from the tops of breathtaking buildings. The road again shook and I pondered the subterranean scene on Lower Wacker. I thought it cold and wet and dark and mostly filthy, loud as hell, pigeons or rats furrowing amongst half frozen trash, shadows dotted with random violent hermits cupping flames beneath torn soda cans, breathing deeply, and ready to fly.

A woman pulling a dirty suitcase while pushing a stroller came to the corner, turned to her baggage-laden husband, and said, "We should have never stayed here the extra three days." I'd seen them exit the Hyatt a minute prior.

"Why? I've had an okay time, haven't you?"

"I mean—I'm living, I guess."

"Do you know how that sounds?"

"What?"

He repeated himself sharp over the traffic. I wanted nothing to do with it. Unhappy people at home are unhappy people on vacation. Anybody who has lived or worked in a ski town can explain this to you—not only are they having a bad time, they're spending a large portion of their savings and using all their vacation time to do it—sends peeps tweakin'. She breathed deep and said, "However it *sounds*, I could care less—it's honest and so straight to hell whatever it is suppo*sed* to sound like. I can't stand us anymore." The wind unfurled her hair and I thought about how years ago, toward the end of the Civil War, in similarly twisted conditions, prisoners of war stood on this very spot, freezing and starving—I imagined emaciated inmates looking over a spiked wooden barricade, struggling with all their will to make it another day, some Confederates from Mississippi maybe, shivering like hell and scheming: 'How in hell er we gonna' make it outta this Fort Dearborn n' get on south?'—and in the end, make or break, what exactly had it mattered? They were all quiet now.

The light turned green, and I went north. A gust blew my shades off my face and I caught them on the way down in one fluid movement—they were back on the brim of my nose in less than two seconds. I wasn't sure where I was headed—I just needed to move. Doing so into the severing wind, I felt like the viscous of my eyes was freezing, and turning into glass. The cold was acute. Tears shot out the sides and I imagined a warm prairie of native tall grass rustling in the humid summer wind, but it didn't help. Before the middle of the bridge a man shrugged his shoulders and went: "Ay young blood, can ya drop me a bone, man? Spare some silver, maybe?" No answer. A dump truck and the 151 charged north, side by side, and one of them jammed through a deep pothole before coming to a halt. Flat-grey, half-frozen waist exploded in all directions and I felt the span recoil from the collision. The sidewalk was slick to the point that my stomach felt abnormal. I stopped in the direct middle of the drawbridge. The faint sound of a drummer banging buckets met my ears as my hand sliced the midway gap of the rounded brown railing. Frozen flags cracked in the wind and as I looked out traffic jammed and an ambulance blasted its air horn mere feet to my side. Siren deafening, its northbound endeavor got nowhere as anxious faces worked upon a felled being in back. Motivations dense in intensity, I imagined the drawbridge collapsing or being bombed, everybody falling under the icy water, quiet and weightless and free. I rubbed my hand on the slushy railing and breathed. Sight went over the edge to where I pushed a puff of white down to the potential fate lingering below. It spied a McFlurpy thrown upon the jagged ice of the River. It looked like a frog green chemical spill—not very appealing—and eyes now east toward the mingled waters of the Chicago River and Lake Michigan—white stretched on to visual infinity and the mind went: so you gonna' say anything when you take me away?

A woman in a manicured black power suit and a coffee colored storm coat passed a second man seated with his back against the massive, riveted, retractable beam that forms the foundation of the bridge. She walked northbound, black briefcase slung over her right shoulder, charcoal boots advancing a slender frame diligently into wind.

As she passed the lifelessly rigid figure, neither took conscious ware of the other. A red, swollen, immobilized hand clung apathetically to a coin dabbled cup, balanced atop twisted knees. Upon stooped shoulders sat a hat-covered head and a gaunt, sunken face—a face that along with its sad, drained expression, seemed on the verge of suffering defeat after a long battle against some intracranial vacuum—an internal black hole whose sole purpose was to collapse the man's skull in upon itself. I wondered: did you really give it your best shot? I'm not judging—it's just that I'm curious.

The webbed mesh of the brown crate he was seated upon weighed against the trussed supports of the drawbridge. I thought of the men who long ago fired the beefy rivets firmly into place. I thought of those who had designed the bridge, where they were sitting and what else might have been on their mind as they went about the business of working an intricate blueprint onto a blank sheet. I thought of those who forged the engine designed to lift the bridge at the sight of a ship, and before them, those who had mined the ore. I imagined what their lives might have been like, what their relatives might be up to, and whether or not they spend time pondering the oft unacknowledged output of their forbearers—and then—then I thought how the entire whole of what is, what was, and what will ever be shall bluster to dust, including the earth itself—swallowed by the sun before being exploded and sent back through time, every single fucking speck of history, exploded at light speed via a deafening, super-bright supernova—a runaway thermonuclear explosion deluxe. I thought about all that in about one-half second, and I felt crazy.

"He's either on something or he needs to be," said a man walking past.

"What can I say? He didn't do his homework."

"Neither did half our clients. I mean—just think of all those hundred year bonds we sold—we planted all those land mines and we won't even be alive to seem them explode." Out shot a unison conspiratorial laugh of no restraint—I continued across the River, and amongst hundreds of people coming and going a man lay dead-like outside the radio studio window of WGN. The midday hosts went on with the show and I marveled at the way cold infuses itself from concrete to bone and from bone to soul. A fixed face wretched like its soul had frozen and shattered and thawed and frozen thousands of times over—as though the perpetual state of fluctuation evoked a sort of gratification within the uncertainty of each moment—it was now in statue stage, a real spectacle of sorts. I stood still for a moment and the mind went: all things shall conclude. This is the inevitable part of existence. And what am I to make of it? This all would be much easier to stomach if I could simply get caught up in all sorts of trivial particulars, and constantly go crazy about them—how nice somebody tied a meaningless bow onto a crackpot award, anything really—never seeing or thinking of what is, happily skipping, dithering static distracting me 'til I die.

I pressed my eyes, saw a white flash, and moved. Across the street, in front of the Wrigley Building, a man seemed happy upon receiving a great kiss from the snow-traced lips of the woman that he loved. I looked to my right, and before the dramatic entrance of Tribune Tower, a thoroughly neat man with a kind smile and an immaculate woolen overcoat dropped his pen to the ground—despite being a fair ways young, you know, not over seventy or anything—he was showing some major signs of Parkinson's disease—shaking bad, this guy. He bent slow, balance precarious, black ball point inches from the tips of gloved fingers and, despite a stringent effort to hold steady with his cane—hickory bending hard, mind you—the edge of the stick slipped out from under him. He fell sideways upon the snowy ground with a muted thud. A blur of people went walking past and I stood still, pretending not to see, fiddling with a bag strap, digging in my pocket for an object I knew not to be there, and thinking: the pinnacle of life is indeed death. He looked up quick and caught my eye. I nodded and tipped my cap. He grinned, sort of, and his face went: goddamn fragile perseverance!—fuck it all, I'm carrying on. He seemed to really appreciate that I let him do his thing without making him feel weak or different. I felt bad as hell for him, of course, but what can you do? Just wait your turn and promise to stay strong and mostly kind for as long as you can, I guess—never taking shit from anyone. What else is there?

"Alright, just stop," I whispered to the self, "End these thoughts for a minute—fucking walk and be chill." The mind rolled onward and as I strolled I pondered the percentage of people who'd recently been sitting in one of these stupid meetings where everybody is asking questions trying to sound smarter than everybody else, trying to get promoted: greatest masters of the obvious in the entire fucking universe. I hoped the fraction low but had my doubts.

A good horde of attractive women strode south and I watched them walk. They were all pros. I figured they could get many things from many men if in the mood and continued north. Across from Atlas Galleries, a big man gazing up into the snowing sky smiled at his girl and went: "Damn. I love this city,"—she fully agreed, and I felt good. Just past was a boutique that sold sexy lady undies and such, and a man with very thick glasses and science-like style was peering at one of the mannequins with a look of profound yearning about his face. A mass of saliva stewed in the corners of his mouth in a bubbly froth, and I could tell by his stance that the cat was wicked starved and liable to act real crazy in the company of a fine smelling feline. I looked at him squarely and hoped he hadn't a cellar with a stack of used hand towels, laid out according to date—I thought it a coin toss.

A few paces forward, ice crashed down from high upon a building and struck directly upon a Styrofoam coffee held by an older black fellow who'd been walking carefully up the slick sidewalk, minding his P's and Q's. Cup O Joe exploded and: "Shit!—you alright?"

"Hell—wow!" he paused, checked himself, and, "Yeah, I guess I'm okay!"

"That was *nu*ts, man!—damn close—can't say ya had a bad day now, huh?"

"Hell, son—had a heart attack in '95, cancer in '98, so, you know, any day I'm on this side of the dirt, walkin' 'round—it's a good day, lemme tell ya."

"Let the adventure continue."

"Ya got that right, young man—have a nice one for yourself now." I continued, happy to have not witnessed a bad accident and snow filled the air. The Mag Mile was busy. Thousands of voices spoke of all subjects, and it seemed a heap of British were in on holiday. I caught some French and South American accents as well, and plenty of window shopping went on at the high-end joints. It was that odd time of year, in the months after Christmas, when retail gets desperate. Santa and his elves were chillin' and none of the marketing majors seemed quite sure how to impel consumers to buy—it was too early for summer clothing, people already had enough winter gear and the spring blossom seemed miles off—how *do* we get these people in here buying?

Some stores shone white light upon seemingly unattainable items guarded by men with guns. Others resorted to paying mildly-desperate people minimum wage to stand in the dirty snow, smoking cigarettes with signs displaying red percentages placed over their necks, numb hands offering papers nobody wanted, and still others went with hyper-sexualized images of sexually ambiguous teens wearing their clothing with expressions that did not quite seem to grasp just what in specific they were in the process of not giving two fucks about. It felt rather corny if you really stripped the hustles to their gist and stared out for a minute—I mean, what rot!

Crossing Erie on the yellow, a father yelled to his young sons: "C'mon, let's make dis," the whole crew eager to get inside Nike Town. A fit further, three kids who probably should have been in school designed downbeat lessons as they went banging the fuck out of buckets on the northwest corner of Michigan and Ohio—passionate faces scathed frantic rhythms as a line of frustrated cars trying to turn left implemented the horn section.

I walked on all the way past the Hancock, thought of going to the Lake, but figured it would be a good idea to pull together a little extra loot in case the check fell through. I had to have some dough to get down with Joey—he would cover me if I didn't, but, you know, nobody likes having to get covered. I looked in my bag for some old coins, crossed to the west side of the street and turned back south. A perturbed, badly soiled and soaking white man laying longwise upon the concrete steps of the First Presbyterian Church spoke to himself as the towering gothic façade and strangling dead ivy cast deep, cold shadows that seemed intent on diving down, enveloping, and swooping him through the forbidding ingress, quieting his feeble voice forever—move!

A trio of fashionable women laden with shopping bags walked toward 900 North Michigan. "Did you hear that retail was up 1% last month? That's great news, isn't it?"

"Well, it is, but at the same time, it isn't. See, there were so many sales last month that the 1% was at such a discounted profit margin that it didn't really help the bottom line very much." Tone fused with expression and allowed me to assume if she hadn't picked that up straight from a headline, it was from her husband, and she was now upset that his company credit card held a smaller limit for her to waste on countless inconsequentialities.

"But it helped me! Hehe!" her friend smiled, holding various bags at shoulder height. "Holy gosh, I need to get a bigger bag and conglomerate some of this! Let's skip this and go buy something in a quaint place on Oak Street."

I moved along, purposeful eye contact with a thousand separate sets and keen observation of countless more all newly registered to rest deeply in my mind. I was about to turn west on Chicago Avenue when a wide-eyed man stepped up and went: "Excuse me, sir? Whur is the Sears Tower? We just got into town and we haven't been able t' spot it."

"It's southwest, you know, you're heading south now, right?—so just roll on across the Chicago River and down t' Adams, alright, which ends at the steps of the Art Institute—you know, two huge copper lions, weathered to green, maybe some guys bangin' buckets, couple other hustlers, tourists everywhere n' shit, big proud joint—can't miss it, go if you can—so you go west on Adams, which is right, obviously, and then continue under the L at Wabash, again at Wells n' bam, couple more blocks and there she is, the tallest building in North America, castin' shadows on all sorts of beautiful, crazy folk, just like you."

"Isn't it called the Willis Tower now, anyway?" his wife asked.

"Not as far as anybody from this joint is concerned."

"Well okay, great—thanks!"

"Ain't no worry."

"Say—you couldn't like, maybe snap a picture of us, couldja?" he pulled his wife in tight, "We always hoped for one together on Michigan Avenue with the snow like this, with the Water Tower in the background n' all—and, well, as luck would have it—" he looked into the fluttering sky and raised a gloved hand with a grin.

His wife added: "This is our first time in town since grammar school—we're up from Cairo, and the kids are way back home for the weekend, gettin' babysat."

"Surely—I'd love to."

"Only thing is it's a film camera, a manual one—you gotta—"

"It's good—pretty much all I do is rove about, light on my feet, using one of these—that's all I've done for years now." I grabbed his camera and set them up with a horse

107

carriage in the backdrop, snow diving in nice, Water Tower in view, and I just let them do whatever—didn't say 'smile' or anything corny like that—they whispered close and shared a kiss, and I took the picture without them realizing. It was nice to not get that instant, digital satisfaction. I thought I caught them being real and in love, and I hoped that they would go on to live good, full lives. A light speed progression went on through the good, bad and in-between times before envisioning that photo being displayed at a bittersweet memorial service, friends viewing them through my eye and merry of what had been. I handed back the camera, wished them well, shivered hard, and on with a smile they went.

I hung west on Chicago, and walked down to Rush. The 511 hazardous incident team rolled north in no particular hurry, washed shiny red and clean, and I entered the Currency Exchange on the N.E. corner. The man beside me in line sneezed and I pondered if I should say 'bless you'—I decided yes but too much delay and so he sneezed right then, again, and so I said so pre the glance that asked: why bother? Up at the glassed window, a teller's voice shot through a speaker and said: "Like I said, sir, we can't help you—this isn't the correct paperwork."

"You know how long it took me to get over here?"

"However long it was, sir, it don't change that you got the wrong paperwork."

"This glass bulletproof?"

"I don't know, why?"

"Cuz we gonna' find out later—maybe t'day, maybe another." The man crumpled his things and stormed out of the store, leaving as much slush upon the floor as his quads could muster. I thought: there is very little unfettered self-reflection in a society so focused upon blame. I felt like sticking a blade to his throat and posing: is the paperwork right or wrong? And who brought it here? Did you think to call first and ask what you needed? And so with those three answers, why exactly are you threatening this woman?—and then, just as he tried to figure it out and didn't reflect correctly, I'd simply shove the tip of the blade from the soft bottom of his jaw through the top of his head—but that would have to be a pretty big blade, I thought, nine or ten inches—how would you have concealed it?—is this really a feasible fantasy?

"Excuse me, sir? S*i*r! Can I help you?"

"O I'm sorry." I stepped up to the counter, opened my bag, and removed a Ziploc containing two Pound coins. I had forty of them. "Can I exchange these here?"

"No. We only do paper money."

"Shit, really? You know any joints that do coins?"

"Just pawn shops or coin collectors really—you'll always get shorted a little."

"Really? Damn. Alright, thanks." I had figured to rake about $120 off those eighty Pounds. "You shouldn't have to be doing this in the first place, man." I squeezed a coin in my hand and thought back to the trip where I got them: I applied and got hired at a British tech company for sole sake of traveling to London. The Pound was particularly strong at the time. They had a Chicago office, and for the sixty days before traveling to London, I grew a maniac-savage beard and left my hair wild. I then flew to London with three very serious women from the Chicago office—I was the kid of the group, by far. We had two days to kill before the first meetings. They made big, detailed plans for expensive meals with our international co-workers. I ditched and got off the tube solo for sake of fulfilling my plan of roving until robbing multiple banks within twelve hours of my arrival. I had specked London on Google Earth, elected to choose depositories spread away from police stations and close to public trans, and figured: ride the tube to the end of the line to places like Brixton, where they wouldn't dare think a Chicago kid took a corporate job simply to fly across the sea on the company's dime for sake of filching thrice off one specific institution not to be named, yep: dress flawless, wear gloves, arrive at rush hour, unfold three pre-printed, non-fingerprinted notes with very simple, direct instructions—non-threatening: 'PLACE MONEY IN BAG NOW, PLEASE'—hand them to tellers, no speaking—you're thinking me a Brit, ain'tcha?—and now stacked, head to private bathroom with electric razor, shave the beard, chop hair, hit hotel and carry on to tech meetings of profit and yield for one week before having old British roommate wire the goods to Chi. I figured bam, get paid in Pounds, hit that exchange rate, take care a' mom and pop, building taxes for Grams, some goods for my sis, maybe drop the cousins an entrepreneurial advance and use the remaining scratch to get the publishing business started before again heading out into the wide, wild world. But no—it didn't happen. I stood in line, eyes looking over the scene, heart roasting and mind going: the difference between saying and doing is fucking wide—miles wide, boy, and I walked out of the first bank, feeling rather disappointed in myself. The plan was too soft and amateur. I asked myself: even if you had gotten stacked to a degree—would there have been any damage done to the institution? No— and so on the whole, you would have failed—you may have attained a perfunctory personal victory via basic strong-arm tactics, but any chimp ill-concerned for repercussion can pull that move. The money was fully insured. Nobody would have blinked but me. Examine, man— examine the multi-tier involvedness which thereby allows this institution and others like it to gradually take from the people—with efficiency so cool, in fact, that the practice is not described as thieving—it is given words such as banking, education, or governance.

I walked a long straight line on that bright sunny day, and, eyes seeing everything, asked the mind to begin working up, step by tiny incremental step, to more complexity, more elegance, and more adaptive perfection in how to wound such foundations.

23

I walked out of the Exchange and felt cold. The previous memory got me feeling like a hot tea. Further west on Chicago, a white businessman in need of a cig approached a loose conglomeration of shufflers posted outside the Red Line stop. A man smoking hard with his head low went: "The doctors—they was all speakin' in past tense—n' 'en I knew." Businessman interrupted and asked to bum—got told two for one. He quickly paid, placed the Ports into an empty pack, and walked on. The provider addressed a friend and went: "Yo you hear? They raisin taxes on squares again!"

"Shi—tha's why you pay $300 Joe, t' get your twenty cartons, G, up onna Illinois-Wisconsin border, man, jus over."

"Why all the way up there?"

"Cuz the man still finna rape over in north-wes Indiana," he said, hands comin' down in half-horizontal Karate chops, framing his manhood and adding emphasis to his opinion, "Ya gotta go way up man—do so n' you could make two stacks jus sellin' loosies—I done the math, G—ten packs a' carton times twenty squares a' pack makes two hunded squares a' carton—n' then times that by twenty cartons."

"So how much that is?"

"Fo'thousan' squares man!—two for one all day!" he said, throwing his hands apart all crazy.

"Shit—throw in some one for ones when people is desperate G and we be makin' margins—"

"Right? We be gettin' them studio sessions in *no* time!" They met fists and I imagined them back in the hood: slumping hustlers hawking loosies in fading daylight in adjustment to inadequate, erratic earnings and an ever rising cost of living—thinkin' a dreams, lookin' at pussy n' wantin a' drink. They were giving life a go, man, some way, some how, so good for them, I thought, good for them.

> "Nother day
> All day
> I say
> Okay
> Let's go
> Let's roll
> N' show why
> You gonna' grind
> Those dreams, G—
> You gonna'—"

The businessman, smoke in his mouth, leapt over a puddle in the middle of Chicago Avenue and, a touch low on breath, he interrupted the fresh rhyme and: "Hey, you know, I'm only here for the afternoon, and then I fly out. I'll want more than two, but I don't need a whole pack. I was thinking—how much for five more?" He bartered seven cigs for a five spot so as to cover his afternoon. I watched him and thought: the way somebody ashes their cigarette is like a sneeze—it's an unconscious gesture of sorts. Everyone has their own style, they really do. His small talk went: "So, you guys like, uh, live up the street from here?"

The man, counting tightly-rammed Ports from his pack, took big puffs and smiled without once removing the drooping cig from the corner of his mouth. Fat white snowflakes flew past his dark face, and he went: "No nigga, we from down the street—you ain't from here, is you?"

"Actually, no, Minneapolis—I'm here on business."

"Shit, boy—so is *we!*" he went, to a chorus of jiving laughter and cool-like low-fives. I smiled and crossed the south. They'd reminded me of a collection of loopers I've known for many years—good people, man—fuckin' grinders—36 all day.

I glanced up to the sight of a single bird flying flush against the grey sky and driving snow, soaring between the buildings, and wondered if he knew enough to long for summer, or if he really didn't mind. I adjusted the coins in my bag, picked through my writings, and wondered: will everything I've been working for wind up failing, or blowing up in my face? I figured fuck it—if it does explode then so be it, because I would much rather explode and go for broke than wean away like the feather detached and abandoned by the body still soaring high above, fluttering to the ground, only to be devoured by a teething dog. You're never going to be happy with that ending—most nobody is, and yet on they go, dreams drawing ever thinner, one complacent day after the next—I say whatever it takes, man. Whatever. It fucking. Takes. Go at it no different than those cats on the corner.

I walked back to Rush and went south before entering a joint that sells all sorts of tea. The gig was crowded. Tea was popular. A balding man with slouching green slacks and an oversized, under pressed dress shirt with a green tie tucked between the first and second button was disturbing people waiting to sit. There were no tables available, and he was reading the Journal, drink in hand, standing up, despite being in full control of a four top on the solo. The masses' expressions were quite the: 'Ahem, sir—do you mind?' type, and I personally hoped he stood at his table for the duration of the queue, enjoying the fact that he had the foresight to arrive first, and so be gone with you now.

A chubby mother seated nearby was loading her already fat five year old son with mounds of potato chips—tiny kid getting loaded up with chocolate milk and coffee cake at ten in the morning—more sustenance than *I* consume, a grown man. What is wrong with this woman?

A group of four middle-aged women, two tables away, were dead in the middle of a book club meeting. Their criticisms lent obvious credence to my assumption that none of them had written shit, ever. "Of *course* he has issues!" Such was the sentiment spout from the mouth of one well-dressed lady and into the ears of the three surrounding in regard to the author they were discussing. "Um hum, of course! Um hum, yep, *d*efinitely," they cackled in return. An old white bum with a hauntingly gaunt face began staring through the window, mere feet away, making her visibly uncomfortable as she ate her crisp orange carrot sticks. He held the line for a good duration, and she became further unsettled.

At another table a man's eyes were staring off into the corner of the room, fixed tensely upon some distant image, some memory. His wife pulled him back to reality when she went: "Did you get a chance to wash the floors last night?"

"Yes."

"The bathroom, too?"

"Yeah."

"What about the closets?"

"For the fifth time, dear, and not a single time more—yes, the floors have been washed and they're all clean, okay?" he was really trying to stay calm—eyes shifted back to his papers and out the window again—thinking of the one that got away, maybe, the only one who ever truly set him aglow—perhaps thinking: you know what? Fuck being safe. Safe? What good is life if you spend all your time being s*a*fe? Wow—I've really come to hate safety, haven't I?

"So then, did you also wash the strand attached to the light in the pantry?"

"Did I clean the goddamn strand of beads attached to the light in the pantry?"

"Yes—did you go over that?"

"No, but I just might wind up hanging myself from that strand if you keep feeling the need to ask—really hun, I just might. Jesus Christ! Be quiet for a minute, wilya?"

She shot back with: "It's just—I'm starving. We need to get out to a proper lunch because I am absolutely starving."

"No, you aren't—you've eaten over one thousand empty calories in the past hour, I heard every lip smack, which is precisely why I'm behind on my work—again." The argument escalated and they shared a look that seemed to say: the closest state to love is hate, and that's why you shouldn't be surprised to hear me say—do you know that I could honestly kill you? Both in their late-thirties, they looked entirely frustrated at the life they'd consigned themselves to. She sat stewing in a sedentary rage of sorts, rolling her fingers along the tabletop, tumbling them anywhere really, in an adrenalized but deliberate fashion, sound of which functioned as a fulsome ode to her non-liberated frustration. The man sipped his Joe and each iridescent slurp seemed to carry the weight of five thousand days' discontent—he looked at her and his face shifted at an internal insight that might have gone: this isn't a love story—this is a torture-suffused jail sentence! I wanted to say: hey, either dive all the way in and love each other for who you are or fly gone—if you keep trying to straddle the rail like this, it'll be ugly in the end—but in all truth, I didn't care what happened to them.

The line to order moved slowly. I picked up and read the paper for a lick and quite naturally the universal situation seemed to be a continuous spree of vengeance-spawned blood-letting. The bum came in from the cold to wait for a seat. Two little kids across the way, no older than six—much to the mortification of their mother, mind you—began referring to him as: "Hey grandpa! Grandpa!" I reckoned their Gramps to be a wild cat for such confusion to exist.

Up on the tele, the perfectly fucking tidy news reporter struck a bleak tone and posed: "Reports show the rise in spending is the weakest it's been in months—consumers battered by a slumping housing market and a credit crunch cut their spending last month to the smallest amount in a half-year—consumer spending on technology devices edged up .2 percent in December, the weakest showing since a similar increase in May. Individual incomes also grew just .2 percent last month, the poorest showing since August. Both figures fell short of economists' forecasts—"

And so here we can easily see just one example of the forever constant and needless push for people to always consume more—the stigma shrouds *less* consumption, conservation—buy, buy, buy what you do not need—no, not good—this is the precise mentality that so successfully enslaves the masses. Slack-jawed faces stared dead into the screen, and I wanted to scream: 'Yo! Fucking wake! Liberation awaits, man, free yourself! Shut the shit off and move around! It's more fun than you think, I swear.'

The accidental session of news watching caused me to feel monstrously detached from the world. One story essentially described a mass of humanity picking fights over arbitrary symbols, and the next focused upon violence in schools, particularly another handsome young honor roll student to have been blasted from the face of the earth for no particular reason. There was, of course, a public furor enacted upon the release of this news— yet, at the same time, well, this all seemed very lost on me. Truly, it did. I didn't feel a part of this at all—the guns, the intent, the public reaction and style in which it was reported—with panic-seeking, propaganda-infused overtones galore—it all seemed—it produced no feeling within me. Most everything in the news is so negative, I'm telling you—they should have a section that covers all the people who hold doors for old ladies or something—the world isn't as bad as they make it seem—at least not in Chicago—I mean, despite the ever-present threat of violence and thievery, there are some kind and courteous people out there, many thousands of them. I turned away, feeling like I was getting poisoned via staying connected—*lite*rally poisoned to an extent—same as I feel after wasting a span gazing at irrelevant hearsay on the internet—it's a sickening feeling, three hours later, when you get up and the day has passed you by, and it dawns on you: that's it—it's one less, and I can never get it back—and th*a*t's what I did with *it?* I imagine what I'll feel like when I'm dying—what I'd give for just one more hour t' fuckin' live, *man!*—I image I'll go over all those hours I've wasted and ask the doc to put me out of my misery, because I'd deserve it.

I blocked it out by focusing on the people—most seemed to be speaking too loudly for my taste. "You know how you really want something and you don't get it? I h*a*te that feeling!" Seated across the room were two trixies around my age, one married, one not, and if ever I was forced to endure their never-ending Valley Girl voice inflections for an extended period, I would need to float far, far away.

"So, do you have FTP access to the server, or not?"

"Wah?" it went on somewhere else.

"They say the early bird gets the worm."

"Well, I'm a mid-morning bird—I know how to live off crumbs," said another man to the chorus of dry, rolling laughter.

A woman brought a meal to a man and: "O no, this is what you ordered me? I don't want to eat this many eggs, and you don't want me to, either—not before a road trip, no way."

At the counter a father tried to furnish three dollars on his daughter for coffee, and she refused to take it. He really tried to insist, and I got to feeling like he didn't have much dough. His left leg was atrophied, badly so. He gave in to her rebuttal and gimped on over for cream. His pants were shrunken short and the shoes he was wearing reminded me of the ones we had to wear in elementary school—those all black, very rubbery types of gym shoes that seem to last a cool five million unevenly paced paces—he was sporting a pair of those, along with a crusty pair of blue/black socks. I wished three silly dollars hadn't mattered a great deal—wished I could have just slipped them both a hundred and walked out.

The plump woman who'd been feeding that puffed up, blonde-headed baby a horde of shit skimmed ahead of me with: "I'm sorry, did anybody turn in a toy?"

"What kind of toy?" asked the bony, bald-headed man working the register.

"A mouse."

"A fake one?"

"A fake one, yes, it belongs to my son—it's his favorite."

"Nope, all we got back here are real mice—they come in waves," he came back with, and the woman stomped off, glaring at my non-concealable chuckling.

"Yo man, that was good—just hit me an Earl Grey and I'll be out of here."

"$3.95"

"For a tea bag and water?"

"Yes—sorry, I feel you—not my prices." I gave him my thermos and final five spot, and when he turned, plain as day, I snatched two tuna sandwiches and an Odwalla Superfood from the display case, and placed the sum in my bag. The action was unhurried, and in plain view of all in line—yes, people, this is exactly what I *should* be doing—pennies have fallen to pence and every opportunity to acquire food from corporate chains that gouge the public needs to be seized upon. I mean—free Lake Michigan water and a tea bag in my own thermos—$3.95?—all without paying the producer a living wage? No. Not happening. If you didn't play like that, neither would I.

Tea in hand I hit the pisser, ran hot water up and down my arms, dried, and on my way gone, I looked at the old bum and said, "Hey, come outside for a minute." He followed 'round the corner. I gave him a sandwich and said nothing. He looked really happy, but so sad in a way, too—his face was just gutted, man—you could tell he'd held a ruinous penchant for substance for ages—mind wondered on how it had all gone down, if any *single* thing would be different in the world had he never been, and my body split south.

24

I walked around for minute, in no particular hurry, just drinking tea and thinking—thinking about what it is I will ever manage to do with myself and at the same time hardly caring at all, just eager to see what was going on. I took in a lot of sights and wished I hadn't recently broken my camera. I felt thirsty and figured I deserved a drink—a cheers to Bowler and the pre-arrival of Joey, anything really, but first I wanted to check the price of a new SLR. T'was a beautiful storm and I felt like capturing it. I thought maybe, if I got the check, I would be able to afford one. I almost went straight to a small camera store in the south Loop, but I first rolled into a large chain store in River North. I figured to keep my options open. I have a rule: never fuck with mom and pop shops—never, *ever*—they're already overtaxed and stretched thin by regulation. If you want to make a move, roll to a multi-national chain that exploits its workers for minimum wage and then gouges the public for superprofits—an easy way to determine this is to check if a large portion of their products are: fabrique en Mexico—if so, tis in accordance to NAFTA rules, thereby slashing American jobs, paying Mexicans hardly enough Pesos to eat, and charging struggling everymen several hundred percentage points of extra margin to obtain that which should have been produced here and sold for less in the first place—once you spot your mark, make your adjustment, and move along.

I walked into a store you can probably guess. The ceiling was high and bright and spying eyes were everywhere. They seemed to be selling a billion bright and edgy things. It was a bad place to go if disconnected—I immediately understood why so many suffer headaches. I made certain to browse at several expensive items, asked questions brimming with confidence, no slouching, proper enunciation, good potential customer, yes, I might just pay in cash—you take cash, yes? You make commission, too, yeah? Good, let's talk soon—and I then moved on to the camera department. Before I set to browse a real Columbia College-type manager got in my face and went ape about how to take great photos with each camera, some whole fucking manual he memorized, it seemed, and I eventually told him to suck back for a few beats. I said so thrice, nicely and legit, but he couldn't help himself—he went on with more unsolicited advice before I stopped him and said I would not buy from the store unless someone else helped me. He gave me a dirty look, so I said: "I just don't want you to lean in to deliver the tip of all tips and accidentally poke out my lens eye with any of the metal sticking out of your face, okay?"—that was how I put it, blunt and honest, with a white fucking smile. You wouldn't stop it. Further, let me see your work, cocksucker, and if it's any good, you can still go gargle rusty bottle caps for all I care. Don't give regurgitated photography advice as if it's your own, man—I read those books at thirteen—go die.

A girl then came over and told me to let her know if I wanted to see something closer. I told her I appreciated it. I eventually asked to see a new Canon. She snagged a box out of the case, removed the camera, and let me fool around with it. It was a standard film SLR, 20/55mm lens, and I was certain it would snap nice. I put it down and: "How much is it again?"

"Six fifty."

"Damn—I'll be honest—that's a little bit of a stretch for me right now."

"It's not cheap."

"I can probably—I'm waiting on a check—next few days I should be good. If you make commission or anything I'll be sure to come in and say you helped me."

"O don't worry about it—I won't be working here by then. Today's my last day, actually."

"Congratulations!"

"Thanks—I absolutely desp*i*se this place."

"Yeah?"

She leaned in and said: "Every single manager is a lying prick."

"No kidding?—in that case, who wouldn't be happy to quit?—well, curiously then, I mean," I removed my beanie, smothered the camera, and, shades dipping down my nose and eyes looking directly into her own, it went: "Would you be interested in walking to the other side of the store so maybe I can walk out the front door with this thing? If you write your number on the back of your card, I'll be certain to make it up to you when I'm better off and such."

"Are you serious?"

"Of course I'm serious—I'm as serious as I've been in many moons." She broke out laughing, shocked and exultant.

"You're crazy man!"

"Well?" I said, leaning closer—neither of us moved for a moment and: "It's a simple matter requiring only the barest collusion—why the hell not?" I asked. "Look deep inside and tell me—what does it matter to you? Do you feel this store treats its employees fairly? Do they provide a living wage for all they make? Is there any concern for when you are sick, or are you simply viewed as a disposable body? Seriously now, I want to know—what difference would it make to you if I walked out the store with this camera right now? What difference?"

"Well—I've never been propositioned like this before, I know that much. Heck, man—I could get in big trouble. The last thing I need is a record. I want to be a teacher."

"No, see—take this as a lesson in candor—you couldn't possibly get in trouble—is there any microphone recording this chat?"

"No."

"Fine then—there would be absolutely no proof available to implicate you. As far as they know, we're speaking about F Stops. What is it, anyway? 3.5?"

"Yes." She must have thought I was a real fucking maniac.

"First off, don't get uptight. This isn't some internal test—take me as a painter who can't afford paints—feel me? I need them—make yourself a part of the experience—I guarantee I'll capture the is and take some beautifully raw photos, and therefore, in some way, the action will be a benefit to mankind—I'll give you your pick of the lot, blow them up and frame them nice—the whole bit. Plus, if anybody stops me, I'll simply say that yes, I stole this, I'm a thief, and I'm busted—I'd never rat on you or anything, not in a million years, and I know by the look in your eyes that you believe me, as you should. So yeah—stroll maybe? Simply put the box in the storeroom. I'll wait a minute until you're plenty far and split—nobody will ever notice—like I said, it's for the good of man."

"Yeah—you."

"That's not a lie. Not a single statement in this entire conversation has been a lie. You've realized how many hundreds of thousands of people are, and forever will be, used by management as simple exploitable labor—there to be stepped upon and shoved about at their whim from now until the time they quit, get fired or retire, they will be used. If finished being another digit in the game, why are you still playing?" She didn't answer and: "Like I said, this is a lesson in candor—here," I handed her my number, "Call me if you'd be up for a drink sometime—I'll owe you. Put me in the directory as that honest thief you once met."

She gave a casual look about the room, grabbed the box and said, "I can't believe I'm about to do this," and, smiling, she strolled on.

"I love ya for it," I said, and she was gone. I was immediately aroused to know the camera was in my possession—it was a go—and with so my heart went pow many times in a row—mind said: what to do? Don't sprint to the gate—relax, take your time, and breathe—it's all just a game, big fucking deal—their policies represent the most crucial theft in the first place, don't sweat it. I stepped away from the area, placed my bloated hat into my bag, moved back to the plasma TV section for a quick minute, initiated several bogus scenarios to the salesman regarding wireless digital transfers of large files between the plasmas, my computers, my servers, printers, modems, guestrooms, restrooms, my heated four car garage and gazebo, and, after getting the tech guy involved in the conversation and vexing his brain, too, I obtained their business cards so as to implant a false swank status into their frontal lobes before smiling an all-knowing thank you and walking out with my new eye, feelin' goodly stoked.

25

Scathing power chords and Johnny Lennon's voice screamed: 'Yeah, yeah, *yeah!*' through my mind as I mingled into the helter skeltering snow and proletariat flow, quickly changing neighborhoods, never to visit that joint again. Wow. That was a score right there, I thought—a real fucking plus for the day. That girl—I knew she was down—she was fed up, man, tired of playing by the book—all she needed was a taught little shove to make her realize it. The only problem was, most everywhere I look I see parasitical-type men, thriving at the expense of all forms of life—am I one of them? Sometimes I fear the answer is yes, and for this I want to die. The lovely answer to this desire is that indeed one day I shall, so be easy.

Now I really deserved a drink—a smoke, too. The wind had picked up, and despite changing back into my roaming duds before leaving the office, she cut cold through me. I covered distance quickly, route odd and twisty, Grand over to Milwaukee, back east on Kinzie, past the chocolate factory, beneath mad Metra tracks and again over the River with that beautiful, oft photographed view of the Sears and raised train bridge looking down the north branch from there. And on I continued past the busy docks of the Merchandise Mart. The Mart stood stout and unaffected by the storm and, as I rolled behind her, a group of guys unloading boxes ripped through the general small-talk one could expect to surround the relationship between hurried delivery drivers and burly dock workers.

I cut south on Wells and passed the main entrance of the Mart. People felt beautiful in their natural flow, all shapes and sizes, all kinds of eyes, expressions awash in varied anxiety, the sound of the horns and whistles and yells and whispers, footsteps of a thousand different tempos walking toward the endgame as the L went roaring furious and angry only slightly above it all, "Sun-T*i*mes; Tribune! Sun-T*i*mes; Trib*u*ne here!" a man screamed.

Snow fell from the track as the train roared south. Tiny white diamonds slipped down my neck and bubbled into beaded ice water. I suddenly felt the cold wearing me down. I tried to imagine a summer Saturday night, a hot one, deep in humidity, shallow in breeze—the type of night where you know a heap of motherfuckers are going to get laid or shot—I imagined sitting on the stoop with my mates, stagnant air abounding, deep laughter emanating from bodies damp with sweat while lightning bugs, round breasts and sirens bounced lightly through the sweltering night—it didn't help. I can usually stir an inkling of inner heat via memory, but the cold was too deep.

I stood stationary on the Wells Street Bridge and looked at the buildings. Just what are people doing on the other side of all those windows? Is anything being made? Anything of worth? I thought of how much of our means of production has fled overseas—how much has fled and why. All these realty and mortgage companies, banks, title companies, insurance companies, credit-rating agencies—these fucking call centers—this is where a good portion of the jobs exist—on paper! Producing paper, moving paper, affecting emotions in a positive light via customer service—so what are they actually producing? Nothing! Fewer and fewer enterprises make anything we can actually use, capital goods—careers are abstract—what do you do?—well, if you have forty minutes, I'll try and explain—all these huge, beautiful buildings downtown—and what do they house? Cubicles with phones and computer screens—fifty thousand monkeys sitting in rolling chairs, dialing numbers and telling stories that seek to impel you to buy more paper with paper you've borrowed on paper in hope that somebody will then purchase that paper for more paper in the not too distant future.

I passed Wacker, leaned on an iron girder and thought: reality built on combustibles burns down and blows away—Chicago learned that after the fire. That's why they rebuilt it of brick, stone and steel—it wasn't made to be easily fucked with. I dipped in the alley before the Beejive Shoeshine Shop, right by the Washington stop—I stepped into a little cut by this hidden old time building back there, and set myself light on my feet. The smell of dehydrated pee was noxious. I exhaled. The view to the snowing sky was all smoke and buildings. I exited the alley as I came and walked north. The storm had changed moods and fat soft flakes fell slow and soft to the ground. A Brinks truck was double parked outside of a sandwich joint, and several people loitering seemed to be scheming. I wanted to hint that the time to start shooting should concur with the earthshaking rumble of the L thundering westward on Lake street—use any possible advantage. The thick snow made identification difficult—it was a good time to pull the job, but they were all dreamers.

A spry young woman went: "That sucks—I'm back from the road and you're out on it!—he's a good guy, good traveler—you'll have fun," into her cell phone, and moving eastward, an old weary woman wearing a blue babushka went climbing up the filthy steps of the L stop at Clark and Lake—wrinkles wrenched into an expression of unrivaled willpower, one weary step after another, as a line of recently disembarked passengers streamed hurriedly down the steps beside her.

"Hey! Where am I supposed t' go when they up there Tag Maghalin it, huh? You want me t' go n' drive over the motherfuckers? Beep that horn one more time n' I'm gonna' dent yer fuckin' forehead like yer fender! Feel me?" A whole line of cars were jammed on Lake on account of two Indian cabbies in the midst of a non-understandable argument after a minor fender-bender. A black cabbie had finally gotten out of his vehicle to explain that he was sick of the blaring—rage was a good look on him, truth told—dude looked like he could make a decent living fucking people up.

A tight little chick stepped out of a wedged Impala, looked back at the big ole stylish gal who dropped her off and shouted, "Thanks again—holla!"

Moving along a man went: "And then I hear from Petie that he calls himself my friend, okay? Friend? The only time I meet with the guy is to call him out on his bullshit. Friend? He's a real shyster—cuts corners all the time, puts people at risk." His aura was that of a classic: so much to do, man of power—a legit and straightforward one—a hardworking

Chicagoan—he went on speaking in a leaned forward fashion, much dual handed nonverbal action and consistent vowel emphasis—I hoped he owned a company that produced a good, quality product, made in America, and helpful to many. His overheard positive outlook made me assume he'd always treat his workers fair. He had a big smile and a lot of freckles—something about his style said if he owned a restaurant, they would always play great, old time music.

Okay, I thought: so now I need film—I figured I'd give a last go at cashing the Pound coins at a bank. I hung a right on Dearborn and stood by the Goodman Theatre for a minute. Two city workers leaned hard, sweeping snow off the sidewalk as a group of high school kids flowed north—each of their respective styles maxed-out to accentuate a field trip to the Loop. Across traffic, a long line of lamps lit the left side of the James M Nederlander way. I cut through. Dripping icicles descended the steps of the black fire escape on rear of the Oriental, and two men tumbled out of the 'Fire Exit' stage door. One lit a smoke and spit hard, almost falling down. The brick walkway was slick—they were movers of some sort. It was a shitty day to be a mover.

I came out of the gangway to the view of the Chicago Theater. Someone famous was to be there in a couple of days. To my left a crazy fool was leering into the Channel 7 News window, possibly looking to make some of his own. A line of busy people rose to street level from the Red Line. I turned and walked south on State. The bike rack outside the dorm of the School of the Art Institute of Chicago was crammed full of different, cool vehicles.

Further southeast, behind Jeweler's Row on Garland, an old, grizzled black cat went, "Sup Dog?"

"Glad to be alive, feelin' fine."

"Alrigh, alrigh," he said, and I strolled on amongst old time gem dealers sneaking crooked-glanced cigs. Across the way, a burly delivery man in black jeans and a late eighties Chicago Bears Division Championship sweatshirt was gettin' after it—heaping boxes upon a manual lift and whisking load after load down the alley from his double parked delivery truck. I decided to try a different bank than the one I originally had in mind—I recalled they didn't deal in foreign currency. I rolled back over to State Street and immersed myself in the torrential flow. A fat black man was excitedly explaining to a young black lady: "Tha's twenty five thousand dollars of potential *in*come! I already signed up six people today alone!" while showing her a slew of various pamphlets and sign up sheets. After a moment of hesitation, she made good her escape. I continued my walk to the sound of a creak-wheeled pull cart powered by a white haired madam skirting along slow and steady to catch the 145 express to Ravenswood. She reeked of can-do, rugged self-alienation—it smelled very pure and American.

I turned west on Randolph and passed the entrance of the Oriental Theatre. A mother looked very happy as she walked a red carpet beneath the flashing lights of the awning, and stepped through the doors—on the way to spend an afternoon at the show with the daughter she'd lovingly raised.

Just then diesel and dust rose as brass bells tolled half noon—two hands turning round a fat gold sun with wavy rays pointed dead north, and the dozen pigeons that pinnacled the spire flew gone at the first gong. The lips of an adjacent man screamed "Streetwise!" but his actual voice got drowned out by the never-ending construction of Block #37. The bustle was immense and the distinctive smell of Garrett's popcorn dominated the area.

Continuing west, an uneasy man got his hustle on holding the door for folks at the *Mac* Donald's on the ground floor of the green and grey Art Deco building that forms the NE corner of Randolph and Dearborn. A car blared and slid across slick steel plates covering a huge hole in the intersection. T'was nearly an ugly accident involving the traffic director—he was angry and shaken—somebody hadn't listened to reason.

I crossed south to Daley Plaza. A well dressed black man holding a white girl in caring style, said: "Look, the Goodman Theatre!" They both seemed very happy. I passed the glassed lobby and spied the Picasso. The Chicago Temple building shot like a golden bullet to the sky and the wide shoulders of City Hall flexed in the distance. Three flags on poles flapped in the wind: the Chicago, Cook County, and that of the United States—a POW flag hung dead below the US flag, and I thought of all the guys from Chi, captured by the enemy in wars throughout history. I imagined them hungry or filthy, dying to get back home for a walk on the Lake on a sunny day—what they wouldn't give for a great inhale of fresh breath before looking east into the level plain of blue, and diving in. I thought it probable that a whole slew never made it and figured it would be good to never forget that.

The voices of soaked, busy bodies cut through parental orders as a clan of kids used the long slab of metal at the base of the Picasso as a makeshift slip-slide into a snow drift—their happiness served as a nice contrast to the mix of cold, depressed people working addition and subtraction for fines incurred via deplorable behavior as they exited the Daley Center. Continuing south, a real fucking nutcase stood with his face pressed hard to the steel pole at the bus stop across Washington waiting for the 20 east to eternity.

Across Madison, I dipped into Chase Tower, and entered the bank. Wrong time of day to go, man—Friday at lunch?—far too loaded—I figured to wait it out for a second. Back in the building lobby, I took a seat at one of the leather chairs facing the long, south windows, and looked out. Snow continued to fall, and I organized my bag. To my left a conversation came: "I feel like I'm married to a military recruiter from Myanmar, man."

"Independent thought fully banished?"

"It died with the honeymoon."

"One day you'll wake old and creaky and realize you wasted many good years, and you'll long to expire."

"Or kill—what do you think I should do?"

"I think you should cheat on her sometimes man."

He looked out and: "I'm just so *tired*—I'm not even interested in other women—all I want is to close my eyes for a long blink, let light beam and discover this relationship was all a dream, that I never actually let it happen—but I did, and it's ruined my best years. I'll never get them back now—it's over, Jake—I'm on the verge of growing old."

I cut them off, looked to my right and an aged man sitting beside me looked about ready to die. He appeared broken in every way aside from the great care he placed into slicking his ghost-white hair just so. My sincere hope was that his thoughts were happily satisfied, though I held much doubt as to the likelihood of this holding true. I could feel his despondency. I figured I might as well wait in the bank—these cats were bringing me down—I waited a long while in a coiling line to learn they wouldn't exchange coins.

I exited east and walked to the corner. From Monroe and Dearborn Street, looking way south, I could barely see the old clock tower at the south end of Printer's Row. It was a real white-out when the wind blew. The cold cut into my back and I moved toward the camera store. People trudged up short of breath from the depths of the Blue Line Monroe stop, careful not to slip on the steps. Across the street, 131 South Dearborn ascended reflective and glassy, firmly contrasting the building just south and its hard vertical lines of cold black metal standing out against the snow.

I crossed Adams and walked toward the Federal Building. A horde of reporters and photographers appeared ready to stick microphones and flashes into the face of a newly accused politician who would then play the game of denial—it was all so predictable. They would write damning stories and nothing would change.

It was then that I noticed all sorts of shoes lining the courtyard—they were covered in snow. I read a sign that stated all the shoes belonged to civilians from Iraq. They were the kicks worn on their feet at the moment they died—they were the shoes of the dead. More than two thousand pairs lay quiet and still. I leaned against a black steel support of the Federal Building as the L rumbled mournfully over Van Buren, and gawked. All the different styles sent me imagining the echoing footsteps each pair might have produced. A woman of high fashion stepped through the scene, lines impeccable, with several bags in her hand—the expression on her face while marveling the finality showed that she had been disturbed by the sight. It was something, man, it really was—all their dreams, bam—just gone. And who were they? I pictured people bartering kicks in a sticky bazaar by the Euphrates, haggling with a sweat-stained merchant, putting them on right there and walking away, satisfied with the negotiation—I bet they never assumed they would wind up blown to bits while their shoes lived on in Chicago, getting snowed on, and generally unnoticed.

I turned and walked fast with my head down. I passed by the DePaul student center and couldn't believe how many of these soon-to-be lawyers had spent a hundred stacks to seem so afraid that the time to make independent decisions had actually arrived. Almost to the camera store and a man yelled: "Ay you motherfucker! I been lookin' fer you!" A train roared over as a big Greek with hands like hairy hams choke slammed a black dude to the concrete on the west side of Wabash. He picked him off the slush like a sopping scarecrow, held him against a brick wall and slapped him sharp with his thick right paw. Several people turned. I watched, unsure if he was about to tear into his throat with the maddened tenacity of an untamed tiger—I hoped for one of those cartoon fights where all you see is a big dust cloud with some legs and arms sticking out. Half-frozen muck slid down a pair of white sneaks as the Greek went: "So you gonna' stop fuckin' round on 'eis, or is Spiro gonna' have t' pay ya a house call? It's yer fuckin' choice—don't tink we don't gotchu in our fuckin' address book." He spit it real harsh-like and menacing, crazily really, words firing steamily out his mouth— the black man was on his tiptoes, wheezing a bit. I slowed and several additional people walked past as if nothing was happening, heads tilted away, focused on the next objective, go, go, go—I thought of the daily, panic seeking headlines of corporate, online media as written by lazy intellectuals—now what did we learn in Sociology class? Precisely what socio-tendency does this scene represent?—it's called fucking life, homeboy, life in the Chi—catch a clue, it's nothing new. They're so soft compared to real people, man, compared to the world. They couldn't tell it like it is if they stood up and tried.

I loitered long enough for: "Man, why would I play witchu man? You think I'm fuckin' crazy man? I tole you man," he leaned close, "Men inna middle jammed me up bad, man. It's comin', man—I'll even hitcha some collateral."

"O, well den, if it's really in yer budget, maybe we'll work somethin' out—no *shit* you'll hit me some fuckin' collateral! Jesus Christ—why ya tink we been huntin' ya down for? I want all ya got on you, right fuckin' now."

"Just calm down a sec, man—shit man—let's talk a sec—" I was humored. His bloodshot eyes shone the wheels blending some crazy twist of a story together at light speed—

The big Greek leered at him after his excuse, and: "Hell, I don't even know why you're mixed up in dis to begin wit. Answer like dat—ya coulda been a great lawyer, pal, coulda had yer own practice even—coulda called it Shinestein n' Sons." They exchanged a look that seemed to acknowledge that in the end, they might try to kill one another. All told, neither seemed to care all that much—nor did I. Aim straight, boys—that's my only advice— aim straight and shoot to kill.

26

I stomped my feet clean and entered the store. Inside was a great sight—all kinds of cool, random old shit that was still useful and beautiful. The place smelled like a darkroom and I would gladly spend a couple extra dollars to support them. An old man came up from the rear and went, "What's the commotion? Is there some idiots fightin' out there?"

"Not yet—they're more in the threatening death stage."

"Well what then? What can I help you with?" He was eating a homemade ham sandwich, chewing very fast. I liked him. It was apparent he'd tell you to get fucked rather than allow for his time to be wasted.

"I need a few rolls of Kodak Professional film and batteries for my camera."

"Alright."

"But I have an unusual request."

"What is it?"

"Can I pay in Pounds?"

"The currency?"

"Yeah. I got two Pound coins, forty total—I'm a little jammed up and can't get them changed anywhere." I handed him the bag and: "They're legit."

"Listen, I'll tell *you* if they're legit or not." He took one out, flipped it in the air, slapped it on the top of his vein-lined hand, and, after shooting the close glance of a watchmaker through his blue eyes: "Okay, they're legit. Ay, Jimmy!" An old Indian fellow came from the back. His accent was deep. There was no way his given name was Jimmy. I liked that the old man called him Jimmy: "Take a look at the paper, wilya? What's the exchange rate on the Pound?" He looked at me close and: "You know, I was in love with the queen at one time—ten years after the war."

"Power can be a very attractive quality."

"You're a smart kid. I got a lot of ladies over the years, knowin' I was the owner of a camera store—knowin' I was an entrepreneur."

"I don't doubt it, sir, it's a great store."

"Ya think?"

"It's local and real and filled with knowledge—I won't be in Kansas City and walk into a sterile duplicate. That's nice to know."

"What do you have against Kansas City?"

"Nothing really."

"I was only kidding."

"O. So how long ya owned it?"

"Three generations."

"Congrats."

"Thanks, son. It's been a love and hate relationship—ever been to London?"

"Once."

"What'd ya think?"

"Too many cameras."

"Agreed." Twenty tics went past, he finished his sandwich, and: "*Well?*—c'mon Jimmy—what is it already? You should have it memorized every day considering how long they colonized you people."

"Can't find it. Don't go so crazy!"

"Don't provide attitude to my tone which did not exist!"

"Vatever! Okay! Is $1.8." I enjoyed their playful relationship.

"Are you sure?"

"Vat it says."

"And that's today's paper?"

"Vat it says!"

"Okay," he looked at me and nodded, "Lemme call my guy and see what he'll give me for 'em." He dialed fast and had a curt conversation. It worked out that he'd get $1.6 per Pound—$128 for the total. As a consequence of having to go through the trouble to sell the coins, he demanded a profit of .2 per Pound. I agreed this was fair, and thereafter left the store with $30 spent on film and batteries, and $82 in cash. I walked south and smiled. Crazy old grinders—they know how to do business—everyone got what they fucking wanted—he made a $16 profit, I got my film and cash, and the fucking pawn shop made their sixteen bones based off the same .2 by eighty Pounds. I felt good. This is capitalism: loose, fluid transactions in small, independent joints based on a combination of speculation, need, mathematics and reason—if you went into a corporate chain and tried to haggle like that, some robot would look up procedure in a big blue manual before telling you that in accordance to line 3,235B, the answer is *no*, sir. See, these stores, their methods of production, procurement and sale represent capitalism hijacked via government sponsored elimination of competition via massive tax breaks for large, lobbied-for companies who thereby bulrush overregulated independents, leaving little option for consumers or small businessmen. I say so because for the small man trying to compete against other larger enterprises that are able to afford those costs, it is simply not possible to sustain. And why is that? How does it continue to happen?

I thought: are independents simply too independent to organize? Why should it be that the better you do, the more you're penalized? The harder you work, the more unfair the tariff—what sort of tarts concluded this to be just? How are you deemed radical to expect to keep a fair portion of what you earn, and to have the right to be logically heard on where taxation is spent? Do you recall why this country was founded? What finally set people off? Sense means nothing to these people, power means all—give me the money, and shut your mouth. C'mon, sir—be a good patriot, really now, let us kill who we want, spend here, gorge there, and give fat handouts to our favorite players—no worry, we'll get to you eventually—we're aghast, in fact, to have to ask for what is yours—we figured by now you would be broken and worn enough to hand it over without having to ask sternly and demand like this. I mean—hasn't our attempt at a gradual tearing down of your head affected you?—do you not own a TV? Did you not feel us seeping deep inside the people? Have *they* not worn on you, either?—the hordes of programmed yes-men seeking to subject you to the tyranny of the majority—have they not yet hijacked your sense of individual self-destiny? Did you not participate in the education system? Don't you understand how you're supposed to act? You are to make your moral and economic decisions based, not on your own self-interest, but on what the government considers the general well being. Why, sir!—slowly, methodically over time, word by word, one example after the next, you are to follow us until finally, without having comprehended the essence of constant doublespeak, you should now be ready to roll over and beg for everything! We and our pet corporations have a claim upon your earnings and rights, and our claim precedes yours—we'll leave some in your pockets, but whatever we provide you for yourself is for us to resolve—some will have to give up a bigger piece of their pie because we're hungry for more. Why, sir!—have we not reached you? Can it be possible that an idea has mined inside the mind and started a little fire? Did somebody pull you aside and rub two sticks together? Let's get you some water—I think I see a little smoke—the last thing we want is for you to know what it feels like to burn. Let's get you some medicine—we assure you this is not predation.

I crossed Roosevelt and headed down to Printer's Row. I looked back northwest and spied the Federal Prison rising through the snow. A crazy concrete triangle with slits for windows, its construction was a rather brilliant idea to torture prisoners on the beautiful sights and sounds of the city—criminals forever perched high above, trapped in cages and O so close to all that they miss. I wondered if you took the City Council, the House and Senate, the full Congress, lobbyists and meddling corporate men of abstract influence—if you actually analyzed who had skewered individual rights or taken bribes to advance agendas counteractive to the interests of those who'd placed them in power—just what percentage deserved to be locked in that triangle?

I cut my gaze and walked toward the pub. I needed a pint, bad—I was feeling pretty hot about things.

27

A tired mug slashed by a dangling thread of soggy, twirling grey, hurriedly turned the corner on Dearborn and vomited a churning orange mash upon a dark-bricked façade. The area immediately smelled of acid. I walked ahead, entered the pub, reserved a table with my bag and approached the bar. "Guinness and a whisky please—something cheap, neat."

"Sure thing." The Latina girl that served up the drinks was hard, but cool and classy in a way, too—she had that low key attitude where she could jive from rags on up to riches, but in the same breath, she would be prepared to slit your fucking throat if ever you crossed her—she was a Chicago chick through and through. "I'd take her serious if I were you. Watch your mouth. Don't push it," was what I overheard on my way to the bathroom. I entered and ran warm water over my face and hands. This felt very fine. The voices of the two men seated at a back table snuck through. "I know fa'sho dude in Edgewater got *o*unces a' blow at his crib, pounds even."

"Maybe we should roll up n' rob his ass."

"I mean we should at lea*s* th*i*nk about it, man—I mean shit—c'*mon.*"

"It helps that I got me a 'lil throw away in case I gotta blow somebody's head off, a Kimber 1911. Maybe we can hit 'em up n' enfranchise, ese."

"File the serial number off a' that—but go deep, man, a few centimeters past where it stops bein' visible, even—you might need t' spend on a sandblaster, but do it—they got special chemicals that'll raise them numbers out of nothin', I swear."

"I already did—n' I only touch it with my R*ee*bok gloves."

There was no mirror and upon the wall above the sink was scrawled a perverse diagram and 'Vote for—' subject's name scratched out with a sharp blade. The clean steel sheen of the bathroom stall beside the urinal was heavily pockmarked where a long litany of angry motherfuckers had given it a stiff right hand before taking a piss, and thinking things through.

I exited, collected my drinks, settled in the corner and sipped a little of each. The warm taste of cork lingered on my lips before getting overwhelmed by cool beer. Lighting was dim and attendance spotty. The main crew was a group of construction workers who lined the bar. They'd been cut early on account of the storm—all seemed glad to be inside a warm, dry place, drinking.

"I tell you guys we got another job?"

"Yeah?"

"Big ground-up work in Kenilwert or whatever it is—a fresh build for dis bigwig advertiser. I'm surprised we got it, t' be honest—we went over the plan n' I musta' rubbed 'em da wrong way for some reason, guy started j*a*ggin' me right off da bat—should be fun."

"Nice. What's his wife do?"

"She's an artist."

"Ain't they all?"

"Heh—yeah, right," he chuckled and turned to another cat: "Ay—'sides work, I hardly seen you da last month. What's a' story? You seein' some fuckin' broad?"

"He couldn't get l*a*id in a woman's prison wit a h*a*ndful of p*a*rdons!" another man yelled.

The whooping settled down and: "I was fer a minute, not anymore."

"So where'd ya meet her, anyways?"

"At da toll—I just like, noticed her one day while going through da toll."

"Whudaya mean toll?"

"I mean da fuckin' t*o*llbooth."

"Was she inna car next t' ya? Were you guys waitin' t' pay n' you hollered over at her? Kudos pal, I've definitely wanted to pull that—"

"I'm sayin' she w*o*rks at da tollbooth. She works for da highway er whatever."

"You mean she makes ch*a*nge? You serious?"

"I am. I'm serious. I—"

"How the hell didja pull that? I mean what'd ya—"

"I don't know. She just made me change one morning—two months ago prolly. And you know, I'd seen her a couple times before, but this one time—this one time I stuck her wit a twenty. She was countin' da singles n' between counts she licked her thumb. She licked it all slow and eyed me up, kinda. I woulda ignored it, but when she dropped 'em coins in my hand, I don't know—she kinda paused n' 'ey were just all warm n' stuff—two nickels n' a dime. Like, I mean, they were warm from bein' in her hand. They held her warmth n' she

124

just looked at me." It was quiet for about five seconds—that's when they all busted out pretty hard.

"I'm done sharin' 'eis business witchu if you guys keep it up!"

"C'mon already! Finish da story or you can get on outta here."

"Fine, fine—so I introduced myself, right. I asked if she normally works dat booth during the weekday morning rush, n' she does. So I basically rolled trew dat same booth every morn for about tree weeks, n' we carried a rollin' conversation the entire time."

"Fuck off."

"No, serious—I always tried t' pay with a twenty or somethin'—a fifty once, even, you know, so we'd have extra time to chat. We eventually ended up goin' on a few dates n' whatever, but I didn't really get into her. Terrible cough—plus she smelled constantly a' hard currency n' all she had were tollbooth stories."

"Like what?"

"Fuckin' I don't know, man, I can't put my finger on anyting now. She had some weird ones. I'll give her dat much. Problem was she was pretty infatuated with some guy who worked for IDOT—guy drives a snowplow er some shit. She found it a big deal. I was comin close t' winnin' her over, but the jag drove her back home to Franklin Park when we got that big lake-effect blast a few weeks ago. He towed some old woman's car outta da ditch onna way t' 294 n' she was all impressed. I could care less—I got an I-Pass now, anyway." They all had a big laugh together, and breathed easy. Their smiles looked especially white compared to their dirty, wind burnt faces. I imagined them through the years enjoying that sort of general shit-talking fused with intrinsic relaxation as earned by laborers lounging idle in the late day shade, palates eager for a tallboy. They were hard workers, you could tell. Every time they threw back a swig I could see all their hands were gnarled. They reminded me of all the guys who've worked with my pop at the machine shop—deafening steam presses pounding out plates on hundred degree days, while industrial chemicals and the smell of burning metal fill the air—I thought of the people back at NVH Online freaking out because it was sixty-five degrees in the office, as if penguins were about to swoop down from the ceiling for a Nordic festival of some sort. Soft. So fucking soft it's sick.

Right then a twitchy maniac walked into the joint—he walked in, looked at everyone fast as hell, and walked right out—back to his car: a red, rusty, early 90s Oldsmobile sitting on the west side of Dearborn. Judging by his demeanor, he either went back to his car because he had forgotten his wallet, or he went back to get a fucking gun, and he'll be good and ready to blow everybody's head off upon his return. His eye, cheek and chin looked as though long ago he was slashed about the face in a sickening spasm of violence. Back inside, he ordered a drink, and sat alone—t'was a wallet—he looked ready to kill though, he really did.

Two tables away, a well dressed black man who I assumed to be fairly financially well-off carried on in a desperate sounding conversation regarding the possible sale of his 1987 Toyota with one hundred and eighty seven thousand miles that he claimed to be: "A slick little coupe—really." Minus everybody that has everything, nobody has shit.

"Smoke?" posed a Norseman-like fellow of considerable size.

"Inna minute."

"Whachu smokin' now, anyway? Ultra Lights?"

"If I wanted a' smoke Ultra Lights, I could just move to Gary n' breathe for a living. I smoke Reds. Might as well get your money's worth 'cuz they've got it pretty well figured out, right?—dey make billions in taxes when we buy 'em, n' billions in Medicare payments when we get cancer—perfect fuckin' storm."

"Speakin' a' that, hey—put on the news for a sec, wilya? It's about time for da weather—der's gotta be five inches out der." The bartender flipped the channel. In shot a common, monotone commercial where a lawyer stares blankly out of the screen and speaks like a broken robot, case full of books in the background. A man slammed his fist and: "Lord how I am sick a' hearin' about Hampton Shagazy financial tapes. I just might go broke so I can greet dat obnoxious bastard wit a fuckin' choke-slam," he said. The bartender was soon engaged in a fairly heated debate on the topic of how shitty it is to live in NW Indiana. The mutually agreed upon sentiment was that living in NW Indiana blows.

The news came on with: "Well folks, we have a real *rid*dle on our hands with this system. See all this Gulf moisture rising north? And do you see this Alberta Clipper crashing south? Now you combine th*a*t with this arctic lake br*ee*ze, and what's happening is a *cla*ssic setup for—" the meteorological dialect went sky high as ole boy flipped through animated slides and spit probabilities that equated to a weatherman's wet dream.

"How many f*u*ckin' graphs is this guy gonna' sh*o*w? Just tell me how much we're gonna' get already!"

"Pipe down! Some people like this shit, including me." I got a giggle from the interaction—Chicagoans would understand. The likely scenario went: snow through the afternoon, another few inches, blowing snow tonight, clearing, colder, damn frigid temps, warm sun and stiff southerly wind early tomorrow, a Gulf push, nearing forty and sunny toward late-afternoon before another big Artic swoop begins with wind building before more snow, bottom again dropping out to near zero by Sunday morn. Nobody flinched. A man walked past the window, cold and defeated-looking, pushing a shopping cart filled with misconstrued knickknacks and fringed belongings, heading to nowhere and everywhere all at once, and I felt nothing. The bartender shut the TV off and offered $20 for the juke, on the bar. It was a nice gesture. People were glad. I was the closest one to the juke and she suggested I pick the first few. I put the money in and looked through the options—the place got real quiet—it was an interesting form of soft pressure—stepping up to a silent jukebox while a crowd of raw, eager to drink fools lingered in the rear: t'was a perfect setup for a snap judgment. I could only imagine being a singer—no thanks. I selected a Chi classic I felt would set people in to booze. Out shot the sound of a piano man laying some sickly quick licks on the ebony and ivory, and the lyrics went on about a stretch of road called: LSD.

A big burly dude raised his glass and nodded at me, "Fuck yeah," it came, "Good fuckin' call," I nodded as he set out in a deep baritone: "And there ain't no road just like it, anywhere I found, runnin' south on Lake Shore Drive, headin' into town—just slippin' on by on LSD…" I took him for the foreman—guys were asking him a bunch of questions about the project.

I loaded a good line of tracks, and back at my seat I worked on the whisky. An elder seated beside me was drinking something harsh and reading '*Walden*'. He met my eyes, and I said, "That's a good tale for the times."

He smiled and: "I've read it before—many times, actually. It's my go to whenever I need to laugh at all the people running about—all who've gone ahead and indebted themselves so deeply to external opinion." He took a drink and: "So you've read Thoreau's essay on civil disobedience, then?"

"Yep."

"What do you think he would say now? If he got a chance to see how far things have gone? What would be his first question?"

"That's a good thought," I said, "I guess, well—he'd probably be wondering how people allowed it to happen—don't you think?"

"And do you know the answer to that?"

"I do, but, I don't—I mean—there're so many distractions—it all comes so fast. I'm heavily tuned out, always have been—no TV, no real link to advertising, almost no electronic use. When I go to people's houses and these commercials constantly fire in with a million cuts and crazy music—it's pretty weird in a way. It trips me out."

"Is that an acceptable excuse for why millions refuse to advocate private autonomy and self-determination rather than the state ruling over the individual?"

"No—no, it's not. I'm just saying you can see how it happens—people are so caught up in so many things—continued survival, mainly—very much goes unnoticed."

"How old are you? Mid-twenties?"

"Thereabouts—I have much to learn, sir."

"You have the right attitude, anyway—but I will say that in my seventy-three years here on earth, what I've seen quite consistently has been a gradual tearing down of individual rights—a gentle series of incremental infringements—hence why it's been very effective. They knew it would be best to avoid a sort of 'gotcha' moment to be sprung on the people, thereby avoiding a larger backlash. The way it has worked over time is you catch a little blurb on the tenth page of the paper that some small right has come to pass, and few notice. It happens every so often, like a new camera going up, and then, eventually—you wake up and notice every inch of the city is eyed up—the problem is, who's watching? The most corrupt central command you can imagine—but it's only so they can to take care of you, right? And another way we remain distracted is the government promotes an archenemy for you to fear, because if not, it becomes the enemy itself—can you name one time in history in which we did not have one?"

"No."

"The enemy distracts from the fact that the state wants you to handle the least amount of your personal business possible, so they can get their grubby mitts on every slice of business. Preventing such is the ideal I most accept dying for. They're takin' care of us, alright—don't forget that," he said. The glance with which he turned back to the book indicated the conversation was terminated. He was a serious old fellow. Looking at him read I thought: you can feel the rising action like a book—there's a worldwide vibe, a hunch in stomachs across the great diameter that things aren't going right and that we're sliding quicker than we ever thought possible. It's not a good feeling at all.

At the bar it went: "I tell you some motherfucker tried to run me off the road the other day? Guy drivin' a delivery truck—no reason at all really. I was drivin' too slow to get nowhere, I guess." I thought: all it is—a bunch of different people pissed off about different shit, trying to exert power over one another because they can.

The guy who'd nodded to my musical selection walked over and: "Hey kid, thanks for the good tunes—good day for a drink, eh?"

"Fuck yeah, sir."

"So what do you do? Sit here n' write stories about nutty iron workers n' stuff?" He was glancing at my opened sketchbook.

I laughed. "Sort of—you know. I uh, I walk mostly—I help as a literacy tutor, sometimes, at this joint on Lake Street, but not often—I write and take photos a lot, you know—I roam pretty hard for the most part, grinding cake here and there."

"You puttin' somethin' out yourself?"

"Tryin' to."

"Solo?"

"Minus select people involved, yeah, solo. I know a load of talented, real kids who need a cool avenue to get their shit out there, you know? We need to do it ourselves and send it out before people who don't comprehend life water it down to acceptable levels of public consumption, thereby making it weak or irrelevant."

"Sounds pretty cool, kid."

"I don't know, we'll see—it's good to be alive is all I know—so you give the guys the afternoon off? They seem pretty grateful."

"Yeah—I ain't havin' my guys up weldin' no girders today. Ain't worth it—too dangerous, plain n' simple—my pop got wrecked in a work accident—ain't never worth it. We can always work fast n' safe onna next nice day." I looked in his eyes and snap-reflected on the insane amount of effort my father has put forth in effort to provide for me, my mother, and my sister—other hardworking people send me thinking of it more and more, his effort, his will to bestow his best crack at life as a crack on me—and the more I think about it, the more I feel I should be giving back to him by now. For all his effort, I should be the one giving back to *him*, enabling *him* to take a fucking seat for once, to sleep in for once, and to take as many deep, unhassled breaths in a row as he goddamn feels in the fucking mood to breathe. Almost losing his hand, smashing a shoulder now held together by metal screws, every day on the edge of disaster—the man deserves a choice aside from uncompromisingly arduous manual labor for sake of sustained survival.

I was suddenly so irritated with my progress on things, that I almost got teary-eyed from hot self-anger—the sentiment manifested itself in my flying mind, a sharpening of a continuous struggle to let the man chill pinched tight in the middle of my chest. I bit my knuckle and: "Yeah—I respect that you gave 'em a break. What'd your pop work?"

"Steel—Indiana mills—three generations. It ended wit me. I just seen my old man suffer too much—dat n' the fuckin' mills mostly closed down, anyway, as ya know. Luckily m' pop pushed me into engineering—lets me plan n' analyze builds as I'm doin' the work. I was a city inspector for a while, but it just got to be too much. I'm glad t' be back onna sites wit my hands in it."

"Too much?—monotonous paperwork or whatever? Too much what?"

"If you're not involved in corruption, you're seen as an enemy of those who are—such has a tendency to get ya axed—know what I'm sayin'? I got tired of it, ya know?—it ain't a fun line t' walk. It's terrible—you'll see some guy ya somewhat respect fully backing X, who's known to be corrupt, just to push his own agenda—and you're like man, you're all the same! If ya look at federal employees, you'll notice a large portion have da top a' der ass located at the midpoint of der back—der's a reason for this kid, trust me," he said. I laughed and he continued: "N' what's worse is den dey all want ya t' kiss that ass n' call it a love story! I wasn't raised t' play dat way. I can't be workin' some gig dat, fer all intent n' purposes, I got zero respect for, n' at the same exact instant, be loaded wit stress n' have absolutely no time t' myself. Dis will not work kid, no, never."

"That's good advice—glad you bounced then—enjoy the snowy afternoon, sir."

"You too, kid—just wanted t' say thanks again fer dem good tunes—we gotcha a shooter over here if ya like." I went over to the bar and knocked it out. The old man who'd been reading walked out with a nod. Back to my seat, people did their thing. Men came and went and the view out the window was dreary, cold, snowy, blustery and downright gnarly—this made me glad. I inserted the batteries in the camera, loaded some film, and worked on the piece. After a good span filled with effective observations, I thought: this, man—this is exactly what I should be doing all the time—paper against pen, man—it's one of the best sounds in the entire fucking world—a sharp pen against crisp paper and the faint smell of newly exposed ink mingling with that of freshly brewed coffee, whisky and falling snow—t'was my exact sense of smell that very moment, and for such I held love.

Two men sat down and: "What's new?"

"O, just wondering when or if the public will ever grow weary of omnipresent, thankless wars in foreign lands while domestically, education, infrastructure and economy are in collapse."

"It'll end."

"It's just beginning."

"I hope you're wrong."

"Me too man. Me fucking too."

I dipped out the back door for a little smoke and as the snow swept in and the L roared past, the mind went: yes, man, there is no time to dawdle—you must always be seeing—fuck all those classrooms and teachers and suggested writing styles—focus upon roam-writing, that style, like, just being out here—you simply need to be going, man, seeing what is, and letting it ride—wafting and writing and seeing and breathing, you'll feel free.

I sat back inside, shivered through a verse and continued writing with: 'It's funny to think of how somebody I hardly know may congratulate me whence this shit is printed and out there—they'll congratulate me on my 'success' when really success for me is right here, right now, alone and not giving a fuck about what anybody thinks—a voice is screaming out the door, half-muted by a gnashing snowplow and sounding desperate. This is what is. This is existence.' I suddenly felt practically homeless and starving and not really inclined to care. 'What is currently good at the moment is a much longer list than what I am allowing myself to feel—don't be a baby. If you don't come from money, such forced deprivation is the only way to produce quality product and open a business without borrowing. Embrace the rawness and don't stress opinion.'

I stood from my work and went up for a drink. In through the door strolled this easy bruising, negative sideburn motherfucker with a mouth like a crooked slit in frozen, lumpy flesh—an overall aura of a mechanized being in a blue uniform—he cut straight to the bartender, ahead of me, and said, "Yeah, listen, I'm in a hurry—have 'em whip me up an egg n' roast beef sandwich wit a side a' whatever, okay? I mean—whatever you can throw in for me on that as a city worker discount, I'll take it—but yeah, make sure they use four eggs, okay? I gotta get back to headquarters, pronto."

I thought about walking outside and waiting for him so that upon his exit I could ask him just how it is that *any* city worker should be en*ti*tled to a discount. I wanted to say, hey, you ever consider: the administration that pays you—these people are robbing us *b*lind! Quite literally, every year it's higher ta*x*es, fees, more permits, tickets—maliciously squeezing every last *d*ime out of the people, and getting us t*wi*ce by encouraging bus drivers to run camera-equipped red lights so as to accumulate tens of millions of dollars in penalties that are in turn paid for with a*d*ditional tax dollars—squeezing the necks of people who've lived in the same home for eighty-seven motherfucking years!—squeezing them out of the homes their forbearers built with their bare fucking hands!—and you know what we're wondering? Where in the fuck is this money? Have you ridden these roads? Old ladies breakin' goddamn tailbones tryin' t' drive t' church—city discount? You have that gun on your fucking side so you stride this private, overtaxed, overregulated local joint, barely making it, and have the absolute gall to ask for a city discount? Get fucked, boy!

Everything about him seemed robotic—the way he stood, the way his head moved from left to right, up and down while reading the menu items scrolled artistically upon the chalkboard—all his movement occurred at ninety degree angles, it seemed. Just like his way of thinking—I'd bet almost anything that his method of thought is all up and down, right and left—no spirals—no beautiful spiral of thought from which he could reach the beautiful state of asking a why and conquering the quest of discovering an autonomously reasoned, ungoverned because.

Rollicking along with further poppycock, his hands clung to a belly of hard, porpoise fat—he eventually grabbed his sandwich and began chewing. Into my head shot the image of thousands of malnourished chickens in cages: a chicken farm, an enormous slaughtering room, gigantic in scope and size and intent, and thousands of tortured, sleep deprived chickens—their screeching reverberations clamoring against concrete walls with horrifyingly desperate, emotive overtones, claws torn off bloody in stone barriers and eyes shocked that in fact, yes, we *are* trapped!—mutilated beaks shattered yellow and red, loose skinned legs swept into the corners by the rubber-skinned hands of feather plastered, authoritatively speaking, day laboring slaughterers. This image popped into my head when observing the cop and his intense, intricately measured-out attack upon his slimy sandwich—it was as if his mouth were fused with the weeping uterus of a chicken, and all he kept screaming was: 'More eggs! The people in charge want more eggs, goddamn it!'—wailing with the proper acoustic consistency to ensure the foul would come to possess the mandatory stress level needed to fulfill a laying rate that coincided with his venomous appetite before it crashed sideways in exhaustion, and died.

I took a pull from my drink as his partner jumped in, and went: "So where my boneless pork at? If you don't get it to me quick, man, you gonna' have t' gimme it on the house." His basic M.O. seemed the type where all he does is eat, complain, take big shits, and snore—he got his sandwich, turned and caught me staring with violence in my eyes. We held each other for a good span of seconds. There was no intimidating him. His pupils said he would have shot me in the back until the trigger went 'click' and gone on eating with not one blink of hesitation had it been only the two of us. It was written all over his face, man, I swear to God. There is a very fine line between cops you root for and cops you hope will get killed—and the same goes for people, really, for ordinary citizens.

A Mexican busboy was mopping the wooden floor toward the rear of the bar. The hulking public nuisance looked at him and went: "Hey, son, I want that floor so clean I can eat off it."

A hard bass line played in the background, and voices grew quieter. The kid didn't reply and: "Hey Billy—you think there's a surcharge if we eat off that spot when he's done? Will we have to tip him?"

"You can eat off it now if you like, nobody's stopping you."

"What was that?"

"I said if you feel like crawling down there and eating your eggs, it's all good, sir—nobody is going to complain. You can use my napkin if you like."

It got real fucking awkward for a second, and nobody said anything. A couple of rough guys at the bar darted dirty looks and time slowed down. The Latina approached and called attention to the total. The men paid full, dropped their sandwich wrappers on the bar, and walked out. The busboy stood a little taller and I wanted to say: what happened? Did you come alive? Don't allow yourself to be disrespected like that. I'll never stick up for you again—this is your place, you people pay the bills—you should be ashamed to allow an outsider to walk in here and cheek off to a hard working employee like that, uniform or not.

I got back to writing and the twitchy motherfucker walked over a hit of whisky, and left without words. I knocked it back and my blood felt warm—I felt it running through the veins in my neck and arms and noticed my hand was shaky. I was feeling pretty edgy. I reached in my bag and from my work pants I grabbed the stack of folded COWS from the front pocket. Many problems seemed interconnected. I walked outside and had several conversations:

"That's just the way it works, man, like one ton of copper ore produces twelve pounds of copper—just math homie."

"Totally."

And:

"Think about it—would you buy a new car without knowing what sort of engine it has? Without knowing exactly what will be responsible for impelling you to your next destination? What if it doesn't have enough horsepower, man? What good will it be?"

"I see."

And:

"If you were to find yourself choking in a steakhouse, I trust you would prefer to be assisted by somebody with knowledge of the Heimlich Maneuver rather than having a random fat man belly flop upon your stomach from the highest available chandelier, expelling the lodge only to kill you via crushing your vital organs via undue pressure—know what I'm saying?"

Silence in understanding, and then: "Indeed."

And:

"The investors aren't just getting by—they're financially launched into the upper crust, the flammable gasoline burning hot upon the surface of a deep cold sea—education has never been a priority here, feel me?"

"Clearly."

Twenty minutes went past, I shook the snow from my clothes, threw the COWs in the trash, walked inside on numb feet and, duty done, I ordered a last drink. I flipped to a page filled with a recently analyzed list—the inscription represented the top fifty investors of PRPB, 'Prime Re-education People Brokerage', the education corporation that owns NVH Online. I looked at the names and thought: these fucking plutocrats have been getting rich on a bait and switch for years, man—poaching victims on miscellaneous false premises, plum and easy—poppycock dense to the point of seeping out their pores, thick with the scent of stale dishonesty—time for an adjustment. I had a pretty good scheme in mind, but it was going to take time. Most top investors were other corporations, or banks. I would have to actually speak with CEOs and board members—have to pose as a false stock analyst from a false investment company and drop certain realities, but only after certain fundamentals were set in place—fundamentals that would assure I get to teach a lesson in crime focused on returning the favor.

I dialed the phone for a dry run, and after speaking with several internal operators, it went: "Allen Richel's office."

"Can I speak with Allen please?"

"Is he expecting your call?"

"I have no idea what he's expecting—how can any one person know what another is expecting?"

"Please hold." She came back with: "Will he know what you're calling in regards to?"

"It's regard."

"What?"

"What I'm calling in regar*d* to. Please don't pluralize regard. It's incorrect and terribly annoying."

"Are you serious?"

"For the most part."

"Can I ask where you are calling from?"

"Of course, you just did so."

"I *said*—can I ask where you're *c*alling from."

"Yes, you've done so twice now."

"Are you looking to sell something?"

"No."

"Why are you calling then?"

"To conduct psychological warfare."

After a short pause a shaky voice went: "You are an *i*diot! You should have a big *E* painted right on the side of your head! Do you know that? A big, giant *E* painted right on the side of your head is what you should have!"

"Why?"

"Because you're an *i*diot!"

"Just making sure," I said, and hung up the phone. This was going to take time— months, maybe longer.

28

I finished my drink, went out, and moved—walking north, the wind ripped between my wide spread fingers with unabashed fury, like its sole desire was to tear them off my hand, one by one—I appreciated the effort and put on my gloves. The tingling in my knuckles made me feel that all I wanted was to go back to the office and smash Fryer's digits with the hammer, one by one, until he would finally come to admit the faults of what he was doing— the problem with this: he's only one small fish in sea of many brothers. If he were eliminated, some other eager imbecile would migrate to lead the school in no time. I threw my camera over my shoulder, cut east on Congress, and walked north on Wabash. The Trump dominated the view, and when a miraculous split second of sun shone through, I snapped—the soaring reflection looked majestic and otherworldly compared to the faded brick buildings that lined the west side of the tracks. Such set a phantasmagorical backdrop as three tourists unsure of where to turn looked at a map, and were promptly propositioned by the two nearest hustlers. I find it funny to observe the body language of people when approached by bum-like individuals at the onset of their hustle. Seems most have a tendency to become very much uncomfortably stiff whence put on the spot and asked for a bit of what has settled in the bottom of their pockets—quite afraid to simply say no—as if it were they who had stolen from them. The bums were persistent and professional, not unlike the government, I thought, in its insistence that it always deserves more, and more, and more—and why?—because I just do, I fucking need it, son, so give it here.

The Green Line to Harlem groaned 'round the bend as I walked upon a thin pathway of trodden snow and flicked cigarette butts. Up a ways, I brushed off and sat upon the edge of a gigantic concrete flower pot in front of Roosevelt University. I tied my boot and watched the people for a moment. Many seemed happy that it was a Friday, and the smell of fried chicken filled the air. I felt good for them—the people, I mean—not the chickens. I honestly wanted to stop each and every one of them, and personally wish them much enjoyment: 'Time is flying, man, have you noticed? Days are fading fast—funny how they just keep coming 'til they're through—I hope you have a blast this weekend—I hope your life is perfect, whatever that means to you—I really do.' I had a few smiles, watching them go, their different methods of movement and styles of dress—I opened the sketchbook, inscribed some comical factors of my surveillance and thought: some of the funniest, smartest kids I've ever known have been lifties and caddies. I suspect the reason lies in the mutual habit of silently observing human behavior on a mass scale for long, sustained stretches of time.

I set off and back across Van Buren, the Brown Line to Kimball lurched 'round the bend as the Pink Line moaned past on the opposing track—the whole of the action felt burdensome—all that steel moving those people and dreams and sorrows, crashing in perfect rhythm over the gap in the tracks—bam bam, bam bam, bam bam—a rusty fucking heartbeat for the many eyes spying out steamy windows at the history that those of long ago had come to erect, wondering perhaps just what in fact it was that life had in store for them. Up north, dark clouds flew past a spire, and again the world went grey.

I continued north on Wabash, and across Jackson, a twisted man exited a crusty food and liquor store, ripped open a warm flask of Gordon's Vodka and endured a horrible-looking mouthful before wiping his lips with a dirty coat sleeve. Slightly up the street, I turned down some guy around my age who claimed to be taking donations for a fund to cover people who'd recently had their homes foreclosed on. I understood there were many tales of woe, millions maybe—I felt for them, but still I said no. He kept on going, though, and eventually demanded, as if it were my contractual 'duty' to help everyone out. It finally came: "Are you trying to blame me for the faults of others?"

"Do you not feel a sense of responsibility to serve the great collective?"

"If you're referring to the great collective of undereducated, uninspired, lazy bastards who prefer to sit back and blame others for their lack of opportunity and foresight—a sense of responsibility for those who willingly acquired loans they had no means to pay back in order to procure substances they did not need while at the same time, having to pay lenders for their own under-analyzed mistakes—so essentially paying double—while at the same time, the majority of this quote, collective, does little or nothing to improve their current situation besides putting on a sad face and extending their soft hands rather than standing tall, tightening their belts, immersing themselves in self-education, acquiring hard skills and getting to work, then no, I fucking do not."

133

"That's a rather cold attitude, don't you think?"

"I was unaware that accuracy could have a temperature." I spit and, "How many organizations, for years on end, have been selling people product that they hold little to no use for, at prices they could not afford in the first place? Is it my fault people bought them? Why do you think such businesses are failing? The entire economic circle has been flawed for years. Credit is finally used up. This is a necessary correction to out of control consumption and poor consumer choices. There is absolutely no reason for people to be surprised—none at all." He looked at me like I was some devil, and I felt like sticking him one right in the fucking mouth to shake him from his general naiveté and unawareness of basic economic principals. He really irked me—nobody is owed anything except the effects of their own mistakes or successes and I live my live according to that principal. Do I dare demand you alleviate problems I've caused myself? I'd rather fucking die than be so soft. "Yo, I know you're trying to do good, man, I do—it's commendable, what you're doing—but you also need to understand it's not your right to demand payment from anybody, ever, less it is for goods or services of your own rendering. You can ask, but don't ever demand like that. A handful of generations ago it was hardly certain that people would live to see adolescence— you sir, live on a fucking rock spinning around its axis at a thousand miles per hour as it slingshots through a chaotic universe—there's not much room for error, and when people make one, I don't always cry for them. Safe travels."

I crossed Adams and dipped in the alley north of Miller's. A shadowed man in a nearby slit smoked an entire cig without ever once removing it from his mouth. He seemed pretty hard. I lit a last drag and an adjacent sign said the Prime Rib was available all day and that it was a helluvaburger—the air smelt painstakingly good if you were low on dough. I opened my bag with the intent of eating that second tuna sandwich, but it just didn't look right. I took off my glove to adjust my belt and accidentally felt inside the waist of my pants—my hip was pretty bony. All I'd eaten so far was that toast, and in truth I was lightheaded, but still, I couldn't do it—I squeezed the sandwich, creamy mayo oozed out the sides and I retched at the sight. Further up the alley the scene saw a young black skater cut a fine line through an oily mire—he pulled a sweet grind on the oversized yellow curb and splashed upon the slushy ground. I tightened my belt and moved along.

Back to Adams and westbound I saw a woman who was so cold and wet and hungry and lonesome and poor—she was wrapped in a soggy wet blanket, head jammed tightly inside—I wanted to take her photo, but I just didn't have the heart. It was really a horrible sight. I shelled her that tuna sandwich and continued on to the sound of booming horns—a bus driver was reading the paper and hadn't noticed the light go green across State. I took out my phone and checked the time. Quarter past one—it was almost time to head back to the office. I dialed Will Zybarsky: "Yo G—what's good?"

"Get my message about Joey Calandra?"

"Yeah. Good shit. I'm in."

"Word. You subbing today?"

"Nah, they didn't call me. I'm sittin' on the stoop, dressed in a lot of layers, drinking coffee, watchin' the storm—I'm prolly gonna' puff one and paint in minute."

"Cool—well listen, it's been a whack day—I don't know how far I've walked, but I'm done with it. It slipped my mind that you borrowed my bike. You didn't crash or get her stolen, did you?"

"Nope."

"Where she be?"

"Grant Park—far southwest end, by the sculptures of headless bodies—a little east of them, actually, toward the Lake."

"That's an odd spot."

"It was a weird night. I wedged the lock key above the rails of the saddle. Just call me if you can't find her n' I'll give you the specifics—I'm tryna finish this song I'm puttin' together—you around tonight?"

"Not sure."

"Word."

I hung up and started jogging—should have called at the pub—I now had to double back to Roosevelt and go east. I blocked the world out, and churned—got there in fifteen and, past the headless bodies, I spied her beneath naked branches reaching dark and twisted against the white, snowy sky. I felt like a tired cowboy finding his horse—it was a big relief, and she looked beautiful. I threw the security devices in my bag, carried her to the street, licked my lips, brain a little buzzed and body eager for some urban skiing, and, after slipping into her toe clips, we went nowhere—the rear tire was flat. "Motherfucking Zybarsky! You tall fuck!" He probably hadn't realized. I checked the rim, expecting it to be destroyed, but it was fine. This was a big letdown—I really wanted to ride. I threw the blacked-out top tube over my shoulder and, out of spite, marched fresh tracks north through the middle of the park. Not a soul shared the scene, and as I cut through to the open south fields, I stomped one posthole after the next and breathed deep with each step. Wind built up steam from far across the arctic meadow and struck me with force as the city rose before me like a monolithic fortification.

I imagined the buildings as peaks and floated back upon moments lived after ripping the mountain with good mates—days where you wake to the sight of shrill, brooding peaks on the horizon, mind eager for hour after hour of life alone with the wind—where nobody is trying to be more beautiful than the next person—because there is no next person—and you head somewhere on high to focus on dreams for a minute, a place where there is no audience minus the vast, untamed tracts of land cowering below—and you fucking go—just owning it—living it—and at the end of the day you all come together and need to nip some whiskey just to cool out, you're so stoked. Yes. This was far less enjoyable. I felt worn, hungry and wet. I recalled the many times I had been in this same field, just one of thousands, jiving to notes both high and low in the midst of loose movement, oppressive heat, sweat and intoxication—so many memories, same field—MJ raising his trophies—there were endless recollections to choose from. Either way, it felt very different now—t'was the way it once was, and the way it shall eventually be—silent and empty minus the haunting wail of the wind, no more people, their music, or friends. I looked east past LSD at the Lake and she just stood there, hulking white with blank emotion—her breath made me feel fragile as hell. I began imagining what I'll be thinking when approaching the mystery, cut east to Columbus, and walked all the way back to the office.

29

I locked my whip to the rack outside and an adjacent, skinny Latino man holding half a taco was sweating profusely, mouth twisted and watery: "I tole ju, I'm bery Caucasian when it come to spicy foods—I tole ju I didn't wanna order from der," he said. His girlfriend giggled, I spun through the doors, and walked to the elevator bank. The button was already lit and the only person standing there was Tim Kramer. He looked at me funny and in my head it was: what in fuck do you *want*, man, just come out with it already! Not everything has to be so calculated—spit it out!

"Hey Anthony—just to let you know, I didn't mean to snap on you earlier."

"Word."

Momentarily quiet, he picked at his ear, and posed: "You know anybody by the name of CW Martino?"

"Not principally, but about a week ago, in fact, I think I heard somebody by the elevator bank answer their cell phone by announcing that name."

"W*e*ll? Did you get a look at them? Who was it? What'd they look like? You recognize 'em?"

"I never got an official glimpse—I was tying my shoe."

"Could you tell if they were speaking to a student? Were they talking about the program? What did the conversation concern?"

"Gambling—horseracing and college basketball—fixing bets, manipulating odds— shit like that."

"*G*ambling? Fixing *b*ets? I don't get it. Would you recognize his voice?"

"There's a chance—why? What's the big mystery behind this CW Martino character?"

The doors opened, and we stepped onto the lift. He pushed twenty-three, leaned in with a very serious face, and said: "Alright—I'm going to let you in on something. Don't go repeating this to *a*nybody, you hear? The only reason I'm letting you know about this is because of your overwhelming enthusiasm for the program, and I don't want what's been happening to people to start happening to you. Then again—how many enrollments do you have this month?"

"As before—none, not a one."

"Well, maybe it's happening to y*o*u, too—you never know."

"What? What might be happening to me?" I wanted to make myself sound 'vehemently concerned', but it was not possible to pretend. I probably sounded bored. I didn't care—looking at him, Tim Kramer was only vapor to me, just waiting to dry out and turn into dirt. I couldn't imagine working, for years, like some people had—putting up a whole show of false sentiments every single day post-analyzing hundreds of different people, and thereby ejecting this false individuality so as to fulfill the desires of how they hoped you might feel, all in part to be deemed 'employable' by the fore. It was truly nuts to imagine that people do such things—how could you even look in the mirror afterwards?—my face would smash straight through the glass, I'm certain of it.

"Well, reliable information has come to light that leads us to believe that a man who goes by the name of CW Martino has been contacting students after they send the application fee. This Martino guy has been calling them directly and sabotaging their entire education!"

"What sort of reliable information?"

"Remember the whole TL Bowler conversation this morning?

"That amazing unpeeling session?"

We stepped off the elevator and: "Yeah—he called and left a message—I dialed back and when he answered, he went *off!*—got out of control on me, if you want to know—

told me this Martino fellow dialed him up and underscored how expensive the program was, to the exact dollar, interest included. Martino also provided unspoken details involving the curriculum and how it's fairly basic and all that, and then pointed the COW in the direction of self-education, recommending he rent books to read for free while working hard and living frugal and things like that."

"How'd he lose control?"

"Bowler told me I might get hurt one day." It was hard not to smile.

"Why?"

"For being a *sales professional*, apparently,"—he still didn't get it—the fact that in the end, what he was doing actually had a negative effect on some people. It was hard to hold back. "It's an inside job, obviously." I smiled internally and thought: nobody in this office has any sense of who or what I am, or what my motives might be—this of course is a huge advantage. It's amusing to think of how frighteningly easy it is to fool people. "My guess is it has to be somebody in financial aid—somebody who works with numbers. I mean—I wrote down what he told me, his reasons of sudden disinterest, capturing his essence as fast as I could—I even tried to use my objection toolbox to wrench the situation right, but it just wouldn't work—that's when he said I might get hurt someday. He had all the price points figured out and was real angry that I hadn't provided the hard data."

"Have you told anyone else?"

"Gloria and Mr. Fryer—they're really concerned about it."

"Don't worry, I won't say anything." I walked into the bathroom and took a glance in the mirror—I looked fairly nuts. The lifestyle of garage living and incessant roaming was finally taking a toll. I felt I needed to lie in a hot shower for a long time, and sleep underwater. Snow had saturated my sweaters, and I was chilled pretty bad. I took down my shades and the eyes that stared back were aglow. I walked into a stall, locked the door, and just stood there for a minute. Two people came in, unzipped, and:

"Do you think Mr. Fryer is looking to fire somebody?"

"I don't know."

"Not knowing scares me."

"Me too."

"Something's set him off since the Rah Rah—he's been comin' at people all day!"

The general conversation of enslavement continued and I checked the time on my phone: t'was 1:58—seventeen minutes until the Reality Check. I had much to do. The duo left and I ran warm water over my red, pained fingers, shivered, and walked into the admission's arena. I was immediately met by Caroline. "Don't you know you're not allowed to wear sunglasses in the office?" I didn't respond. "Where's your work clothes?" Silence again. "How'd the dentist go?"

"What?"

"The root canal—how'd—?"

"Fine."

"Can I see it?" I opened my mouth. "There's still a big black hole back there!"

"We're trying a holistic approach—brain waves."

"Really?" I walked away. I headed over to Kristen's office and peered in. She wasn't around. Upon her desk was a large, unopened box. This had to be the delivery. Without hesitation, I took off my biggest sweater, put it over the box, and made for the stairwell. I opened the tape with a blade and sure enough, I was in business. Aligned alphabetically, I took my check, flew back to ground level, came up on the lift and, without witness, I returned the box to her desk in under four minutes time. This was a nice stroke of luck.

Back at my desk, I sat back in my chair and breathed a huge sigh of relief. Voices droned on as I figured they always would, like some sort of horribly polluted, glowing river, forever gushing infectious babble downstream—no longer would I subsist within earshot. I mean, this was it, man!—I was finished working for halfwits. I looked at the ceiling and smiled—all these silly jobs and slogans and products that were a waste of raw materials to begin with—"Wow," I whispered, "I'm actually done with them—I'm actually, fucking, done." I opened the envelope and read the total: $1,119 after taxes and fees—I made a fist and felt a fully crushing desire to complete the project and break into the world with a style that would allow me to partake in massive adventures that reach far beyond the realm of normative expectations and possibilities. I looked around and thought: imagine sitting in a cube surrounded by such duplicates as years of prime strength silently drain from the body— duplicates mainly indifferent to what is minus little victories such as sneaking a glance at amusing YouTube videos while on the clock. 'Have you seen this video?' Do you know you're slowly dying, and wasting away?

I placed the sketchpad into my bag, went through my desk, made certain no personal items remained, and my hand pitched everything else—all their silly handouts and diagrams— bam, into the trash they fell.

I almost left right then, but up the hall it went: "Just ask him why he doesn't have more phone time. I mean he obviously has enough calls, but maybe he's not choosing the correct talking points." I leaned back and thought: these saps, these poor saps! The voice started coughing as though its scarfed lunchtime meal had consisted of mouse hair with a side of head lice. It came 'round the corner and went: "Hey, Anthony."

"Hey, Petra."

She coughed and: "Hey—listen to this application letter, you'll die."

"Mind if I read it for myself?"

"No, here—it's probably better for my cou—" I grabbed it and began to read. The one hundred percent, exact translation, went:

I am aplying for college that I am strving to better for myself my career path my families future for two year degree that complition I will have confident to have high skill and decision making backed education which then eliminate hesitation caused by guessing rather than knowing and to acheve more throughout career and life by removing a option ceiling that seperate experience and education allowing me to take advantage of my full me and to go beyond press operator require at least a two year degree to move up on management and I want a oportunity set a exsample for other but for three future learners and to lead and show them importance of college education first hand rather than saying and this is what I hope to be able to demonstraight on the three children who are the three future learners I told you about and if you would be kind enough and willing to give a hard worker a chance and that I won't let you down at all and do all my homework as on time as possible but sometimes be rarely late on assignments if I need to help my oldest daughter learn.

Thank, you.

Gus Ferguson

I removed my shades and: "What's your deal, Petra?"

"What?"

"C'mon—do you really think this guy should go to school here? You have a ton of enrollments this month, I mean—he needs basic literacy lessons—many, many hours worth— isn't it obvious? Why push him through? Don't you understand what the result will likely be?"

"O, don't be a spoilsport—so he's not a certifiable genius, so what? He won't get any dumber from this program."

"Maybe not, but he'll be pushed toward bankruptcy and become far more angry."

"You really think so?"

"If you had to give him your home address before enrolling him—would you do it?"

"What does that have to do with anything?"

"A logical consequence of this premise would be either: A) you do, because he'll be so thankful to you that he might send you a gift—or B) you don't, because you figure he just might want to torch your crib after realizing what happened. So yeah—would you give him your address, or not?"

"That's a stupid question."

"Is it? I mean, think about it—the people up washing windows—doing this, that— you think they want to be doing so? Hell no! It's called surviving, man—it already involves heaps of complexities and sometimes all it takes is one more needless payment to sever the rope."

"He's clearly undereducated."

"That's my whole point! What are you not following? He needs to secure a whole basic foundation of skills that this curriculum does not provide, for free!—you can play pretend and skip that truth here, now, but it won't work in the real world—there's actual societal derogation that occurs as a result of low-literates buying degrees, trust me—it all steamrolls in an avalanche of ignorance of sorts, thereby enhancing the distress of the lower register." I mean—if I were unable to see such things, I would feel eradication of self via gunshot to be the best deed I could do for the good of humanity, straight up.

"Give me back the letter."

"No."

"I said give it to me!"

"Do you comprehend my point?"

"Do you comprehend mine? I want to help him become brilliant this year!"

"Are you playing with me right now? Or is your mind a repository with no intelligence behind it whatsoever? Which is it?"

"I can't believe you just said that to me."

"You're a prime mover of these problems!—you and your inchoate, embryonic thought patterns. You might have great numbers and go on free vacations at the end of every year, but you're a dunce, plain and simple—you're a clown." I wrote his number on my palm, crumpled the letter and tossed it to her feet. She was shocked, legitimately. "Okay, now bend down, pick it up, and leave the area. Very good."

She stood, and, "You know what? I'm not even going to get mad. It's obvious you're jealous. I'm done trying to argue with you rationally. It's not possible!"

"You're saying this to *me*? That *I'm* the irrational one? You just symbolized the whole world for me, I'm not even kidding." I took a deep breath, held it in, and: "Do you realize that right now, this moment, this very exact moment in time—do you realize that it has already become a non-moment? A was that no longer is? An is that just was?"

"Why are you telling me this?"

"Just because—" I needed a tangent based on infinite silence to avoid flipping my lid right there. It was time for the Reality Check.

30

She stormed off, I situated my things so I'd be ready to leave, grabbed the camera, walked up the aisle, and yes, the scene out the window was madly beautiful—I then snapped a photo to prove so. I joined the circle beside Doug—he looked at me with a very serious expression, and said, "Just think about the Russians sending up real space monkeys. They must have been shitting their pants!"

"Who? The monkeys or the Russians?"

"Well, both I guess."

"Yeah, that's pretty fascinating."

"Did they consider 'em full-on Cosmonauts? Officially or whatever?"

"I'm not really sure, Doug. Great question." You fucking maniac!

"Thank you." The guy's admittedly been on the verge of going belly up for twenty years—eternally seeking a way out of debt for his family, or so he says, and such are the paths his mind most often wanders: the official rank of monkeys in spaceships.

"Do you like reality checks, Doug?"

"They make me nervous."

"They should—really." Seconds ticked on and everyone huddled tight to learn a new lesson. It was just like grammar school, or high school, I thought: education is not—or rather, *should* not be perceived as a sort of unwarranted clamping down of clout upon the mind, therein causing the owner of that mind to be powerless to contemplate beyond these presupposed parameters—no! Education, quite obviously, should ensure the complete opposite—it should ensure a thorough burning of walls—it should represent a steady demolition of the practice of implanting conclusions, and instead instill a brazen, codified intuition concentrated upon the ingredient of genuine problem solving and innate rationalization rather than current, problematical situation, wherein education, *grades* are spotlighted upon memorization, learning by heart, erudition by rote—and all without comprehending the reasons why a remembered deduction has come to represent a certain because. Minus specific curriculums, the general education system of the United States has very little to do with the actual teaching of how to think at all. And that—that is why many intelligent people I know were usually poor students on the books—because they didn't give a flying fuck about such nonsense!

Face grave, Mr. Joshua marched toward the group. From what I gathered, his evolution to a leader was a slow and subtle process. It was rumored that he began as a lowly advisor, only to be brought to tears in such meetings—literal, weeping tears via the Reality Check in regard to his performance. Such sorrows must have pinned hard within via warm outside praise of eventual success, and now, being in charge, such has melted out and cooled into a plastic, smiling mask of implicit blindness minus total sums of certain numbers. That's all it was for him—numbers: how far above or below goal folks were, and how much time was left before they were to begin again. Looking at him now: blonde spike atop a chiseled face that aimed into a square jaw—he stood like a proud member of the Aryan race. T'was in my mind a forgone conclusion that had he been living in the Motherland seventy years ago, after being slapped into compliance, perhaps, he would have ordered many showers for the good of the state.

His cool blue eyes gave a good look around. Against the wall, Caroline and Kelsey stood with the dull excitement of two thirty watt light bulbs attempting to illuminate a cavernous hall. Mr. Joshua breathed in and then explained that it was again time to listen to and write down endless snippets of nonsense spewed from the mouth of a supposedly shrewd senior manager who seemed to have done little more than memorize enough clichés to sound diminutively intelligent.

Just then, as though parting the Red Sea, Rich Knaffey split the rear of the circle. Expressions offered poignant respect, as if he were a lead chair of great orchestral maturity, and: "Alright," he said, "Who here is a college graduate? Go ahead and raise your hands—go ahead, all the way now—alright, so about one third of you. I know it's been some years and all, but think back on that moment—the moment you walked across that stage—has there been a more stirring moment in your entire life?" Considering I could have gleaned the vast majority of the academic information I discovered in college for free had I chosen so, I felt enormously guilty that my parents worked as hard as they did to grind all the dough it cost for me to float through college for four years. I was the first one in four generations of my family to attend and graduate from college. By all accounts this fact was supposed to mean something, but it didn't—the whole process felt remarkably hollow insomuch as the actual education was concerned. I had a fine time and all, don't get me wrong—I bounced around and linked up with a wild combination of kids from the Chi and ole country-type farm folk whose parents had already trained them to think rationally. Our loose crew read books of our choice, enjoyed time on the porch, and rarely attended class—we analyzed, laughed, discussed, fought, roamed and ran relentlessly through the woods in mind-altering states: such was how we learned most. Thus, when it came time for my commencement, I told my parents I did not want them to come—I promised that I would one day produce an individual work representative of the erudition family and friends imparted to my mind, and to not waste gas money driving down to the graduation. I felt they had already wasted far too much cash on the very minuscule quantity of knowledge my government-approved professors and curriculum had imparted upon me, and moreover, the entire route down I57 is an enormous speed trap, so forget it. The fact that my father had slaved in a machine shop for thirty-five years in order for me to walk across an artificial stage to shake the hands of individuals I respected far less than he—as a overture to a so-called pinnacle of ach*i*evement, no less—this was beyond embarrassing for me. I still can't believe I wasted his hard earned chop like that.

"I was weeping when I accepted my diploma," I invented. Knaffey looked at me like: O, you again. "I almost missed the dean's hand on account of"—how drunk and annoyed I was, frankly, and when I grabbed hold, I squeezed it real hard, as though about to fall over, nauseous at the thought that I'd actually gone all the way through with this fucking joke. I mean—the whole idea that one must *pay* in order to obtain knowledge is due in part to the fact that purchased, outside affirmation of knowledge is deemed all-important, with self-affirmation or an original presentation of intelligence purposely defeated and downplayed in an effort to ensure enrollment at high priced educational initiations as a mandatory prelude to overall 'suc*cess*'—in order for true innovators to ever be given a chance, this must be verified as a farce!

"Who else cried?"

"I will—I'll tell you that much, I w*i*ll cry," Kelsey said.

"Are you enrolled here?"

"Yes, Mr. Knaffey."

In possession of an innocuous smile, Knaffey placed his arm around her shoulder, and: "So here you see, folks, proof p*o*sitive and within our midst is an example of how people will feel after finishing the program. Americans, no matter how smart or cleaver, cannot get their foot in the door of a fresh career without the little piece of paper we so happily distribute. Now, if this is the case, why are enrollment numbers slu*m*ping?—why are they not growing as fast as we n*ee*d them to be? You see, it's because of this problem that we don't know what conversations are going on in boardrooms right now. PRPB investors might be saying, 'Well, NVH Online is their biggest earner by far, and they're not doing the things we w*i*sh they were doing right now. In fact, well, they're almost—is that a plateau? Is that graph illustrating a plateau for God's sake? Maybe we shouldn't invest a more prominent figure—perhaps their total worth has pinnacled—maybe we should take the money and run.' Now what if investors said this? Who would be to blame? The job of obtaining new business—to whom does it belong? Who is the link? The conduit—who? Who is in the trenches each and every day, unpeeling the onion and extending offers?" He glared about, holes for eyes exhaling an obscene heat in this pressure cooker of false pretext—fire inside feeding on the energy of leftovers like an old boiler choking down faceless, oddball chunks of coal and emitting a blurry haze of purple soot as the only divulgence suitable for the existence, exploit and destruction of whatever sense of independent thinking that was at one time in p*o*ssession of those surrounding.

Doug inched forward and: "We are?"

"What was that? Come again?"

"We? It's us, right, who—um—"

"Who wh*a*t?"

"We build—um, trust and we, uh, establish, uh—"

"You build *t*rust, establish rap*po*rt, *a*nd you unpeel the damn *o*nion! See—this is what I mean. Right now, if I'm one of the institutions who own stock, I certainly have at least a little bit of concern. It's not to the point that there's a lot of negative media attention around our numbers right now, but if this continues, this trending toward plateau, this drift toward non-variation, non-gain—if it continues, well, we might not be injured now, but we will be, certainly so. It's simple, okay? Go with me—try to understand, alright—our stats aren't there. We're still making tens and tens of millions of dollars per quarter, but that's not why we're here—this is a hit and run, alright?—we are to hit the floor running and keep on doing so!—until our legs fall off, or damn near. And we've been running, don't get me wrong, okay, we've been running and gunning since the onset, but we've gone from a forty point per game triple double to suddenly hoping for offensive rebounds and subtle put backs. You know what this is? This effort? Your effort? It's not good enough! We're not jamming it home—when you get these prospective students on the line, damn it, you need to dr*i*ve it home! Re*me*mber—none of these things are good for our stock—our board, our investors— they're ready to bet on the under. And you know what happens when investors and management bets on the under? You know who's the first to go? You, folks. People. Like.

You." He paused for effect, and faces looked uneasy. "But on the flip side, investors are a forgiving bunch—so long as abuse doesn't go too far, they're rather eager to absolve. If we go on a tear for the remainder of the year, or even the next quarter, all is temporarily forgiven. People are again buying large volume and loving us. We're an education company, remember? The likeability factor is always a key to investment—it's a key element of what is always being monitored, and people like companies that promote learning. Does the public like our image? Do they approve? Of course they do!" He walked over to me, smiled and said: "People remember, don't they?—what it felt like to cry when they walked across that stage—investors appreciate that we grant the same opportunity to others. I know we always express joy at our career placement rate, but what is the first job graduates are offered with their new degree? Anybody?—the first job they're given is a chance to claim, publicly, how intelligent they've become—a chance to describe, with proof, how they've acquired this intelligence—by graduating college—the most accepted way in existence." He clapped for himself, four little clicks, gave everyone a good look, and said: "Go get 'em guys, and thanks for the invite to the meeting, Mr. Friar—like I said before, I see a lot of potential in this group, a lot of future leaders—especially Kelsey." Her cheeks flushed, and Knaffey quit talking. He, Fryer and Gloria whispered on the side for a moment, and a small white spade of unknown fodder flew out of Gloria's mouth and landed on Knaffey's shoulder in the midst of their conversation. Mr. Joshua again came to the middle and began talking. His face grew redder as his mouth motored ahead, but all the sounds were blocked from my head—all I thought was: you shall disintegrate, man—soon you shall end.

I couldn't listen, I was finished—but I knew what he was saying, the gist at least: he partook in what has been a large push in recent years, from all sides, toward the acceptance of information without independent assessment. Squeezed tight in the middle with few actionable angles reside the freethinking people. Countless institutions such as this insist we obey. It is becoming immoral to question—immoral and un-American. The idioms are slowly fusing together and it's a brilliant scam. You likely see it every single day, working itself from the top down—people become infuriated when their authority comes into question—when someone asks for specific reasons why—as though there is no right to demand reason. Freethought is treated as babble from the mouths of curious children, and quickly ushered aside. Large sums of those in charge, especially within bureaucratic systems, spin inquiries into insinuations that the asker had no right to poke about, and so the point is thereby irrelevant. It would be better if their press secretaries began meetings with: 'You are not allowed to pose any questions we are not competent enough to answer—alright, fire away,' and off runs a cycle of absurdity firmly rooted from the very beginning—from the very instant a child questions the reason of a lesson and the teacher replies, 'Uh, like, because I *say* so, that's why—that is what is in the textbook—can't you see it?' I remember getting that answer, and thinking: just what do you mean by that? It took a few years to recognize: it means you're the problem, one of them—slow down, search for stringent reason and study the motivations and subsequent results of an entire event, and give the kid an answer. You see, in all truth, children are brilliant—they amaze me. The purity with which they're capable of thinking—the ones who refuse to accept: 'Because I said so' or 'Because I'm older than you' as logical answers—when their minds are prime, unpolluted sponges—before the monotony of the machine has worn their broad, interested intellect to mush—before they've submitted to the idea that living their lives as cogs or wheels is logical—before all that crap poisons them, they're nothing short of: staggeringly brilliant. This is why you see many parents become so frustrated with their own children. It is the parents who've given up—they've given up years ago—given up the desire to think on their own—the desire to be fucking amazed. And then you see their kids—the way they are in love with knowledge—in love with all the world makes possible for them—and they're standing there, these tiny little people with raw, all-encompassing minds, unpolluted by prejudice, non-seduced by secularism, ready to love, ready to fulfill undreamt dreams, ready to sprout into pillars of passion to which the word impossible is laughable—and then we ruin them. We tell them not to question, to sit down *now* and do what they're told—and kids—they know when something doesn't make sense—you could see them yearning to say no, but what do we do? We rout their rebellion, we defeat their dissidence—we saturate them with mind-altering medicines to promote proper be*hav*ior. We need to teach them to rebel—need to tell them that it's okay to run wild and free, and help them follow ex*act*ly what their heart feels is right—to follow their soul to wherever it wants to take them—to say fuck you to anything they feel is unjust or plain wrong, and to never claim their own reasons to be: 'Because I said so.' I want to teach them to laugh—to laugh right in the face of the authority figure who attempts to authorize unjust action—but that's not what we teach in this country. It's what we *used* to teach, but we're teaching it less and less on a generational basis. For the most part, teachers are paid to instruct students to o*bey*—to obey and jump on the bandwagon against all who refuse to, despite well formed reasons, and enjoy first hand lessons concerning the tyranny of the majority.

And the delusion, although simple at the surface, is extraordinarily calculated—quite simply, it's the refusal to admit what *is*. Some call it political correctness, but beyond that, it's an effort to wrap a discussion of what *is* under a cloak of indecency—under the premise that those who discuss what *is* are non-morals, and therefore, are not to be taken seriously—their conclusions shall be discredited—and that is exactly the way what *is* shall be spun into what *is not*—such originates in the premise that the discussion of what *is*—is in itself, evil, if indeed the conclusion of the is be too different from results generally desired by the true powerbrokers. Foundations who use this line of reasoning never admit what they're doing. They've either self-deceived to the point of believing their own false logic, or they've used this tactic enough to realize: when policy is called into question, a quick solution is to quickly question this individual's right to ask the question, and attack them personally from atop a false podium of assumed moral highlands.

Alright, calm down. Forget it, you did what you had to do and you're leaving, c'mon man, inhale, exhale, breathe—inhale, ex—

"Is something wrong Anthony?" Did somebody just say that? Am I hearing things? I removed my hands from my eyes, and it took a moment before black silhouettes distinguished themselves. Damn—Mr. Joshua was speaking to me—everyone else was staring.

"I'm sorry, what was that?"

"I asked if something was wrong—are you nervous to make the call?"

"The call—yeah—I was just, uh, reflecting on the script."

"Good. That's what I wanted to hear. Are we ready?"

"Most certainly."

In an attempt to forge the line between free speech and incitement, I figured I would play a game of cause and effect, because remember—there is a big difference between talking tough, and thinking smart.

I stepped up to the speakerphone, looked at my palm, and dialed the number. The phone rang. "Uh-huh."

"Hi—is Gus Ferguson available?"

"You got me."

"Well Gus, this is C.W. Martino with the Gallop Poll, and you've been chosen to participate in a brief cause and effect survey, results of which shall soon be published—do you have fifty seconds at your disposal?"

"I 'spose."

"I'll jump into it then—cause: you're about to spend fifty thousand dollars on school loans for an education that, in the least, shall fail to incorporate lessons that instill the slightest comprehension of rational thinking methods, such as the scientific method, into your curriculum. You'll be given a heap of pointless homework, not unlike sorting junk mail that, in the end, shall serve to waste plenty of your quickly fading time on earth. You will then be forced to make a payment for such, heavy interest included—for the next three hundred months of your life. Now what's the effect?"

"I don't understand."

"You should. Contact your admissions advisor at NVH Online once you've built your answer. Good day."

I hung up the phone and people went crazy. Fryer stormed toward me—I almost thought he was going to take a swing. I was ready to slip a right when it came: "Are you out of your goddamn *mind?*"

"Are *you?*—don't you understand what happens when you sell diplomas to people who read at a remedial level? Do you not see? The whole fucking country is falling apart because of shit like this! I was a literacy teacher to a guy with a degree from here! A guy who couldn't read and went broke because of this shit!—he was a student of mine—you s*o*ld him a degree. That's the only reason I came to work here—I just had to see it to believe it!"

"We are ap*pa*lled by these comments!" Friar screamed.

"Bull sh*i*t you're appalled—what was stated was nothing more than matter-of-fact truth. If your stance is that you're appalled by the comments, then you're in fact appalled by what is. Understanding the difference is imperative to comprehending actuality."

"Be quiet!"

"I don't think so!"

"My name is Mr. Joshua, and your name is listener!"

"I thought your name was Mr. Fryer."

"You know what I mean, goddamn it!"

"That was my student!" Petra screamed.

I stepped back and: "Listen, people—stop thinking collectively and see what is. Who here doesn't at times, aspire or fear at levels that exceed logical possibility to an extent? Most do, most certainly do, especially those in need, and this in turn leaves them susceptible to such hope infused, light at the end of the tunnel-type scams—and what's happening here— you're feeding off this basic characteristic of human nature and twisting a non-viable solution into a fixed idea that is proposed to be best suited to resolve a lack of education—do you not see any problem with what you're doing? Does anybody see what I'm talking about? Or are you just crazy? Are all of you crazy?"

"You're nothing but a provocateur, a problematic personality—what? You think you're some luminary or something?"

"You don't need to be a luminary, Mr. Joshua, to see the fact that thirteen months down the road he'll fall in a hole when stuck with fifty thousand dollars of debt and a *Virtual Diploma*. Yeah, he's a real success story now—learned nary a thing, didn't take a si*n*gle test to earn that degree, not one! But you know, he's got that piece of paper—got that paper that pr*o*ves, yup—so now what? What will probably happen: cat walks into the local factory—hey, guess what! I just earned my degree, you know, I went to co*ll*ege and all that, I want to interview for a management job. Alright fine—and they take him through an entire slew of analytical questions and assessments and what happens? Boy ain't so quick—he had no comprehension of how one should think critically before he enrolled here, and, fifty stacks later, the case remains the same—been told what to do his whole life and never asked a single question. Maybe they ask the guy for a writing sample to serve as an example of his communiqué prowess. What happens? Guy can't complete a single paragraph without several veritable flaws. 'Um, uh—my *v*irtual *pro*fessors didn't make me take tests, they didn't ask for writing samples, they said'—'Time's up pal, sorry, but don't let the door smack ya on the way out—thing has a tendency to sl*a*m.' And it'll take every ounce of energy to avoid breaking down as he walks through the door of his home that afternoon. His beautiful children will sprint to greet him, jump, wrangle upon his legs, scurry into his strong arms, and yell: 'Daddy, did you get the job? I know you did Daddy, we love you so much. You h*a*d to have gotten it—didja get it? I wanna play baseball on a t*e*am this summer—one with uniforms and real equipment. I know it's expensive, but, ya know, since ya got a de*g*ree and everything—wow pop—I might play in the big leagues some day.'

"And you better bet the poor guy will swallow the biggest lump his throat has ever held when he says—'Yep, I got it guys! I love you so much, too!' He'll say something like that, but in reality, he's tasting blood—eating his lip to keep from breaking down before his family—'I'm going to take a walk guys,' he'll say—'Should I pick up some ice cream?' And they'll scream about chocolate or vanilla or waffle cones—'I want nuts!' 'Me too!' 'Chocolate, vanilla, nuts and waffle cones, coming right up!' He'll say, smiling the panic away for a brief moment. 'Congrats baby! We're all *so* proud of you.' His wife may say, 'O, and yeah, this came in the mail for you today—it's from Sallie Mae.' And the guy will open the letter and for the first time he'll appreciate the h*e*ft of the loans he took to pay for this bullshit education. He'll sit down at his computer, go to Google, search for a loan calculator, enter the equation of 50k at 11% interest for 25 years and realize—O, I have to pay $490.06 per month for the next *300* months to settle up for th*i*s education*?* Hmm, what does that come to? O, a nice round figure of $147,012—far more than my current net worth, but you know, I have this piece of paper that says I'm su*c*cessful now—this paper that pr*o*ves! And as soon as the guy realizes he's fucked his entire family beyond reproach he'll blink lids over red, angered eyes, pat his son on the head, say: 'I love you boy, I love you so much. If anything ever happens, I need you to take care of your mother and your sister—but don't worry, nothing will happen, but just in case something d*o*es happen—just know that I love you. I'll be back in a jiff—I need to grab that ice cream!' And the guy will grab a pencil, scribble instructions about unmarked bills and a bomb upon an unpaid heating bill, walk to the bank, the same loan-sharking bank that issued him a predatory loan they should have known he could never pay back—same bank now asking to be bailed out for its stupidity, by *me*—and he'll hand the directions to the teller, get arrested, go to jail, and tomorrow, tomorrow when you open the Sun-Times, you people will read about him and you'll say: 'What a rotten criminal, I hate criminals—I hope they lock him away for a good long time!'—well you know what, people? Fuck. *That!*"

"We're gonna' have a big talk!" Joshua screamed.

"I don't think so."

I strode off, and headed for my things—I heard his voice yelling, seeking to regain relevance. I grabbed my bag, dipped into the stairwell, and bam, just like that, it was over.

31

Back out in the world, I grabbed my ride, tossed it over my shoulder and moved toward the Currency Exchange. I wanted the check cashed quick, green and in my hand, with all necessary association with NVH thereby slashed. I imagined them placing a hold on it, screwing me over somehow, and so I didn't waste any time. I walked, a bit dazed for a few blocks, and "Holy shit, man," I said quietly, "That place was a genuine madhouse, and I'm done with it. Those were *act*ually people, and that's how they live life." The snow had slowed some, with thinner, sun punctured clouds replacing the heavy overcast of before. Two seagulls circled the dim orange ball and a weird transient with greasy grey hair crossed Chicago Avenue through this slanting light and spit thrice upon reaching the southern shadows—he cast a scornful look upon me and through puffy drifts of white he lurched on.

I entered the store and the line was shorter than before. Standing there I thought: God, I feel so good, I feel like I just had so much weight lifted off my shoulders—like when I'm in the mountains, and nothing can touch me. Up at the booth, the woman from before was waiting to help me out. I stepped up and: "So, you get them Pounds cashed?"

"Yeah, I did actually—good memory. Some cool older fellow helped me out." I signed and handed over the check—"Can I just get green for this?"

"Of course, but they'll be a fee—your bank would be cheaper."

"I don't keep an account, but thanks for the tip."

I handed her the check and "We'd normally take $25 from this, but I'll do it for $21. You have an odd face."

"Cool—make that stack out with fifty twenties and give me the rest in a separate pile." She did so and I rolled the stack with an old asparagus rubber band, and threw it in the top pouch of my bag. $98 was leftover from the $1,119 minus the surcharge, and I figured that would be my cake for the weekend. That combined with the $70 left over from the Pound exchange at the camera store was plenty for a roaring good time if you did it stingy.

I walked out and as soon as the cold hit me, more than anything, I was ready to grab a big bowl of hot soup with good, hearty bread—I was eager to be warmed by a thick mush from within. I walked south to Grand and State, turned west, and headed to an Italian place I knew to make good Minestrone. I sat in the side room and the waitress was real liberal with the crackers and such—she gave me near half a loaf of homemade bread, and by the time it was all mixed together and cool enough to eat, there was hardly any liquid left in the bowl. It was a delicious meal with nice soft beans and all that, very filling. I ordered a coffee and asked for the bill. She'd hit me the Joe for free so I tipped her five bucks and apologized for the crumbs.

A local social magazine was sitting on the adjacent table, so I took a glance. It was a nicely constructed magazine with quality paper, and all the people in the photos were chic as hell—not only models in ads, mind you, I mean the whole thing, from cover to cover: everyone was primped like they were about to be gazed one last time before being buried in the soft earth. The mag held a large section that featured random socialite parties to have recently popped off across the city, and from each party there were several prints of decked-out fabulists having a gay ole time. I hate to generalize, but really, the vast percentage of them looked stiff, or plain daft—like if you had to hike in and spend a week with them in a huge cabin in the middle of nowhere, all the gear you could ever need strapped tight to your backs—great coffee and smoke and booze, plenty of firewood and musical instruments galore, sounds of which were set to reverberate around huge, climbable mountains with heavenly clarity—I was sure most would somehow manage to have a bad time. They were geared to go out just once, everything provided and planned, adorned in delicate costumes, with the principle purpose of the trip: to be seen having such an *amazingly* great *time!* that their faces would be on the verge of melting off—and then they'd cross fingers, rush to the rack and find their photo published in the next issue of this trendy tabloid, and say, 'O, that Joe fucking hobnob takes *great* photos, he's a great photographer, really—I look spec*ta*cular in this picture! Maybe we should hire him for a project.'

Fucking soft—I snapped it closed and tossed it to the end of the table. I took a drink and looked around—it was a nice place for a coffee and soup. There were a lot of old black and white photos on the wall, and nobody stressed you. I sat back in my chair and a girl came through the door. A cold gush of air swept through the room and a clump of snow fell from her shoulder. She was wrapped in layers, but you could tell that she was lean and nimble. She spoke with the hostess and they obviously knew one another. She asked to look at the schedule, and slowly the two scarves wrapping her face unwound. I was interested to see what she looked like, but she hadn't turned 'round. She walked to the bar, grabbed a toothpick, tucked it tight in the side of her mouth, dropped a scarf, bent, faced me as she did so and I noticed. Fuck. I hadn't noticed anybody like that since I'd noticed her the first time, five years ago, walking up Church Street in Evanston on a nice, sunny day.

"Yo!—Melissa!" She turned but didn't seem to recognize me—I flash-thought that I had the wrong person, but such was impossible. A sagacious bird with long brown hair, her style was extensively efficient—she didn't push the issue too much or come off as trying too hard, no—she flowed unprocessed—nice and easy, chill and smooth, every garment had a usable purpose and nothing was wasted—I could tell just from her stride that it had to be her. As she walked forward, a faint outline of a faded flower on the inside of her left wrist was visible. I imagined her sitting cross-legged, waiting for the L maybe, up above the street, sun heatless and gleaming, hair wild with the wind, pen drawing upon her body—tongue half in, half out, just like a little kid.

"Anthony?"

"Yep."

"Holy shit man!"

"I'd say." She stood before me for a second, and smiled. When you won't be seeing somebody for a long while, you catch yourself memorizing the lines on their face—she hadn't changed. I leaned in and she gave me a big squeeze—I noticed she smelled like oranges, and we just stood there for a minute. We'd had quite a time together, from time to time, back in the day. "Didn't you recognize me?"

"No man, not at first—you look sorta, um, rugged."

"I look crazed."

"A bit."

"It's cool, you can say it. Take a seat."

"What are you doing here?"

"Eating soup."

"I mean in Chicago—I thought you were in the mountains."

"I was—I've been back for awhile, just trying to get things going—you?"

"I work here."

"Yeah? Nice—great bread."

"I know—I eat my weight every day I'm here."

"Are you starting a shift now?"

"I'm supposed t' fill in for someone in a few hours, but it's not for certain—I came in to get my check. I'm a hostess, but sometimes I waitress, too, so I fill in randomly all over."

"Cool." It was quiet for a minute, but not uneasily or anything. It was comforting like feeling the warm belly of a furry dog on your cold feet in the crackling stillness—low flames rising over red coals, nobody hassling you over a goddamn thing.

"Where do you live now? Same place?"

"West."

"Apartment? Same roommates?"

"I uh—I've got a solo pad."

"Nice."

"It's alright."

"Ever finish that book?"

"Not yet—I was working for an education company until I walked out a few minutes ago. It was complete nuthouse for the most part."

"What was going on there exactly?"

"It's hard to explain, but truly you would not be*lie*ve the perpendicular plane of pietism that betokens each morn, man, you'd have to be there to accept as true or understand it. Just *so* many riotous falsehoods for sake of mind control disgorged from maws reeking of this creepy sense of meticulously crafted, false spontaneity that should have left any free-minded individual feeling heavy-hearted and above the irrational logic employed by supposed superiors, you know? The level of hypocrisy was insane."

"Sort of the way you can't help but laugh when you hear the General of an invading army addressing that country's home grown insurgency as terrorism?"

"Pre*ci*sely man! Exactly! If somebody invaded America, everybody and their mother would be out in the streets, shooting until the last man—and that's why it was mad, like, nobody seemed to think anything was wrong at *all*! Few found anything the least bit odd—at best, people were like, 'Well, should somebody get fucked over, what can I say? I'm only doing my *job*.' It was quite sad, it really was. There was no individual discretion over right or wrong at all—zero questioning of authority or sense of open-mindedness—a great swell of useful idiots subverting a mass of their own kind without so much as a blink of an eye on either side—the entire system zombified."

"So no sense of responsibility for the way things are?"

"And gladly so."

"So really it wasn't *too* unlike the verve I observe throughout my everyday is."

"I guess not."

"And how's that make you feel?"

"Like a pint, with you."

"Or several."

"Yeah. Fuck yeah. Do you have anything going right now?—I can't believe you're sitting here," I said. She was a cool girl, man—a flash-reflection on our shared experiences set me thinking how often you find yourself speaking of how wonderful life will someday be, and fail to realize how wonderful it currently is. It was sort of like that—we shared a lightning strike-fused friendship based on a random, shared experience of the world we live in, and I had missed her a good deal.

She shrugged her shoulders and: "Nope. Where should we go?"

"Somewhere cheap," I said.

"Obviously—by the way, when's the last time you saw the all in every this?"

"You mean amplified?"

"Do you remember when we ate the earth on those beautifully sunny days, and everything changed?"

"Yes, positively—why?"

Rosy cheeks pulled the corners of her mouth into a wry smile, and her hand snagged a purple zippered pouch from her bag. She opened it and: "Voila!"

"You're crazy, man!"

"Been holding onto these in wait for a random snowy day—it's just a little, you know, something extra—just a little boost." She opened her eyes wider and: "Shall we slip through the shadows on the furthest parameters of sanity?"

I started laughing and: "I thought I just returned from there."

"Shall we?"

"We'll see—I need a minute or two before diving into that with you." I watched her return the pouch to her bag, and all the contents were aligned just so—pens and markers and notebooks and a little ratchet set—organized all proper-like, in nice little rows. "You help me relax, do you know that?"

"Because I'm weirder than you?"

"Probably."

"There aren't many." She set the bag on the floor and: "So why haven't you phoned me in the past three years?"

"I've hardly phoned anyone in that time."

"So I'm just anyone now?" Fuck! Her question hit me like a cold slap. She pulled her hair behind her ears and I remembered how we'd sit, feet buried deep in the warm sand, toes penetrating to the deep, cool point below—and that sun: lacing through lurching poplar leaves—and that br*eeze*: its casual enunciation of all things living to all things alive—ears seduced by every sound as eyes gazed 'round—look at this breeze blowin this green!—damn—it'd be nice to live forever sometimes—yes, yes indeed—it was when sitting cross-legged at the lakefront, mellow correlation of voices between waves and wind warbling through my ears and into my mind that often I realized time alive upon this earth is both precious and beautiful. 'Enjoy it,' she'd say, 'Your time, your mind, and all that the two combined shall come to discover. Tis your life to live and try and die, and never allow a soul to tell you otherwise—just let it rip.' She was young, three years younger than I, but mad wise with a humble old soul, and a thousand times more peaceful or beautiful than I could dream to be.

"Did you ride here today?"

"Of course."

"Even in this storm, huh?"

"Work to eat, eat to live, live to ride, ride to work—besides, you know I've always been in an affair with the earth, Anthony."

"I know, MD—say, you don't have an extra tube by chance, do ya?"

"I do—700c—need one?"

"I do—that'd be huge—your self-sufficiency was always alluring."

"You'll be there someday—don't think I'm about to change it for you. I saw that bike out there and I swear I thought it was yours." She flipped the toothpick around in her mouth, picked the magazine from her end of the table and: "What? You read this rubbish?"

"No, but sometimes I look."

"Me too—"

"So do we get our whips and slam these streets?"

"She still got one gear?"

"Yeah—me."

"Then yes boy, let's go—let's get up and blaze through this city of ours."

32

Outside, Melissa glanced at our rides and: "How can you not love machines so pure? You sit and you pedal and you go—one gear, amen." I changed the flat, hands still warm via the endless functionality of liftie gloves, and after I filled up the new tube with a gush from a CO2 instant tire inflator, Melissa said: "You can buy me a drink for that." She kicked her shoes clean, slipped her toes into a footcage and: "So you in the mood to ride some personally glorified Kinglines, or what?" I nodded, stood tall, threw my leg over the top tube and we set off moving, back east on Grand.

My meditation immediately absorbed every ounce of discernable change in the surrounding scenery. Every swerving vehicle and darting pedestrian, every crack, crackhead, pothole, snowdrift, concrete chunk and thundering snowplow flashed through me and was measured in milliseconds—and back into her saucer blue eyes, the world floated away: "Careful, it's icy," she said, "Don't go cracking your head open on me now."

"Yep."

"It's a good day for fenders, glad we got it covered—nothin' like a dry ass after a wet ride—you want to mash around for a minute and then head to the pub?"

"If you'll be warm enough," I said, freezing my ass off.

"I'm good." She put her head down, drummed hard and cut south on Wells. Her long brown hair flew wild and untamed out the back of her helmet, and heart rising, body riding, world flying by, I found myself hoping I wouldn't have to die—wouldn't have to age, or ever break down, every muscle fiber forever contracting in a miraculous spasm of release— I thought back on old times of racing city streets and descending rock lines into graffiti coves—waves and wind pounding and spraying hot mist, a delicate haze enshrouding a panorama of architectural bliss as green earth is set alight—exhale—and in smoke I see unrealized dreams spiraling into space—questions shed—how many futures dead? Stars of the Milky Way total the neurons in my brain—and now back we race—can't escape your face—old poetic motion lands me in a dark, windswept grove—life in the breeze—thunderstorms and peace—breathe, just breathe. The moment felt very reassuring for me—that it was possible to disconnect and move around and have nothing else matter minus how fast you could go. I looked back and: "How do you feel?"

"I feel really good!"—she yelled so over a thousand sounds, smells and visual shifts of the city, and as the L banged overhead, her body glowed through sharp lines of light severing the procession of painstakingly crafted iron tress work in trim, unadulterated streaks—and how many times, hammering onward, did I twist back and spy your eyes and grin wide at the wise, cleanly honest expression on your face as the scene flew by? The L screamed like a stiff old mare as we rode a thin, frozen line of slippery rivets on pressurized, wet rubber over the frozen River—Melissa cut through the red at Wacker, slammed east on Washington and leaned south on LaSalle. On we rode through deep, darkened couloirs of architectural bliss, hearts beating barely on the other side of our skin as the wind pounded in. I took a deep breath, exhaled vapor, and churned harder—she looked over and: "This is as close as I'll ever come to feeling like a rock star," and as soon as she said so, she split jammed traffic in a razor thin cut beneath the ever rising rafters of plush offices packed to the gills with profit graphs, leather chairs and wireless everything—I thought of spending my entire life sitting stationary behind these panes, blood clots clumping purple within unused legs, and on we raced.

A thunderous roar shook me and my eyes grew wide at the earnest face of a firefighter guiding his enormous screaming truck northbound in opposing lanes, bobbing between any and every imaginable being, sound cavernous, girder beams resonating his finely tuned mind frame on the way to an emergency blaze though the Friday afternoon, heat island rush, while his mates got battle ready in back. We chased on, observing the miffed, mewl-strewn body language of middling middlemen roving to and fro—meteoric, behind schedule strides and a culture of isolated microbes roved about the metropolis on mid afternoon expresses to nowhere.

MD again took the lead and we flew past a lonely-looking old man whose hollow eyes penetrated my head in a split second as he leaned against the frozen limestone wall of One North LaSalle—I thought of what dying alone might feel like, cut across Madison, almost clipped a traffic director, and my stomach began to twist, turn and tumble. I imagined the incredible sense of longing that would come at the moment you realize, yes, believe it: you thought you had something more to say, but you have had your last conversations with all for whom you held love, and the tale that was you is through—had this been realized, how many volumes of words would have spilled from within? How many sentiments have gone unsaid? How many unmoved motions died in stationary waste? How many silly grudges have gone unforgiven? It was terrible to think about, it really was. The insanity of being alive and not knowing what lingers ahead—how much easier it is to believe that yes, yes I will simply do right, at least more right than wrong, and there shall be nothing to worry about—my God how much easier existence is for those who chalk up reality to an omnipotent deity and its unfathomable whims—how much simpler indeed! But again—recall these frantic whispers as you fall—recall the most in-depth thoughts and moments of transcendence—you have already eclipsed these concerns—accept your eventuality and enjoy every moment, mate—breathe, exhale, and be.

We leaned left and mashed east on Jackson, beneath the shadows of the Board of Trade—we caught the stoplight just perfect as crazed brokers exited colossal doors with

152

expressions that said it all: another five days of highs and lows come and go, and now it's time to forget buying and selling and holding onto, and get mine—blow what be on the mind into another time via crashing waves—the upper surge of infused substance soon to come, yum—just a little bump—because you hear me? I'm someone!—I move funds—try and raise some and I'll sling your many zeroes—and it was those precise, dark circled expressions that reminded me why I love regular fucking heroes.

I passed an empty maroon cab on my left, his rear wheels slipping just a bit as he cut over and beeped his horn in an attempt to attract a touristy-looking trio standing confused-like on the sidewalk, looking skyward. MD hammered past a electric blue taxi on my right and as we crossed Clark I slipped a pedestrian and pothole in a fluid double move, skidded a little and slashed an asphalt gash as we burned on, just making the light east across Dearborn. A wave of people crossed the street behind us, a fleshy sea barricading an approaching iron army—I sat back in the saddle as MD rode tight beside me, smirked, and gave me knuckles: "Good shit."

"Hell yeah!" I leaned back, watched her ride and thought: there are very few people who, despite knowing them very well, remain mythic in your mind. The wind seemed to cut through my eyes and exit my ears—my entire head felt cleared. Melissa looked over, tiny shining diamonds dotting her eyelashes and eyebrows and: "Just imagine you're pushing headlong into a blissfully warm, southerly wind—" she sat back with no hands, spread her arms wide, closed her eyes and: "My skin is warm with the breeze and sun." The middle of me was uncomfortably numb, but I didn't mention so. We split to opposite sides of an indecisive vehicle and she yelled: "Maybe after some drinks we can stroll the Art Institute for a minute."

"What about work?"

"What about it?" I nodded and she cut four lanes of flowing cars across State—my calves burned as I clenched my jaw and dug deep to make sure her timing was right. Head to the ground, I reflected racing skis through stick straight tree trunks in slanting sun, shadows and pine becoming one, and as we caught the light with our turn north on Michigan, the fat old sun tried to break through a thin layer of dim clouds in a fit of near misses. A skinny, hushed streak broke through and blowing snow shimmered in the air—I looked at the sky, a tiny sliver of blue framed high above the buildings, and tell me, won't you please?—why I became and how I'll leave? MD pulled beside me with a look that said: spinnin' 'round this universe, spinnin' 'round this crank, life can be alright sometimes, wouldn't ya say?—and a little low on breath, she said: "The undeniable fact is that exploring is not dead."

"Thank God."

"You have a place in mind?"

"Yeah, let's cut out west—Adams to Damen and north from there. We'll hit a little spot up near Augusta—it should be pretty lifeless and they have a good juke."

"Lead the way."

I leaned west on Adams, Art Institute at our rear, and the sun finally streaked clean—the world turned bright and serene, with fresh, unmuddled white covering most everything—I turned 'round and the sun looked like a star in the middle of her constricted pupil, and then I remembered that it was—her presence had me internally euphoric like gaining speed uphill, and my mind burned on, world flush with depth, and as MD's sun-drenched stroke churned her wheels I felt sick at the thought that nothing will last. The snow would be filthy with black oily residue in a few short hours, just one step closer to melting into oxidation rainbows—same as everything else, man—same as her, same as me—and lost in her blue eyes I screamed back from the other side and surmised: imagine what you'll be thinking when approaching the mystery—all I am: all I'll ever be? Won't know 'til ya go and if so then never—so you better hold on, fucking tight—forever—

Palmer House tourists struggled to catch a cab in the cold windy street and a man outside Miller's begged for change—one leg, one arm, no feet, smile ceaselessly bobbing to the beat, the beat, the beat—streets—not summer streets, loaded with overflowing sweat and electricity, but brutal winter ones, with hard earned fun—a little black boy with the back of his head etched ala le skyline darted across Wabash in a near miss, proudly sporting a T that paid an ode to B96 hits—and engines roared and horns blared and gears wailed and tires squealed—though not quite as loudly as the shadowed madman screaming in the alley—a blind businessman drenched in sunlight slowed his stride and the tic-tac of his stick from side to side to coincide with an automatic voice sounding atop Adams: there will be a delay—no dismay, all is okay—and as the alto sax screamed clean and unbroken I rode through and pondered: just what percentage of you is woken via the constant eclipse of this mild form of madness described as the is? Take it in while you can, man, all of it at once—because that sneaky motherfucker is always creeping just a little bit closer, my friends—he soon gonna' come whisper in your ear: 'The end'—'Is near?'—'Is here'—and all those fears—just what the fuck was the point of ever being afraid?

We exited the tracks above Wabash and sweat streamed out my pores, and as exhaust entrails diluted sun rays, horns blared back and forth to each other as irritated faces raced their killer cars to the next red light and nerves got set to do it all over again. Melissa yelled: "I'll always get really blissed-out when moving my body, even if I'm arthritic and worn." The newly blue sky had me salivating at the world. I'm most happy when I'm out here, I thought, most enthralled and set afire—movement, man, movement—is there a greater love? We approached a tight jam at Clark, the legends of this city again impelled to build, and traffic squeezed into one lane, making way for a growling crane as it lowered a rectangular sheet of iron the size of a bus, directly above westbound traffic in the far left lane. Lookin' at sun-blasted asphalt between a bus and a dump truck, dancing shadows of exhaust entrails blurred the air—scalding diesel pistons fired with the compression ratio of solid fuel rockets and shook the earth as dirty sweat bled into my eyes—we burned past the long line of traffic and I thought: most everyone just beeps their horn and steps on the gas, in such a rush to do nothing at all—forever running amuck in the infinite now.

A man in a hardhat barked orders and we bombed on—MD kept tight on my rear wheel as traffic came and went, mostly shaving our elbows at three times the speed limit on slick, icy roads, eager again for access to all three lanes. We blazed under the L at Wells, and up past Franklin my eyes scanned a man huddled tiny and frozen, balled up against a trash can on the SW corner, cowering in the heartless shadow of the tallest building erected on the continent. I asked my head for quiet as we tore across the Adams Street Bridge—we hugged the right side and rode what looked like a tidy sea of rusty, serrated razorblades shimmering in the full bright sun—a no fall zone for sure. Any four season cyclist can tell you these bridges get mad slippery after a winter storm—my rear tire went skating all over the place as drivers gunned the gas and cold wet rubber hummed the iron grating in an effort to beat the light at the pedestrian walk across the span. I stood out of the saddle for added stability, and as racing cabs cut off buses to catch a fare outside Union Station, the whole span shuttered beneath the collective weight. On the walkway, a semi-usual dude was banging buckets in fine, upstart rhythms, occasionally pointing a drumstick at another all day sucker immersed in an impassionate operation, marching on like a line of stone faced clowns exiting a carnival after another laughless night on stage, and wobbling toward the train. We stalled for a second, waiting for a bus to move clear of Riverside Plaza, and I said: "People look so worn out."

"Because they are."

"No shit." We squeaked around the filthy back end and hustled past Canal—Old St. Pat's went by our right, standing proud and traditional, home to huge weddings and funerals, and above the Kennedy Expressway, breathing through my mouth I could taste the mercurial haze rising from many lanes of jammed, frustrated traffic, eager to get home for forty-eight hours of unbound instants. Soon into Greektown and past Halsted, the smell of carbon was overtaken by that of mustached men with gold necklaces and perfect hair cooking huge slabs of lamb and I felt like could eat about ten gyros.

We cruised past Morgan, hugging the right side of the street, and traffic eased—we kept an even, crisp pace past Racine, and as respected old buildings of the West Loop streamed past I said: "You aren't the least bit chilly?"

"Imagine a humid summer afternoon where sixty thousand foot thunderheads linger over the Lake like a bumpy blanket left to soak moisture in a sauna."

"That's not working."

"Just move and lose yourself in it, Anthony—you used to be burly—have you gone soft on me? Think back to our long rides through the wind and the beating sun—and the times when the butterflies beat us up the hills." Head down, my wheels flew over low light skipping slanted across polluted liquid cresting a pothole—we passed Whitney Young Magnet School, and an opposing park space, where multicultural kids dashed for a deep pass thrown by a scrambling QB. Brown spiraled through blue until a throng of bodies dove into the snow in the corner of an invented end zone. I smiled, glad to see high school kids engaged in recreation instead of jacking old ladies—we rode past some mansions and across Ashland. On the SW corner, the Mexican Consulate saw a consortium of uncertain faces huddled in tight, fast talking groups: seeking information or discussing what to do post discovery. Up ahead, a spellbound flagger directed us to turn our bicycles into the Consulate parking lot to pay twelve dollars to park. There were no other cars around, and his deadpan face made direct eye contact with me while a gloved hand waved an orange flag in perfect figure eights—cat was zoning hard.

Across Ogden and under the southwestern swing of the Pink Line, the United Center rose to the right and Malcolm X College stretched to the left. Even on warm summer days with everything abloom, the area produces a very abandoned feeling within me. The harsh wind blew Readers against the chain link fence of the UC's south parking lot, and the only other sounds were our wheels compressing snow on the road and the Green Line roaring west in the distance above Lake Street. We passed two old churches just shy of Damen, put our heads down, and swung north. Melissa put the hammer down, and tearing through sunlit west side streets, I felt free—alas I often long to feel like the wind—blowing however softly or fierce—affecting the entire surface of the earth at my whim.

As we approached Madison I noticed a man standing alone in a lot on the west side of the street: smoking and looking up to the bright sky as he exhaled, he looked like the dark trunk of a lodgepole pine standing stoic in a silent field of white. Sun at his back, he formed a perfectly vertical, rigid silhouette—we rolled on, and just past Madison, Main Street Wine and Sprits and the surrounding area was jukin'—as the city workers had mentioned earlier, the

Bullies were playin' the fuckin' Knicks tonight, and all the dudes who were set to get out and hustle between three and eleven were getting liquored up real hard. A collection of people were openly passing a blunt to the right of the structure, and many folk loitered about, tellin' jokes, laughin', smoking squares, glaring out or just standing quiet, red lips drinking out of brown bags.

"Is that the place?"

"No, it's not."

"I hadn't hoped so." We passed an old church at Washington and another at Warren, where a big round man with a mustache, blue knit cap and nicely pressed pants shoveled the steps with a glad look on his face. Moving along, the sky was clearing hurriedly, earth smelling divine, and just ahead, soaked in the soft light of an early February afternoon, empty white land stretched east before Lake Street. "They're going to try and turn this tundra into a whole neighborhood later this year—the developer just got approval."

An advertisement showing a person of every race looking happy and carefree was already graffitied with gang insignias, and random trash littered the scarred landscape. We rolled on past and she said: "I wonder who'll live there."

"Who knows—a lot of people have gotten high, fucked, or been killed in that field, though. It's been empty all the way since getting burned out in the riots—a wide empty stretch in the midst of all this madness, for almost forty years. I bet it's the first step that will eventually see lower income people get booted out of here over the next couple of years—if gentrification maintains its pace, that is."

"People are not fuzz or change in someone's pocket that can be moved from one place to another just like that—not without irregular results, at least."

"No kidding, they're talking about tearing down Cabrini, and all the other projects along Orleans—once the developers sweep in that will be it—they'll get kicked out onto the streets with no place to go, and then people will wonder why other random neighborhoods become way more violent—they'll tear down an entire hierarchy and everyone will turn into lone sharks."

"I would never feel secure living in a building owned by the government."

"Right? Sometimes there ain't a choice." I looked back at the road, snuck a pothole but caught a hard little ridge hidden under snow, and the worn cork grips on my bullhorns eased the shock wave in my numb hands, but I was still left with that early season, fastball-in-on-the-hands-type pain.

"Damn—that was loud. I thought you bent the rim for sure."

"That's how it goes, right?—ya ride through all the crazy shit at full throttle and then eat it when you're chatting, and taking it easy." We rode on and under the Green Line, further north, a bright blue GD was painted on an empty warehouse sitting forlorn and unattended—in contrast, a blood red, upside down pitchfork was sprayed on the boarded door. We entered the Industrial Corridor, and looking west down Fulton, brawny masonry buildings lined the road. A train whistle wailed and a blue Metra engine powered solo toward the loop—another GD marked the railroad bridge and: "There's been a lot of Gangster Disciple graffiti going up around here this winter—even over toward Western and Chicago, and further west—they're creeping in on Spanish Cobra and King territory—it's gonna' be a long hot summer, boy, substance fueled and violent—a good time to be a poor, unaffiliated white boy, sitting back relaxed and watching them go."

We rode on quietly, eyes enjoying all the little nooks of the next few neighborhoods as the crisp winter sky entrenched the dome beyond our domes. Melissa stalled at a stop sign to let a dog and his owner cross the road—she was the kind of girl that would go out of her way to never kill an earthworm—always tiptoeing around them when after a mid-spring storm, hundreds popped from the ground and flopped about the sidewalk after maximum earthly saturation. Equally considerate to all elements of being, she took great care to swerve around a pool of dirty pigeons fighting over moldy white bread in front of a boarded up, foreclosed property that was still sort of stoic-looking, protecting its winter lawn in haunting stillness as the rest of the world carried on. The icy cool breeze set me in a weightless state of inner numb as a black man dressed in all black pushing an empty shopping cart in the direct middle of the street went hustling eastbound on Grand—he was set against a brilliant sky of steel and concrete too bright to stare upon, thus causing him to appear like a radiated hunter-gatherer on the search for a useful artifact somewhere along the fringes of a post-apocalyptic society. We rode another mile north, cut east just a hint past Augusta, rode for another block and got to the joint. "That was great," she said, "My mind's thought explored rivers of ink and forests of paper on that ride, man."

"O yeah—I'm ready for some warmness and feeling mityfineee—howbouja?"

"Ditto." We locked our whips to a well worn black U rack and entered the pub.

33

The place was mostly windowless, and it held a rich, long acquired smell of many subtleties, like a kind grandmother's apartment maybe, with many old-country spices baked deep into the plaster. It was dimly lit and the decorations were unsystematic to the point that you felt like you were about to have a drink in a crusty old shed—they had an old time, redheaded Camel girl smoking in a poster by the pisser alongside portraits of weirdos and a coo-coo clock, a decent amount of stained glass and a myriad of additional bullshit—all in all it was a cozy joint. We walked up to the bar and a battered old dog with a skinny tail and kind face gave us a good sniff before tottering back toward two old men seated at the last set of stools. He laid down, stiff and decisive, and the bartender asked what we wanted to drink. I was shaking a bit, so I ordered two cheap beers and warm whiskies. The guy brought over the beers, slid MD's helmet out of the way, set two shooters on the grained wooden counter, and as clear glass climbed brown, he went: "How was the ride? Pretty raw? What was the best part?"

"Constantly moving." We clicked glasses, and knocked it out—"Whoo," she said, "That'll warm ya up."

"I hope so."

She squinted, took my shades off, leaned close and said: "Your face looks like you've either been thinking or smiling a lot," she touched the corner of my eye and: "You grew some crow's feet."

"Good—I hope my eyes are ancient-looking some day—ancient as fuck from all they've seen," I said, putting them back on.

"So I take it you've been smiling?"

"Thinking, mostly."

"About what?"

"Who knows—I need a slow button for these synapses, though."

"Wearing down from the inside out?"

"You know?"

"Yeah." We were about to sit when she whispered: "Who's this far-out Asian randomite to my rear?"

I looked and the guy behind her was hacking into his coat sleeve, nose leaking like a sieve. "Donno—why?"

"He's wheezing like he has the goddamn bird flu. Let's sit in the back."

We posted up in the rear, next to the pool table. The place was more crowded than expected, with two sales guys firing at the eight ball and gabbing along: "Shit, he makes *what?*—if I was makin' that much money, I wouldn't dr*eam* of taking a day off, you know, in case something went wrong,"—the next shot was a scratch to the corner pocket that ended the game and: "That guy up front was Japanese, by the way," I said, "The bird flu is primarily a Chinese problem."

"How do you know?"

"I read the news."

"No—that he's Japanese, I mean."

"It's his style, Melissa, his pants mainly—they way his crotch is flaring out. I've looped for many years: Japanese men tend to have a meticulous golf swing and wear pants that frame their crotch when they execute a proper hip turn—communism keeps the Chinese too restricted to be so bold—after a good shot they immediately turn and walk stoic up the fairway, proud to have represented the state." MD smiled and Billie Holiday's voice floated from the juke. I didn't know what song it was, but I was certain the pipes were hers. I threw my bag under the table, blew a warm gush of air into my hands and: "Do you know what song this is?"

"It's 'Fine and Mellow'—a beautiful track, one of my favorites," she said.

"I can see why."

The dusty tele above the bar was muted, but the images droned on with several commercials about upcoming celebrity reality television shows, and: "You know, it's just not possible—at least for me it's not—to go swooning over a whole team of celebrities who would likely be plastic cunts to know in real life. I mean—who gives a fuck?"

"I've always been shocked to see what percentage of people's lives revolve around shows—it's really enough to make my head explode—you have a clump thrust onto a stage in front of a national crowd that goes bonkers for people who are nothing short of glorified karaoke singers—people who never sing any of their own songs, and then, after they win, when they get a big contract and *do* have to sing one of their own songs, it's always some lyrically blasé unchallenging nonsense containing no substance whatsoever. I mean—that's what it has actually come to—it's like: boys and girls—get out there and open your eyes! Damn!"

"It's hilarious."

"I know, right? I'd rather watch a show about that Japanese guy—if he's really Japanese, that is," she said.

"Either way, he's drinking warm vodka with a cold violent look in his eyes—he probably follows a crooked path and seduces strange women with sundry tactics. I'd waste a minute on him."

We drank quietly for a little while, and she looked at the back wall and said: "Wow, some of these paintings are fairly perverse. Who's the artist?"

"Probably some guy who walks his golf course backward before every round."

"You think?"

"Nah." In the back corner were some prints from the Renaissance, and after looking out in silence, I said, "The skills people have are insane. I mean—truly fucking insane."

"I know, right?"

"Especially the realists—a lot of these modern works are bullshit. I mean—so you drew a half-assed picture of a big nail, twenty feet tall, and it represents blah, and now all the bookworms want to sniff your cock. Real people know real art, man—I don't even know what that means, precisely, but do you know what I mean?"

"I do," she said.

"Like Degas—when I look at some of his paintings and drawings of guys just kickin' it in a smoky room, light sort of low with a lot of hidden shit going on—that's love, it really is. He makes you want to be right there, in that painting—you just know he would have been an interesting guy to drink a scotch with—I wonder where he is."

"He's dead."

"That's what I mean."

"Like in heaven or hell?"

"Anything at all, really—whether his consciousness has lived on in some form—I get stuck wondering about that sometimes."

"It lives on right now, through your interpretation of his work, does it not?"

"I 'spose, but—I meant as far as he knows." I removed my shades, accepted the room was dim enough to not bother my light sensitive eyes and said: "So how's everything been?—on the real, I mean. You still livin' life your way or what?"

She finally took out the toothpick, cracked it in half beside her ear and: "I feel monstrously electrified and simultaneously tormented by it all to a degree that sets my full internal into a self-inferno."

"Good, you haven't changed." I took a sip, shivered and: "It's good to know you're still a lioness on that bike of yours—shredding those hot, do or die lines through traffic, just like the old days."

She took a drink and: "Don't paint it like that—you could still put the hammer down and smash me if you wanted—you never get short on breath, ever—how is that?"

"When my head is taxed out, feeling fast and strong plays a large part in getting me through the day. If I ever fail to stay as raw as my body is capable at a particular age, I'll feel sick at myself—it's just the way my conscience works. It's weird."

She sat up a little straighter and: "Seeing your eyes—you really *do* look like you aged a little bit—but in a good way, you know?—via doing things, not wasting away—your face has really changed in some subtle way."

"My eyes get more violent?"

"No."

"Too bad."

"Have you?—been doing proper things, I mean?"

"For the most part."

"What have you been doing, anyway?"

"It's hard to say."

A stocky-strong, bearded Russian madman dressed in a well tailored grey and white pinstripe suit with black slicked hair and equally shined shoes—he walked in, clapped his hands once, real sharp-like, and in accented English he yelled to his thick friend, "I ready, I ready for anyting! Anyting, boy, I ready!" and it appeared that hell, he just might be—they sat at the bar and set off drinking.

"I mean—what do you do with your days, mostly?"

"Stroll thousands of strides and think millions of thoughts."

"Still?"

"Yeah."

"So I take it you eventually quit that IT job and went west, yeah?"

"Yep."

"You took my advice."

"Hell yes."

"I was only a sophomore in college then."

"I know."

"Do you remember what I told you?"

"Of course I remember—it's one of the best things anyone ever told me: be frugal, go straight-edge for a bit, save all you can, continue to write, to create, do not allow yourself to become bogged down by the false expectations of a society that in all reality you hold no deep concern for, and go." I was just out of college when I met Melissa—I'd followed that American dream, planned path: high school, college, corporate job, money, spending, more money, accolades, and so forth—I didn't do it for long, but I did do it for a time. I hated it the whole way, and her advice helped push me to be real.

"When did you go?"

"Not long after the last time I saw you."

"On the Lake, wasn't it? In that graffiti cove near 57th Street?"

"Yeah—we had that little fire and ya told me t' forget other people and go live."

"That was a great night."

"Hell yeah."

"Did a day finally come where you just couldn't take it?"

"It was a lot of things—I was pretty green, you know, naïve as hell about the way things worked in the business world—nobody in my family worked a corporate job—they're all artists and hustlers, blue collar peeps, handymen and loving mothers, so I didn't know anything about it at *all*—I might as well have been Canadian, you know? So I finished school, fucking barely, but on time, and then I got hired at that gig and—"

"But why'd you decide to apply there?"

"I don' know—I wasn't all down to go t' college in the first place, right, and when I was done, this joint was touted: 'One of the best places to work in Chicago,' you know, that old story, and I was like, okay, fine—I didn't have any money or ideas minus the fact that I knew all I wanted was to roam and write, ramble through the woods and random cities taking photos, but again, if you refuse to use credit, and you don't come from cake, you have to work hard to make that happen—plus my family was all proud that I might get a 'real' job and all that, so I gave it a shot and they hired me. I didn't know squat about sales, let alone high end technical sales, and so they taught me a heap of details and paid for me to learn. After a five month crash course they linked me up to sell to the government—to state, local, and education sectors—so after making countless phone calls and building relationships, people started buying heaps of expensive shit from me. Institutions spent more and more, many millions of dollars, and I eventually started making money, you know, quite a stack for me and my background—people in management were like: 'Where in the world will you ever make 25k in one month again? You should be on cloud fuckin' nine right now.' And they were right, I mean, as far as that total being a lot of money—but it was just like—who cares, man? All I could think was: this is the people's money, literally, yours too—everyone who pitched in on taxes is getting jacked by this company and all like it—management drooled as the frantic push by purchasing departments to expend every last dollar of use-it or lose-it budgets cultivated a great take off the state—grown men and women would run up the halls, Melissa, bragging about what percent they charged people—literally cheering out loud about how many 'Geeps' they attained."

"What's a 'Geep?'"

"It's a slang term for gross profit."

"And now people wonder why states can't pay their bills."

"Right? And when I beat them at their own game, they acted like I was a fucking hero! People knew my name and they fucking cheered me for embracing the waste, eventually showering me with awards. My desk was close to the kitchen, so I was always stuck breathing the horrible smell of disgusting people microwaving processed slop they intended to shovel into rubbery tummies—and they'd all walk past and tell me: 'Great job, Anthony,' random ball of shit tongued into the side of their mouth as they carried another plate back to their cube, hands set to cram more company provided doughnuts and bagels down their necks before tackling additional action items—it was a real eye opener—there were all sorts of slogans that impelled employees to embrace the waste and the overall push to consume the peoples' gains was insane."

"There had to be some necessary spending."

"There was, and this company—their product may have been expensive, but at least it was quality—I saw many competitors ship straight garbage to people at even worse rates."

"Did you gouge people?"

"Yep."

"How'd you feel about it?"

"Fucking disgusted—but at first, I was like, well, at least I'm not on the corporate side, gouging regular schmoes—then I got to thinking and realized that gouging the government defines gouging regular schmoes—such is how deficit bloats. I wasn't taking the thought process deep enough until one night I had a dream and was terrorized by the muted sound of purportedly little men fading into nothing—a tiny hiss, air leaking out of frozen wheels, mouths speaking out just enough for the masses to understand they weren't alone—just enough to understand how hard they'd been leached off—the sound of all that paper being counted and handed out, note by note, by a million sets of dry, cracked hands, like my dad's, and the industrial gush of a heating duct in a federal building droning in the background, nobody speaking a word of why it was wrong—shuffling feet did their duty, and moved along—and I wanted to yell out: 'Hey, we work for we—this is the basis of being free—I think many sectors need reminding,' but I was late for an assessment on my vocal chords—I was in this weird future world where you had to pay to be able to think and speak."

"After you hadn't called in so long, I figured you'd gone."

"Yeah, I had—going up to the mountains was good, man, very freeing."

"Did you meet good people?"

"Yeah, the best, many kindred souls—we all stayed at this joint we called le hotel Africano and I thought about you quite a bit, out there—you would have fit right in. We lived a minimal existence based on movement, and had a good ole time—all livin' that transient town truth where ya live ya love and ya leave, that's what ya do."

"You had to have some decent cash left from the tech company, didn't you?"

"I ripped through it pretty nicely."

"On what?"

"First a guy in Denver scammed me for a fucking lemon Chevy Blazer, and then, after that went kaput, I made sure everyone drank the best booze and ate good soup after climbing the tallest peaks and going as fast as was personally possible with what was left."

"How much can one really spend on booze and soup?"

"A good amount—I just wanted that loot gone, man, so it went. I felt so cleansed, walking to the train with a big zero, after giving the last sum to a random bum in Denver."

"And so why'd you come back?"

"I had to earn enough t' print the piece—but according to proper principals, not via selling things t' people who don't need 'em."

"So where've you been working?"

"The worst places possible."

"The worst how?"

"I've only worked for companies that produce horrible product and then wrong people by deceiving them into procuring such at over-inflated prices—I work to make the company lose money and then further exploit the jobs as a tool that allows me to write and be creative while the internal destruction carries along."

"Are you being serious?"

"Yep."

"I mean—I'm not sure what to say about that."

"Say anything, or nothing—I mean—that's what it is, how I'm getting by."

"Where'd you get this idea?"

"Skiing."

"What were you thinking?"

"I was rambling down the continental divide, last one of my mates to take the drop—I was the most scared n' least talented—we'd climbed high in windy, frigid conditions, all our gear strapped to our backs while tight-roping this three foot wide, no mistakes allowed, knife-edge ridgeline in gale force winds that put us down on all fours and sent us straddling an imaginary fence nearly 13,000 feet into the sky—and when we finally reached the point that had seemed unattainable a few hours earlier, the spot from where we'd jump—that tiny, uneven platform of snow, ice and rock thrust into the sky with what seemed like the entire world spread out below—I clicked my skis onto shaking, weary legs, gazed out at the world, and left alone I screamed a scream immediately devoured by the sheer vastness of the scene, leaped—and in the momentary silence before my body blasted into snow and went thundering downhill attuned to the sculptured rhythm of a trillion heartbeats before, the thought came to me—thinking about my uncle Ronnie—his slender, wasted body, all fucking mangled in a wheelchair, and my Uncle Frank, lungs immolated by acid—good ole Frankie—my dad's brothers—both of them sitting in my grandfather's living room, in their wheelchairs, bodies sparkling clean after Gramps cleaned 'em up—that's when it happened—while flying free down that mountain, making huge GS turns and laughing with tears in my eyes, feeling divine as I cut through bright light, hit a pillowy knob, felt air for a jiff and then hit soft landing with snow padding my beard—mind reflecting that horrible fucking feeling I got when we'd all piled out for a cheap buffet, and while my pop was filling my uncles' plates, I heard some guy make a remark about Frankie and Ronnie having dandruff. 'Don't they wash their fuckin' heads? Just look at all that sh*it* on their shoulders, man—fuckin' *sick* is what *that* is.' That's what I heard him say, this pale and obese, white trash, Gary Indianan cunt in skin-tight jean shorts and a candy apple red, mesh tank top—he said that, aloud, to an equally rank friend of his—loud enough for my uncles to hear his observation. He sat down at his seat and went on leering at them sitting all zigzagged and rigid in their wheelchairs, with a smirk on his face. *Ooh!* The wicked things I'll do to you!—even as a child the thought screamed through my brain and led me to shake—I imagined calmly pushing my chair away from the table, tottering over, big smile on my face, and now directly behind him, standing height that of his sitting neck—hey little fella—hey—and next I'm perforating with one smooth slice, twisting his jugular like string of snapped blue shooting hot red, his eyes quivering as I spin it 'round the blade like the spinning moon around the spinning earth—ain't nothin' gonna' slow it down, nope—I sat still, squeezed that knife in my hand and all I could think was that I'd laugh—I would laugh my *ass* off at how far the blood would squirt from his neck after I plunged the full length out the other side—I wanted to take their shame away once and for all, you know? I was in third grade, I remember it distinctly." I sat back in my chair for a moment and Melissa didn't say anything. Her face hadn't changed and so I wasn't sure what she was thinking. "What?"

"You have a lot of hate inside you—I would have never guessed it."

"You're right, I do—and I know that probably sounds crazy, but as a child, my grandfather lost his leg playing in a south side freight yard—he was waiting for his dad to get off work at the slaughterhouse, and his foot got stuck in the railroad ties. After trying desperately to pull him out, his brother held his hand, eyes wide and voice screaming as the steam engine charged through and severed his leg below the knee—it was a miracle that he lived in the first place, that I'm here—and to see him, my tiny grandfather, all one hundred and forty pounds of him, wooden leg and all, carry—on his fucking back—Frankie and Ronnie, one at a time—forty year-old, full-grown men—to see him carry them into the bath and gently, painstakingly wash their slender, wasted bodies—visions that planted the fucking roots of humility—day after day, month after month, for years! And to hear these fucking pigs say that! To hear those fucking slobs make those comments and to know that *they* heard it! *My* uncles! Ooh!—I'll never get over that—that rage—like Frankie—he was the m*a*n— my dad's older brother, always looking out for the family as they got bounced from apartment to apartment, all over the city, from one crazy neighborhood to the next, taking care of Ronnie, my dad's youngest brother—brain damaged after a hospital error during his birth— working one odd job after another, anything he could do to make ends meet. I mean—my dad and Frankie shined shoes in dangerous taverns for a couple extra pennies, anything—some summers they went up and worked the fields in Wisconsin while my Grams stayed behind— just the boys, living in a one-room shack like indentured servants—and to look at the old black and white photos of Frankie in his prime, when he was raw as hell and grinding all he could—he was unbelievable, Melissa. A great boxer, people wouldn't fuck with him, but he didn't start unnecessary trouble, either—he just looked after the family and did his best—so strong and able and talented and wise—he eventually took a third job on a night shift, just so he could pitch in a little more—and that's when he got brain damaged, working a horde of hours in an unventilated room with synthetic chemicals, at Menith—and to see him then, after the insurance company got out of the claim and the family scraped some change together, sued, and lost again to high priced corporate lawyers protecting the business—fucking educated people in nice suits patting themselves on the back for preventing a poor, hardworking family from getting a goddamn *dime!*—not a fucking dime to help with the loss caused by them!—I imagined the group getting drinks after the case, shaking hands at a job well done, 'Cheers to your nothing, suckers—we take all, give nothing, and we never will—here here!' The whole lot huddling like a ball of sticky worms in a hot Styrofoam container to discuss the intricate nature of the case, so maybe they could have an easier go at the next sucker—and then there was Frankie, fucking ruined, just sittin' there rigid and having t' live with it."

"That must have been horrible."

"It was—it was fucking horrible—and like anybody who's made the transition from healthy to handicapped, accepting the new reality as such was never fully feasible—life and its memories were to be forever structured as before, and after."

"So I take it you didn't stab the guy at the buffet?"

"No—my uncles' blue eyes grew wide at the same time mine did, instantly darting away before rolling in acceptance of their own predicament, sort of embarrassed at their inability to stand up and tell the guy to get lost. I was just a kid but felt like they looked up to me so much, you know, it was fucking weird—they always gave me this silent vibe like I was to be the only man who could live on in full capacity, so never be weak—that's how they looked at me—and so I led the charge to shake off the mockery with a laugh, sticking an extra plate under my shirt and poking fun at the prick—but each time I made them laugh, they breathed a bit harder, to the point of struggling—such heart wrenching sounds, their twisted frames made—and I laughed with 'em n' all, but really all I wanted was to cry out like: what the fuck, man?—so I eventually glared a stare at those fools that explained: if you dare mock this helpless person I love so dear I will fucking kill you, right here, right now, happily riveted to a surreal enjoyment of the moment you breathe your final, blood-soaked breath. I think the guy knew what I meant, I swear—he stopped looking and I bit my tongue till it bled and tried to relax—my pop rolled back with their plates of food all organized according to their likes and dislikes: 'What's up Anthony?'—Nothin'."

"It had to inspire you—seeing them live that way."

"They motivated me to get out and push in the first place—seeing them all banged up for all those years—it was like, all the raw athleticism they never got to use was poured in me, you know? Like in the main room of my grandparent's house—the entire goddamn wall was a huge mural of mountains and forest, from floor to ceiling—and all the time, voices barely comprehensible—Frankie would have to hold his nose closed when he talked, and he was still very difficult to understand—and they'd be like, 'Anthony, see those mountains? We're gonna' climb them someday.' And I was just like, 'Yeah, you know, definitely'—but in my head it was like, damn guys, you're never going to fucking climb anything! You can't even move across the room because these greedy crooks fucked up and ruined your bodies and faced no repercussions! So eventually, when I was working at that Computer Technology Wherever company, they all died, all three, right in a row, one in each month: Ronnie, Frankie, and my Gramps, all gone—that's when it was like, alright fellas, fuck this, it is damn well time to climb high and go fast—so that's how it worked out there—I'd leave town before dawn, get set to climb high, so many paces, counting in my head, fifteen thousand in a row, all uphill, some good tunes on, alone with the sky, and eventually, three hours later, I'd get up top, catch the sunrise with 'em, let out a fucking scream and we'd bomb it together, arcing and beautiful and free. It was pretty deep at times—when you're out there alone, completely by yourself with nobody around for miles, man, I swear you can hear the hearts of history beating at your side."

"What did they succumb from in the end?"

"Ronnie actually crushed himself to death with his own body, collapsing his lungs from how crooked he was—Frankie died from other complications of the retardation and paralysis—and my Gramps, after his oldest and youngest sons died, he was just so exhausted after their fight was over, you know, both mentally and physically, that he just got pretty quiet for a little while and went."

"Were you upset when they died?"

"Only when reflecting on their hardships, you know?—I think they lived to the point that they were so thoroughly worn and exhausted that dying silently felt divine. Near the end, I was sitting with my pop and Gramps while he was playing an old slow lick on his organ, and after he finished the song, he looked up at the mural, and in this tired, distant voice, he went: 'Get your tickets—'—and all I could think was no shit Gramps, no shit."

"He sounds like he was a great example."

"Yeah, he was a great man, kind as hell, and no complaints—strong until the final breath—they all were. Nobody tried to go numb on drugs or off themselves on account of the pain—they just ate it, man, fuckin' sober n' with a smile."

"What pops in your head most when you think of them?"

"Their great sense of humor through it all—that and they fucking loved Chuck Norris, long before it became hip to do so—whenever he knocked someone out, Ronnie would look over and go, 'Aww man!' and Frankie would start laughing real hard in this seized up way where he didn't even make a sound." I took a drink and the memory was overtaken by the crazy way the distressing sirens of ICU patient vital signs mingle seamlessly with the sound of hospital-wide lullabies designed to ease fresh new souls into a world of utter chaos. I shivered and: "In the end, at my grandfather's wake, my dad was so sad all he said was, 'What does it matter, he doesn't exist anymore anyway,'—he didn't mean for it to sound so cold, you know—it's just, his dad was his hero, just as he is mine—he loved him dearly and hated to see him suffer, and so when I saw him kiss his hard, cold head, and a tear fell from his eye and onto his dad's silver hair, I got to thinking of how hard my pop has worked himself—the way he's come from nothing, all on his own—a lot of dudes would have up n' quit—felt sorry for themselves because of their harsh past n' spent their life getting drunk, but no—he's busted his ass in the same machine shop since he was a goddamn teenager, taking his lumps with a good sense of humor—his best shot at life as a shot on me—and thinking of all that, never had I felt so much anger in my entire goddamn life. Fucking very serious anger at how the machine had finally worn them out, you know?—very serious and burning, calculated anger—seeing Gramps get buried beside Ronnie and Frankie, all of them laying there tight in those humble, shallow graves, sleet crashing sideways on that windy winter day, my grandmother sobbing to the point of not being able to stand—in that moment, something changed. I was just like: fuck *this* man! Straight up—I'm never working for these sorts of people again, unless it is to ruin them. So yeah, after I figured some plans at altitude, that's what I've been up to—but now I'm done with that, too."

"What sorts of places did you work for?"

"The first place I got a job upon returning was actually the insurance company that was supposed to cover Frankie while he worked in the factory."

"You're serious?"

"Yep."

"How?"

"It was a long process, but I waited until they were hiring managers, learned a slew on my own, and got the job. They wound up putting me in charge of a whole bunch of independent agents, a mistake, obviously—"

"What the hell did you plan on doing?"

"In reality, I remained completely uncertain about what my intention was, even after getting appointed to the position. I 'spose somewhere deep inside I'd always dreamed of getting hired, creeping in there via any available method, really, remaining after hours, and physically destroying the entire place—every server, back up device, fucking computers, printers—every desk, every drawer, every paper and pen—ruining the entire business, quite literally, finishing it off just before dawn, and exiting the Tower, satisfied and light for sake of the flourishing implementation of my family's revenge. But that's not the way it was—I walked in and, like most everywhere, all it was: a load of everyday people doing their best to provide for their families, and held hostage by an intricate system of politically correct rules penned by upper management. It was horrible."

"I don't get how you were hired to begin with—lots of people study hard. How were you able to get your foot in the door?"

"I basically set TNT on the hinges and lit a short fuse."

"But how?"

"I incorporated a company, one with a title that insinuated it could employ all sorts of specialists, you know, so I could claim to fill any role I chose and subsequently allow additional false personalities to boast about my prowess in filling that role, therein getting me hired at different organizations—and in this specific instance, I put out an ad seeking high level business managers—in response I received many resumes, picked the best candidates, interviewed and asked complex questions over the phone to fill a nonexistent position I would never hire for, you know, so as to decipher trends in their solutions, analyze and expand on such. I then asked to review their educational documentation from their respective colleges, did so, and subsequently changed these same documents to possess my name—I then used this collection of knowledge and material to get hired at the insurance company. It was that easy." She looked at me with a blank face, so I said: "Melissa, when someone is moving toward a goal of vengeance, it becomes all consuming and all containing. There is nothing that stands in the way. It was simple forgery, but at the same time, I had to be on point—if you forge documentation that says you graduated Magna Cum Laude from a certain business school, these people expect you to possess Magna Cum Laude business knowledge. The possession of such knowledge is still mandatory—but you have to earn it yourself, without anybody patting you on the back or pushing you to possess—which, I believe, is the way it should be in the first place. I felt very qualified to fulfill the position and I would have done a good job for them had they not impaired my family. In short I guess I self-radicalized to an extent."

"So what exactly happened?"

"Even after I got hired I had a lot to learn—they had intricate tests on policy and individual health plans that I had to pass, and I had to memorize crazy material, including all the specific problems the company would rider, you know, exclude from coverage: fuckin' heart problems, fuckin' hip problems, fuckin' any problem that was a problem for the most part—in reality, I knew a lot of these things, but I had to see it first hand, how it worked, you know?—how such companies wiggle out of having to pay what was really owed—and in my head, I had this whole vision of all these powerful managers crushing the people, but it wasn't like that, either."

"How's that?"

"Even in such a huge company, there were only a handful of people at the top who held sway—it is they who decided to form policy around extracting superprofits—in truth, there's plenty to go around—people's heart problems *should* be covered. What prevents it is pure greed shared across several industries—like the calculated ritual of a math teacher sharpening pencils and cleaning the chalk board at the end of the day—it's hard to explain— prices don't come down because competition is colluding to fix wages and values to secure the highest possible margins for everyone involved. It's an intricate, interconnected system, and that's why it's proven impossible to break—because honest competition doesn't really exist." I took a drink and: "In the time since the incident with my uncle, the company had switched from group coverage to only providing individual plans. In the end I figured the only way I could make a difference was to expunge certain portions of people's records before paperwork was sent to underwriting for analysis—and what I did, after an agent sent in personal insurance forms for approval, I mean, the agents didn't care—they weren't paid based on how expensive people's plans were—they got paid for how many people they signed up—so it made no difference to them if our estimate was cheaper—in fact, the company actually got more business on account of my activity."

"How?"

"The agents were independent, right—they worked with several insurance companies, all with different, albeit similar options—and so, after dealing with the individual in need, the agent would then send their records to several companies, including Peltip, and the company with the best plan at the best price is generally what the person desired—so, after I received certain people's records who were having a difficult time getting affordable or effective insurance because a previous condition that was certain to be ridered, I would scan the paperwork at lunch, rid the problem and reprint before sending to underwriting—as a result, their estimates came back far lower, with the condition covered because it suddenly didn't exist."

"Didn't the agents wonder why the price was lower?"

"You know, I thought they would, but I suppose people don't tend to ask many questions when business falls into their lap—at least that's how it seemed."

"How many people did you do this for?

"Not many, less than two handfuls—the last being a girl named Meredith born without an anus, and desperately in need of a take down pull through procedure that would have cost her father six figures had I not completely eradicated the old record and started anew—the problem was that a previous surgery was in need of a fix, but she was now too old to be covered on her parent's insurance, and when she wanted to get covered on her own, her ass was excluded—to be frank I don't even know if it worked. The agent told me the story, and so I called her dad directly to spill what I was doing and why—that it was all a crapshoot to some extent, no pun intended."

"What'd he say?"

"He was fairly stunned t' get called by some guy tellin' 'em: 'I'll obliterate the record, you sign the papers and get them to me di*rec*tly—that way I'll push it through to underwriting without even letting the agent realize, and if he calls you, tell him you got insurance somewhere else—I'll have her covered by Friday, so schedule the surgery for as soon as possible. Maybe you'll get away without having to cover the cost and maybe you won't—it's not a guarantee, but it's the best chance you have, sir, so I say go with it.' He asked if I was serious a dozen times and jumped on board. He told me I was a saint and all this shit, and after the insurance was approved, I left, dead in the middle of the day, and never came back—in some way I felt like I was on the verge of reaching some final vindication, but not quite—not one that could help my family, at least, but fuck it—I figured I'd make those boys exist forever via the random goodwill toward another in dire straights and this was the best idea I could come up with."

"I don't know how to respond to that, but it makes me glad—but sad too, though, in this horrible way."

"I know what you mean. When I walked out that day, I finally broke down about it all—I'd kept it in for years—all the fuckin' Christmases when my dad would give his brothers a nice new wallet with a little cake inside, and they were all thankful, like they were about to walk somewhere and spend it on a good-looking gal and have a good time—I—yeah—fuck."

I cleared my throat and she asked: "How'd you go about quitting these places?"

"I didn't say a word to anybody before, or after, the time I left. I went poof-wild, like a ghost, and never again made contact. At the places with the biggest bastards I asked everyone what they wanted for lunch. Said that it was on me because I'd won fifty dollars on a scratch off that morning and so get everything ya fuckin' crave: sides, drinks, all of the above—and then I just never returned."

"God that's funny—didn't they try to call you?"

"I hope so—after getting hired, I always changed my contact information to be the direct line of a previous manager I'd already gone poof-wild on—so I don't know. If so, the image of them slamming the phone on one another is a strange sense of unrealized satisfaction, like being the author of a book that made somebody go crazy many generations after your living departure—it really slays me."

"Damn, you're out of your mind, kid."

"A bit."

"You must have learned a good deal about the economy and different industries, observing all this."

"I did—and the number of crap companies producing crap product astounded me."

"Like what exactly?"

"I don't know—it was all schemes! Quite a few, all horrible, perpetuated by companies filled with dirty, muckraking motherfuckers—I was at venture capitalist firm where the people were basically loan sharks, and they had these damn lists of businesses that had recently been denied loans, right, and so they'd call the owners, listen to their plight, and then they'd say some shit like, 'I understand where you're coming from, Jack, because small business owners need to be a little *tou*gher than most—and that's why we're speaking to each other right now—what we need is action, by both of us, to*get*her—what I'm going to need you to do is—' carrying on in this real philanthropic tone the whole time, you know, because they were so fucking giving, in fact, that they were about to rip 'em as deep as possible with a high interest loan that would increase exponentially in a very short time frame and likely bury the guy—they'd talk fucking Sam's Bait Shop in Timbuktu into taking an emergency hundred thousand dollar loan, right, five times more than needed, at an impossible rate—some big shots would talk the guy into using his little home on the lake as collateral and have him sign his life away because—'We under*sta*nd that owning a small business is the American dream, sir, and you're so close, just *so* close to making it,' here's a fucking anchor to chain around your neck, let's take a final dive at success together. It was fucking brutal. They talked amongst themselves as if they were actual producers of some sort, you know?—it was garbage. All I could think was: hey, by the way, you've produced nothing—*nothing!*—ever. Not a single creation minus debt, waste and trash. Make sure you stomach that before you die."

"So you went over hard numbers with a few people?"

"Yeah."

"For how long."

"A few paychecks."

"So really, you'd eek a few checks, make changes, observe, write and move along?"

"That sums it up Ms. D, on the button—I'd observe salespeople who made a strong habit of belittling secretaries, with a usual line being, 'I can't talk to him? So then, it's *you* making this decision?' And then the person would gather everybody around, put the phone on speaker and say, 'I'm sorry, I didn't realize twelve dollar per hour employees were allowed to make the sorts of decisions that impact the future sustainability of the company. To whom am I speaking again? I thought X was the CEO.' And then everybody would laugh about how little the person on the other line must have felt in that moment—they would just fucking laugh, dozens of them—fucking g*row*nups, man! Hence why I have no compunction about what I've done, not in the least."

"And this last place?—this place you left today?"

"Maybe the worst of them all, so far as the depth of the hustle—some seriously crooked shit going on—a full mix of moral, religious, nationalistic and educational lies spun tight into a single, running script so as to fulfill huge math equations of interest collection and unsound investment. The bosses liked to command from the front like the Centurions and this allowed them to build the mentality of all the rank and file people into that of little soldiers working together to build a Great Society of certified dimwits. It was literally insane."

"Were any of the people working there nice?"

"A lot of them were, actually, nicer than most—but it was that robotic nice where you could spit on their face and they'd say: 'Thank. You.' like a droid."

"I don't like that."

"Nor do I—it was like, how many pharms are you on, people? Jesus."

"Did the experience expose you to a new frame of mind?"

"Mostly it helped me solidify old thoughts—to see how deeply the whole structure of American life is based on keeping you 'locked in'—locked in by borrowing unnecessarily large sums of money for things you don't need—the unnecessary in this case being huge school loans for an education that teaches little in the way of cognitive thinking, reason, or actual problem solving. Fifty stacks on memorization and busywork at eleven percent interest—"

"Then the clothes, car, and house, and second car, and then, then after you've piled up enough bills to be a real 'man' or 'woman', then you're to haul off and hitch the most standable stiff you can find, pop a kid, teach them the same wasteful lifestyle, and together you all grind it out for the rest of your lives, make a proud face, and die."

"American dream right there, girl."

"Many people don't wake from that mindset until it's too late. They realize they're just expensive walking coffins—that they've been dead their whole life, and poof, it's over."

"You're right."

She had a drink and: "Wow. That's some story—that was a revolution, in fact—what you did."

"No it wasn't."

"Sure it was."

"Why? What is a revolution, anyway? I mean, how'd you define it?"

"By the book, Anthony: as an individual stand against injustice despite a conscious attempt by authority or popular opinion to influence or manipulate that stance as erroneous or improper."

"And so how does what I just described qualify as a revolution?"

"Easily—all revolutions are really a culmination of hundreds, thousands, millions really, of distinctly unique actions by distinctly unique individuals, the success or failure of which all depends on the number of revolutions per minute occurring at once, with your own personal revolt against injustice being one more storied notch to further the cause." She took a drink and said: "So you never printed that book, huh?"

"Nope."

"But you're still working on it?" I nodded and: "Well are you getting close at least? What's your gut feeling?"

"I got a feeling in my stomach that finally, after much time and effort, after roaming and capturing thousands of tiny moments, tiny thoughts—they're finally coming together to form a piece I shall feel satisfied with."

"Can I read what you have?"

"When she's ready."

"Maybe I'll catch fire."

"Fuck that—you're already burning. You strike me with those embers every time I see you."

The dry sound of the cue ball breaking the rack cracked and: "What I'd really want to read are all those little books in your bag."

"We probably couldn't be friends anymore. Not if you read that shit."

"You think I'd hate you?"

"You just might."

"What for?"

"A million things, at least."

"What do you feel like, when you look at all the work in a pile like this?"

"Mainly I feel awe at the number of meltdowns that have occurred along the path, both witnessed and experienced, and then I get a chuckle."

"And so you're trying t' wind this all together?"

"Yeah, it's alright, I'm havin' fun—it's like, now all I have to do is split this into two hundred thousand words—in a row?—O—I have a long way to go."

"Do you feel confident in it?"

170

"It's almost like sometime long ago I completely forgot what I was tryin' t' say—all told I want people, if they care what others think or live gripped by external pressure—I want to let somebody see that none of that matters—and if *one* person decided to live for what they loved and say fuck all else, then there, it's a success for me. I want to live up to the beauty in my head—what I see every day, what leaks in there—but the thing is, after a seemingly endless array of efforts have come up short, I've begun questioning if my mind can live up to reality—know what I mean? The actual world is totally unbelievable."

Cool bubbles of water ran over my fingers as I grabbed my glass, and she said: "Still looking to put it out solo?"

"Yeah."

"Why not shop it around?"

"Because I would never sell the product of my own mind to another individual who would then hold power over what I created—I think it is plain nuts, in fact, that so many people do so—sell to people who just sit back and buy creations so as to then pretend as if it is truly theirs—people who then change around and water down to the point that it *is*—and not only am I not for sale, window shopping is prohibited. Good sums of these industry fools are little thieves who'll tell you the work ain't worth a damn, only to sew certain bits of it into their own half-baked narratives—all in an effort to get their photo into that corny magazine we saw earlier, dressed just right. I didn't come this far to be told what to do—quite the opposite. I don't care so much how many people read my work versus knowing it got done my way, alone, without anyone telling me to do so."

"All anyone does is grow up to be told what to do, it seems."

"I can't stomach that path."

"I respect that—is it about this? All the jobs and everything?"

"Nah—there's a regular plot to it n' all that shit."

"Then what is it?"

"Basically an effort to incite widespread indignation with what is to the point that if your previous actions make you want to jump off a building, it'll either yank you back, or give you a tight little shove—or so I hope. I got a lotta' work t' do, n' hopefully many unbeaten beats n' unbreathed breaths ahead with which t' do it. It'll be weird though—in a lot of ways I don't talk to anyone, let alone everyone."

"Just make sure you don't find yourself so wrapped up in something that once gone, there's nothing."

From the booth directly behind MD it came: "If I hear you bitch about one more thing, I'm gonna' spit right in your face—how about that for love?"

Melissa raised her eyebrows and whispered: "Did you hear that?"

"Yeah—I think they're talkin' about gettin' a divorce."

She leaned closer and: "What do they look like?"

I spied over and: "He's white, a little pasty and soft, but with a face that hints at a freaky side—my guess is he likely chases poor foreign girls whenever he can. I imagine he seeks to impress them with a very calculated exhibit of American showmanship—and she— she's an immigrant, possibly Malaysian, and my blind, unsubstantiated assumption says she used him for citizenship, and he used her for sex."

"He sounds like he's ready to kill her."

"He probably is—I'd bet he's been socially awkward and on the verge of a collapse his whole life, with no self esteem, and now, after enjoying a brief period of rule over this woman, he's coming to realize that he'd rather strangle her than lose his sole source of supremacy, thereby reverting to his pathetic withdrawn existence of high tech hermit perversion—plus she's about to take half his chop—it's no wonder he can't accept that their arrangement has run its course."

MD looked down at graffiti etched in the old wooden table, squeaked a finger around the brim of her glass and: "I hope I'm never one of these people who get through the night by fantasizing about how loudly they're gonna' slam the door in the morn."

"I'd rather open it and get shot in the face."

"Agreed."

"You're my *wife*, goddamn it—I gave you that ring so you better love me!"

Melissa leaned in and said: "One should earn love, not simply be granted such—in fact, non-conditional love is earned as an effect of many conditions, and is therefore imaginary."

The woman and her heavy accent continued: "I can make it mut mor difracul for you—mut mor difracul, O yes. I have a great royer, a very powraful royer—aw judges know h*ee*m, and he look so f*i*t in Jockey short—so f*i*t, O God." I took a good look at the guy so I'd recognize his face if I saw him in the papers—thin lips twitched a hint before retorting to each statement—just enough to tip that he was about to slip off his rocker in a real bad way.

I cut my gaze and: "You know, MD, it felt good to be riding beside you, hearing your voice somewhere besides deep in the memories of my head."

"Agreed."

"It's been a long time."

"I know—it seems like a lifetime."

We sat there for a moment and watched the people. A loud pale fool crashed through the door and nearly fell over—his lower leg was encased in a cast and walking boot, and the scratches on his face made him look as though he'd crawled many miles from a wilderness of thorn bushes and termite mounds. He ordered a snifter of cheap gin, killed it, and ordered another—his speech said he must have been boozing for many hours. He then gimped up to our table, looked at Melissa, smiled and said: "Suh wha do y*o*u do for gri*n*s?"

"All sorts of things."

"Such *as?*"

"I avoid spilling details about myself to people I don't care to know."

"Well do ya want a stick a' gum at least?"

"Nah, it's cool, I have a lot of gum in my life right now." She looked down at his leg and: "What happened?"

"Broke m' humerus."

"Not too funny."

"No, it ain't." But really it was, with the way he was standing so drunk and so crookedly angry—plus the humerus is an arm bone, but there was no reason to correct him and dispel future humor based on his incorrect appraisement. He bumbled off to a spot across the room, along the wall, and set off drinking.

"Well, he gave it a shot," I said.

"At least he wasn't a jerk—kept it clean—thanks for letting me handle that."

"I thought he was gonna' go dirty on you for sure—thought I'd have to choke-slam him through the window."

"He's a pretty big guy for that small of a window."

"I'd do my best to stuff him through—neck first if possible."

"I wonder what he's like on a date."

"Fucking horny, I'm sure."

"Do you think he's just looking for a bang buddy?"

"I think the hole in his mattress is probably overflowing—can't you picture him sitting in a bathtub of cold, dirty water for hours on end, playing tug of war?"

"Must you?"

I took a drink, looked at her and: "Can I get a stick of that gum?"

"I don't actually have any." She laughed nice and loose and I thought: as a man, you'll always miss being able to kiss certain girls at your whim—how could you not? "So do you hang mostly with the same crew of mates as before?"

"I do."

"They still the wild bunch that I remember?"

"Yeah, it's good—I don't really socialize with people I'm not willing to lose everything for—maybe on the quick, if I have to be at a party or something, but in terms of openly getting to know new, *hip* people and such—I'm still fairly antisocial. I'm fortunate to possess a wide swath of mates I went through a lot of shit with, you know, growing up together, traveling, living in the woods, whatever it may be—we'll be down 'til the day we die. I'm really lucky, actually."

Melissa grabbed at my hand and: "Are you okay? You're really shaking—aren't you wearing a base layer of some sort?—you never caught chills like this before."

"I'm fine—it's just an accumulated coldness from past days that I need to shake—I'll be right back." I stood, looked at the guy against the wall with a raw hateful gape so he understood there'd be serious repercussions if he didn't leave Melissa alone, headed to the head and ran warm water all over my hands, arms, and face. There was no mirror and the walls were painted dark red, like the blood of a dehydrated hiker in a barren wasteland, sipping his own piss, searching for shade and waiting to die. The lock on the door was broken, and one of the old men banged in and back out in a jiff—it was a one person facility. He slurred over to his ole mate and his dog that he planned to buy them a big lunch and dinner every day for the rest of their lives after he won the Lotto that evening—his voice was pretty haggard, and he seemed to fulfill the myth that people and their dogs begin to resemble one another over time: they were both dirty, furry, and rough. His pal told him he had no chance, to burn his ticket then and there, and I figured the two of them had spent most their lives smokin' cigars n' cigarettes n' talkin' shit like that. They made me smile, but made me feel empty as hell, too—it was all winding down now. I walked out as the bartender went, "Think Bill wants some water?"

"Nah," the old man said, "He's fine," he dripped a little beer into Bill's mouth, gave him a pat and "Yeah tha's good shi, ain't it boy?"

He smiled at me and: "What do you feed a dog that big?"

"Everything the bastard wants, tha's what!" He laughed all crazy and it gave me a kick—Bill yawned, pink tongue folding in two right at the tip, and he lay tight against the bar, round brown eyes peeking up at his master as he entered the bathroom. I sat back at the table, and MD was massaging her hands while looking at one of my journals.

"Want some lotion?"

"Sure." She poured some on my hands and: "This has a funky stench."

"Real aloe smells like plant intestines, not that Bath and Body perfume smell." She flipped through a couple more pages and: "I hope you don't mind me spying through this."

"I don't."

"There's some crazy random shit in here."

"Ja mon."

"And you have nice handwriting."

"Thanks, that's a real compliment."

"But on certain days it seems to get more jagged on a sentence by sentence basis on account of the extreme amount of substance you consume in passing hours."

"Another accurate observation."

"I remember you said you'd write me letters if you ever went away."

"I did."

"I never got 'em."

"I never sent 'em."

"Why not?"

"I just didn't."

"Do you still have them?"

"I don't, actually." In truth, I always do my best writing when it's for specific people in specific letters, and in this instance, there was only one letter—like forty thousand words long, written tiny as hell, not a lick of white left on the sketch paper, several detailed drawings, and the substance focused on far too many insane subjects to send through the open mail—I remember being in a lift shack, like two months into it when I added: 'As you may be able to tell, I'm taking a good amount of time to write you this letter.' After a while I figured it would be best to not send it—it's just—if you go and send a letter like that, the other person is then stuck understanding how much you care about them, you know? When you spend days trying to write good stories for one single person, by hand, it gets like, a bit heavy— that's why they invented books—so you can copy pages and bind them together, and pretend what is written is for a bunch of schmoes you can't stand. So instead of sending it, I relaxed alone in the woods and lit it up—in the quiet crackling I earned an honest yet hollow feeling via creating for someone the best you were capable of, only to roast the produce hot and smoky, never a single reader and no digital copies, just as the Great Mother shall be when the sun grows large and consumes her in a firestorm.

She continued reading and an old man came through the door. I took a drink and he greeted a white haired fellow in the front of the pub with a big hug—they shared a look that seemed to say: 'Damn, it's good to see you!—life is really flying past, ain't it?' I took another drink and absorbed the bittersweet feeling. It hit me deep, man, I'm telling you. Neil Young raised the stakes through the jukebox—hitting the opening riff of 'Cowgirl in the Sand' just as Melissa turned my book closed, set it down, and with a serious look about her, said: "Actually, just a second—I have to pee." She headed off, and the men up front approached the bar. They seemed like wise old fellows who always progress at the same speed, neither rushed nor lethargic—never wasting a move, like they knew their eventual total, and were trying to hoard as many as they could. They reminded me of two chaps well beyond their prime strolling up to a golf course, set for a late fall round as scattered skeletal leaves and the impending doom of a long shrill winter linger in the air—the ephemeral nature of the opportunity to spend time together was evident in their hard-bitten facial expressions as they set in on their first whisky.

MD returned to the table, sat, put her hands flat, took a breath and I said: "Let your mind run and let me know what trails it chooses."

"Well lately, and really, it's not just lately—perhaps I took a brief period of time to get away from incessantly questioning my existence—but lately it has happened again: I've returned to questioning, and I do not think I can stop."

"You know what they say—one day you'll be wondering how you got so old just wondering how and then it'll be time to split."

She placed her fingers to her temples and: "Seriously—it's really crazy to think of the fact that I am, that I exist."

"It's the craziest."

Her head moved up and back, hair followed in a wave and: "It's just—I love my family quite much—my mom and dad—and thinking of the fact that they won't exist one day is just too much to fathom."

"What has you on these thoughts so much?"

"I don't know—I had a close call last summer, and I've been stuck on it ever since."

"Feel like chatting of it?"

"Not really."

"Did you crash on your bike?"

"Don't worry about it."

I looked at her quiet for a second and: "So you know, I'm not trying to be awkwardly personal like observing the insides of a ladybug as she walks up the opposing side of a window pane—I just want to make sure you're alright."

"Let's just leave it alone for now."

"Cool." In the past she was prone to these wild giggling fits that set her all ashake—somewhere deep in the expression of her face said an incident had agitated her innocence into a mix of wary disenchantment.

"But you know how I'm feeling, right?"

"Without a doubt."

"I mean—the whole human experience is fully dependent upon the self—so when you get stuck on the contemplation of the non-existence of such, well—it's aversive, quite possibly the most aversive topic you're capable of creating. A grasp can never be realized in full form—not by me, at least," she said, "The brain working to prove its non-existence and determine the subsequent result as evaluated against various existing mystic hypotheses is too contrasting a scenario on innumerable fronts." I looked down at my drink, at the swirl of bubbling brown liquid brimming the glass, noiselessly spinning, bubbles as stars and black as the cosmos, and I felt tiny—I closed my eyes, took a breath and embraced the black. "You ever think, Anthony—what if when you die, we all do?—and that's it."

"So long as the possibility wouldn't change what you're doing today, you're living life your way—tis a good target to shoot for."

"How do you get there?"

"All that matters is what someone has done and if they really meant it—if you do that, then you just have to look at it like: it's cool, I existed, so no worries."

"That's true."

"Before I turn to ashes in a slow burn, I intend to love as many moments as I can, ya know?"

"I'm with you, trust me," she said.

175

"Don't you feel you've lived for your passion? You're passionate of all you do"

"I've lived for my passion, yes—self satisfaction. This is the greatest individual gift I have ever given myself, Anthony—to remain immune to adolescent insecurities and breakdowns via searching for self contentment and disregarding outside opinion." She took a drink and: "I didn't fully realize what it meant until I was in high school, in creative writing class, and my teacher suggested I reread my work aloud, so as to get a better understanding of the flow. The woman was unawake on so many fronts that in my head I was like, okay, you're giving me a D because this is too advanced for your soul—I'm not even going to argue because I don't care what you think."

"And didn't that set you free?"

"Yes but, see—it's the deeper eventuality of me that has me worried—I've had trouble sleeping in the past year on account of the fact that I have been having all sorts of terrible nightmares about dying. They've been horrible Anthony, truly so. I've been waking without the ability to breath, neck deep in a quagmire of death and nonexistence." She rolled her fingers across the tabletop, raised a dark eyebrow and: "It's something—just how often these dreams have been overwhelming me—that talk of your uncles has me thinking about it again."

"What's frightened you?"

"I don't know—its like, once you've burned down those walls, the house can never be reconstructed—the ultimate safe-house of an assumed personal infinity—once you've torched it, you'll always be out living amongst the elements, shielding your face against one pitiless storm after another, fully marveled by the ever charging cycle of beauty and horror and everything in between." She took a firm sip, set the glass on the edge of the table, looked at me with those profound eyes and: "Once you step outside and start pondering the death of those who were closest, you feel—I feel like a mammoth puzzle on the verge of blasting into unseen particles to be dispersed randomly across the multiverse, trillions of light years apart, all traveling in squiggles and loops, relentlessly outward, at the speed of light. I imagine myself and everybody I've known blowing up and away and into the blackness, and I hope somehow it shall all be blown back together again, the result of some relentlessly erratic, cosmic wind, piecing together the mathematically impossible, chaotic equations of yore—blowing them back perfectly, just the way they were."

"Yeah—if you get stuck thinking about it, topics like that, well, it can be hard on the mind. Trust me, I know—"

"I don't think it can happen." Nobody said anything for awhile, and I finished my drink. Neil's long jam soared high and low and moved my whole body and soul as MD gave off the peculiar sensation you get when you glimpse somebody's face fill with knotted fear as the rationality of questioning personal infinity sinks past blindly assured acceptance and the mind begins to grapple with the plausibility of nothingness—there is a distinct expression of horror that grows with the reflection that all that was is perhaps destined to be naught: I know because I've often looked into the pupils of my insane eyes via their reflection in a polished knife blade at the side of a fire when thinking such things. I took a good long look at her: sitting there, long brown hair falling neat and straight past her eyes, down her shoulders and across her chest—her legs were crossed and a slice of candlelight was striking her face from the side while her blue eyes read whatever her slim hand was writing upon a napkin—I'd always loved her wild, exploring mind, tormented as she was, and I'd missed the entire experience that is her, *abun*dantly.

176

She stayed quiet and my eyes observed the long wayward grain of the table upon which her hands were placed—a culmination of a hundred years growth held this horizontal placement of self—and from what forest did you sprout? Who were the men who fell you, shipped you, cut you, stained and pieced you together all over again? Altogether, history owns me—it's impossible not to see. She swung her dark hair from her blue spheres and: "I'm forever glad I can explain these things to you—how sick I feel at the thought that I'll never conquer my own mortality. A lot of folks can't handle it if someone provides an estimation that shatters their panorama of sanity."

"Any time, darling—that's what I was thinking of you, just a moment ago."

She sat quiet for a moment, breathing easy and: "It's just—it's a tough thought—that maybe we're lone animals on this earth walking round, fluttering down—and maybe the only reason we're so crazy is because humanity is the single species with the mental capacity, consciousness, and cognitive ability to pretend it's not the case—you ever think of that?"

"Yeah, I have a phrase for that: if this whole experience depends on your mind, how can what is, be what is, if what is cannot become what was—you know, post the final quenching of such? When the mind goes, how can any of this come with you?—the thought that maybe it won't, I mean, it's a deep fuckin' sector of reflection—I know a lot of folks who've almost drowned there—including me."

"Say again?"

"How can what *is*, be what *is*, if what *is* cannot become what *was?*"

"Because, well—maybe—not to sound like a little kid, but do you think anyone is out there, you know, listening to us?"

"I can't say—but I'd almost prefer that there was no God, just so I could get a good laugh out of everybody who kills in his name."

"You're not laughing already?"

"Not really—I'm more sitting quiet and still, feeling good and warm when I imagine all of their fundamentalist banter buried quiet beneath black, burned boulders."

"What makes religion difficult to believe for me is that I could picture myself making up similar lies as those that found the basis for most religions for sake of controlling people for my own selfish reasons." She took a drink and: "Ever wonder if you were alive in another form before?"

"Yeah—if so, I kinda think I was a dog, hangin' out with some cool fellas, runnin' 'round, takin' a dip in a lake from time to time, relaxin' n' eatin' all I could."

"Really?—I always thought maybe I was a giraffe."

"I could see that—you're nice, ya always loved salad n' you are long n' lean." She kept writing and: "It's good to see you moving that pen—are you still letting it ride?"

"Yeah, but reading your journal makes me feel I've been skipping out from writing the little in-between details of what is going on in my life, you know, the gritty, day-to-day realities and such—what the people on the L looked like last night and the emotions in their eyes, what I strove t' do today and whether I did it, you know—the general standard of my regular haps n' happiness. See, I've been doing loads of technical writing for my side job, and reading this," she said, holding up my Moleskine, "I feel very much in the mood to write simply for me, like, I'm talkin' real life, the shit that's happenin' every day—the conditions, circumstances and stipulations you and I strive to not stumble upon, and the associated struggle to overcome," she said.

"That's a good way to put it."

"Yeah—it'll feel best to be free to roam and write whatever crosses my mind all of the time, just taking life as it comes—I'm sick of writing and editing law briefs for an irritable attorney."

"Some people can just crank it out, you know? I'm not one of 'em."

"What do you call all this?"

"I call that a mélange of gallimaufry miles away from a readable project, yet still as close as I've ever been—I don't know how these authors do it, the real ones who crank out a book per year, sometimes two, on all sorts of random, intricate topics, no less—I don't have the discipline—all this is mostly leaning back under a tree or having a pint on the stoop or at a bar, and scribbling a couple lines along the way. I can't just write from nine to five—I need to be living crazy fucking experiences and having fun, as currently I am. I'm no pro."

I had a drink, she smiled, ran her thumbs across her eyebrows, inhaled deeply, and as she let it all go, her posture relaxed. "Feel like a martini?—on me?"

"I'm not gonna' say no—God knows if they'll even make 'em here."

We walked up and she ordered two gin martinis, extra dry, and the bartender took great care in pouring them just right. He looked happy to have executed the rare challenge and she left him a nice tip. We walked back to the table, clicked cheers, and she went: "How'd that olive taste?"

"Like the sweet nipple of a beautiful bare breast to have just swam a tepid, salty sea, hard beneath the water."

"Shut up!"

"Ah-ha! There it is!—that beaming, complex smile."

"Yeah yeah, you got me."

"Don't pretend you haven't missed my silly bullshit."

She laughed, slapped her hand on the table, took a small sip and: "That sounds like a cool niche of a place, actually. If it were warm like that, I'd just feel like taking a dip and sitting today—sitting outside in the sun and wind and allowing my mind to overtake itself in random thought and contemplation, getting wet drying off over and over again, yes—I'd be underwater, thinking: I am free and clean after having swam relentlessly in this sea of seas—I shall return to you from which I became—I shall return to this vast empty place without names, yes." She smiled and: "In some ways it's easy to see how a long stretch of dedicated outdoor time would send the subconscious on a wild, productive ride of untold, voluminous rawness—I camped in Glacier for three weeks awhile back."

"Hell yeah. How was it?"

"It was, frankly, beyond words. I'm certain a day shall come when it all comes pouring out of me, but now is not the time." She was quiet for a second and: "Damn Anthony—we have such a great time together. I've missed it."

"Right? Just wait until it gets warm again, it'll be great."

"I think it's supposed to be fifty next week," she said.

"Wow—fifty degrees?—that's a goddamn heat wave!"

"I know—it'll feel like eighty."

The record changed on the juke box and: "The Velvet Underground?"

"'*Heroin*'—good jam for sure." Melissa started to braid her hair into two long strands, grinned and: "My dad used to play this for me when I was a kid—he played loads of music for me, just him and I together in the basement, and something about the experience put me in love with all sorts of random ideas, like going to iffy pubs and ordering high class drinks, deep cuts hummin' in the background, you know, just hanging out alone with the beat and looking at all the weirdos."

"Well, here you are, successful in your endeavor." I set my drink on a coaster and sat back. I thought back to meeting by the Lake—and there she would be, sittin' beneath a copper beech tree, proud and grown with skin like an elephant, lounged and saturated, readin' somethin relevant: 'What's news?' 'I live—I'm alive, independent and free.' 'Ain't many better ways to be.' And never once did I tell you, never once did I say, all the thoughts that went screaming, round and round my brain. She took a drink and I spotted her one, single freckle, located just above and to the left of the nail on her right index finger, and it made me smile. Looking at her, I couldn't help but notice that her stick straight hair was longer than ever—such drifting delightful and carefree on the warm, southern summer breeze—this may be the image I painted most when reflected upon her, and thus I noticed and smiled at its length. I felt an old desire come aglow: to hold her tightly and have her beautifully long and straight brown hair fall delicately about my face in that cozy, welcoming manner it always seemed to—forever.

One of the sales guys playing pool scratched on the eight ball and handed a fee to his opponent. He re-racked, leaning over and exposing designer socks that just screamed success, the whole bit, hung the triangle from a post, dialed his phone and stood in the corner by all the cues—and it made me a little sad, the hopeful smile he made when he got his girl on the line, five beers deep—the way he yelled: "Hun, the new job is incredible!—people already love the product and we're gonna' be rich, baby, we're gonna' make it—I say fuck that Civic, baby, you're gonna' be drivin' a new M3 in fuckin no time, fuckin' no time at all, baby! After a few months I'll have enough saved to move you up here and we'll get a nice place and a sweet HDTV and a garage to park the new car in and it'll be a blast hun, a blast! We'll go out to the nicest places all the time and have more money than we know what to do with!" I don't know exactly why for certain, but I felt sad as hell hearing him yell that shit over the sound of fifteen or twenty people drinking beers—many of them seemingly yelling the same type of hope or dream into phones or across tables, aisles, at the bartender, the doorman—I imagined them all stretched to the financial max for no important reason, where any little adjustment to their earnings would be devastating, and all I could think was that it's all such nonsense, such complete and utter nonsense!

I almost felt like I was going to faint for a second, so I went to the bar to get some water. A lady sitting nearby needed a drink—the tender ignored her and served me first. She seemed to be your standard fifty year old woman with over-dyed, red hair, who smokes Misty 100's while drinking at a bar, alone, at one in the morning on random weekday nights, looking for dick. Are you aware that the world shall soon crush you? Nobody seems to be.

I again sat, handed MD a water of her own and: "That woman at the bar was visibly irritated when he served you first."

"You saw that?"

"Yeah—it was a perfect example of why physical beauty is a short lived form of power—she should have never tried to fool herself."

"Good catch."

"Day after day, incidents like that cause me to feel more and more separation from the general public. Each time I walk or ride through the city I overhear so many snippets of conversations that I gain a sense of the general feel of society and it's all fucking worry, Anthony. I find myself floored by the percentage of individuals frazzled beyond tranquility—

and not temporarily beyond, but permanently so: it's all worry, hurry, entitlement and pointless little power surges. Very few take the necessary and beautiful time to *breathe*. It's like, breathing is great, man, so take a moment to do so, because a day is gonna' come when you'll be all dried up. It's like, rule number one, don't sweat the small stuff, rule number two, nearly everything is the small stuff, ya know?"

"Like I said—fuck that Civic, baby, *fu*ck that Civic!" the man yelled, "It's gonna' be a cakewalk—now that I've mastered the front of pretending to care, the rest is easy."

I leaned close to her and: "Ever see all your words as a faint breeze with no succinct meaning?"

"Yeah—it's called dying," she said. I took a drink and that pervert-looking, broken cat along the wall disappeared out the door and some other, equally corrupted oddity took his place. Melissa took a long sip of her Martini, nearly finishing it, licked her lips and: "What do you really want to do in the end?"

"I think I've decided that all I want in life is to be in love, ride my bike, and drink good coffee."

"And climb mountains and such."

"Yeah."

"And race down them."

"Yep."

"And roam with pens and paper and a camera and whatnot, eating mostly breads and grains and fresh, local foods, while meeting people and drinking beers and sometimes being super quiet for huge stretches of time while getting high and having really raw sex."

"Yeah, all that stuff occurring at mostly the same time is all I need—you know me well."

"Any back up plan?"

"To live in the woods most of the time, saying little."

"Then you'll begin to speak the words of a man who spent too much time alone."

"Fine with me—I'd rather go crazy in a solitary stupor than get worn out by nonstop claptrap."

"You can greet that routine cheap as hell if you escape the craving for false necessities."

"Exactly, Melissa—just eliminate all that is unnecessary, all the insincere upgrades, just buy one thing once, one quality object at a reasonable price, something with lines that will always suit your style, your comfort zone, one that fucking suits its purpose and wastes nothing, and that's it, you have it, you possess it, there is no need for more, no need to clutter, no nee—"

"Imagine the faces people must make when dying from indebted stress at an unexpected age after having placed such an emphasis upon th*ing*s. It must be horrifying, Anthony—it must be sick. My question is why do so many prefer clutter to clean, open space? Space you could fill with your body at any time you wish."

"You think that's what most prefer?"

"I do—it's like when you walk into somebody's place and they're like, 'O, sorry if it feels crowded in here, I'm looking for a bigger place right now, actually—I need to get a bigger pad,' and you're like, um, no, what you need to do is stop purchasing such a large sum of crackpot bullshit, that's what you need—you represent just another consumption orientated lifestyle, just—"

"Trading your time for every new, flashy item available," I said.

"Yep."

"Your greatest resource."

"Yep."

"The undeniable foundation of all you shall ever come to create."

"Yep."

"For a certain amount of dollars per hour."

"Yep."

"I say get fucked."

"Forever and ever."

"Yep."

"Because to then in turn work more and more hours at a place you loathe to repay the debts of the unnecessary as interest accumulates at an exponential rate—to do that is suicide for the soul." I took a drink and: "I know it's not easy, Ms. D, but you have to promise me you'll stay strong and enjoy your life—you won't be seeing another one—your story is that you were, and, ultimately, that you will not be—forever doesn't last, you'll see. So don't ever go weak."

"Agreed." We clicked glasses, tipped our drinks and: "I'm feeling rather relaxed right now," she said.

"As rightfully you should be."

"Want to get the fuck out of here and breathe the air?"

"Absolutely." I stood and: "Wait—I can't find me hat."

"It's in yer hood."

"Good eye, Ms. D., good eye." I pulled the wool over my crazy hair, finished my drink and bundled up. I felt warm for the first time in a good while—no tingling in my fingers or feet. "Damn—you know, I never explained any of that shit to anyone before?"

"Nor have I."

"Thanks for hearing me out—today was the end of a long, twisted road. Thank God I ran into you."

Melissa winked, wrote something on the front cover of my sketchbook, handed it back to me, set her pouch on the table, and: "Anytime, man—so are you game to split this delicacy?—it's not much, just a little boost, you know?" My eyes met the wood grain below the purple cloth and I imagined the future: years of growth rushing in a river of immortal connectedness—immeasurable in its depth and emancipation—blast into pieces and set yourself free, boy, explode and go and go—a silent nod saw her slip a soft bit of this and that into my hand and I gobbled the full sum straight off, and washed it all down with a big drink of cool water. I took a deep breath, rubbed my face, looked up and exhaled with that wild anticipatory feeling of sitting back with friends, eagerly aware of the action's impending consequence. "There's no turning back now."

"Nope."

"Let's go."

34

We stepped out and I immediately shivered as super cooled water dripping from an icicle no thicker than a strand of hair hit my neck and rolled between my shoulder blades. I popped my hood, looked to the sky and the sight of snow coated limbs twisting toward the fading sun was comforting—every single thing depending on that same, finite energy seemed to erase any sense of privilege over other organisms. I took a big breath and exhaled at the blue sky above—and damn man, *damn* it was fucking blue at that moment—that top-of-the-mountain, high altitude blue that gets you feeling that no matter what happens, things will somehow manage to be alright in the end. "I can't wait until those Redmond Lindens flower sweet in the humid summer shade."

"Right?" She sniffed at the air and the quixotic look of her face made me laugh. "The earth smells so sterile right now. I need spring to set me free with waves of green as the city goes exploding with vibrant and crazy people—I need that bloom to remind of how little seeds have within them the entire history of their species—how it's been that way for a million years before me, and how it'll remain so long after we're gone."

We walked a thin trodden path east toward Winchester, cut south, and dipped into the alley. I reached in my bag, opened the case to my glasses and: "Smoke one?'

"Surely." I sparked a light, fought the wind, and the sound of a helicopter whorled overhead. "Is that the Ghetto Bird?"

"Does it say CPD on the bottom, in Old English lettering?"

"Yeah."

"Tis then," I said, pulling my head out of my shirt after finally getting it lit—"Makes me want to listen to Black Sabbath in a way, and really get into it."

"Is it around here often?"

"Only after serious crimes—but it also seems to fly loops around the West Side after school gets out—I think they implemented the policy after that kid got beat to death with a golf club and a few others were shot a couple weeks back—what time is it?"

"Not quite four."

"Yeah, that's probably why then."

"It feels like we're in a war zone."

"We are. There've been nearly as many violent fatalities in this city since 03' as there were in Iraq and Afghanistan combined—fathom that. If you don't call this a war zone, I don't know what is." She took a puff, and her face looked pale. "You alright?"

She exhaled white and: "I can never quite get used to it—the fact I'll have to end—like all the thousands of people who've ended in these streets."

"You're not going to end like that, Ms. D., trust me."

"What will be, will be—these people kill one another over which way the bill of some tacky haberdashery is tilted."

"Life is cheap in the eyes of some."

"You mean most?"

"I 'spose its close."

A businessman with the face of an explosive little league coach passed the end of the alley, and yelled: "How do you have ten list hit twos, and no list hit ones? There's no excuse!" He snapped closed his phone, stubbed his toe into the curb and took a hard spill.

I held my laughter, MD looked at me and: "I keep overhearing these conversations that seem to deal with supposedly immense, complex problems that in the end will most certainly wind up as non-entities."

"The day he screams to the point of bleeding out the ears, he'll realize something went wrong a long way back, and then it'll be time to die." He walked off and I noticed something on the ground where he'd fallen. I walked over, scored a twenty he must have dropped and showed Melissa. He returned a moment later, looked around for a second and stormed off more frustrated than before. "You're a good girl, man, you understand how to be in cahoots with somebody—how to keep a secret—most the world is a bunch a' snitches." She didn't respond and: "Do you think it was immoral not to give it back to him?"

"No—it's part of the game, part of the fun. If it were a thousand bucks it would be different."

"I know—we'd be on our way to the casino."

An old scrapper worked his way east, gaping manically for any substance of worth as he came upon our position. He was pushing a tin brimmed handcart through piles of snow when Melissa took the twenty and gave it to him. His face glowed with appreciation, and I took a drag and leaned back, northeast wind charging hard and blowing the embers of the cherry bright red as faint white exited like the effluence of a smokestack. He gave me a funny look and: "You can have some, sir, if you like."

"Nah, I better not—I'll get too cole." He dug in another bin, crushed a couple cans, added them to the haul and: "Sometimes, after a big snow like dis, you can hit a real homerun inna blue bins 'roun here—plows make big driffs n' trucks can't make it inna alleys—lotta' tin piles up right quick." He peeked in the next set of bins, looked back and: "I wouldn't loiter 'roun here wit tha fo too long—tha's when 'em slick boys show up inna unmarked whip n' bus yo ass."

"Good advice, sir, I appreciate it." He nodded and then used what appeared to be every muscle fiber in his angled, emaciated carcass to shove his cart directly into the throes of the torrid wind, hands and upper appendages sucked tightly through his sleeves—an outline of ten bony apexes clutched the handle from somewhere near the core of his storm coat-covered torso. His sleeves slapped around him like a dog-eared mountaintop flag snaps around its meek, skeletal flagpole—such reminded me of the American flag stationed atop Peak One in Ten Mile Range after bearing the brunt of countless Arctic orientated storms in a long, malicious winter. The heatless light of the fading sun shone upon his windswept, crease-lined face—but ay—with elongated eye contact, his communicative expression seemed to say—tis just another day, and fucked as it may, this be my only way. Wheels got jammed in a rut and he readjusted, breathed deeply, tilted forward, mined an exhausted sort of energy from somewhere deep within, and his soiled sock heels went slipping out of thin-soled shoes with the extolled effort exuded in a crack at manufacturing renewed momentum, and living another day.

"You think he's right? You think we should leave with that?"

"Nah, he's accustomed to getting profiled—we'll be fine." The iron bars over the windows on the building next door were worn by age but still forbidding. I wondered how many times throughout the years they'd succeeded in keeping random creeps on the outside, and if they'd ever failed. I hoped the family who resided there had many weapons and well thought out plans on how to protect their wellbeing. I passed the handcraft to Melissa and she took a drag, closed her eyes, and exhaled white. Taking a moment to breathe, my eyes shifted skyward and were thereby enveloped by a pallid blue reflection and polychromatic sunlight.

"Sure is blue right now."

"I was just thinking that," I said.

"If Mother Nature could speak with mankind I think she'd say: I'd be so beautiful, without you—and I would have to agree."

"Either way, lucky are you and lucky am I, spinnin' 'round this clear, crisp blue sky." She made a pass, I took a drag and: "Sometimes it is hard to fathom how everything has come to be just so—in saying sometimes I mean always, of course."

"Which is why all you can do is live." A middle-aged bum with a cane limped southward on Winchester, old haversack thrown over his back curving his torso trickily askew. Melissa's foot crunched onto a fresh paw print in the snow and she said: "Chicago is so beautiful right now. Want to walk around for awhile?"

"Hell yes."

We slipped onward and: "Are those the same boots from five years ago?"

"Yep, they're finally worn in."

"Took long enough."

"It's a good feeling, like wearing in a groove on the space bar of a typewriter or the sight of marble steps rounded off at the edge and no longer sharp for sake of paces compiled, one by one, into the hundreds of millions, like the main staircase in Union Station."

"Walking on the soft snow like this reminds me of how we'd walk down that little path to the beach, sand of the early morning cool beneath our feet." She took a breath and: "Say, can I hold your hand?"

"Of course you can," I said, extracting it from within my sleeve, extending it toward that of her own.

"Cool—just wanted to make sure I still had the option."

I smacked her on the shoulder and: "Nicely done."

"Come here," She entwined her gloved fingers with my own and squashed the ten of them deep within her coat pocket.

She kicked through a puff of snow and I said: "Ever find out if you're anemic?"

"I'm not anemic."

"You have icicles for fingers when it's eighty degrees."

"You should thank me—I'll start charging a cooling tax if you don't watch it."

"Spoken like a true Chicagoan—you should run for City Council."

Her drag came out her nose and: "I need it to suppress my—"

"Whooping cough?"

She got it all out with a steaming exhale and: "Spies never have a cough, never need to sneeze, none of that."

"That's why they are spies, dear."

We went back and forth a few more and she finished the handcraft with a casual drag, extinguished it in the snow, threw it in a trash bin and: "Thanks, that was," she gave the thumbs up with her opposite hand, "Totally cool."

"Sure thing—want to walk west?"

"Alright—don't be shocked if that gets me in a goofy mood, though."

"O? You've come to the right place—moohahhahhehehaugh!"

"You're crazy!" she said.

"Nah, it ain't true—doc says I'm fine."

"I wouldn't trust that quack—you need to catch a second opinion."

I laughed and: "Whudaya feel like doing?"

"Wanna have a contest on who can fit the most pieces of gum in their mouth?"

184

"Depends who buys the gum."

We walked to Damen and cut north to a Mart on Evergreen—besides being tagged with a blood red *187*, the store front impelled you to by cigarettes, phone cards, Lottery tickets and paper towels. Taped inside the door was a printed image of some guy who'd recently robbed the joint. Whoever it was had done a plum rotten job of obscuring his face—there he was, in plain view, a little white dude with a shaved head, pointing a gun and eating a lollypop. We entered, grabbed a pack of gum, and got in line—the little girl at the register addressed her father: "Look at the cow on my carton of chocolate milk, daddy! Doesn't she look cute?"

"That's nice, honey."

"What happens when a cow runs out of milk, daddy?"

"When dairy cows' production declines, honey, most are slaughtered, and their skin is fashioned into leather. Then, hides of their calves, the baby cows, the boys—they're frequently force fed an extremely high fat diet and subsequently slaughtered for veal, and then their skin is transformed into especially high-priced calfskin products, like your mommy's brown boots."

"*Ew!* Is that true, daddy?"

"Yep."

"Even the ones that make chocolate milk?"

"Even those, little lady."

They exited and the radio of the cop ahead of us cracked to life with: "Hey, let 'em know I'm comin out the back, okay, so they don't shoot me."

"Units, 1410 is coming out the back. Again, units involved in the mission on 18th street, 1410 is about to come out the back. Do not engage." I thought: if I were a cop, I'd have some serious conflictions, man—to put your life on the line every waking moment for people you can't stand, like they do, is damn valiant. A lot of cops are bastards, but a lot of them are damn alright, too. It's just like anything else, I guess, fucking teachers, auto repair shops, heaven and hell—

He split and Melissa asked the Paki: "Say, do you sell Animal Crackers?"

"No, just Elf Cracker."

"Forget it then." I paid, we split back into the sun and she threw me a couple sticks. I snapped off my first bubble and we walked back to Thomas and cut west across Damen. A real strange bird walked past and Melissa said, "There is something remarkably unwholesome about a thick boned, six foot five, unshaven man reeking of tequila, walking around in an Easter Bunny costume on a random afternoon for no particular reason."

"You never know what's on the mind of those passing in the shuffling madness—only thing you can do is embrace the chaos and carry along."

Doing so, a pregnant woman walked past and Melissa yelled: "Congratulations!"

"Thanks! Thanks a lot!"

We paced on for a bit and: "You didn't know her, right?"

"Nope."

"Just making certain," I said, "That was cool of you."

"That's the way it has to be, man!—I just hope she wanted it, right?"

"She seemed like she did," I said, 'Don'tcha think?"

"Yeah, she was excited—the way she was holding her belly was very nurturing."

185

We leapt over a big drift on the sidewalk and: "It's great to see a beautifully cool woman expectant—you can only assume the world shall somehow be enhanced."

"It's true—I can't even be*gin* to imagine what kind of thoughts will be racing 'round my head when I set out for a long Sunday stroll with a b*a*by in my body—in *my* body, a b*a*by. How crazy!"

"I know, right?" And suddenly I felt a longing to have children and see myself live on—to see my father and grandfather and his father before him become reborn in the form of a child of my production—how truly insane!

"I imagine breastfeeding in a rocking chair, warm beside a fire, snow slipping from the sky in silence, mind and soul stretching far beyond my current comprehension of calm amazement."

"I'm sure!—it's crazy to think, like, bam: there they are, a fresh new person, created, seemingly, out of nothing, and ready to take it all in—nature is utterly mind-blowing," I said.

A couple squirrels hissed at one another from opposing trees and: "But imagine what it would feel like to have a child who's a complete bastard—like if your son or daughter turned out to be a dirty rotten scoundrel of a person—how disheartening it would be! If such became the case, I'd have to feel that in some way or shape, I'd failed."

"Right?"

"I mean, Gasey had parents," she said.

"They must have been awkward as hell."

"Or as a less extreme example: imagine how disheartening it must be for a parent to have their daughter desiring, 'I wanna be like that dumb bitch,' seeking to model their persona according to the latest, assembly line-manufactured, pop culture icon of no substance or worth." She shook her head and: "I'd be beside myself."

"If that happened, I'd drop everything and send her far up into the mountains right away, to get a real take on things. Make her live like Pocahontas and eat maze all day—then we'd see how many twenty year old guys were texting her about gettin jiggy on her pink iPhone."

"You better pray you have sons."

"No shit—whoever they are, my children, if luck be on my side and I happen to have some healthy ones—those kids are going to live a wild existence, man, truly fucking wild and unordinary—exposed to the wilderness and all sorts of literature and minds of all types, flanked by dozens of crazy uncles and never shielded from the world and its cold realities—made aware of the power of creation and witness to thousands of moments that hold the capability of sweeping their breath away—Lord how I hope—we'll go camping and climbing and skiing, all the time thinking and seeing and dreaming—should that day come I'll be a glad, glad man.

We crossed Damen, passed an old man and his wife, hand in hand, walking east, and in the distance church bells were ringing. "Want to walk on the sunny side of the street?"

"Surely." We slogged across a snowy lawn to the north side of Thomas and, flooded in sunlight, we continued west. A man wearing a winter cap with ear flaps who'd just shoveled his stoop sat upon the steps, smoking a pipe and sipping a drink—he was a dependable presence in the neighborhood that makes you feel glad, like the little old ladies who always do their best in keeping their little yards crisp and nice, their gangways non-slippery and shoveled. He blew a long white stream of smoke into the sun, met my eyes and: "Afternoon, sir."

"Good day," it came back, in a thick eastern European accent—he had the hands of a sturdy working man and the bright, aware eyes of a reflective soul satisfied with life. We continued along, and from across the street, the sound of scraping shovels emanated as several homeowners tidied their comfortable bungalows just right.

"They're really getting after it, aren't they?"

"Because that crazy old guy'll probably assassinate 'em if they don't shovel."

She smacked her glove in her palm and: "That's why you need silent, strong types like him to help keep things in the neighborhood straightened out."

"Very true."

She smiled and said: "Chicago always comes together and works as one after a big winter storm—it's a beautiful thing."

"Right?"

"The real spirit of the people shines through as folks dig out and carry on—total strangers go all in for each other, shovel-wielding loners spend all day walking and digging, walking and digging—people's entire measurement of self-health is arbitrated by how they felt while: 'Diggin' out from the big one last year.' It's a birthright."

"And part of the reason I feel that if Chicago fought Los Angeles, LA would get knocked stone cold."

We continued west and an oft observed, raw, shaved-headed European dude driving his personal backhoe seemed to be embarking upon yet another unpaid madman project that would make life easier for people in the neighborhood. It was good, this project, all of his others—they seem to keep him busy and at least part way separated from what seems to be his natural destiny of killing ignorant and inadequate people in as malicious a nature as he could possibly conjure. We passed, he nodded his head, I waved hello and then glanced at the old mansion on the SW corner of Hoyne and Thomas—an old coal chute on the side of the building was welded shut and: "Can't you just imagine, big burly guys at the turn of the century, dirty as hell on a beautiful white winter afternoon such as this, horse carriage parked on the side of street as they delivered a load of coal to whatever baron lived there at the time?"

"And just think—they're all gone now, no longer thriving in the space between nothingness and eternity."

"I know—it is so fucking weird."

The air smelt like burnt wood and: "It's gonna' be a good night to have a fire."

"I'd love to just chill by the flames and dig the catalytic compassion."

"Hell yeah, that's the dream—to sit back in a rocking chair, music charging, surrounded by raw images captured by my own eye and drenched in moderate fulfillment of my favorite vices as the fire burns on."

"When's the last time you went camping."

"Fairly recently."

"Last fall?"

"A little after."

"Where'd you go?"

"West of here."

"Rockies?"

"Not quite." We approached the alley and halted at the triple toot of a horn. A loaded-full, banged-up pick up truck with vertical wooden extensions of its bed made us ware of an impending presence, crept past the building, swung east and thumped up the street—it was driven by the same individual that I have seen parking that truck in alleyways across from gangways in all sorts of ways for fucking years—parking as abruptly as possible and tumbling out the red-rust door in worn boots while sharing a cig with whomever the passenger may be—usually one of two or three fellow Latinos with whom he is always riding and exploring and discovering second or third or fourth hand treasures and piling them tactfully into the beaten bed—climbing out the cab with the wide-eyed awareness of explorers of old, explorers who, in habit, as is the habitual nature of man as an animal, seize or capture what already was and claim it new—not only new, but completely their own—and with a half-broken Winston passed from mouth to mouth, lip to lip, inhale, exhale, mad camaraderie between these gruff Latino males—the truck tumbled on, jolly and free and bursting with the sound of horns and strings and up-tempo, lasso-throwing harmonies galore. "Shit like that helps me relax," I said.

"In what way?"

"Just seeing random grinders havin' a good time doin' whatever, you know? You can sense they've been tellin' jokes all day, n' makin it fun—know what I mean?"

"Yeah," she said, long braids framing her face, "I guess you have to do what it takes to secure a waking moment that does not involve shared space, shared interaction, or shared congestion—it's hard to break free from all binding powers of shared human contact." She pulled her hat tighter and: "Walking neighborhoods like this after a fresh snow puts me at peace and in the mood to live in a place with a yard, Anthony—a little comfy yard for me and my family friends—a spot with a big old tree or two and room to run around and fuck about and be left alone—give me that and I'll die in peace, for sure."

A shadowed man limping up the tire rut in the snowy street was bouncing an old, beat up league ball to himself—he grunted with each wind up and swore a little after the release—he had to throw it quite aggressively in order to produce the necessary rebound, and as he passed, I looked into the light and pictured an enormous hand engulfing the earth, winding up, and hurling us as a split seam fastball, east versus west, straight into the deafening sound of the sun. I closed my eyes and thought: why is it so easy for me to see what will be when the world is stricken from the record?

Walking up the stairs of a nice little crib just shy of Leavitt I overheard an old mailman give advice to a young apprentice: "See now, ya have t' remember now—A to Z is gonna' be key—it'll bring ya excitement when unlockin' a multi-resident mailbox—you know, when you got tha key, man, at the end of a long, gold chain—ya got the power n' ya release that whole side—fill all those slots wit all that mail, man, one by one, n' ya leave it right there, just waiting to be opened—tha's something, man, that kind of anticipation."

"If you say so, Rick."

"You get that A to Z stuff down pat, own a comfortable set of shoes for every type a' weather n' keep a sense for which dogs are kind n' which are killers, n' you'll be set fer a good long run a' this shit." We turned south on Leavitt and across the street a thin woman without eyebrows who looked to be stricken with cancer paced outside of the live-in hospice of a hospital. She was really soaking it in, man, the beauty of the day, eyes alert and yearning to stay—we shared a little smile across the tracked asphalt and I felt sad as hell for her—the way her body was eating itself and slowly fading away was painful to observe.

"I hope she lives forever," Melissa whispered.

"Me too."

"Life is crazy—everything matters, and then you die."

"The process is relative for all that is—we all use ourselves up and turn t' dust."

We continued on and passed a guy out by the church, smokin' a cig, leavin a message that went: "Ay brother, uh, sorry I missed ya man, but thanks for the call—I don't know, hit me up when you can—everything's doin' good, shorty's adorable, cute, mother's restin', n' unfortunately, I just figured out I came down with a cold this morning, so I can't even hold 'em, but anyway, I'll talk to ya, hope you're doin' good—I can't believe we fuckin' did it, man, but we did! Later."

"And from the end, the beginning begins," MD said, "That's cool to hear."

"Yeah, it is," I said, "This is a weird spot—I often walk past and this is where the ambulance drivers and nurses come to smoke. There's no smoking on hospital grounds, so you see these guys who've just dropped a body, and then they come here by the church and shoot the breeze like they just got done mowing the lawn or something."

"Maybe that's what it's like for them—maybe it helps them cope."

"I'd never have the stomach for it—I'd be stuck after hours on that whole person's life, all they fuckin' dreamt of, n' the deep horrible sorrow of falling short." A screaming ambulance from west on Division swung south on Leavitt and lunged into the lot. It was escorted by a cop and after a three point turn, the paramedics swooped a dude on a gurney into the building, and the officer followed. "Probably got gatted, huh?"

"You think?"

"Maybe—cop's there to take his statement as a victim, or take him in after he's fixed. Looks like it'll be awhile, with all those IVs dripping in."

We continued north across Division, Melissa making fresh long strides, her face catching the light just right, and as we passed some government housing that included frozen sneakers swaying from the phone lines, a tubby ruffian addressed three random scragglers with: "I'm serious now—I got a bad feeling about t'night, man—if we fuck dis up we gonna' be in a real fix, boy, n' I ain't finna get cut down cuz a' yo mistake."

He flung a whole bag of Mac Donald's wrappers into the street and out of earshot, Melissa said: "How do you *not* pick that up, like, as a human being?"

"Generational ignorance."

"I wonder what they're planning."

"Maybe it's a surprise party—you come home, turn the lights on, one guy points a muzzle in your eye, and the other three yell 'Surprise!'—and then you fork over all your best shit n' get pistol whipped."

"You think?"

"It's not unlikely—I almost got jacked this morning, in fact, I almost forgot." I rehashed the story and: "It's unbelievable to think of how violent people are—and what's worst is the violence is most often directed toward people who have done little or nothing to provoke the aggression."

"Yeah—I, I know."

She got to looking pale again and: "What's wrong?"

"No, it's nothing, I'm fine."

I heard snow crunch, turned back and noticed that two of those guys were trailing us, a quarter block behind. I paid slight mind, and carrying on, the dead fingers of a tree tapped against a no parking sign as the wind whistled through the other side, between the metal sheet and pole, and the pitch forced out sounded like the scream of a woman in severe duress. We passed an old elementary school built to stand more resilient than military nerve centers of many countries, with massive limestone pillars gleaming white in the sun, and further on, electric buzzing shot from a window of a garden apartment. "That's a cool peace sign," Melissa said.

"Yeah, but it's foolish to put that up."

"Why's that?"

"It leads to the assumption that they don't have a loaded shotgun under the bed, or a revolver in the nightstand, like all the smart old timers around here."

"That's a sad way to think."

"Maybe so, but it's true—anyone who puts an electric peace sign in the window of a garden apartment over here is asking to get jacked. They just moved in a couple weeks ago—I noticed from a vantage point nearby."

"They probably have little of value beside oils and incense—why bother?"

"They'll take the sign then—take and sell it to a different hippie—these fools will take anything that isn't bolted down—like that new restaurant on the west side of Western, for instance—a crew went through the front window and made off with the entire safe within one week of its opening—one week! They thought they'd be hip and not put bars on the windows—bad idea."

"I thought it was up-and-coming over here."

"This neighborhood has been up and coming for a hundred years—tis far better than it was, but you shouldn't go around putting peace signs in the window unless you're baiting people you'd like to kill."

"How was it worse?"

"You couldn't go to Wicker Park and hang out for God's sake. When my pop was a kid, man—he and his brothers and mates got chased around here with baseball bats, fuckin' chains, huge gangs of guys going after them for nary a reason. They held down the corner of Hoyne and Augusta. After Frankie got retarded he wanted my pop to wear his leather coat, his best possession, right, and almost immediately, some Latin Kings tried to jump him for it over on Iowa and Damen—it was three on one, and after these fucks pulled the hockey maneuver and were wailing on him, my pop heard 'em say, 'Les take his fuckin' coat, mang,'—he knew he'd die before he gave up Frankie's coat, so he cracked one of them in the balls, took off, and another guy started shooting at him—cat missed, and so I exist. He worked hard to make certain I'd have a nice, secure childhood, and got us out of here, but when I was a kid, I spent a heap of time at my Gramps' place in the summers—my ma's pop—he delivered soda and spritzer to all the pubs around here for this joint Polonia Bottling Works, and it was plain nuts, man. He knew all the maniacs who hung in all the little clubs on Western, the little European joints where they don't even let you in without a fuckin' password—he'd buy 'em all a round n' they'd unload the shit for him, and he'd sit back n' have a beer n' shoot the breeze with crazy owners who went by names like 'Mumbles' n' shit. He took me along once in awhile, and one time I got real scared when some Puerto Ricans stood in front of the truck and refused to move—they were screaming at him, saying they were gonna' beat him down, callin' 'em a pussy old man n' shit. He reached under the seat and said, 'Don't worry, Anthony, they make more than beer in Belgium—I'd never let anyone monkey witchu,' and he pulled out this little .25 Browning semi automatic with a pearl handle and gold trigger, and convinced 'em to move. It was very comforting, knowing a big strong guy who loved you was looking out for you, and that he would never let anything happen, ever—you know? When I rode with him, he never put the windows down, even when it was hot as hell, in case a vato loco tried to throw a brick or bottle at us for no reason."

"If you mentioned some shit like that in a campaign, you'd be disqualified."

"Right?—it was a valid concern, it really was—still is—Gramps would drive to this little discount joint west on Augusta for all kinds of random shit, near Humboldt Park, and we'd roll up there in his big blue Lincoln, you know, in the middle of summer, and these people looked at us like they were ready to rip our heads off—but he was never scared."

"So because of all that, these people shouldn't have a peace sign?"

"No, they shouldn't—they should be more ambiguous—adorn the façade with minimal ornamentation alongside a tidy wariness that suggests if anyone sneaks in there, they'll soon be laid to rest."

"That's a weird way to think."

"That's the way everyone in our family has always thought—my great grandfather was a part of the Czar's army, and after he escaped the revolution, he was so scared the Communists were going to come after and murder him that he slept with a .45 at his side until the day he died."

"How'd he die?"

"He got shot dead."

"By the Communists?"

"No, in the street—a single blast, right through the head—over on North and Clybourn, outside some place called the Barrel House."

"Really?"

"Yep—story went that somebody knew he'd cashed his Social Security check, and he let his guard down for a second, and that was it—poof, gone—so it's inherent, that way of thinking—in all my mates, as well—we all think alike: continued perseverance is to be treated as the highest sanctity—disallowing people to fuck with that involves many subtleties. You must always be thinking the thoughts of the enemy."

"You have many enemies?"

"Everyone is my enemy, until they prove otherwise."

"That sounds like an exhausting mindset to maintain."

"It actually keeps me pretty fresh." We walked on and dormant brown ivy strangled stone buildings, awaiting another summer and the chance to strengthen its grip. Wind hissed through the dead fingers of brown bushes and: "How'd you feel last fall, as the cold wiped the color from the earth and turned everything into a grey mash?"

"I felt better than I do during most falls—I was ready for that summer to die."

We approached Pierce and outside an intermediate care Manor, squirrels fought high in an old oak tree. An excited dog sat below, refusing to follow his owner, mouth salivating, attentive ears listening to the whistling wind and inter-rodent bickering as his eyes watched impatiently for a stroke of bad luck. A little black boy walking past with a Spiderman backpack smiled huge and went: "Look ma!—tha looks like the dog from the dang commercial! He waitin' for one of 'em t' tumble down so he ken eat 'em!" He seemed like a happy little kid and his ma had a great smile and so they got me feelin' glad.

"Could you imagine if, when you saw someone broke, some mother and her kid like that, who are obviously struggling from a financial standpoint—could you imagine if you had the means to be like: 'Here, I want you to use this for whatever you need, and I hope you have a great afternoon.' I wish that could be my profession. I need to make it so. The only problem is coming up with enough loot to give lots away and still survive. I have to think of something." We cut east on Pierce, passed a series of fine crafted buildings on the north side of the street, and I said: "Whoever tags '*Forgive*' all over this neighborhood must feel guilty as fuck about something or other. I wonder who it is and what they've done."

"Maybe it's JC."

"Can't be—rule states Jesus' penmanship would have to be faultless—this tagger doesn't loop the G properly."

She snickered and we passed several beautiful mansions where all the beer barons lived during prohibition, turned back south on Hoyne and: "I love the way everything feels so fresh right now—I wish I had my camera."

"I have one—want to snap it?"

The Blue Line rumbled toward O'Hare and: "Love to." I passed it and: "This is nice—new purchase?" I nodded, we walked along, and: "This is an artsy neighborhood."

"Meaning there are a handful of artists and hundreds of additional kids whose mommies and daddies pay their rent so they can play artist?"

"Yeah, that's true—but I meant it more in terms of how all these buildings were constructed."

The corners of a black iron fence protecting the passing property spun into intricate globes and: "You're absolutely right—every last detail of these buildings possesses artistic intent. They didn't erect thin sheets of Chinese drywall and try to gouge you for half a million dollars, like these new, so-called de*velo*pers—everyone who worked on them were specialists—they were built to be unique, and to last. It's impossible to walk these old streets and not feel like man has devolved."

"Their size and originality is insane."

"It'd be pointless for me to own one. I'd wind up sitting on the porch the entire time." We went to cross Le Moyne and a guy chatting into a Bluetooth driving a green Acura rolled the stop sign, nearly trimming my toes. I gave him a look like: yo, relax pal, and he flipped me the bird.

"What a prick."

"Probably just spent fifty stacks on a degree in visual communication." He floored it east like a big man and we continued to stroll. "Observing a four way stop for a minute helps ya realize the sequence is compromised half the time by they who cheat. It's a good metaphor for the world—holds a certain element of accuracy, MD, it really does."

"Well, as was proven long ago, nature forbids man the irrational. Eventually the irrational perish—that is nature's undeniable law. His day'll come," she said.

"Think he'll get what he deserves?"

"Everyone does."

"Not quite, Melissa—not even close, actually."

A non-efficient human being took six moves to get a rusty bucket out of an adjacent parking space when all they really needed was three and MD tried to focus the lens toward the sky. "I can't seem to get this right."

"It's cool, be confident—trust your eye. If you write like you take photos and take photos like you write, you'll be all good."

I shut my eyes with the click of the camera, and the sound of the shutter set me back in a cove and observing the impetus of my bliss beneath the blue skies of a hot July afternoon—she was looking through her lens and our blue/green lake was warbling in the background, bowing elegant to the city that I love—I looked at the people as she snapped away, and you know how it is: everybody has their own little spot on the Lakefront that is th*eirs*—the spot they seek to escape or embrace the thoughts in their brain: "I can't stop thinking of hanging on the warm, sunny shore. It's been forever."

"It'll be here soon, Anthony, we'll make it—soon we'll be on our bikes on a nice humid ride along the Lake on a clear spring day, set alight beneath bursting spring trees, listening to Zeppelin screams—" She again snapped: tiny pyramids of white atop red hanging spheres—the Crabapple tree on the west side of Hoyne bowed under immaculate weight.

I heard snow crunch, turned back and noticed those two cats from Leavitt were still pursuing. We'd walked nearly eight city blocks since passing their spot, a full mile, and the one—wearing a red coat, red Nikes and a red Phillies cap twisted left—he cast a hard stare in an attempt to intimate my glance. The fact that they'd followed us for so long was worth noticing. "Hey, put the camera down," I whispered, "Those two dudes from Leavitt n' Crystal are still creepin'—walk on my inside shoulder and move a little faster. If they try n' front just take off running toward that brownstone adjacent to the alley and I'll fight 'em to the death, okay? They'll have to kill me for this bag—I'm not giving it up alive."

"What if they have a gun?"

"Run faster." Her face turned anxious and as we approached Schiller I went: "Don't you carry a knife or anything?" She pulled a blue Precise V5 from her pocket and removed the cap. "Indeed the pen *is* mightier than the sword."

"Or at least damn irritable if situated in a vulnerable position and thrust violently inward."

"They should start placing that advertisement on the box—is that all you got?"

She nodded and I reached into my pack, showed her my specialty, handed her an extra knife I carry, and said, "Don't worry, follow me." We turned east and I slipped the hammer up my sleeve. We walked a handful of meters, stopped under a bent oak tree strangled with dormant ivy, faced where they'd be coming from and, as they passed a set of bushes and approached the sidewalk, I stood in front of Melissa, tapped the hammerhead through my sleeve against a weathered copper fence protecting a huge abandoned manor, and stared. They slowed, glared, and turned back north to where they had come from. We stood for a moment, and my heart was pounding hard—I could feel the hot blood racing 'round my veins and I thought it no surprise at how red dotted patterns paint the walls at such great distance at crime scenes involving sharp blades—the heart is a hellova pump. I took a long, deep breath, grabbed her hand and: "When you're walking around in this world of hunters and prey, you might as well be a hunter, or at least damn ready to play that game. Being alive, quite technically, is all you have, hence the reason those who try to embezzle your entire life force should make the acquaintance of many gruesome follies. You have to let 'em suspect that perhaps you're an ace predator in your own right to help 'em move along."

"Why'd you tap the hammer like that?"

"So they knew I had a metal object in my hand without seeing what it was—I look just odd enough for them to be unable to assume the object is not the muzzle of a gun, see? Having a crazy face that insinuates a conscience independent of care for repercussion allows for a longer life—these people rove on the look for the fattest or kindest sheep to slaughter, and then they do so—that's the game. This city is festooned with fools who prey on presumably weak targets, like people who travel alone or those who are small in stature—or women, of course. That's why you either need to move in packs, or be a lone wolf—make it seem like you're part of the same game—make their head inquire thrice if you're worth it. Lions don't eat lions, if they can help it."

"Yeah, but how many people walk around with modified hammers hidden up their sleeve?"

"Not enough, not nearly," she smiled and "Well, kiddo, whudaya say we take a seat?"

"Sounds good to me." We continued east, past an elementary school that had recently seen a woman raped in the playground on her way to the Blue Line, and I laughed aloud at the thought of knocking those fools out cold, and cutting their ears off as compensation for wasting my time—I figured I'd sever one each, one ear and one eye in an effort to keep them forever imbalanced. "How do you always seem so happy?"

"How can I not be? I'm alive now, and I'll be dead—I accept—enjoy breathin', MD—we're all so amazingly lucky, however temporarily. Goddamn me if I ever start taking that for fucking granted, because it's great." We crossed Damen and entered Wicker Park. All the bums n' addicts were hangin' out by the south entrance, playin' chess or dominoes, some yelling at each other, per usual, and the space looked very beautiful, dressed in fresh snow as low orange light lit all the brownstones and oak trees across the meadow. I was feeling damn good so I pitched ten bucks to two dudes at a concrete table and told them to grab a drink. They smiled, we walked on and: "Funny how the park's inhabitants are always segregated just as the city: rich whites to the north, colored bums to the south, and all sorts of weird madfolk of various races lingering in the middle."

"I know, right?" We crunched through the snow, brushed off and took a seat at one of the benches surrounding the fountain. The Blue Line raced toward the loop and a bird sung in the background. Weathered copper leaves stretched to the sky from atop the two-tiered, sculpted fountain. I tried to imagine it misting in the summer wind, the courtyard filled with life and running laughter, but I couldn't quite develop it. All the plants in the pots were dead, and I thought of the older fellow I'd seen planting at the advent of the previous spring—my hope was that he was still 'live n' breathin'. "You feel warmer now?"

"Yeah," I said, fighting a hidden shiver. I took a big breath and exhaled white as a clan of kids ran through the east field, enjoying a game of tackle football in the fresh snow. Tufts of white fell from the extremities of a huge oak tree swaying in the breeze, just shy of the basketball courts, and: "There's an old black and white picture of my dad and my uncle Dennis, as kids, standing in front of that tree. The trunk is twice as thick now."

"Your dad had another brother?"

"Yeah."

"What's he do?"

"He's a bum—a user and a violent con man, straight up—which makes me respect my Pop's work ethic and stringent morality all-the-more. There were no excuses or complaints to keep him from greatness."

"Did you ever meet him?"

"Not more than a handful of times." A cold, glinting gust of air sliced up my pant leg, and I thought about how as a kid, after the few Christmases he was around, we would drop Dennis in the middle of fucking nowhere, man, by some crazy abandoned factories on Elston—I remember thinking: any person who would consciously choose to exit a vehicle here, now, as their proper volition—if you make this choice, man, of all options available, you are an absolute maniac!—and my pop would give what little bread he could spare, forty dollars or something, a big pinch for us in those days, right, and I would always find myself thinking about, well: how in Dennis's mind, he was running though a meticulous breakdown

194

about how far he'd make that forty dollars work for him, how th*i*s time, this time would be somehow different than all the rest, this time he'd finally get his shit together—but at the same time he'd be craving that fucking booze, man, craving that fucking hard, hard booze and infused within him would be that *need* man, that need for just one drink, just a sip, and in search for such he'd probably walk into some roughshod, run down joint chosen straight out of some long unknown derelict directory of dilapidated dives existing solely in the minds of the earnestly desperate, subsequent to which, after having drank the full charitable allotment in a single sitting, fighting his way off the premises and falling wasted and flat broke into some undistinguished gutter, I imagined him waking enveloped in a bandage of miscellaneous fast food wrappers in the broken light of an arctic orange sunrise with nothing more than a stale sliver of my grandma's bread crumbled in his pocket. He had nobody to blame but himself, and I will feel zero pity when he dies.

"Hey, check it out—there's a fly on your leg! I wonder how it survived."

I watched it set for some seconds and: "A creature I would have been quick to kill as a child—I'm more apt to let enjoy its life as an adult."

"Maybe it's the opposite for some people." Saw-toothed grey clouds bled red on the edges in the west whilst being blown south by the cool northerly breeze—the shadows cast were complex and intricate like the face of a mountain. You could see the lines, the avalanche chute—fuckin' drops you might take if you had nothing to lose. The Blue Line to O'Hare hooted the horn and roared past Honore along Milwaukee in the distance, and an old water tower rose rusted and sun drenched to the northeast. MD snapped a frame and I smiled at the way a photo always represents a moment in pure silence. We sat quietly for a long stretch, and the sun lingered half a hand above the horizon. People came and went, and it seemed like the city would have a lot of energy that night. "Hey Anthony, thanks for looking out for me back there. I was scared."

"Don't worry about it—that was nothing. I doubt they were going to do anything, but I just wanted to be sure, you know, safety first. I always assume that something will malfunction on a trip this undulating and lengthy, and I do my best to make sure it ain't me or someone I care for." Her pink lips parted just a shade as she smiled and: "Let me see that camera." I looked at her through the lens and she tried to keep a super serious expression— the color had returned to her face and I made her wait forever before snapping—she finally broke down and laughed and with the snap the moment was burned into a physical history of being.

We sat quietly for a long span and: "Do you feel an electric relaxation beginning to tremor?" I looked into the dark centers of her blue spheres and they had grown from the inside out. I took a breath and closed my eyes, and in an instant all that had been rising came crashing down—music of profound cadence and depth sent flowing rivers awash in painted leaves as the sky screamed majestic overtones of late fall prime—I drift away and my body thunders across a ridgeline, placid lake lingering below with a color wheel of a hillside rising proudly before submitting to crisp, clean air. Damn—and in my head I breathed deep and couldn't speak—I fell back to a sunrise in the cool fall air and thought: I'm 'live n' breathin' n' happy to be so—the perpetual presence of birch trees in these woods adds contrast via their straight white trunks against the dark granite rock of the jagged mountainside—and O the beautiful black skin of sugar maples weeping with temperate rain water—the sound of her running through proud folds of bark and into the green, soft ground makes me want to stay awhile—O the echoes this steep walled canyon must have reverberated and heard over the years. Native peoples perched high upon little known ledges, feeling the cool stone beneath their fingers and pondering a billion brilliant queries as to the hows and the whys and how comes of the world as they stalked their prey in the opening, fire red light of day—and then, twelve hours later, bodies in the same space, reflecting what was, minds clear and wide as a cold mountain river raging with snowmelt, feet sturdy upon rock still hot after dusk. Where did you bring me? And where does this leave me? Back upon a solstice moonrise and saucer blue eyes that when spun together shatter my mind—thinking I shouldn't be thinking the thoughts that have been constantly eclipsing my mind—sunset—moonrise—how high?—saw your eyes—love—love breathing—I need so little to sustain me—primal instincts torturing me, neither waxing nor waning—a single full bright evening—sleep, sleep, sleep—breathe, exhale, breathe—please see this stirring green valley from behind your panes and feel no pain as you enter an ancient gorge cut by a winding river whose name is unknown—shadows shift continuously as the sun beams through the branches of topmost trees, blazing red upon a distant ridgeline through which this river began to carve, eons ago—slicing through great mossy walls of damp bedrock, molecules moving atoms day by day—inhale the breadth of color change within a single tree—green at the shadowed bottom, red and starved for energy at the top as orange and gold fuse the middle—trying so hard and failing to hold onto the warmth as the cold wind wipes the color from the earth—to die on that forest floor—in the middle of a colossal mash cascaded in all the colors of life departed—I charge on and over an unknown hillside to discover an untouched, pristine protrusion of rock whose existence had always been confirmed in the form of an inner mounting flame, the mind's eye of possibility—the sun beams warmth into my chest and I am grateful—a shaft of light brightens a bank-full river charging to the sea, slipping away, drenched in the cool, deciduous exhale of the wise valley below—O sweet enormous forest, delicate goddess, beneath my vision, essential mother—recall the frantic whisper as I fall—think, soar, ask why—sweat blue mist and sing for eternity—flooding summer storm, winter wind, shine on. Please. See. Everything.

I opened my eyes to the bright world and: "Yes, feel it."

"And where is your mind, Anthony?"

"Afraid that all I'll wind up doing is complaining about the world without changing anything."

"That's a very good fear to hold close to your heart—I fear such each and every day."

"Are you afraid to die?"

"It scares the hell out of me. The end is all I can see."

"That's an accurate observation, MD—all you gotta do now is cool out and live."

"Easier said than done."

"Just relax, it'll come—because what I do know: you are the earth and the sun, the wind and sky, all together at once, even after you die—and so open the self to this vast empty space—the scene so large, your mind is erased—take in, give back, breathe deeply and say: everything is everything—tis beautiful, ay?"

"It's a mind frame that's hard to maintain—so many distractions, leading me astray," she said.

"Give me your hands—move with me now, just release: what's your favorite thing about a rainy day?"

"The rain."

"Okay—so it let inside you—do as I do," she took a breath and: "We're postin' in the trees, the switch blowin' in the breeze—the surging sea had made our bodies feel light and free—weightless and floating upon the turquoise water of a white sand shore, head exposed to the southern summer trade winds—a keen participant in the ten million year tradition of west blowing east—and I saw you smile when we rode 'round the bend at Diversey—grass and trees so green, and the Lake—that deep haunting blue with clouds so tall and sun-bright white that you feel like Everest standing there, lingering in the sky just past the city—and you looked to the west and rain beset your eyes—an enormous outflow pounded warm and wet, under sunny skies, while Evanston looked black as night to the rear—and steam soon rose low over the land—sent tanned faces teeming with sweat—and we again moved and rode through shadows as wooden arms reached long and free for exalting sunlight, and I was happy enough to cry."

I looked at her and she looked at me in a way that said you don't always need to say, 'I love you,' for someone to understand that you do. "Close your eyes again," she went, "Where are you?"

"Flying high through rural Nebraska and drooling out the window as an empty stretch of sky hangs over an empty stretch of land, black on black, occasional lonesome light bulbs winking past as the train wails through the biting winter night."

"Same ride reborn—"

"Okay, yes, out the window it's all lilac, full purple bloom, grass growing full and green, and O how I appreciate the blueness of the skies, the green in the living, the wind in the wooded—not more, not less, on this day than the last—a moth and occasional robins flutter impulsive through the air as daises sprout and a stiff breeze blows through bud-strewn oak trees—I blink and two rabbits are chasing through the big blue world—children jumble atop jungle gyms and hawks circle a field, mice hidden, refusing to yield—and there they go: fences, fences, everywhere fences—only question: what kind of sense is?—all of this wire, wood, brick and steel—an occlusion of caliber whose fissure I feel—imaginary lines criss-cross my mind—shall they ever be crushed?—not in my time—and then come the coal cars, thousands and thousands, brimmed to a pinnacle, screaming past, just waiting to burn." I took a big breath and: "Your turn."

"Colossal rhythm rolling quietly in my mind as the fire crackles blue and orange in a hot metal ring—glacial melt sling-shots through rock at a pace that belies the fine, soft smell of the forest—with the afore word the fire stirs and breathes a brighter light—it's all coming into me now, and spilling back out—I breathe deep and smell that organic material that took all those summers to grow—burning—absorb the duality of these sounds: fire and river, mankind at its root, crackling and crashing a descent through a lush, sub-alpine forest that is dense with streams, waterfalls, loose rock, fir trees, giant cedars and all sorts of wildflowers—ah yeah, Anthony, this fire is so nice and warm—and this river, always flowing—every second, raging—and I'm thinking: when I'm back in Chicago, in traffic, and when I'm dead and gone—raging, man, she'll be raging on—slipping down a mountain that will stand forever, unyielding, supporting it all—until the sun finally consumes enough of itself to grow swollen and engulf the globe, she will stand."

We sat for a good while and watched the world go as we climbed the peak in a dual internal world and summited engulfed in a calm silence of mutual recognition akin to being born into a mind of perpetual momentum, forever needing to flow.

After what seemed an hour the wind blew a plastic bag across my feet and Melissa went: "When the weather begins warming I'll feel grateful."

"Yep."

"Remember dancing and hanging out in misting rain as sirens wailed and horns blared through humid, midnight, summertime air?"

"I wish we were on that stoop right now, in fact, sitting back while the rains cooled off an otherwise steamy evening."

She took a breath and: "Last season's warmth wasn't right—something really terrible almost happened to me late last spring, Anthony, and I never thawed out. What I remember most was the next day, the day after I almost ended, actually. After everything was sorted out early in the morning, I took an inexhaustible stroll, from slightly past dawn 'til beyond dusk I walked. In the morning, shadows casually withdrew as I moved through different neighborhoods—I felt impossibly alive at present, brilliantly so—perennials were popping in places I never expected them to rise, and the sky felt crisper than it had in a long time. The breeze sounded and smelled magnificent: filled with the scent of newly living things—the aroma of tilled dirt and green, flexible leaves, freshly cut grass, flowers—this magnificent northwest breeze blowing all these smells through various neighborhoods—upon me, into my mouth and nose and my body—my mind—through my widespread fingers and onto the paper I occasionally stopped to write upon—it was everywhere. Spring had come to bloom and I had so many beautiful colors in my mind that I became speechless—so many subtle intricacies of brilliance leaching in—and a billion questions of being arose like the ever pending continuation of an ice flow—every reflection pouring through then and there, like our great mad lovin in the sweet fall air—and I walked east until I sat and stared into the dark, restless waters of the Lake—and gaping upon the level plane of blue, I questioned if it thinks: can you feel me as I feel you? Cool breath thrust upon my skin as my mind contemplates thee—can you feel me? The dream I dreamt that evening, Anthony, when I finally slept, was the first one in the series of me—dying. I was laid out, perfectly still, eyes open, able to see, unable to close my eyelids, and people I knew kept streaming past—and I was very sad to no longer be—I saw you and remembered the two of us tan and lean and strong and entwined in a raw pure release beneath blue skies and blowing green, reaching deep—and I thought: don't let it end, please—but it did, exactly then—it was over—black and quiet—and then I woke. I've felt frozen ever since." She leaned into my side as the sunlit blue sky held its breath, and after time ticked by: "I had a revelation that day."

"About what?"

"About a million things," she said, "I'll be weeping while I'm dying, just knowing everything I am might be over—I'll be bawling."

"Well, that's not going to be for a long fucking time." Large, silent tears rolled down her cheeks. "Damn—what's wrong, Ms. D?"

"Nothin'."

"C'mon, something's been bothering you this whole time—what happened?

"I've become afraid to die."

"Why?"

"I got attacked that day, in my place. Someone snuck in and tried to get me."

I felt the odd sense of suspended calm of an inner city neighborhood in the initial seconds of a blackout on a hot, steamy, mid-summer evening, before the searing rage is unleashed. "What the fuck do you mean, somebody tried to get you? Are you fucking kidding me?"

"No—it happened in my old place on Halsted."

"And you're okay, I mean—what the fuck, man! Do you know who he is?"

"Yeah, they caught him, I fought him off and screamed fire and he panicked and ran and the cops caught him hiding under a car. It turned out that he'd raped six other girls in the past few years. He didn't, you know, get what he wanted—I was the only one he didn't get."

"Jesus fucking Christ Melissa!"

"I remembered when we met, you know, not long after your friend Shannon got killed—I remembered you told me it's best to yell fire if something like that happens because the majority of weak humans would be too timid to come to your aid and confront violence head on." She looked into the sky and: "I just haven't been able to, um—I guess feel like myself since it happened—after almost getting violated in such an unspeakably primal manner—my nerves and emotions are, uh—I don't know. There're no words for it—just a real deep feeling of something wrong inside. You wouldn't believe how close I came to crying when I saw you at the restaurant earlier today." My stomach twisted and I thought of old deeds of evil heaping up to the heavens—our great friend to many, Shannon, Shanny Mac—a girl compassionate and kind to all—my mind burned through images of her running at full speed down the track and over hurdles and helping handicapped kids carry their books between classes—I would watch her and those kids, little innocent guys who reminded me of my uncle Ron—how awed they were, you know, to be helped by such a selfless and beautifully kind girl—I understood what a big deal it must have been to them, you know? I could feel it—and taking her to a dance, her mother and father and grandmother and brother all standing in their wooden walled living room, gazing at her proudly, and in my mind I was thinking: do I even deserve to take this girl out for a night? I'm such a rotten scoundrel at times, don't be an asshole around her, whatever you do—and later, in college, talking to her at the gym, both during workouts and when she worked there, and to notice a certain janitor, always standing in the background with that mop, squeezing the handle and staring—how many times did our schedules interact?—in the bathroom, after class, changing before hoops—you were always in there, mopping that floor, and after I said hello you just stared at me, soundlessly, and after awhile I just stared back—I told myself just because you feel it, doesn't mean it's there—but then when my friend Stevie B stormed in the door and said it: 'It's Shannon man—she's been murdered!'—and standing in the background of the news report, loitering about, that same motherfucker, there you were—that same ugly face one could not imagine laughing out loud—to imagine him squeezing her fucking neck like he squeezed that broomstick and swept the dust into a pan—that such a worthless thing could so easily kill the greatest—the feeling was insane—he took a legend off this planet. She was so cool, and calm—the girl you wanted to take to a great party, know what I'm saying?—and to have her meet the end via an incredibly ugly, dirty kind of vicious killing that changes you forever—to know the last thing she saw were those black lifeless eyes leering—just as they did when they walked by as we sat on the porch—not mate meeting mate, but predator meeting prey—and I felt the jigsaw piece fall into place—hate beginning to contaminate—and bam, she was gone, yet another beautifully sweet breath exhaled and forever lost in the expanse.

The sound of my teeth grinding snagged me from my flash reflection and: "I don't know what to say, Melissa. I really don't." Wind hissed through the dead, gnarled garden, and the time to leave had come.

35

We walked away, light on our feet, and Melissa spoke of her dreams—to flourish, independent and free and successful on account of her own internal drive—no help, no handouts—just alive and released to learn and train and experiment and strengthen—big breaths and long strides unhassled by outsiders and no more interruptions on the path to being all she aspired to be. As she spoke of triumphs to come, I couldn't lose the image of a spiraling hollow point of an irate bullet—maybe I should just do it?—send them crashing through blameworthy craniums—take up a job maiming them—as many as I can get my hands on—all the creeps who sneak on innocent souls as they float off to sleep: O to be the source to extinguish your life force—and remorse? I think it be more like elation. Is killing the killers first perhaps as necessary as the fire of the furnace for the creation of steel? A long series of terribly violent acts cascaded in my brain and: eight hundred and thirty seven—"I should not be counting off my paces to that degree," I whispered to myself. By the time we got back to the bikes the sun was below the horizon and the icicle that had dripped down my neck was draped in shade—a trim clear strand with a frozen droplet of water swollen out at the very bottom, suspended in time, yet destined to fall.

"I think I should show up to my shift," it went, "They treat me pretty right," as she didn't want to jam up the friend she promised to fill in for if needed, and figured it would be bad karma to hang her and the eatery out to dry. My tire was again flat—I couldn't ride her there, and so we shared an emotional hug, excited of many good times to come, and as I squeezed her tight, I felt like a cold surge of old worries came pouring out of her, melted hot in her head and cascading down through her feet as they hung above the ground. Her eyes burned red, but in a strong, released sort of way that alluded to many warm, clear future days of passionate existing. Her arms dug into my back and her body felt lean and sure of itself—from the moment I met her I'd held her in the highest esteem and wished for nothing minus a life filled with the greatest of feats—and to imagine that a man tried to steal her away from herself with his bare hands—I had to slow myself down for a second, I really did. I squeezed her tighter at the thought and smelled her hair—the scent was reminiscent of when you walk in somebody's apartment after they've departed and breathe in their essence—tears start welling up in some supernaturally spontaneous style that makes you smile n' breathe deeply n' laugh mellifluous n' free n' clean at the madness of it all—an insane sort of acid churned my stomach and I forced myself to stay positive.

I watched her ride off and walking away, paces compiled, miles, so clean and clear, lived for thirteen billion years—and every so often I strolled past an elder, eyes meet—hello, hello—we greet, and to myself I smiled and swore I did, that they realize, that I am, that they are, that all is, and no need to be crazy or ill-tempered or mean, because right now is all there is, all that's ever been, ah yes, tis a new moment of a new day, son, and you're alive and breathing, healthy and clean, the miracle of life that is me continues to be—and off I strolled, grinning a grin, happy that I am, happy that I live—but then the flood crashed through the levy and burned my chest as I began to drown.

I slid my hand across rigid lips and my mouth was bone dry—I pushed my left thumb across my eyebrow slow and hard—I had thought the ride was over but really it was just beginning: "Holy shit. This isn't good. Calm yourself, man, fucking relax." My heart started roasting: five hunded degrees, high altitude beans, a feeling of insane mystic caffeine burning through me—the windows were opening and the breeze was strong. An explosion of emotion took root within—it was about to be a real steep slide. I put on my shades to escape the passing faces as I churned through what felt like a flat earth society with some occasional low-voltage fools scattered about alleys—twisted bleak brush banged against bricks on the cold invisible wind as a bundled baby was pushed past in a stroller. The chill had affixed his mouth to a position of awkward rigidity, lips swooping inward, flesh bloodless and white, and this reminded me some haunting final moments spent at the side of the dying—the visions gave me chills as the mind flooded with the moment you find yourself drawn to every crease and crevasse of a person's face, every shade and refraction of a person's eyes—when the mind begins racing: what will you look like when you're dead and dying? Smile—please smile.

I shivered and got the deep sense of closure one gets while descending on edges after working from sunup to sundown, continually exposed, upon the uppermost slope of a frigid mountain on a bright, windswept day, as the dark unforgiving night comes plunging down from outer space. I next passed a bundled woman resting on her stoop. Illuminated by a harsh street light, she was gazing upon a tuft of white hair, crying softly. I walked on for a couple hours and the City, man—her streets drew me in real serious-like—straight into a crazy embrace filled with varied smells of human sorrow, shrieks of raw elation and self-imposed solitude. The Mother exhaled continuously and let it be known that indeed we have a ways to go before raw lonesome nights cease making themselves known via tapping hello the dead, crooked fingers of wintertime trees on the midnight breeze—just who is behind these panes, these panes?—the City, she screams, all hours of the day, many fates, and every time she opens her mouth she draws me closer, spinning me hard and setting me loose—all that's happened here, ups and downs, mate, forever—millions of families with stories that span the spectrum of memory from sorrow to ecstasy, what will be will be—allow it to come to you, freely—and taking several moments to consciously breathe, I slowed things down and swallowed—try to be all right with it all, involved—get a new nugget a' gold as often as you can, man, and things'll turn out alright—you're just another dude perusing this scene, man, like uncle Dennis, wherever he may be, a kind old lady or the most crooked men on the City Council—carrying on over a predestined edge, one foot off the ledge, all equally susceptible to eternity, just wondering, probably, when and why and where that time is gonna' come— and what post breathing that time will mean—and sirens screamed through the early Chicago eve as warm glowing windows melted snow and sent streaks streaming down—who is dead and dying, and who for them is crying? Upon whose cheeks do tears streak like snowmelt upon these panes? Large drops dove into half frozen puddles as the earth subtly amassed the large drink that shall finally allow her to breathe after a long, windblown winter. How long before she exhales? How long before green prevails? And when shall you sweep me away?

I passed a neat brownstone with shoveled limestone steps, and in the upstairs window a little kid was peeping out. His brown face was smeared against the steamed glass, and I looked at him and thought: beautiful how ya come in, pure and fresh in that gorgeous green, lush empty field, but almost immediately the bricks start building around you—a societal alliance rushing to constrain all open-ended beliefs and viewpoints—building around the young individual at a furious pace—frantic hands stack tall a windowless, concrete and stone building, built thick to the point that to call a single block of this restrained conviction into question serves as such an inharmonious injunction into the non-vacillating worldview of human inhabitants of this blue spinning sphere, that a volatile mixture of incensed panic and rage shake at the realization that a gaping green field of non-hypercritical supposition could be such an unexpectedly horrifying place to chill, and capable of exploding the foundation completely—and so it stands, until finally, at the end, after the walls have moved steadily upward and inward, the once young and open-minded individual is slowly suffocated, laying in the fetal position upon a cold, concrete floor, arthritic and scared and unaware of what might have been—ready to be thrown into the cold, hard ground, and buried silent—unless it somehow sneaks in: that neutron bomb of possibility which leaves the bunker in tact but blows the mind apart—when suddenly you realize that there was no bunker in the first place, and for the first time since birth you're standing stark naked in that field, grass greener, sky so immaculate blue and limitless that in a way you realize your mind had never fully comprehended the insanity of its existence at *all*—and from here being alive shall never feel the same.

I walked on, exploding at the thought, and at a distant intersection I closed my eyes to take in a group of cashed fools producing beautiful sounds beneath the low voltage hum of a lonely streetlight—they were a sweet mix of roughness and elegance, like a slim brunette violinist with sad eyes playing sharp and undisturbed, lounging in a tree limb of an aging ash tree, high above a humid urban street scene of midnight chaos. I watched them sing and one man played a horn as the others snapped their fingers, and I thought: you go out as you come in—all of us do, whether it is realized or not—we all go out in the same exact fashion—at a single point in time, a single place, too, multiverse stretching for trillions of light years in all directions—delicate breeze puts you on your knees as you wonder how what is has come to be, and simultaneously you realize the query is answerless—and you're gone—so yeah, sure thing guy, give me your job application and I'll put down my personal references and five words that describe me. Get bent.

I laughed at the thought as it came, world dark behind these shades—addiction and paranoia invade as I stand tall and act brave and yearn for self control to maintain an unbreakable stance of defiance for that which I am tired of defending: sanity—I accept the fate and this acceptance exhausts me. It puts me down in a deep place—histrionic feelings of heavy breathing and incongruent reasoning brings me to my knees—I ponder what is wrong and nothing comes—unsure if I am breaking or broken or freshly woken—perhaps all three are causing this brain bleed—save me—I understand why people ask God to do so—it is really quite simple to yell the request and consider it golden and true—you need to find that inner calm, boy, that deep peace that is admittedly evading thee—

I kept walking, mind flyin' down many simultaneous roads, all of them twisting and peppered with blind, sharp curves that epitomized the hyper-stimulation of my soul until I descended the ledge in a slow motion freefall—back to the ground and eyes facing the blue, open sky—lotus position—solitary mission—of nonexistence—stringent wisdom says this be what it be for everyone—the free verse collision continued until I exhaled with: "You have a lot of work to do, man, and hopefully many unbeaten beats and unbreathed breaths ahead with which to do it. Yes man, let's go."

36

Feeling hollowness in my legs, I was reminded that I had walked and ridden quite a way since leaving the garage that morning. The time was nine o'clock and I felt ready to sleep for many hours. Inside I felt fine about life—I replayed revolutions again and again—and after being released, so many things, memories, distant and near—a new born strength that begged to not get infected with worry for what might be, for in many ways, it already was and is inside me—I walked quiet atop a snowy sidewalk, examined all the different footprints and: "Fuck those tired eyes, ay boy? Fuck those tired eyes—fight on for a moment here and breech the precious territory on the borderline of sanity versus delirium. See, you need to realize that a day shall come in which you will reach the end of your endless potential—and if my fucking Pop is still trudging along and grinding every grind he can grab hold of with the tenacity of an old untamable guard dog with ears peaked high and eyes set wide, then how the fuck am I going to try and say I'm tired? Nonsense man, complete fucking nonsense—I have no right to be tired yet, none at all." I passed a man with his hand out and thought: all who live off the donations from others rather than their own creation—is it possible that all your life you have purposely avoided doing anything truly productive?

I felt thirsty and almost called some mates like Zybarsky and my man EP, or my boys IJ and Vidler, Dr. Soap, the MC, Brian Thomas or Johnny Whispers—any of a number of good people to sit and carry on with really, but I figured if I quit my job to work hard I should do so—interaction could wait 'til tomorrow. I stepped into a place for coffee, sat and pulled out my old sketchbook for sake of tightening the outline. I tried to push Melissa out of my mind, and the initial warmth of brown draining down my throat and into my stomach was soothing. I removed a sweater and to my left was a professor—over-tanned and over-dyed was the fitting description of his epidermis and hair follicles. His maze of style was casual yet stiff—a non-casual sort of guy obliged to breathe easy on account of his accompaniment—his face hinted at internal analysis of his effectiveness every second of it: so very calculated. "I must be a curator of tears," he said, to which the response of his two students was subtle awe. "*No*body places the sort of pressure on themselves the way *I* place pressure on myself. I get a lot done, I'm a scholar. Did you walk here? I can walk you home." He was trying to lay the mack on a wide-eyed undergraduate in a fairly merciless style.

I desired quiet and they soon departed, but a different screwball seated on the other side got to hacking off. He was on the 'Critique List' for some goddamn publisher and was in the process of explaining to a different bore what it feels like to have his opinion: "Matter on such a profound level." The guy went on like a goddamn wind-up toy and: "It has been an active day today—a very, *very* active day." He wiped his mouth and: "My entire body feels discombobulated—see this?"—stretching with hands bowed above head—"My brother's ex-wife taught me that one. It helps to unwind. I wonder if any place makes a good cheesecake around here." Will you please shut up?

The book reviewer exited the scene, and there I sat, on the brink of inventive infusions galore—amazing though—he was just the sort of guy whose opinion could not possibly mean less to me, and yet *he* is the person chosen to review hundreds of books and perhaps criticize each aspect of original creativity as his sole representation of creation. What a joke. I took another drink and out the window, an old hustler was pressing overpriced proletariat for what they could spare. A tall, klutzy woman crossing North Avenue approached and fumbled her belongings upon the ground. Eager of the opportunity for a little victory, he pounced upon the felled items and returned them, thereby forcing her to dejectedly file through pockets for a handful of change. Across the way, a gang of young, expensively clad wives roved with expressions that insinuated they had either left a great sum of personal production undone, or that they never held the desire to produce anything minus wet cocks of rich men from the very beginning. Up front, the girl at the cash register kept saying: 'I hope you have a wonderful n*igh*t!' to all the customers, but the timbre of her voice was so sour I wished her to merely smile kind and quiet and allow folks to carry on.

Two tables away, the decibel level slowly escalated until: "I still don't understand why you got fired!"

"God babe, like I told you, I got caught up in some politics—you know how it goes! Don't act like I wasn't trying."

"Don't you understand? Our money is dying!"

"You think I don't see? Jesus!" The woman gobbled down a handful of prescription drugs and continued to whimper of various misnomers, occasionally re-applying eye-shadow in a sadly sickening display of self-pity. Meanwhile, a small group of forty-something's in the corner of the room rattled off an entire catalogue of illogical reasons as to why they will be rich someday, and at the same time, refused to examine the natural ceiling of human ability— most specifically that of their own. Their actual plan was to initiate a line of hot pink accessories manufactured in Bangladesh under an invented French name and come up with a cool logo—I held hope for the idea to crash to the ground in a scorching fucking mess. I took a breath as an old, true blue skinhead waltzed past the window. He wore a black leather jacket with a lightening patterned SS patch sewn upon the sleeve, stone-washed jeans and red laced, steel-towed combat boots—his wardrobe meshed well with the static look of blind hatred engrained upon his biting face. Not more than three paces behind came woman with an angry, misshapen mouth and a limp. Her body language was closed off and she held her hands flat upon her frozen ears as she spoke aloud to herself—this fused with a half-assed red dye job of a crooked bang-line to give her an over the top aura of lunacy. My eyes moved to a thin black man crossing the street who was nearly run over by a car that refused to slow down and I thought: when will my luck run dry?—all these maniacs, everywhere, roving about—and here I am, living as well—I don't get it sometimes, man, I really don't. I have no idea what we're doing here. And written tiny in green ink upon the wall beside me was:

'Art will always live on in those who create and appreciate.'

Who is the author of this truth? I wondered—
"What did you guys do on your first date?"
"Our first date lasted for six days. We were fairly engrossed with one another from the very beginning," it came from a woman up toward the register. Her friend responded with a question regarding the best status to state on her Facebook page for sake of attracting men, and then:
"But how do I hide my downfalls? I have lots of downfalls—cookies, cakes, hot fudge Sundays, iced cream, hot pie—yeah, I have loads of downfalls." She laughed sadly as an eyebrowless woman waltzed past the window, and placed snug upon her head was the pink hat she earned by participating in a cancer walk. Flanking her gaunt shoulders were her husband and adolescent son. All three of them appeared proud but worried—my hope was that she does not die soon. But we're all gonna' die, boy, each and every one of us—from

silence we came, and to silence we shall return—I reflected Melissa's thoughts, all of her words in a flash of feeling, and I felt like an explosion in the sky.

The female voice of a life-long smoker shot through the radio of a cop waiting for a drink with: "We have a report of a missing person: Agnes Abramowitz was last seen wandering the 4000 block of W. Irving Park at nineteen hundred hours—subject has Alzheimer's Disease and is out without her coat." Imagine that—just as your cup brims full, a dirty drill bores a hole in the bottom, and an entire lifetime of memory goes poring into the dry sands of an inescapable desert—tis a terrifying thought man, it really is—to become the walking dead—to become a simple sculpture of addition: (X) beats per minute by sixty minutes per hour and twenty four hours per day, perpetually droning forward with no perception of who you were, where you are, or that you are—a sort of horrible pacifist version of the night of the living dead, minus the actors.

I shivered at the thought and a small girl entered the room with her mother, and she—she being the little one—she removed her beanie and let the world know she was stricken with cancer. Is there anybody unaffected by this disease? Lord! Her mother's overtly large shades looked very cute and funny on her little face—but horribly sad, too, as light beamed off her bald head, making her appear white as marble. God she was tiny—and her eyes so blue and large after removing the glasses—and back on, 'lil pink lips grinned not quite carefree as two tiny fingers struggled to hold the frame upon the bridge of a nose too minute to support them. Damn.

Is there life after death, or death after life? Observing the mother and her staunch effort to avoid coughing in the direction of her 'lil girl and her weakened immune system, I didn't know what to think. Reflective black mirrors concealed her cheeks, but I could see she was grimacing in pain as the poison injected to kill the poison collected in small, hateful black balls took hold. She pulled her beanie on, writhed nauseous and: "That's a cool hat," I said as she walked past, and a small, temporary smile was soon swallowed by the overwhelming complaints of three overfed college students swooning over a fashion mag at an adjacent table. The fucking madness of it all was too much to bear. I opened the old sketchbook and wrote:

'All I ever wanted, was to be like other girls
Dancing and laughing, hair spun in curls
Please won't you take, this poison out of me
Swore that I would grow big and strong
You lied to me mommy

It is so easy, to be a hero on paper
If you could trade places, what would you do?
Would you step down off a' your throne
Trade all your hopes and dreams
Dive into her body and swallow her screams?'

I shook the thought off, picked up the paper and looked at the stats. Inside it said a few notches were etched in an ever-growing number—names of the dead went ringing in my head, like an old song forgotten but never really said—the galactic harmony of rockets racing and bombs blasting blurred the words—I thought of all the tales of woe, all the families, man, and friends, too—it was a big fucking number with a lot of crazy notes on both sides of the line. I opened my eyes and the man who had filled the table across from me was speaking of integrating operations—he was in his sixties, and after ending the call, almost forced to out of sheer proximity, he made some small talk on the tune belting out of the speakers: "It was just Mozart week on WFMT."

"I know—it's nice."

"Pure genius," he said.

"Hell yeah."

He raised his cup and then descended his face tight into the screen of his computer. His son walked in and: "Hey hey! Jimmy-boy! Want to see the system I just streamlined?"

"I'd rather see your wallet—I need caffeine and some food. In fact, you know I don't like the coffee here, dad—I prefer light roast—I can't believe you wanted me to meet you here." The father reached into his back pocket and: "Can you just give me a twenty? I need some gas, anyway." The son, ten years older than me, it seemed, went on like he should have won the Pulitzer Prize for criticism long ago, grabbed the cash like he was in a big rush and trudged off with an impatient gait.

The pop caught me spying and: "That's my boy."

"I gathered."

"Looks like me, no?"

"Yeah."

"He's gonna' be a successful guy, I'm sure of it. He's very bright."

"Yeah?" I almost mentioned that he seemed to me like your typical whining, overprovided man of incessant nonchalance for taking handouts and complaining about the quality, but I didn't want to ruin the guy's life. "If he's really smart, next time he'll buy you the coffee, and appreciate your presence."

"Excuse me?"

"No problem," I said, "Have a good one." I'd had enough so I dressed, repacked and walked outside just as a little brown pup tied to a bike rack got scared as hell and ducked low with a whine as the L charged over—"No worries, mate, you'll get used to it."

A man on a phone yelled loud over the roar: "Just a blur, these days, in a way, with work, training, saving, eating and sleeping intermittently between everything—how've you been?"—and the steady click clack, click clack, one two, three four, click clack, click clack, five six, seven eight, pounded seconds away from his life, southeast toward the Loop.

A dark haired girl drove an old black Bug through the intersection, just beating the red, smile upon her face as she took a big swill from a plastic water bottle, head bobbing to a beat. I walked south on Milwaukee and in front of a bookstore a roughneck and a lecturer were engaged in a heated philosophical debate. "I'll jus remain affixed t' my streetwise orthodoxy n' you do your thing," it came. Two men with guitar cases strolled past them from across the street: feeling free, said their facial expressions, as their voices discussed the set list for an impending jam at the Double Door.

The illuminated windows of the L streaked through bare trees and further south, a guy in his forties had taken a bad spill, and the white furry face of his Malamute was stained red along the mouth from licking the small but deep gash on his forehead, and hanging tight at his side. "Ya alright?"

"Alright enough—this guy tried to chase a squirrel while I was standing on some ice and down I went."

I walked on, and after seeing that guy all wet and mucky, I felt in the mood for some fresh duds. I hadn't purchased a fresh shirt n' pants in a minute and mine were a good ways soiled, so I dipped into the next store—I looked for some flat-fronted slacks and a plain top and this proved impossible. A good number of people were shopping but one guy kept looking at me real funny. "Can I help you with somethin, dog?"

"O—I was just looking at your shirt—but not just the shirt, really," he said, flirty as hell.

"C'mon man, don't be comin at me like that, alright? I mean it—have an alright day and move the fuck along."

"What? Are you a homophobe? That could be a hate crime."

"Why? Because I hate the thought of your tongue in my mouth? Get lost."

A sales guy walked up and after some banter it came: "What in specific are we looking to add to the style portfolio today?"

"Man I just need some useable slacks and a shirt. Something made in America if you have it."

"Well this Burberry Prorsum, gold jacquard silk blend military shirt is $795, and these black taffeta Slimleg Trousers with side tabs are only $595."

"No no—I mean, listen—I'm just tryina' spend a couple bucks on some plain, usable shit—do you have that, man, or not?"

"I mean—not in the way you make it sound—maybe try the Army Surplus store."

"Alright, forget it, thanks anyway." I left, persistent push to capture interesting and original images across new landscapes again shaking my creative inclinations to the core, and as I continued southbound, a young man confined to a wheelchair gazed upon his wounded reflection from the corner of an earth brown eye in the cold, black marble façade of the adjacent building—his expression, much like the northern orientated wind into which he was wheeling himself, was bitter and sullen and brimmed with despondency. Our eyes met and the feeling exchanged was rather lonely. I pushed past another set of eyes: glassy and wounded and bloodshot and pleading: what to do? I can't really tell you—and high tension rails frying freezing snowflakes buzzed above me as I entered a mart in search of a snack. An eight year old kid shaped like a grape went: "Mommy, can I get some ice cream?"

"No baby, I tole you—no ice cream until you're over this cold."

"Can I get an extra bag a' potato chips then?"

"Sure baby—are you already done picking out all your sweets?"

"Yeah."

"Okay—let's go home now—let's go home and watch some TV." The next man in line refused to leave the store after being told by the cashier that he could not purchase liquor with his LINK card—they were at a nonnegotiable standoff, and so I left without getting anything, appetite temporarily suppressed. Further south on Milwaukee, waiting for a bus, an elderly lady shot a disapproving gaze at a young woman with a softball butt shielded by a woolen checkered miniskirt. The young gal dragged hard on a clove cigarette and hacked mercilessly, gaudy red high heels shuddering in dirty slush—her hyper-sexualized, loose persona made the older lady appear extra-grandmotherly. I leapt over a slush puddle and cut through the bright light of a Laundromat, and in the near corner, waiting for his clothes to dry was a middle-aged man with a slapdash goatee, wearing a cheapjack coonskin cap and playing a Ms. Pacman video game, obsessively. I thought: the human race is not one wit crazier than before in its history—we are just more numerous and news is more quickly and widely reported. All in all it's the same mad buzz spinning in fucking circles as was the case many millions of moons ago.

Two sets of rubber tread tore down the wet street and nobody was around for awhile. My steps shifted from muted to echoing as I paced through varied depths of snow and ice, and all the used furniture stores were closed, front windows shielded by rusty iron gates to prevent lice-ridden couches from getting jacked by varied desperados. Every sort of store claimed to have the best deal in the universe—all their fucking signs blotted my vision. I passed a used jewelry store and a joint that sold plus sized negligee as the snow along the curbside piled into black stained spheres that crackled through the still night under the pressure of my boots. I passed the Wendy's near Division as a bloated, balding white boy in his mid 30s pushed through a group of fidgety pigeons before squeezing into his whip and diving into a garbage bag worth of slimy, fast food, lungs all short of breath as he started the vehicle, and clunked on west. Remaining in the lot was an extremely heavyset black mother and a single child, hopelessly begging for change.

An ambulance and a fire truck screamed past with a furor—flying on the way to save some person this evening who likely did not think that they would indeed need saving when the morning imparted its lovely purple hue upon their newly woken eye, and yet here and now their fate screams upon my ears with the firm fluidity of a babbling brook rippling through a mountain town during the late spring runoff.

A scraggy man of struggle rode his bicycle northbound, opposite of me, wind whipping his face, left foot lurching down after his right, every ounce of energy he could muster squeezed into the endeavor on microscopic, millimeter sourced measurements—he rolled past with enough sustained momentum to only just avoid falling over, spinning his way toward God knows what.

I passed the Noble Square Apartments, and a man strode up to me with uncertain intent. I raised my fists a little he went: "Don't worry, you ain't gonna' get robbed man."

"No shit."

"You lookin f'love man?" and out twitchy lips and spat into a coarse palm came a threadbare bag of coca, "You know we gotta do it like Miami 'round here."

"I ain't with that white, man."

"Shit—no? You think you can do me a favor, though? I mean, this my *las* bag—I'm jus tryina' be rid of it. You think you can like, jus buy it maybe? As a favor, I mean?"

"I mean—no, obviously not." You had to give it to him—he asked for the business, confident and without blinking. I know a lot of sales managers might have liked a cleaner version of him on their team.

"C'mon, *man*—you know how you get t' feelin' after 'em superjets have gone on n' shi—*right?*"

"Don't be houndin' me, man." I walked past, nice and tall, looked quick behind to make sure he wasn't tailing, and in the blocks thereafter I felt heartened via witnessing a series of polite exchanges amongst complete strangers traveling to and fro. People held doors to stores, made room and took turns so that others didn't have to step in slush—a young Latino let an old black woman get on the bus before him and a couple of properly raised kids said please and thank you when directing a request at their parents—such a common, simple theme like wide-ranging courteousness goes a long way toward keeping people sane, I believe. Earnest smiles set my mind and body alight like an ecstatic firefly lost and found in the turbulent trade winds of finite consciousness with no choice other than to flame, go dark and flame again—try and glow bright, boy, as often as you can, because if you get caught up on that dark side and don't work on beaming bright, it's gonna' be a dirty, twisted slide—it can happen to anyone really.

On I walked until: "Excuse me, excuse me man—you got anything for me?"

"Do I *got* anything for you? No, I fucking do not."

"Can't you spare something? I need you to help me."

"Is that right?"

"Yeah."

"Only you can help your self, man."

"I can't man, times are—"

"What? Times are tough? You're younger than *me* man!"

"Yeah man," he said halfheartedly, "Nothing has been easy. Everything—" I felt like telling him what a soft cunt he really was to be begging like that—an at least averagely educated white kid in his early 20s seated comfortably in unfrayed jeans, clean Nikes, and a multiple hundred dollar North Face jacket—asking *me* for *my* fucking help, cell phone in his lap, just sitting there on a bench with a limp hand extended in a style that insinuated: I deserve—I deserve the fruits of your labor because I'm sitting here in the cold with a sad look on my face and nothing is easy, so pay me. I imagined him taking handouts from his parents for his entire life, complaining that th*is*—it's not what I *really* wanted—so and so got th*at*, and I wanted it, too, to tell you the truth, but thanks anyway, I gu*ess*—I felt like kicking him in the throat and beating him down right then and there—just pounding his legs until I was sure he wouldn't be able to walk for a couple days.

"My contribution to society has been nil, thus would I dare expect my share of society's reward to be anything more than nothing at all? Nope. See, the fact that you expect help from people to which you've provided nothing—this makes you a disgustingly weak little boy, so fuck yourself." I spit at a high velocity within one meter of his feet and walked on.

For one reason or another, that kid really annoyed me—I was consumed with anger over his approach until the driver of an IROC Camero flying south on Milwaukee flung something out the window: I picked up an old cassette case sitting in a slush puddle to view: 'Hey Now! Rich's Xmas Tape 1992!' The set list was loaded with 80s death rock and started with 'Cadillac Hearse' by Radio Werewolf—I figured 1992 to have been rough for ole Rick. A decade later, he'd grown tired of listening to it. I walked a bit further and decided to catch a drink down Milwaukee, but dipped into an alley before the Ohio bridge to drain my overactive bladder. I got spooked and almost peed on my foot upon noticing what looked to be an old man with white hair, dead and rolled up in a bloody carpet, thrown in haste against an adjacent brick building. It took a moment to realize it was just an old mop that must have been used to soak in red paint, rolled in a dirty rug and set outside—it really spooked me, man, no kidding. I took a breath, stared up to the still, black sky, and the rising moon, drenched in sunlight and beaming out above the Sears Tower, seemed more hospitable than my garage.

I continued south, and waiting to catch a green at Grand, a bus splashed up. A smattering of desperate-looking motherfuckers exited all bleary-eyed, and a modicum of Newports went crackling into their lungs. I tight-roped an adjacent curb, and to my surprise a group of five Amish women and one Amish dude exited the bus and eyed me all conspicuous-like, wary of my shifty-looking aura or some crap like that. I wondered what they were doing in Chicago, in that neighborhood right then, and then I began thinking a million weird thoughts, such as the entirety of not-up-to scratch things I've done and will continue to do, and whether those Amish women entertain erotic sexual thoughts to some degree. This one who looked as though she had been raised in a cupboard until the age of thirty-six was giving me the eye something fierce, I kid you not. The guy seemed a bit steamed that she was looking at me and I didn't want to cause strife, so I finished my tightrope two-step, J-walked the intersection and dipped into a pub that advertised package goods.

37

I took a seat at a barstool, and the gal in charge went: "How's the night find you?"

"A bit cold but damn alright—can I have a Guinness?"

"Surely—want to start a tab?"

"Nah, I'll just pay as I go." I opened my bag and put my money in my pocket, big roll in one, little in the other, opened my sketchbook, set my bag on the ground, and a balding man with small ears dressed in a well worn suit seated further up the bar struck a conversation with the tender as she poured my beer. His hands dipped below the ledge where a frantic attempt to remove his wedding ring failed on account all the weight he had gained since last it had been removed. The finger looked like a swollen purple sausage pinched shut by a petite golden washer. A crooked blue vein near the surface of his white neck twitched as he smiled and slyly wrenched at the tiny sphere like a prisoner trying to tear a ball, chain, and bloody iron clasp away from an abraded ankle.

I looked about and she delivered the pint. It felt good to sit alone and have a drink, nothing planned out, open sketchbook and pen ready to go as life rolled along in random style. The place had a door on each end of the room, and a guy toward the west end of the bar went: "Ya know, Becky's my liver n' onions—always gets me through my day n' makes sure the sheets are clean."

"Dat's nice, Billy, dat's goo—"

"But dis other one, man—u*mm*—she's like steak, man, steak n' lobster n' ice cream all at once."

"She'll taste good Billy—but she'll give ya heartburn."

"Dat's why I got my TUMS," he said, raising a glass of whisky, "So I don't feel nothin'." A real heavy guy walked in the door at the east end of the room and made his way toward them. "Der he is finally—dat's Racquetball John."

"He don't got da build of a racquetball player."

"He don't play racquetball." The guy who knew him stood as he approached and: "Ay! Racquetball Johnny, man, what's goin' on?"

"Save the smoke you're going to blow up my ass for my autopsy. You got my money, Billy, or not?"

They had some things to sort out, apparently, and after the balding guy on the opposite end of the bar finished another drink, he gave a final tug on his ring and addressed the bartender: "I just reenrolled in school to get my masters degree in being an entrepreneur. Forty-three years old and I'm actually doing it—it's a very prestigious program: Northwestern."

"I thought that's what starting a small business is about." It was a great answer on her part—to learn real truth, he would have been better off forgoing student loans and borrowing ninety stacks to have a go at something, hands-on all the way, hustling every actionable angle, making things happen in the real world, do or die, and skipping the process of taking loans so as to hold hands in group projects with other latent slaves to an 'education process' that skirts 'doing' at all costs—I almost expanded her point, too, but didn't bother. He was exactly the type of guy who'd go on to get hired by some government agency regulating businesses according to tenants written by authors who'd never owned one, nor worked for one not supported by tax dollars—complete portraits of economic ignorance placed into positions that require demonstrable application of such for the sake of all. I mean—are we trying to fail on purpose? Good God—what do you expect will happen when such people encourage banks to give loans to everybody with a pulse so as to ensure the world shall be 'equal'?—the first lesson in kindergarten should be that it ain't, kid, and the only way to secure a place for yourself is through prudence, hard work and humility—that shortcuts might work for a minute, but they'll eventually come crashing down like a mildew-ridden, plaster ceiling. If the reins of government were given to true, independent business owners, and everybody left them alone, they'd have this joint running smooth in no time. But instead, they, the millions of people who've lived life and provided for themselves via their own ingenuity, are being ordered about by what equates to a few hundred silver spooned buffoons—how they are allowing themselves to be squeezed blue with such impunity by what are basically weak, non-callused hands devoid of skills minus signing bills that essentially read: 'Because I say so,' I'll never know.

The guy belched twice and carried on about his new collegiate program, and: "Are you in school?"

"Every. Single. Day." It came, "Every night I work behind this bar I learn from a few wise, varied folk, and then I mix that by taking note of all the people I don't want to be like—you learn a lot that way." What a cool chick, I thought. I looked at her and laughed— she was trapped. It wasn't busy enough to bounce rapid to other patrons, and the guy didn't take the hint. He went on about his Ivy League undergraduate degree, the difficulty, the competition, the 'profound satisfaction' and such—I thought: instead of constantly mentioning you attended Yale in an effort to propagate your assumed level of intelligence, how 'bout pronouncing something humorous, original or interesting? Simply repeating the geographical coordinates to where you sat like a stone within four walls of the consortium is a fuckin' bore, man.

The dark haired maiden stepped over to me and: "What do you do for a living?"

"Roam around, climb up the earth, fly down it and think about shit."

"What's that pay?"

"Keeps me sane."

The guy looked over and yelled: "Like they say—in an economy like this what you need to do is stay in school—stay in school for as long as you can!"

"Is that right?" I asked.

"Abso*lutely*."

"And acquire all that debt because?—why not sit day after day in a big field surrounded by complex books from the library and end the habit only after the mind has become swollen enough to bleed out your ears, for free?"

211

"Well what would the point of that be? You wouldn't even earn you de*gree* for God's sake! I went to Y*a*le and have had a tough climb. *Yale* for God's sake! Knowledge without the diploma is worthless."

"Please, please cease believing such riotous falsehoods. Your reality is limited only by your own lack of imagination and industriousness. I swear to fucking God, this entire place is out of its *mind!*"

"In what way?"

"I'm sick of accepted wisdom being that unsanctioned self-education is some sort of impracticable plot to be frowned upon. The whole fucking cycle, most of it, is designed to make money!"

"Making money? You honestly think that's what the education system is about?"

"Across the board, the price of education has skyrocketed multiple times beyond inflationary rates so as to become impossible for middle class people to send their children without taking loans—why is that?"

"They're building new facilities, they've appointed more international teachers, better dorms, you know—"

"No, not in the least—it's well beyond that. The price of education, relative to inflation, has more than quadrupled in the past decade. A few select groups of people are making heaps of money off this—unqualified people involved at the university level enjoy inflated salaries, and folks in the financial sector have made billions via interest for sake of investing government debt into harebrained, get rich quick schemes—all to churn out broke, addicted, immoral morons for the most part, who then get hired at near pointless companies, compile more debt and run them into the ground, further pushing us into a two class, have and have not state that imports everything."

"Is that what you write in that book of yours?" the man asked. I didn't answer and it came: "Well, whatever you write, the way I figure it, if you keep at it, maybe one day you'll have a whole bunch of loyal fans."

"I live comfortably in deep obscurity and I always will—I don't want to have fans, I just want to be left alone to live and die."

"You sound like an old man." I didn't say anything and: "Before going back to school, I was an unemployed academic. If you think you're going to make a living being smart, think again—that's why I'm going back to school—to learn how to do things on my own."

"That sounds like an oxymoron to me."

The guy went on about a slew of shit: "And further, what my studies taught me was that most everyone longs for some associated narrative to their lives. Don't you?"

"Mainly, I long for something beside the exhausting, relentless toll of daily routine for something I do not love. I want nothing of it," I said.

"I'm working on a book on that subject," he said, "But in this market, it'll probably do terrible."

"Not if its worth a damn—and if right off the bat you recapitulate the initial proclamation that you're writing a book with the supposition that it'll do poorly, and include a readymade excuse in the very same sentence, well—you don't sound like anybody I'd be interested in reading. You sound soft and weak, and I wouldn't root for your success in the very least."

"Are you serious right now?"

"Fully," I said, "I cannot stomach people who announce their intention to do something great and include excuses for its likely failure in the opening stanza. It shows you're unconfident in your work—and if you, the craftsman, are indecisive and hesitant to chat about your quality, then your product is likely doomed. Don't blame it on the economy—check your premise and fucking blame it on your self." I terminated the conversation, closed him off and thought: what's with these new, soft ass Americans?—every opportunity to control our fucking reality, no big fucking chief controlling our desires, and still—how many act upon them? What percentage? Realize you can wake tomorrow and study anything you like, for free, so as to grow into anything you want from the ground up—and yet what will people do? Complain to acquaintances about frivolous incongruities initiated by other unimportant acquaintances. Sit in traffic. Hate reality. Gain weight. Yell for no reason. Feel jealous of those who work hard and succeed. Take no initiative. Wait to die so as to finally start living in heaven.

He again got to speaking at me and so: "I'm just saying, man, if you try to blame outside circumstance as the reason you'll fail to accomplish your greatest of goals, then you never possessed the proper level of self-respect to achieve in the first place—if not for the current availability of 'the economy' as the focus of your flaw, an alternative would have been created in its place—there's always some excuse. I don't care about your excuses. I would hold such elevated respect if only you stated: 'My goal, X, has not been attained just yet, but I'm still plugging away.' Alright?"

I dipped way deep inside, and ten minutes later the bartender walked over, pushed a long straight strand of black hair away from a blue eye and: "I'm not sure if this is a compliment or a cut down, but when I saw you walk in, I thought you'd be an idiot—you drove that guy out of here, and I appreciate it. He comes in here every once in awhile and bugs me until he runs out of money."

"No worries—I've assumed bums on the street to possess a less cognitive mathematical mind than a second grader, only to play them in chess for five dollars, and lose to a perfectly executed Queen's gambit within twenty moves, so I feel where you're coming from."

"When's the last time you played chess against a bum on the street."

"All summer, pretty much—they're not quite full-on bums, though—they're like math bums—left-brained calculation addicts, if that makes sense."

"I've never met one."

"If you hang at the chess spot on the Lake just south of North you'll get to know what I'm talking about." We shot the bull for awhile: "And so we never elk-hunted again."

She had a good laugh and: "You have some funny stories."

"They're all made up."

"Really?"

"You'll never know," I said, and she poured me a whisky on the house after I left her a nice tip, and went on tending to the other patrons.

A couple came in and the man went: "No, sit here—there's a bit of a draft in that spot because the wind cuts through the stray bullet hole in the window."

I gazed round and spied a burly, middle aged dude whose pocket knife probably smelled like garlic drinking a pale-looking brew in the back of the room. He was seated beside a man with a similar sort of seriousness about his bearded face—his choice of reading material was: The Articles of Confederation. He mumbled something, words blunted by his thick Chicago accent, and when asked to repeat he lowered his specks and: "I said if people came through time n' took a look at dis joint, dey wouldn't know where da fuck dey were."

"No shit," his friend responded, "If da founding fathers came back they'd be construed as domestic terrorists, n' placed onna a watch list."

"In a fuckin' minute—they'd be branded intolerant extremists for refusin' t' accept the preposterous demands of inept double talking thieves who claim their right t' take as patriotism instead of patronage. It's fuckin' incredible, actually."

"Frankly," the man began, "Of da many tings I'm sick of, I'm most sick a' people I don't even know pourin' my dough into third world hellholes—it results in no change minus der fascist leaders growin' fatter via corruption."

"And we keep payin' for it—us and Western Europe: governments preach prosperity while the public is carryin' their belongings in bundles n' plastic bags—mostly on account of government theft, no less."

"It's like askin' me t' do aerobics in fuckin' bondage—t' work my ass off n' give it away t' crooked corporate n' government alliances the way we do. Dis country has become a mirror image of what its original settlers were fightin' against—everyone's afraid t' call a spade a spade—my kid's doin' good in fuckin' school n' they downplay it as much as possible. They don't put up test scores on the board no more in case it shames some a' the kids."

"I'll tell you right now: if I wasn't shamed into doin' better at school by my nuns I woulda been up shit creek. I thank God they shamed me so hard. Every test I was at the bottom a' the list they circled my name in red, right there for everyone t' see. Eventually I didn't wanna be there no more. That's all there was to it."

"Third t' last?"

"Ay, I wasn't last, alright?" They had a laugh and the man continued: "But seriously, all I can say is hide yer dough, hide as much as ya can n' be frugal wit it—at the end of the day it comes down t' you and nobody else—in a system a' government manipulation you're either a cog inna wheel or yer out of the car, right?"

"Yeah—out gettin' run over n' left for dead."

He set the book down and: "You met my old scientist friend Bart Klein, right?"

"Nope."

"He moved way out in the North Dakotan prairie n' quit payin' taxes altogether. Lives completely off the grid now—he don't even own a phone. Communicates via mail n' courier only—spends all day immersed in self-preservation on his piece a' property."

"Sounds like an intelligent bastard."

"Yeah, real hard worker—it ain't been an easy time, but he's left alone now."

I wondered if this will become more prevalent—civil disobedience and self sustained realities such as was the case before all were subjected to a thousand page tax codes so as to pay for killing peasants and protecting cronies in far off lands of stone. I hoped for such until: "I smashed my mail lady—great legs on this one. Girl walked seventy miles a' week," Racquetball John interjected from the end of the bar, "She tried t' play hard t' get but, well, that proved a hard thing t' do when she had t' swing past the joint t' deliver late fees on m' bills every day, know what I'm sayin?!" a bunch of drunken high fives rung out all sharp-like and "Ay bartender, three drinks n' some change please?"

"Sure thing."

Behind me a man spoke of his wife and rubbed his temples before he looked at his friend and went: "You know how it goes—sometimes you just want to crash your car into a wall at ninety miles per hour and take a long walk."

The friend seemed the sort of cat who might consider canned sheep tongues classy dining, not the type I would go to for advice on my wife—he was an unbalanced-looking fool with crazy wandering eyes and a halting mustache, and soon it came: "We were mackin' some barely legals, actually, until Stu got us kicked out n' blew it, man."

"Bogus—I haven't had a barely legal since I was barely legal, really."

"Yeah, I'm tellin' ya man, they were hangin' before my eyes like North Shore jailbait—they were real young and supple, real innocent. If I wasn't livin' at the Y at the time—I'm tellin' ya, man, heh heh heh, I'm tellin' ya she woulda tasted sweet as sugar—"

I flipped my sketchbook to an old random page and drew a sawtoothed combat knife beneath ink on pulp that went: "You look cute, obviously."

Sun struck her smile, and, steeping a teabag between delicate fingers, she said: "I know you love me."

"Yep, you're right."

"And so what shall we do on this wonderfully sunny, and for the first time in a half year, seventy degree afternoon?"—t'was an old interaction with Melissa, written several years ago as we sat in the shade feelin' okay, watchin shifting baby leaves dilute sun rays on a breezy, spring afternoon. I noticed my handwriting had changed a bit in the time since I'd written it, and remembered the western breeze that carried the smell of a million trees exhaling all at once, a sigh of relief and amazement and horror at the fact that they had come to be—a human sort of cognizance, if only for a second—shock at the fact that again they are bursting alive above the scene, rattled to the core at beauty of the view fused with the prospect of dying and being unable to carry the experience in some lasting fashion—these were the conditions that day as we took turns talking and being quiet as bright light beamed down from an open sky. "Sure is nice," she said, "The smell of leaves pushing through initial flowers as birds sing fresh, happy songs of rejuvenation. O how good it feels to be in spring, Anthony, really—I'm reborn."—try as it might, my imagination could not seem to get the color right.

Two men went out the door for a smoke and I caught a chill so bad I felt like I'd never be warm again—t'was a chilling of my outsides from within, and I blew hardy gusts into my cupped, bloodless hands when at a table just behind me it came: "I mean—you *actually* bel*ie*ve that humans were formed in the Garden of Eden? You bel*ie*ve that shit, Anderson?"

"Unequivocally."

"And how old do you believe the earth is?"

"I'm not sure—probably about five, six thousand years old maybe."

"Despite all the geological evidence to the contrary?"

"That—all that wasn't written in the Bible, those geological findings."

"So no?"

"So no, I don't believe in those numbers."

"Despite all the scientific evidence?"

"Yes, despite all that."

"And what about the civilizations that existed before the Bible was written?"

"What do you mean?"

"Where do they fit in terms of your God's grand scheme? The Aztecs, Egyptians and Romans, the Cherokee and Sioux—are they not in quote, he*a*ven, because they existed before the time of Jesus Christ? Are they not in quote, par*a*dise, because they existed apart from Mohammad? Were there no good people back then because they did not possess supposed parameters of behavior with which they could be judged and executed, written by, quote—God? Should their history be negated? Their society? Is this conundrum invisible to you or what, Anderson?"

"Well—I'm not totally sure. I guess I never thought about it. Some call that the age of ignorance."

"As opposed to now?" He took long look across the room and: "I just want you to remember this in your dying moment—I want you to think of me—think of me and know that the Bible, the Koran and Torah, all religious books—they are merely books of stories written by random people over hundreds of years—written by humans fundamentally no different than any other, no different than you and I, and not by the hand of God. These books are nothing more than chronicles of unfounded fables supported by rabid, desperate fans who are so deeply afraid of the possibility of a non-infinite personal reality that they often reach a stage where they are frantic enough to kill in the name these false fables—think of me and this conversation so as to earn at least one moment of personal honesty with reality before you fade into black, Anderson—I'm sick of you trying to convert me." The guy split and I thought: I ponder those exact ideas, but I choose not to scare people with them—I possess many thoughts I choose to not scare people with, in fact, including myself.

Trying to smile but feeling a little empty, I had another drink. So yeah—how will it be without me? Is that what man of old used to think? How's it gonna' go when I escape me? Will that deep, crushing black be all I'm gonna' see?—I grasp how folks turn to their Gods to ease these daydreams—and so God fucking damn it all—me as well—goddamn me straight to motherfucking hell—if there is such a place. "How's it goin, pal?"

"What?"

"Are you using this stool here?"

"No."

"Mind if I take a seat?" This Anderson guy was all set to cramp my style.

"I mean—there's a bunch of other stools around, man."

"So you mind then?

"If it doesn't matter all that much, I'd rather you choose another." He sat down and I thought: who comes up on a guy at a near empty bar and sits right next to 'em, on purpose, and doesn't expect a problem? Nobody I'd like to know, that's for sure. I didn't say anything or even look at him too close because if he would have given me the wrong vibe, well—in all honesty, I was in the mood to strike with retaliation monstrous and disproportionate to the cause of the problem.

He didn't start in on me right away, and I was relieved. Out the door, air brakes released and a big diesel engine roared up the snowy road. I watched the ballgame for a minute and after the 3rd period ended with the Bulls down sixteen, it came: "Did you hear what the fella said to me awhile back?"

"For the most part."

"What'd you think of it?"

"All I want is to watch the Bulls, write and relax right now—cool?"

Apparently not—he talked for a good while, and if you've been writing lots of dialogue, people will begin speaking and you literally begin to picture handwritten sentences funneling out of their mouths. All the ums, and pauses, and stutters, and incomplete thoughts—you should try it some time, really. If you try to visualize individual words churning out of individual mouths, you begin to realize how incomprehensible most verbal communication would appear upon paper. Let someone speak, listen very closely, and picture letters, thousands of sloppily scribbled letters discharging their chops. After you've practiced this with some unceremonious characters, the next time you actually speak with someone who makes decent sense, you'll appreciate them that much more. It finally came: "Man lost God as soon as he started telling other men how to find him."

"Technically, man invented God—thousands of them throughout history. In a sense it all began with one man telling another how to find him, so you're incorrect."

"What do you mean by that?"

"It means I was serious when I said I was not in the mood to talk to you, man," it went, and he shot me the parvenu look of repugnance I fully anticipated. "Believe what you need but don't bring it to me."

"You haven't been reborn, have you?"

"I'm reborn about fifty times a day, man—reborn and burned down to the ground before slipping into sweet fucking dreams."

"That's what I thought, as well—but then my house got re-possessed—I made some bad investments, my business and marriage fell apart, and so I became a born again Christian."

"What for? To pretend that you screwed up your business and were married to a gold digger because you hadn't been praying enough?—if you really feel like being born again, quit lying to yourself pal."

"Ex*cu*se me?"

"No problem."

He gave me a twisted look and: "All who belong in hell will find their way to the inferno."

I didn't respond, slid over a couple spots, and turned my attention to my work. I looked back after a minute and dude was still sitting there, leering at me, and so I told him to cut the shit for real and he eventually did. Up to the tele, there were only eight minutes left in the 4th now, and the Knicks were giving the Bullies a beating. We turned it over and a man near the door slapped his hand against his table and: "Goddamn it! This fuckin' African! Fuckin' looks like he should be inna bush wit a machete in his hands!—guy's makin more per game than I make inna year t' keep dribblin' the goddamn ball off his foot, n' he's gonna' cost me a hundred bucks if he keep it up!" Time ticked down on the shot clock and I thought: life—it is slipping away for this guy. Can he feel it?—the fact that it will be ending? I don't quite know what to make of it. I flipped to a new page, unable to concentrate and: wow, my head really works that way?—t'was my self statement after contemplating the weakness of suicide versus Ronnie crushing and slowly suffocating himself to death via laughter. I looked around and thought: it would be interesting to lecture this room on the philosophical possibilities of First Cause and subsequent effects upon individual existence on a theory by theory basis before ending it with a sharp gunshot from the jaw through the tip top and dropping stone dead then and there.

I took a big breath and almost felt like I was about to go down backward over the stool when a couple of well dressed guys around my age came in the west door, sat further up the bar and: "How's LA?" one man addressed the other, "You must be learning a lot—" of pussy shit like ass kissing until your lips bleed so as to be told your writing is worth two bits.

"I am. It's incredible," he said, and he went on to describe all the amazing people for whom he races to retrieve coffee and pastries: "I'm working my way up the depth chart—you know how it goes with writing out there." He went on to say that so and so was just *so* hilarious in real life, and XY and Z were all hot for him. His buddy nodded and I got to thinking that it would be a good idea to build a cave below the surface of the earth so as to avoid contact with society for the next fifty years. I quashed a good group of beers in the next thirty minutes and got to feeling pretty affected. I tried to get goodness to wash away twisting rage via kind thoughts and such, but the fire was burning too hot and bright. As time ticked on, the bar filled with a bunch of loud people around my age and I felt nothing like them at all. I felt way older, a few centuries worth, at least, and soon a few groups of 'hip kids' came in, disheveled in just the right way—clothing crooked and factory made worn-looking, but cuffs spanking new, each cavorting about with such individualized flare that it only served to highlight their conformity—and it seemed to me that now that they had their tattoos, they were supposed to *be* somebody, supposed to represent some ca*u*se—but the likely cause they represented was that of another inexperienced cat with expensive ink thrust through their skin and no clue of an independent, self-realized identity. Maybe I was wrong, who knows? At least I hoped so, I really did—and so I sat there drinking, bewildered to an extent, and as I looked out at everyone all I could see was flesh melting off their faces and white rickety skulls jawing on about nothing. Sometimes life is just so—so many words for naught. Everyone laughed and I thought I heard their teeth clinking together like a serial killer's wind chime, and so I closed my eyes and tried to go black and breathe sanely but instead met the image of Melissa's face twisting in fear as an unknown man lurched in on her. I pushed my lids with my palms until a white flash bright as an atom bomb erased her eyes with a shockwave three times hotter than the surface of the sun that saw people on the other side of the planet waving flags and cheering wildly at news of her vaporization.

Another brew slipped down my neck and I shivered hard as more people came and went, breeze cutting through the room, drafting me, and after another shiver and the sight of brake lights beaming red though frosted glass, I wondered where my uncle Dennis would stay on such bone chilling night. I've thought of him a lot in my life—an inordinate amount, you might even say—it's just: to think he's been out there cussing and hustling, for all these years—I mean, do you ever cross my path, man? Do you think of dad, Gramps and the guys? I look at all these bums trying to see if it's you and I never know—what will become of your soul, man? And in this instance, I was reminded of him by the sight of those brake lights on Grand Avenue gleaming through the window—they reminded me of a painting he once sent me, after my pop and uncle Norm got him out of a big jam where he was about to get killed by some people he owed. The image in oil on canvass went: furious red-eyed bats verging on smashing through spooky blue church windows, eager to swoop down on cowering figure. Around the edges he wrote things like: 'Life is an illusion,' and 'What begins will always end,' along with additional haunting slogans to send to a ten year old kid, right, and to top it all, on the back of the painting, all sorts of weird people from the halfway house he painted it in had signed things such as: 'Flowers will bloom again—Gloria Tinsley,' and: 'Big Earl Davis—room 216,' and 'Maryanne, I still love you, whether you want me to or not—Rich from the 3rd floor,' and forever I have wondered who such people were and what would become of them—how I fucking wonder, man, forever.

A real haggard broad in a conversation with Racquetball John went: "Have I mentioned I'm the Vice President?"

"The Vice President?"

"Yep—I am the vice president of naughty trouble."

"Who's the president?"

"You are."

"Well, *shit!*" he went, mouth smiling, cheeks red as hell.

I took a deep breath and caught the image of my eyes in the bottom of the pint glass as I ended my drink and got back into the sketchbook. A redheaded girl who'd slowly worked her way into my vicinity began talking to me. She was alright and such, but I was feeling nuts and not keen to share myself when it came: "See, I sell commercial real estate."

"Is it everything you're breathing for?"

"Well, yes, but not quite—eventually I want to complete grad-level work, you know, work up to that level."

"Right."

"I'm working with a new property located in an exclusive, gated community."

"I don't know that I'd be interested in such a community. I'm the type of person those gates are generally seeking to exclude—my friends and I."

She laughed and: "I'm going back for my MBA, also—I figure it won't hurt to know more about business than the next guy."

"Cool."

"Yeah, it's just that, I'm getting to the age where, I like, need to get married fairly soon, and I want to be sure everything is locked in place—good insurance, two functional cars, a comfortable house, you know, a life with no uncertainty, so I'm able to like, provide a stable life for myself and family. I'm almost there, I feel."

"Um hum, yeah, that's important—it's good to be responsible and such." My mind was silently spinning out of control. Well I suppose it was not *all* that silent—it was quite loud on the inside, but outside it was a silent plunder to the depths below. My heart beat quickly as she reshaped her hair and inched her breasts closer to me. She was nice and all, but the more she went on about her pragmatic approach, the more disjointed my reality seemed to become—she was making me feel like a total nutcase without even trying—I switched to whiskey rocks and felt how it would be possible for me to, if things didn't work out to my liking, wind up sort of like Dennis. It was a pretty crazy feeling in a way.

"And I feel like, I'm still, developing, you know, the mindset of accountability, like, where I'll be able to jump in and have kids right away, you know, I don't want to be like, thirty-two and still looking, you know, for compatibility, and then, have to like, get married and have kids immediately per se—that's my quandary right now. Are you involved with anybody at the present moment?"

"Hmm. Involved. No." I was tweaking fairly hard. I drank a heap of water and got real fidgety.

"Are you A-social?" I honestly couldn't answer, man. I felt like I was having an asthma attack as again the entirety of what Melissa had mentioned pulsed through me like an explosion post static coming alive in a dark, broken sky. I breathed out and felt like hypodermic needles held by cigarette smoking detached nurses were bleeding me dry from my most prominent veins while I attempted to lift as much weight as I possibly could, all at once. "I can be A-social sometimes, too—I know how you're feeling right now so don't worry, you're okay." No, you don't, and no, I'm not. Further, whatever happened to being soft spoken? Has this once highly regarded personal trait been vanquished from actuality for the sake of selling more prescription drugs or what? I couldn't muster an answer and: "Is it something I said?" She was all self-conscious now.

"Not at all."

"Something I *di*dn't say, then?"

"No, c'mon—I just need to chill solo right now, but good luck n' all. I hope everything works out fine for you in the end."

"I think maybe you need to get cheered up—I felt that way myself, earlier today, and I thought about going to the Signature Room, but it was just too cloudy—I want to be able to *see* if I'm going to spend the money to eat at the top of the Hancock—I was supposed to take my friend Mindy, in fact, but we got in an argument. I mean—it's not my fault that like, everybody likes me, but, you know, I'm kind of a kick ass person."

"Gotcha."

There was a long silence and: "Are you a Quaker?" she asked.

"I eat Quaker Oats, that's about it."

"No, not a Quaker, I meant a Buddhist."

"I don't know man."

"What are you thinking about?"

"I don't know, nothing really, you know—just—my own shit."

"Something is on my mind, too."

"Cool."

"Want to know what it is?" I was hardly listening, mostly focused upon keeping a decent finger and foot-beat to '*In Memory of Elizabeth Reed*', efficient overtones of which were charging out the jukebox, "Fine, I'll tell you," she said, "I'll let you know what's on my mind, but then you have to tell me what's on your mind, too." She spoke of many things, including: "My knives!—my brand new granite counter tops are actually capable of dulling my stay sharp knives."

"That's some pickle."

And wrapped it on: "But you should do that—it'll look good on your resume."

"I bet."

"Okay, so, what're ya thinkin' about?"

"Honestly, it's nothing—really nothing at all—I'm not tryin t' be rude, really."

"But—"

"I'm just trying to relax and compose myself, okay? Can you ple—"

"You prom—"

"I have absolutely nothing constructive to say." She waved me on and, "If you must know, I was just thinking that if somebody blew up this room right now, I mean if somebody was fed up with all the things that had been feeding them up for so many years—all the random little things too numerous to name—if somebody was fucking fed up to a point that they were literally on the verge of imploding and thereby determined that the best solution to this little problem of theirs was to do so outwardly—to walk into this crammed full bar here, dynamite and ball bearings and rusty fucking nails galore strapped round their waist—if someone was looking to crush for the rush—perhaps the fanatical rush to be*lieve*! I mean—I certainly be*lieve* in—a bigger than you and a bigger than me—but yet I don't kill as my way to you me to see the unseen. And why? Because they who do are primitive human beings— and so if this somebody walked in here, screamed praise to Allah or whoever and pushed some little black button hidden in the pocket of their overcoat and sent us all to bits, brains all over the walls, organs, blood smearing shattered pint glasses—maybe you'd try and find survivors and all there is, fuck—half a body in one place, a faceless head in another, fucking arms, the bomber's ribs might be driven deep into the side of someone's body as other wounded people went moaning and screaming in pain, partially blown up or horribly burned, faces shredded, skin hanging off like liquefied cheese grated by shards of hot flying glass and sole survivors of obliterated friendship circles left bloodied and weeping upon their knees, faces inflicted upwards and fists demanding answers from a smoke-filled room—and what does one feel whilst dying in an explosion, anyway? A white flash of pain and a single, white hot reflection before the pressure wave concussion comes rushin through and obliterates you into indiscernible oblivion?—who can say?—and so if that happened, all the ideas—all the ideas I have that I think are so great, the ideas I think will in some way or shape, matter—all the ideas in *your* head, too—well, they wouldn't matter anymore, would they? As if they had never been, *blam*—all which you cherish, just—*blam!* Just the way each and every day several thousand people around the world are blown up by governing organizations or shot by madmen or stabbed by lovers in fits of jealousy—and the only thing to come of it is that they represent some number in a death toll to which you, I—to which we're all completely detached. But for them, for those people, their everything, all they were or had ever planned on being is no more, and I knew nothing, no details of the beauty in their head—just as it would be over for us—over and without distribution or the desired exchange of our own ideas and dreams, you know, if some maladjusted marvel of ferocity decided to make it so as a right of his or her free will—but it wouldn't even matter because even if we *do* spread our conceptions, all we're going to be in the distant future is another number, some finite figure within the four point five billion year lifespan of our little sphere of fresh air floating through the colossal vacuum—know what I'm saying? I'm going to be a number, just like you, just like all of these people who pretend this isn't so," I said, looking around, "So I ask you: what would it even matter if this place exploded?—it's a fact that, whence viewed as a whole, is nearly unstomachable and capable of breaking you—feel me?" She sat very still for a moment—blank expression entrenched on her face, not speaking. "You asked me what was on my mind—I'm thinking of all sorts of crazy things, like—if you don't want to know what somebody is really thinking about, don't go around asking."

"Glad to meet you, anyway," she said, and she stood, placed her navy-blue pea coat over her shoulders, and walked over to a small group of friends who were having a big ole laugh about something or other.

I turned the other way and in the corner someone was saying: "Let 'em fuck with us—let 'em! Do you know what would happen to them? We would make them a grease spot. You understand me? A grease spot!"

At the bar it went: "I said I wanted some more."

"And I said you're cut off."

"Boo!"

I exhaled for what seemed like forever and thought: okay man, easy now, easy—just breathe, everything is fucking fine. I closed my sketchbook, finished my drink, pressed my temples to the center and walked quick outside for some fresh air—seeking asylum from my brain, just feelin so strange, I saw a man up the street make an angry face at a imposing figure and demand to know: "Why you be steady trippin on me, *B?*" The guy responded in jagged sign language and I figured a mute who has not been able to utter a single solitary sound in forty years is bound to have some pent up aggression.

I smiled, took a super deep breath, exhaled white and tried to relax. A man walking past nodded at me and I said: "Cool dog man."

"Ey I appreciate it—hava' night."

"Yeah man." The fuzzy fellow wrinkled his nose and gave me the crazy eyes, letting me know he'd die for his master, right then and there, before plodding his ice speckled paws up the block—his face was not unlike my dad's description of a dog he and my uncles found while working as summer laborers on that farm I mentioned to Melissa. Found near the property, he was a wild bastard, thick furred and protective as hell, and they had a tough time taming him after bringing him in, so they named 'em Frisky—he was the best part of their lives, for the most part. Long and short of it: over the course of the summer, a rural door to door salesman would not stop *hound*ing them about buying a goddamn vacuum cleaner—nary enough money to *eat*, chowing bowl after bowl of farina, yet still, the relentless bastard kept showing up to sell the vacuum, convinced he'd talk them into it. My grandfather was too polite to tell him to beat it in the menacing fashion that was necessary, and so eventually he came back yet again. This time, the kids screamed for him to stay in the car. They yelled and waved their hands in the stark summer light. But no, he thought, I want to talk to your father about the nifty invention again, and make some cake—the man got out without realizing that Frisky was loose and angry to see him on the grounds again—such was the warning the young boys were yelling—and just as he stepped up, Frisky ran around the car and gnawed the guy's leg all hard. Guy dove back in his whip, eventually kicked the dog off and started screaming that he was going to sue the family, bankrupt the already broken and such, and shortly thereafter he came back with the sheriff. Gist went: instead of taking my grandfather to jail or suing, they decided to shoot and kill the dog. So, just like that, with the cop and salesman watching, my dad and his brothers were forced to tie Frisky to a tree, and give him their final hugs and kisses goodbye. He must have known something was up because, as my dad puts it, just as the sheriff stepped up with his rifle, Frisky began charging, full force until the slack was up, and his whole body flung forward as his neck lynched rearward—*wham!*—legs flying out—*wham!*—body racing full bore and being snapped back in an effort to break free—raw animal instinct anticipating impending annihilation—over and over as the sheriff popped him a handful of times with a bolt action .22, you know, grazing him the first couple times, real gory and drawn out, and when Frisky finally went down for good, my dad and Frankie and Dennis, bawling, sprinted off to hold him as Ronnie sat crookedly, crying in his wheelchair, and as my pop lifted Frisky's head off the dusty ground and kissed him, his collar broke loose—he was that close to getting those motherfuckers. I always imagine their faces, holding that bloody dog, watching those guys drive off down the dusty road, duty done—the image does something crazy to me, man, it really does.

I came back to reality and a few groups of people walked past, in high spirits, it seemed, to be spending time together, and I looked south toward the Loop rising cold and rigid in the distance, with streams of white smoke streaking from the tops of sparsely lit buildings. The wind blew and ice crystals tumbled down the sidewalk as though infused with the soul of a born-free animal—so yes, plant this seed and pass it down—instill such within all you love—born free you must work to forever remain so—a wonderer—how the fuck couldn't you be? Why the fuck shouldn't you be? Roam—the mountain is there so climb upon it—the mountain is there so fly down it—breathe—breathe in and accept—and this—my God—why is accepting limits so fucking difficult?—the breeze struck me in a strangely subtle nature that had me feeling as though I were dissolving into everything all at once—relax, breathe—see what is and accept—eons—fucking eons of time that come at you like seconds—charging up the long standing ridgeline of the mountainside into the black sky, drenched in shallow pale sunlight absorbed and cast off a moon not quite full for sake of the fact that the shadow of the planet upon which I reside is stealing a slice of luminosity— billions of people on the other side basking in rays as I view their sliver of shade upon a rock revolving a larger molten stone in a vast empty space—and on we go, spinnin' 'round at a thousand miles per hour for sake of remaining in place upon this Magic Gravatron and crunch, crunch, upward and onward and into the star speckled sky, thousands of feet on high I dissolve into the vision of Orion and climb on—and though this is happening now just as every second I have ever been has been exactly right *now*—no past, no future, only present—I am—the hands of the Hunter into which I feel myself soar—born in a high intensity nuclear fusion reaction millions of degrees and thousands of light years preceding me, with a sound so deafening it eclipses comprehension—one hundred and eighty six thousand miles per second times sixty and sixty again and then twenty four by three hundred and sixty-five and another fifty thousand further, all in order to realize: twinkle, twinkle, little star, I just now grasped how far you are—crunch, crunch—I tightroped the curb and became tiny again, and damn it felt nice—moonlight glossed the snow atop a parking meter and lit the granules into miniature stars and I felt quite free and unwounded by time at the moment.

I thought of my work and it went: O this medley of effort—how I long for it to transfix itself into an assertive representation of life that shall outlast me—so alright, do or die—and if I do not get done, I will not only be the one doing the dying, I will be the one doing the killing, too—so grind motherfucker, grind—think of your family and don't lose track of the fact that you have a date with the end, always creeping as she be, and so if you had one final hour, what would you do? Take one hour from everyday, even one half, and break it down with full submersion into that which you love—do so and in the end you will have lived free. I thought of Melissa's advice and walked back into the bar feelin released and eager to hit the road and get back to base camp so as to catch some zzz's, wake and start fresh again—it was then that I sat down and it occurred to me: my bag. It was fucking missing.

Blood withdrew from my limbs and slid into my chest cavity, seeking to protect my organs from the impending meltdown. I made a big scene real quick, looking frantically about, and after giving everyone a close once over, I snatched my sketchbook from the bar and bolted into the night. It took nary a moment to realize, yep, this is actually happening— all my work is probably gone.

The next hour involved a blur of futile searching and leering at people until: "Holy fuck, man—I'm fucked!"

"Are you okay? Need some food?"

I pulled my head out of a dumpster and: "I'm not fucking homeless, man—and don't ask me if I'm okay. You don't even fucking know me—got it?"

"Just tryin' t' help, buddy."

"Well I don't need any help—and if I did, if I did need it, I wouldn't want it—I'd rather die cold and alone at the fault of my own, facing bravely the problems I've caused without complaining. Okay?—whether you mean well or not, just get the hell out of here. Fucking hear me? Get the fuck on out!"

The guy split and I looked into the next set of trash bins. The dual positives: the trash had been picked up that day—I could see straight through to the bottom—and secondly: it was cold—had it been summer all the dog shit and rotting organic matter would have been roiling in humidity and thousands of well fed flies would have been shitting on my forehead and trying to lay eggs in my eyes like I was one of those malnourished sub-Saharan kids, too weary to swat. I looked in another dumpster and nothing. Fucking nothing! "You stole the bag with the least worth to you and the most worth to me, man—both sides of the action, totally pointless! My whole horde of negatives was in that fucking bag, man. You should have never had them with you, Anthony. Fuck! You're an idiot, man! Goddamn motherfucking cocksucking whore bitch motherf*uc*kers! *Ooh!*" I flipped over an empty bin and the mind went: years and years and *yea*rs of capturing minute moments via image and word—scribbling in dark, weird places in deep hazes and just like that, just poof, gone, so long—like fuckin' dying. T'was all I'd valued, really—I looked to the sky and felt totally broken all of a sudden. I felt like jumping from a forty story building and crashing through a parked car before opening the back door and taking a long walk.

"O the precious hours!"—a crazy violent surge of the type that has a habit of sneaking up from time to time and reminding me that indeed I am my father's son, and within me exists the potential to dip into an immense stockpile of viciousness that, after generational prevalence, there remains a mass of significant quantity deep inside me—such swept through real serious-like and: "Sure, everything's fuckin' okay, sure—" over and over I said so as I held my knuckles out at shoulder height and pressed with maximum pressure upon the jagged brickwork of some slapdash mason from the turn of the century, and made not a peep as the skin gradually tore away. I trudged up the alley toward the next set of trash bins with blood dripping off my fingertips and peeked inside: nothing. Wow. Minus the words and negatives, I lost my grandpa's hammer, an extra knife and the camera—I could care less about the camera, except that it held that last photo I'd taken of MD at the park. I pictured some sick cunt developing the film and lusting over that image, personal as it was, and I felt rage at the thought. I jumped around at a sound and in my head it was some guy with my property, but indeed it was just a plastic bag blowing down the frozen road.

Why? Fucking why are you so stupid? All I had needed was some fresh air—I figured myself covered but forgot there were two doors to the establishment—guy snatched and dipped out the other side. So now what? All that heart-felt writing and thinking, so much time, a ton of random experiences with random people, all taken down as beautifully as my mind could manage—fucking gone. Fuck! I smashed over another group of bins, cursed hard and a woman smoking on a balcony startled me with: "Are you alright, sir?"

"I'm just a little irritated with my whole state of existence, that's all."

"I'll pray for you."

"Please, don't bother." I turned and felt numb via the unintended sharing of my intellectual property at a scale that consisted of the total output of my whole mind and soul over the past seven or eight years—the maddest shit—the totally insane trains of thought that were so fucking broad and intense tangled up—the shit you'd show nobody—not because you were scared or doubted it, but because *fuck* people!—feel me? Why share the live fucking rawness with them? That which flamed when roaming the earth blazed out of your skull via the fucking hugeness of it all—ten billion streams of shake-inducing thought roaring through as you squint down at your hand and try to explain a tiny bit of the firestorm roaring within, all the time knowing that you could write and burn a thousand pages, and it'd never hold a match to that feeling right then, there in the world, at that moment, being who you were, one and gone, that single breath and beat, that sun, that wind—that *feeling—bam!—gone!*—and so that's what I missed.

I walked beneath an underpass and unspecified, freezing beings lounged among the rafters. I asked if anyone had tried to sell them a backpack and it wasn't so. I searched about for several more hours, peeking in dumpsters and entering posh establishments to warm up and spy all the patrons before getting back to it again. I returned to the original spot six times but to no avail. By the final time through the door people turned to me as if I were about to start killing—faces gawked and whispered shit I couldn't discern—probably something like: 'Is that the guy?' 'Yeah, that's him.' 'What a crazy-lookin' guy.' 'Yeah—I think he's crazy—he looks even crazier than the last time he was here, twenty crazy minutes ago.' 'That's what I just said.' 'O yeah, I know.' 'If you know so why'd you ask?' 'I was distracted by this crazy guy.' 'O yeah, him.' I searched the bathroom and I thought back on what I had gotten done—all the years I'd spoken about getting it done—all the ideas—all that fucking time spent thinking, writing, throwing it away—thinking, writing, throwing it away—little fires building into a great wall of heat—all my insights, my visions, the creation of my own original concepts—the amount of time spent clarifying, edifying, perfecting, polishing, improving and, well—I ripped punches into the door of the stall with my bloodied hand and yanked on it until it fell from the hinges—I walked up tight to the mirror and talked some hard shit at the reflected image of my exhausted eyes before storming into the desolate street—

A doleful sense of finality settled in and I became vicious. I went ahead and walked the entire way back to camp, straight through the lonesome madness of the West Side and down Chicago Avenue, holding tight to the sketchbook, which was all I had left—my temperament seemed to become more hard and violent with each pace. Every alley and fucking corner seemed to greet me with shadowy, lurking figures, facial expressions insinuating mal-intent melding with a physical capacity to see the threat through—eyes holding a gaze that above all else seemed to represent the raw sort of expression that yes, I've done this before, and I'll do it again—motherfuckers smokin' in the slits, a single cherry fading in and out like a distant star in empty space, wanting nothing, yet pulsating, waiting to explode. I walked past cracked-out, sprawled-out Joes, homely motherfuckers listing upon light poles, shadow of their over-stretched, fuzz-balled beanies casting a pan of indiscernible blackness into the space where a face may or may not have existed. I strolled long strides, full of intent and met crazed, bloodshot eyes with an unspoken statement that served to reverse any uneducated assumptions into a firm concern of: is he really worth it? Hood raised high and ready to die—as paces compiled, I smiled at the internal notion that I wanted them to, that I was eager and pleading, a hunter deceiving, most surely believing that whoever dares try and eradicate my vivacity would conclude as a formless tragedy: beaten and bludgeoned and mangled beyond responsiveness or recognition. I felt no fear of dying, no care of pain—fully sane and logical and determined that not a soul minus my own shall ever be capable of affecting my will—go ahead and give me your best: kill, kill, kill—I'll renovate the thrill.

Past Ashland, there was hardly anyone around—it was a real depressed stretch of impoverished urban America and in my head I felt like every car that rolled down Chicago was about to pull over and light me up for no reason. After Damen I didn't see a soul, and as soon as I passed Western and got back to camp it struck me: my keys. It took quite awhile to pry the aluminum garage door high enough to squirm inside—the effort made a lot of noise and still nobody looked out their window or called the cops. Once within, I dug into my rucksack, put on many layers of fresh clothes, lit the heater and warmed my hands and feet. Illuminated by the flicker of blue flames, I put my head in my hands, opened ye olde sketchbook to a random entry, and it went:

> 'All I own is thoughts and words
> What I've spoken
> What I've heard
> All I own is sights and sounds
> Where I've gone
> What I've found
> All I own is nothing at all
> Just like you
> After you fall
> So breathe today, so deep within
> The fact that you have always been
> Always been and never were
> Every ounce of certainty you'll seek
> To wind up forever unsure'

I sat real quiet for a long time, and once in awhile a little piece of mortar tumbled down the crumbling brick wall. My throat constricted like I was about to cry and I thought: I am going to sleep now—strange to see how I can envision myself one day feeling tremendous relief at the prospect of never waking again. It was closer to dawn than midnight when I climbed into the tent, thought my last thought, breathed my last breath, and went black. It had been a ramble of a day.

38

I woke and the sound emanating from the goddamn radio did not make me feel comfortable at all. In fact it was about the worst song that could be playing, whatever it was—some super repetitive, dual piano, harp and electronic jam fronting the droning sound of a semi-violent orchestra, all in purposeful off-time synchronization and overlaid with ill-timbered shrieking tones that made me feel every bad thing I'd ever done was going to stare me dead in the eyes as I'm dying, and then my head will explode and sound like that song. Dark waves, man, horrible and crashing, dark waves of reflection.

And the morn—my how it arrived in a flash—I felt as if I completed little more than a single, protracted blink, during which time the world suddenly became bright. Had it all been a dream?—a sensory experience that did not exist outside the mind when silently yearning for the fat ball of fire to light the morning sky and save me from the dark frightening night? I lay there for awhile, watching my breath steam above my lips while wondering what Melissa would have said had she paid a visit: "So this is how you live? You camp in this garage, nearly devoid of possession—an accidental neo-luddite held lukewarm by the lullaby of your heartbeat and it's faintly lurid, graceful triumph of the coiling gale as the echoing sediments of formerly life-filled entities incessantly rage within your eardrums—all to avoid playing the game?"

"I guess so—that's a damn accurate description of it. So whudaya think?"

"I think your freakin' *crackers*, man!" I imagined her smile and the sound of her laughing big and loose and:

"Keep it down, Melissa, Jesus—you'll get me tossed, cackling like that."

"Nice hatchets."

"I thought you'd dig."

"It smells like a man in here—it's cute."

"Cute? I don't know—you sure you don't mean: acute? This joint's fairly rank, I admit."

"Does it ever feel weird, being in here?"

"I mean—I get to feeling a little nuts, being here at night—when you hear the cold wind sneak through the aluminum door with a whistle, and it's just you in the quiet, alone with your thoughts—I get to feeling a bit nuts, you could say."

"You know what? This is going to be your year."

"Only because I made every other year mine by constantly working at it and dreaming big and fucking *do*ing it—I mean how many people claim they will be published someday? So often I'm at a pub and I hear: 'You know what? I'm gonna' write a book someday'—and I was that naïve kid once—20 years old and dreamin'—but what a process it took to learn things don't happen quote: someday—they need to happen *every* day to build into that someday—only via discipline and mad tenacity and leavin' it all out little by little does someday come to be—hence this will be my year because I fucking earned it.

I imagined she'd enter the tent and say something like: "Can I join you?"

"Um hum."

"Like all cozied up right there?"

"Um hum."

"I think I would like that." We'd chill for a minute and she'd continue: "No one will ever get you like you I do, don't forget it."

"How could I?"

"It's pretty cold in here—you should get a space heater."

"I don't trust space heaters—half the time some fool goes up in flames it's because they couldn't put on another layer, and the heater sent the whole crib up for *grab*s, man. Plus it's easiest to write cold shit in a cold place, truth told."

But that didn't fucking matter now, did it?—all the time it had taken to fabricate many thousands of sound, durable descriptions was squandered away. Alas no, losing my work had not been a dream—for the dream to which I'd woken involved a shootout behind the garage—in my final breath, my gun refused to fire and my assailant was free to creep deep on my eyes before pulling the trigger. It was awful—I was unable to move—a paraplegic on the verge of being gunned down—the man marched close enough to kiss my face, held direct eye contact and smiled just as the flash from the muzzle of his gun blinded my vision and woke me from my slumber. Laying there alive, I figured things could be worse.

Truth told, I had thought about inviting Ms. D back to the garage when we'd been together on that stroll, but I just couldn't do it. She would have understood my frame of reference, I believe, but still—I wasn't exactly proud of the joint. I planned on being proud of what came out of it, but seeing as that was gone, I mostly felt like torching it. Either way, I needed a hot fucking shower and some food, so I got dressed and split. And the trees this morn—black bark weighed down by dense white, what is living and breathing now in a prison of pristine vigor. It was below freezing as I headed to a nice gym and finagled my way in for a hot steamy shower and some work on the heavy bag to ease my anger. I walked in, told the girl I'd left my padlock there on my previous visit, she pulled about fifteen locks out of the lost and found, I spun a pretend combination on all of them to no avail and, after apologizing, she handed me a fresh towel and told me to enjoy my workout. I brought a different backpack with a second set of clothes, and as I ripped into the bag with loud pops, it felt good to be out of the camp, losing my mind somewhere else. An hour later, I left a bit more relaxed, nicely warmed and clean as could be.

After reentering the bright world I ate three green bananas purchased at the gym, rolled back to the neighborhood where the bag had been stolen and repeated the same routine as the previous evening—nothing came of it. Toward the end of the endeavor, while waiting for a light to change I heard a rough-looking Island guy waiting for a bus who answered to the name of 'Jamacko' yell to a friend: "Sh*ee*t mon—he tried t' f*u*ck me over all last year, n' now I'm still workin there, n' he's not." He leaned in on his friend's shoulder with a chuckle and: "See mon? The big boss, gone—you spit at the sky and it'll fall in your eye mon—trust me mon." As I carried on, I calculated my karma and figured maybe I was due for a windfall of bad luck, anyhow, bearing in mind the tally of all the little wrongs I had committed in previous years. Old lessons had me feeling like some wise elderly owl was staring big yellow eyes down from a wasted tree limb, not blinking or uttering a sound, following me everywhere—those huge eyes—if you tried to run his head would spin 'round with you, all casual-like, sight beaming to infinity. Fucking shit—that goddamn feeling of being spied on, invisibly, every second you breathe can make you feel like a real lurch sometimes—mad superstitious and constantly keeping score, one good for one bad, so that maybe in the end you can wind up breaking even: purgatory, here we come son—it can't be much different than this, I assume. Once you let it in, man, no matter how illogical—that crazy Catholicness—it's in, man, forever—at least for me it is—whether you'll be knocking fists with JC, saying: 'What's the w*o*rd, homeb*o*y? I began believing you were a figment of our imaginations for a minute there—' or not, those goddamn Catholic lessons get you keeping tract of your score like those old ladies who've been sitting in the same green box seat at Wrigley for seventy years, keeping tally on a losing effort from now until infinity.

After a while, I gave up for good and went to where my bike was locked. I removed the wheel and headed to the L so as to get the tire repaired. I was sick of walking and at half noon, the day had warmed rapidly. The temperature was in the high 30s, and after such a prolonged cold snap, the air felt rather balmy. Arterial streets were respectably clean and people were out and about, drinking coffee and doing chores, jogging and walking dogs and bicycling and embracing the thaw with gusto southerners would not comprehend. The city had a renewed sense of vigor—it had been feeling quite frigid, raw and unnerving—downright desolate at times, as Chi City oft manages to feel when the wind turns raw and daylight is fleeting. Yes—I'm in the mood to crush you, little friend: t'was the feeling this beast had bestowed upon my body of late.

I passed two men tending to some electric lines, and one shut his phone: "Was that your girl?"

"I swear to God her voice cuts through me like fucking nails when she drinkin'."

"It's only noon."

"Well, she's already at it, whudaya want me t' say?" He exhaled steam and: "God, I got no desire t' be here on 'eis horrible fuckin' job minus the fact that by doin' so, a day may come where I no longer have t' keep doin' so—ya know?"

"Beats drivin' around, smokin' cigs n' lookin fer scrap metal—don't it?"

"Barely—I fuckin' hate electric."

"Why you an electrician 'den?"

"Just pass the fuckin' long nose pliers, alright O'Bryan? Stop askin' questions."

I kept on and waited to cross a light as a fire engine and ambulance screamed west on Division—I was surrounded by two attractive women and a business man in his late thirties, speaking loudly into his phone. He'd exited a silver 7Series BMW and took his time looking at the ladies as we'd approached the red light. He struck me as an annoying little snob, mainly from the sound of his voice and the way he spoke so loudly of his situation for sake of impressing those surrounding—he must have been talking to a business partner of sorts, as he went on about how good things had been of late, and he then said he was about to dip into the bank, located directly across the street—"Well, you'll owe me—I raced to get here and they're almost about to close." The desired discussed withdrawal, if you can believe it, was to be $75k, in cash: five hundred 100s, and five hundred 50s. I mean, fuck man! My stomach dropped when he said it, and when the light changed, I remained where I was. He walked, still talking on the phone, dead into the bank across the way. Wow. My heart began to hammer hard as I examined his shape closely—he was wearing a tight-fitting pair of black slacks and a mock turtleneck—I scanned his outline for any bulge that might indicate a concealed handgun and saw nothing. Wow. Wow. Wow. I watched him fill out paperwork through the window, raised my hood and walked a couple addresses north, kitty-corner to the one and only exit. Fuckin' seventy-five stacks man, in loose cash—that whole first nugget, right there man, right *here*—waiting in the hands of a man I already couldn't stand. My heart went racing crazy—after what had just happened—the thought of having to show up at that new insurance company on Monday—to start over like that, from zip—my God. It would take so much time to write a book from scratch again—if I didn't have to work, I mean, I could be done in a year, if I did, well—it could be five—six or seven even, to write it perfect and raise enough capital to print—goddamn—is it right?—would I curse myself for generations?—I made two fists and touched my knuckles to my cheekbones and pushed inward—those calcified fucking hands, all those shots on the bag and lessons from my dad— just one, man, all you would need is a single cold ass shot and good night it would be—a fat stack with plenty of slack to help me and the family—but what's the first lesson pop ever taught?—that it would be wrong to take from a private citizen in the first place.

The man walked out, still on the phone, holding two fat manila envelopes in his left hand—I mean where is this fucking guy *from?* This is Chicago, man! People get offed for sixteen dollars and a pack of Newports and this cat speaks openly of a $75k withdrawal for sake of impressing strange women while never assuming there to be a potential problem stalking that same story? You're out, walking on the street, right now, with that sum of money in your hand like a lose football, talking about a sushi chef and some random whore you're trying to mack despite that fine handsome wedding band on your left hand, and here I am, walking behind you, fucking three feet behind you, blessed with the power for a one shot knockout and *bam!*—I just walked past you, all this on my mind, and off you go, into your sedan and on to your next destination, no sense of the of the struggle of good and evil that just played out on your own fate, and alas I do not know how I feel about it. Did I make the wrong choice by not sticking this dude? The honest truth is that I did not know. I really didn't. That was a test by God is what that was—a test by something. With all the shit going on, the temptation to take down that mark was serious. My karma would have been wrecked forever, would it not? It was a test, man, I'm sure of it—during one of your lowest lows you were bestowed with a huge score, just sitting there on a platter, ready for the taking, and you didn't dip to the dark side—I thought: you're either a semi-good dude or a total fool, I honestly didn't know.

I leapt over a puddle and the line to get a car washed extended way up the street, and all the Mexican dudes wiping them down were hustling fast as could be, happy it seemed, whistling and singing as the sun poured down on a bright, profitable afternoon. I walked on, grasping inner peace as snowmelt poured from rooftops and elongated icicles occasionally crashed to the ground. Matted soft snow had packed into ice and white tree limbs trickled back to their darkened ways with an assist of the beaming sun, evidence of yesterday's storm gradually expunged. As I walked, my boot became unlaced. I knelt upon static pigeon feet once paced in wet concrete and tied to the sound of a dribbling basketball coming from a recently shoveled court. I peered over as a son crossed over and drove past a father, missed the lay-up and, after ole boy scooped the rebound and headed to the top of the key, the kid yelled, "I got past you there, pop, I *s*moked you!"

"No son, you didn't—I was still in your head," it came with a smile, "Hard t' finish those drives with me yellin' *boo* in the back of your brain, ain't it?" he said, smiling, tilting his sun-drenched face to the side, low-dribbling through a puddle, pulling away from several animated reaches for the steal, slapping the hip-check away like Jordan did Starks with the clock winding down, driving, pulling back, crossing over to the left hand, between the legs and: "Whachu got son? You playin' that Le*Bron* D—whacha need t' learn is that's why I always take it to you like Michael would," and back to the top of the arc he head faked and came with a hard drive before pulling back at the left elbow with a smooth cross through the legs—he faded from seventeen, extended his fingertips over the outstretched arm of the up-and-coming young blood, follow-through arching across blue and: *net*—"Game!"

"Dang, dad! But only by four—I swear I'm gonna' catch you someday."

"You gonna' get me, trust that, but not yet, son, not quite yet."

"I can't get my hand on that damn fade away."

"Well, when you do, it's pretty much over for this ole boy. You know I gotta savor these wins—you gettin' physical, kid. I'd take ya t' lunch, but I don't know if I needja gettin' any taller."

"Can we?"

"Hell yeah—let's do it." They slapped five, shared a half-hug and strode off—and as they did, I marveled at the thought that my pop attended that same joint, forty some years ago. I pictured him running around the same schoolyard, worried that the family was set to get evicted from another crumby apartment in a matter of weeks—but he'd adjust, they'd all adjust and trust in sustained hard work to raze what may have been a deep obstruction to feeling at ease—I thought of such and took strength from the memory.

I re-laced my other boot, stood to go and noticed a beaten old Rosary jutting from a pile of ice. I kicked it loose, grabbed a handful of snow with my gloved hand, washed it clean and put it 'round my head—I figured it had to be a bit lucky to have stumbled upon in that moment, and I damn well needed some.

Another half block east, I passed a group of teenage entertainers soliciting donations on the sidewalk via the feat of jumping rope in a tumbling aeronautical assault of flips and summersaults—the best part about it was that the 'rope' was a young black boy no older than eight—two long-armed kids held his hands and feet and whipped him around like a string of burnt spaghetti as the others took turns double-dutching mere inches from his face—it was hands down the best form of child endangerment I'd ever seen, and I donated a handful of change to further the cause.

Across the way I noticed an older black gentleman struggling to push a rusty Lincoln Towncar to a joint on Wood that does emergency tire repairs. I figured if I helped the old guy get his whip out of a drift at the advent of yesterday morn, I might as well continue the trend. I sprinted up on the rear bumper and began pushing without an introduction. He smiled a real clean set of teeth and: "Wow! Thanks! Thanks a load!" I didn't respond, and after we moved her the necessary two hundred feet to where the Latino workers were hustling to fix the front wheel of a rusted-out low-rider, he said: "You strong boy! I was strong in my day, but shi! Ya pack the wallop of a big man in a normal frame—tha hat you wearin give ya extra power?"

"It was my grandpa's hat."

"*Aw!* Lotta' good energy in tha hat then! You know I ain't never given my grandson none a' my hats er nothin' really. I got a lotta' hats." He touched the brim of his black leather dime cap with a black leather glove and I felt he likely took great care of his possessions, few as they might have been.

"Yeah, give him one—whether he'll appreciate it now or not, I don't know, but he will someday, if he turns out alright n' shit."

"I will. I really will. Alright now—be easy. N' thanks son—ya didn't have t' help out like that. It really meant somethin' for me."

"No worries sir." I left and thought it odd that I lied about that being my grandfather's tam hat. The statement came out before I had time to think of why I would say such a thing—in truth I'd gotten it from a resale shop. I don't have anything that belonged to my grandfather—he had nothing to give but love and effort really, so, I guess in some weird way I wished it had belonged to him—I must have subliminally made myself believe that it had, I guess. It suited his style, and if he had owned it, he would've worn it, so it was as close as I could get to having something of his, in some weird way.

A family of several Mexicans stepped from a blue minivan—the driver had this wicked skinny moustache and his hair pulled all slick-tight in a glossy black ponytail—he walked around the front of his car, flipped a quarter into the air, caught it, slammed it upon the top of his hand, peeked and at the same time held secret the result of his guess, and jammed it into the parking meter before walking off with the remainder of his crew in the general direction of the secondhand clothing gig just up the block. I blew out a nostril onto the ground and passed a nail salon where all the women waiting to be served were watching the show 'Let's Make a Deal', and the thought of many thousands of similar people sitting around watching the same bullshit exhibit was depressing enough to make me die. A brute of a man waiting for his woman to finish looked as though he were having an identity emergency after his large male Rottweiler leapt upon the rump of a well groomed male Shih Tzu and pumped hard while emitting a rancorous effusion of yowling hullabaloo from a frothy mouth. He pulled taught the choke chain and yelled: "We don't ma'fuckin *swi*ng tha way, *man!* I'll fuckin' abandon yo ass if you keep rollin' like tha—stop fuckin' wit tha thingamajig n' pay attention t' me! Damn!"

He yanked 'em back hetero and I continued east, hiding my laughter as I sauntered away from the salon—after a few beats a very hard-looking King and three additional Puerto Rican schmoes wearing black and gold gave me a hard glance as they rolled a Cadillac Escalade westbound on Division. The snow-reflected sun beaming off the driver's shaved brown head and inked arm was very contrasting to his shiny white SUV—the windows were down and he was blaring some typecast *gangsta shi* that went nigga this and nigga that, my dick is fuckin' long and my rims is crazy huge n' shiny too, and in case I forgot t' mention, I gotz a fist full a' dollaz n' my bitch is badder 'en yours, but I could still have your bitch if I wanted, n' I'll fuckin slap your bitch twice before I have your momma grill me steak in lingerie n' bend her over the hot stove n' wit mad crumz still stuck on the corners my mouf—n' jus fo kicks I'll blast all your homeboys straight t' hell if you don't give me props n' call me tha hardest nigga of them all—you know, the track went something along those lines, real fucking tasteful, and all I could think is that it would be so refreshing to hear classical music or jazz blasting from a car filled with gangsters, just once before I die—I didn't cower to their look and I felt this enraged them. I thought: what if they rolled up on me and I just unloaded on them? Would my violence really change the world for the worse? The media would say this or that about me, and according to 'law' I would be guilty of a 'crime', but what do I care? Do I honestly worry one iota for what anyone thinks of me so long as I'm personally content with my actions and know them to be just? Of course not! The people out here in the streets know the reality, the way innocents are pushed around and bullied, and they're sick of it!

I imagined the definitive sound of six steel-jacketed bullets slipping into a revolver before the stainless steel wheel clicked closed, and across the way, set to the backdrop of a payphone etched up and down with pitchforks to mark alliances between Peoples and Folks, an old Latino man in blue jeans and a faded 'Repeat the Threepeat' Bulls sweatshirt was picking through a trash heap. He added two new items to his shopping cart and sat upon a patch of melting snow, back pressed against crumbling brick as he thought of something. I walked on, passed blood smeared on snow that showed somebody had walked past Rite Liquors at the wrong time, and the sound of an air drill and a hammer hitting iron mixed with the smell of a body shop—a young black girl passed, dragging her hand across a chain link fence—her fingers rebounded like those of a court room reporter detailing in shorthand the gruesome details of such a girl's violent death as glistening snow fell from individual links via shuttering metallic reverberations.

I passed a light pole with the back panel ripped off, and an indiscriminate mass of crap was jammed inside amongst the wet wires. Across the street, three suspicious Caucasian fellows sat in an old gold beat up Chevy Caprice as a fourth man worked on switching license plates. At the next bus stop I picked up a paper sitting on the bench and skimmed some grimy stories: a 50 yr old woman whose throat had been slit, a 39 yr old man who had been clubbed to death by unseen assailants, a young mother who'd been raped in broad daylight by two men in a public park in front of her husband at gunpoint, a young child who had been taken to the hospital with PCP and crack in his system, a drive-by shooting that had killed two men and wounded two more, highlights of a corruption trial, and on I read of an old man just up the street who was found beaten and stabbed to death yesterday afternoon—so yeah, just another day in the Chi, right? The last yarn was only a small blurb about how a caretaker came in and found him tied to a chair, body somewhat decomposed, and obviously dead for a good many hours. Now this occurred on Augusta, right, just on the other side of Western—so that means

232

this poor old man has been intermittently interacting with my grandmother for years—a steady cornerstone of the neighborhood—ruthlessly murdered within the walls of his own home, his family's home—and the killer is just strolling around here, free to take more lives. Ingesting to a story such as this, it becomes hard not to root for an ethical man with the brutal will to begin hunting people down. I mean—why not?

I blocked the thought and in the distance, a hideous concrete CHA building with not a single window on its west side rose twenty-five stories into the blue sky beside a sign that implored me to swallow some Hennessy and another that showed some redheaded slut in a tousled blouse who insisted I 'act naturally' via drinking a particular type of Vodka so she could seduce me. I thought of this country, some of her images: windblown wheat on a family farm sun dyed light like the hair of the young American boy toiling alongside it—I lifted my eyes skyward at the sound of the police chopper and flipped what was into a hawk hovering above, great span spread wide, body totally still on the surging wind as eyes explored lush foliage for a fresh kill.

I was brought back to what was when brakes creaked a hulk to a halt and a diesel engine thumped over the sound of cooing pigeons—a Dodge Charger with blacked out windows blared its horn, swerved around the truck and booked its open throttle through the intersection of Ashland and Division, nearly exploding three pedestrians whilst avoiding the red light camera that was installed for sake of increasing public safety. Now waiting for the light to change, the man next to me addressed a friend: "To be honest, there is pretty much no way I would ever go to that reunion. Though I can see how it would be fun in some ways, I really don't feel like explaining myself to people—I don't feel like listening to people trying to brag about all they've been up to in the past twenty five years or what they own because frankly, frankly I'm feeling more reclusive than ever. I don't feel like seeing Ward Wakefield circle the room while spouting every detail about his life. I don't know why exactly, but I think that would really irk me."

I smiled, imagining what this Ward Wakefield cat might look like and what he's up to these days, crossed Ashland east, and just as I entered the Polish Triangle, among mounds of melting snow, trash and human excrement, a random maniac loitering by a tree stepped up and tried to sell me hash. I went ahead and explained that I wasn't interested. He followed up by offering me coca instead—as if exclaiming that I was disinterested in hash was some code word for wanting cocaine. The man in question was extremely large and a deep black hue— one of his eyes was a bit lazy, which really caused him to look like Biggie Smalls in a way. I wouldn't have smoked his hash even if I had possessed the superfluous funds to make the purchase. His demeanor insisted he might just stick two fat fingers into a deep, warm place, and roll a black sticky ball into a high class bag before trying to sell it as the 'Realest shi you ever tasted—no lie'. I looked back after passing on the offer, and as he loafed his dirty sagging pants past a thousand pieces of gum marking black blots upon concrete and various propaganda taped upon light poles, the dealer turned toward a trio of teenagers awaiting the #9 south to 95th and whispered what I assumed was the same scenario. I honestly thought about sneaking up and shoving a slim blade deep between two vertebras in his lower back before releasing a torrent of spinal fluid and blood and calmly walking away, I really did. The knife I'd lent Melissa and my mini hammer were lost with the backpack, so on this morning I had to bring an eleven inch Frank Beltrame switchblade along for the ride—I tend not to carry that one because the cops, if they so choose, could drop a weapons violation if they pull it off of you—either way, it was the only knife I had left and I thought of thrusting the beautiful, gleaming tip deep into his torso before twisting the rosewood handle clockwise and whistling a nice, happy tune. Several facets of his aura produced rage within—I pictured him returning to kick it with his friends, telling stories all loud about how he 'Made moves' that day, nigga, 'I was hustlin' like a *ma*'fucka' when, in reality, here he was, tryina catch the ear of some fourteen year old kids who might not know better, and possibly wreck their life so he could make a buck and talk like a big, self made man. Glide within the eye of your is and see who you are with untainted perspective—if the sights seen on the ride say you have to change things, do so—but no—this man, in many circles, is construed as cool for 'Makin it happen, son'—hence why, in many respects, modern thug culture is so fucked up it's not even funny, I'm telling you.

I took a long calm breath and held a blue railing while descending disgusting and broken red steps past a sign that said: Blue Line—Division: 1200N/1600W—a hint of dried blood stained the right side of the wall in a speckled pattern one might expect after a ripe grape were stepped upon by a fat greasy toe on the scorching salt flats of the Nevadan desert. I removed a glove, ran my fingers across the cool ceramic surface above the blue railing, passed a long forgotten, destroyed bicycle framed by Wendy's wrappers, and the woman in customer service window went screaming: "What? You was jus tryna transfer? N' whachu got left on that card? O you gotta add two fiddy on there baby—it ain't a free transfer no more."

"Shit, you gonna' owe me two bucks now!" a man yelled at an associate—I blocked the commotion, spun through the turnstile and dipped all the way down below.

39

"So she came in and was like: 'What on earth are you doing right now?'"
"Whudja tell her?"
"I mean, nothin'—I just said I was trying it on, you know, it was a new brand."
"She buy that story?"
"I'm not sure—I hope so, at least. You ever do that?"
"Yep."
"You too? You've really masturbated with a condom?"
"O, definitely not—I thought you meant lie to my wife."
The guy acted self-conscious as hell all of a sudden, and there was a long awkward silence before he looked up the dark tunnel to sight the next southbound train to the Loop, and said: "Now listen, don't go besmirchin' me over this story man—I mean—hell, just forget I said anything, wilya?"

I walked further down the platform, unwilling to be a part of the unease, and a discouraged dark haired man went: "So how much that gonna' shrug me? Another stack? What's the deal here? You told me this stuff was all under warranty. What? You're breakin'—I said you're breakin' up, man—I'll call you when I—I said I'll call you when I'm above ground, alright? The train's delayed—I thought all that was supposed t' be covered, anyway—hello? He*llo?*" He hung up, took a deep breath and looked for light down the dark track. Still nothing. I lingered for awhile, just zoning on the overall crustiness of the train stop—white I-beams discolored by rust shot from a red, worn floor into a filthy shattered ceiling that saw paint and plaster chipping away in huge flakes. Concrete walls growing God knows what sort of organisms looked as though buckets of carbolic acid were thrown upon the topmost sector before scalding the surface with a corrosive runoff, and congealing in the middle of the track.

I looked about as a loudmouthed girl whose calves were nearly too fat to fit into her Ugg boots pushed a bright red bulb of gum through one of the bored holes that outlined the insignia of a pay phone receiver in rusty iron as though some sharp shooter of old sent a several clips of .32 shorts through the side in an artistic display of marksmanship to be forever envied. "I hear that if I exercise more, I'll lose the weight real fast—it's just that I hate movin'. We haven't even set the date yet, anyway—n' besides, the last thing I want is t' get all thin for the wedding n' have him get the impression that I'm planning to keep the weight off, O no," she said. She held up and tapped the bottom of a Cheetos bag so as to devour any leftover dust before tossing the wrapper down on the tracks.

Her gibberish was soon overtaken by a man with a deep voice that changed tones in rolling waves as he went singing:

> "S*ooo* you think you got a h*a*ndle man—
> But then ya start to understand—
> You're *looo*sin'—
> Ah *haaaaaa* you're looosin'—
> A little ev*vveeee*ry *day*—
> There's no way t' stay sa*aaaaaa*ne—
> Said ya think you got a handle man—
> But then you start t' understand you're looosin'—"

I looked past him and near the stairs an unhygienic fellow with a big grin held a sign that said: 'Too dumb to steal, too homely to trick, too honest to run for office—donate please, anything will help'. I noticed his handwriting was decent until being distracted by a woman who went: "It was supposed to be eight roses and six lilies, but he got me a pink and white bouquet instead. I mean, he kn*ow*s how I feel about pink! What is wr*ong* with him?" I sensed a hint of a control freak in her basic actions such as constantly searching for that *one* last comment to make, that final jaded splice of an opinion—searching and finding with the efficiency of a Phoenix missile carob Northrop Grumman and its answer to the Soviet threat—

"I guess he's just not into details in the way you are—details are *every*thing."

"I'm glad someone understands." The guy to whom she was speaking was a typical opportunist eager to say whatever was necessary to get a fresh piece of pie. He was rosy cheeked white boy in his mid-forties who was dressed like a bit of a bumpkin, and he spilled incessant complaints of the delay. He went on eating his pita chips while mirroring the girl's grievances in enlivened style. The cold had fatigued me, and so did my observation of the rigid, predictable language of the duo at hand: she tried to come off like a cool woman, but bubbling below the surface was the soul of a life long complainer coming to terms with many angles of deep personal disenchantment for which her present status provided no remedy.

I walked farther down the track, passed some putrefied yellow bullshit splashed upon the base of an I-beam, and breathed. Five moments passed as a prickly fellow with stark white shoes crept about. I could tell he wanted to speak with me—it was much the way a young child walks cautiously toward a dog, and needs several moments to build up courage for one small, insignificant pet. He was peeping at me out the side of his eye while involved

235

in a head down, hands clasped behind the back style of slow pacing. I finally obliged and he came out with several unremarkable stories about absorbing too much sun whilst fishing for bluegills from a rickety canoe on the Des Plaines River, and his overall fondness for spending time on the water. He told a handful of crude jokes and I nodded silently—you know how it goes—whether you're in the mood or not, each trip below ground is a new adventure—sometimes you're forced to endure people, and other times you luck out: this was just one of those days, I guess. He rolled up his sleeve and: "How's this look?" It almost came: horrifyingly permanent, but I caught myself at the last second.

"Damn," I paused for too long, six full seconds, but it took that long for one huge, imperceptible breath to seep from my nose and keep the expression on my face from changing. "Fucking sweet man, I mean—damn. Super-tight artwork man, that's all I know," I said, looking at all these skulls with flames coming out of the eyes tattooed on his forearm. So dude strode on, farther up the line, looking at every single woman from head to toe, thinking of God knows what. I wanted to ask him if he ever contemplated what would it feel like to slit your own neck—to actually breech the tip of your Adam's apple with the slender edge of jagged glass in one unhurried slice—laidback—what would that even sound like? Mouth wet with the taste of hot blood pouring thick and red, streaming downward in mismatched streaks before slapping the ground with authoritative coherence of the fact that yes, yes I'm dying—I'm dying here, now, and despite the fact that I always knew doing so was my unquestionable destiny, I was never able to quite believe so—lest not until believing is no longer possible—what would it feel like?—fuckin' riddle me that, you mustached marvel of predatory indecision, fuckin' riddle me th*a*t.

I moved further down the line and over the soft smell of a freshened-up woman with dark hair, it went: "Shi, lookit them legs righ there—not a varicose vein *on* them ma'fuckas *man!*—I'd start at her ankles, man, kiss up them inner thighs, man, all slow n' shi, kiss her bellybutton n' shi, kiss her armpits n' shi, have tha pussy goin' without even *tou*chin' it man, *mmm*—I don't know if she a mother, a babysitter, nanny or what, man, but d*a*mn she got a fat ass! *Shi*," he said, "If she need a breadwinner you kn*o*w I be finna step up t' th*a*t. My mom*m*a*!*"

"Shish—stop talkin cr*a*zy boy!"

The man was leering at a black woman in her young forties, standing beside her husband, some twenty paces away. She placed a stick of gum between her lips, walked a set of red high heels toward the trash can with the wrapper, and he said: "Keep goin' baby, tha's yo speed right there, m-m-*mmm*—you feel like startin' your day with a little sway? Mmm—*damn!*—don'tcha jus love skinny minis wit apple bottoms n' full lips like that man?—godd*a*mn, son! You seein' this man, or wh*a*t?!"

"Dude finna peep you lookin' at his girl, man—I ain't finna get in some shi cuz you fuckin' hot for her, man. Chill wit tha shit already—she high class n' she taken."

"I'll knock his fat ass flat n' give it to her r*i*ght, man, *shi*—I walk wit a lotta confidence in that area, I ain't playin'—tha three inch gap righ there is jus *a*xin' fo me t' dive in man, head first, mo*u*f *o*pen."

"Man you jus t*a*lk at a girl n' she gets pregnant. You got four shorties wit three women—ain't tha enough already? I mean—if you don't know you crazy, you crazy."

"Ain't my fault them hoes was sweatin' me so hard—tha's on them, man, them shorties is th*e*y problem now. I did my part, n' I'm makin' money fo 'em—they gonna' turn out alright on they own, man—I got faith in m' genes—I ain't even stressin' tha shi no mo."

An incorrect appraisement of the past inevitably leads to a misconstrued orientation in the future. Over. And over. And over again.

I set my bicycle wheel down and surrounding me, many faces peered up the line to see if the train was coming, when in truth it was a pointless endeavor considering you feel the ground shake long before the tunnel becomes bright. Of course there was no roar, and as all the goddamn absurd conversationalists spouted on in perfect clarity, a woman wearing musky perfume trudged past with a tired look in her dark eyes as a chunky white man wearing crusty black corduroys hacked and spit a slimy green discharge directly in her path before leaning haphazardly upon an I-beam. Beneath my smiling surface, I was boiling—maybe I should work at a think tank, I thought, maybe I should work on trying to compress the kill chain. As the delay carried along, all sorts of people built up on the platform, and as I tried to imagine their collective worldview, all I saw was chaos. Complete. And utter. Fucking. Chaos. That with a lot of sad and hilarious bullshit mixed in between. I took a breath and thought: find peace amongst this madness please, I'm beggin' you brotha.

A fit black man in a charcoal suit came down the stairs and after grasping the delay he swore and sprinted street side in search of a quicker solution—between the rails filthy water congealed a mass of old newspapers, fliers and cig cartons. Two poor old ladies went on: "Las summah, Paysmall had a big sell off, n' I went n' bough me fo pair a' shoes."

"Um *hmm*."

"But two a' the fo broke apart 'fore fall was through."

"Um *hmm*."

"So I figure maybe tha's why they was shippin' 'em off—in the end it wasn't really a deal at all, they jus madeja feel like it was at the time but, you know, the quality was low."

"Um *hmm*—" she blew her nose, "How's Clancy? He holdin' up?"

"Just about."

"Um *hmm*."

Her strong hand held a sparkly shopping bag that read: 'Life is short—utilize your taste!' I felt sorta bad for her and thought the container likely cost more to make than the product it contained. I then spied a couple pudgy city workers standing near by, one white, one black, and the white fool was using a walkie-talkie. I crept on their position for sake of gleaning information regarding the delay, and he went: "February bums me out man."

"'Cause it's Black History Month?" The black guy cracked.

"Heh, nah, I was born in February. Valentines Day, no less—really annoys me." I was about to ask him a question when he continued: "Every time I hear one a' these schmoes complain about the train I just wanna say: 'Fuckin' madmen built the motherfucker with their bare hands over a hundred years ago and it still stands, so fuck the hell off'—ya know? All these people waitin' here, lookin' at us like: ay guy, ay what the fuck? You wanna know what the fuck? Stop throwin' your fuckin' garbage on the tracks n' all the other tings you people do to wreck it for yourselves. All we're doin' is cleanin' up your mess half the time—what the fuck's wit *you*, in *fact*?"

"Ay," I interrupted, "How's it goin'?"

"Pierce m' neck wit a butcher knife, n' when it comes out the other side, I'll provide my opinion—that give ya a clue?"

"Somethin' bad happen?"

"Ain'tcha been waitin' here fer an hour wit everyone else?"

"I only been here a minute."

"Some fuckin' freak jumped onna fuckin' tracks n' got severed in half up past Logan Square. You know how crazy this place is?—it gets into people."

"Not good."

"No, it ain't—n' it happens all a' time—fuckin' weekly, in fact. All these slickseeds who jump in fronna' the fuckin' L n' make their final act t' be a pain in everyone's ass who's tryna get somewhere—these people who force da goddamn train operator t' witness sucha' fuckin' gruesome event n' have fuckin' nightmares about the fuckin' expression on their face as they leap headfirst onna' tracks n' have a thousand tons a' steel slice 'em in thirds, like cantaloupe—people who impose anguish on some young paramedics who gotta come down n' scoop the fuckin' segments while firemen hose down the track: I hope they all burn in hell, these fuckin' leapers—I hope they fuckin' r*oas*t." He spit and: "If you ever wanna off yourself, kid, come up wit somethin' that don't fuck up everyone's day, alright?—it's still gonna' take a minute, if that's what you were wonderin'." I walked away and continued to wait. It took another twenty minutes before a train to Forest Park rumbled in the distance, and I thought: people of all races take solace in ocean waves, and your iron grumble is my deep sea release—fuckin' CTA howling like a rapturous osprey: gotta get out of this city and catch the real thing someday, because I'm rusting out.

Mucky pools of water between the rails rippled and thick paint strips waved on wind pushed through the tunnel in advance of the train. A sarcastic cheer came up from the crowd when the high pitched whistle began: *wooooooooo!—wooooooooo!—wooooooooo!*—I could tell right off by its speed that the train would not be stopping. It was already filled to the brim with folks from earlier stops and was running express to the Loop. I looked to my right and as the tunnel grew bright I spied a sign that asked peeps to not lean over the platform—I inched up and stood with my toes past the blue rubber safety line, shut my eyes and imagined what it would be like—in the background it came: "So think you got a handle man, but then you start to understand: you're *looo*sin', ah *haaah* you're l*ooo*sin', a little e*very daaaay*—there's no way t' stay s*aaa*"—the reverberation of massive steel hurtling down the tunnel was otherworldly—the blast wave of pressurized air hit me before the train actually passed—I stood there, rigid and dark, picturing the glistening wing of a dragonfly in the dawnlight, hoping nobody pushed me from behind, and as it roasted past, mere inches from my face, I marveled at how uncompromisingly insane a person would have to be in order to throw themselves into the path of that screaming beast. It was a soft move man, I don't care how bad things were—it was, and forever will be, a bitch-ass move to go out that way.

A chorus of boos and complaints came up from the crowd, but I wouldn't have gotten on that train, anyway—waiting a few moments longer was better than jamming into that microorganism infested, steel coffin with throngs of bulky, aggravated bodies of various health levels I could not stand to imagine. I bounced my wheel on the ground and could not wait to get back on my bike. Eventually another train rolled up—feet shifted upon concrete, and on I strode.

40

The entire car smelled like a big pool of yellow piss that had frozen and thawed with each trip above and below ground, for weeks. "This is Division. D*i*ng. D*o*ng. Doors closing." The train lurched forward and soon streaks of light beamed past the blackened window—I stood just inside the door and the noise while charging southeast beneath Milwaukee was deafening. There was one attractive woman on the train car, and all the men, married or not, were taking turns looking at her. People adjusted and I got pushed farther inside the car, up against the opposite entrance—I took a wide stance on the disgusting floor and tried to block my gnawing hunger as I looked about: fat creamy bastard taking up two seats as skinny old Asian man stands braced against a pole—sickly faces leaning to the right as we tear 'round a bouncy bend—upside down pitch fork etched in steel door beside a broken heart and: 'Disciple Killa'—fat boy picking nose now, hard look into his droopy eyes sees him turn away—car #3018, how I fucking hate you—a man with his fat ass pressed against me answers phone:

"He*lo*? Sup. I said s*u*p. W*u*h? I'm onna train. *Wuh?* I said I'm onna tr*ai*n! Why m' late? I said didja ax why m' late? Cuz a' the train. I said cuz a' the tr*ai*n! Naw. I said n*a*w! Where you at? W*u*h? Hole on, I gotta another call. I said hole on! Hello? Sup. W*u*h? I'm onna train. I said I'm onna—" way to a deep fuckin' place in order to evade your mush mouth and an impending migraine. God fucking *damn!* Forget what I said about never jumping—fuck! I pressed my face tight against the window and the sound of the train roaring through the tunnel had me feeling as though I were constricted in a manmade wormhole that, in a single instant, had me bound and surrounded by fools who were destined to labor in tweak-factory from now until the end of time—no matter how bad you wanted to die, everyone lived forever, and there was no way to commit suicide. The motherfucking obtuse cunt of a character carried on and: "He tole you t' tell me I gotta pay 'em by *when?* Nigga need t' *chi*ll on tha—he might own tha crib n' be m' landlord n' shi, but I'm *in* there man— it's gonna' be a real pain in his ass t' get me out. R*i*ght? I know. Don't nigga know I'm a grown-ass man? I ain't payin' 'em 'til I *feel* like it!" You're a grown-ass fool, at best. Shut. The fuck. Up.

I pushed farther into the car, in a near panic, bicycle wheel held high above my head, clanging off a map of the subway system and an abortion ad, and the weird white guy who'd been pacing at the Division stop looked at a wounded woman standing beside me, and said: "Hey—you in a movie or somethin'?" She shook her head no. "Commercials?" Again it was no before she buried her broken out face in her blue nylon coat. I could see him getting really weird without permission if alone with a woman with no chance for repercussions. She looked as though she had any number of diseases, man, and looking at the open sores along her mouth, I got all scared to breathe for second. Stash-man raised his bushy salt-n'-pepper eyebrows and kept looking about, restless as hell, hardly able to contain his desire to speak to anybody on anything while she looked to be freefalling back to horrible sobriety after a session of roasting poles for dollars, bushy logs sticking out of that ashen face as it bobbed, high as hell off whatever household goods happened to be around, until all the pickles in the jar were slumped, wrinkled, and satisfied. An old man coughed and I shivered hard. Dude sitting across the aisle unwrapped a Whopper. It was evident after two bites that he was a lip smacker, finger licker and tongue flopper. Soon someone initiated a ruinous methane attack, so I had to breathe through my mouth for a minute. I exited the car at Chicago Avenue and entered another, closer toward the front of the train. It would have been easier to walk between cars, but every time I do so the people on the next car look at me in absolute revulsion—especially as a white guy. Black guys walk through the cars and people look up with expressions like: O, okay, just another desperate shine with a story walkin' through the train—in my experience the looks were: O, wow, this crazy wh*ite* guy is comin' through?—he must be about set to kill everyone.

The other car was just as crowded but people were nice and quiet. Several people silently listened to music or read, and besides looking out the window, I began paying attention to people's shoes, socks, their gloves—how worn they were, whether they chose fashion over usefulness, and after doing so I imagined the likely style of the apartment in which side by side they rest after a long, hard day. I became quite sad on a number of occasions, simply observing shoes or old jewelry—like this Spanish woman seated across the way, for instance. Her nails were painted very neatly and everything, but her shoes were so shoddy. She rested them very ladylike, right beside one another on the wet, filthy floor, and the way the brown leather was salt-stained and ruined by the elements made me sad as hell for some reason.

I took a breath and was soon heartened to see that a guy toward the back of the car was reading '*Siddhartha*'—he was almost finished with it, only a sliver of pages remaining, and as I got to gazing at his shoes, the next thing I knew he began berating a man for accidentally elbowing his ribs as the train lurched 'round a corner—all I could think was: you did not retain a single, solitary lesson from that tale, man, not one, and my guess is that such will be the same with the majority of your life. Herman Hesse is rolling in his grave right now, I'm sure.

I blocked the world until the wail of high voltage electricity was drowned out by tranquil street whistling as we stopped at Grand and Milwaukee. A few folks exited and back moving it went: "Hi, this is a message for Tony, I think you said you live off the Orange Line and—" this relentless homosexual cat sitting at my two o'clock was hollering at every fool in his phonebook, leaving long, awkward messages. Dude's style was fairly slick and I was surprised at how desperate he sounded—his stiletto boots were shined to perfection and his fingernails were quite clean, thereby fulfilling several stereotypes. Toward the back of the car two miscellaneous bums were having a drunken yet surprisingly factual conversation about traveling at the speed of light and ensuing consequence. A father snapped a photo of his two sons sitting tight together on one seat, feet barely over the edge, and I imagined them both decades older, showing that photo their own grandkids: 'Hey, take a peek at me n' your great uncle on this old time train car'—but then I figured the CTA will likely be using the same cars even then, and the envisioned interaction was moot.

At the next stop I again changed cars, and was now in the very front of the train. I pushed into the middle and the woman sitting to my right flipped open her book to page 68 and got on with reading some crap that went: 'The field of marketing attracts many extraordinary minds, and for good reason. A career in marketing can be very lucrative, in fact—' another girl to my left was reading a graduate study on bullying written by some schmoe whose name I could not read. Great, great, great. Everybody in this car is already dead. On the whole train: dead. Already dead and alive again, so like I said, I'm feeling fine. "By the time I get home and by the time I work out—" this woman, her voice was booming: "Gerald convinced me to buy a bigger TV—it matches the wood just perfectly! It'll take us a couple years to pay it off, though."

"Yo," a man said, closing the paper, looking at his wife: "I read my horoscope and it said I got a huge hidden fortune—it's in the Federal Reserve, just waiting for me."

"Well you better hurry n' snag it, they're about to spend it in China."

"It's spent," somebody said, as the L lurched 'round the bend.

I opened my sketchbook and got set to draw the scene when I heard the man who had been sweating that forty-something classy black woman at Division say to his friend: "Man, I already m*a*ke money, man—I make $2,900 a m*o*nth!" He adjusted his diamond earring between with his thumb and pinkie, his coke nail catching on the piercing for a second, and: "I don't even have t' come in if I don't want to—I m*a*ke money, man, government pay me for m' three shorties already! I m*a*ke money, man!" No son, you rec*e*ive money. You are not the creator of this wealth, and the fact that you do not grasp the difference shows just how far the delusion has gone—it is this precise mentality that is breeding an entire nation of dependent losers across every race, gender and ethnocentric boundary, period. It's unbelievable to me, how fucking soft that thought is.

They were playing some sort of a card game when from the mouth of a dejected business man it came: "Didn't you hear the automation? There's no gambling on this train."

"Well you gamblin' righ now boy, steppin' up on my bi'ness like dis—we best part ways, both guilty, cuz I ain't finna lose no b*e*t." He looked at him like: you gonna' get slit slow if you don't step back.

His friend sat forward in his seat, infringing their two faces and: "Yo he a body snatcher, G, don't fuck wit 'em. I seen him pull dude out the window of a Jetta after talkin' shi like he was recreatin' his birf—m'man hurt 'em real bad. Don't even meet eyes wit 'em again." He sat back in his seat and the face lingering on the other side gave him a look that held a level of brazenness like: I'll stomp until your head is smashed or stab until the blade breaks. Let me know whacha want it t' be cuz I. Don't. Give. A. *Fuck*, son!—it was a look you had to notice, and the guy shut up. Dude looked about ready to butcher an entire animal with a flake of flint in his pocket, straight beastin' man, a legit threat that was best to avoid. I envisioned confronting a guy like that, and pumping off rounds into his chest before stepping away feeling like I sprayed chemicals on a cockroach, not a care in the world.

"You lucky we onna train—p*u*ssy-ass f*a*ggot-ass b*i*tch-ass nig*ga*!—fo *real Joe!*" he yelled, pointing his forefinger like a barrel of a gun, poking it closer to a anxious forehead with every insult—thing was, he had real small hands, like a T-Rex, but he was still a big body, and angry as hell. He shuffled the cards all rough and: "I'm lookin' for a fresh g*a*me, which one a' ya'll wants *in?*" I almost suggested Russian roulette, but I didn't quite have the moxie at the moment. A news anchor-type passenger with puffed brown hair and an uneasy, intellectual face almost looked ready to pose: 'Why are you engaged in hate speech right now, sir?'—what are you f*ee*ling inside?'—why is he engaged in hate speech? Because he's a crazy motherfucker who's feelin' crazy right now! It's that simple sometimes! Anyone with their finger on the pulse of humanity can tell you so: Looney Tunes ain't just a cartoon—it's a quarter of the flats on the block or the cabins in the woods in one way or another. Stop acting so shocked—if you can't report things as they stand, unafraid of the stark ugliness seen in the depths below, start taking a goddamn cab or work from home.

I turned my back and walked way up to the front of the car—I looked down the track and took a peek into the quarters of the main squeeze—the operator of the train was great, man, really solid. He was the youngest operator I'd seen in awhile, like twenty-one, at best. He was a lean black cat with a big smile, and I enjoyed the kid because it seemed like this was ex*a*ctly the job he has desired to work for pretty much his entire life, probably had mad train sets set up to scale, little trees along the track beside stores, Hotwheels all set up, waiting patiently at the crossing and whatnot, and now, here he was, driving the L, loaded with people—he loved it, you could tell. I was glad for him—he looked his brown eyes up the track with great tact and seemed to revel in the responsibility of getting hundreds of commuters to their destination safe and sound—a self-satisfied, hardworking kid, I hoped he forever remained such. When not as crowded and filled with greasy oddballs, I enjoy riding across the earth and kicking back to the steady exhale of wheel upon rail—mind traversing a wide, jagged path, providing proper antithesis to the long, straight and unyielding track upon which the body is riding—a train ride can be comforting when not shared with folks who make you want to spew.

I exited at Jackson, and the calmative sound filling the arched tile ceiling was that of male and female street performers singing 'Autumn in New York'—they didn't sound exactly like Ella Fitzgerald and Louis Armstrong, but who could? Either way, they were damn good—the woman was full figured and her eyes smiled as she held nice sonorous tones with an expression that held the composed confidence earned by a life long church soloist: bustin' those pipes in the house of the Lord loud and clear to cheers and tears so as to cleanse sinners back clean each and every Sunday—the guy was bit older, right around sixty, and he held a real subdued personification of humble eloquence as his fingers roamed the ebony and ivory keys relaxed and easy while his deep personal voice hitcha strong.

Their sound faded out as I strode down the stairs and cut into the tunnel that connected with the Red Line at Jackson and VanBuren. The air smelled musty and a surge of diverse faces streamed past, some taking their time and others sprinting to catch the train I'd just departed. I passed a bunch of ads and a few folks sneaking prohibited cigs before making their next train—at the direct middle of the tunnel, perhaps the most whack-ass jam hub of weirdness, ever, an MC spit rhymes and juggler twirled random items in hope of earning spare change while additional grifters did their thing. A 'lil Mexican kid in green snow pants coasted a BMX tactfully between the comings and goings of all other pedestrians, and seventy steps later, I rose to the Red Line just in time to catch an approaching northbound train.

I stepped on just ahead of a black woman with bulging dilated eyes when it came: "O my God! O my *God* help! Somebody help me! Stop the train! Please somebody *he*—" the woman in question forgot to mind the gap between the platform and the door and her foot was wedged in between. "Please! Don't let the train start—help!" I dropped my wheel with a clang, spun back and immediately tried to wrench the foot loose—she was pretty heavy, and as I tried to lift it out, I thought for sure the train was going to start moving and cause me to witness a bloodbath other than the dark red blot between her legs staring me dead in the face. As I tried to wrench the moon boot loose, I looked closely and couldn't figure where it was stuck—my hand fit all the way around and it actually began to feel as if she were stepping upon me on purpose, it was quite weird. I squeezed and tried to lift, and her foot felt ready to explode—it was jammed into the boot like the tenth, final clown compressed into a subcompact car—she fell back on a middle-aged white man who supported her weight and tried to pull her back to the platform. He leaned on another man, who supported his weight just right for a second and, suddenly, that man turned to walk away, and they both fell out of the train—the woman whose foot was in my hand, and the man supporting her. It all started and ended so quickly, and she never thanked me—it was quite odd.

I stepped back from the edge and to my chagrin the guy who had been holding her up shouted: "Goddamn it! My wallet!—they took m' damn wallet! Hey! They pickpocketed me! Hey hold the train! Don't even move, Ms! Don't even! They took m' damn—"

A big argument got underway and the woman in question castigated the man for being: "A *racist-ass* cracka *bi*tch ma'*fucka*," who was insensitive to the fact that she had:

"Almost died," and in my head it was like: goddamn Anthony, you need to get high up in the mountains, man, seriously. This is just too much, all the way around—this place is shortening your life every day—don't pretend you can't feel it. I can see how the next place may never feel like home to an extent, but man—people fighting life and death on the street over $20 every minute like this *wears* man, I swear t' God!

The guy hollered all crazy and got security involved, they got the cops, and again I was stuck on the train's schedule, waiting for an incident to get squared away. He tried to bring me in as a witness under the assumption that the person trying to get her leg loose had seen something, but in truth I only saw mashed salt smudging my gloves and a man standing behind him at one point, then walking away—the actual theft had gone unseen. They were a team, out working a hustle, there was no doubt, but of course it was impossible to prove—I was certain of it because I had seen her walking with the other man, the two of them whispering in the tunnel, discussing strategic visions versus operational reality, and he was now nowhere to be found. The woman in question had a face of long lost credibility—it was evident she was eager to leave by how fast she spoke under questioning, and in a way I felt she was most worried that the longer she waited, the more her partner would have already spent before splitting what was left, and lying about the total sum found in the wallet. Through her explanations, she acted like she was going to a party with an improv cast—everything was so over the top: "Tha's ma*lar*key officer! Everything he's sayin'! Tha's all a buncha ma*lar*—"

The guy who'd been robbed looked exhausted as hell, eyes sunken and posture slumped while explaining the story to the cops—all the passengers were irritated with him: "Maybe you didn't even h*a*ve your wallet in the first place, Christ guy! I got th*ings* I need t' be *do*in' right now!—this is the middle of my freakin S*a*turday man! You're really screwin' me up—you know that? You're really scr—" and really, perhaps the saddest part was they had robbed the most busted motherfucker around—I mean, of all available, what a terrible choice. Dude had these horrible generic jeans on, ones he'd worn for untold days, you know, Grams wouldn't use 'em as a kitchen rag they were so thin—his knees looked bony and arthritic and his thighs gaunt as he sat, ice cold, it seemed, explaining his side of the story—and so what'd they get?—a wallet that, despite containing little money, was probably a centerpiece to his existence, with a couple beat up photos of people he loved, OCD-styled receipts for ten cent combs and fuckin' tins of Murray's Pomade aligned according to date. It was enough to make you want to die man, I swear—I felt really good for not knocking that guy over earlier, because even if he were a affluent jerk holding a huge sum, at the end of the day I'd have been yet another worthless punk who, at the root: took what isn't earned so as to pretend that it was.

We eventually got underway and the train limped through the chilled tunnel, past CTA workers in thermo-gear, hammering the day away, grinding it out n' doing what it takes, making a living, living a life, guiding us onward—a flash of spark from the third rail—a Polaroid—momentary infinity—the echo of their eyes—the unseen, heartless wind—momentarily seen, infinitely understood—their faces—stark white blurs—and after several stops, we rose above ground before Fullerton, where I spied fresh graffiti working its way up several icicle-lined fire escapes in artistic style, framed bright by the gleaming sun—and boy was it nice to see that blue overwhelm the black. It was dark down below, empty visions eroding my strength. Now flying through naked trees, I looked down on the neighborhoods: people out and about, lovers and kids and grandparents and drifters and bums and comedians, family men, sluts and mothers and brothers and sisters who'd die for each other, everyone in their winter clothes, shopping or saving or scraping, trying to have a good time for the most part—and looking down man, I felt pretty good again. I felt like you do when you're on vacation and you run into a stranger from Chicago—you know they're probably alright, that they've been through it, and if you had a drink with them, you'd be in for a coupla good laughs. I gazed at the Brown Line rumbling beside me, at faces, deadpan and laughing, unknown lives three feet away—faces I saw for a second but will remember forever—all of us bounding back and forth on an electromagnetic tether, clicking on up the track toward whatever lies ahead. The cold fresh air blew in through the doors at the next stop and tasted fine—I exhaled, breath rolling onward in a white cloud before I rode further north, got off, and made my way to the bike shop.

41

Nearly to the store, a rad little girl exited with her pop—she was all of eight years old and took the liberty to launch a solid ten inch curb on her new, mini BMX with a registered speed of: fast as she could. You, my friend, are fucking beautiful young soul, and you make me happy to be alive.

I walked into the shop and it went: "I don't know anybody who's dying wish will be to have had the opportunity to work for a few more minutes."

"And therefore you don't know anybody who loves what they do for a living."

"In fact—you're right, I don't."

A husband and wife were looking at some of the varied merchandise, and a woman who worked there stepped up and offered: "You don't know any bike mechanics then, do you?"

"No in fact, I don't."

"They're a happy group of crazies who revel in solving problems—some would die angry if a project were left undone." She flashed a disarming smile and "Let me know if you have any questions about anything."

"Great, thanks."

I looked upon all sorts of cool machines hanging—waiting, it seemed, to take you however far you felt like going—at any speed you chose, in any direction—what a great invention, seriously. Despite their beauty, I thought: machines are unemotional at their root—it is man who gives them their personality. Each bicycle could easily be a hunk that rusts in a sedentary family's garage or the weapon upon which the earth is sliced and landscapes are seen as you voyage to whatever destination you deem apt—it is the operator of the equipment that offers the variance. "Are you and your boss still arguing?" The wife asked—

"We've enacted an armistice." I waited patiently as he went wild posing heaps of queries to the girl who worked there, just over and over and on and on, going hog wild, right—then, unprovoked, he began talking about law, about how after so and so gets his summons, well, after so and so sees *that*, we'll see what he has to say about this *now*, won't we? "I mean—he told everyone he got the scar after surgery for a brain tumor, but in reality we think he got his head bashed in for coming on to a guy he thought to be gay—we have two witnesses. Can you imagine what that sort of information is worth to someone?!—I mean, as his wife's divorce attorney—just *imag*ine what that is worth! Insurance fraud to cover for *per*sonal fraud of th*a*t sort—he's a real Blue-blooded, old money guy, I mean—he would absolutely *die* if that news ever got out—he will, with absolute certainty, settle with me so quick his head will sp—" on he went, and I thought: lots of folks make nice livings for themselves as bottom feeders, they really do—it's just waking the next day stomaching yourself that I find to be the impossible part. After I stared at his face for awhile, well, it all of a sudden seemed to morph into static—a full wall of lashing static with all noise and no substance—and after this I thought, easy boy, easy: all noise shall eventually become silent, and I felt glad.

I walked to the back where the workshop was, saw the guy that ran the joint, and after some small talk as to how things were, I asked for the tire to be changed. It was a good bike shop run by good people—they'd always been fair to me and gotten things fixed right, sometimes not charging me labor, and so now, no matter how far I am when a problem arises, I always try to give them my business—hence the L ride all the way up there for a simple tire change.

I sat back in an old yellow barber chair beside a wooden wall at right that held random useful shiza for sale: chain grease and pumps and wrenches and such, and as I waited I spied a cool poster beside my head: in the bottom, written in blue it said: Velodromo Comunale Vigorelli—above the lettering was a brilliant flow of action that saw two Italian sprinters on the brink of barreling off the page and flattening the viewer on pure vintage track bikes. I imagined it hung in some humid alleyway in Milan in the mid 1930s, strong fast guys stretching, getting ready to race and spying beautiful women waving fans upon tan faces and old men sipping off fat jugs of red wine as they placed bets, high up in the stands, excited to watch a race on a nice, sunny summer day—crazy that they were all gone now, most of them at least, or certainly well past the stage of physical prime. "You have to use this energy now, man, while you have it, I swear t' God," I whispered aloud to myself.

A mechanic in an oily black smock handed me back my wheel and: "You had a jagged pebble of sand hidden between the rim and the tube, that's what kept giving you that slow leak to a flat, man."

"Thanks a ton, really—I probably wouldna found it."

"Any time man!" he said, friendly as hell.

I walked to the register, and the other owner snuck away from: "The cook at my place in Connecticut makes the b*e*st huckleberry hotcakes you ever—" for a moment and came to ring me out.

"How ya been?"

"Good, good. You guys?"

"Good. Real good." She gave me a cheap total of like ten bucks and: "Hey you know what?—we should put you in the system, finally. That last time, when you forgot you had those parts here for the whole summer, we didn't have a way to get a hold of you." I gave her my number and last name and with a chuckle she said, "You're not related to a Dennis Riedie by chance, are ya?"

"Why?" I was shocked to hear his name come out of her mouth—I responded: why?—because I assumed he'd fucked them over at some point in the past. Whether I'd claim lineage or not depended upon the story. I closed my lids and pictured a pair of wild, obsessive eyes like John Wilkes Booth coming in there and raising havoc.

"O there's just this random guy with that name who's come here once and awhile for a real long time."

"What's he like?"

"Um, I don't know, he's kinda like a rougher guy—he's got this bike that he rides around everywhere—I've seen him riding around forever, but he comes in here and has us work on it from time to time—like I said he's been coming here for quite awhile."

"Huh." How crazy—my uncle, who I'd barely seen—had he been going to the same bike shop as me, for all that time? "And you say that you've seen him riding around here, like—often or over the years or—"

"No I'd say often—often over the years."

"When's the last time he came in?"

"About three months ago, maybe in late October or something."

"Hmm. That's funny because, between you and me, I have an uncle who's kind of a bum who rides his bike all the time, or so I hear—mostly after he winds up at the hospital after a big crazy crash, my dad hears from my grandmother, and then he tells me, but either way, you know."

"It could be him—he never gave us a phone number and I'm pretty sure he lives over at the Y on Paulina, actually." That news was nearly as odd because I hoop it there on occasion with my boy Zybarsky.

"What's he look like? Like, a haggard guy or like, real worn down or something? What's his—"

"Funny—now that I think about it—sort of like you, in this odd sort of way, but with darker hair—he's in real good shape for his age, I mean, he rides everywhere. He's real gracious and proud of his bike."

She smiled and: "Wow—that's something, you have no idea. My pop will probably real surprised when I tell him this one. Maybe it's not him, I don't know—but still—if he comes in again, tell him maybe, that I come here, too, you know—if he's got a nephew with my name, I mean, it'll be him, and if not fine—but if so, maybe I can see him once more or some shit."

"O, of course—I will, definitely."

"Take it easy!"

"Yeah, I'll be talkin' t' ya—thanks again," she said. I walked outside and initial sunlight beamed warm and diffuse into my chest as the earth held her breath. I thought: wow, how wild—I can't believe Dennis has been going to the same bike shop as me for all these years, and I've never run into him. This is too weird—I've probably ridden right past him dozens of unknown times—on the Lake, in the streets—who knows? I thought of all the weird guys I see riding their bikes on the Lake all day, all through the year, and I tried to figure which one was him.

I turned on my phone and dialed my folks' house. My pop answered and "Hey, Anthony! How's it goin', my man?" A man boisterous and open in personality, with direct, thunderbolt displays of emotion, talkin' to my pop always helps me relax. I pictured his hand holding the phone, a hand that only comes to possess that sort of power after molding metal, day after day, for forty years—I imaged cuts and nicks and a couple of swollen spots, and I felt real proud to be my father's son in that moment, as usual.

"I'm good, real good pop—how're you? How's ma and the kiddo?"

"I'm good, they're good—your ma's out with Auntie Sandy, Janice and Nancy, Carol and a few of the other girls, and the kiddo went for a run after finishing a big project for school."

"Nice crisp day for a run—good for her, I'm sure she's enjoying it." That made me glad—my sister always tries to enjoy life as she goes, and doesn't take anything for granted—the thought of her listening to some tunes and jogging on a sunny afternoon made me real glad. "Be sure n' tell 'em all I say hey n' hello n' everything."

"I will. So what else? How's the writing going—think you'll be done soon?"

O yeah, that whole thing. "Yeah, I mean—I just have to keep busting on it. I guess—there's always an excuse, right? I'm behind where I should be, but yeah—I'm gonna' get it done, pop. I swear t' God I'm gonna' smash it out all over again."

"All over again?—I thought it was almost done."

"Well—it is done in a way—I just have to work harder and faster to make it better than it was, that's all—it'll get done."

"That'll be great, Anthony—whatever comes of it, we'll be proud of you—remember, everyone has to make a living, some way, some how—maybe this'll be your thing."

"We'll see."

"Options are pretty dry these days—whatever you do, work hard at it and you'll survive, at least somewhat—never be too proud t' work a job if it's a good n' honest wage."

"Thanks pop, I know—it'll work out—I'll have those property taxes covered for you n' ma and then you guys can just relax for once."

"Just you worry about yourself, kiddo, don't go worryin' about us—we'll be alright. I got all I need, Anthony, you guys—your mom and your sister—so long as I got you guys, I can care less about anything else."

"I know—I'm just sayin'—how's work n' everything been?"

"Good—I mean, a little slow, real slow, actually, but you know, we're above water—it's hit and miss—a busy week, a slow week, you know."

"Yeah."

"We're lucky we've been able to hold on for so long—when you look at manufacturing—there's a lotta' joints that haven't made out as good as us. Who knows how long it'll last for, but when you look at it, if I was workin' somewhere else, I could have lost my job ten years ago, easy. You know—you started talking before I could mention it, but grandma called—"

"Grandma in Chicago?—it was her birthday last week, eighty-six."

"I know—amazing isn't she?—it was grandma in Gary who called though—she called about Dennis the other day."

"Really? That's *so* weird because that's partly why I was calling—I just went to the bike shop I normally hit and they had Dennis in the system—his name I mean. He's apparently been going there for years—comes in a couple times per season—can you believe th*a*t? He's been going to the same joint as me all this time—I mean, what are the odds? What'd grandma have to say? He crash his bike again?"

"Dennis died two days ago————————————Anthony? Hel*lo?* Are you there?"

"Yeah. I'm here. Just hold on a second." I put the phone down at my side, bit my knuckle real hard and nobody said anything for a long stretch. I cleared my throat and: "So, I mean—is there gonna' be a funeral or a wake or anything?"

"There's not going to be any service, nobody's got the money for it. He's already buried, in fact. They put him in Potters Field yesterday morning. Like I told grandma—it don't matter if they bury you downtown on State Street or in a hole in the middle of nowhere. When you're dead, you're dead. I went to see him the night before he went and—"

"What do you mean? You *saw* him? Are you serious?"

"Yeah—I drove down there and—"

"Why didn't you call me, dad? Gosh, I could've come with!"

"He wouldn't have wanted you to seem him like he was, Anthony. He was having a hard time breathing, you know, it was pretty bad—the funny thing was, as bad as it all was, you could still sorta tell he was a good lookin' guy." Nobody said anything for a minute, and I just watched the people going past.

"I can't believe it."

"Well, you should—you knew this was going to happen, at some point or another— I'm surprised he made it as long as he did." I imagined the guys whose job it was to bury him, the things they might have been saying when they put him into the ground—maybe they wanted to hurry the hell up and get home to their families, or go out for a drink—either way the dirt came down and there he went, borne into the earth and hastily interred without identification. Wow. He'd reached the place between now and eternity, and whatever was there, it had him now, and that was it. It hardly seemed real in a way. "He chose his life— how it ended is what he chose. I remember when Frankie got messed up—he was just in that chair and he would have given *any*thing to be up and about, making a living for himself, doing right, and there was Dennis, totally healthy, able to be anything he wanted, and there he went, throwing it all down the drain, day, after day, after day. If anything, he was a great example of how to n*o*t live your life. Deep down he was a user, n' that's all there is to it."

"I know dad, you're right—it's just wild, is all. I mean—that's it, that's what he chose and now it's over."

"Yep."

"Where was he at? What hospital?"

"This place on the south side. They found him on the street a couple weeks ago and he was at a different hospital at first. When he came to, he was fighting with them and had to be restrained n' shit—I think he knew it was pretty much over—his kidneys were failed and a whole bunch of other stuff was all messed up. He wasn't conscious when I got there. What can you say? It's a sad story, but that's what he chose. If you want to be sad for someone, be sad for Frankie and Ronnie, who didn't have a choice. Be sad for them, not Dennis." I could tell that, inside, he was still pretty sad about it in a lot of ways. Dennis was his younger brother, only by a speck, and so growing up, they ran together like crazy—he just never took the proper road, and I think it drove pop mad at times, wondering why Dennis chose to live that way. Eventually he had to live his own life and forget about him. I guess that's how it goes sometimes.

"This thing is nuts," a man said, speaking of a new personal electronic device of some sort to the woman on his arm, and as they walked past the wind slipped through the trees I imagined the entire sum of it reaching its destiny, thereby showing how nuts things truly are. I took a second to observe the snow of yesterday's storm—I observed tufts melting slowly upon the sidewalk, and as soon as one melted away and changed form, another fell into place upon the precise spot the other had melted—and from the end, the beginning begins, over and over and over again.

"Man. I'm sorry pop. I know you guys were real pals back in the day."

"Me too—what happened to him is just another reason you have to make the best of it—once we start tickin', there is no pause. Once you're going, you're going, and when you stop, you stop—if you want to make something good for yourself in-between, it's all up to you—remember that."

"I know—I won't forget it—what'd grandma say?"

"Same thing: 'I told him that drinkin' was gonna' kill 'em'," he said, in this very humorous grandmother tone—"'I was right, wasn't I? I told him that liquor would be the end of 'em, I told 'em, but you know Dennis—it was his way or the highway.'"

I laughed—we both laughed—it was a solid grandmother voice—I matched it: "'O that drinkin', sonny, that drinkin' 'll getcha, it will.'"

Pop chuckled and: "It will though, that hard stuff is bad news, Anthony."

"Yeah, well, so it goes, right?—well listen, pop—I love you, man, you're the best."

"Thanks Anthony."

"Hey pop, you hear that rumble?" I held my phone in the air and said: "An old Lincoln just drove past on Damen here—black one, a '65 with suicide doors, hardtop—if I ever make it, I'll buy you one and we'll go cruisin' together."

"You sure it was a '65?

"Pretty sure."

"That's one of my favorite cars," he said.

"I know."

"That's the kind of car where you get in it after a long day of work, turn up the tunes and it's like: it's all good, man, it's all good." We laughed, he paused for a second and said: "I remember I was sittin' on the stoop with Dennis, when we lived on 107th and Racine—Frankie was still in the hospital, and the week before, when grandpa went to sit by him after he got off work at the factory, someone broke into his car, and stole all of his tools. He came out and he couldn't believe it. Like the sky was falling. They wrote a little blurb about it in the paper, a hardship blurb asking for the tools to be returned, no questions asked, and some weeks later a guy pulled up in a big black Lincoln, just like the one you saw—he got out, this big guy in a black suit and he said: 'Is this the Riedie residence? Is your dad home?' And Dennis ran in, grandpa put on a flannel and limped out, and the guy said, 'Come with me, Mr. Riedie, we're going to Sears—I want you to get all the tools you need for your work.' Some guy just showed up like that, after reading the story or hearing about it, like an angel—he took grandpa to the store and bought him everything he needed, and more, all Craftsman, all the best stuff, filling up the shopping cart, paying in cash, and then he dropped him off, and never once did he tell him his name. I'll never forget my dad's face when he came home that day. Never. That guy was a saint, man, he really was."

"They're out there." Neither of us said anything for a minute. I brushed soft snow with the side of my boot and: "So you just chillin' tonight?" I asked.

"Yeah, I might chill down in the basement, have a brew or two, light a fire, you know, just relax for a minute and whatnot, maybe ring uncle Norm and listen to some tunes."

"Cool." I figured it'd be a pretty in depth night for 'em.

"You?"

"I'll probably see some of the guys."

"Cool—keep your eyes open out there."

"I will—and hey—I just want you to remember—Gramps would be proud of you—you made stuff real easy for me n' ma n' the kiddo with how hard you worked. I'm sorry about Dennis and everything. I'll be talkin' t' ya pop."

"Love ya Anthony—you take it easy."

"Yep."

42

I caught the #50 south to Augusta to get back to my bike and was there within forty minutes. I put the wheel on and realized I hadn't thought of the fact that my key to the bike lock was in the bag with everything else. Slick move, real slick—I was going nowhere. I turned my phone back on and dialed EP over the hopeless click of a car trying to start and not turning over: "Ay what's up man?"

"Do you have a power saw, or something that can cut through a bike lock?"

"Why, you see one you wanna snatch?"

"Yeah, my own." I explained the haps and the fastest he could be there was an hour or so—he was in the middle of a woodworking project but had a tool for the job. I had some time to kill, and so I figured I'd walk over to my Grams' place over on Walton. Like my pop said, she had turned eighty-six the previous week, and so I figured I would stop over and chill for a minute, say hello to the woman who started it all—the woman who bore the woman who bore me—I just felt like being around some family, you know? I gave her a buzz, told her I would swing past in fifteen and asked what she needed from the store. She said nothing, a lie, I was sure, I told her I didn't have my key, and she said she'd unlock the side door for me, and to come on up when I got there, but don't get her anything. I figured I'd shoot over to Western to hit a little European deli and grab her milk, a little coffee cake, big pickles, potato pierogis and few additional items I knew she liked to eat.

I walked about twelve blocks and the day had cooled a little—the sun still shone through blue and the time was half two. A well groomed UPS man delivered on time, boxes tucked under his arms as he rushed up the stairs of a nice brownstone and rang the doorbell—a woman answered with a big smile and he tipped his cap after the exchange before tearing off in the truck, just like a commercial. A young man strode past with an irritated gait—his arms were long for his torso and his entire coat sleeve was ripped like he'd just gotten in a tussle—and as he approached an elder woman, he strode upon the shoveled portion of the sidewalk, thereby forcing her onto an uncertain sheet of ice. Dude showed no respect for a senior and what she'd seen—the times so raw and rough through which she'd breathed—I felt like strapping him onto a table and grinding a straight-edged razor into his collar bone, taking a thin path until the sound of cold steel cutting calcium muted the screams. I mean—the terrible feeling in your gut after you pull a low class move of some sort—do these people not feel that? Does it not sit there for days, gnawing at you?

Nearly to the store, shadows shifted on sunlit brick as a huge King Crimson Norway maple on the corner of Oakley saw a few pesky leaves cling to their limbs long after the accomplices had died and been stomped to dust. A friendly white guy with the body of a drinker took a long drag of his cigarette. He exhaled a white swirl into the sun, waved at an old man and said hello to a passing couple—he was the type who generally smokes cigs on the corner and engages in running conversations with everybody who lives in the area. A neighborhood where you still see nuns from time to time, two of them gave this man a funny look when he yelled to a blue collar fellow across the way: "Ay, you see that goddamn game last night? I know, right? The defense ever hear a' passin' the goddamn puck t' yer own team fer once? Jesus Ch*rist!*"

I cut south to Iowa, continued west, pulled open the door to the deli, held it for an old man, and entered to the same scene as always—it was all Europeans, crowded but quiet as everyone went about their business, squeezing fruit, smelling vegetables and looking close at all the fish. I had run errands here for my grandmother for many years, and it always struck me that people who'd lived under the Iron Curtain—it was like their offspring came out of the womb with that same dejected look on their face—that look you saw in historic photos of people waiting in long rainy lines for moldy bread in Soviet Russia and such, little kids even, they all looked the same—as if it took several generations of American citizenship to shake the fear that a ruling Oligarchy could embezzle your ration cards if heard openly contesting state policy. It's a terrible face, man, like they always expect the worst to happen, simply for the sake that it is possible—only after many generations of no hope do faces start twisting so sour that an entire society looks obsessed with aggression. The guy ahead of me spoke all close and quick to the Ukrainian checkout girl—I imagined it like: "Man behind me with positive face—he can not be trusted."

"Yes, I know this—I've been vatching h*ee*m very closely—this man, he is not broken." They were probably talking about an omelet recipe, who knows—they're all so harsh, Eastern European languages, every one of them, that I always assume the orator is breaking bad news of some sort—a guy could be asking a girl to marry him and it sounds like he's giving execution orders. I placed the items on the counter, had my money ready when the total came, paid, accepted my change and moved on without incident—her face severe, I could tell she'd been satisfied by the exchange. They're all ruthless as hell, all the checkout girls at this place, it's unbelievable. They serve an old grandmother or a priest one second, hand out low end hard liquor, Polish pornos, condoms and cigarettes the next, and their expression never changes: they're back in line somewhere, no umbrella, waiting for that damn bread.

I walked outside, cut past a cut that weird fellows sit in and live in all summer—and sometimes, on real hot days, if I happen to grab something at that joint, I'll buy this real horrible malt liquor that they sell for less than two bucks in these awful 40oz plastic bottles— they sell it warm, and I always buy a couple and leave 'em there in that cut in the blasting sun, and when I swing past again, a couple hours later, they're always empty, discarded about the area. I do this for sheer amazement—I mean those guys must feel like the inside of a crustacean's asshole after slamming that shit, but down it goes, to the very last drip, each and every time. You want it? You got it.

I cut through an alley where pigeons fought over slices of white bread eaten from the inside out, passed an abandoned factory where a rat shot from a crack beneath a big steel delivery door I hadn't seen open in my lifetime, and I paused at the vision of a little park on Western, the one Gramps always took me to. Large butterflies with widespread wings painted upon that factory wall were faded after decades of wear but still inspiring—even gangs refused to tag signs over those butterflies—it was crazy how nothing had changed. My last memory of my grandfather was from a set of monkey bars on the northeast end—they were the old kind, with actual repercussions if you fell, made before kids were treated so dainty—I got to the tall point in the middle, nearly double my height, and I froze with fear. I yelled for

Gramps to come help me as he sat smoking a cigar on a bench, watching me play—his body was riddled with cancer, and as he pushed though the pain, hustling as hard as he could, I fell and busted my head on the concrete just before he reached me. I looked at the spot and thought of how he hugged me real tight in that moment as his eyes burned red and angry at reality.

I shook loose from the thought and cut into another alley from there, heading east, toward the tip of the Hancock rising black in the distance. A lonely train whistle broke the temporary silence of the cold shadows, and pigeon wings clapped together as they rose into the sunlight. I dipped into Grams' gangway from the alley, opened the big black side door where a handwritten sign said: 'Keep this door locked at all times!' and left a boot print on a pile of mail. I picked up and flipped through and the bills kept coming. I got to thinking: O yeah, he's not alive anymore—I suddenly felt why my Grams never wanted to adjust—because even if the sender were People's Gas or Commonwealth Edison, she felt good upon coming home and pronouncing my grandfather's name, aloud, on the final Friday of every month.

Before I went up I dipped into the basement to make certain nobody had crept inside when she left the door unlocked. I opened my switchblade, looked in all the sheds and the coast was clear. I removed two carbon marked iron plates from the old time stove, stuffed in all the junk mail, all that bullshit from Jewel, Dominick's, local aldermen and everyone else, and I set it alight with matches she kept down there. A couple bags of dry leaves I'd collected in the fall were placed in the corner, and so I jammed a bunch of those into the stove, replaced the plates and stood there for a moment, listening to the blaze garner strength—all that organic matter that took so many sunny days to grow, all that color—burning black.

I exited the basement, gazed up the stairwell and spied the 'lil chair Grams rests upon when going up with a big load—yeah, how I love this woman, and how lucky I am to have spent such a great slew of time entrenched happily at her side. Up top I placed the coffee cake I'd gotten for her on the big squared-off banister head, and knocked. A little voice called from within, "Just a minute, just a minute—" the chain lock slid and the deadbolt clicked: "Hi, hi," she gave me a nice hug and: "Come in, come in, come in,"—she seemed so little right then—as though she'd have almost no impact on this massive world of unknown endings and forgone conclusions minus her kind and respectful interactions with the whole of it: "What's all this?"

"Just a couple things I thought you might like."

"You should have come here first—you could have rolled this in my cart!"

"It's no trouble, it's not that heavy."

"Trow 'em on the table. How much do I owe you? I wanna be square with you."

"Nothin'."

"Anthony—don't even be silly, you'll make me mad! How much?"

"Two bucks."

"It was not two!"

"Honestly, it was three bucks."

"Are you sure?" I smiled yes and she shuffled her little slippers off into the pantry to get some dough and paid me four crisp singles. "So we're all square now?"

"Yeah Grams."

"You sure?"

"Yeah—I gotcha some milk, juice, pickles, bread, eggs, an apple n' some other random stuff—take a peek," I said, emptying the bags.

"That was not three bucks!"

"Don't worry about it!—it was close enough."

"Anthony! You yatsek! Trow your bag in the corner—it looks heavy. What can I get you?" I took a seat at the kitchen table and she immediately went to the fridge, opened the OJ and poured me a glass. "I think you need some juice." Man did I feel relaxed to be in her presence, in that apartment right then. It smelled like everyone in my family, all at once, and it was a real nice feeling—it put me at peace. Watching her go about the kitchen, I thought: what a great, kind woman. She has taught me much about being alive and living it right. It's a great fucking blessing to have a long list of family members for whom you hold heaps of respect and gratitude. She asked me to get a blender down from a shelf high in the pantry, and as I walked in I clicked the light and looked at a penciled in growth chart of myself etched into the doorsill. I looked at a handful down low, and I couldn't imagine myself standing there, that small, with my same heart and mind within me, all that time ago. It was something. "Was there any mail down there?" she asked, as I used her step-ladder to reach up top.

"Yeah, I brought it up."

"Who was it from?"

"I don't think any of it was personal—it's all bills n' stuff, check the table." I looked around for a snack but all she had were Fig Newtons and I wasn't in the mood.

"Say, you couldn't do me a big favor, could you? Before tomorrow morning?"

"Of course, anything—what's up?"

"I was gonna' go to five o'clock mass, but I caught a chill and I'm not feeling too hot. Do you think you could get me a church bulletin? I like to read them—plus I think they might put grandpa's name in it this week, but I'm not sure."

"I'll be right back."

"No! I don't mean no—"

I evaded her grasp, shot down the stairs in a flash, exited the side door, looked both ways, walked north toward the street and, just as I came out of the gangway, a guy in a tan coat with a raised hood, baggy blue jeans and Timberland boots tried to open the driver's side door of my grandmother's old silver Cutlass in a fluid move, walking west after having tried the car before hers, and not breaking stride. The car was maybe forty steps to my left and so his view was blocked when I came out from behind. I saw him try the car before hers, assumed it was his, but then he fucked with the Cutlass. "Ay! Why you fuckin' with that handle, man?!" He turned back quick with my statement and I put my hand in my pocket. Feeling the handle of my switchblade, I thought: I'm not even gonna' bother boxing you—if you even try and step, you're gonna' get that skin sliced fuckin' pink and wide, bitch—I don't care if this car is worth eight-hundred dollars—it's Grams' hard-earned whip and she's not putting up with your bullshit anymore, none of you—I'll gladly risk my wellbeing for this insignificant shit—I'll stick my fingers into your eyeballs and peel your face off from the inside out. Fuckin' city of animals man—hungry, filthy, desperate animals. Everywhere you look, that's all it is—animals of different races out on the hunt. Dude went jogging away when he saw I wasn't playin', and I yelled a few things I thought would prevent him from approaching her vehicle again before running off for the church bulletin.

Past a rusted fence that had bled a carroty color into concrete over many decades, two minutes later I was back up the stairs when it went: "You're back already? Gosh that was fast—I can't believe it! I didn't mean go now for goodness sake!"

"Yeah, no sweat—it was good that I did." I set the periodical on the table and thought of how, at this stage, walking to church, what amounted to a block and a half—this must seem like a mighty trek for her.

"I heard someone yelling out there, a minute ago. I went to the window with my binoculars, but by the time I got there I didn't see anybody. I wanted to make sure you were okay. Jack's son caught and beat up a couple burglars last week and they're in a bad gang. People think they're gonna' come back and make trouble on the block before he testifies Monday—everyone has to keep their eye out right now."

"It was probably just a cab driver or something."

"I don't know, they sounded real mean." It cracked me up, the image of her sneaking up the front window in her puffy pink slippers, binoculars in hand—the little spy! She was a proud CAPS member for many years—all the little bi-weekly meetings about what crimes had gone on in the neighborhood—Grams was always in the know, man, no pulling a fast one on this gal. I was glad she hadn't seen me yelling at that guy, though, she'd have worried about it for a week. After helping her with a small smattering of additionally miscellaneous labors, I said: "It's pretty cold in here, Grams."

"I know—I was cold when I woke up. I was under so many blankets. I think the heater's out. I looked but I couldn't tell."

I bent down to look and saw half-burned toothpicks piled beside the heater where she'd tried to light it. The old Moores heater, a big rectangular hunk of iron the size of a tow truck's engine block, was cold to the touch—I dipped my finger in the earthenware she'd placed atop the grille to help add humidity to the room, and the water was chilled. "How long has this been out for? Why didn't you call me? I've been out in the cold so much I'm a little used to it and didn't notice at first—it's way too cold in here for you, Gram."

"Just since this morning—I didn't want to be a bother, you know."

"O please, you know better." I lowered the metal shield, struck a match, lit a toothpick, moved the safety to the side, pushed the ignition, stuck the flaming pick through a little hole at the bottom, switched the gas line full open from pilot, spun the thermostat to full blast—h*issssssssssssssssss* and: "1927 ain't got shit on me."

"What Anthony?"

'Vshrouwh*ooo*sh!' A huge line of burners flamed blue and: "I said it wasn't lit. It'll be warmer in a minute, no worry." I took a breath and it was all gas—I coughed and: "This thing is like a bomb just waiting to go off, you know that? Don't even try t' light it again if it goes out. Just call me and I'll come do it. You'll wind up blowing the whole goddamn block up if you make a mistake." I closed the shield, examined the burn for a few seconds through the protection glass, warmed my hands and relaxed as the white ceramic coils began to glow red. The heater was like having a controlled campfire in the kitchen—it was really comfortable whence you got it running right, and it threw an unbelievable amount of heat. I got off the ground just in time to stop her from trying to remove the cap from a jar of blueberry jam—she was trying to make me toast and I could *see* the pain in her face as she twisted to no avail and I thought: she doesn't deserve this—she's been a nice lady her whole life. It was cold in there, and as a lifelong seamstress, the arthritis in her fingers was killing her. "Gram, don't worry about that," I said, taking the knife from her, "I'll do this."

"Are you sure?"

"Yeah."

I popped open the jar and she said: "Okay, I'll check the mail den." She flipped through the items, "You still have the same number, right? I tried calling a couple days ago and it went to the message."

"Yeah, I got the same one."

"That m*ess*age—my lands!—you sound so dignified! 'Hi, you've reached—'" she went on, imitating me, talking in a voice that made me sound like a diplomat. We had a good laugh about it—

"I know, it's phony as anything—it's that way for business and junk like that."

"I think you sound nice!" she said. I looked up the hall, the light flooded in from Walton, and I pictured everyone in my family walking down it at one time or another, coming to eat a hot meal, at this table—coming to eat with her. And looking at her I thought: it's terrific seeing my grandmother every week—and in sharing her unvarying presence over the years—observing such, I felt in touch with the power of aging—the way time defeats all comers is humbling. I mean if your mind is sound and cognitive, still sharp as ever really, even when in your middle and upper eighties, keeping things keen and sly, as Grams is, well, I suppose it must feel mad to sit with a sharp mind while at the same time observing and perhaps more importantly *feeling* the effects time has had on your joints, bones, muscular capacity, flexibility, lungs, just everything really—it must be mad to admit that physically, your best days have long since passed, and never again shall they return to a form that in any way or shape resembles your personal definition of prime. I looked at her smiling there before me, and I wished I could wave a wand and make her young again. "O, before I forget, come here a second." She dropped the mail before opening it, shuffled to the bedroom, pointed to the top of her closet and: "What's in that green box?"

I climbed up: "Hats."

"What about that blue one?"

"More hats." She pointed at another and it had all these cards and letters I had written as a kid, both to her and my grandfather. I couldn't believe it. I showed her one and: "I think I could draw better then than I do now! That's pretty damn good!"

"Ain't it? I thought you'd get a kick out of that. Now look underneath it all—is anything there?" I lifted all the papers and at the bottom was a little book. The brown cover was made of felt and worn very thin—it covered delicate fiber paper bound with a leather string. I held it at an angle against the light glaring from the hanging bulb and looked very closely—I could see the face had once held intricate designs of bare trees, but the embossing had been worn shallow and the color was all earthen brown, with no distinguishing divide, so it was hard to tell how it looked. "That's it! That's what I wanted to show you. I was hoping it was in there, but the box was too heavy and I couldn't lift it. Boy I wish the cover was still nice. It had such a nice cover at one time."

"I have an idea—want to see something cool?"

"Sure!"

"You have a pencil and a blank sheet of paper?" She brought me a full size sheet of plain loose-leaf and a pencil—back in the kitchen we sat and I wrapped the paper tight around the book, and got to work. Ten minutes later, after rubbing out a graphite rectangle, we had it. In the bottom right, in fancy cursive it read: Class Autographs, and the remainder of the page was a beautiful series of bare trees and root systems of equal depth.

255

"Wow! That's just the way it was, I can't believe it!"

"Cool ay? Uncle Norm showed me that trick once long ago with an arrowhead fossil he found inside a broken stone, up at the lake house. He made a print of it like that and kept it with me for a long time." I flipped it open, and above a little stamp on the bottom of the first page that read: MADE IN USA, it went: Schoolday Memories of: and there below it was signed: Louise Solik, Class of 1934. Her writing was preserved impeccably, and the handwriting itself was great. On a page called 'My Favorites' I looked beside Sport where she wrote: 'Swimming, Tennis & Golf.' I chuckled because I knew she couldn't swim, as her mother was too scared to let her learn, and the image of her playing tennis or golf, which I knew she hadn't, just seemed so ludicrous to me. A couple pages further along was a nice drawing of a sailboat on a lake at sunrise, illustrated in rich oil crayon, and beside it was note from my great grandmother—I did not understand the language, and beneath she signed 'Mama'—I showed the page to my grandmother and: "What's it say?"

"It says: 'May God bless you through the years, love Mama'—she was so nice."

"Well you took after Busia, that's for sure—everyone still talks about how nice and hardworking she was—this book is crazy. I can't believe how good the condition is!"

"I thought you might like to see it."

"Are you kidding? It's amazing!" I flipped through the pages, and to think that she was just a kid when she got the book, younger than me now, in this same building, this same apartment, my great Gramps sitting right here perhaps, in the same damn chair—and how the world had changed in one lifetime!—you might say the world changed more for people born in the early twentieth century than any generation in history—two world wars, political and social upheaval of unseen proportions, the rise and fall and potential re-rise of communism— from few paved roads to the current intricate system—actual ice in the icebox, as Melissa had said—the insane technological achievements of a single lifetime!—and here I was, holding this little book that transcended all that. I flipped the pages and read what people wrote and, at the root, people's desires were mostly the same. All of her 'chums' had wished her a nice life of good luck, success, health and a loving family, things of this regard—I flipped a page and on April 5th of 1934, an indiscernible person had written: 'Love many, trust few, always paddle your own canoe—many happy returns in the future, your chum,' and then the writing faded away. On the four edges of the page, written clockwise from the top left, with one word in each corner, it said: 'For. Get. Me. Not.' I asked who had written it and she didn't remember. She encouraged me to keep browsing, and of the many things I noticed, people's handwriting was far superior back then, and the majority of people who signed the book had drawn something nice on the page—flowers or trees or a sunset, the Lakefront—intricate foliage cloaking poetic verses—people were quite artistic and positive on the whole. I flipped to the end and the last six pages were signed by boxers—it said their names, weight classes and records. "What's this?"

"Daddy took me down the street to the fights at the Chicago Stadium and he insisted I get those—he thought they'd be worth money. O I was so mad! They sweated all over the pages and I still had more friends I wanted to sign in there." She started chuckling and I found the image of her getting dragged to a raucous drunken scene at the Stadium with my great grandfather to be very amusing.

"Jackie Fields signed this book? You saw him fight? He's in the hall of fame."

"O yeah—that's the only fella I remember. They all went real crazy for him. He was from Chicago." Her eyes looked real blue and young at the moment, hair spun in pink curlers, barely visible below a cute brown winter cap. "It was a wild time," she continued, "But I didn't like it—it was scary, watching those guys sock one another so hard like they do. Why would anyone ever want to get socked like that, all those times?"

"You know, for money, for pride."

"Ah, who needs it—they all looked like pitted prunes after a few rounds, anyway." We laughed and: "Say, did you light a fire downstairs?"

"Yeah."

"It smells good—you throw in some leaves?"

"Yeah."

"O that smells nice."

I made a couple open-faced strawberry jam sandwiches and some bread and butter, and we kicked back and ate as the room warmed. I poured more water into the stoneware placed upon the heater, and she began opening her mail. "Who's this from? This writing is so tiny I can't believe it. That's how they getcha t' be late on the bills—they write it so small so you won't know what the heck they're talkin' about."

I took a glance and "It's from the county treasurer."

"Taxes?"

"I think so."

"What? They wanna raise 'em again? The property tax? There's no way! They gotta be crazy!" I didn't have the heart to break it to her, she was barely hanging on. She'd always run the building to make just enough to cover the expenses. When family wasn't living there, she rented to struggling families of strong moral standing, but it was becoming impossible to come up with the money to cover government theft under this policy. "Daley. What does he expect me to do? Pay three more per*cent?* Daley can go *whistle* so far as I'm concerned! He can go whistle!" It was the closest she could come to a damning insult. It was funny but sad as hell in a way. "Where does he think everyone's gonna' go? Now if I don't raise the rent, I'll lose the building. And where will my tenants go? Some crumby neighborhood that's dangerous for the kids? He's a crook. They're all crooks." A lonely train whistle broke the temporary silence and a fire truck blasted its horn somewhere nearby. My mind ran: feelin' so at home with sirens wailin' one after another up Western and down Chicago—there is a certain strange comfort found in chaos. Accepting that life is generally fucked and not bubble wrapped in a TGIF sitcom storyline relieves my stress—I glanced at her rusty chain lock hanging unattached and floated back upon hundreds of childhood memories that took place within those very walls, and I felt insane. "Maybe I'll have to sell the building finally."

"Don't even say that, Gram." I imagined some rich guy buying it, some punk developer who got his start off his daddy's money—I looked at the old oak door and in my head I saw him walk in with shiny shoes, looking at everything and: 'O, what is th*is* crap? I need you to dump this, that, pitch this, get rid of that crap over there, and what's all this?—rip this shit out, you can b*u*rn this, so far as I'm concerned, and for God's sake, whatever you do, get rid of all these stupid crosses all over the joint—I don't know what kind of superstitious old coot lived here, but I want all this cleared out, pronto!'—all the meager possessions owned by a genuine and kind person—and then he'd redo the joint, rent it out to a bunch of yuppies and say he *owned* it. He'd go eat with some associates at the Trump Tower and mention, offhand, that he'd 'developed' another building on the West Side, over on Walton— the smug sonovabitch would go on eating a meal that cost more than my grandmother spent in a month, and in a way, I'd want to kill him dead. Not that it would be his fault per se, as he would be the annoying free market result of a condition perpetuated by government itself, therein making it a false free market, actually—either way, that image irked me hard.

I closed my eyes for a long blink, opened and watched her strain to write a check to the government, like an old pianist fighting against the closure of her fingers' ability, she wrote it as legibly as possible, with a cold, shaky hand—I went to peek out the window, and there, in the corner, on her sewing machine I saw an envelope that read: 'To be opened after I go—' My stomach dropped upon seeing it, and I wondered if maybe she had not been feeling so hot—did she think something was wrong? Christ. Why would she even write something so crazy like that when she seems fine? I imagined her taking great care in drafting it, handwriting as nice as her worn hands were capable, same hands that wrote in that brown book so long ago, and I wondered what she had written. I mean—gosh. One letter, summing up all you felt—the last letter! Ever!—and written as such, with that meaning known to the author as they were penning it—what on earth had she said? And what was going on in her mind as she wrote it? I looked at her, that smile engrained on her face after a lifetime of positive vibrations and—I had to walk into the front room so as to not break down at the thought then and there. I couldn't imagine here gone, I really couldn't—she'd been such a rock for the whole family for all those years.

The floorboards creaked under my feet and out on the street a funeral was streaming past from one of the old proud churches in the neighborhood. I thought: her life, the entire sum of work produced by her being has nearly concluded—surely she has to be satisfied. Despite daily pain and anguish to which at this point of my life I cannot personally fathom, she remains in excellent spirits and in a wonderful mood whereby distributing her near continual smile en route for my eyes, she subconsciously says: I feel no fear for dying, and nor should you—just keep trying your best to do the right thing and everything will be fine. I walked into my grandfather's room, and looked at the ceiling, the walls—my uncle Norm and my pop and I had spent a good minute fixing it up some time back. The walls were all cracked, the electric was bad, and the ceiling had to be redone—we had quite a time on that job, having some beers and listening to oldies and sipping off an old bottle of vodka we found in the basement, hidden amongst my grandfather's tools. Doing work with the guys in the family can be a hellova time, not to mention all the useful tricks you learn as a young blood watching old timers problem solve on the fly—I listened to wild stories, shared a lot of laughs and we did some decent work before it was said and done. I walked back into the kitchen and: "Hey our work is holding up, huh?"

"You guys did such a beautiful job. I couldn't believe it. You all had a lot of beer, though—too much. It's no good for you."

"It wasn't that much. Hey Gram, that reminds me, I forgot something downstairs I'll be back in a second."

I walked out the door and the cake was still sitting on the square railing post, where I'd left it. I unwrapped it, took out the box of candles I bought at the deli, shaped them into a smiling face and set them alight. I crept back in all quiet, and she was at the sink, rinsing my glass with her back turned to me. I set the cake on the table and shut the light. She turned back, startled by darkness and: "What's all this?" she asked excitedly, playing along as if she didn't know.

"Don't think I wasn't gonna' bring cake for your birthday last week! You think I forgot?"

"Anthony! You yatsek! You tricked me!" I set the flaming monster on the table, put my arm around her, sung happy birthday and the whole slew of candles, the whole twenty pack went blazing away, right—and they were *hot* man, they were throwing some real heat—straight melting the damn jam on the cake and one another with the combined warmth and such—Grams said, "Well, okay, I better make a big wish den," and sure enough, sure as fucking hell she took a big deep breath, and blew out every last goddamn candle on the whole cake, just like that, *wham*, they all went out, clean and true, every last one in her single effort—I could not believe it. It was certainly a great, great sight. I broke out in great loud laughter, clapped and almost cried in a way, too, out of sheer happiness, and of course we then split up the cake and ate it and all that crap. I ate almost none of it because I despise cake and felt it tasted awful mainly, but she seemed to enjoy it well enough. After we finished up she said: "I'm gettin' old—can you believe how old I am?"

"You're not that old. You look great, in my opinion—you look real strong."

She swallowed half a Vicodin sitting on the table and: "I feel okay. My hands hurt, though. My hands hurt real bad," she said, looking at them all close. She turned behind and placed both palms on the hot water heater, which was right there in the kitchen, next to the stove, and: "Ah, that's better. They just need to warm up more, is all. Isn't it something that they used to look strong like yours?" she said, reaching across the table and touching my hand. "Your hands are just like your grandfather's."

"I guess I'm lucky then—let me get you something to drink, okay?" I refilled the juices and we sat, relaxing for awhile—we spoke about storms, ice, snow, weathermen, farming, gardening, apples, tomatoes, marriage, aging, pain, hardship, expectations, jobs, money—a whole slew of things, we spoke upon. I enjoyed it man, I really did. I consider her to be fucking amazing, my Grams, and that's all there is to it. I think her sense of humor has been a tremendous asset to helping her age as strongly as she has. When the time comes, I imagine she'll lay not only comfortable, but vulnerable, and ready to see what's on the other side. It's just—the idea of life reaching finality is just so rough sometimes.

I imagined how it might go, her little feet causing two teeny bumps in the covers half way down the hospital bed the and goddamn the haunting image of her eyes as she holds her last breath, exhales and dies—'We love you,' I'll sigh, and slowly, after minutes, that final drawing in of fresh air shall cease escaping, as though unconsciously, after her heart had stopped, her soul doesn't want to go—it'll want to hold that one last breath forever, and the only reason it'll get squeezed out will be because we're holding her too tight, trying to get her to stick around—and everything she saw in her life—from the February of her birth until the last image she views, my eyes, my blue eyes telling hers that everything is going to be alright—it'll all float away for good right then, forever. Man.

I snapped to, looked at her, unable to speak, and I assumed with a hidden certainty: this will be the way that it goes. She caught the sense of strange emotion on my face and so she sat up, chuckled and said, "Do you know that I love you?"

"Yeah Grams, I know—you give me strength to call it weak, you know that? The thought of you makes every one of my complaints feel so weak."

"That's nice honey," she said, "Of course I have an extra key, since you lost that other one. I'll find you the key, sure."

I laughed and: "You didn't hear me, did you?" she shook her head no and: "I said that I love you, too. I gotta hit the road now, but I'll be seeing you soon. I'll come over next week and bring good bread and a bunch of tomatoes and garlic from the joint on Erie and I'll make sauce for us. I'll reduce the shit out of it, real slow, and we can play cards while we wait."

"I'll be looking forward to it! I love sauce and bread, I can taste it already." She kissed her fingers up in the air like she were an old Italian lady and I appreciated her subtle humor—elders who keep it real forever are rare gems man, no lie. "I really enjoyed you coming." We stood, I gave her a big squeeze and: "I always enjoy spending time with you, Anthony," she said, looking up at me with those beautiful blue eyes and that happy face.

She retrieved an extra key and I said: "Ditto Grams—I love ya, you're the best." And in my head I thought of my family and it went: we will always be here for you, Gram, until your last second or the moment our bodies fail. Just say the word and we'll be here for anything you need. We love ya so fuckin' deep it's mad and if anyone ever gives you a problem, they will surely die.

I changed her garbage so she wouldn't have to take it all the way down by herself, kissed and made the sign of the cross upon the old oak door, and split.

43

Back outside, the air had continued to cool and the wind was picking up, sweeping in a sparse arrangement of thin white clouds from the north. I walked the trash out back and as I swiveled 'round and walked down the gangway, the crunch of ice echoed between the buildings. I ran my fingers across cold shadowed brick as is streamed past to the backdrop of ringing church bells—a diesel engine slowly ascended and rumbled low again, with a grueling change of gears—a car alarm wailed, two woman spoke in a European language and an old man whistled soft as he walked toward Western—and right then I thought of Grams having to sell the building—to someone who didn't know the neighborhood or the way the bricks sat and the shadows they cast at that time of day at that time of year—the familiar thud of the side door and smell of the stairway as the warm summer breeze drifts through flowered cotton curtains in the hall—speedy young feet dashing up the steps and the last breaths in the storied lives of men who died slumped upon them—Gramps' voice rattling the plaster as he yelled at the Bears for all those years—all the intimate sounds of the floorboards as he walked out of the room after an interception, seething about the offense—the echo of the symphony on cold, dim winter nights as the old heater blasts red in background—the weight of the glass in the cabinet of the cubby—the click when you closed it and sat with the book you grabbed to read above the sound from the street upon which family had lived and died for over a century—a man wants to buy you and develop you, I thought, looking at smoke rise from the chimney that led to the fire I had stoked—maybe it would be best to watch you burn.

After exiting the gangway, I moved east, toward the bike. The gangway and the sidewalk on the block was shoveled real nice, likely from a cop neighbor of hers who always went out of his way to take care of the entire area and make certain things were in order—I thought I was going to have to shovel when I got there, but it was already perfect. You see people keep things right for many years, and you get to thinking: if someone else lived there, a different family of slobs who made a mess versus one that always went out of their way to lend a hand and tidy up—the whole area would be different to a degree. Hence why it all comes down to specific individuals making a difference in the world—there is no such thing as blanket action—it's all about distinct threads and what they come to represent. I looked to wave hello but the guy wasn't around—either way I'll always remember and respect the little things he and many others did to look after the neighborhood and my Gram, and try to pay it forward in the future.

As I walked on, I kept thinking of that letter, hidden on the far corner of the sewing machine, against the wall. The more I thought of it, the more happy I felt, in a way, that she possessed the mental and spiritual wherewithal to etch a final will and testament, looking back, perhaps, over her life with a comfortable conscience knowing that she hadn't hurt people who didn't deserve it while offering sound advice. I imagined it talked about the pointlessness of bickering over little shit, and the importance of living for your passions—I was thinking of such as I approached the alley just shy of Oakley where, sprayed in black upon the stone foundation of a building in foot high lettering was the phrase: 'Go for it!' I wondered who'd written it and whether or not they had done so—either way, I was glad of their suggestion. The message was much better than the majority of ideas conveyed via graffiti in the area. I was in good spirits and to my left was a wedding—the beginning of a new family—and there they stood, proud and in love after exiting the church, happy before their relatives, youngest of whom stood atop snow piles in dress shoes to catch a view of the glowing couple in the precise spot my folks and aunts and uncles had once stood, happy as they were, many moons ago.

I walked on, smiling at the thought, passed a few handfuls of friendly folk of various ages and races out enjoying their Saturday, and as I approached Leavitt, a young man stood before an easel facing the building on the southwest corner. I'd seen him out there four times in the previous month, composing what was out of nothing—natural light, paints and paper and the image that be—and indeed it was a proud Chicago building, shrouded by naked ash trees and deserving of a portrait by a talented young painter. I viewed the miniature scene of the scene and it was flush—all finishing touches now, he dabbed here and there with a careful confidence the architect of that building would have appreciated—he had to know the building better than its occupants to a degree and, looking at the real shitty car he had driven there, I sensed his reality as not unlike a professional gardener—master of greens at many great estates across the city, forever pained to spend their whole life dreaming of when they'll have their own patch of land and flowerbed to care for, only to never see that day come.

I mentioned the painting was beautiful and he thanked me for noticing. I walked on and recalled passing that house long ago, at my father's side, and as I spoke of the great individual work that had gone into every feature, including crazed mustached Vikings scored into stone, he said: 'Who knows, maybe you'll own it one day, Anthony.' I scoffed at the idea, as it was far and away the most stunning display of individual craftsmanship in the neighborhood, completely unattainable in my eyes at the time, and he said: 'So long as you understand that the only way to get there is through hard, unrelenting work, anything is possible. If somebody gives you a job, even if it's some basic labor job, do the best ya can and keep a positive attitude—negativity will never get promoted—do so and you'll do okay for the most part.' It was good advice—he always said shit like that, though—he always reminded you anything was possible if you went for it—and when you looked at the duality of his reality versus what happened to Dennis, there was reason to believe him.

A guy who looked to be floating off into some fiddler's green walked past, eyes glazed and face pale, and soon I was back at my bike, a couple miles on, where I had last seen Melissa. EP wasn't there yet, and so I took out my phone and thought of giving her a call, but what did I really have to say? I didn't quite feel like seeing her, at least not right then, and I wasn't about to deliver some big sob story about getting my backpack stolen, as it was more embarrassing than anything else, and so I figured it was best to take it easy. I'd call her later in the week and figure it out from there. But still, she was on my mind. In a way all I wanted was to pick her up, gather our meager belongings and head out to a nice little spot deep in the woods, a cabin with a little creek, fir trees, soaring mountains and a nice fireplace, get a kind dog and talk to maybe ten or fifteen people for the rest of my life whilst living out my remaining days under the anthem of disaffiliated leisure. After fifteen additional minutes of unrealistic daydreams, Eric Petrosky rolled up on his dad's old blue Raleigh and: "Yo!" he yelled, with a big smile on his face.

"Hey EP, thanks for riding over here."

"Sorry it took me a minute—I hadda take me a good n' proper n' then rinse my ass n' run the hand afterward—far more poop came out than I can remember consuming fuel for and, I didn't want to waste all the paper on one party."

"As if you ate one of those magic sponge dinosaurs that are supposed to blow up large and fright-inducing after water is sprayed on them?"

"It was fright inducing alright."

"I don't doubt it." He laughed all loud and dismounted the Raleigh, pulled a lighter from his blue jeans, cupped a square and—*in, in, in*—he exhaled a huge, much appreciated first drag into thin strips of shallow light and watched the white clouds roll away towards their destination of disappearance, of fading into nothing. His nails were dirty, chin stubbly, cheeks rosy and hair greasy—his smile was big and: "Ahh yeah," he said, looking at the sky, "What a day, right?" Some people just love to smoke man. It's their decision, stop trying to talk them out of it.

"Hell yeah—has me cravin' spring."

"It's supposed to get cold as shit tonight though. Like fuckin' zero or some shit."

"How was that ride, by the way?"

"Fuckin' aggressive mate."

"Closest you'll ever come to feeling like a rock star?"

"You said it."

"Those are great."

"The greatest—whatever your method," he said, "So where is this fucking thing?—next lock you get, you should gimme the second key."

"Not surprised?" He shook no, I showed: "So what's the prognosis doctor?"

"Alright, I think I'll be able t' cut through it."

"What'd you bring for it?"

He threw his pack against a tree trunk with a thump and: "This. A Bosch portable die grinder—it's pretty nuts, 27,000 RPM's and a new disk, so I think it'll work."

"Dang—you pimpin' it kid—when'd you get that piece?"

"About a month back—pricy, but I been using it t' finish the bike racks I been buildin'. I been blastin' out work like crazy man."

"Mine almost done?"

"Yeah—it's pretty sweet—the drawer is perfect."

"Cool man, I'm stoked—it's the most proper way to display a bike I've ever witnessed—how ya been besides? I ain't seen you in a minute."

"Long days, tired body, okay money, healthy mind."

"I like that—so the wood shop is comin' along n' everything? Full transfer down below?"

He flicked some ash and: "Yeah, that's all I been doin' for the past three weeks, finishin' the set up. There was so much sawdust in the crib I couldn't keep workin' in the front room. Leo had this girl over the other day and there was like two inches on the remote control. It was time to move down to the cellar."

"Awesome."

"The only thing is I think there're rats down there—I ain't seen one yet but I heard 'em squeakin' n' chewin' when I shut the drill—I'm real scared a' rats man."

"It's probably just mice."

"Yeah, hopefully—but I gotta show you this other leverage invention I came up with the other day—it's just an idea, but—I think it might be pretty good man, for real—like, really—a bank filler man, no lie."

"Now you got me all curious."

"It's pretty all right man—I wanna see whachu think though."

"Hell yeah!—you're a modest kid—this sounds nice and serious."

"We'll see—so how you been feelin', Riedie? Crazy bastard."

"Ah, a little hot right now, burning in a way, but alright man, pretty good."

"That's good—it's good to be on fire because the more I walk around and look at people, the more I realize that never once did most anybody get to the point a' playin' with matches." A posse of hearsay spreading, prim pregnant mothers pushing designer brand, dual toddler buggies up the sidewalk reminded me of why I could never live on the North Shore. One duo lagged behind because a kid in a green full body snowsuit whipped a red saucer sled at a parked car and the mom lit into him. He didn't seem concerned of her opinion that he should act more like she and her sisters did, and he dove on the ground, hollering at will. The mother, overwhelmed, held her belly and EP said: "Fun day in the neighborhood, eh?"

"Yeah," she sighed.

"And it looks like you have another little bundle of fun on the way, eh?"

"Yep." She was not in the mood to be speaking to EP at all.

"This is why we're still single," he said, waving a hand at the kid rolling along the wet, salt-laden snow adjacent to the curb, "But really, you're doin' a good job with this little roadrunner. When're ya due again, anyway?"

"March seventeenth."

"Whoa! Saint Patty's Day! Shit, is it a boy?"

"Yeah."

"Well, he'll probably be pretty nuts then, huh? You're about to have some competition, little man! Keep up the good work," EP said to the kid.

"I will! And guess what! I'd never been sledding before, so like, this was one of the best days of my life!"

"Proper!"

They trudged down the street—she on the sidewalk and he through the deepest snow he could find in every single lawn—mother promoted that son hurry up in an effort to catch up with her friends and he took a flying leap onto the red disk in the opposite direction. I smiled—fragile mothers without brothers who have boys are in for a real surprise man, straight up. "So you go out last night?"

"Yeah—I tried to call you, actually," EP said, "There was a work party with the guys from the old shop—you coulda came if you wanted."

"Good times?"

"I get too crazy, man, when I drink fucking scotch—that's all I'm going to say about it."

"That's pretty much all you drink, man."

"Hence my problematic reality."

"What went down?"

"We hadda buncha drinks, n' eventually these girls came t' dance and whatnot—one had this sexy dirty way about her that only a fucking lunatic can love—she had stretch marks on her belly because she'd already had a bunch of kids—it was horrible—but she didn't care, she was just dancin' all crazy on a buncha older dudes n' shit—I stood there, looking out at these guys drooling on rubbery tummies, thinking: this is what happens when you do not pursue your fucking dreams and you become a fucking corporate slave—you have to find outlets for your frustrations—and always, nearly always the outlets wind up being one disgusting choice after another. I eventually came back home to the woodshop and worked 'til fuckin' dawn—just knowing I don't want my life to go down like that was all the motivation I needed." He flicked a fat ash with his forefinger, took a firm, crooked-faced drag on his Turkish Gold, exhaled the entire sum through his nostrils, and said, "Fuck it all." He finished his cigarette, flicked it into the street, approached the lock, pulled a pair of safety glasses out of his pocket like a true shop rat, turned on the grinder and let it rip. The noise was astral, and as hot sparks hammered the ground and melted snow on contact, I thought: if your whole crew flew back in time, who of your mates—who amongst them would have been the trapper? Who would have been out there, solo, forging a life from the wild? Who would possess the innate manual dexterity and sheer lunacy to hack a path of continued subsistence from wild, untamed lands filled with humans and animals who wanted to kill you? Such are the men you'll likely have the wildest time with, and EP is such a man. The kid was constantly toiling on one of several inventive ideas: adjusting, improving, finishing or beginning fresh—up with the sun he'd use a pipe wrench to undo a knot in the drawstring of his PJ pants and get on with it.

Right then a cop rolled up and blipped his siren right quick. I turned, EP shut the grinder and he rolled down his window: "Ay, c'mere a minute. Whachu you guys think you're doin' over there?"

I walked up and: "It's my bike sir, I swear. I lost my only key to the lock last night." He was an Irish-lookin guy with dark hair and dark eyes, a typical Finnegan, and he gave me a glance that said the majority of conversations he has on duty are filled with fabrications, and he wasn't in the mood for my bullshit.

"Ya got anyway t' prove it? There's been a ton a' bike thefts around here lately, as usual. We roll up n' your buddy is usin' a grinder on the lock—whachu think that looks like t' me?"

"I get where you're comin' from, n' I appreciate it. If we woulda been two different guys on my bike right now, I'd be glad as hell that you rolled up like this—um—O I know!— I have my initials etched into my seat post, below the visible line inside the frame. If I take off my seat and they match my license, are you good with that?"

"Yeah that works—smart idea, actually."

I did so and he split, and about ten minutes later, EP busted through the lock and it clinked to the ground. "Nice! You the man!"

"Fuckin' a' man! I didn't think it was gonna' go for a minute! That was a great lock, Riedie—too bad I had t' break it. I didn't think I would take nearly that long."

"Right? So what's the plan?"

"I have t' get back t' the wood shop n' finish the rack I been crankin' all day—I'm up for anything afterwards."

"Nice, who's it for?"

"Some guy, he ordered one—my first official order other than you guys."

"Awesome man—see? You're doin' it EP. Despite all the risk, you quit your gig to focus on what you love and you're doin' it alone—you worked hard as shit t' get t' this point, be glad. What's the time by the way?"

"2:25."

"Alright, cool, I'll hitcha in a couple hours then. I'm gonna' roam for a minute, if my legs got the juice.

"Word—I'll catchu." I knocked his fist and off we went.

44

Toes pushing into clips, it felt great to be on the move. I rode Damen to Chicago east, Milwaukee south to Halsted and again east on Washington. I charged into the wind and beneath the many tracks of the old Northwestern Station, the world felt dirty and wet and cold—all the slush was black and exhaust visible, and the city seemed to be poisoning me—but still there was the rush, man, the feeling you get when tearing through it: a wave of excitement and hatred for it all at once—as with many things, indeed. Over the River the grated bridge was slicker than ever—I looked down past where my thin tires spun upon the streaming iron lattice carrying me east to where cracked ice and water flickered with the wind—cars bombed past and to my right the huge limestone face of the throne known as the Civic Oprah House stood proud in the sun. I wanted to go back in time and shake the hands of the men who built such a thing, and I thought: O to be an eighty story giant, sitting relaxed and looking out from that chair as I dipped my feet in the River running below—I'd smoke such a big pipe that you'd need all the poppy farms in Afghanistan to come together in harmony to produce enough tinder, and through my insatiable appetite, finally the tribes would achieve peace—I'd fly in the elders and thank them individually, raise them up in my palm and show them the world from the vantage point of an ogre—we'd pose for a picture taken by a blimp, and upon their return, they'd instantly be considered the wisest men in the village, because they had puffed down with me—I sat back in the saddle and laughed, relaxed at how stupid and childish my mind could be, spinning no-handed up the street on a bright, random Saturday.

And hence go, roll and shred through the air of relaxed lucidity via freeform movement—all feel with no hands—lightening speed, hurricane breeze and no concerns. Just fuckin' float, man—past Dearborn, State and Wabash and at Michigan: 'Your Ad On This Bench' says the shit has hit the fan and you still won't admit it—a man laid there before the statement, half exposed from a green sleeping bag, sipping off a jug of red wine like it was a fine and understandable thing to do on this particular afternoon. I turned left and thought: I'm going north on Michigan because I want it—the 174 Express hissed in my ear and I imagined the realities of the individual commuters on board—I snuck past on the inside, just shy of the River, crossed Wacker among hammering traffic, and over the bridge a kid was lookin' at me, eyes big brown saucers pressed tight against the rear window of an Audi and mouth gaping open some six inches away—he seemed to be dreaming what it'll feel like to grow big and strong and ride this way—mighty fine, quite okay—and on I charged and got that rare feeling—when you realize that if you choose to run as fast as you can, nobody will catch you—I felt out of my body in a way—taking big risks with super thin, no mistake lines—the type of fully-committed lines that cause one to feel as though you're floating, watching from above—drifting along, sitting on the edge of some invisible seat, the helicopter pilot in a ski movie perhaps, holding your breath at the prospect of witnessing perfect execution or untimely demise, knowing there is no space for in-betweens. I took a breath and couldn't help but smile as I passed a long line of fifty thousand dollar cars stuck in traffic, leaned back in the saddle, catching bright rays on my face—I gazed up and thought: even if you leave, someday you'll come back to this city. You'll come back and love it and hate it and love it some more, the individuality, the beauty, the horror, the madness of heaping masses of nature combined with metropolitan wonders my mind couldn't have imagined in ten thousand years, yet here, here it is, already thought of, already constructed for my sake, for the sake of all who currently are and all who shall someday come to be—and thanks, thanks to everyone who pounded a single nail, spun a single screw, planted those flowers, that tree, the one who thought of cutting down but decided let them grow just so—this city, my home—so warm, and at the same time—so fucking cold.

Right then a cab almost hit me, and the guy apologized with his eyes before snapping across three lanes and booking west down Ontario. I looked up and felt like the grey car ahead was melting into the road and the ground and the sky were also dissolving into each other—at the same time I kept thinking about the undeniable fact that indeed the sky and the ground don't melt into each other at all, at least not before the earth melts into itself miles beneath the sea, see? And the loud, vociferous tone of a rust-spotted, revolving axel of a dump truck adjacent to my ear spawned the thought that if this globe were not twisting round itself as fast as it be, all would simply be up and gone and floating away, and life would not be—but no, breathe, I try to remind myself—I'm just a random fool seated upon a bicycle rolling up a road and whistling on my way to the Lake—all is well, fine and okay—I zipped onto the sidewalk after Oak Street, cut subterranean into a tunnel and under the Drive a man and his sax ricocheted beautiful tones off thick stone walls—I nodded thank you to his crazed joyful eyes as I passed, hung a left at the end, climbed up the ramp and bam, there she was, stretching out from white to blue—the long shadows cast by skyscrapers rising against the fading sun stretched east, over the Lake. The translucent sky and tranquil water melded together in a sort of fragile, distant, blue-green event horizon, providing the sense that if the wind blew too hard, the whole panorama might shatter. The calming sound of water placed me at peace—time to fly boy, time to fly—I turned south and around the Lake Shore Drive bend that begins at The Drake, the path snaked east and so did I, eluding large chunks of asphalt blasted onto the trail by union snowplows tearing up LSD so as to ensure plenty of work for union road crews the following summer. Around the bend the path was loaded with snow and ice, and after negotiating such it was due south. My fingers were cold and I balled them in my gloves as cars whizzed with such force on the other side of the wall that I could smell and taste the salt as it was crushed by their wheels—I thought: in each one of those cars there is a man or woman at the wheel who, for better or worse, is trying to get somewhere, both now and forever after, and I hope it works out alright for 'em.

I imagined the same scene under warm humid skies: the Lake crowded with boats and loads of people walking and running and biking and swimming, many just sitting, alone with their mind and the view and current concerns while others spoke with friends or lovers of minor hilarities or future dreams—but right then, at that moment, it was only me, me and a bundled Rastafarian juggling red plastic balls, but soon I was past him and it felt good to be alone in such a huge, ceremonious space. World class buildings rose to my right, newfound giants, upward into blue, the entire sum rooted deep into blasted bedrock, hundreds of meters below—and looking up at the many thousands of windows passing by, I wondered if anyone were looking down at me and pondering my existence as I pondered theirs.

Ohio Street Beach in the distance, I hammered dead straight on a slanted slate designed to take the foamy wash of pounding waves back to the Lake from which they came—she fumed cold breath upon me, skipping across the smoking iced surface and cutting into my skin—I suddenly felt weak and stiff and vulnerable—afraid to push myself in a way—I breathed slow and deep and thought of all the times I'd ridden that stretch, all the different weather and different sets of friends—when I was at my best, the times in the humid morning, blood rushing fresh after rest, all alone at sunrise alongside other people seeking isolation with speed and the washed out beat of the shore—you ripped here before, man, at a good solid pace—so c'mon, let's go—churn those poisons out: the exhaust you breath and ignorance you see, all the shit that you hate that gets inside and impedes peace of being—if they cut me open, would black sludge be the scene?—why sometimes do I feel it breeding?— keep pushing it out, man, please—if you don't, you know what you'll become?—don't let that sunny side up and die—not now or ever after. To the right buildings possessed personal variety like the vales of a mountainside, and back I flashed to Frankie and Ronnie's eyes, their inanimate, useless appendages producing genuine hatred for stillness and deep sadness for all who're stuck—I grit my teeth through the burn and imagined my cadence pulling tight a steel wire around the necks of those who'd maimed the blameless on purpose—one thousand top gear revolutions pulling the sharp steel strand one thousandth of a millimeter tighter—on I'll fucking churn, until finally the wire is pulled so taut it slits through on all sides—one layer at a time until s*lurrfp*hli*pp*—the final is slashed with a pop, like the tip of a hook through the moist, bloated middle of a fat folded night crawler—isolated ends of the body twitch wildly with the insert, and as thick black blood and mucus shoot out with the entry of the barb, my suspicion that the insides of those who hurt the helpless turn to slime over time is validated.

I shook loose from the thought and at my left a man stood alone with handfuls of bread, bating dozens of seagulls into a frenzied whirling twist of white wings and yellow beaks floating against blue. They screamed free, I put my head down and counted aloud with a sustained wind at my back—groovin' at rapid clip, I climbed a ramp, curled through a little park area, avoided two pedestrians, crossed Illinois, and as I continued south over the frozen Chicago River, LSD hummed steady above me. A huge hazardous abandoned hole where the two thousand foot Spire was supposed to rise sat dead west of the Drive, collecting whatever debris the wind felt like sending inside. In a way this failure was comforting to me—the chasm was serene as compared to what the additional hustle and bustle of wheelers and dealers would have seen. I zipped a downhill stretch past the harbor, frozen and motionless as opposed to when all the yachts sit bumping music in sultry sun as people drink and smile. The path turned west and Chicago rose with the sun to its back, a goliath deity, broad and diverse, complex in motivation and sole possessor of all the unseen stories running wild through her shadows—one after the other, too many to count, stories wobbled on, and as the path turned south I put my head down and counted one, two, one, two—my tires clicked over the cracks like steel wheels over intercontinental track and pumping on, my body felt strong—I was reminded of times of old—the feeling of living in a mountain town on the verge of a huge dump—when the tourists are gone and the entire populace is free to go big in coming days—when the silent impact of snowflakes at dawn somehow comes to possess that cold metallic echo of a shotgun shell being pumped into the chamber as expressions go: are you ready for this?—fuck yes—and climbing high into the exposed sky in maddened conditions—wind raging sideways, tryin' t' make you starfish the whole way down the mountain, the crew carries on—like ducks flying south for the winter, mates take turns leading the charge and creating the initial postholes to be followed and stepped in by counterparts—counting paces like the lead goose in the V must count each tired wave of his wings—only thing to do is keep counting down until you're there, and fly.

I drummed on with the wind, Lake shimmering beyond still barren trees, and I didn't think of anything for several thousand revolutions—past Grant Park and around the Shedd Aquarium, small clusters of people took pleasure in each other's company under what was arguably one of the most dramatic urban backdrops in the entire world. A small number of bundled joggers and lonesome cyclists came and went as I passed a silent Soldier Field, and a trace further south, the old toboggan hill saw all sorts of happy kids and engrossed parents having a hellova time together as they whooshed down the slope. Some short seconds later, the Gold Star Memorial Park went by the wayside—and looking at a family of five laying flowers and wiping their eyes, I thought of all the officers who had died in uniform over the years—the sons and daughters who were deprived of their presence in gratifying everyday moments like the one just seen on the hill.

The path leaned left, bent back right and went straight behind McCormick Place—cold in the shadow of that black rectangular beast as Burnham harbor stretched to my left, I passed the non-functioning waterfall on her back wall, and farther down the trail, the migratory bird and butterfly sanctuary was empty and barren. Sustained and quite strong, the only sound I heard was that of crashing waves being overtaken by wind between breakers. Deep beats thumped fluidly and blood ran through me: precisely that many less till the end—no, fuck off with that thought—nothing will reach me, certainly not weakness—grey ground flew beneath my tires and my breath steamed—I looked left over the half frozen expanse, tried to shut my brain and it went: I am barely fuckin' sane man, still. What did it feel like for those who chose to ride off the edge?—they who crashed through the ice and floated down with open eyes as the sun and sky grew dim to dark from then until forever more? I thought of two wise old fellows I grew up looping for: ole Mick and Parlson—what would they have to say, if eyeing the scene? 'Look at this—how beautiful!—it looks like God came down and painted this view himself.' 'He didn't need to come down and paint it,' Parlson might reply, 'He's already here,'—extreme peacefulness etched on his face in the moment—same look he held as he walked up the fairway with a half smile, eyeing dying leaves, late in the fall—his acceptance of what is with such absolute faith that I envied him: belief, deep untouched belief—and even if this faith is in nothing, so long as it gives you faith in the fact that you must strive to make the absolute best of now, whatever the now may involve: make the fucking best of it—do so, and via sheer aftereffect of positive tenacity, life will always be beautiful in a way. Don't worry about anything besides that, man, honestly—it's just as it was when the mountains and moon sky melted together as the ultimate truth—it's all gravy man—simply has to be—so don't ever get down.

Weight lifted, I sung freethought cantos on various subjects in assorted tones to nobody in particular—I sung out so loud it felt like the first time the bottom of my lungs had been cleared in ages—looking out to the point of visual infinity, it went: "Yo boys! You hear my voice calling out? You hear my lungs belt it loud? Or am I just lost in the vacuum?" After twenty more minutes of mashing southward under similar routine, I got down to 57th Street and Promontory Point. The spot is ideal in the winter, as hardly anyone comes around—I swung left onto the peninsular islet and passed an old Jewish gentleman sitting on a bench with crossed legs as symphonic overtones came from his portable radio. Fingers on his chin, he looked out at the city and held an expression like he could be debating what he would eat for dinner, or on the verge solving a conundrum of the physical make up of man that had evaded science for centuries, despite many thousands of minds devoted to the quandary. I rolled out to the end of the path before it looped 'round the back side of a stone building, dismounted and carried my whip down a snowy knoll to the rocks. There I sat, upon the farthest, tallest point of the old retaining wall I could find, feet hanging cold and bloodless above the water. A distant foghorn moaned and ice blanketed stone—water the color of several billion post ripe vegetables went slapping amongst itself in accordance to the violently rotating blades of a blender, and again the sound of large chunks of ice slicing themselves into slivers slashed into my eardrums. The air tasted like the smell of rain through a luscious sky and above me, atop slippery rock, a Latino family consisting of six adults and three children posed for photos—they took turns snapping one another in front of the Lake as the Loop set the background, still gigantic, seven miles north in the distance. Next the young men, four of them, all around twenty years old—they posed for a final picture with facial expressions that reminded me of an old poster of matadors, seemingly ready for anything, whatever bull life would throw at them, they'd be waiting to take it down—*snap*—their image was frozen forever, and onward they strolled toward the many miles they'd yet to roam upon these twisted, open roads.

Nobody was around for a few moments, and I sat peacefully until being startled by a woman who snuck up on a real blubbery fella with a phone to his ear. He looked to be thinking of something real serious as he stared into the void and waddled up the path—she darted in and tickled the shit out of him, deep under both pits from behind, and he shrieked crazy high pitched and folded over helpless—no different than he might have in the third grade when poked during a silent period by a goofball kid, seated behind him in class. He coughed hard and caught his breath and in a big deep voice said: "Why ya ticklin' me when ya know I'm tryina call in t' my sports show? Are ya crazy? I agreed to walk out here witchu in dis cold, n' now—now you're gonna' make me sound like a weirdo fruitcake if they put me on when you're ticklin' me—I use my real first name for God's sake! I got a reputation for callin' dis show—people across the city know me—they're gonna' tell the crowd to give it up for West Side Frank, n' it's gonna' be me, giggling high-pitched like a milky funboy cuz my crazy wife is ticklin' me, n' I'll have t' wait two months before callin' again!" They had a big laugh about it and: "Seriously—cut it out already, Jill," he said, "You're gonna' make me chuckle just thinkin' about it." She about fell over, she was laughing so big and loose—he grabbed her hand, she slapped his ass and they walked on, back toward shore—a married couple in their early fifties, and I was glad to see them out havin' a good time, n' taking it easy.

Ten moments later: "Excuse me," this Eastern Bloc accent came, "Can you take a photo of us?" I said sure, asked how they wanted it and she said, "You know, the view,"—for sure, I know—and *snap*. The husband made a happy face but seemed conscious of not looking weak whereas she did her best to look as stunning, cunning and chic as she could. They were both wearing black shoes, black pants, black leather coats, gloves and black beanies, too, and after they walked away with a military gait, I thought I'd taken what would be used as a profile photo on a social site involving ex-KGB husband/wife international assassin teams for hire.

The scene spread empty, I pulled the old sketchbook from my bag, inked an empty page and sat looking out, breathing and going over what had recently been, mentally. Sun beamed sideways, in and out of clouds sliding down on the north breeze, and I was in the mood for nothing minus the intrinsic enjoyment of a moment alone with the view. It felt good to get centered for a second, nothing pulling my senses awry, nobody selling or suggesting, no smart phones or texting—and so I sat for half a hand of sun, eyes mostly closed as I dove deep inside and swam beside as much positivity as my mind could derive from distinct memories of family and friends I love. I shivered and: don't be cold, I thought—the fragrant earth exhales sweet as dew evaporates on the blasting morning rays and in this divine state, the wind holds her breath as I begin to bake. I tried to stay strong inside like a monk on a mountainside, looked up to the sky and spied a hawk floating perfectly still as puffy sunlit clouds soared above—full grown and glorious, his eyes beamed for prey as wind rushed beneath his spread wings at sufficient speed to fly against what was without movement—in a blink they swept back with a primal scream from a hooked beak—the current meditation of levitation turned calm to vicious in an instant as he dove like a red-tailed bullet, talons cocked like the hammer of a gun until they sunk into the back of a squirrel scurrying along the rocks—he rose up on the wind, spread sideways against the huge open sky, father working to feed mother and son, one creature continued, another destroyed, cycle of life as untamed now as in every generation before. I thought: stay strong man, right down to the last fucking second. We're all going back to her, mate, this fucking Mother of us all—hate her, love her, whatever your feeling, it don't matter—we're goin' back to her—remember so as you travel across and walk over old roads and bridges built sturdy as stone by men now buried beneath or burned into her skies. Be grateful that you be and dream free.

Vague tones rose louder, and I turned to see the old Jewish man and his crotched Kippah moving toward the end of the point. I can sit silently in public locations while listening to symphonic overtones for hours on end—and all without hearing a single word anybody says—but most importantly, without caring. The distinct sound of WFMT's Saturday afternoon opera intensified from his radio and the timbre and emotion of a woman's voice produced a great feeling of sadness within—a deep sort of sadness you feel when a person you love fades to the earth—when you think of those you love who're here now, and you imagine a time, perhaps near to then, when you won't be able to drop in and say hello anymore—the many Saturdays at my Grams' place listening to those operas hum in the background were drawing to a close. The man ambled leisurely onward, and the reaching voice of the Italian woman flowed high and low, dramatic and slow about a subject I could not ascertain—it possessed a haunting depth of closure that has to be earned—so sad, in a way—sad and beautiful as hell, too—the type of sound I'd hope to enjoy inside my mind when fading out.

Her voice eventually lost to waves and wind and I tried to sit quiet and reach peace, but the faint sound of flipping paper got on my nerves. I closed my book and noticed it hadn't been my documents that caused the sound—a few meters away, on the next level of rocks, a folded up envelope was thrust between two boulders. I retrieved, noticed it was opened, removed a folded page of loose-leaf inked on both sides and read:

'Yo yo yo man, saga man—the dynamics, of my life, are fuckin unreal—I can't even get into it now man—it all becomes so fuckin unreal that you just can't articulate it. Man, fuckin, ugh—imagine that you think that you might have fuckin AIDS, and you don't get the test results back for two weeks, and you called twice, and you haven't gotten a return call. And you look at your wife and your fuckin baby, and you're thinkin about that every day, that you might be dying a slow death in front of them, and ruining their lives. You know how our imaginations are—those fuckin imaginations run wild, man, they play out every fuckin scenario down to the last, diminutive details. Motherfucker. Then you find out that—you're okay!—and you put out all these promises to the Lord Almighty—you know, that you're gonna' fuckin clean up, and appreciate what you got. And three days later you're fuckin the shit out this Mexican American, hot chick, from your regional office that's down at a meeting you organized. And then you're getting cock grinded by her employee, this black chick, at the bar, and then, then you're negotiating times to fuck her later, because you got a hotel room with the other chick and you're stuck fuckin her brains until the next morning comes—and so you fulfill your updated schedule, and two hours later you're going home to your wife in Cincinnati smelling like the other chick.

Wow—I guess, I mean, what a year, man, what a fuckin year—I've become like a fuckin dual personality fuckin monster, fuckin philanderer—fuckin dirty drunk—fuckin everything, man—adulterer—web of lies, man, fuckin tangled in 'em—unbelievable, man. It's dirty man—I've been comin out if it—it's like, ugh—it was fun and all sometimes, but at the expense of like havin a normal family and keepin a wife happy n' being a respectful father and all that—it's like I replaced it all with—with—fuckin, I don't know, man, I must of fucked—I can't even believe I'm sayin this, but like, eleven, maybe twelve girls this year—gotten head from like four or five more of 'em—from fuckin Bangkok t' Chicago t' Moscow t' Saint Louis t' fuckin Ho Chi Minh City and some other place in Vietnam—I just—I just feel like a fuckin dirrball, man, and it's just all gonna come fuckin crashing down—my wife's just gonna find out, have a nervous breakdown, grab that .45 and shoot me in the face. Whoo. Hopefully that doesn't happen man, but uh—I'm not gonna be as dirty this year—if I live—if the web of lies doesn't close in on me and strangle me to death—fuckin dual personality, man, holy shit—I just wanna be normal, man. Wow.

Anyway—hope you're doin well, man—happy New Year to you—it's always good to hear from ya—it's always good to hear from somebody I can fuckin' bare my fuckin' darkest soul to, and there is no fuckin' judgment, man—it's just understanding, and a little bit of laughter. So, alright man, take it easy—and do me a favor and burn this after you read it.

Your friend,

Eliot Black'

It was a mighty random letter to find at that moment. I felt real relaxed after reading it, knowing some guy named Eliot Black was out tweaking somewhere on all this shit. I felt like a million bucks, more or less. It was risky, I thought, stuffing the letter back into the envelope, to have even sent such information to Chicago, through the mail—he was lucky it didn't go undelivered, sent back to the return address and into his wife's hands. News reads: man shot in face with .45 in fulfillment of self-prophesy via his very own pen stroke. I figured I'd burn the motherfucker and help Eliot in his effort to start over. I turned my back to block the wind, noticed two guys walking toward me, lit the bottom corner and held it between my fingers as orange flames rippled up the side. White faded black in my hand and one of two big men walking up went: "Sup."

"Ay."

"We got smoke, if you got fire."

"Yeah?"

"Yeah man."

"Cool—I gotcha."

"Cool—mind if we sit witcha then?"

"Nah." They were about my age, maybe a shade older, and after nobody said anything for a second, I went: "I'm Doug Bible, by the way."

"Cool—I'm Bo n' this m' man Blue."

Sometimes you just shake someone's hand and you can feel their whole history—he had real strong mitts and seemed like a solid guy, and I wished I hadn't lied about my name. "So how you guys doin'?"

"How can ya be less than perfect if healthy n' alive on a day like today?"

"You really feelin' that good?" I asked.

"I mean—mostly—'cept we walked on out here t' puff on this n' chill a minute n' m' man Blue didn't bring no fire like we planned. You straight savin' the day for us, man." He had a bright smile, and I could tell him a positive persona by the lines of his face—he's had some good laughs, I'd bet.

"No big deal."

I passed the lighter to him and he couldn't get it going. He shook it and tapped it and shook it again—four more flicks still nothing. Blue said: "Give it here man—I'm a whiz wit tha shi." He removed his tan wool tam hat, buried his head in a blue pea coat like a turtle, capped the hole with his hat and promptly popped out, mouth smiling and shrouded in smoke: "Tole you I'm a whiz wit tha shi," he said, and so the three of us sat, not saying much as we looked out north toward the Loop, and smoked.

Blue lipped it for a bit, passed to Bo and a minute later it went: "Yo—yo Bible—yo *Bi*ble m*a*n!"

"Bible?—O yeah, right on man I'm zonin'—thanks." Goddamn fake names—they never fail to throw me off—like a puppy eating a banana for the first time, the texture just can't be anticipated.

He passed the handcraft and I took a couple pulls. The familiar taste of a Swisher lingered on my lips. I exhaled skyward and in the distance a group of six kids were in the midst of a full body barrel roll race down a snow-coated knoll. A false start argument ensued between the two winners after they bottomed out and Bo went: "So you stay down here man?"

"No—I'm back up toward the border of Humboldt Park."

"Lotta' affiliated R*i*cans over there man—fools peddlin' dope all over the place, just lo*o*kin' t' jump people."

"Yep."

"Ma'fuckas'll pull a blade on you every t*i*me."

"Yep."

"I'm a locksmith onna side, n' every time I gotta go over there for some gig I get glared hard as hell man, like I'm a ma'fuckin' *Vi*ce Lord from Austin up tryina make moves n' they hood n' shit. Happens *every* time man, I swear t' *God!*—they look at me like a nigga can't be out workin' legit—nigga always got t' be up t' somethin'—know what I'm sayin'?

"Just like most white boys are preppy fraternity brothers or fuckin' rednecks or stiff-ass IRS employees or serial killers—there's always some stereotype."

"Like what I said about Ricans in Humboldt park, even—people'll say tha's a stereotype, too, but it ain't—I didn't say they *all* bangin'—I said a lot of them is—there's a *di*fference—jus like by us, down here onna south side—there's a lotta' blacks bangin'—not all of us though—but still, there's a lot. N' that's why I hate the way I get looked at up there, everywhere really—in Chi, it's impossible t' wash your hands of it—someone's always tryin' t' front, no matter what. It happens in a second, man—car rolls up all slick—niggas ain't about to check references man, know what I'm sayin'? Ain't no time t' say: 'I been singin' in a church choir my whole life, man, n' I'm only here t' help a ma'fucka get in his whip cuz his drunk ass locked the ma'fuckin' *keys* inside, a'ight? I ain't here t' compete n' sling no Blue Magic in your hood cuz the man be bringin' the heat t' mine, *a'ight?* I'm a workin' man—leg*it*, nigga, tryna' earn n' take care of m' family, so lemme go about m' business like a man would'—ain't no time for that." I could see in his eyes he'd had a lot of face-offs in the style he'd just described—he was damn sick of it.

"I never fucked wit any a' tha shit b'cause m' dad always preached that prison can't be no option," Blue interjected, "You'd need t' grow a ma'fuckin' *croc*odile tail t' keep all 'em *dip*sticks outcha' *ass*—" I busted up and, "I told myself as a kid I ain't goin', sho 'nuff." He looked out quiet for a second and: "It'll get better when we older though—all the fools our age'll be dead or locked up, n' then finally none a' the young G's'll fuck wit us cuz they'll finally figure out we was never in the game like that. Then all you gotta watch out for is gettin' robbed."

"That'll be sweet," Bo said, and we all had a good laugh for a second. "But these thugs man—you get to our age, a little older than them on average, even jus four, five years—we got a little more experience so we can look at 'em like: c'mon, man, for real?—you really tryina do everyone like this? *Still?*—n' then they look at me like: I have a right to my way of life, right?—but that don't mean it ain't disgusting."

Blue sat cross-legged, shook his head and: "It's all about sellin' dr*u*gs, man, tha's all it comes down to most the time—drugs n' drug money, n' the power attained wit it. Everyone's tryina get a zip a' the best shit n' sell it so they can buy hot sounds n' kick it wit bad bitches, you know."

"It's not surprising though," I said, "It's terrible, but when somethin' becomes lucrative, it gets violent—even in commercial commerce, things get violent in a different style, via lawsuits n' trade wars and, eventually, real wars—many wars throughout history were economic in nature at the beginning—so when there's a lot of money involved, on an individual, street-based level, with too many people tryin' t' sell the product to a small customer base, people have t' physically establish their territory constantly defend their selling points from competition, and thus continuous violence becomes the necessary n' deterministic coefficient of the equation. Just nature bein' nature man."

"Cuz they don't c*a*re, man," Bo said, "They hollow inside—born hollow, raised hollow, they st*a*y hollow—these young bloods are stone ma'fuckin' k*i*llas at six*teen*—half the kids I know wanna be a black market executive in they own right—you look in their eyes man and there ain't nothin' there but an intense crave for power—that's who I fear."

Blue snapped his fingers, raised his eyebrows and: "Ay you remember Ernie Weatherspoon? From apprentice class?"

"Yeah—he tall bogus, dude's a buster—fuckin' washout."

"No you thinkin' 'bout Mike Ivy. Weatherspoon was a real friendly fella."

"Kinda had like a round face? Guy who had all them jokes 'bout horseradish?"

"Yep."

"O yeah, I remember now—chill dude man, real nice guy."

"Well he n' some other ma'fucka's I can't recall—they went down t' some house party dude was invited to, and before you know it, they threw 'em off the roof and his whole body bust like a watermelon, man."

"Who?"

"Ernie ma'fuckin' *Wea*therspoon, *man!*—some young fools mistook him for another dealer n' threw him off a roof wit no warnin', n' he all busted up now."

"They ever catch who did it?"

"Naw, but his cousin say if he ever find who it was, he gonna' find out what they love most, you know, besides themselves—n' when he find out, he gonna' slaughter it."

The brutality of the threat didn't make me blink—it was a basic, matter of fact part of life in the world—hence why you don't fuck with people. "When I'm walkin' the street, if I see somethin' odd I start thinkin': the guy over there, lurkin' in the shadow, threatenin' t' be a threat—he gonna' try n' hurt me, n' he's able. Soon you begin conjurin' some real violent offensive moves man—I mean, tha's jus life, I guess, but still, it's a lotta' stress over time, livin' n' thinkin' like that—when ya spend so long keepin' sho that edge is sharp it feels like it be finna get brittle n' break. Always havin t' watch out cuz ya never know who's lurkin' in the frozen shadows, bidin' their time in a moonlit hunt—it wears ya down, man."

"You basically have to be prepared to kill, or get killed, to fight on the street—same now as ever," I said, "If you're not, you walk away—run if you have to—straight home t' chill on that fact that it's better than being dead, severely injured, or in jail."

"Or on the run."

"Right, of course—none of these options are good—they are, however, the accurate effect of that cause. It's a dangerous, crazy fucking world out here, man."

Nobody said anything for a long minute and my face felt cold from the wind. They seemed to be bummed about that Weatherspoon news so I went: "So how you like locksmithin'?"

"It's cool, Bible—I'm real good wit tha tricky shi. Always have been."

"Whachu do Blue?"

"I'm a Smith too—tha's partly why I'm so tight wit this fool."

"Cool."

"But tha's just on the side—Smithin's for tryina stay above water, you know, tryin' t' work up a 'lil stake is all. Our main thing is we sing—in church man, in bars, train stops man—but las summer we got into a coupla' fests where people went dancin' on the street— the wild, body-filled street man," he said, standing, face happy a hell, "People was out movin' on the product of our lungs—dancin' sweatin' bodies, alive n' set free, tumblin' through the streets in varied stages of lucidity—all kinds risin' high to the tuneful harmony of love n' bedlam—go, go, go—shit, you know, Chicago always does so—those scenes was *live* Bible, straight up, but still, we do any gig possible, small n' large—tha's how we catchin' on."

"When we ain't Smithin'," Bo added, "We tryna go big—legit."

"Man I dig—so you two grow up together then?"

"Yeah—see, my pop—he knows how t' throw a barbecue man—lamb, all the best meats—it's your birthday?—anything you want—he a hard worker, man, a provider."

"Nigga takes it to the bank every day, jus like mine," Blue added, proud look on his face. "Our pops was friends, still is—tha's how we first met. It ain't always like that in our community—we lucky we got great examples."

They gave each other knuckles: "N' seein' pop get older, man, seein' the way he ain't slowed one step—doin' what's best for m' ma, for me n' my bros—at the end of the day, I'm just tryna do the same, feel me? I jus gotta keep on keepin' on, man—keep pushin' like mad like him 'til the end."

Naked branches clicked together on the wind and: "Ever think maybe if your pop didn't have it as hard as he once did, you'd go soft?"

"Yeah."

"Me too," I said. "My pop—no one was t' stop him—he was on a mission when it came to makin' a life for me n' my family."

"Mr. Bible don't play no games?" I shook no and it came: "Is he a worker or a company man?"

"Worker."

"My pop too—n' tha's who I'm dedicating my LP to, my pop."

"Cool."

"Cuz he also taught me if you don't take time to appreciate things you'll go on toilin' n' grindin' until one day you gonna' be like: wow, that was a lotta' wasted energy, wasn't it?—and off ya go. Know what I'm sayin'?" Bo looked at the sky and: "What happened t' ridin' a cool fuckin' path, n' havin' the travel down that path be the point? Like—enjoy the process, man, the everyday *grit* n' shit—it's all the little jivin' grimy effort that makes the work legit—if you ain't findin' fun for yourself in those little moments, man, it's gonna' pass ya by n' *crack*—ya die."

We finished the burn and I felt light and released—it was good to be reminded, first hand, by two random cats without a lighter how many miscellaneous folk are out striving to realize passions and fulfill idiosyncratic dreams in the beautiful, hard knock way this country allows for. I feel such splendor, watching people go all out. I closed my eyes within my shades and thought of sitting right *here*, in this very spot, with Melissa—light cut through wafting leaves as the sounds of summer evening radiate from the bodies of locusts clinging to the underside of topmost branches—throngs of people, happy and free, taking a moment to breathe as we sought to believe in the eternal positive sonata of the soul. It had been a very lush summer for Chicago, with warm humid temperatures and powerful, rolling storms. Growth had been spectacular, morning smelled divine, and as we sat listening to the wind through the tall grass of the late summer shade, a flock of forty seagulls were eyeing and annihilating insects between blades of green twenty feet to our right—a red and black caterpillar crept toward me, munching blades as his body rippled forward. Melissa said: 'Maybe this little guy realized: hey, the birds will stay away from this person, so I'll take my chances with them—being squashed is better than being eaten.' She smiled as the wind blew through her hair and: 'I think I'll put him in my shirt pocket and ride him to a safer place, yes.' She insisted we ride way north near the Uptown basketball court on the shore before she set him in long grass near some bushes with: 'If you make it to be a butterfly, and ride the wind south to Mexico for the winter, think a' me once in awhile as you flutter on!' I felt so happy, thinking of that moment, I really did—many people would have thought it ridiculous, but I loved that helping a random caterpillar in its quest to some day fly mattered to her. 'Enjoy it—your time, your mind, and all that the two combined shall come to discover. It's all you from here on out—tis your life to live and try and die, and never allow a soul to tell you otherwise, so let it rip'—let it rip, let it rip, let it rip—the phrase echoed off her lips as a I sat there thinking: God, this girl is legit. I was about to leave: "So hey, thanks for the smoke guys—enjoy the night—"

And Blue said: "Feel like one for the road?"

"Uh, well—yeah, sure—if you're kind enough to offer, why not?"

He walked up the knoll past the path so as to shield the wind with the walls of a stone park district building as he prepared a handcraft. Bo and I sat there all crunched into ourselves, trying to hold heat with discourse muted and view soaked in, and Blue was back in a blip and his phone was ringing. He had a short, indiscernible conversation and: "What's the word son? Was that our man about the Bulls tickets or what?"

"Nah, that's my homegirl," Blue said, "She just wanted t' let me know she got me some a' my favorite snacks n' shit—I gotta snag a couple things she forgot—she a down ass broad fa'sho—been hookin' it up on the proper with big love since day one."

"I'd expect nothing less," I said.

"But what about the *tic*kets man?—Kobe's comin' t' town tonight. You think he'll come through?" Bo rubbed his hands together and: "I been waitin' t' boo his ass all *week!*— ya boy ain't gonna' scram on us with the cake, is he?"

"M'man always used to hook me up with food—his grandma'd make 'em peanut butter double-deckers, throw 'em bunches a Hoho's n' shit n' he'd share 'em like a ma'fucka. He straight—if he can't get 'em he'll hit us back no problem."

"Cool."

"So what's up?" I said.

"Whudaya think is up?"

"Another 'lil session?"

"Fa'*sho.*"

"What's the status on the apparatus?"

"Proper greenery, you gonna' be jovial—my skill guaranteed like graffiti on a boxcar, G." He took a thick chain out of his pocket—and for a second, for a second I thought he was gonna' try and sell it to me, but then he put it on. He noticed I'd looked at him funny, and: "I can't really go walkin' with this 'round m' neck over where I stay at. I'd wind up getting stuck for it. I jus keep it in my pocket until I'm chillin' somewhere, n' then I enjoy it."

"Cool."

Bo raised his eyebrows: "What'd th*a*t shrug you?"

"A lot, man—plenty," he said, breath steaming over his head.

"Tha's a beauty, a hard-earned beauty."

"I know man—I wish they'd just make more gold n' drive the price down."

"They'd never do that—they'd lose profits, Blue!"

"Actually, even if they wanted to, it would be impossible because the only time gold can possibly be made is when a star explodes," I said.

"Is that for real?" Bo asked.

"Yeah man. During a supernova, neutrons strike iron at unimaginable speed and, in a sort of insane cosmic alchemy, gold is formed. That's the only way—the true root of what you're wearin'. There is a finite amount upon the earth."

"Shit I tole you this chain was ill man, didn't *I?*"

We all had a laugh and: "I never thought of gold as finite. You jus think they make it, you know?"

"Right? They form it, that's true, but it's not made—it's just as few people think of how long it took deciduous forests to die off and sink deep below the surface of the earth, and subsequently, how many years it took for the earth's pressure upon that organic matter to concentrate it into dense, void-black, crude oil."

"Or the next step—the step of extracting it from the earth, right?"

"Exactly—and how many minds combined to conjure the design of the equipment to discover, to drill, to extract, to hold, to ship—"

"And then you gotta draft gasoline from there, right?"

"Yep—plus the infrastructure to make its use possible and—"

"People assume it's simply cooked in a vat, like soup—"

"And even if it was soup," I said, "How much effort did it take to grow the potatoes? Who tilled earth and the planted the seeds? Who harvested and loaded the pickings into sacks? Who transported them? And when they got to the manufacturer, who loaded them into the capital equipment driven assembly line responsible for dicing and dressing and feeding them into the can? And how many minds throughout time made each step of that process possible? How many millions of minds were responsible for one tiny improvement after another for sake of increasing efficiency to the point that the earth can sustain—"

"Nope, jus go the store n' it's there—as if the aisles be the fields n' the cans be the plants."

"You buy the can, take it home, shed the lid, pour it into a bowl, stick it in a microwave, select a period of time you desire yet another monumental machine you had no part in creating—select how long you want that to operate, you press start and energy from a hulking coal or nuclear fired power plant comes flowing over vast tracts of land via high tension wires maintained by madmen, and sixty seconds later, after millions of molecules have been sent stirring by invisible energy that reached you at the speed of light, the soup is steaming. And then, someone has a single taste and they say, 'Ah, this soup sucks, too many beans—and so they pour the whole bowl into the toilet, pitch the can in the trash and off they go to flip more TV while debating what next they should buy on credit."

"Like even when we layin' tracks, you know—I mean those thoughts are mine, those lyrics and beats is mine, right, but still I'm harmonizin' through a microphone I didn't think of or create, and my voice boomin out speakers that I didn't build, and it's all overlaid with beats I put together on a program I didn't write, n' then I'm recording the whole gig on digital, dropping post production—*wow*, man."

"There is a complete and total disconnection with the process of creation for the vast majority of society, to which repercussions exist. Who thinks past the first level, let alone the next five, or ten?—and I'm not sayin' ya have t' be the person to build or think of all the products you use, but before you look at somethin' n' say, 'O wow, this sucks,' ask yourself—what have you produced? What of your own? What plants have you grown and harvested, avoiding the ever-present risk of insects, too much sun, too little, too much water or shade—helping them live through it all to allow you to eat? What animals have you caught, killed, cleaned, dismembered and cooked? And if you're cooking, to what do you owe the fire and utensils? How much of what you use did you have any single role in besides handing over currency to a cashier of some sort? The honest answer, for me, is not all that much. And that's why I'm not apt to complain very often. Because I'd be a fraud to do so."

"Let's puff this man," Blue said, twisting the finishing touches on his Swisher.

I nodded with a smile and Blue displayed the finished product. "Now that's some quality work, my man," I said.

"I tole you I'm good wit tha tricky shi."

"I wonder who grew it," Bo said, "This some home grown or smuggled in by a cartel?"

"Well, I know who gonna' s*mo*ke it," he said, dipping into his coat with a flame.

We passed the vibe and as it faded out, Blue said: "Ay Bo, let's head on high to focus on dreams for a minute—Bible, you up for a track?" I nodded and in a harmony slow and undulating, they burst out:

> "*I'm thinkin' bout good times——*
> *I'm thinkin' bout sun-ny days——*
> *I'm thinkin' bout far off pla-ces—*
> *And smilin' fa-ces, yeah, I'm driftin' away—*
> *Said, I'm driftin' away, hey, hey, yeah—*
> *I'm thinkin bout old times when we—*
> *Ran through the streets—*
> *Football in the park invitin' everyone ya meet—*
> *Kids with open hearts, and wide open minds—*
> *O how I long, how I long for those times—*
> *I'm think 'bout good times—*
> *I'm thinkin' bout sun-ny days——*
> *And smilin' fa-ces, yeah, said I'm driftin' away—*"

They carried on with several beautiful verses that made me happy—the subject matter was genuine and tangible, very Chicago, and as their voices flowed a-cappella, they lifted me high like I was breathing that oxygen-loaded, spring-mountain air. Again I felt cleared as I looked out toward the Loop and soft orange light shined on the apexes of surrounding manmade mountains—the beautiful transfer of their pitch from high to low fast and slow struck me—they went on singing and I felt an infinite realm of pristine opportunity lay before us—life was raging celebration, a good time had by all—an erupting party with no unnatural power, with every non-essential item in the household to be burned for light alongside a tearing jam session with everyone involved—no matter how it goes, man, stand strong with the internal beat and remember mankind at its root: fire, water, flesh and song— even in your weakest state, feel too good to believe it and overcome.

After a pandemic of improvisation of gradually amplified beauty, they wrapped it up with a long high note held until breath was gone, and I felt honored to receive a great private performance by some old school cool dudes at an unbeatable venue. We all wished one another well—good health and proper luck in the future, and off into the unknown we strolled.

45

Rolling back north, the cold wind was ruthless. More clouds swept in, thin and clean, and the sun's escape was muted and without drama as it was engulfed by the impending storm long before slipping beneath the surface of the horizon. The sky looked swollen and bruised, and as the fractured Lake churned darkly against the rock and concrete shore I put my head down and generated mounds of energy in order to progress just slightly faster than if I had been walking. It was a dead gale in my face, and as my eyes stared split second upon the black visual infinity of the Lake I shivered hard. Flurries strengthened into snow and my slicks spun silently along the soft path—wheels transformed into non-machined, white deep V's conducting soundless motion minus the steady· exhale of condensed breath as I go go go—my nose was super cold and my lips bled a bit, and after spending the past three frigid days mostly outside from dawn 'til dusk, I developed a deep permanent chill the likes of which I had not felt in many moons. It was an arduous ride and it took nearly an hour of woeful revolutions to get up toward Chicago Avenue.

I left solitude and cut back under the Drive to society, and in three blocks passed every size, shape and race, so many faces and nationalities—I dodged a pothole and beside the middle of a double bus, time slowed—the accordion reverberated like a black cancerous lung and I pressed on, barely evading the front end as it swept back into traffic. Past a coin shop, I saw a disturbed young man chase after and stomp a bird to death and felt the urge to stop and stick my long, slim blade, deep into his eye while asking: 'Why? Why did you have to harm for sheer sake that such was feasible? Do you now see how awful it feels?' I cut north on State Street and snowflakes evaporated upon the vertical stainless steel exhaust pipes of a blue garbage truck in swift sizzles as horns blared. I imagined a battered steel toed boot pressing a grubby gas pedal as I spied the filthy fumes roaring out the exhaust pipe: we have to come up with a better way, I thought to myself, and I damned my mind for lacking the scientific wherewithal to conjure its own credible solution to the problem. A block later traffic jammed as a semi-crusty white guy on the back a city truck with a cigarette hangin' from the side of his mouth exhaled a white cloud before passing the square to a black partner of equal esteem—they rode standing upon opposite ends of a bumper, setting horses in five meter increments as for a lane closure. The white guy got the cigarette back, took a crooked-faced drag and looked out at traffic with a rotten face that said yes, you're waiting, you're waiting on us and we're not gonna' move any faster, so have a good one.

I cut past them and over to Marino Park, the Viagra Triangle as it's called, for sake of snagging a hot drink from a little café before making my way back to the West Side—I needed something to help heat me up, pronto. I ordered a Joe from the little stand as Mediterranean guitar flowed from outdoor speakers and a non-active fountain supplemented a brick lined triangle of movers and shakers—the smell of unaffordable restaurants filled the air as who's who of Chicago's socio-economic upper crust jived on surrounded by scattered Midwestern whores wearing four hundred dollar shoes and not knowing how to walk in them. A crazy-looking white woman who only a few moments prior I witnessed looking sadly into a store window, working hard to make herself presentable—she rolled through the park, humbly begging, and I pawned her a lonely, crumpled buck.

I leaned my bike against the trunk of a bare honey locust and it felt good to be drinking coffee and breathing easy. I took a seat next to an outdoor heater and warmed my hands as a man went: "We have proper market in*tel*ligence, certainly—it's just that some of our relationships are *so* good we don't ask for what we should—this year, in order to optimize certain market vulnerabilities—hey, wait, let me call you back in a moment." An extremely busty, assy and classy black woman strolled past. Her hair was a braided work of art and each stride was very deliberate. The surrounding audience took notice. The cultivated white chap and his tight suit stepped up and spewed some verbal diarrhea in her direction but to no avail. She looked at him with a silent expression that said: I'm the real deal, kid, so don't even bother.

I sipped my coffee and smiled wide, in love with her immediately—it warmed my insides on the way down, and I took a minute to etch a sketch of her illustrious lips when it came: "Yo R*im*, you writin' *rh*ymes over there?"

I looked up and: "Who's Rim?"

"Aw shi, my bad—I thought you was someone else—you got a straight ma'fuckin' *tw*in who's always writin' *rh*ymes n' shi—I thought you was h*im*." He walked on with a slick hustlers gait as the steady click-clack of horse hooves pranced past State and Maple with young, snow-swept lovers kissing silently in an elegant ebony carriage. I looked at the classy outfit of the man handling the horse and the happiness entrenched on the faces of the couple in back, and I thought that right then, at a time identical to this lush romanticism, somewhere in Somalia, waves of Arab men were coming out of the bush on horseback, foaming at the mouth as they approached a village of semi-nomadic farmers set to be a new subject of profane sexual violence—women are getting gang-raped in front of crowds that include their husbands before being carried off like a unrecognizable black insects and devoured by a swarm of large army ants as the sun beams heat through a spotted blue sky. And then—then I thought of how that village would be torched: thatched huts set alight while men with guns waited outside, ready and eager to cut down those who would run screaming in primal panic out the door—blood would stain the dirt and some would remain huddled together, a last moment of desperate love exchanged amongst the flames rather than running out into the gauntlet of a torturer's tryst—and days later, relatives would return to recover bodies burned so bad they weighed just a tiny fraction of their old self, and life as we know it would go on. I shivered hard and thanked God for not being born where torturous killing is a part of your everyday—fighting tooth and nail—killing, mutilating people—displaying heads on spears to terrify people in towns in accordance to manipulated worship. The things some believe are incredible and only possible as a result of countless centuries of generational brainwashing to profound depths—and so I wished I could show up and ask: do you not recognize the embers of irrationality glowing brightly within you? But indeed the answer might come: 'The Word of God is like a weapon. God is a great weapon. The greatest, in fact—remember that,' and I would be dead and gone before I could blink. Chicago's rough but, you know—it's mild compared to that shit.

A cop walked by with a fresh Joe and radio crackled to life with: "I have a known location of a wanted man—subject is eating at Kung Pow Mandarin Chinese restaurant on 86th and Kedzie, and is wanted on a warrant for assault stemming from a retaliation incident with the ex-boyfriend of the subject's sister. Subject's name is Derrick McCoy, an African American male, 25, six foot, 170 lbs last seen wearing blue jeans, a black puffy coat and a black winter hat—no priors." He was precisely my size, weight and age, and I immediately connected with the man in question, for the occurrence of someone fucking with my sister would certainly result in something far worse than an assault—I had nothing but respect for his motive.

280

I waited until the officer walked out of earshot, dialed 411, pushed zero for the operator: "Good evening, directory assistance—city and state please."

"Chicago, Illinois."

"Go ahead."

"I need the number to Kung Pow Mandarin Chinese Restaurant on 86th and Kedzie."

"No problem, sir. Would you like me to connect you with no extra fee?"

"You bet."

The phone started ringing and: "Kunpowchin*ee*," some guy said, fast as hell and nearly incomprehensible.

"Hey sir, I don't mean to bother you, but I think my cousin is eating there right now and I need to talk to him—it's a family emergency."

"You cousin work here?—no, this is family own Chin*ee* restaurant!"

"No he's *eat*ing there. I need to talk with him. His phone is broken. Just yell out for Derrick McCoy—he's a black guy wearing a black coat with a black hat. Just get him on this phone with me, sir, please."

He muffled the receiver and I heard him yell out for the man in question. A moment slipped by and: "He*llo?*"

"Derrick?"

"Yeah—who is this man?"

"Listen now—this is about the incident with your sister's ex-boyfriend. Someone snitched on you and the cops are coming t' scoop you at this Chinese joint right now. I just heard it over a policeman's radio, so I figured I'd try and tell you before you get pinched."

"Who *is* this man?" He asked in a real low whisper, "Are you playin' games wit me? Someone putchu up t' this? Stop foolin' man."

"All that happened is I heard your story dispatched on the radio, and the cops are coming. Let me guess—you're six feet tall and wearing blue jeans, a black coat and a black hat—someone who knows where you are is a rat. I respect that you looked out for your sister man, but you're gonna' get snagged if you don't bust outta there right now. Just, you know—never hurt good people, alright? Good luck mate," I said, and I hung up. It was a corny line to end with but I didn't know what else to say. I wondered what he was thinking—getting a call from a random white boy he didn't know about a highly personal situation like this had to shatter his head a bit, right? He'd never know me and I'd never know him, and that was that.

I again dialed my phone, checked my messages and it said I had two fresh—first some cat named Robert Reinstrudle called. The message was deleted immediately as soon as it was determined to be work related. He was excited about something or other—I didn't even come close to hearing him out. He was from that insurance company I was supposed to start the following Monday, and I almost fell into a panic at the thought that now I'd have to show up. I had completely disregarded the idea upon quitting NVH Online, but now, with material gone—fuck—just don't think about it right now. The second message was from JC—he'd tried to ring several times and was annoyed I hadn't answered. He told me to meet him at an old spot of ours by seven o'clock or he'd string me up in a real obscene way. I slammed the Joe, got on my whip, blazed down State and cut west on Chicago, passed the red-bricked projects between Wells and the River where street light cast delicate shadows upon numerous people sleeping soundly upon concrete cradles and others prepared to spend their Saturday night in a frenzied fervor, devouring Beijing Cocktails and hardcore Haitian plant shit and washing it all down with the unseen contents of the brown bagged bottles held delicately at their side.

With a grin my heart bumped beats temporarily unphased by the eternal conundrum of life and motherfucking death, and down the stage of diffused street light rhythms rolled into the cold, quiet night. Same goddamn mystery lurking 'round the next corner for me along with everybody, one of them, just waiting to swallow—so no reason t' worry man, just go go go. Before the River cars crushed into one lane, and as two refused to make room for each other, a white man rolled down his window with: "Nice car! You like art? Man I'll slit your neck above an untouched canvass and make your wife a fresh new design—don't start beef!"

I slipped beyond the jaw-jackin' easy as could be and snow iced my beard as if I were skiing—past the concrete factory on Halsted, steam rose in a profuse cloud above the sound of industrial production. Beyond some dilapidated buildings and under the Metra tracks, the smell of baking bread got in my head as I passed an old time bakery at my left. The road was snowy and if not for my fenders my body would have been a mess—I progressed steady but cautious and was passed by a brother with breakaway speed reminiscent of a man on a mission—if he showed up to race at the Velodrome he alone would be worth the price of admission. Cat almost got clipped by a cab as he hung north on Milwaukee and I continued west before crossing the Kennedy, continuing past Ashland and dipping the wrong way up Paulina for a few blocks to where JC said he'd meet me.

I got off my bike and it hit me that I had no way to lock her up—duh. I asked the European valet driver if he would mind keeping an eye while I asked permission to bring her inside. "Is no problem," he said, wiping a tuft of snow from his shoulder. I waited patiently for him to approach me, and after explaining the situation, the bartender was cool with it—he'd poured us hundreds of drinks over the years, often hitting us cut-rate tabs in exchange for fat tips and so when I asked if I could stash my ride he waved to come right in.

I ordered a drink and a hypermuscular Mongolian man sparked a square in the corner, standing stiffly as he leered blankly into an empty space on the wooden wall. "Hey, there's a smoking ban now, buddy. You ain't visiting Ho Chi Minh City—get outside," the bartender said. He leered at the tender as smoke steamed from his nostrils, and exited with an expression that vexed me—it was a look that said he might pull a Glock from his pocket and unload upon returning to the room. Time passed and he didn't return, and I felt real comfortable to be drinking in a warm familiar place with good music, dim lighting and about a thousand bottles of liquor along the wall. The same cats were working there, doin' their thing, same lean Mexican dude with the traditional fade of a lead busboy hustling quick trips, efficient and courteous and serious of his work. The joint held a real old time vibe on account of all the Motown, swing, big band, blues, gospel, jazz and doo-wop on the juke, and the ornamentation was real 40s-like. The room smelled like celery salt and I was thirsty—Marvin Gaye's voice flowed easy out the speakers, and all different sorts seemed to be feelin' slick off the same beat—tell me—how does it feel? To be? Pretty fuckin' alright—right?

A man who didn't fit the scene came in and sat next to me and I told him the spot was reserved for an ole mate—that we were regulars and whatnot, and he asked if he could keep it warm 'til he got there since it was the only open stool. Again, I thought, here we go. He ordered a drink and didn't touch it. He then walked away for a moment, still within sight, turned back, away, back again and slightly away, fiddled with his slacks, almost approached a woman and didn't—and the whole time he kept such a staunch eye upon his glass I felt certain he possessed an innate paranoia of being poisoned. His demeanor—wary and defensive and distrustful—and after observing such for a moment longer, I then began to ponder whether

282

perhaps he de*ser*ved to be poisoned, and further, if I should be the one to do it. And that's why it's best to be easy, man—if you're too careful, people get ideas.

I watched a commercial and counted the cuts, how many scenes were spliced—I counted, to my amazement, twenty-four splices during a thirty second ad. People have no attention span, man, nearly none at all. Dude sat back down and: "So," he said, "What do you do?"

"What the fuck do *you* do?"

"Well, g*eez*!"

"Nah, I'm kidding, see—I throw people off for a living—I'm an attitude adjuster, like, you thought you wanted to speak with me, and now you don't. So yeah, hasta mate—vamoose and the likes."

"You're funny—are you still in school?"

"Every day."

"I finished a very long time ago, twenty years, but I'm still in education." A silenced commercial flashed images of old folks living comfortably alongside a green percentage indicating how much their savings had increased since using a particular investment firm and: "What are you putting toward retirement at this point?"

"Black lungs and a bum liver."

I was not in the mood to converse with this fool. I looked at him like: why are you forcing yourself upon me like a British businessman upon the supple ass of an underaged Bangkok boy in an infested motel with rubber mattresses? Incredulous to my vibe, he responded to a muted news report of a shooting rampage at a college with: "This is why behavioral contracts should be signed before one gets admitted to college."

"Be*hav*ioral contracts? All these Mr. Fixit motherfuckers saying that in order to enroll in college, a be*hav*ioral contract must be signed, and you—you're one of them. I mean, my Lord! Do you honestly think anybody whose intent is to blow twenty people away is going to give a fuck about a behavioral contract when they know the repercussion to that crime is either life in prison, death via lethal injection or suicide by cop? I'm sure they'll be real worried about that goddamn contract while sending hollow points through people's heads at twelve hundred feet per second. I'm sure that contract will really be weighing on them."

"How about gun control?"

"I'd like you to be the guy who knocks on people's doors and says: 'Okay, we just wrote a new law, so before I leave the premises, you're going to have to give me all your guns.' Sure, okay—and further, gun control only serves to keep guns out of the hands of honest citizens—again, if somebody is comfortable with an element of malicious action that includes overlooking the criminal repercussions of robbing or killing somebody, just how is the lesser crime of illegally possessing a weapon going to serve as a hindrance to this action?"

"Then take the guns away from everyone completely, make owning a gun punishable by long stints in jail."

"The previous argument is still relevant, and further, doing such would put you at the mercy of the state—Imperial Japan, Nazi Germany, Fascist Italy, Soviet Russia, China, North Korea, Myanmar and Iran in their current form—they and countless others all disallowed personal ownership of weapons as a precursor that allowed the ruling elite to suppress dissidents in a violent style without fear of repercussion."

"Well what's your suggestion? Why do you think all this is happening all of a sudden?"

"It's not all of a sudden! My God! Read up on history sometime, okay? Humankind, since the very beginning of its existence, no matter the race, no matter the country, creed, or gender, so strictly speaking in reference to the hominid species—it has forever been brimmed with the occasional, and sometimes not so occasional madman or madwoman who is hell bent on inflicting the maximum amount of damage to the greatest number of innocent victims in a given moment as is possible. Say all you want about mass murder and warning signs gone amiss, but madness on horrific scales shall never cease to exist—tis a sad fact, but historically sound and destined to repeat itself for endless generations to come."

"But how anybody can make a conscious choice to slaughter the innocent in such a way—I mean—how it saddens me!"

"It saddens me, too, man, but in some strange way—I feel pretty numb to it. I'm saddened, of course I'm *sad*dened and everything, but I'm *cer*tainly not shocked by it. How anybody can be quote, '*shocked*'—when somebody is being interviewed by a local reporter and you see them explain how fucking *shocked* they were as the newscaster is broadcasting *live* from the *shocking* scene—well, that stance simply amuses me. If somebody walked through that door right now and started blasting people, well, I'd feel no shock at all. Not a sliver. If I walked into the alley to take a piss and somebody was getting robbed or raped, I'd feel no shock. I'd certainly try to *do* something about it, but I wouldn't feel a sense of shock, that's for damn sure. This is the way the world is, and frankly, that's the way it has always been."

"False."

"What do you mean, false? F*a*lse? Have you ever studied the history of human behavior? Do you know anything of the brutal past of your own species? It mirrors the brutal present! *False?* Wake up."

"Well, if *I* walked out into the alley to take a piss and somebody was being raped—I would *cer*tainly feel sh*o*cked by it."

"Well, you shouldn't be—the ones who feel shock are the ones least likely to react fast enough to do anything about it. In fact, I'd bet almost anything that somewhere in this very city, someone is being raped, robbed, or killed right now. Right at this exact moment— *now—bang—dead.* Several, likely—I'd bet anything, but, well—I never bet on games I pray I lose."

"Your mind is too warped."

"No—it is too honest. These are the facts, pal, the pure, indisputable facts, and these facts are in distinct correlation to the nature of mankind. People are hate-fueled maniacs, at least a fair portion of them are, and if they are hell bent on killing the innocent and in the process they keep a low profile until one day, seemingly out of nowhere, they explode, well, gloriously kind and peaceful people will die. This is how it works—period—like the Boy Scouts say: always be prepared. If what I say makes you sick, then fault the world itself, for what I am explaining—such is the is, mate. I've seen it happen with my own eyes and I changed forever. I woke. I've woken several times, in fact. Once you wake you don't go back to sleep, ever—all that happens is that you become ready for the next time."

The majority of people refuse to look past their nose, let alone think critically about how what we do today will effect tomorrow. On the whole, humans are—pretty dumb. They're alright when it comes to non-complex regurgitation, but they're downright dense when it comes to explaining why a situation is as it is—and I know that statement is a sweeping generalization, but it's true. Every time I try to prove that generalization false, I wind up proving it true. You probably know what I mean.

I walked outside for some air, tried to phone Joey so I could boot this guy from his spot but to no avail, came in, sat on the stool and a real estate commercial on the only television in the joint flashed the image of a proper manor with a slashed red percentage superimposed over the well manicured lawn. The man sitting beside me said: "The social order will come to faultlessness when even the most useless and pitiful members of society reside in an abode as such."

"Why would they deserve it?"

"What would that matter? I mean—what's the difference?"

"Precisely my point—the difference is monstrous—because they who loafed would have to depend on others to foot the bill—and so what would be the prerequisite of all that labor?"

"The needs of the other people, of course."

"Exactly!—understand: your needs are not my motives, man. Nor should they be. Yours, nor the government's, nor my neighbors' needs supercede my own. So long as I'm not wronging people, my motives are mine, and they are to be left alone, period. I mean—my contribution to society has been nil, thus, would I dare expect my share of society's reward to be anything less than nothing at all? Nope. And so if attempting to cure the societal order via bestowing such an abode upon all dwellers, it is only via the previous motivation that the backbone of wealth can be created—and such is a backbone of well-organized, authoritarian theft that I, and most others will forever refuse to comply to, so fuck off with that plan."

"That's a strong statement." I didn't reply and: "I earned my doctorate degree studying basic tenants of social fairness."

"Very good."

"And now I teach."

"I do not doubt you."

"Do you think I'm joking or something?"

"Nope—fuckin' facts all the way here, straight shooter—I do not doubt you."

"The way things are today, someone is going to have to give up a piece of their pie so that someone else can have more."

"What if that someone grew all the ingredients by their lonesome and cooked it in their own stove? I don't own much, but I take pride in what I do own because I earned it—how could I take pride in eating other people's pie? Why would it be my right?"

"Because life isn't fair—the rich are ruining everything."

"When's the last time a poor person gave you a job? Never. And further, it's a bad habit to pile people into the category of economically *rich* as though they are to be derided for perhaps living frugally and earning a strong wage via unsurpassed effort and talent. I mean sure, I find some wealthy people bothersome, but not necessarily more than any other class of people, and the dislike is not as a result of how many zeroes round out their salary—it would mostly be if they cheated their way to the top or treated their workers unfairly—and then you'd have the chance to not support that product."

"Maybe they inherited the money—maybe someone gave them a business."

"Well, yeah, things are obviously easier if somebody fronts you capital or hands over a profitable corporation with a good reputation—but that's why it's about what happens afterward—maybe they invested wisely, or improved the business model on their own intellectual merit—and maybe you would have invested in crackpot ideas or pissed off clients via ineptitude, thereby driving the business into the ground—who's to say? Just as you shouldn't glorify everybody who grew up poor and made it, you should avoid unnecessarily faulting all who grew up rich."

"Do you know there's a revolution under way?"

"Is that right?"

"O yeah. Things are changing."

"What do you mean by that exactly? What do you even mean?"

"I mean things are changing."

"Changing to wh*a*t, *why*, and for what objective?" He sat there blank and: "You don't even know what you're talking about for fuck's sake! Are you a republican? A democrat? An independent? A constitutionalist? What are you even t*a*lking about? What is the philosophical root of this statement? It's real easy to sit here and say you're a revolutionary—if so, you're leading a revolution to *what?* From *what?* How would you describe what is right now? And where is this revolution taking us?—how will it be financed, and where will this money be spent? And what basic tenants of individual rights will change under your plan? Get to work on all this shit, man, seriously—my whole family is fucking tired out and we want to live in our new house, up on the screen like you suggested. Start busting your ass so I can get in there and chill the fuck out, pronto—but get me another drink before you get cracking with the plan, alright Jack? I'm fucking thirsty pal, real thirsty—hungry too, in fact, what name is your tab under? Mind if I get my friend a whisky as well? He'll be here shortly and he's a real thirsty fella." The bumptious cunt looked at me with a smug smirk as his hypothetical axiom fused with reality, and I felt such frustration within—you give someone a real word, hands on example of their very own 'fairness' theory, they grasp the infeasibility, and then you're the dick. Mainly, I don't understand how people expect that they deserve things without working for them. And further, after obtaining these things they didn't deserve—after coming to possess they feel some sense of respect derived chiefly from that which was unearned to begin with. This disgusts me, in fact—I wanted him to feel what it's like to pay for that attitude.

"I know what you're doing."

"I should fucking hope so! Christ man!"

"Do you really want the drinks?"

"If you want to buy them, yes, I do—experience what it's like to become a fresh victim of proletarian drift."

He ordered, paid and: "Alright, here you go," he said, sliding two whiskies over—"And now you can't say that I didn't live according to my own ideology."

"Yes, I can—you lived according to mine—you chose to buy those drinks—it was a choice. Had I forced you to purchase them, against your will, with a distinct consequence for you to face had you not, then you would be living according to your ideology."

"That's only semantics."

"Semantics are everything pal—semantics designate what is." Human history is a story blind tragedy—a story authoritarian control, suppression and subjugation—often under the pretext of the benefit of mankind—and such is what his ideals would eventually perpetuate. I felt he likely held his doctrine in good faith, but the fact that he so plainly misunderstood or did not analyze the underlying crux of what such a philosophy would entail so far as its enforcement was concerned was agonizing to me. Please seek to understand the historical ark of repression few seem to grasp and the reasons why it came to exist—if you don't, it'll happen again, every day, a little splice at a time until nobody will comprehend what has happened, and life will be miserable.

I ran my hand over my tired eyes and: "I know this is not a big deal to you—that the entire instance is a very tiny incongruence, but really, really I believe that the great global imbalance of now is a compulsory result of a great colossal sum of such incidents going unchecked. Do yourself a favor and correct your hypothesis now, accurately, and continue to do so in forthcoming situations—else prepare for that one last final glance at your face in the mirror wherein the image staring back at you will be that of a complete and utter fraud."

"That's how you feel? About seven silly dollars?"

"Just as long as you know it'll eventually add up to a trillion dollars worth of bullshit, man, I can care less," I said.

The guy closed his tab and split and I noticed a few uppity guys in their early thirties gaze like I was weird for having made any statements at all. Guess what: I don't give a fuck—you people are so doped up on manufactured remedies for the human condition that I refuse to recognize you as such. You feel sad? Depressed? You want some medicine? Go out and live, homeboys. Go for a walk in the wilderness or hug your goddamn family and share some laughs together. Soon they went back to their Palm Pilots, not interacting together whatsoever for five full minutes, all four of them immersed in a virtual world, browsing Chinese goods, updating their Facebook status and tweeting that they were in the room with a real madman, some bullshit like that, and I removed the old sketchbook from my bag and drew what I considered to be a miserable draft of the scene. I compared the two and figured I must have recently contracted diabetes, blurry as it was. Fuck it!

I walked outside for a moment, clutching to the sketchbook, and sat on the icy curb. I phoned Joey again to no avail, and the entry went: 'Ah yes, back to the root—writing by street light at seven past seven and—' I cleared my mind until my hand was too cold to continue, and dipped back inside. Short seconds after sitting it came: "Yo motherfucker, gimme your shit, quiet and quick." I turned, stood, went in for the handshake and Joey pulled me tight with a big hug—if you're his guy he lives and dies for you, period. I suppose it can be said that one can discern a large bit of information about people by taking the time to take a good look at who their friends are and what they are like—such as how honorable they are and so on—and if that's the case, JC makes me look better than I am in a lot of respects. Either way we had some catching up to do, and I found myself feeling quite fine and ready to go.

"How the fuck are you, crazy bastard! Thank God you're here," I said.

"Great man, I'm fuckin' great."

"You're one of the only people who make me feel small, you know that? You're a regular giant of a man these days—the Bulls could use your help in the post—fuckin' Knicks killed 'em last night."

"What can I say? My ma, God bless her—she never let us eat fast food as kids n' I kept on growin'—say, why you sittin' here like this?"

"Whudaya mean?" I said.

"Are you tryina get snuck up on? Only a fool sits with his back to the door."

"What are the odds of there being a problem?"

"It only takes once man, that's it, so why risk it?"

"Fine, move to that table in the middle, it's cold over here anyway."

I shivered from the draft as a train of five smiling strangers all held the door for one another as they entered the bar—I took a big pull from my drink as street-lit snowflakes dove through the doorsill. Joey looked at me with a contented expression and said: "Ah man—it's good to be home, lemme tell ya."

"Goddamn right—so, I mean, being over there—everywhere you been—is the grass greener?"

"Comin' home feels pretty fuckin' lush—as wide as the world is, and as much of it I hope I continue to see, there's still nothin' like comin' home to the cold Chi and seein' your mates after a long time gone."

"We all missed you, man—it's never quite the same."

"There's no place like this man—I've been all around the world and there just isn't. I know its cliché, but ya need some time away from the good things, especially even, because when you're away—that's when you realize how good they are—whudja get me t' drink anyway? Whisky?"

I slid the brown-brimmed glass that professor bought into his hand and: "Remain true to your addictions."

"I've never quit anything I ever started, man."

"I'm glad you never tried coke or heroin."

"Me too, man, me too."

"Why didn't you?"

"I've always kind of suspected I'd die the very first time I tried it."

"Well stick with your gut. You have plenty other habits you can die from."

"Like being crazy."

"Exactly."

"Cheers Riedie," he said, "It's great to be alive," and our glasses clicked together with a warm receptive resonance—a familiar inauguration to many disastrous evenings, we were off and running. His mouth twisted into a craggy grin after he threw back a jigger of hot whisky, and: "Ever feel you're destined to die a death of a hundred thousand self-inflicted wounds?"

"Every single day."

"I mean, how many loud laughs have we had over drinks? Ten, twenty thousand?—thank God, right?"

"Most people spend their money on things—we spend upon experience."

"It's all ya got in the end, so why not?"

"And even still, who knows if you even get to take that along?"

"Which is all the more reason t' keep doin' 'til ya die," he said, "What happened to your hand?"

The scab on the knuckles I had dragged along the building after losing my bag had cracked and blood dripped: "I tripped over a potted plant."

"If you beat someone to death, keep it to yourself, okay? Don't spill the beans to me, man, because I don't want to know. If you did, or ever do kill someone, just man up and keep quiet about it—take it straight to the grave, okay?" He blew a gust into his red, freezing hands, took a napkin to his soiled feet and: "You gotta be a goddamn triple jump master to not ruin your shoes on nights like this."

"Yep—not a good day to work for Streets and Sanitation."

"Man, when *is* a good day to work for Streets and Sanitation?"

"Fuck if I know—did you fly straight through to O'Hare?"

"Yeah—nice flight, no problems—I sat next to the Air Marshall."

"How'd ya know? They're not supposed t' say nothin'—you see an outline of his piece on his body?"

"No, he was wearing the shiniest shoes on board."

"You think that's the tell?"

"Absolutely—military habits die hard."

"I thought you were supposed to go to that bachelor party in London before you came home."

"I did—last week." I gave him a look like: well? "Everyone says they won't cheat on their wife, but when you've got some twenty year old Venezuelan girl who looks like nothing you've ever seen before whispering that accent off full lips into your ear that if you come in back and spend twenty dollars, you'll get anything you like—I mean, minds change man, minds change real fucking quick. And I almost got robbed that night."

"In London?"

"Yeah—I was on my phone, smoking a cigarette in this cut and this guy comes up to me, right—he didn't display any weapon at all, right, and so he just came out with it like, 'Okay bloke, hand it over,'—like I was supposed to be scared of him because I was an American overseas or something."

"Whudja do?"

"First I started laughing, but then I got pissed. I was like, hey guy—is this some gag? You think you're a tough guy? I live on Western Avenue, okay, in Chicago—a city where streets are prowled by hard-up humans that act as armies of angry stray dogs, eager to devour all you have—a land awash in weapons and disjointed anger to the point where you may be knifed in the small of the back for the slightest of crookeyes—a place of cold winter nights and hot summer days that see hordes of hot, frustrated fools hangin' on the corner as sweat goes drippin' off prison-big muscles before evaporating on cracked asphalt as sirens wail through the hazy sky—you're going to have to come at me a little harder than that, son. Come see me when you figure out how to rob somebody proper—I'll be ready for you."

"You said all that?"

"I thought most of it and told him to get the fuck out my face before I straight k*ill*ed his ass. I was about to cut him real bad, you know how it is—the only problem with owning a real nice knife is you want to see red on it sometimes." I laughed and: "I pulled it out of my breast pocket and was like; 'You wanna *do* this mother*fuck*er?' and he fuckin' ran like he was at an Olympic trial of some sort. It wouldn't a' mattered if he did rob me because in the end we hit a casino and I lost most my wad on an unemotional blackjack dealer at $50 per hand."

"Who's the manufacture of that spring loaded blade of yours again?"

"Persuasion Arms Company."

"I thought they closed."

"Nah—arms companies don't close, man. There are too many people seeking vengeance and too many thrill killers out there for arms companies to close. Only time they'll ever close is if a competitor devises a more efficient and less expensive means to kill other human beings, which they haven't." He took a drink and: "By the way, a girl I would love to undress just walked in here—simple, natural beauty leaves me contented—fucking always Riedie."

"Hell yeah."

289

"That ass would be highly delicious," he said, licking his lips.

"Go say hello."

"Nothing corrupts me like sex, man."

"You and the rest of the world."

I looked over my shoulder as she sat at a stool at the north end of the bar and removed a heap of reading material from her bag before getting into a bottle of beer. "Should I go say hello?"

"If you're going to interrupt a uniquely sexy girl poring over a pile of books, you better have something good to say."

"I'll wait a minute."

A waitress with an unsociable mouth and vatic round eyes approached and: "You guys need anything? The orders have to go through me now that ya moved from the bar."

"Yeah," JC said, "Can you shut the TV?"

She shook no and I said: "Are the millions of desperate advertisements fighting for that same steadily shrinking disposable income giving you a headache?"

"Yes."

"Seriously now, I'm in a hurry—what do you guys want?"

"I'll have a Guinness and whatever my man wants. He just came in from Romania."

"Where's that? Asia?" she asked.

JC's pupils restricted and: "It's good to look at countries on a map to know where they are, and what the hell they're shaped like—geographical ignorance is a major turn off."

"I wasn't trying to turn you on in the first place."

"I'm just sayin', is all—maybe spend some tip money on a globe tomorrow." She gave him a real sour look and: "I'll have a Johnny Walker Black Label, neat."

She walked off and: "How much do you think it would cost to get her teeth fixed? I don't mean it like an asshole or anything," I said, "That's just the true question scuttling through my head."

"Are they bad?"

"Look see," I said, as she addressed the table behind us with yawing vocalism.

"O, yeah—it's gonna' cost more than she'll make working here, I know that much. Dental work of any sort is a fortune, practically."

"I know—I've had this black hole in the back of my mouth for three years now."

She approached our table—I thought she'd heard when it came: "What'd you want again?"

"Johnny Walker Black, my lady."

"Before you waste your time hitting on me, I have a boyfriend, okay?"

"Relax toots, your self-flattery is a bit amplified—I'm just shootin' the bull is all, relax," Joey said, "Curiously though, what'd your boyfriend do to swoon you?"

"He wrote me love poems based on astrophysics metaphors. We both obtained our degrees in mathematics—chaos math."

"Well do me a favor n' suggest to the bartender that he add more Scotch and subtract all the ice from that next drink, wilya? The last one was drowned out like a bag of cats."

"I don't do requests."

"Well how about demands?"

"Zing!" She split and: "She's nice and bubbly. Good grief," I said, "She must be new—I would never hire a girl like to serve drinks in my pub. We should have stayed where we were. That bartender Chuck was in a better mood."

"What's with all these stiff, right-brained girls 'round here?—Christ! Accountants n' statisticians—don't girls draw or play the goddamn guitar, sing or bullshit with people in a laid back sexy style anymore?" He raised his glass, finished a good sum, set it down and: "Whatcha know offhand about astrophysics, anyway?"

"The knab gib is the opposite of the big bang."

"I think they do a dance in Romania called the knab gib where everybody crouches real low to the ground."

"Makes sense." I took a big drink, "How was Latvia, anyway? You were there before Romania, weren't you?"

"The people I met were about as friendly as a pack of wild dogs, actually. When I wasn't working my ass off I was pretty much constantly blasted and roaming."

"How were the girls? Fairly sophisticated?"

"They had very dejected attitudes, for the most part—hardly any positive girls out there at all—but very clever."

"Did it get you thinking of all the cool, lighted-hearted American girls you've known in your lifetime?"

"Sort of—it certainly got me thinking that many American girls never had to work very hard in their lives, and when they do, when they graduate some bullshit college program and get some bullshit office job, and right away they're complaining that the workload is bullshit—these Latvian girls would walk in there and spit on them for how soft they are, and they'd deserve it."

"I've seen hard-edged cleaning ladies drone through the cubicles looking at such girls with that sort of expression."

"No kidding, right? I mean—they have a point. I did meet this one girl out there who was real serious about getting off man. Real serious."

"I'm glad."

"Nothing like great sexual encounters to help pass the day—I spent time with her for a bit and things were pretty good. Real smart girl, but real ruthless, too—if you ever married her you'd never quite trust what she'd say about you when alone with the kids. She'd be trying to subvert you the whole time in one way or another. Through her I realized when you're late for work because of raw sex—you don't really care that much for repercussions."

"I said I didn't want that, ma! I don't care! I don't care! *No!* I don't want that!"

The two kids of the young family seated at a table behind us were raising hell. The mother was on her phone, paying no attention to the situation at hand: "O you have to *see* my new baby!" she said, like she bought it in a boutique.

"See that?" Joey asked, "You ban smoking in the bar and next thing you know the place is a goddamn nursery. I guarantee if I were wolfing cigs you wouldn't have the smell of dirty diapers or the sound of spoiled babies muddling the room like this. You have to think about cause and effect—each and every possibility before making a decision to ban smoking—I mean sure, people may have healthier lungs in the long run, but what good is that gonna' do when ya got five, ten screeching kids in the pub and a migraine to boot? Blood pressure rises either way you look at it—I want that shit rising on my terms, man—my fuckin' terms."

291

We sat quiet for a minute, drinking and listening to old music, and the aggravated father ushered his family out of the establishment and apologized for the chaos. He looked annoyed with his wife, I finished my drink, licked the whisky off my lips and said: "Maybe we should step up to the plate—open a novelty pub that doesn't allow anyone under 21 no matter what time of day—no televisions or personal electric devices at all—only music—and the only food we would serve would be bread, oil and cheese."

"I guarantee no one would come."

"I know—that's the best part. It's just—I've never understood how people are so easily entertained by television when directly out their front door resides the wildest show on earth."

"Not everybody lives on Western Avenue, man."

"I guess not."

"And if you want to open a novelty bar, we should open a joint that serves lavishly expensive white Russians mixed with real breast milk—you'd have rich weirdos streaming in from miles around—it'd be a totally organic business."

"You're a maniac," I said.

"No, I'm simply looking to fulfill a prearranged market loaded with them—there is a difference, however narrow."

"If we owned a bar, would we die, or go bankrupt first?"

"Die, definitely."

"Yeah—"

"Wanna ro-sham-bo for this next round?"

"One of one."

I lost and: "I hope you're prepared for a long evening," I said.

"Of course—being prepared keeps me alive and out of jail—but I can't get down as hard as we did the last night I was in town."

"But you had a good time, right?"

"I'll be havin' a good time in a coffin pretty soon if we keep havin' those kinda good times. I'll be in a coffin real quick." The last time he'd been in town his right leg was in a cast from the knee down. We went to a pub we don't normally visit, and from the moment we entered, the bouncers were oozing with hostility—they were huge, drunk, hitting on all the attached girls and yelling at patrons for tiny infractions—the type who forgot that rational diplomacy is the number one method of maintaining control, and the only reason they hadn't been thrown out of the establishment, was because they were on the clock—yet another example of the morality police being the biggest cheaters in society. We had a whole crew there, and after a few drinks, as JC walked out of the bar for a cigarette, his drink accidentally splashed a bouncer when he set it down. Dude followed him outside, to talk to him I assumed, but then I looked out the window and saw he'd jumped Joey and cold cocked him from behind, and was dragging over an iron bike rack to smash on his head as JC fought with another employee on the ground. I pocketed a heavy whisky glass, zipped out all quiet, and after the crash a big body landed blunt end down, temporarily inactive—we finished the other guy, left that spot and celebrated heavily, never to return again. Fact is, if a friend of mine is accosted, it is my business—always has been and it forever will be, you know, all for one and one for all—it's an old saying that always works, and all our mates comply. All told, it was a very ugly night, in a beautiful way.

A short Mexican dude walked in from the freezing night and pulled me from the memory: "Tamales tamales! Tamales tamales!"

"How much for the whole damn thing?! How much for it all?!" Joey screamed this crazy as hell, far more manic than was necessary.

"Wait a second, hold on!" a man yelled from a booth on the side, "Other people need a chance to order here too, ya know."

A few more parties took out their wallets and JC winked at me: "See, without him even realizing, I just helped that guy's sales right there, maybe even tripled them—I was never gonna' buy the whole thing, it was never my intent—you know how my stomach is with Mexican food—but buy screaming this, all the people around here feel this man is holding a finite product, something warm and delicious they may not have the opportunity to obtain—and so all of a sudden, they want some, too—that's all advertising is, in a way, from a man selling tamales from a satchel to the highest national echelon: it's all about getting people hyped about shit they don't even want."

"I told you it's never the same without you—class move man," I said

"Ja mon."

I had a laugh, the man fulfilled a dozen orders, came over with the tamales and: "So ju really want all of them mang?" Joey explained the ploy, and the man understood and appreciated. "I chud have my friends go in some places and try dat treek."

"Make sure they're wearing a three piece suit—it's instant credibility."

The guy had a laugh and added two chicken tamales to my order of three on the house. I noticed a man had returned and: "How 'bout the Mongolian cat in the back lookin' like he killed about twenty-seven grandmothers—he buy any?"

"No, I tink he mean mang—he make bery crazy face when I ask if he hungry, like maybe he chud eat me—I no want bother heem."

"Unhinged?"

"Ese is non compos mentis, amigo—loco—biolent like a Corinthian."

Two real preppy girls came in and Joey raised his eyes to the guy for him to hollar at them—"C'mon man, say it: Tamales tamales—"

He did so very nicely but quickly, embarrassed almost and in a polite, high pitched tone, and they looked at him like: do you, honestly think, that *I*—that *we*—would ever, in your wildest dreams, buy a tamale off the street from a guy like *you?* It was a hoot man. They walked away like the whole initial presentation of their persona to the room of powerful single men had been hampered by the occurrence—they were tampered goods now, tamale chicks: "Ah man you're making my lips bleed, they're so chapped I'm not supposed to smile this large," I said, "That was great—they were pretty nice ay?"

"O yes, bery nice, bery beauteeful—now I will be walking home on tree feets!"

I nearly spat my drink out. JC gave him a $20 and said: "She probably looks nice in negligee—it's sexier to hint at what might be rather than lettin' it all hang out like some crass flabby flasher on a spring break video."

"Not many modern girls understand how to mix classy and sexy—it either comes off as too forced or too easy, not that mellow, flowing, no big thing in-between that lures you in for an anticipated hello," I said.

"Ya have to be a little old fashioned to pull that off, which is great—it's like, let me be a little chivalrous, you know? You don't need to arm wrestle me because I hold open the door or insist you walk out of the elevator first."

The tamale man finished making change, Joey gave him a nice tip and off he went into the dark cold night with a low key jovial vibe. "Damn, I'm pretty hungry."

"It's good to be hungry—this confirms you're not a glutton. If you really want to be serious, you should spend most of your time hungry on purpose—not starving, but just a little bit achy—it'll make you realize how soft most of this country has gone, and you'll understand why we're no match for China's discipline."

"Don't talk about it, Riedie, it's too depressing—gimme one a' them tamales."

JC took a satisfied bite and then, just prior to delivery, some pumpkin-butt, penguin-bellied broad with a pretty face and a shaved head sneezed sideways, all over the waitress and our tray of drinks. She was almost about to force them on us, but the glasses held dozens of spit bubbles, and she split for fresh ones. "So how's the international gig man? Still dig it?"

"I don't know—maybe I'm just maladjusted in some strange form that prevents me from working with people—but how could I not be?" he said, wiping his mouth, "Yet again I'm working for a foundation where you'll practically get sacked for not laughing at certain jokes and shit like that. I've been involved in too many fake laughs in the past six months to stand myself Riedie, far too many. You ever see yourself living a private life of the mind?"

"Sometimes, man, sometimes—hence why we should start our own school."

"What would the focus be? The curriculum—what would be the major crux of it?"

"Staying loose—I swear you need to start a whole fucking school just to teach people how to stay loose these days. Half of society consists of stiff stuffy negative nags afraid of their own shadow—people who haven't cooled the fuck out since birth."

"I guess I'm just becoming more of a loner as time goes on," he said.

"I don't mind loners—I would rather hang out in a neighborhood with a lot of weirdo loners than one infested with hipsters who attend Columbia College."

"You know how it works with those fools man—they're so conformed in their non-conformity that they've begun to conform."

"That's why I like how during certain times of the day my neighborhood seems to divulge a hidden slew of lone crackpots lurking up alleyways and gangways with a deceptively quick pace—it's real easy to mix in unnoticed. But about the job—I mean, you're doin' well—you don't dig it?"

"It's cool in a way, traveling the globe and hustling in different countries, learning of different cultures and making adjustments on the fly—I've learned heaps, but still—like my boss—he's an email tough guy, you know, just flat out ri*dic*ulous man—I look at him in real life situations where he calls his parents and complains and I'm just like: are you kidding me? Are you f*uck*ing *kidding?* This is who I'm working for? It's impossible! It's really quite impossible for me to respect any person who has nearly no ability to fend for themselves and who is incessantly dependent upon their parents to take care of every aspect of their continued survival—and that's what these guys are like, proper degrees or not—big fuckin' babies collecting monthly stipends—I can't keep trying to earn profits for this guy and others like him. I'm out there, making beautiful moves on the fly only to be paid an imbalanced margin for what I've produced from scratch and—it's just—I can't do it anymore Riedie, I just can't."

"It'll work out."

"Fuck having it work out—in waiting for things to work out, I feel that something horrible has been happening to me: the world is turning me into a realist, a realist who accepts the world's standards as realistic, horrible because the average realistic standard of living life to its fullest is deplorable, in my opinion. It's this job that's doing it to me, meeting people all day long and actually selling them, trying to get them to buy something, a product I despise— that's my fucking job, what I do—pure insanity. I mean Jesus fucking Christ, man! Is this really what I've grown up to do?"

"For now man, just for a minute—soon enough you'll be promoted and—"

"And? If I take the ten percent rise I'll get triple the responsibility for that which I already held no care for, and get taxed more, so what good is it? By those standards, I'd prefer to remain a common drudge." He took a big drink and: "People come home barely alive after a fifty hour work week at a job they loathe but are told to be grateful to own, and flip through terrible shows beaming from an enormous television they could not really afford in the first place, pleading: take me away from my reality."

"Fucking new American dream right there, boy."

"I mean—how is this—*this*—I mean—this is the realistic choice? I mean—wow. Fucking *wow* man."

"How are your co-workers?"

"Well, the fuckin' wind up is most of them spent their childhood inheriting money, man—they went to proper English boarding schools before continuing at Oxford n' shit, The London School of Economics, Ivy League the whole way through—I'm dealing with people living in the echelons above reality. We don't relate, okay? They've been so sheltered from getting dirt under their fingernails it's miraculous. When it's time to grind, all they do is complain—and then there's me, the son of an electrician from Chicago with two raw-ass older brothers, smashing all of them. They're so soft it's sick—the rich and powerful are much more self-pitying than the poor—and for me, teaming with these people becomes unrelenting in its distractive nature—it's like, just be quiet, leave me alone, and let me work—I will produce, and you won't."

"I love it."

"The only time I worked as a partner with one of 'em the guy went in and blew a whole deal I'd spend four months arranging with this Sultan out of the UAE in a single meeting. That's what happens when you start leaning on shit you can't lean on—because technically, there is nothing to lean on aside from self. Fucking nothing, fucking nobody—so you got t' be strong is all."

"What went wrong?"

"He basically didn't jive with the guy—he annoyed the Sultan so bad with his elitist attitude he wrecked the whole project in an hour. There's only one guy I respect in the whole joint, a black guy from the Netherlands. He's a cool guy, don't get me wrong—but a perfect mold of what I won't want my life to be twenty years down the line. At this stage, every decision and comment has become another crossroad in a career of yellow lights—he has to bite his tongue so much he's gonna' wind up going mute."

"Right."

"But he has to—he's got a family, I met 'em."

"What's his wife like?"

"She's a promiscuous witch for the most part—and so now it's too late for him to go all in on an unknown in some respects. This place pays him a decent wage so he has t' go with it—as far as the rest of 'em—God they're arrogant. It straight killed them when the next time I came back from the Arabian Peninsula after two weeks with triple the deals they garnered in two months out there—but it's because they don't know how t' be grimy, man, they don't know how t' slog through bullshit n' talk to real people. They're all by the book, no hustle, no street vibe—and when I beat them they look at me like: well, I still have more than you, anyway, so beat that. And in my mind," he said, leaning in: "In my mind it's like: you might have more money than me for my entire life, but in the end, at least I was self made, man—you know? In the end I'll be able to look in the mirror and, however it works out, at least I'll be able to say that my reality rests squarely upon my own fucking shoulders— that nothing came free—that I wasn't some trust fund baby, country club raised and adroit in the art of passive aggressive grumbling—I mean, fuck *that!* Fuck those soft bastards!" He rocked back, smiled and: "I swear it's the same lesson I learned at sixteen, bloodied n' tired, filthy after cuttin' raw chickens at Hickory Roasters and tellin' jokes with a bunch of Mexicans at five in the morning for minimum wage before the crowd came through: the poor fucks serve the rich fucks, and the rich fucks are most often the ones in shoddy moods."

"Just keep fucking grinding, mate, forever and forever more until the result of years of frugal living and steady constant work leads to a laid back reality with near infinite options for travel, exploration and good times."

"I know—I long to have my time belong solely to me n' the fulfillment of my deepest desires—and hence why I've been grinding this grind every day, man—I'm getting it in so I can go big, man, that's all there is to it—but: I've had days recently where I come into the office and I'm completely unable to speak with people. I simply can not do it."

"And?"

"And that's why I'm going out on my own this year man—sink or swim, Riedie, I'm doin' it. I'm tired of makin' everyone else wealthy. It's time to use my mind, creativity and steady persistence for me."

"You don't know how glad I am to hear that—you know what you want and you're going for it—many do but don't—lying to yourself on this subject will fucking *kill* you in the worst way m' man," I said, "You'll rot from the inside out. How long you had the idea?"

"A minute—it's pretty good, I think—I'll get into it a different time after I iron out all the kinks but, I mean—I was lucky enough to be born in America, right? I figure may as well take advantage of it—may as well give my best shot at being an entrepreneur. The beauty of frustration and dissatisfaction of self is what will get me there—being dissatisfied with oneself is a tremendous asset, at least for me it is—it keeps me pushing to get better via trying harder every single day—and that's why I'm glad my life has been a struggle in a lot of ways—it took me a long time to learn things just don't happen: *someday*—they need to happen *every* day to build into that someday."

"That's the perfect way to put it, JC—I suppose that most people in the world, especially the corporate world, are realistic in the traditional, safe sense, of settling for a soft, comfortable lifestyle, rather than slaving in anonymity and devoid of commercial success for sake of eclipsing outside judgment at the detriment of their true inner passions as you have. It's why so many people have meltdowns, man."

"How can't you meltdown if you've spent a huge sum of life living for other people's opinions?—other people's dreams?"

"The majority, quite literally, of all people, and the time they've lived upon this earth, has been spent in this exact fashion. It's quite nearly unfathomable—they live their lives doing things they're not really much concerned with or interested in, you know, they just get along with it and do so because they wandered into it, and then they wait for the weekend, and push repeat. I mean—what good is it if one fulfills their seventy five year life expectancy if all it lead to was 27,000 nights of quiet desperation?—soon you'll be out there doing your thing, JC, so have a good time and don't worry about it—a good percentage of the people who'll die inside will be those who were never true to what they really wanted—they just—can't—quite—break—that fucking chain—and they finally—ugh!—they get cracked by the ball from the inside out—hence why I will never give up a large swathe of time for something I don't love, period."

"That's what I'm sayin'," he said, "You're a good example, man—these people, including me, need to invoke some recklessness, man—the sort of recklessness they'll miss later—when they're settled in n' wonderin' what could have been done in life. You know? What could have really been done? Imagine being stuck wondering!—and then it just ends, you know? And they don't act because of external pressures—so fuck what people say, good and bad—because in the end, it's only you. If you're not satisfied, what's the point? And granted, it's necessary to be realistic to some degree, but it's more necessary to be out of control, truthfully, I swear. I need to make firm plans that will enable my life to become fulfilled, or ruined, you know, like the flip of a coin, every penny you own on either red or black, based upon my own effort, for me, disassociated from external control—all in on myself Riedie—that's living, it really is—and that's why I'm puttin' all my chips in the middle next year."

The sound of crashing glass and serrated laughter reverberated through the room—a tamale chick bumped into the waitress and she dropped our second set of drinks. "Unreal."

"Were those our drinks again?" I nodded and: "When a nigga get antsy, people get shot. I'm thirsty as a ma'fucka'—she better recognize," he said, white as hell, and I busted out laughing. "Who's the viceroy of this joint? Can we get a friendly waitress who ain't jinxed?"

A real bothersome girl who always seems to be drinking at this place stepped up to JC with: "Hey you! It's been a long time!"

"We've only met once. Technically, this is the shortest we've gone without seeing each other. It was twenty-four years last time."

"So you're still a smart ass?"

"Yes I am."

"What are you guys talkin' about, anyway? You two always look like you're up to no good—you're not very approachable."

I nodded and: "I'll be back." I slid toward the bathroom, stepped over the spill, took a piss and the thought in my mind was that dying will be crazy. I looked into my eyes as they reflected off the flush control and stomached that the full realization of one's own morality is a haunting, personal thing—got to treat it with respect and do your best man, that's all there is to it. Breathe man, relax, enjoy yourself and fucking come to terms that you have been created and do exist. Relish in it and go with the flow as you make your own waves downstream—I warmed my hands, wiped them on pants and spied what that sexy girl was reading upon my return to the table. I met JC with: "Ready t' puff a bit?"

"That'd be positively mint."

"Can I come with?"

"Nah."

46

I grabbed my gloves off the table, JC snagged his coat from the hanger, walked past the jukebox—a rare one with real records, mind you—and after asking the barkeep to watch my bike, we dipped outside. I couldn't find my lighter and the only other guy around was that European valet driver. "Yo Jackson," Joey said, "You got a spark?"

"Vat are you vanting?"

"A lighter—c'mon, I know all you Eastern Europeans smoke, help us out partner." He handed over a black Bic, "Can I bring it back in a minute? We're good for it," he said, handing him a couple bucks. Dude nodded like: if you know anything about ethnic cleansing in Serbia, then you understand that you fucking *bet*ter bring it back, son—and we walked on down the street. JC roasted, passed, I took a long, slow drag and gazed up upon white, triangular clouds racing south past the soaring full moon like forbidding Chinese stars thrown by a giant hand at the vital arteries of some distant monster, and exhaled. "This tastes great."

"Yes sir—I handled my business in case you didn't get anything for me—did you?"

"No."

The moon disappeared and snow continued to slip from the spotted sky in a silent, gentle rhythm. A beat-looking drunk cat in an old Pirates cap walked past pushing a shopping cart topped by a slushy haul of scrap metal and a ragged case of MGD. "Ya'll got anything extra fo me?"

"Not tonight man, sorry." He took a drink from a bent can and pushed on. We continued to move and a sign mentioned that a neighborhood watch was in effect, but I saw no prying eyes minus huntsmen and prey. A filthy car honked twice before exiting an alley, and accelerating up the block. We dipped in the same alley, settled in a dark spot past a dumpster and continued smoking. "Why'd you bring your whole backpack out here Riedie?"

"Don't wanna lose it."

"That'd be a gut shot, ay?"

"You better believe it." I took another drag, exhaled and: "I'd been crankin' hard on the piece of late and—just reading it all, going over all the wild times over the years—it makes me wanna never have t' die, ya know? It's crazy that we're going to."

"Don't ever take it for granted, Riedie—the good health of yourself and those around you—there're plenty of chances to fuck it up."

"I know—it's insane when you think about the fact that none of us are dead yet. None of the boys, I mean."

"With the way we live? That what you mean?"

"With the way we live—we should all be gone. We all should have been gone years ago, one way or another—people we know get pretty faded."

"Fuck it," he said, taking a drag, exhaling into the streetlight and: "We've all had a real good time together, so don't worry about it—when it ends, it ends. Don't pretend like it's not going to—there is no book to which an infinite number of pages is possible—so keep goin'—don't try n' hunker down at the starting line t' pretend doin' so will prevent you from reachin' the finish—enjoy the course and the people cheering you on, man. I'm not scared of anyone anywhere—if you end me, you end me, man—congratulations, but guess what—you never reached me. Never, man—and the older I get, the more it seems people become afraid of their own shadows—like the big secret nobody knows is that in the end, your own shadow sneaks up and stabs you in the spine."

"I think a lot of times it does, man—people finally realize what kind of shadow they've been casting for so many years, and they break down in shock of themselves, and then it's over." The world was quiet for awhile and I thought: it would be so easy, in a way, to go to sleep outside and never awake—just float into black—forever.

The wind blew delicate, hollow ice crystals sharply up the alleyway, and we chilled quiet for a stanza or two, next to green graffiti on an abandoned building that said: '*Property Value*', and a few doors down, the back gate opened and released two fair skinned females with sexy gaits—they crunched up tire rut in the alley and one said: "Hey, what are you boys getting into?—smells good over here."

"Just takin' a breather with an ole mate after a long time gone," JC said, "Where you on your way to? I didn't expect to encounter anyone easy on the eyes in th*is* spot."

"She's headin' t' heaven and I'm off t' hell—we're off to meet our men."

"Husbands?"

"Boyfriends."

He passed her the smoke and without hesitation her red lips enveloped the tip—she took a modest drag and held eye contact with him as she exhaled through gently descending, street-lit snowflakes. She was a well dressed, no-nonsense woman in her early thirties—a little bit older and right up his alley, literally.

"It's mighty cold out here, boys."

"Ain't so bad," I said.

"His opinion is skewed."

"Why's that," she asked.

"This fool walks through the woods like he's Hans Christian *And*erson! Every time I'm shakin', nose leakin' like a junkie's ass, it's not that bad, supposedly."

"No gloves, no hat—hasn't a woman ever taught you preparation is everything?" she asked, taking another long luscious drag with eyes closed. She held it deep for a good span—her hair was long and dark and it matched her eyes when they opened wide and her body leaned back like: *whoa*. "Well then," she said, passing the baton to her friend, "That's the real deal, kind sir."

"It's the new heavy. How's it leave ya feelin'? Comfortably numb?"

"And then some. How 'boutchu darlings? Are you boys properized?"

"We're tuned out of our minds."

"Live around here?"

"Somewhat."

She looked at Joey, up and down, very deliberate-like and: "My, you're tall. And that topcoat is the real deal. I like the way you dress—you're very dashing."

"I'm an Irish-Italian multi-generational Chicagoan—whudaya expect?"

"That background makes it sound like you're an active member of the civic spirit of the city—Chicago means a lot to me—is my assumption true?"

"O definitely—my entire existence is a lexicon of running corruption." She had a good laugh and they shot the bull for another few minutes before JC said: "So maybe I'll see ya around sometime 'er somethin'—I'll show ya a nice time on the town if I do."

"Could be—what's your name, anyway?"

"Joey—Joey Calandra." She gave him her number without being prodded and they split. "Wow—she was interesting," he said, watching them walk away. She gave him a nice look back and waved goodbye with a black leather glove before turning the corner and dipping out of sight.

"Definitely."

"I was just a little late for jumping the gun on that introduction."

"So you were right on time then?"

"I guess that makes sense," he said.

"Yeah I thought ya did well."

"Why didn'tchu talk to her friend more?"

"I don't know—didn't think of it really—she didn't strike me, I guess."

"She said she was a sex therapist man!"

"That doesn't mean she knows how to fuck—either way, she hogged the entire magnitude of your fine roast."

"I have a few more twisted," he said, opening his pack of squares, "Let's spark another n' take a walkabout—I hardly tasted my own creation."

"You were too busy lustin' over the menu, mate."

"Blame me?" I shook no as he placed her number in his inside coat pocket and we carried on in the opposite direction. We came out the alley and turned up the street. Nobody was around and we had to leap over the onset of each curb to avoid dunking our feet in salty sludge-water and the snow fell harder, enveloping the world in white and eliciting a sensation of quiet tranquility. "Muhug*harr*r—muhug*harr*r—*mu*hug*harr*r!"

"Jesus Christ man, you alright?" JC leaned against an ole crib, with his right hand positioned as though it was about to slip the tip of a sawtoothed blade into the soft stomach of an arch rival—and through quivering lips a vile pile of yellow bile slicked the bricks.

"I told you my stomach can't handle Mexican."

"It sounds like you're pushin' a fuckin' baby out of your mouth!"

"Shut up man," he said, laughing and belching and spitting all at once. "Just shut up alright? Ya just had t' force those tamales on me, didn'tchu?"

"Force? You were practically drooling looking at me eat 'em. You alright?"

"I'm fine man, I'm fine—don't worry about it."

"You just sent twenty bucks worth of whisky to an icy death."

"Relax already Riedie—I'll get the next round." He passed the handcraft, still leaning over, cleaned his mouth with a handful of snow, composed himself, blew a gust of heat into his mitts and we walked on. He was shaking so I let him borrow my gloves and: "Goddamn acid reflux—let's just circle a couple more blocks so I'm sure I'm cleared out before we go back inside. I don't wanna make a scene in there." Looking at his tall torso walk all slow, pained and hunched over, hand pressing his sternum, it was hard not to laugh. I held it together and he straightened up after a few hundred paces and moved on as if nothing had happened, good as new.

I took a puff and: "What was your best puke?"

"Too many classics t' pick one—yours?"

"It's still from third grade—Mrs. Malzachezowski's class."

"Wow, she hated me—she was a serious woman."

"Well yeah," I said, passing the baton, "She was a survivor of a death camp—hadn't told a lie since 1945 when she pretended to be dead in a pile of bodies—she probably still asked forgiveness for that white lie, crazy as she was."

"Remember how she made us sing America the Beautiful every morning and shit like that?"

"Of course! She constantly inundated us with horror stories of what living under an authoritarian, fascist government was like and encouraged us to not take freedom for granted—very ethical woman, but wicked mean when she wanted to be."

"Typical Jesuit, Riedie: very honest, very smart, and very mean—and so?"

"She yelled at me so hard for not doing my homework three days in a row that I puked a hot liver sausage sandwich all over the whole coat rack like a sprinkler, all the way left to right, after recess, and at the end of the day, when people went tweaking, I was like 'Huh, that's pretty lucky, they got every coat but mine.' The smell was awful."

"That was *you?*" I nodded and: "And you kept it quiet for almost two decades?" I nodded again and: "Well when it's time to commit a crime and keep quiet, expect a call."

We strode an easy stroll listening to occasional stoop-speak generalities, hit a quiet stretch for a minute and: "So you seen any a' the guys lately?"

"I saw EP earlier."

"Madman activities are always mandatory with that kid—he's a real firebrand."

"Sho is."

"What about WZ? You seen ole Dubzy in a minute or no?"

"He was supposed to be around tonight but I ain't heard from 'em yet." We walked for a minute longer, were about set to loop around and come back to the joint when it came: "No. Fucking. Way."

"What? What Riedie?"

I looked around and: "See that fuckin' van with the hazards flashin'?"

"What about it?"

"Yesterday morning, I was over by Chicago and Noble and the motherfuckin' punk drivin' that thing and his boy fronted me with a pistol."

"You serious?"

"Yeah, I forgot to tell you—so much has happened since then."

"Suburbanites think this shit only happens in the movies—in reality, it happens every day—fifty times more than it gets reported in the news."

"No shit."

"Were they black?"

"No—white and Hispanic."

"Good, then we can kill them and if we get caught the press won't twist it as racial—not that I'd care what they construed it as, but still, I hate that shit—I don't even see what color someone's skin is man, I swear t' God—I just look in their eyes and if I don't like 'em, it's on." He pulled his blade and: "What do you wanna do? Slit the tires?"

"No—you know what? Let's fucking torch it."

"Fuck—you sure? It's double parked man. They might be back real quick. You sure it's the same one?"

"Dead positive—see that drunk driving sticker on the bumper? It's the same fuckin' one—they're affiliated, I guarantee it—dude was asking me if I was a Gent before he flashed the piece—they'll never suspect a coupla random white boys for a crime like this." Joey inhaled a drag on his Davidoff, and looked out at surrounding brownstones.

"I wonder what crib they're in. We have t' make sure they're not spyin' us."

"Let's get movin' then—and don't leave any cigarette butts around here—they'll run that DNA five years from now, when the crime lab gets through the backlog of sex crime evidence."

"They don't have the budget for that."

"Either way—don't give the option. You game or what?"

"Whudaya want me t' say?"

"Embrace the madness a revenge-orientated experience shall create."

He took a drag, flipped his right hand over in a nonchalant fashion, exhaled and: "Fuck it—I always loved bonfires, anyways—where should we get the accelerant?"

"Anywhere—just not a gas station."

"You take me for a fool? You think I'm one of these people who'll pull into the local Amoco, fill an empty gallon, license plate on video, and then, twenty minutes later, a set of wheels belonging to a known gang-banger is burning blue? I'm sure there're some bad detectives on the force, man, but c'mon—even if they couldn't pin it on you, they'd probably sell the information to the prey—don't remind me of such obvious tactics."

"I'm sorry, man, it's just—you've been living in Europe for awhile. I have t' make sure your exit strategies haven't got soft."

"Soft? Me?—fuckin' *me?*—soft? Fuck you, man. If you ever want to go one on one with rangy string criminal thoughts, you'll lose. Trust me."

"I'll never hold fear so long as you're on my side." I suggested we jog Paulina some blocks to an automotive repair shop and peek in their dumpster. We crossed Cortez and got to the joint that advertised: breaks, tune-ups and emission tests. I concealed my face and spied inside the garage for a second to make certain nobody was in late, chopping a new Mercedes, boxed to export. Coast clear, we dipped in the alley, approached a blue dumpster with '*OH SHIT!*' tagged on the side in white, and after flipping open the top my nose and eyes went spying for near empty aerosol cans, lubricants, paints, oily rags, and other industrial flammables. There was a strong scent of grease so I climbed in and found a slew of good shit down at the bottom—a can of WD-40, saturated plastics—pretty much a little of everything we were looking to find. I emptied two Jewel bags, added the haul and tied them tight so nothing got wet from falling snow. "Alright, let's hurry before they leave."

"If you want to act gangster," JC said, "Do so in just fashion—rob a scheming bank nonviolently and give half of the loot to a handful of people who've been notably wronged— all these cats who go around sticking muzzles in the faces of innocent victims for sake of stealing their last five bucks, pistol whipping them, and then making a rap song about related activities are about as gangster as a fucking maggot, I say." Jogging back at a quick clip, JC looked at me earnestly and short of breath, said: "Now you're absolutely *pos*itive this is the same vehicle, right?" It was a serious question but all the snow on his head made him look like a fragile old man and I laughed. "I'm not kiddin' around now! I don't wanna torch some old lady's car for Christ sake!"

"I know—yes, I'm absolutely certain—same three stickers, same rusty hitch." The van was parked illegally in front of a hydrant, and this was another reason I figured it was alright to torch it—had it been parked right against other vehicles I would have opted out because the damage to other people's property would be unavoidable. It was a perfect situation. The block was quiet as we approached the van and we couldn't figure what building these people were in—then it struck me: maybe they were in the van. "I'll knock on the window n' peek inside before going for it so we don't accidentally commit a homicide— be ready, alright?" JC nodded, we both took out our blades and I knocked on the side panel. Nothing. I wiped the snow off and peeked in the window and the coast was clear.

Just then JC said: "Hold on, hold on—walk across the street, c'mon." I followed him and some short seconds later a cop drove up the road at a decent clip.

"That was close."

"I can hear a Crown Vic or Chevy Caprice comin' from miles away—cops n' cabs, cops n' cabs—chargin' up Western all my life—I have the whole range of their transmissions memorized. Alright, how do ya wanna do it?" he asked, walking back toward the van, "It's pretty wet, with the snow coming down. You might have to break a window and light it from the inside. Opening the gas cap and jammin' lit shit inside will either die out or blow up in our face."

"Yeah, you're right," I said, "Keep a sharp eye—I'll bust the window out with the blunt end of my knife."

"Wait a sec," JC said, and he walked up to the front door and opened it, casual as could be.

"You've got to be kidding." He winked, I climbed in, looked around, reached under the seat and: "Well look what I fuckin' found," I whispered.

"O *shit!*"

"Looks like I got me a new throw away." In my hand was the checkered walnut grip of a Ruger Security Six police revolver with a four inch barrel: "This is the same fuckin' piece they displayed yesterday." I lit the Bic and there was some crusted red on the hammer. "I hid by an old fuckin' boat in a lot on Noble when they came back 'round the block n' I saw a dude in a suit get pistol whipped—this is probably his blood." I opened the chamber and it was loaded. I pushed the plunger, six hollow point .357 Federal rounds fell into my hand and I clicked the wheel closed. I held a cold lead round to my temple and: "Un-fucking-believable man—one of these babies was this close to rifling through my head and ending everything, *pow*, just like that."

"What kinda fool keeps a loaded handgun in their van and doesn't lock the fucking doors for God's sake?" My heart pounded and I thought: who is going to die this evening? Who will they have loved and who loves them? And why will they die? Because an immoral man like the driver of this van will choose to make it so. This gun in my hand will serve as the source of execution—I held it and examined the way it had been made, the artistry involved—it's always interesting to think of the person who designed such objects, and to wonder the reasons why they chose to make them just so—the fuel of one man's power, the end of another man's line. I felt like doing worse than burning—I felt like lurking quiet in the back seat and blasting the motherfucker's head off just as he turned over the engine, I really did. My hand was shaking with rage as JC said: "Alright now hurry the fuck up—and keep those fuckin' rounds in there until we're out of here clean, Riedie. This thing is double parked for a reason. If dude comes 'round the corner with a crew you best be ready—you already seen these motherfuckers be playin' for keeps—I'm not about t' get cut down like some fuckin' Swede out here."

"Alright, get across the street and keep a look out—light a cigarette and stay casual." He stuck one in his mouth and: "If you see someone comin', start coughing real bad."

"I cough real bad by accident when I smoke sometimes, you know that."

"Start sneezing then—I'm not gonna' be able t' see you from inside." JC lit the square, handed me back the lighter and walked casual across the street. I shut the door, slid the rounds back into the chamber, clicked the wheel closed and climbed into the back seat with the Jewel bags. It's such a different feeling, being out in the city, armed and ready.

When you know deep down your ethics are sound and no matter what, no matter how bad your situation was, you would never accost an innocent individual, you start feeling real fuckin' righteous all of a sudden. When you walk your grandmother around the block with a piece in your pocket and three or four thugs walk past with a hard vibe, you start feeling like: c'mon man, really, start trouble with her, I fucking want you to—it'll be my pleasure, in fact. See, there's a reason man invented guns: no matter how tough and courageous you are, there's always someone bigger, badder, and less honorable—if unarmed there may come a point where you'll be at the mercy of these maniacs. Why would you walk in fear when you could walk *as* fear? Know what I'm sayin'? There's just no comparison.

I cut open and emptied the bags of plastics and oily rags on the back seat. There was a heap of random bullshit all over and the interior was cloth—leather would have been harder to ignite. I stacked old Styrofoam cups, about ten empty packs of cigs, a coupla empty cardboard cartons n' some soiled towels into a little pyramid and rolled the down the windows a couple inches so the fire would be able to breathe. I sprayed the whole pile and seat with most of what was left in the can of WD-40 and left a trail to the driver's seat as I climbed back up front. I was about to light it when I heard JC start sneezing uncontrollably. "What the fuck man," I said under my breath. I ducked low and peered out the window in time to see five guys comin' down the steps of an adjacent building—and there they were, those two punks from yesterday, tellin' jokes carrying on like regular ole fellas. I almost started coughing from the fumes so I tucked my head in my shirt, took a deep breath, heart pounding, gun in my hand, body suddenly petrified as I prepared to face what I assumed would be a kill or get killed situation. They went back up the steps after finishing their cigarettes and as soon as the door closed I lit the flammable trail with my left and watched it float quickly across the floor and climb to the pile on the seat. The shit went up quick as hell and I threw open the door, locked it behind me and cut across the street as fast as I could manage without running. I handed the piece to JC and: "Stick it in the pocket of your topcoat. It doesn't fit in mine." We looked back and a warm glow filled the front windshield and smoke was already surging out the crack into the silent evening air. I didn't feel guilty at all, rather I reflected on my most peaceful, happy moments as a child, spent alongside family in front of the warm resonance of a fire. Music bumped from inside a brownstone and JC smiled huge—we cut an alley to the next block as soon as we could and hustled back to the bar in a blur of nervous, adrenalized movement. I addressed the valet driver, waiting outside: "Here's your lighter back—sorry it took a minute."

"Is no problem," he said, happy, relaxed, and European as hell: "It serve good use for you?"

"Yes sir."

"Very good then—have great evening gentlemen."

47

We entered, sat at our table and didn't say anything for a minute. I shivered and: "Yo keep your coat on, obviously—after we leave here we'll ditch that."

"I thought shit was about to go real wrong for a second there—was that them?"

"It was—fuckin' perfect job lookin' out man."

JC nodded and: "Think it went up or what?"

"Absolutely—there was way more WD in that can than I presumed—flames climbed up the back seat in a huge wave straight out of 'Backdraft'."

He laughed and: "There's something to be said of the theory that most arsonists stick around to watch the fire—it was hard to keep walking, Riedie—I would have loved to stay for the roast—fuck those guys, anyway. Karma got 'em."

"If we work as the dirty fist of karma, what's that make us?"

"Just."

"You think?"

"Yes."

"So you don't think we earned bad karma with that maneuver?"

"No—honestly I don't. We got a weapon off the street and destroyed a vehicle that had been used in robberies. We should get a fuckin' award, if anything."

Across the room a crazy mustached fella was talking to the girl at the bar with the books and JC said: "Well who would have guessed it?"

"I could be mistaken, but I believe Alex Paul is correct when he says mustaches give men the courage to take cavalier action at inopportune times."

"Who's Alex Paul?"

"Arguably the nastiest tele skier in Summit County."

"Does he have a mustache?"

"When he feels up to it."

"That guy looks like a fuckin' chimney sweep for God's sake! I shouldn't a' waited," he said, slapping his hand lightly upon the rosewood table.

"There's a fuckin' million man, n' you just met a good one in the alley by chance—don't worry about it. She's only readin' self help books, anyway—I looked."

James Brown came over the juke with: "Are you ready to *jam?*"

"Yeah!"

"I said are you ready to *jam?*"

"Yeah!"

"If it sounds good say yeah!"

"Hell yeah!" Joey yelled, and I felt good as hell sitting there, havin' a drink with such a good mate at my side for the first time in a minute as succulent funk filled the room. Fuckin' life man—this is what it's all about, I thought, at least for me it is—it's all about what's in the grooves and who's dancin', you know? Fuck everyone else.

The waitress delivered four drinks, two whiskies and two Guinness and: "Hey, here ya go guys—sorry for the delay."

"No problem."

"I didn't mean to be rude earlier."

"Neither did we."

"I thought you guys left until I saw your bike was still here."

"Nah, we were just—hangin' outside for a minute."

"Well I hope you guys have a nice night."

"You too—but hey," I said, as she turned, "We only needed two."

"The pints are on me," she said, smiling, "Enjoy," and off she strolled to other patrons.

"Funny how things work out," JC said.

"Yep—when luck's on your side, it's just that easy."

Sirens were vaguely perceptible and: "You think we should split and get rid of that thing?"

"No let's just relax for a minute. We'll leave in twenty—be cool."

A burly black guy covered in snow came in wheeling a bunch of beer cases and after his second trip I said: "Ay were you makin' deliveries on Jeweler's Row yesterday?"

"I *was* actually—you work over there?"

"Nah I was passin' through n' I noticed your Bears sweatshirt—it was a classic."

"Shit I worn tha thing prolly three thousand *times* man. Tha's funny."

"It's a tough night for your gig, man—keep dry, keep warm," Joey said.

"'Eis ain't nothin'—I been heavy haulin' since before you was even born! In the old days I had me a job doin' *see*-ment work, precast work—now *that* was rough—at least with this I get t' warm up in the cab n' listen t' sports talk n' snag me a laugh from time t' time—know what I'm s*a*yin'?"

"Well have a whisky then," I said, "She just gave us an extra," I said, sliding it over to him and: "So what do you keep for protection?"

"What makes ya think I keep anything at all?"

"My grandfather was a delivery driver—he taught me a lot of things."

He smiled sly and: "I got a Judge."

"The five shot Taurus that can take .410 shotgun shells?" JC asked.

"The very one."

"Good choice, sir, that's a mean motherfucker."

"I know—it allows me t' be a r*e*al nice guy, no matter what—I don't gotta waste no time actin' tough." He laughed big, winked, raised his glass, knocked it all back in a single go and: "Thanks a lot fellas—take care now," he said, and he split with a grin.

"It kills me," I said, "Raw guys like that all across the country are out in the cold, grinding in streets that are one wrong turn away from taking their lives, and then they just hand 35% of their dough to little thieving cowards without making a sound."

We eased back with the tunes for a minute and JC went: "How was the road trip you took last summer? I can't believe I haven't seen you since—can't believe we didn't even talk about it yet. What was the best part?"

"When you're grindin' man, time flies," he waved me on and, "The best part of traveling across the country all last summer?—besides camping in the mountains under the stars and such—it was nice to see the great number of random entrepreneurs who've said fuck all else, I'm going to give it a shot and earn my living as my own entity—allow the chips to fall where they may. It was nice to see, man, it really was—for this is what America allows: the right to decide. Spread evenly between these cities, towns, mountains, valleys, streams, prairies and fields is the fucking freedom to choose how you'll grind it out, and that is a fucking beautiful, monumental thing."

"The United States, as founded," JC said, sipping the whisky, tasting his beer, "Is certainly one of the most rightly principled states in the history of the world. The fact that, if ruled as it was written, this country provides no stringent control or demand upon the what, where, or when you choose to do, or not do anything of your own sovereign inclination so long as these activities remain within a certain acceptable blueprint of human behavior lends credence to any and all who consider the initial supposition incorrect—even in the UK you have to be born into the aristocracy in order to come to rule—it feels like a caste system to me, everybody bowing to the queen."

"The opportunities this country provides for greatness are too innumerable t' name—the beauty of America is that every day, the free choice to walk into a library and cram for hours upon any subject, philosophy, or theatrical work you choose grants itself to each and every citizen—you can rent books and take them along as huge, vast tracts of protected lands stand tall and ready to be climbed upon and hiked through, mind exploding, free of charge. Just how am I supposed to feel sorry for somebody who made the choice to sit stationary, burning their eyeballs upon television shows and falling victim to foolish trends and advertisements?—they had every opportunity to break loose and become self-actualized. The same guy burning his eyes out on reality shows could have been practicing guitar until his fingers bled and writing lyrics to explode the listeners' head, every day a little closer to becoming a self-made rock star. Therefore, by no means should it remain their right to punish me for their poor life choices and lack of individualistic drive. I say let them shatter, let them fall—because anyone who tries to claim my personal sovereignty as susceptible to the whims of such a cooperative will meet with serious problems upon attempting to implement its sortie—fucking period, end of story."

"The fact that so few do choose to live like that is an indictment. I'm not sure of what exactly, but it's an indictment of something very wrong. I mean—traveling the globe and living all these places as I've done—especially in Eastern Europe and the Middle East, China and Venezuela—it's helped me see: I've enjoyed *lots* of privileges by being born here. Just being able to have this conversation objectively and openly is a privilege—it's not a privilege for the true right of man, but it is whence weighed against modern worldwide actuality. Billions of people Riedie! Billions of explosive minds are controlled by simpleton yes-men adhering to autocratic orders to strike to injure or shoot to kill all associated with independent thought for the sake that reasoned thinking poses a risk to irrational governance—and they do it! They throw their fists and pull the trigger, man!—thousands of times per day, all across the world, without ever asking why—without even caring!"

"So how do you stop that?"

"I guess that's the question, right?"

"I mean—why is it that the same people jailed under the old regime are often jailed under the new?"

"It's because they stand for free thinking."

"Exactly. They don't want the sharpest blades out on the loose, cutting through and exposing the bull."

"I simply cannot fathom how the irrationality is so mainstream," he said.

"To rule the minds of adulthood, the initial step must be to rule the minds of adolescence—thus, from the very instigation of cogitation, thought control takes shape in seemingly insignificant ways that, when compounded over years, renders freethought impossible due to the fact that the people cannot even comprehend that they're brainwashed."

"What I'm beginning to appreciate is that most of the political rallies I observe seem to be nothing more than large arenas filled with impromptu screaming for change by a myriad of drifters without a plan. This isn't precisely true, but it is damn well beginning to feel that way—like the political process is most represented by those concerned with sounding right rather than making sense—the entire crux of deep philosophical standpoints are subject to change on the whim of a mispronunciation."

"I think people are confused," I said.

"Con*fus*ed? Don't even get me started. I think people have absolutely no idea why they are as they are—absolutely none. Walk around a bar and listen to people talk—what do you hear? Snippets. Little political snippets of regurgitated propaganda from MSNBC, CNN and Fox News being spewed into the air by uncertain sounding voices grabbing for some sort of collective assurance that they're not quite as fucked up and desperately misinformed as they feel. I'm telling you Riedie, the more I walk around open areas with attuned ears, the more it seems like the world is losing itself in a deafening chorus of self-conscious sentences that in the end do little aside drain meekly into nothingness. Self-certainty can only be earned after many silent hours of well analyzed reflection—the fact that it so rarely occurs is fuckin' pathetic—"

"Most men are mice."

"They're either mice or lions who believe that being a lion simply means roaring loudest—and this is another reason why the youth of today has little ability to make a stand and protest, little ability to declare that: hey, this is fucking *bull*shit, man, so fuck yourself—because ideological aggression by the powers that be have besieged the idea of self-determination over time—the idea of everyday people invoking personal responsibility has been slowly eroded so that many aspects of everyday life need to be regulated—many people make money off of this philosophy, and over time, it has leached into the heads of the masses and made us far less self-sufficient—negligence has become a corporation, a national fucking motto: if you can get away with it, push forward and keep quiet," he said.

He took a big, relaxed drink of his whisky and: "Well it certainly doesn't help that people see that philosophy from the top down," I said, "I mean—how is it that you have two parties walking over us hand in hand for all these years, and nobody rises up? This whole country was built on people rising up over oppression, and now?—now a large portion of people's days involves ensuring such subjugation carries on unchecked."

"You mean through little, seemingly insignificant actions?"

"Exactly—by being the sales guy who hits a person for as much as you can, every time, despite knowing your product is rubbish—they talk someone into buying something they know will not benefit them or their family, and then, post transaction, they pat themselves on the back, proud of their coercive prowess. I mean—this is what is referred to as success! Perpetuating the actions that fuel the oppression is called fucking success man!—and such is how ordinary people become oppressors themselves, and build an entire societal atmosphere of corrupted repression of common courtesy. There're all sorts of examples, but in the end it comes down to an individual choice of what power you seek to answer to—and very few answer to honest, humble decency, man—far less than half."

"Every peddler I see, man, most of them, most of these street soliciting, hawking bastards for whom the question of: why? is outlawed as unrightfully straightforward, too prime to earn an answer of merit—and the problem: they're asking for pennies, a spare buck here and there, no big deal, all told—I don't mind hitting them on the side from time to time—at least I know where the money is going—but then when a beast asks for billions, nobody seems to pose any question at all! It's much easer to pose this question to the bum on the corner who demands payment for that which is undeserved versus the man who dresses in the costume which presupposes yes, I deserve, I deserve all this and more, sir, and if you refuse to give, we will take. And the whole place, man, the whole entire place obeys. It's fucking sick. I pay, you pay, we all pay this sort of assumed superior who in turn forms the false foundations of intersections across the city and country and world of supposed rightness, mainly obeyed and traveled upon by the masses as a sort of frenzied superhighway, perfect and serene with all the appropriate shops screaming past on the sidelines, but really, really they're nothing more than latent pedigrees, rare breed, primeval lineages whose main priority is consumption and defecation—over and over and over again—we plant and harvest the crops, cook the dinner, *and* we pick up the waste, all of it, barehanded, while at the same time tilling the fields for what will surely need to be a bigger yield the subsequent year. It's like *hey!* Wake! Stop feeding these thieves! Stop allowing yourselves to be gorged upon!—why do we feel so fucking obligated to issue blank checks on our dignity as a country in that the less worthy, the less logical, the less accurate and reason-capable human beings are the ones existing in positions of power?—how is this so? It's—it's amazing! History's tendency to repeat itself—this most tired of all clichés—how I hate and despise its accuracy." He took a big drink of his beer and: "So what is it? Are independents simply too independent to organize?"

"That's funny Calandra—I said that to myself just yesterday. I don't know what it is—maybe the education system engrains a sense of wanting to grow up to be a mini tyrant so you can boss around all the mice searching for a spare crumb—not that there're many spare crumbs in the first place."

"Hopefully the bailout will help."

"You can't create money out of nothing, it always leads to collapse—there is no physical value supporting the worth—it's not like Ford, or GE, where they produce usable things people need, and then people pay a price for the stock based upon the presumed quality of the product—the bailout equated to printing money: if there is nothing to stand behind it, from where does the value take root?—you can just throw ink upon paper and claim it has worth. That's why in Zimbabwe it takes 16 million of their dollars for a loaf of bread—you get fools in power who look at the budget and are like, 'Damn, we need more cake for that stadium I was going to name after myself—go ahead and fire up the printers, boys, n' tell 'em t' ink up about six billion,'—and that's precisely why it's all going to fall down, again, only harder—just wait and see."

"I hope you're wrong."

"Me too, but I'm not—if you need evidence: for every dollar a working person saw as a result of the bailout, the banks saw $40—they made trillions on the way up, and now that they have to give back the imaginary gains created via inaccurate accounting, the same people who caused this are in charge of fixing it, and distributing cash—I mean, of course the Treasury is in favor of the bailout—all the former chiefs, and the current chief of the Treasury worked for one of these banks for thirty years before being appointed to a position with even more power! I mean—if you place former CEO's of banks into a position where they can print money—what do you think is going to happen? Jesus Christ!"

"Talk about a conflict of interest."

"Not for them!—and then, after the economy takes a dump, crime will go way up and the state will use it as an excuse to clamp down even harder."

"Do you think the collapse was proof of the failure of capitalism?"

"No—and I've thought closely about that argument: because if it were truly capitalism, those banks would have been allowed to fail without an infusion of public funds—and after they did, reckless practices similar to the ones that got them in trouble in the first place would no longer be applicable for sake of ensuring the continued existence of others in the industry—as it stands there was no significant consequence to foolish actions." I took a drink and: "Rich international corporations dominate the government via buying favors and the average individual counts for absolutely nothing, not a thing—you and me: we're nothing. Our families: nothing—just working widgets forking over payments. In essence, property rights don't really exist anymore. This country was founded so its inhabitants could earn a living as they chose, right? This is what spurred innovation—that one could create product, earn money, buy property, and be left alone—that's where the liberty stems from—from the right to possess private property and to do upon such whatever you choose so long as it holds within generally accepted parameters of law. That's how it worked—but now, even after purchasing land, you are subjected to the arbitrary whims of a corrupt government to charge you however much they feel, on a yearly basis, with no recourse when they decide to raise the tariff unfairly high—and if you choose not to pay, you go to jail, and your land is repossessed—so again, there can be no liberty without private property, which again, there is not. The people are losing. All we're doing, essentially, is renting our land from the government. And this is why the true innovators have to lose allegiance to both parties and start anew, according to the original principals of checks and balances and a government that serves the people, not one that steps on our necks and shouts orders—in fact, I don't want to talk about this anymore. I'm getting too heated."

We drank quiet for a minute, and he said: "Do you ever feel that perhaps you're destined to radicalize?"

"Mainly I wonder how I haven't already."

"Me too." I looked around the room and he said: "The press can talk about the right and the left all it wants, but there is an enormous middle. Giant swathes of individuals understand what is going on and why and recognize how desperately rational adjustments are needed—people who get that you can't write checks forever, despite there being no funds, okay?—the practice is a basic precursor to paying the fucking rent on time." He took another drink and: "When you've been consuming more than you've been producing at an extreme rate for an extensive swathe of years, that which you've built on paper holds the tendency to blow down—the entire calamity is so hysterically simple." He shook his head and: "It's crazy to think of all the men who have given their life for this country, man, it really is—hundreds of thousands of men, millions really, younger than us, who have already lived and died, man, their entire story wrapped up on a neat, hidden package, contents forever unknown. I think of the numbers and wonder what they'd say if they stepped out here now, and took a look around? Would they feel it was worth it?"

"I hope—we have to work to make it so."

"There was a time when people were unbound to reach their full potential," he said, "But then they allowed themselves to be walked upon and stole from, and it is now the thieves who wrap themselves in the flag and call you unpatriotic if you seek to take responsibility for your personal liberty: if you seek to keep a fair shake of what you earn and demand input on where what you have given is spent—if this is your demand, you're viewed as a potential problem. There is plenty of money in this country—we have the largest GDP in the world and collect the most taxes, and yet simple community projects go unfunded, and the claim is that they need *more* to get it done—how is this possible? Do you know what percentage of money government collects is actually spent here upon the people who paid?"

"Is it less than half?" I asked.

"Yes, by far—can you believe that? Far less than half is spent upon they who gave. So when you think about it all at once, it's amazing how skewed things have become."

"And compounding the problem is the fact that, minus military hardware, we've devolved from an economy based on making real things to one in which Washington defines interest on credit card debt as consumer spending, and then adds the sum to the GDP as additional collateral so therein we'll be able to borrow more from China and give it to Pakistan. I mean—when and why did we downgrade the standard so severely?"

"And meanwhile you have three hundred million Chinese men of military age, hard as nails, living on white rice, doing pull-ups and shooting targets for a living—and still we keep borrowing from them—the goddamn Chinese have a higher savings rate than us. The fucking goddamn Chinese! Just what will Americans say, Riedie, when they finally send these men to collect the money?"

"Probably: 'Like hey, angry Asian dudes, why don't you just like, ch*ill* for a minute man, like, you know, you don't have to be like, all harsh n' stuff, like, I know we've been borrowing from you but relax, we'll get you your loot like, kinda soon so like, why don't we get baked together and watch some TV or play video games or something.'"

"Right?" he said, laughing with a distressed expression: "It's fuckin' sad but true: we're owned and influenced by foreigners!—that's how indebted we are. It's pathetic, man— you look at the Chinese, these frugal, logical, calculating bastards—and to imagine they technically own half this country because of how soft we've become—to understand that they are one of the biggest contributors to both sides of the political spectrum so as to ensure a win/win situation and a fuck you to the people—a people so gluttonous and distracted that they drone on like the hum of burnt transformers outside a power plant—to admit what is makes me disgusted."

"Yeah but it's our fault—maybe the argument has never been rightly presented, but people *need* t' be active in their agenda—everyone says: 'O, it's a terrible state of affairs, nothing is made in America anymore, we produce nothing, it's awful, just awful,'—but then the next day, when these same people need to make a purchase, where do they go? A big box store—Walmart, Target, any number of them—and so what it comes down to is people have to put their money where their mouth is. The media is always so excited when large chains show positive earnings, right?—but why? What percentage of the product sold there is made in America? Where did the boots-on-the-ground labor of that product stem from? Southern costal China—the manufacturing floor for most of what winds up rotting in our landfills, six months down the line. Seriously—I'd like you to find me a single article of clothing at Walmart that says: 'Made in the USA' on the fucking tag. Just one. I fucking dare you. And the same thing happens when new age American entrepreneurs come up with a fresh inventive idea—they run to China or India or Bangladesh or Vietnam for the manufacturing quote so they can make the highest margin possible—and I'm not hating on them for doing so, indeed this is their right, and their choice to do so should not be regulated—all I'm saying is that the reason this happens is because, for the most part, the American public puts no pressure upon producers to assemble product here. If more Americans took an active role in purchasing American-made products on purpose, free market pressure would dictate that more products need to be made here—it's that simple. It's a stupid fucking cliché, but people need to actively put their money where their damn mouth is, seek out American products and, assuming the quality is there, they have to buy them for the current reality to change. And— and I know this is asking a lot—people also need to examine where the labor is based— buying an American car doesn't mean shit in a lot of cases because they're manufactured in Mexico according to NAFTA regulations—so sure, five fucking big shots get their pockets filled on this side of the border, but the labor is foreign. The free market is the greatest regulator of all time: if people suddenly refused to purchase product manufactured overseas, who would be forced to thrive?"

"American manufactures."

"Exactly—like printing a book for instance—if I ever get my act together and finish one off, I could either get it printed overseas for a handful of cents per copy, or I could spend more to have it made here, in a state where manufacturing had been struggling, according to eco-friendly practices, as a private matter of principle. If the time comes I'll choose the latter, and put my money where my fuckin' mouth is, just like consumers need to—and maybe that won't matter to the average reader, but so long as I know I lived according to my own principals as a producer, I win—feel me?"

"Yeah man, you'll get it done—this day will come—you said it's coming along real great on the phone—what's the status?"

"I have a lot more to do than I thought, but hard work will see it through."

The waitress asked if we needed anything, and I shook no. We closed the tab, took decent care of her and sat quiet for a minute. I was enjoying the heaving impressionistic stride of an old Art Tatum lick, and I imagined how terrific it would have been to live in old Chicago, rolling down to the Three Deuces Club on State Street in a big black Lincoln on a Saturday night in the late 40's, war won, with a cool dame at your side and fat roll in your pocket. Man—I'd of had quite a time boy, you could put your money on me. The beautiful dream was broken by what I'd qualify as barely an acquaintance approached and said hello. "So yeah—whacha been up to?"

"Forgetting my troubles, starting some more," Joey said.

"Anything else new?"

"Nah."

There was an awkward pause and: "Well, I just bought a duplex for like two hundred and eighty thousand," volunteered the mouth of this metrosexual crackpot, "And really, really I'm thinking that within five years it should go up to about three seventy or thereabouts—I feel good about it, you know, my interest rate is fixed, but to fertilize its topside opportunity at the maximum pestilential level, I'll have to borrow more money. I don't want to but, well— all I have to do is put a new roof on the garage, get new couches, leather couches, a few nice chairs like, calfskin or something plush, you know, and then, well—I need to get a pool table, resurface the driveway with concrete, brick if possible, upgrade my plasma, get a flat screen for the bathroom, a stainless steel refrigerator, granite countertops, a grandfather clock and, possibly, if I can get the loan, lease a new BMW 7 Series.

"I—"

"O—and my wardrobe, I mean—I need new suits and slacks and shoes. I'm just not sure where to start—if I get all that done by next summer, I'll be happy."

"Sounds chill," JC said.

I took a fervid gulp of my whiskey, rounded ice cubes glinting in fractured light as I gazed at his blurred auburn face through the bottom of the glass, and asked, "How long do you think it'll take to pay all that off?"

"I mean—the rest of my life, unless I win the Lotto."

He went on for awhile, details of which I will spare for sake of avoiding an aneurism at the instant a re-speak of his story should occur—dude eventually split and JC said: "You hear that guy? I mean—what is *with* these people, man? I don't even know 'em, *and* I ignore

312

him—and what do I get? His entire goddamn economic profile—like I'm supposed to give a flying fuck!"

"Not impressed?"

"I'd be more impressed if he hadn't a penny and walked hard streets at weird hours serving vigilante justice dressed in black. You don't need to rattle off some list comprised of everything you own for me to respect you. Chill the fuck out."

I finished my drink and: "What about principles such as thrift, prudence and living within your means? What about the simple joy of making due? The joy of not wasting?"

"People become what they witness to an extent—and many parents didn't show their kids those things, Riedie, hence why we were lucky."

"You're right—our dads were blue collar guys, man. They taught us to be content with hot food, a roof over our head and a loving family."

"And that's why, as a nation, we're losing—everyone wants to be a motherfuckin' wasteful, gaped-at movie star—working-man hands and quiet stoicism died with fuckin' steam engines."

"When people are bombarded by marketing since the inception of cognition, it's hard for them to avoid consuming such nonsense—they've all gone to the same schools, studied the same text and been sold the same dreams—there is very little freethought, with the way all is connected."

"Fuck being connected."

"No doubt," I said.

"If you are, it's mostly to a bunch of shit, anyway."

"You're right."

"I mean—have you spent time around stupid people, Riedie?"

"Yes."

"You can get them to do anything for a couple carrots, damn near."

"You're right!"

"And then you get millions of idle, stupid people with no money, skills or options surfing the internet for fifteen hours a day, watching people get their heads sawed off or brutal porn mixed with more war and it's like—shit, this idleness mixed with the internet is gonna' be the death of us in the end—it's just too much, man, humans weren't meant to stomach so many horrible images."

"Remaining forever connected will result in a slow crucifixion of the mind and soul, man—every pointless click on the mouse is a slice of time shredded from the fabric of finite reality. Get out there and go!"

"Speakin' a' which, let's bounce."

48

JC decided he was going to take the Blue Line up to surprise his pop and bros with a hello before he had to split town, but first we'd take a ride. It was still early, just shy of eight, and as soon as we stepped outside, the smell of burnt synthetics filled the air.

The valet driver flipped his coat collar and: "Need flame again?"

"Nah thanks, we grabbed some matches—what's up with that smell?"

"I think there was fire few block down—many screaming truck go down road fifteen minute ago—funny how fire happen on such wet night."

"Yeah that's odd—well we're gonna' take a ride—if I hitcha couple bucks will ya make sure my horse stays inside?"

"Yes," he said, as I handed him a bill, "This is only business I have tonight—vatching bicycle and lighter rental—is very productive."

I laughed, thanked him and we walked up the street to hail a cab. It was still snowing, and after a few moments wait, a struggling machine rumbled to a halt. I opened the back door, and in a British accent JC said: "Titch of oil for your gears gover*nour?*"

"No man, she cool man—she sound rough but she run like panther man." The driver was a young cheery Indian fella dressed with a fresh hip hop vibe—blue feathers hung from the mirror, the back seat was decked out with red lights and I liked him immediately. "Don't break if ain't fucking broke. That how it go, no?"

"Close enough," I said, "But seriously, what's with these gears man? It sounds like I'm sitting in a cicada—she ain't gonna' crap out on us, is she?"

"You are sitting in very serious Mothership man—don't feel nervous for her. She could T-bone Abram tank at a four vay and you vouldn't feel pain."

"Well does the heat work? It's straight freezin' back here," JC said.

"O? I thought seats vould still be varm after vat happened hour back."

"Why's that? You have some fat fool farting up a storm back here?"

"No man, I had me voman back there man—I vas on zat flim flam man—zis, zat vay, sidevays, ready to skeet up in there like, mmm-*mmm*—zis is going to be ripe!" I straight busted for a minute after that one—I was nearly in tears seein' how happy he was about it—dude's face was straight glowing.

"Was she a fare?"

"Yes man."

"Was that the first time?"

"Yes man."

"Christ—whose side were you on, his or mine?" JC asked.

"Ve vas all over place man!"

"Was she clean?"

"As a vhistle."

"So it's been a good night I take it?"

"Very good except for last fare—he vanted me to drive to Visconsin. I said no vay and he vas big tweakball man."

"What's your name?"

"Diep."

"Well listen Diep," I said, "You got time to take us for a spin on Lake Shore? Up, down, through the Loop and then right back here? This kid beside me takes the types of journeys you begin by making peace with everybody you love before you leave. The style of sojourn you expect to get hurt on. The style of sojourn you *hope* to get hurt on. The type of trek that, if you happen to die on it—then you do. That's why I want ya t' take your time and let us enjoy the ride, alright? I won't be seein' this kid for a year, maybe longer. Here's twenty bucks toward the fare so you know we're not fuckin' witchu—you up for it?"

"Yes man, for sure man."

I pulled the bill back just out of reach as he was about to take it and: "But you got to let us smoke—not cigarettes—we just want to chill on a ride and pretend like we're rich and you're drivin' a limo—this is what we do before one of us is gonna' leave town for a stretch— we'll make it worth your while."

"Yes sir man. Vatever you vant—but if pulled over I know nut-ting."

"Of course not—but just take your time, we're in no hurry—we're not gonna' smoke until we make a stop, anyway." I instructed him to drive over near my Grams' crib so I could get the piece out of our possession. JC slid it to me beneath the seat so we didn't spook him— I used my hat like a bag, placed it in my backpack and had him stop a block away from the actual address for sheer paranoia sake. I scurried down the snowy sidewalk, cut into the gangway, dipped downstairs and unloaded the rounds before hiding the trophy deep amongst my grandfather's tools.

Back in a flash, Diep turned up the bumps, JC sparked some smoke and we sat back, each looking out our respective windows, soaking in the view. He passed me the baton and I took a real nice pull and exhaled—cold air streamed through the crack in the window and I was feelin' wild as a young woman's voice said: "O, this is so wonderful—I jus love you guys!" after winning a prize on GCI, voice booming over the speakers—I smiled, happy for her, and Diep's Mothership grumbled on—at stoplights she sounded like a frozen Panzer snowed in on the outskirts of Stalingrad—a steel tomb with supplementary head room. We rolled Oakley south, passed an old gangsta crib just north of Grand run by Insane C Notes— situation told via many large green signs and a statement of: 'God made love—God made pain'—and the stop sign on the corner had been recently tagged with a gold Satan Disciple insignia, thereby fueling the feud and hinting of further violence to come. Some people will never cool out and coexist—it's just not in their DNA. I thought of those days in mid-April, when the warm weather sends natives stirring from their enclaves, hungry tummies, eager to hunt, and bass goes bumping from low-slung whips and all the punk bitches rob the innocents to pretend like they're legit—I was glad it was winter, cold and quiet. Even still, the prevailing calm veneer of a neighborhood at rest can disappear in a flash—one must always be ready. I took another drag as we rode beneath tranquil white branches, happy to be on that beautiful Saturday evening, and I proceeded to breathe deep, opening the doors of perception—street lights streamed past to the backdrop of shadowed brick and half-buried parked cars—Diep turned the bumps louder still, and soon we were flying east on Warren, engine roaring past the UC as wind tore into my face hard enough to make my eyes water.

The lots were full and I wondered if Bo n' Blue made the game and were inside booin' Kobe. I smiled at the thought, and through the Loop in a flash, we got to the Drive and: "Diep! You're a madman!" JC yelled, smiling huge and groovin' as the Mothership roasted a soaked, slick LSD past cars driven by people with stories far longer and twisted than our own—I asked him to switch the radio to a college station in the low 90s that always pumps hard Blues on Saturday evenings and he complied. He wasn't familiar with that style of music and he liked it immediately—it made him think of his father, mother, brothers and sister, back in India, he said, breaking their back every day so as to continue living tomorrow. I told him a lot of people love The Blues and after a few miles of driving he said I could add him to the list.

JC passed and smoke lingered upon my lips, a kiss, and when I inhaled it felt sensual, beautiful, everything I hoped it would be—and what am I? What am I becoming? Am I truly a writer? I feel maybe I am, but that's all, just maybe. And in my head exists a myth: a myth of my own self as a world changer, a problem solver, a decent comedian even—you name it and I've dreamt myself as such—a blacksmith, an executioner—but really, what am I? I'm a mild addict, slightly alcoholic, skiing, street-riding caddy slash photographer who has slept on the floor for five years since college with no possessions aside words now gone, and photos. And fuck those photos anyway. Sometimes I just want to throw all of them in a pile and burn them, just burn everything I have—every last best possession in a dark cove, saturated in gas—bursting into light like the van tonight—the full motherfucking sum roaring hot before I walk and walk and walk until fall over I do, fall over I do and I die and never was I—leave behind not a single shred of evidence that I lived at all. Just one in a million, a billion, a *tri*llion lives lived and died to have never made a sound, no whimper, no cry, no O me, look at I—just was and died, sitting back, enjoying the ride.

And so on we rode—all the way central to north to central to south, consuming the duality of American reality. Off The Drive and turning back at 57th street: "It's hysterical," JC said, "The entire world seems t' believe the majority of Americans are rich—I'd love for them to come to the Chi and take them for a long drive west on Ogden, a long drive south on State—they'd be shocked man, I swear. Things just ain't like they used to be."

"Fuck it, they never are—even the way you think things used to be ain't exactly right—it's all torn up n' jumbled in a swirl a' reflection—romanticized n' glorified n' still not quite as beautiful as it really was—life's the wildest, man, it really is."

JC took a drag, looked at me and said: "Don't worry Riedie—we're gonna' make it to the top. Some way, some how, we're gonna' get there man."

We rode on in momentary silence minus the soulful old cadence of Robert Johnson: 'I got t' keep movin', got t' keep moving'—I exhaled out the window, listened to the road, watched the buildings fly past for a minute: 'And the day keeps on remindin' me, there's a hellhound on my trail, a hellhound on my trail, a hellhound on my trail'—it kept jamming on, that old time, barely audible recording, and I thought of an old picture of him I'd once seen, staring like a ghost into the camera, long slim fingers spread over the fret board as a cigarette dangled from his mouth—I shook my head, looked at JC and: "What a track," I said.

"Hell yeah."

"Listenin' t' songs like this—sometimes I get to thinkin' that maybe we're both nothing but a couple more leaned back motherfuckers cruisin' on dreams of makin' it to the top, pretending for certain that it'll become so, without so much as defining what 'the top' qualifies as, and never inspecting the insane topographical map for the most logical, nontoxic route to the precipice—and then I need to breathe."

"That ain't our style, Riedie, and you know it. We can either play it like we were fuckin' born t' fail n' destined to lose, or we can wake every day with the agenda of proving otherwise—we gotta bust through the forest foot by foot, fightin' bears n' shit—n' if they eat us, so be it—we're gonna' be self-made motherfuckers—self-made or self-destructed."

"Or maybe a little of both."

"Hopefully so, I 'spose "

"You really think we'll make it?"

"Hell—we have the world by the fuckin' balls—we're young, driven and free—even if we don't, I'll be damned if I start complaining about things."

"Agreed."

"N' besides—I remember when we were younger—we used to listen to tracks like this n' say whatever happened wouldn't matter one way or the other—as long as we were still listenin' t' tracks like this n' holding our ground against the steady flow of bullshit, we'd have won."

"You're right man, you're right."

Diep eventually pulled the Mothership back to the joint after cutting through the Loop. I gave JC a hug and: "Alright man, be easy—have fun with the family and tell 'em I said hello."

"I will man, we always do—it was great seein' ya—I love ya like a brother, Riedie—be safe n' I'll catchu soon—don't worry about the cab, I got the rest of it man." He sparked a match, lit a square, I got out and they drove off, clanking up the quiet road. Watching the tail lights fade in the distance, the reality of my situation and all that'd happened in the past two days suddenly hit home and I felt cold and tired and wet and despondent, totally insolvent, with full on panic pouring in—this was supposed t' be it, man, I'd already put the work in and this was supposed to be a celebration—I thought about going home and starting over, but the whole objective was so mammoth in scope it almost made me vomit— the idea of sitting down with hundreds of blank pages and a pen, and starting from zero all over again was horrifying. What was hardest to stomach was the reality that I'd have to go back to work man, go back to doing something I didn't love so as to fulfill what I did. I pushed my hands against my eyes, saw a white flash and thought: realize that whatever it takes, you need to get this motherfucking piece finished, else go down as one of the most infamous posers your mind holds capability of conjuring—whatever it takes man, you have to get done.

My mind began tearing ahead on the length of the future struggle—it was going so fast I had to take a knee and embrace some big in and outs, nose to mouth—but I could not do it, man, there were no breaths to be had, zilch—this is all within seconds, mind you—I could barely breathe so I told myself: all I am is all I need—I dug deep into years of memories and maintained my sanity with the old conduit of: so long as you live right—so long as you don't lie or wrong people on purpose and without reason—so long as you encourage people to follow their passions and never bring them down on account of petty, jealous reasoning, you'll be able to die comfortably. Just try for that man and you'll be alright no matter what.

"All I deal with all day long are dramatic bitches!" a man yelled into his phone as he tumbled around the corner, nearly falling over me, "Then I get off work and cram onto the L with dozens more, and then, then when it's all said and done I come home to the most dramatic bitch of them all!—and right away she starts in on me about not being happy enough to see her, that I'm too old t' need t' go out—on and on—I should have never gotten stuck in love like this, ya know?" He teetered half-gassed up the frozen walk and I shivered, happy I wasn't him. I blew into my hands, put on my gloves and as I stood, the normal hydraulic fluidity between my endoskeleton and joints was altered into a sort of sack of jagged skin on the verge of being punctured by pointy, rickety bones that creaked with every movement. A check of the time revealed it was only nine—I could have swore it to be four in the morning. I checked my messages, sort of hoping Melissa had called, but alas she had not.

I thanked the valet guy, went inside and in a flash I was back on my bike, lost in the thoughtless pleasure of motion, like snow work, headed for EP's and what I hoped would be some random, mild insanity. It's goddamn beautiful to have mates that say, 'Make certain you give me no notice at all, just show up and stay for as long as you like'—and when you happen to, it's great—the idea of camping right then left a cold, lonesome taste in my mouth, and I really hoped he'd be home. I passed that fully mashed geezer who'd been drinking

MGD and collecting scrap—he was spewing hunks in an alleyway, looking ready to go comatose on a cold bed of concrete as I rode on. With each revolution time continued in its usual inescapable style that has me waking and wondering of the everlasting nothingness lingering beyond my experience of such—everything that seems so massive in my head—my experience and those shared with others: nothing more than a fucking hiccup in eternity. I passed a black feline making his way through a different alley, silent paws printing upon white, contrasting like bright red roses lain upon green grass ahead of an old granite grave stone in a small town cemetery at the side of an unknown road as warm spring wind cut in above the dead, smelling alive—it's funny how intertwining thoughts of family and loved ones and success or failure blend into a fine point deep inside and represent a desire to thrive and hold onto the experience forever—I can see how some people grow so tired, holding on, when in fact what they are holding onto is a primal struggle in and of itself—I can see how hands and expressions grow brittle—as does the inside of the head—it takes more than focus to not grow tired.

I almost fell and thought: but how does one prevent this? Maybe you have to keep that wonder of the world—those same wonders you held as a kid—the growth of trees and snow and thunder—the height of mountains and depth of oceans—all that puts you in your place, really, like standing alone in open desert sands, with that ball of fusion blasting in the blue sky, heat just a reminder: surely as I won't burn forever, you, my friend, will surely die—and a drop of sweat drips from the chin and upon footprints of different little creatures and their ways of eking by, alive, only to evaporate and be blown to oblivion the next instant—you must release all the little things that don't count: because that's the shit that will wear you down, man—frivolous complaints splitting your brain like the sound of cluster bombs shrieking down through blue—man wasn't designed for that shit—he was designed to live loose—but you can't love living too much, either—not to the point that you become afraid to lose it—because you can see in people's faces when they've come to fear such: everything changes, in a way.

I figured I'd stop n' snag a few brews, so I brought my ride inside nearby mart, left it up front, grabbed some Guinness and got in line. The clerk took his time eyeing two Asian girls buying chardonnay, telling them how nice they looked and such, and the next guy stepped up and was greeted: "Ver is your Budviser man?"

"Not today, Amir," he said, "We're gettin' down with some good."

"Nice man. Ver is your chick man?"

"I already tolja I don't kick it with her like that no more."

"She vas nice man."

"You leered at her every time we came in here."

"She vas bery nice man."

I stepped up and he rang my order without even looking at me—brown eyes and white smile had already met the girl behind me—he was a real whorehound, this clerk—I would have never guessed it. I put the brew in my bag, cut down Potomac for a few blocks, hopped a curb and dove into a gangway where EP's ivy-strangled, red-bricked coach house stood buried in snow like a secretive haunt known only to elite heroin addicts in small town Siberia. The only give away of life in this case was the sound of power tools and smell of cigarettes radiating from a veiled stairway beside a broken stone wall that led to a cellar. I put my ride over my shoulder, negotiated the icy steps, opened the hefty rust-strewn door, moved through a pitch black room toward a rectangular vision of light and: "EP! Yo! EP! Yo man!"

"Ay ole mate! I can hear ya man! Come on in!"

He was barely audible over the crackling snarl of a ban saw. I set my ride in the first room, opened the door and was met with blasting punk rock, whirling sawdust, and the vision of a crazed shop-rat, concentrating as if performing open heart surgery with a Turkish Gold hangin' from the corner of a clenched mouth as he cut a pristine piece of pine according to his predetermined specifications. He shut the saw and took off his safety goggles. I threw him a brew and: "Sorry for yellin' man," I said, "I didn't wanna startle and have you lose some fuckin' digits with your hand so close to the blade."

"Thanks for lookin' out Riedie!" He was real jazzed—I could tell he'd been mashing hard for hours—nonstop since he'd defeated my lock. He wiped collected dust from his eyebrows with a rag and: "So how you feelin' homeboy?!"

"Fuckin' good," I said, "Fuckin' great."

"You wind up takin' that ride?" I nodded: "Solid?"

"Very solid—very random."

"So whacha been doin' for the past two days otherwise?"

"Just roamin' mostly."

"Interesting things occur when roamin'."

"You fuckin' said it kid." He cracked his drink, addressed a huge Craftsman tool chest splashed with a hundred different stickers, and soon his callused hand was digging into an old red steel case containing drill bits. He adjusted an Irwin Quick Grip holding wood on one side of a work bench, measured, marked with a pencil and set his safety goggles upon on the plate of a well used old drill press—he inserted a new bit and I stepped up and wrote 'EP Rules!' above the two main switches in soft sawdust. "What's with all this Hot Shot spider killer man?"

"It kills on contact," he said.

"Yeah but why do you have so many cans?"

"I fuckin' hate spiders man."

"I thought the problem was with rats."

"Yeah, so did I—and I thought heard one behind the drill press earlier, thought it was a rat for sure, so I grabbed the level to beat it to death and when I peeked back there—it was a giant spider that was making the noise man. I had to walk out of here for like fifteen minutes before I came back, I sprayed so much shit on that thing."

"How big could it have been?"

"Too big to talk about—let's not mention it again." I leaned against a large table set against a brick wall that held many bike mounts in various stages of completion. His woodworking skills were really something—hand crafted and designed to hold beautiful cycles horizontally, out from the wall, they were part trophy mount and crown in their own right, beautiful and useful as they were. "Ay did you decide which kind you want yet?"

"Yeah, the one with the drawer."

"Stained or natural?"

"Maybe natural—you get that white pine so smooth it feels nice by itself." He dipped and held a two inch paintbrush above a can for a moment, and allowed excess fast drying polyurethane to drip clear, back into the can before running black bristles smooth and efficient across the sanded surface of a recently completed design. Spread about the room industrial orange buckets held hundreds of wooden bits slashed away as large pieces were reworked into alternative forms. There were additional, smaller tables in the area, each of which was loaded with an incredible number of random devices which EP employed in ways known to him alone—looking at all his work I thought: this kid's a straight up crackerjack—he can put anything together. "How'd you get so good at all this shit man?"

"I don't know—some of it I was born with, but still, we grew up at the end of a huge generational gap—there was no internet when we were kids—we didn't spend our childhood online, consumin' n' producin' n' tradin' gobs of electronic drama with faux friends that people count off like pins in some goddamn bowling score—we were out there, man, runnin' wild to an extent, making up games n' cavorting about, playin' ball, hoopin' n' gettin' in trouble until we were too dirty n' tired t' carry on—so we finally ran or rode our separate ways, ready for dinner, ready to clean up, eat n' change into black clothes for nefarious nocturnal activities—but when I wasn't doin' that sort of stuff, I was in my dad's woodshop, tryin' t' make things. There was not a single virtual thing about our childhood, Riedie, we had t' entertain ourselves—it's no wonder I can't relate to most of these kids."

"No shit," I said.

"And they're not even that much younger than us!—it's so different now—kids have a thousand 'friends', right, but who's gonna' be there on moving day?"

"Not me."

"Who's gonna' pick you up when your whip won't start? Or help you get an oxidized nut off the fuckin' bolt in the dead of winter when you need t' change your tire? Is it gonna' be one of these jokers on your web page, or the motherfuckers you lived n' died with—laughin' n' cryin' n' boozin' n' smokin' the years away as slowly we went from curious pups to rabid dogs?"

"Fuckin' cheers t' that, man." I drank a significant amount of my beer, and in the corner was enough used sandpaper to have stripped a locomotive, and enough wood stain to transform its graffiti-laced freight train into a long line of wholesome, English-chestnut themed dining cars. I took a deep breath, felt weird immediately, and wondered how many brain cells he'd lost, painting in this unventilated room.

"Hey look at that die grinder over there, Riedie—not the portable Bosh we used on your lock, but that quarter horsepower, old motherfucker—look where it was sold and who made it."

"Kmart?"

"Yeah, sold at fucking Kmart and made by the McStraw-Bedison Company in Boonville, Missouri—back when chain stores sold reliable shit made in the States—me n' my dad have been beating on that thing for thirty years and it still works like a gem."

"That's a fucking relic man."

"I know—they're not in business anymore, but their woodworking tools still run like mad—if that thing had an hour counter, it'd be well over ten grand."

I walked over by a wooden egg crate shelf and checked out the goods. One crate up high held a heap of little leverage designs he'd been fabricating out of nothing. Many of them were very ingenious and innovative, from small and intricate to large and powerful—but if he were to have sent a resume to an engineering company, they would seen: EP, high school graduate, mechanic and shop rat—and bam, it would have been pitched to the trash immediately. So often he mentioned the tasks set before him and so often the toil needed to fulfill was extolled—the only result possible to these habits was that eventually, he'd make it happen. I was proud of him, truly. Continuing to look at his inventions, I was authentically taken aback by his raw ingenuity—he'd build what were sturdy, high end leverage devices of

320

diverse use, by hand, himself, out of wood, rope, rubber, plastic, using elaborate, multi-use pulley systems. "EP man—what the fuck is all this? Are you kidding me? How long have you been working on this?"

"Pretty much constantly," he said, polishing off his Guinness, "When not working on the mounts. Another beer?"

"More steel in the US is used to manufacture bottle caps than automobile bodies, and I think you're half the reason why."

"Why thank you—that's a fine compliment."

"No problem—I'll take one, of course," I said. "So does this work over here have to do with the invention you were talking about?"

"Maybe."

"Do I get to see it?"

"Do you want to?"

"Are you kidding?" Music charged in the background as he walked over to the opposite end of the dusty room, moved a huge sheet of plywood and, on the wall, behind it, a small white sheet that looked to be a soiled pillowcase protected the item in question. "Fuckin' slick presentation man—all this for me?"

"You like that?"

"Of course!"

"Now you can't say anyting about this—it's not patented yet."

"Who the fuck ya think you're talkin' to? I'll be takin' so much shit to the grave they're gonna' have t' stuff me into the ground, the fattest folks there, with their bare feet."

"I know I know—I just had t' say it—okay, you ready?"

"Of course! I can't wait another damn second!"

He grabbed the sheet at the bottom, seized it off the wall and: "Voila!"

"Well Jesus Christ man!"

"See, it works like this," he said, demonstrating. "It's just a prototype."

"Wow—I'm speechless!—you know how many people will want to use one of those?"

"I told you it might be pretty good for real."

"I can't even *think* of someone who wouldn't find that useful."

"Well—priests and nuns wouldn't need one."

"Yeah but those are dying trades—this is some big time shit you've made." I checked the ins and outs of it and it was legit—he'd put a lot of thought into it and it was something my mind could have never conjured on its own. He'd done serious homework on the market audience and created an original product, from scratch, that would fulfill the needs of man. "You should be real excited about this man."

"I am."

"And you deserve to be—this took a lot of thought and persistence."

"Hell yeah—you have no idea how many failures it took before I got it right. It's not always easy to get things done when you're an all-over-the-place type a' motherfucker like me."

"Yeah, but when you do, it's probably all-the-more satisfying."

"It is—I feel good Riedie, no lie."

"So what's the plan for tonight?"

"We'll see—we're either sittin' here drinkin' n' bullshitting all night or you're in for a real nice surprise. I'll know in about twenty minutes."

"C'mon man, another surprise? I've had enough the past two days."

"Anticipating the plot of your evening to the point of perfection is no good—it's much like a line down mountain, Riedie, n' you know all about that—you don't always hit that presupposed line, man—shit happens and you have t' fuckin' improvise based upon preexisting unforeseen conditions, right, and often—often you look back upon the face and find the ad-lib is what you love most."

"Alright ya got me man. You're killin' me with this shit though—by the way, have you talked to Dubzy today?"

"Yeah he's upstairs, working on a painting and the logo for that product."

"Really? No way. I didn't think I'd see 'em this weekend."

"Yeah he's been grindin' up there for hours man."

"Alright—well if I'm gonna' do anything tonight I need to take a hot shower and get some dry socks from you. I've been enduring the incredible pain that comes when your skin is freeing and dying for hours now."

"No problem—take whatchu need but leave the crazy wool ones for me."

"You got it."

"I'm gonna' wrap up down here and I'll be up in twenty."

"At which time you'll let me in on whether we're staying here or—"

"Doing that other thing? Yeah—you'll know soon enough."

"It better be good."

"Don't worry, it is."

49

I climbed out the cellar with my ride on my shoulder and the brews under my arm, crunched my boots 'round the coach house, shimmied up the steps, turned a brass doorknob and there he was—Mr. Will Zybarsky, facing a canvass with an expression like he'd been lost in a state of creative exuberance since the moment he hit puberty. "Yo! Will! What's good my man?!"

"Yo Riedie!—feelin' fresh—how ya doin' homie?"

"Pretty good, pretty good." He slapped me one, pulled me in with a shoulder bump and: "So what's crackin'?"

"Just bustin' on paintings n' comin' up with a logo for EP's bike mounts."

And speaking of such, several different designs protruded from the wall—I hung my whip on my favorite style, admired her beauty and said: "So how's the day been?"

"I woke with the boot on my car this morning—'sides that mostly gravy."

"Shitty man."

I tossed him a brew, he cracked it, I put the rest in the fridge, did a bunch of pull-ups on their bar in the corner and: "Yeah—just two tickets for a boot now, right?—plus I let this chick borrow my car and didn't even know I got the second one. And further, I hadn't used it in the past three days, so I didn't realize it was on there for a minute, and the fine increased each day."

"You're lucky they didn't tow it on you—they usually snag it the next day."

"I know, all the snow saved me—either way it's seven-hundred bones with juice on any delay—sort of changes your mood at the start of the day—and then they'll say they don't have enough loot to fix the potholes and raise taxes more."

"They're so full of shit it's amazing."

"All I want to know is who's gettin' rich off me. Who are the people stuffing their pockets?—where do the live and what are their names?"

"You'll never find out, man, you really won't." I looked in the ashtray and "What's with all these cigarettes with lipstick traces?"

"I think EP's been seeing some seductive black lung—he denies it though."

"Why would he?"

"Don't know—either she's ugly is or he spends the daylight hours posing as a transvestite while I'm subbing."

"I'm guessing ugly seductive black lung."

"Well I should fuckin' hope so!" he said, "But could you imagine?—me n' Leo leave for work and he slips into a little black dress, clicks down into the woodshop in high heels and wrenches those burly, hairy arms n' on rusty iron bolts n' shit—smokes hanging from his full red lips."

"C'mon man! I don't need, or want, that sort of imagery—don't make me gag, Jesus Christ!" I said, "Where is Leo, anyway?"

"Workin'—he started that new company, he been grindin'."

"Good man, I'm glad—seems like everyone I know is goin' all in on something or other—so how was your Christmas n' shit? I can't believe I ain't seen ya since."

"I know right? The past month has flown—Christmas was alright—but with some of my extended family, it was a lot of: 'So, what *exactly* are you doing? When are you doing this? That? When are you gonna' be finished with blah—' This year they were being serious with me. This year I felt like people were a little more like: 'You've been living wild for a long time, you're lived your life, so when are you gonna' get miserable like us? Seriously now—when are you gonna' be responsible and start getting miserable?' And in my head it was like: so you drive a nice car and know what's going on in every sitcom. Cheers, nice life."

He leaned in and made an adjustment to the eye of a woman with a thin black brush, dipped in blue—her face was like an epitaph—it encapsulated a cutthroat persona, an age old problem of man—the same face that lures you in shall steal your life in the end. "But since I'm a laid off teacher and freelance artist, I don't know what's going on in the world, right? I was getting looks like, well, you don't quite under*stand* where I'm coming from and you won't—not until you're a grown up. But what does that even mean Riedie? You're not grown up until you have a job you hate and have no time and are always on a schedule to meet with people you can't stand and—man! Am I not an adult because paint? Because I play open mics?—because I'm not working full time?—what is it? Sitting there listening to them complain, I felt an insane horror in my stomach at the thought of a dying moment of a life lived devoid of creation. It was fucked, the instantaneous flash to such a perspective. The mind inside my daydream felt terrorized at the realization that it was about to be extinguished before ever having been set alight."

"People who've worked their whole lives for others often have a hard time grasping that one can be productive on their own. They say: 'So, are you sick of being *off* yet?' But really, it's like: I've never been so *on* in my entire fucking life."

"Right? I know whatchu mean—that's my feeling exactly. People see nothin' and they see it so well—I've seen a lot them walking around with headstones in their eyes this season—millions of 'em walking around malls looking for a nice plot to bury themselves beneath—just waitin' t' thud."

I walked in EP's room, admired his minimalist display of a handful of hoodies, flannels and T-shirts, looked in his drawer and couldn't find many socks without holes besides the wool ones he asked I didn't use. Plus the other ones were all white. I don't wear white socks—they're just too ridiculous. I walked out and: "Hey—you have a pair of dry socks I can borrow?"

"Heeled socks a rare commodity with so many paces compiled?"

"Yeah—and they're all mashed with salt and slush."

"Hold on a sec," and back in a flash, "Check it—eight trail-rated pairs—take your pick—I got plenty more in the back if none of these feel right."

"Wow—what's with all this woolen refinement? These are great."

"This is where a good sum of my wealth lays at current, in socks. So long as my feet are warm and dry, I can deal with anything. Plus you can always barter socks—you know, comfortably warm, dry, clean socks for an ole mate in need in exchange for maybe an extra pint and a few whiskies and the likes."

I unlaced my boots and: "The deed shant be forgotten my friend."

"Make every warm step a good cool drink for my throat."

I yanked the decaying rank from my feet, shivered and cleaned the sandy junk from between my wrinkled red toes: "It's nice and fucking cold in here, man, nice and fucking cold."

"Yep—the gas bill was apeshit last month so we said fuck it, layer up—plus I want to be chilly, I want to be hard. EP and I both work better in those conditions."

"I'm gonna' bust a hot rinse to get the blood going—I'm freezing, man, for real—it hit me real hard on the way here."

"Word," he said, eye studying the brush as it mixed colors—I went in, clicked the single light bulb hanging in the room, twisted the warm knob only, hopped in the tub and blasted my body with wonderfully scalding water while making sure to keep my hair dry. Steam rose from my cold clammy skin and I shook like a bastard. The pinkie toe of my left foot was swollen round and purple. I flicked it a few times under the water and hardly felt it. I soaped up, rinsed, dried fast, threw on those great dry socks Dubzy had lent and bundled tight before exiting the room.

Upon doing so, Dubzy's phone rang. He walked in the other room and I felt like my feet were being hugged by nice cozy sheep—I sat back on the couch and felt real nice. I looked around at some of his recent work and thought: this kid has mad skills man, let me tell you—diverse covetous artwork is arising in this house on a daily basis. I looked at a piece of piece of paper sitting on his table and it went: 'I wonder if I have been painting in such volume and of such quality because I have been using so many drugs. I have been trying to quit, albeit unsuccessfully. So unsuccessfully. In fact, in the time it has taken me to write these words I have taken three large hits and have become extremely high. Substance man—why is it that I need as I do?' Will reentered and: "I gave my number to two girls named Courtney the other week, and one of them wants to go out for a drink." He was a real Don Juan in his day, a regular rake for the most part. Women practically threw themselves at him at times—usually beautiful but insane ones.

"What'd you introduce yourself as? Will? William? Zybarsky? WZ? Or Dubzy?"

"William."

"I actually forget that's your real name sometimes, I swear. They both of equal standing, looks wise?"

"For the most part."

"That's good—excludes the possibility of disappointment." He got back to painting and I watched the show. The wall around the current work had been hit with a thousand brushstrokes of a thousand colors in varied length, width and depth—this caused her to appear as though she were experiencing a profound '*Eureka*!' moment. If moved away from the exterior brushstrokes, her face possessed a far sadder, solemn temperament. "Hey who is this playing right now? They sound great."

"Some wild-eyed dude named Louie—I was drinking with him and an allotment of randoms in an elevator control room last week when he said, 'Stick for a minute and check out this track. I bought a fifty cent tape of The George Benson Uptown Quartet, and it's pure.' He was right."

"No doubt."

"It still snowin'?" I nodded and: "I can't wait for another great summer of chess on the stoop n' ground balls in the alley. How's camping been?"

"It's been good, you know, productive, but damn ridiculous at times."

"But as ridiculous as it feels, I suspect if feels very beautiful, too."

"It did, man—I mean it does—it feels pure—purely fucking nuts in a multitude of ways, but pure nevertheless."

"Think you're gonna' move back in next summer?"

"I don't know—either back here or my Grams' crib—probably here."

"Why'd you decide to camp instead of moving in there, anyway?"

"The garage was way cheaper—I didn't want to ask for a favor."

"She thinks you're still living here right?"

"Yeah—I get total solitude in the garage—it's like an urban cave man, it works."

I smashed a good portion of my drink and he said: "Maybe one day they're gonna' be like, 'Yeah, they lived together once, the painter n' the writer.'"

"More like survived together."

"No shit right?"

"So if you're gonna' see this Courtney girl—what's up with what's-her-face? Not working out or what?"

"Our interaction is never calming—it always raises irritation in both of us—at least in me it does." His phone rang—"Shit, this is her calling right now!"

"Courtney or what's-her-face?"

"What's-her-face. Do I answer and tell her I'm thinking about her right now?"

"Only if you are," I said, words garbled in Guinness. I looked at him and laughed: "So you've suddenly found yourself in the point of the relationship where you're havin t' breathe a lot—havin t' step back and take a breath."

"It ain't sudden, man—she's been burnin' through what little cake I have for three months," he said, ignoring her call.

"It's hard to save, man."

"I'm *not* saving—not when I'm paying for two people to eat, to drink, for clothes, transportation—her whole aura screams of the fact that she's a rabid consumer of obnoxious thingamabobs of no quantitative quality. I mean, c'mon man, that's not my style."

"I thought she was a feminist."

"Not with this credit card bill, no way—she's a goddamn horde. I need t' get with a girl who's at least been hungry a few times—somebody in touch with reality."

"You're right. It's terrible to be with somebody who's gotten everything they wanted nearly every moment of their life as a non-result of their own personal production. They possess no perception of what it takes to become self made, man."

"Her presence is not good for my liver or my lungs."

"That's why music is your medicine."

"Well better I start jammin' then, every minute I live, that's what it'll take to neutralize her—it's just—I can't respect her—and further, when you waltz past the dumpster of a Chinese restaurant and it is ninety five degrees outside—it smells like that man, her apartment."

"You're crazy! You were probably here with her n' misremembered!"

"I'm not kidding! She owns so much useless crap it is literally rotting in itself." He mixed some paint together and said: "The weird thing is—I've actually reached the point where I can't stand the sound of her voice. It gives me an upset stomach, no joke—we have these horrifically repetitive conversations about nothing: 'How's work? Fine. How's your family? Fine. How are *you*, I mean, how are you *really*? Fucking fine.' The last time I was with her I remember thinking: kissing, loving, fucking, hugging—kissing, missing, embracing and trusting—why suddenly am I wondering: what in fuck has the point been?—and then I knew it wasn't right."

"Exactly—"

"It's a very interesting feeling to find yourself looking at a chick that once drove you mad, a chick you thought would have your fucking number forever, man, and then suddenly you find yourself looking at them and you're like—*you?* I've been losing my mind over *you?* Just two months ago she filled me with crazy waves like I could spit on her and kiss her harder than you've dreamt of kissing someone in the same breath—but now she seems so ordinary! I found it hard not to laugh out loud when it all sunk in."

"There's not many where you'll look back and, no matter how it ended, you have to say: she once was a true love of mine, and she always will be."

"I know, right? You know what she does? She makes me feel old. She looks at my life like: wow, this is what you do? How you live? And so in my head I was like: am I? Am I alive? I know I am alive, yes, but am I living? Fucking yes, I am. I am alive and living as I as a child held hope I someday would! She's trying to force a whole structure to my world that will never work."

"Honestly—you have to boot her, mate. It'll hurt for a minute, but if you don't, well—in the end all she'll do is hold you back from reaching your potential, and you'll hate her. You'll hate her more and more and she'll hate you, too, so grab me a drink and feel glad to have averted a huge, lust-driven disaster—boot it."

"You're fuckin' right man. Fuck. Lust is wild."

"It's the wildest—but when it ends, you know right away it ain't love."

"I know man—and she told me so last week—she said she loved me and I straight cringed. She said it in this creep style man, all slow with her eyes all buggin' out on me that made me super uncomfortable."

"When, 'I love you,' feels like, 'Please, don't leave me,' it's time to hit the road."

"Thanks for not being a pussy and telling me straight."

"No problem—but if you end up sticking with her, don't mention I said that shit."

"I won't."

"But keep thinking about it until you leave her."

"I will."

"I mean, really—do you think you'll tell her to split?

"I probably should, no? I mean—when she was in my arms n' cryin' last week she said, 'I'm just crying because of how happy you make me,' but shit! I felt horrified man! I was like, fuck, it would be much better if I didn't make you happy at all!"

"Does she fulfill you, man?"

"No—not really."

"So what do you need?"

"I need a girl that, if you married her and had children, you'd spend the majority of parental gatherings neck deep in nonverbal mockery of the other hopelessly rigid, cookie cutting parents on the scene."

"N' that ain't her?"

"Fuck no!—I mean—I need a comedian, an athlete, an intellectual, an artist, a barfly, a nurse, a psychologist, a forgiver—the list is endless to what I need man, but more than anything man, I need a rock, a beautifully original one that, no matter how hard I try, cannot be broken."

"That's a rare stone, B."

"So rare."

"Grab me that damn drink already." He came back with another Guinness, I had a sip and: "I imagine life will be much easier whence you discover the person you desire t' spend the majority a' your time with," I said, "It'll make it easier t' concentrate on your true desires, yearnings, wants n' cravings."

"Right?—isn't that pretty much the point of the search, anyway?"

"I assume."

"So I can eventually be like forty-five—I'll wake holding her in the dawnlight," he said, holding back a laugh, "Birds singin' songs, flowers burstin' open n' shit—n' I'll say, 'As long as I awake with you in my arms, there's not a single thing in the world I would ever dream of complaining about. Good morning, darling—I love you.'" He shook his head and said: "It's just—I could never imagine myself saying that, and meaning it. Never in my goddamn life! That's the real honest truth!"

"Well that's good. It's important that you acknowledge that—don't ever pretend meaning some words you don't stand for. It'll be the end of you—the horrible bloody end." I walked across the room, ran my fingers across the smooth sanded surface of another of EP's mounts and said: "Ever find yourself looking at a friend when suddenly this voice within, it clicks: whoa, it's you!—you're the one I love!—has that ever happened to you?"

"It has," he said, thinning the paint of his brush on a pallet.

"It's crazy, right?"

"It is—what made you think of it?"

"I saw Melissa yesterday."

"You mean from a long time ago?" I nodded. "How was it?"

"We rap on such a cosmic level, it was like I'd just seen her last week—you know how long it would take to get somebody caught up on my whole wavelength?"

"A minute, for sure," he said, laughin' a little.

"The idea of gettin' t' know someone from scratch n' building that trust sounds exhausting to me. After ten minutes I was looking at her like: you're utterly brilliant, mad cool and sexually profound—someone who makes me ecstatic at the possibility of what is."

"Rad."

"Yep."

"She's a cool girl man, you might want to keep track of her."

"You're right—somethin' in the way she moves attracts me like no other lover—I know exactly what George Harrison was talkin' about when he wrote that song, man, so long as he meant what he said, and I think he did. I would rather hold her hand for thirty seconds than fuck some hot, sought after celebrity a thousand times."

"Imagine if you lost track of her and wound up having a son with some ignorant bitch—and as soon as they were able to talk, as soon as the chip off the ole block got curious n' began asking countless questions about the world, imagine how it'd feel when that silly bimbo of a mother begins offering ill-advised, unreasoned answers, and ruining him from the very beginning. If that happened, I guarantee you'd spend the rest of your life wishing you could say, 'Ask Melissa,' every time the kid posed a statement of original curiosity. That's a horrible thought, isn't it?"

"Of course it is, man! It's one of the most horrid thoughts I can conjure! Don't be saying crazy shit to me like that, Jesus." I took a drink and: "I wonder what my family would think of her."

"If she puts you at peace, they'll love her." He moved down and got to working on the shadow of the woman's chest and said: "So how's the book? Almost done?"

"Yeah, it's done."

"Are you serious? That's great! What's it been? Four? Five? Six years in the making?"

"I gotta tell you something man—between you and me—I had my bag stolen last night—it had most a' the work in it. I'm back at fuckin' square one for the most part."

"C'mon—*all* your journals? From before and through college and everything after?"

"Minus that big old sketchbook, yeah, all of it was in there, jammed full—n' it's all gone."

"Are you playing with me man?"

"No, I'm not kidding. Don't tell anyone, either. It's finally sinking in. For a minute I thought it was the most insane dream I ever dreamt, but it's for real—I had to tell someone."

"Fuck!" He asked how it went down, I explained and: "So whudaya gonna' do?"

"I guess start over—push the pedal to the floor and try to kill it from scratch—but it's gonna' take a lot of steady intensity to begin, push through and conclude—it's gonna' take years to build all that material from zero again. It's not good. I feel totally wiped out in a way."

"Only the things that you truly love, will you pursue with that energy—I have no doubt that you'll make it happen, Riedie, and who knows? It might even be better this way. Words of struggle hold intrinsic purity."

328

"So long as they aren't false."

"They won't be—they can't be—so I'm sure you'll hold it down neck deep in your usual submergence of realness, and pull through on top. You're too strong to let this break your dreams, kid—you've probably written more shit since, haven't you?"

"I guess."

"It's what you're meant to do, Riedie—it's gonna' happen, you're gonna' finish."

"That means a lot, man, comin' from you. Keep that quiet, though." I watched him paint for a minute and: "You feel like drawing a cover for it?—the book I mean?"

"Hell yeah man, I'd be honored."

"Alright—we'll work on it then. Maybe I can just tell you how I see it in my head and you can draw it while we play chess—finish in a few sessions or so."

"Sounds good to me."

"Seeing that—it'll be motivation t' fuckin' smash all over again—I'll just sit with it in front of me and force myself to create."

He chuckled and: "You're gonna' be crazy by the time you finish that book, man."

"Probably." I took a drink and asked: "How've your shows been lately?"

"I don't want to talk big, but man, I've been rockin' it."

"That's accurate, man, be proud—you've been working at it your whole life, just like everything else."

"Thanks man—I think the album's gonna' get done this year."

"I'm gonna' have t' buy like ten of 'em, with how fast I wreck my CDs."

"That'll be the most I've sold of anything, technically."

"Beautiful—did you sub yesterday?"

"Yeah."

"How was it?"

"Alright—we had these motivational speakers talk about effort n' all that—one guy was this ex-banger who cleaned up and made it—but there was this other guy, this white guy waiting to speak who looked all weird, right, and in the middle of the first speech he walked over to a group of snickering kids, took this note from one of them, handed it to me and, in this extremely proper voice, he said: 'Um, I caught one of your students with this note.'" He put down the paintbrush, handed me a crumpled paper from his pocket and I read:

'Tha dude wit da peanut or small azz head is not doin or sayin nothing and he look funny.'

"Are you kidding me? Did you write this?"

"No man! That's the note, straight up!—and when he handed it to me I fuckin' read it two extra times real slow just to keep from bursting out laughing—the guy was just standing there with his peanut or small *azz* head, watching me read it, so I said, 'O, yeah, rest assured I'll have a chat with them after class, rest as*sure*d, sir.' What was I supposed to say? The note was accurate as hell!"

"I don't know how you do it—why would one ever forward a note that referred to them as such? I'd have taken it out of circulation and never breathed a word about it."

"No kidding."

"I can't believe they cut back so many positions this year—would you have been all gravy if you were tenured?"

"O yeah—unless you're molesting kids, you're not bootable. And half these people, I mean—they're pretty deplorable teachers in my opinion. All they do is scream, yell, refuse to employ reason or hear these kids out before coming to a logical conclusion—they don't treat the kids with any respect and they wonder why they receive none. It's so predictable—the classrooms become a mirror image of their own insanity—and a lot of these teachers *are* insane by the way. You'd be shocked, seeing it first hand."

"So have you been interviewing places?"

"Yeah but nobody is hiring this year—it's fine, I'll keep subbin'."

"Have you tried the 'burbs?"

"Yeah—don't even get me started, man. I went up to this joint on the North Shore last week, right, and first off, when I pulled in, my car was the junkiest one in the lot by a country mile, alright. These kids were driving BMWs n' Benz's n' shit, like an episode of 90210—it was crazy. So I walk in there—and I probably should have been wearing a suit, but I wasn't—but I went through this whole interview with this fat bastard by the name of Mike something or other—I had to speak with this cat for an hour and 'explain my abilities' to him, right," he said, quoting the previous statement with blue Smurf fingers the length of ET's, "But really all I could think of was how large of an ignorant cheeseball he was on account of his statement that, 'In teaching, the students' happiness is the utmost importance—it is a key to classroom control—how do you feel you compare your own methods to this philosophy?' And as soon as I listened to my voice attempting to explain myself to him, I nearly fell fuckin' ill right then man, I swear. He was disgusting—like when somebody with mediocre talent has been told they are the best for their entire life and in the end, they actually come to believe it—he was the guy who finally believed, man—it was sick. First off, to be a good teacher, one's foremost concern must be teaching *truth*, not the students' happiness. And in my head I was just like: do you have the slightest fucking concept of who I am and where I've been teaching? I was looking at this clown like: I've been teaching in the straight fucking *hood* man, for years, relating to kids who span a spectrum so fucking diverse that you cannot even be*gin* to fathom my frame of reference. I mean—if this guy would have walked into some of the classrooms I've walked into in the past six years—in Englewood n' fucking Humboldt Park, Lawndale, up in RP, down on the South Shore—I mean they would have chewed him up and spit him out so fast he would have been *cry*ing as he ran out the door to his car. Fucking crying man, I guarantee you—they wouldn't have given him one *sliver* of acknowledgement! I've had kids where the only place I was able to gain their respect was on the goddamn basketball court, after school, steppin' out until they were callin' me goddamn Kirk motherfuckin' He*i*nrich—the crazy dark-haired lanky white boy with handles—rainin' treys and goin' t' the hole on these guys only to eat hard ass fouls so maybe they'd listen t' me in history class the next day—whatever it took, man, I did it, I was there every day—keeping my cool when gangbangin' thugs pushed my buttons, tryin' t' purposely get me to end my career on them, breakin' up fights that would make a barroom brawl in Dodge City look soft—and still I showed compassion. There was always a distinct feeling in my stomach when taking phone calls from kids—when they'd call all alone after their parents got locked up, and I'd have to tell 'em t' hang tight, t' be tough and that everything would turn out alright—and trust me, there were plenty of times when it didn't! All the shit I've done! And this fucking book-learned guy is sitting behind a desk with a smug smile on his face, questioning what my teaching philosophy is, and how I measure up to some schmoe who wrote a goddamn paper about classroom control but probably never taught a single instant in an inner city class in his life—how do I measure up to his philosophy? I almost walked out man—I should have, in retrospect."

"If I were a teacher, I would wind up getting fired for insubordination—I'm certain of it," I said, "I don't know how you do it."

"Neither do I man, trust me."

"So that school you were the full time sub at—they didn't hire you at the end of last semester?"

"Nah—the chick came back from her maternity leave and they brought her back in and whatnot—and that class was hard to leave, man—I got real tight with a lot of those kids—quite a few still call me—we got real emotionally bonded when that Kadieja girl got killed by her ma's boyfriend in November. Takes a real man to rape and stab a twelve year old, right? Fucking incredible."

"Human beings, some of them, are just fucking sickeningly evil, Will, that's all there is to it. I do not know if there is a heaven and hell, a God or a devil, I don't know for sure if such exists, man, but really, really if anything makes me feel that such things *do* exist, it's not the goodness in people, man, rather, it's the wickedness—even within myself."

"I know what you mean." His phone started ringing and: "Give me a minute," he said.

He walked into the kitchen and I browsed around—looking at his paintings, at EP's racks—and I felt fortunate to spend so much time around driven, creative madmen like them. "So who was it?"

"My ma—she's in the hospital right now."

"Everything alright?"

"Nah, not really man."

"Why, what's wrong with her?"

"No—she's with my dad."

"Why? What's goin' on?"

"He's getting a blood transfusion—he's like, really weak, I guess. His body is like, running out of nutrients."

"Is he still getting chemo?"

"Yeah—and I want to be like, who deserves that shit, dude? But that's the name of the game, too—we're all gonna' be dealing with some shit like that down the line. The final pinnacle of living is dying—it has t' be—and I wanna die with my eyes wide open, know what I mean Riedie? Like, this is it man—this is how it's gonna' go—tryna laugh at the pain. Because fuck—if dyin's the pinnacle of livin', and I live with my eyes open, I most certainly plan on dyin' with 'em open—wide fucking open."

"I find it very beautiful when someone dies after some supreme struggle to live, ugly as it may be, until the bitter fucking end of existence."

"Well he's certainly on the verge of accomplishing that, mate."

"Is he making progress?"

"When making progress is having nine tumors instead of ten, I mean—fuck progress. The man would kill himself if he didn't have to take care of us—if doing so wouldn't cancel his life insurance."

"You think?"

"Absolutely—the other day he gave me a look like: I'm going t' die soon—I'm gonna' fade into black forever and it's gonna' be a real big and well-earned nap. Take care now, son, I love ya—it was the craziest look ever, man, I'm telling you. Until he got sick, I never realized how fragile sanity was."

"Some say you can't truly find your mind until after you've lost it."

"You're right—I feel a thousand times stronger nowadays, after going through all this with him."

"You are—this has been a long, horrible battle for all of you."

"I guess—I just have to accept it. I mean—he's dying man. He's fucking dying—but it hasn't gotten any easer since I first got the news—I was teaching—the phone in the room rang and it was my ma—she told me, I put the phone back on the cradle, looked at the receiver, hated it, tried not to believe the words it just spit at me, prayed it was all a dream—the kids were all talking amongst themselves, being all loud, and then I just screamed: '*Fuck!*' They looked at me, shocked, and I told 'em what was up. It's best to be honest with children, completely honest and open, best to let them see you, who you are, what you value in a raw sort of way—they love you for it, when you show them you're on their level, so I wanted to tell them why I yelled 'fuck' like I did. Kids are smart, honest—they try *so* hard, they really do, most kids—they try to make you proud and think so deeply, much more deeply than many adults do—they want to be loved so much."

He returned to the easel, painted quiet for a minute and said: "But he's already gone in a lot of ways, my dad, like—he just stares at me with these dead, lifeless eyes sometimes—I mean, I look at him, and I wanna shoot him, like a horse—my fucking father! He's in so much pain. So much pain it is unbe*lie*vable, man. I gotta write him a letter or something. It's just—to see how hard he worked his whole life—all the effort it took to save for us, and now—for him t' know he's spendin' it all on dyin'!—that he's paying outrageous fees to an insurance company—my God. And he always built me up, Riedie, always told me I was the best, yelled at the ump after a bad call n' told me what a good artist I was, pushing me further with constant encouragement," he said, working on that woman's face with extreme precision. "I'd be done with a piece, it'd dry and I'd be ready to make a quick run to the closet with the thing when he'd stop me, take it from my hands, hold it up in the light and say, 'Look Ry, stop and *look* at this—look at how good an artist you are! My God! I don't even know how we're related you're so good!'—he never tore me down or totaled out a long litany of sacrifices he had to make on account of me coming into existence, no, never man, he fucking never did any of that—all the mistakes I made growin' up, all the times he coulda made me feel small about the stupid things I'd done—he never dissed me man, never once—he always gave it to me straight, like a man. But the thing is—in a lot of ways, he never saw what he had, either—he only wanted more. He told me once that I wouldn't be happy unless I was making a hundred thousand dollars a year. I mean—the next thing I knew I was fifteen and I woke up and understood the world better than he did. Better than Superman! And in my head I was like, gosh dad, you've truly not transcended shit about life if that's the way you feel—but then, after I finished college, he finally seemed to relax about all that—finally realized what he had, happy as hell to wake in the morning with my ma and start the day together—he realized what it was all about—just as it was about to get taken away from him. It feels unreal man, I fuckin' swear."

He went back to quietly painting for awhile and said, "Wish I had someone else's brain sometimes."

"Your most original and creative shit spews from your most fucked up mindsets."

"I know man. I know. And I'm there right now—I have been since last week when I had to wheel him into the hospital for a meeting. Needless to say, the sight of him getting the bad news was horribly sad n' final—we sat in the office, told a couple hopeful jokes, n' a few minutes later, the doc broke the bad news. And as she was talkin' about the options, she started lookin' at her Palm Pilot, probably checkin' what time the next poor sucker was supposed t' come in for 'the talk'—but she didn't do it rude, either—she's always been very kind and compassionate, and my dad really likes her—it was just—there are so many other people afflicted, so many reaching out to her in desperation for answers she can't provide that it broke my heart in a way, right? How couldn't it? And so my mind was flyin', flyin' over everything, millions of calculations, thinking, my dad, he's dying, he's going to die, this is it—I mean, what the fuck, right? The doc was going on about hospital care when what may have been the most haunting expression I have ever seen rolled past in a gurney as we sat idle, gazing into the hall—it was an old man connected to all sorts of machines—his face was frozen to an expression that seemed to signify, that in his last moment of consciousness, it struck him—all the things he never got around to doing, and all the silly reasons of why that was. I think my dad saw 'em too, and it was part of the reason he decided he wants to go out at home, with us—he might live longer the other way but what would he be?—hooked up to all sorts of fuckin' machines like the guy we saw?—a machine to breathe, a machine to piss, a machine to shit?—a former fucking human now destroyed n' carrying on with the help of a manmade cluster a' gruesome gadgets, deliberately tailored to maintain a constant despoliation of personal dignity under the guise of denying a defeatist outlook of the situation at hand—see? He's alive! Yeh. Sure. And the insurance company—they would love if we went on 'keeping him alive'," he said, again quoting the previous three words with his blue fingers, "All for sake of filling the fucking pockets of that greedy hospital, Riedie—so he could lay there frozen with people coming in and out of the generic room, going about their business as if he might as well be a plant or a goddamn plastic chair—I mean—fuck that!" I thought of what Mr. Zybarsky must have been thinking—sitting stoic next to Will, the two of them stomaching the news—and it was hard to not get choked up. How can anybody be expected to die without sadness? I do not believe this is possible. The reminiscing—the impossibly poignant, torrential flow of thought in reference to one's greatest moments and passions—and having to accept that it's over—my God.

"You been able t' keep your faith?"

"It comes in waves, every day—up, down and spraying out in between, and then I just pray harder to a God I'm all in on to remain sane." He took a deep breath and: "It's not comfortable," he said, looking up, eyes filled with intensity, "I don't know—something about the whole situation has me real spooked these days, man—I can't seem to shake it. I've been able t' stay focused though, by tryin' t' go big so I can buy my ma's house for her and prevent these crooks from bleeding her dry. Unless my heart stops, man, I am going to create a sickly huge sum of work this winter for her. I'm gonna' live meagerly, create and burn—gonna' keep my head to the motherfuckin' grindstone until the sad, bitter end when the earth steals me away from myself—until then, I'm gonna' bust it so I can lift my ma up n' help her relax. Whatever happens," he said, looking at me serious, "I know I won't go down like I was just waitin' t' thud." He crossed and uncrossed his arms, shook his head and got back to the painting.

I noticed how much Dubzy looked like his father in that moment and had a hard time fathoming Poppa Z would soon be gone. I just got so emotional thinking about how this man worked and saved his entire life, only to spend it on dying. Fucking life man. Life is crazy, but death, death is craziest, the craziest by far. His pop was a brilliant, driven, energetic man, youthful in heart, and here it was, basically over with: Just. Like. That. WZ was about to experience a horrible life event to which there shall forever exist a distinct hitherto and boundless subsequence—in the end it might break him—not completely, but I was certain he'd shatter pretty hard.

"That's a beautiful painting man," I said, and it was—rather haunting—something about her eyes said: everybody breaks the same—not precisely so, but ultimately—it hit me deep in a way.

"Thanks Riedie. It's been pouring out of me so I've tried to say fuck feeling sad, just let it ride. Every day has been a roll of the dice of late—I ain't even gonna' try n' dispute that it ain't."

"Well—to your fuckin' pop," I said, raising my drink, "He's a great man—always has been, always will be—maybe he'll make it man, maybe he'll pull through."

He raised his glass, his head nodded and his face held a small forced smile: "Hell yeah—ya never know 'til ya know I guess, right?" He finished the remainder of his drink in a single pull and I imagined how it'd go—maybe he'd get better, and again wake to face the day upbeat and thriving—but deep down I knew that wouldn't be how it would go. Soon we'd sit on the stoop and pour a little out for him—booze would roll down the stone steps before we put one down, and Dubzy would be the new man of the family with no choice other than to be strong carry on.

EP banged into the room from outside, crazed hair coated with sawdust and snowflakes, and said: "So guess who's playin' at The Metro tonight?"

"Don't know."

"The fuckin' 86 Bears baby!"

"No joke?"

"Nope."

"Can we get tickets?"

"Already got 'em."

"Serious?"

"Yep."

"For us?"

"Yep!"

"You don't know how good that makes me feel," I said.

"Yes—I do."

"You know how badly I need something like this right now?"

"As bad as me, I'd bet," Dubzy said, "I just need t' turn up, tune in and go, go, go."

EP jumped in the shower and I milked my drink as Dubzy finished the painting. "You sure you feel like going, man?" I asked, "I don't wanna pressure you."

"Yeah, I'm sure—I need t' get out n' move—I'd rather live today, not waste away or wait to get wet in a new year's rain—if I stayed here and sold myself on one-half truths, the subway sounds would get out of tune and I'd go crazy. I need to be out there witchu guys tonight, out with everyone striving t' be strong and live right. It's the only way to ensure my sanity."

"Cool Dubzy—it's gonna' be great."

"I know—I think we're all ready to combust."

"And I can't think of a more flammable band I'd like to see right now—they'll show you what it is to burn."

50

We stepped outside with our rides and the murky sky had stopped snowing. A thin break in the clouds exposed an incandescent sliver of glass, the full moon severed into a crescent, and as my deep breath released into steam I felt an insane connection to the earth at present. So many things had gone through m' mind in the past two days and I couldn't name one if you asked me. I looked at EP and Ryan adjusting their saddles and checking the pressure of their tires and they smiled—so much was happening it seemed, all the ups and downs and inbetweens across the years were mended into a single chaotic dream state of constant locomotion, reaching for dreams that stood across oceans, and someday, after constant rowing and nearly foundering, we'd either get there or go under.

We set off moving, north on Wolcott, and I thought of the many instants we exited the crib, threw on something to Rise to and tore off into the darkness of night, eager to explore and roam free while lost in the enjoyment of unsystematic urban decay. We passed a chubby white guy who looked just about dead, laying face up on a frozen walkway, and I said: "What do you think happened to him?"

"He probably read your journals and went crazy," Dubzy said.

"I wish man."

"White homeless guys always have such nice tans—even in the winter," EP said.

"Pothole EP—look out!" I yelled.

EP's front wheel exploded into it and, amazingly, it kept on rolling, fresh as ever: "That's why I build my shit to twelve hundred Newton metres," he said, "And why riding through city traffic on icy roads always feels like a sporting event to me."

Stop lights and stop signs were blowing in the wind, and we mashed due north, dead into it. Dubzy looked over and: "You know, thinkin' about my dad—I would have loved to smoke one—you don't have anything, do you?"

"No, but—I might—we have to take a tiny detour—we have time EP?"

"Yeah but not much—we'll have to smash."

We did so until we stopped at an old book store—EP watched the bikes as Dubzy and I dipped inside. We went downstairs to the scientific section and: "What are we looking for?"

"Unless they sold it, they have the original ten volumes of the 'Book of Knowledge' down here."

"Is that code for something?"

"No—well, sort of, but no, that's the actual name—the 'Book of Knowledge' was an old encyclopedic set of fundamental information that came out in way back when—I had one, when I was a kid—secondhand. It was the greatest thing ever, for the most part—the drawings are awesome. Just keep looking for it."

"Are these them?" he asked, stopping along a dusty old shelf. I opened a volume to page 6547, European moths and caterpillars—a colorful clifden nonpareil with its wings spread wide, and there, hiding inside, was an old fatty of mine.

"Are you kidding me?"

"Nope."

"That's a little insane, Riedie—logically so."

"Yo fuckin' mayhem *is* logical."

"What if someone had bought that?"

"They'd have received a tasty little delicacy to go along with crucial facts, I 'spose."

"God, you're ill sometimes."

"I appreciate that."

"How long ago did you leave that up here."

"Very—I can't believe this book didn't sell yet, man, it's a classic for ten bucks!"

We walked back upstairs and: "Find everything you were looking for?"

"Yes sir," I said, and just like that we were off.

"You'll never guess what this kid just did," Dubzy said to EP, and after explaining we dipped into an alley, straddling our top tubes, and I insisted Dubzy take the plunge. He leaned against a wall that had been tagged in small white lettering with:

'We make the rules'

And sparked a light. Head rising from his coat, he smoked with his usual style, with pure love for substance, with quick, authoritative drags, puff, puff, inhale, puff, puff, inhale, head tilted slightly to the left, spliff held adoringly between the thumb and forefinger of his right hand, brown eyes rolling back in his head and in a final, inspired drawing in of enchantment, a cornucopia of ghost white vapor lingering upon his lips was drawn up through his nostrils—he exhaled for what seemed like forever and smiled lightly.

"That was large," I said.

Cockeyed, he handed me the cobbled-together spliff, and: "Take a taste, Riedie."

"I'm good man, this one is all you."

He followed my advice and said: "Older I get, the more I realize it's all you can do really—try to be alright and call people out on their bullshit—most especially yourself," he said, "And in truth, things ain't been so easy of late." He took another taste and: "Thanks for hearin' me out so much recently, guys, you know, with all the shit about my pop n' everything. I know I been talkin' about it a lot, but—I don't know. I appreciate ya hearin' me out is all."

"Don't even worry about it man," EP said, "We'll always be here for ya." He didn't reply and EP continued with: "You sure you're cool Dubzy?"

"Yeah man." He insisted I take a drag, and as I inhaled a sensuous blend of earth and fire, I transcended myself man, right then, as in many moments before, and a moment later, it felt good to be out, moving through the night. We passed a man breaking bottles on a step, just one of ten thousand front stoop melodramas to be played out on a random Saturday evening, and EP said: "We have to get a move on it."

"Alright let's not fuck about, let's just do it," I said, and we mashed in silence for several miles and let it all out, not an ounce left, forever blessed with that edge—and then, out of nowhere, a cab zipped around the corner, completely in the wrong lane, and it missed hitting Dubzy head on by a handful of inches. "Jesus man! That cab almost clipped you— that would have been real serious man!"

"I thought you were about to die man," EP said, "I'm not kidding!"

"My guardian angel," Dubzy said, "If I have one, is a tired motherfucker." We got caught at a red light right there and a man singing on the corner belted out:

"Let it r*aaa*in warm water
Down on my soul—

Click

Click

Let it r*aaa*in
Warm w*a*-ter down
On my so-o-o-*oul!*

Click

Click

May I n*eee*ver grow old

Click

Never grow weak—

Click

May I never become

Click

A-*fra*id t' speak—

Let it r*aaa*in
Warm water
Down on my soooooooooooooooooooul—"

He noticed we were listening and said: "Looks like you're already wet boys!"

"Yep."

"Try not t' mind ridin' when it's wet like dis—cuz one day ya won't be ridin'—one day ya won't feel it snowin'—so far as you know, ya know?—so let it rain warm water down on your soul—may you never grow old, may you never grow weak, may you never become afraid to speak—let it rain cold water down on your soul. That's what I always says, anyway."

He walked on, singing loud and free, we set off moving and Dubzy said: "You know what? That guy was an angel."

"I knew you'd say that, man," I said.

"Maybe he was my Guardian Angel, in fact."

"You think?"

"What? Can't a white kid have a black Guardian Angel?"

"If you have one, dude's fuckin' black for sure—I feel the same about myself, in fact."

"That he's black?"

"At least partly—a lot of white folks bore me, when I really come to think of it. A lot of black folks I know always manage to keep their spirits up, no matter what—they always seem to have a decent time, even if life is fucked—it's more my style."

We put the fucking hammer down on a long, carving ride of unparalleled fury and EP said: "I love how the steel company makes Cortland so nice between Racine and the River—with the Christmas lights and such."

"Right?"

"I love riding through this corridor like this, late in the dark night when they have the doors of the melting building open." We rode past and from across the street we could *feel* the kilns and blast furnaces radiating heat on our faces—we peered in and sparks flew as a ladle of molten iron was poured into an open hearth furnace for conversion to steel, and there were just a couple of shadowy guys in there, black outlines of men in crazy industrial wear, surrounded by red. The sound radiating from the long manufacturing plant into the atmosphere was ethereal—the sheer amount of energy being used to essentially emulate the pressure in the center of the earth to liquefy metal was profound. "The power it takes to galvanize steel is so wild—I'd love to own this place—I'd build things you wouldn't believe, Riedie, you don't even know!"

"Enjoy it while you can EP," I said, "Because it'll all be condos soon enough. The Cook County tax on industry property has finally risen to the point that it's impossible to maintain a profit—all this leaching is driving industry out of here—and in a city this big, just like a country this big, you need to have blue collar, physical jobs. Some people need t' go t' work n' stamp a fuckin' press or mold metal, man. Not everyone is made t' push pencils n' sell bullshit—some people need t' build. And so they'll close this joint down," I said, evading a wide spree of glass on the icy road, "And there will be a new slew of bitter, unemployed people, who'll go sitting idol, aggravated and thirsty, and after they haven't gotten a job in the next two years, they'll have to go rob those condos, perhaps, which will then give the government the authority to hire more cops to levy more fines and fill more cells, thereby requiring more tax dollars, and bloating the system even farther."

"People need to have something to do," Dubzy said.

"That's what I'm saying—there will always be crime, but a significant portion of crime is need-based, at least a quarter of it, I'd say. Americans are hardworking by nature—if there's a job for them to do, they'll do it. A lot of these midgame crooks, if they had the option, would gladly work some steady grunt job if it would provide a livable wage to raise a loving family. They really would—a lot of people just wanna have a family n' be happy, but it's damn near impossible without borrowing and getting buried. The government robs industry, industry is then forced to rob the people who are then robbed by the government once more—we get hit three times. In fact—I don't want to talk about this right now, let's just ride."

"Sorry."

"No, it's just—these pricks are trying to tax my grandmother's building right out of her hands—tryin' t' put her out, an old lady! Lived in the building her whole life, a place built by my fucking great grandfather, and every year these weasels come up with a magic new number of how much it'll cost to live there—these thieves. It's gone up exponentially over the years while at the same time, city services continue to decline. Bunch of fat little thieves is what they are, and then—then when it's time for an election, they tout the great struggle of what it means to be a Chicagoan, and ask for votes. It's like, no man—you're not living this life, you're causing this life, motherfucker! Know what I'm saying?"

"It seems t' me that every election breaks spending records, gets progressively nastier and remains virtually tied," EP said, as we jumped our front wheels over railroad tracks, "And what changes?"

"Nothing—not a damn thing," Dubzy said, "Just a different set of crooks with the same agenda taking from the people."

"Maybe that's why I can't get into it," I said.

"You weren't born to jump, Riedie, frantically rabid, from bloc to bloc, screaming praises for party leaders alongside whirlwind choruses of followers, man. You're an independent mind who understands that what government seeks is to steal from independent minds—every single side, every single angle, doing all they can to keep power out of reach from those who are true innovators—they're all set against us—a media, government, multi-national corporation alliance that is nearly impossible to defeat."

We cut through the light at Clyborne just perfect and I said: "It's sick how effective they've been."

"No shit."

"I mean, it all comes down to money in the end," Dubzy said, "It really does—people without money don't get listened to unless it's at some speech where they bring up the mother of a kid killed in war—she'll endorse a candidate one way or another, and after a great round of applause, she will then be swept aside, her two minutes of shared mourning over and gone, and as soon as that candidate gets in office, his handlers will be racking their brains to ensure people like her donate to the campaign the next time around, so they can continue to collect more dollars—and together they roll in their power like fat pigs in mud."

"Keep working hard," I said, "And then we can have anything we want."

"Not anything, exactly."

"Kind of—I mean, what do we want? A simple life and to be left alone, with the ability to explore random things—it's attainable man, I'm telling you—all I really want for myself is my own little place with a stoop and a garden. That's all I really need."

"Between taxes, the mortgage and bills," Dubzy said, "You need t' clear six figures every year for ten in a row if you want that in Chicago, in a neighborhood where you're not getting shot at every day—we're gettin' pushed out of our own city, guys, admit it."

"I know—fuckin' nuts, right?" EP said.

"The city makes it nearly impossible to own unless you're a property company collecting rent—and so you can see how clout-controlled mechanisms, over time and protected by the machine, hurt everyday citizens. It's very difficult to afford a single family home in Chicago if you're not a millionaire."

"Let's just forget it," I said, standing up in the saddle and pushing the pace to a mild level of danger, "Let's just worry about enjoying a compelling show tonight—it's lucky enough that we're going."

I was quietly despondent about the fact that what Will said was true—it was a rather helpless feeling in a way, and it left a deep feeling of unease in my stomach. Nobody said anything for the remainder of the ride until we finished cascading those slick surfaces and EP said: "That was a nice, aggressive route." He kicked the snow off his feet and: "It's felt good to just give yourself away to it—to the fact that it's just you, rigged to a chain, and however hard you churn and perfectly you steer is how it's gonna' go."

"Not much different than life I 'spose," Dubzy said.

I didn't say anything in response because my mind was disturbed at a very deep level. Certain realities had sunk in and I thought of the millions of Americans like me n' m' mates, stuck in a sidetracked society on the brink of losing itself—I looked across the street and some old madman was smoking a pipe and combining his nose and his mouth to work as quite a formidable fire stoking furnace and chimney as he looked blankly at frozen bricks, prime opportunity for meaningful ingenuity long since passed. I shivered, thinking it wasn't a guarantee, no matter how hard we worked and driven we were, that we would not wind up in shoes similar to his. He sat in a slushy puree and a dog tried to steal his sandwich. "Whoa whoa whoa!" he yelled, diving atop it like a lineman on a fumble—the dog and the woman walking him carried on as he scarfed it down like a starving psychopath and promptly got back to his pipe.

We locked up our bikes, EP lending me an extra, and outside the venue, a long line of adrenalized eyes wrapped around the building and stretched down the frozen block. The scale at which the sense of anticipation escalated with each pace closer to the door was feverish—the world somehow no longer felt cold and crushing, and I took a moment to soak it in: that rare feeling before a rare show by a rare band—one that transcends the idea of music alone and fulfills a raw sense that all who are there are capable of bridging the gap between contemplation and action. It wasn't hope for the sake of hope, no man—there was an underlying rhapsodic harmony of credible intention in the air—a glaring fucking feeling swelling in the street that the arbitrators of future reality were to be you and me—a fucking taste in my mouth that evades description: like that of a bloodless victory by valorous, driven minds over the wordless power that had held us down deep beneath the suffocating stream of tears released by all who asked why and never sought to kill the because—the future was amendable and there were no predestine conclusions—alarmist indolent worry of the totalitarian stranglehold upon our throats was about to activate in a serious fucking swell of purpose.

I looked at EP n' Dubzy and they shook their heads, almost in disbelief, it seemed, that here we were—after all these years, man, all the close calls—still living and breathing—in a city flat out raw and unpredictable alongside mates best described as living upon a polished knife edge, forever slicing and incising the mind to passion, consequences be damned—there was no restraint, not now, not ever—and thank God because: why bother?—we jumped years ago and fed off one another at an extremely severe caliber—entrusting one another with the entrenched duty of enshrining the entrance fee of an epically untamed existence with the envious commission of pushing each other evermore whence teetering on the brink of colossal entropy. Such had been the cost of admission: quite nearly everything in your life that is ordinary and sane. "We've reached such great heights," Dubzy said, "It's hard t' even think about without breakin' into tears a' joy."

"I still haven't come down. I'll be damned if ever I do," EP replied, "I'll never be reached."

"Fuck right boy." He grabbed the tickets from will call and we entered the building among throngs of keyed up souls of many backgrounds—collective exuberance filled the air and people felt privileged to be there—I didn't see what seemed to be a single indifferent individual on the scene—expressions were filled with meaning—a feeling that when you hit the floor with a mass of bodies and the lights came on—when the hum of thousands of sizzling watts was broken with a single power chord, everything you spent your days dreaming of would suddenly feel possible.

"Troll around a bit?" EP asked.

"Yeah—let's." The floor was smashed with bodies and we headed to a bar in the corner. "Whachu boys want? I got this one," I said, "Scotch?"

"It's ten years after I got my license, I'm still driving an 89 Saab, I'm still broke, and I'm still taking Julie to parties and not having sex with her—yes, I'll have a fucking Scotch, please," EP said. I smiled after watching him make that statement in such good spirits—kid always manages to keep people loose with his self-deprecating sense of humor. EP's a good soul man, a good soul.

The bartender was hot and she knew it but was chill about it—dark-haired, fit, stylish and on the ball, she hustled for everyone's orders all the same, cognizant that she was not the reason people were there, but at the same time giving them another reason to hurry back. She made my change quickly and with a smile, our trio of glasses clicked, skin leaked in the stagnant air and walls streaked with condensation as we sat back and bullshitted at the bar for a minute, content to grab a drink at a concert together for the first time in a good long while. We had some moments to kill before liftoff, and so we eased back and spoke on many good mates of old, their great traits and delirious ways and what in fact they were up to—some had started families, others roamed and still more had gotten lost in the race—mouths traced great memories of their lively faces on past days, and when it all spilled out it seemed much time shared with many names had passed in a blink. It took me back and: "It'll always be that way," Dubzy said, "Where months seem like days and it all blurs together into a life lived and died—it's only gonna' come faster with age."

"Just keep keepin' up man, we'll be alright," EP said. I thought it the right answer but Ryan had a point—all the random scenes performed over a chance weekend—all those people, the many hundreds you see—passing on as if a dream—over and over, no break until the final close—and to never identify the last hurrah before ah hah!—it gotcha!—Lord how it makes me want to run sometimes, that thought—that obvious fucking snapshot of reality—they spoke for awhile and I drifted off on visions of indistinct faces pushing in toward the stage, kids ready to rage who's most common trait was that the anticipation of seeing the band was beginning to drive them mad.

We had more laughs n' I eventually told 'em about Dennis meeting his fate in recent days, and so we clicked glasses and poured a little out. Booze splashed the floor like blood on the street and I figured from then on I'd leave his memory there with it. We bullshitted a minute longer, smashed a last drink among smiles and laughter and pushed into the anticipatory fray. The light up front went dark and through the obscurity, the beat of a drum began in a way that seemed to say: the beat flows 'til ya die, right? Remember that when the downbeat ends and there ain't another night—you don't wanna look back and say ya didn't give it all like you said ya might.

And just like that, the stage burst into light and it was *on*: peaking perfectly in a faultless chaos, the accelerated, polished madness of power chords and provocative lyrics washed over me like boiling tar upon an already overheated body. My eyes scanned the horizon and the arid smell of spilled scotch and sweating, raging hominids rose to the roof naturally, like morning dew burning off in an early summer solstice sun. The lights dimmed and again fired bright, and the main room of The Metro exploded in an undiluted exultation of emotive release—several hundred different sorts swayed in delirious waves of symphonic passion—a sort of infinite languid beauty gone sordid.

A girl's hard, sweat-streaked body slammed into my back and I raised my hand to apologize for the mishap. A pair of wild, animalistic eyes met my own and she suggested: "Always tongue," before banging a blamelessly free face and mocking raw smile back and forth before again disappearing into a vengeful torrent of flying bodies and frenzied eyes like the barely credible lioness I assumed her to be. I looked at EP and he smiled like: yeah, fuck yeah, we gotta keep livin' fast boy, keep livin' fast and never die.

From a second of silence the emergence of flawlessly timed sound emblazoned the bursting room with a rawness that entwined the spectators in a rushing release of emboldened emotion—the identifiable details of that which had coursed within each soul was sent out in a massive wall of heat, up to ceiling, rattling 'round and sweeping down into a churning frenzy by a nucleus of ringmasters whose eminent mastery of vehement ferocity was unparalleled. The bassist and drummer were in a ferocious groove—like the boxer who spent countless hours pounding the bag alone in a dark musty room, conjuring combos in a tenacious flow all his own—there was no money saved up for 'Guitar Hero', no—and now that all the hours and days and years of preparation had led to a stage, every beat was struck with bad intentions—I could see it in their eyes—all those nights, alone with a dream, and now to be here, delivering for those who'd flocked to be a part of it—the veins in their necks flexed with a downbeat that sounded like gunfire—I looked at EP as he finished his drink and screamed: "There is no guidebook to becoming a band like this!" I nodded, aware of their path: cleared, plowed and paved by themselves, with hindrances scoffed at, buoyant and angry, and I understood then why others like me were dancing and screaming: they lifted us high and said never fear dreams—because a life without them is a long, boring death sentence.

The lead guitarist ripped up-tempo solos in Herculean proportions, and up front, a girl was floating above the crowd, flying at times, and as she was thrown high by a hundred sets of arms, she was holding the singer's eyes with her own, a direct energy transfer of the utmost rawness between the two as he held his hand out and lifted it higher with his voice—and as he did so she reached out to him—a mix of pain and elation entrenched on her sweat streaked face as she screamed lyrics that reached a point in her soul that her best friends had never touched—their mutual ascension was exceptional, both meaning so much to each other in the moment—she held his eyes as he screamed on, and by the time she came down to the ground and turned to face me, she was in tears, released in a style so primal and free I was certain she wouldn't forget that moment for as long as she breathed.

I felt myself rise above what was as a fanatical face on stage obtruded a flying body, screamed instigative truths and asked the inhabitants, "Just what? Just what is it that you plan to do? There're so many brilliant minds out here, out everywhere—brilliant kids who understand what the fuck is happening in the world, yet have no say in what is. Articulate people of all races, all religions, different colors and creeds—we all understand and still nothing changes. But why is that? The distractions? The anxieties? What is it? Is nobody being heard? Do people even have a chance to be heard any more? Common men and women—are they? Shit. It seems the answer to that question rests squarely upon what it is you intend to say. Vibe with me on that?"

People agreed: meaning breeched in an echelon of severe open mouthed screams.

"What you say has to fit within specific strategies and exact agendas—else you'll be hushed, not heard." The eccentric singer carried on posing unanswerable questions to which the crowd felt anger for not possessing actionable answers. Gazing the room I internally posed: perhaps I am not the only one feeling so hungry to make a difference—where does the truth lie? Perhaps tonight is the night for the average, puritanical, starchy proletariat to puncture their minds with a punchy bass line and punishing fills on the high hat and kick drum and have the answers cascade into the world with immediately lofty results.

"Never have I seen a species live in such fear of itself!" he yelled.

Nor one with as many reasons to be, I thought.

"And how does one change that? How does one go about teaching better lessons when we live in a place that collects tax dollars to pay for our favorite form of higher learning—dropping high explosives on heads while saying: 'Because I *said* so!' How does one go about making people listen, if this is the reality?"

The crowd milled about as different people shouted different things and my mind traveled several thousand tangents as I felt my heart beat twice.

"On what day will you finally wake from no sleep with your insides on the out, unwilling to continue waiting for answers? We all need to answer!—now!—through action! To be free is all you have. To lose this one sacred will transform your thought into pollution—so go!"

And like a million rocks slingshotted into a confined room with rubber walls, people again were on the move. Bodies were energized and eyes contemplative, like an old man to have just sat down with a bottle of scotch and a pack of cigarettes for sake of spending the next eight hours looking out on a dangerous street, mind pinned on a single thought, waiting for dawn.

Music poured through me and I thought about how crazy the world really is—I figured only an animal with neither fear of death nor fear to kill can hold a sliver of hope for survival. A hardcore melodic track raged in the background and a thousand voices highlighted the details via fused enunciation. The violent transfer of ripping metal power chords and high-pitched, tear-jerking libretto brought out many memories of completely unrelated subjects as a flood of limbs carried me forward, and into a pit of flying bodies— eyes surrounding said: try your best to defeat me—I'll be here all day, still breathing, raging really, just waiting to take you down.

I lost tract of EP and Dubzy in the swell of raging limbs, and after taking some hard spills over the course of a few songs I eventually made my way up to the balcony—it was a real scene man, looking down on the crowd and watching them go—they were keyed up at a level rarely witnessed. Nobody was on their phone, browsing the internet or texting friends— people were engaged, activated, not seeking to evade reality but determined to change it, purposefully, and according to reason—or so I sought to believe. I stared down on all the young thinkers and imagined the management of NVH Online standing in the same spot—Mr. Joshua would leer down with those calculating eyes as Gloria Prendercast waddled to the edge, wary of falling over. They'd spy concertgoers as the precise mold of who they'd seek to contact and tinker with—they'd try to convince them to drown their independent brilliance with a wave of helpless ignorance—but no—standing on the balcony and feeling that heat rise and rise and *rise!*—they wouldn't be able to douse this fire. It was a beautiful sensation and so I thought: how could I give them a taste of their own medicine?

The band ripped into another song after the lead guitarist slid a chord all the way down the fret board, slow and deliberate until the other three on stage exploded in sound, perfectly on key. I thought: this life, man, how it shall be lived is up to me—and so maybe— if I ever get to where I need to be, and complete that which I began so very long ago—maybe I'll expose that school—that whole education corporation. Maybe instead of naming its actual ticker symbol, I'll simply use a basic form of alphabet encryption—that way, I could just call the corporation PRPB and let people figure it out—O yes, how hilarious—NVH Online would follow the same formula, and peeps could determine who the criminals really were if interested. And then, if I were truly crazy, I could invest the money from the initial pre sale of the book into a bet that said that company's stock was going to deflate based upon the information I had released, and allow the tale to become a self-fulfilling prophesy of sorts— thereby reinvesting the money earned as a result of their destruction into a *real* education experience in some way—O what a funny lesson plan that would be.

I took a breath as I pondered what was possible when a younger kid around eighteen stepped up and said: "Awesome show ay?"

"Hell yeah man."

"The 86 Bears are always awesome man—there's no better band from Chicago, it's not even close. They're so real man, it's crazy." I smiled and he said: "I lost my friends in the crowd."

"Me too."

"This is like the kind of show I'd want to meet a girl at, you know? Like—she'd have to be totally cool to be here tonight."

"You're right—you see one you like?"

"Kinda—what about you?"

"I got a girl I dig but she ain't here tonight."

"How'd you meet her?"

"On the street."

"You like—just went up and talked to her?"

"Yeah man—she seemed cool so I said hey."

"I wish I had that confidence—I don't think I have it in me to do that."

"Are you true to yourself man?" I asked.

"I think so—I try to be—why?"

"If you're honest with all you are man, you will have the confidence to speak to anyone from a chick at a concert to God if there is one—once attained, after many days of brutal honesty with the self, you can't be reached."

"That's deep man—I guess I get nervous is all."

"Don't sweat it, you'll be fine."

"You think?"

"Hell yeah man, don't worry on a damn thing man, honest—think of the big picture and float over the rest—so where's the girl?"

"Over there, on the side, the one with dark hair in that black 86 Bears shirt with the fist."

"If you don't go say hello tonight, you'll always regret it. Don't sweat it if she ain't down t' chat man—as long as you mean what you say it won't matter—you'll only get stronger."

"You think?"

"Absolutely."

"Thanks man—that's really good advice—seriously—what's your name?"

"Anthony Riedie," I said, shaking his hand, "Good luck homie." I watched the kid walk over and after a couple minutes it was evident he made a good decision. They were engaged in conversation and singing together, and the sight just about made my night. I again looked down on the scene, took in another mad poetic and prophetic track and my heart started racing—it hit me like a fist, man: I had to see Melissa.

I ran down the steps to retrieve my gear from the coat check, and shot out into the frozen night. My entire base layer was soaked with sweat and I unlocked my bike in a fury. It was a whole combination of things, but the scene had finally unbound my feelings to a point so profound that I desired nothing more than to dash through the night, look into Melissa's eyes and say: 'Hey—I'm not sure if you'd want me to, but I basically feel like living my life for you—and yes, I'm serious.'

I looked through my sketchbook to where she'd written her address and phone number alongside: 'No excuses now! Love Melissa,' and I was off, flying up Clark as fast as my legs could push me. I imagined many things, some shallow, some deep, but more than anything I longed for the simple happiness earned by doing your absolute best for someone you hold in the highest esteem. Past Lawrence and way short on breath, I told myself to relax—just be cool man, you don't need to come in from the night unannounced and talking crazy. Just be easy, say hello and play it cool—and as soon as this thought finished I began wondering if maybe I should propose to her, just random like this—it would take a long while before I could get her a ring but maybe she'd take promissory note. Again I changed my tune to maybe asking her to check a flick, whatever one she was interested in, and now in Edgewater, I cut over to her building on Sheridan, stomach in knots and hands shaking—I was really out of my mind for her.

I locked my ride to a parking meter, entered the lobby and pushed her buzzer like a crazed bike messenger, eager to drop a package and get on with the next tag. "Hello? Who is it?" A man's voice came over the intercom and my stomach sunk. Fuck. Who was this fool? There was no way he understood her like me—he never sat with her at the Lake, for hours, solving the whole riddle of the world before being unable to decide what we wanted on our pizza for the exact same length of time. He didn't know *shit* about her, man—fuck this. The only reason he's there is because I was too stupid to be honest with her. "He*llo!* Who's th*ere?*"

"Who's *this?*" I yelled, confrontational as hell.

"I asked *you* who *you* are."

"Is Melissa there?"

"Who *is* this?"

"Wilya put her on? It's her place, not yours. Melissa! Are you there? It's Anthony! I'm downstairs. I'm not tryin' t' bother—I just have t' talk t' ya!"

"I'll be right down pal," the guy said.

That was it—someone was about to get fucked up hard. I pushed my fist into the stone and my heart was fucking pounding. The door that led into the building from the foyer had no window, so I stayed dead quiet so I could hear his footsteps coming from the elevator. I heard two sets, and I couldn't believe that she'd come down with him. Didn't she hear it was me? Maybe she was going to escort him from the premises and then let me up. I tried to stay calm and *bam*—the door opened and she wasn't there. Two police officers walked out with a serious look on their face. "What's this?"

"Are you a friend of Melissa D—"

I didn't even hear them say her last name—my mind was racing so fast. "What the fuck is wrong man? C'mon—"

"I'm sorry but—Melissa got killed in her apartment last night, on Friday. I'm really sorry. We're just here t' escort the evidence tech." I didn't even move. My ears held a crazy ringing tone like after an explosive goes off too close to your head and he said: "I'm sorry man, she's passed." I don't even think my expression changed, and he said: "There's a warrant out for the suspect, if it's any conciliation—several witnesses saw him with bad scratches on his face and a black eye—we think he's on his way back to Mexico, but they'll be looking for him along the border. We're sure it's him. They'll get him eventually, pal." The cop said, putting his hand on my shoulder.

"How'd he kill her?"

"Don't think about that pal."

"Was it with his bare hands? Tell me man!"

"We can't. I'm sorry—there was no additional assault, you know—if that helps give you peace at all—we think it was a robbery gone wrong. She fought him like a lion." I walked outside and vomited for a while, almost unsure of where I was. What was there to say?

A two day silence over untold miles of blurred vision said it all—and so here I am, back on the shore and looking out after quitting some pointless insurance job—square one, square none—a Monday morning spent talking to an expanse with a sketchbook in hand—to that level plane of blue stretching out forever, until forever ends—man Melissa, I honestly would have taken care of you forever—but I'll see you someday, all of you, I'm certain of it.

The End

Always charging, this colossal countdown—
Raindrops raging down the mountain—
This constant change—
So strange—
Because O God I scared me—
Live hard, I dared me—
Bet me, I did—
And I promise, I'll win—
I bet I'll never die—
You too, just try—
Just admit you're always living—
Admit you always were—
A distant bolt of lightening—
The thunder of the world—
Everything that's frightening—
An ever-changing mural—
And what I am?
A man, goddamn—
One stand—
On this land—
With these hands—
A single chance—
To dance—
Loose and easy—
With all whom you love—
Living free because—
Freedom of being—
Is all that ever was—
And from the end—
The beginning begins—
Be strong, be real—
And never be reached, my friends—

Robbie